Naero's Fury

A Spacer Clans Adventure

Book Three

NAERO'S FURY

Mason Elliott

High Mark Publishing

High Mark Publishing
www.highmarkpublishing.com

Seattle & Portland, Chicago, London

NAERO'S FURY

by
Mason Elliott

Trade Paperback Edition
© 2014 by Mason Elliott. All rights reserved.
Published by High Mark Publishing
ISBN 978-1-930451-09-4
Watch for other titles by this author in the future.

Cover Art by
Frank Miller
frankmillerdesign.com

Edition Notes
If you do not see this edition note here in this spot on the copyright page and on the very last page of your ebook or print version of this title, then you are not getting the final, polished version of this novel that the publisher, editors, and author intended for you to receive. Please contact either the publisher or the author via their emails or websites if you do not see the following update code:

High Mark Publishing Update Code K2428E

1

They danced upon the edge of oblivion, all three crippled starships docked together, lost in the unexplored Gamma Quadrant and spinning dangerously close to the nearest sun.

In Naero's current condition, startapping might yet prove fatal. And the additional distraction of a sudden flare-up of her Cosmic sickness did not help matters, either. Pulsating sores of disrupting, infected Cosmic energy, fed by the Darkforce, erupted all over her flesh, causing her intense pain.

The air was suddenly rank with psyonic ichor, fetid ozone, and putrefaction.

Naero attempted to use her weakened abilities to lick at the star as if it were an immense lollipop of Cosmic energy. Power—both she and their ships all needed power to restart their cores and save themselves.

To pull that off, they had to get in dangerously close to the star.

Too close and they'd all be reduced to a puff of atoms on the solar winds.

If she were in better shape, the process might prove easier, and safer. Yet she and Baeven were both still drained and beaten up from getting them there–spending all of their Cosmic energies to power the unstable wormhole that brought them out that way, on their dire mission.

Naero reached out tentatively with another tiny feeder ribbon, struggling not to open herself up to too much power. She and Om both knew what would happen then. A runaway, out-of-control power surge, building to a huge gigablast.

She struggled to avoid such a fate, almost too late.

Even the small feedback rush that shot into her smallest feeder tendril was nearly overwhelming in her reduced state.

The rush of pure Cosmic force raced through her sick and damaged body, transfixing her, consuming her last defenses.

Such power. Raw Cosmic energy beyond description. Naero gasped and tried to swallow.

That power nearly destroyed and incinerated her.

If she allowed it to suck them in, they would all be disintegrated. Instant flaming death.

Om screamed in her head, but she could not make out his words.

Waves of Kexxian defensive protocols lashed out and melted and vaporized in the face of such naked might.

They struggled against a star itself–to war with and absorb those destructive energies and make use of them.

Om attempted to save them. More Kexxian defenses erupted and ramped up exponentially in expanding bubbles and spheres.

Naero screamed. Her veins, her heart, her brain–every atom of her brimmed with Cosmic force. Her Cosmic disease was both fed by such energies, and destroyed by them.

Even her Dark Beast fell back in sudden shock, bloated and blitzed on energy in a sudden, besotted coma like a drunkard.

Her friends and crew…her family.

They were all that Naero could think of and recall.

With one wave of her hand, she spent most of her power to fling their ships back from the impending destruction, restarting all three fusion cores at the last instant–even *The Star Fox.*

Naero finally understood, too late, as she barely managed to transform into an energy being.

She had managed to save the others even as the star pulled her into its gravity vortex.

Yet somehow, for the moment, the Kexxian fields around her stabilized.

She swam or soared through the intensely hot, expanding energies of the star's surface, as if it were an immense sea of energy.

Then she caught sight of Khai, the Mystic Enforcer, moving under his own power and force of will.

Bright green and glowing in his own energy form, he swung himself around, far outside the fierce core of the star, recharging his sword Yii within the might of the sun itself. Just as Yii had been created in a similar fashion.

Naero struggled to move toward him, still unable to keep herself from slowly being drawn in further, in her weakened state.

He looked her way, sensing her approach. Khai called out to her telepathically.

You're moving too fast, Naero. You'll be drawn into the core. You won't survive there long. I know that fact, better than anyone.

I can't stop myself; I'm sick and damaged. Please, catch me. Help me, Khai. I'm dying!

Khai strained and strove for her, the look on his face suddenly frantic. He just missed her fingertips as she continued to spiral in.

I can't reach you in time! he said.

Naero smiled sadly, as an extreme calmness and serenity washed over her.

Like all Spacers, Naero knew that one day she would return to the stars.

She just had not expected it to be this soon—not while she still had so much to do. So much she still yearned to accomplish.

Naero took no further thought to herself. Her worries and fears were all for those she loved—for those who would remain without her.

A scant few months before, through all the many perils that she had faced, up to this critical moment, no one could have told her that she would stare such a stark fate as this directly in the eye. The most recent events of her life flashed rapidly through her mind as if they were vids.

*

Merchant Fleet Captain Naero Amashin Maeris wondered if she was headed for further training with the Spacer Mystics—or execution.

She stood upon her bridge with her feet planted firmly to either side, her hands crossed slightly behind the small of her slender waist, resting on her energy cutlass, sheathed on its belt swivel on her athletic hips. Her plain, Nytex flight suit and uniform hugged her small, agile form tightly, just the way she liked.

Her eyes were pointed up at the stars above her, as they often were when she was deep in thought or worry. The stars belonged to all.

Naero led her people from the deck of her small, merchant flagship, *The Flying Dagger.* Her refitted bridge was leaf-shaped, like a battle blade itself. Pilot and co-pilot stations up front, crewed by her Second, Commander Enel Maeris and Ensign Sying Lii. Then her captain's chair, raised up behind them, which could rotate 360 degrees beneath the bridge blast screens, which were currently down. She and her bridge crew could see all around them through the clear bubble pod of the normal glasteel canopy.

To her starboard sat Leftenant Commander Surina Marshall, third in command, at her communications station. On her port, Ensign Piper Fae at her scanning station. Next behind them–filling out the last quad of the bridge crew–Ensigns Kimbel Allen and Passaendra Wilde at shields and weapons on the left, and Ensigns Keldo Ramsey and Tarim Martan at jump drives and security on the right.

She and her trade fleet of sixty-odd vessels followed their current orders from the Spacer authorities, proceeding in the direction of Thanor-4–another super-secret world, known only to the Mystics and Spacer Intel. A journey of about one standard week.

After the recent, tumultuous events on Janosha–and her part in them– Naero had agreed to surrender herself to the judgment of the Spacer Mystics and their three High Masters. Thank goodness it would be all three of them this time, and not just High Master Vane of Chaos Wisdom.

Naero had a pretty good idea what his vote would be.

Still, she had given her word, upon her honor–even if doing so did, in fact, lead to her execution.

When they drew closer to Thanor-4, the rest of her fleet was ordered to peel off and trade in the nearby vicinity, to anxiously wait to hear from Naero about how her case turned out.

Naero said farewell to her many friends among the other captains and their crews, including best friends Saemar and Chaela. Many of them had served together during the Annexation War and all of the battles and skirmishes since that time.

Her outcast uncle would continue to shadow them in his own unique, alien ship, *The Shadow Fox,* along with his strange alien crew. His ship could vanish at will and remain undetected. Like Naero, Baeven did not entirely trust the tender mercies of either Spacer Intel or the High Masters.

But she didn't have much choice.

One fact remained clear: Naero's growing Cosmic powers continued to spiral out of control, becoming a danger to all. Either she found a way to learn to control them, with the help of the Mystics…or she would eventually have to be put down, like a dangerous monstrosity. Even she more or less agreed to that now–if things got bad.

If it got to the point where she started killing people and couldn't stop herself–as in her repeated nightmares.

The real truth was probably even much scarier.

Neither Intel nor the High Masters knew what to do with her. At least not yet.

Naero took an emergency call from her ship's doctor in sickbay. That was the place they'd brought her younger brother Jan after the trip over from *The Shadow Fox*. He'd been delirious and remained traumatized ever since Naero had rescued him from a long capture and the horrible torments of their enemies.

"Zhen, what is–"

Naero heard sounds of a harsh struggle over the link.

"N, get down here. Jan's out of control. He's tearing the place apart. Ugh! And us with it!"

"I'm there, Z. Subdue him if you have to."

"We can't. Our stunners won't even touch him. Help! He's trying to burn us!" Zhen screamed.

Jan had recovered well enough to use his psyonics; Jan was a pyrokinetic.

She suddenly had an even worse thought.

What if it wasn't even Jan? What if their insane brother Danner had taken Jan's mind and body over again?

And if she had gotten her Cosmic powers back by now–what if Danner had found a way to do the same thing?

Dan had been more powerful than she and Jan put together. In raw destructive strength, he rivaled the Mystic High Masters.

Naero knew this for a fact from their last encounter.

"Enel, Rina, take the bridge. Pass and Kel, head to sickbay and be ready for a fight. Tarim, get two of your security teams there. Shields, squad stunners, and needle guns."

"On the way, N," Tarim said.

Naero picked the best fighters she could send. "I'm going on ahead," she told them.

She channeled Cosmic energy and used her Mystic abilities to transport just outside of sickbay in an instant.

Right as medtek Trudi Cheyenne came hurtling through the door panels and nearly knocked Naero down. Tru smacked into the opposite wall of the corridor and dropped to the floor in a scorched, bloody heap.

Naero raced into sickbay. The smartroom struggled to put out several fires. Medbeds and equipment had been knocked around.

Her brother Jan fought Zhen and several crew in the far corner.

Then Naero read Jan's Cosmic energy aura–nearly out of control with Chaos energy–and a growing dark haze of Darkforce power.

Like her and Baeven, Jan had his own Dark Beast lurking deep within himself, trying to break out. Or perhaps she was sensing Danner's malevolent presence–Jan's insane twin, still in the hands of the enemy.

Either way–not good.

Jan kicked and punched, and flung three crew aside as if they were nothing. Zhen activated her personal deflector screen, just barely avoiding being encased in a gout of destroying fire from Jan's extended hands.

Naero shielded herself, backed up by Cosmic energy, and swept in to slam Jan against the wall. For an instant she staggered him, trying to find some way to sense exactly who or what she was dealing with.

"Jan, stop it. It's Naero. You're hurting our people, our friends. Is it you, Jan? Is it you in there?"

Jan blinked at her and then sobbed. "N? Is it really you, sib?"

Naero wrapped her arms around him. He clung to her suddenly, gasping and desperate.

Part of him really didn't know.

"It's me, Jan. It's really me. I'm here, and you're safe with me, on my flagship."

Jan collapsed against her and wept. "Am I? I–I thought they had me again, back in their labs. They hurt me, N. They kept it up and they kept looking for new ways to keep hurting me. Unlike Danner...I had never been tortured before."

Naero held him tighter and clenched one fist. "I'm sorry it took me so long to find you and set you free, Jan. But you're safe now. And when we locate those who did all of this to you and Danner, we will make them pay. I swear it."

Jan shuddered and shook his head. More crew charged into sickbay. Naero waved them off for the time being.

Jan rambled. "I couldn't bear Danner, sib. If they had had me long enough, they might have driven me mad–just like they did to him. Sometimes I could keep him out of my mind. Other times I could not."

"We're going to our Mystics, Jan. They can show you how to shield your mind. They can show both of us how to control and use our dangerous powers. There's so much I can tell you, and show you. But right now, I just want you to relax, regain your strength, and know that you are safe and back with me, and among our people. I love you, and I'm going to protect you…with my life, if need be."

Jan looked confused. "Your…flagship? Haisha! How long was I…out of the mix? I couldn't judge time. Months, maybe a year passed. I'm not sure."

Naero made him lie back down on a medbed. "We'll get to all of that, Jan. Too much has happened. Just take some time to relax and recover. After lunch, I'll come by and we'll have a long talk."

Jan's eyes went wide in panic. He looked like he was going to freak out again.

"The machine!" he shrieked. "I just remembered, N. The worst was when they stuffed me into one of those…those things. I couldn't breathe right, and the constant waves of shifting pain, and I was trapped. I–I couldn't get out!" He covered his eyes and whined, nearly going catatonic.

Naero sighed, and spent the next several hours at Jan's side while he attempted to recover and make sense of things. Once he finally slept fitfully, she spoke quietly with Zhen, then conferred with Om and with her crew on the bridge.

While every passing moment brought them closer and closer to Thanor-4 and the judgment of the High Mystics.

2

The Flying Dagger reached Thanor-4 six days later, minus Naero's trade fleet, who parted company from them after Day 3.

The secret planet was a blue, green, brown, and white earthlike with five main continents. Four of these were in close proximity, with one far away from all the others on the other side of the planet. Naero and her people were were on approach, heading toward a small, newly constructed, Spacer Intel starport on the isolated continent–Nashara–the only one that scans showed had any tek.

Although the other four land masses did have small pockets of lo-tek, near-human populations concentrated around a bay, their tek level was somewhere near the Old Terran Dark Ages. Interesting.

The continent of Maedor was particularly intriguing, far beyond its high mountains and vast deserts. The eastern half of the extended continent consisted of dense forests to the north, and equally dense jungles to the south. Gigantic land serpents; barbaric, semi-sentient, goat-like, tribal humanoids. A violent place of what many would call monsters.

All they needed were Ejjai.

Thank goodness there were impassable barriers between them and the near-humans.

Naero gasped suddenly and could not even breathe.

It was as if an icy blade suddenly penetrated her heart.

A bizarre Cosmic energy wave suddenly passed through her without warning. She nearly toppled over. Then she gasped and fell back into her captain's chair.

Even Om, the Kexxian AI trapped in her head, was suddenly disrupted for the flash of an instant.

Jan collapsed beside Naero's command chair where he had been standing and shook with convulsions before he blacked out.

An immediate call came from Baeven. "Naero, did you just experience that strange energy surge?"

Naero shouted over the link, her eyes still spinning. "I sure did. What the hell was that?"

"Naero, I've only experienced something like that once before, long ago, back on Janosha. And if it's what I think it is, perhaps you should turn tail and run–right now."

"You know I can't do that, Baeven. I've already given my word. Why would you even suggest something like that?"

Jan came to and struggled to regain his feet.

"Because," Baeven said. "I don't want to see you banished and made an outcast–the same way I was–with a death sentence on your head."

"I've got news for you, Baeven. If I cut and run now, that's pretty much what's going to happen any way. But on the other hand, what in the hell are you talking about?"

Surina called out from her comstation. "Captain, Intel is hailing us. The High Masters are awaiting your arrival. Somewhat impatiently, I might add. They sound upset."

"If they just felt what Baeven and I felt, I bet they are. Tell them we'll be there shortly, Rina. With respect, of course."

"I'll be the definition of tact, sir."

"Naero," Baeven said, "let me warn you ahead of time. I've got an infinitely bad feeling. If there just happens to be…some kind of amorphous, shifting alien obelisk, statue, or artifact on this planet– don't go near it. Ever. Don't even look at it. Stay the burning fuck away from that damn thing–until you and I have had a chance to talk."

"Seriously, Baeven? The High Masters are going to decide my fate within the hour, and you're worried about some artifact? We don't even know if there's anything like that down–"

Shalaen burst onto the bridge, along with Gaviok, the mantid from Baeven's crew.

"Did you feel that Cosmic power flare, Naero?" Shalaen said. "There is a very unusual, Cosmic power source on the surface of this world, right where we are heading."

Even Om joined in. *Naero, I can also sense it. Anyone with any ability will be able to sense this thing–whatever it is–and it is both Kexxian and Driathan in nature. Very ancient, and extremely dangerous.*

"Everybody shut the hell up," Naero shouted. "For right now, the only place that I am going is before the High Masters for them to decide whether they destroy me or let me live. Once that is finished, I might be able to consider whatever other disastrous choices lie before me."

Yet despite her words, Naero could also sense whatever this startling thing was down on the planet. Her sense of warning was going crazy, and yet this new source of Cosmic power sang to her with a siren's call that was both incredibly seductive and terrifying, all at once.

It wasn't just her Dark Beast that craved to feed upon this vast power–just as it always did with every form of power.

But every part of her yearned to taste of this new power, and drink deep of its sources.

It was *that* alluring.

Even though Thanor-4 nearly pulsed with all of the Chaos and Cosmic energy that lost Janosha had once swelled with, Naero could definitely see why the Mystics were very interested in this world.

When they landed on the surface at the relatively new Intel starport, Naero left her flagship with her many friends beside her in support, her head held high.

Yet all the while, more and more, she felt this new, frightening power tugging at her as if it had a will all its own, stronger than even her own.

She felt it with every step.

What in the hell was this…this thing? It defied imagination.

*

Naero struggled to focus on what she was there to do. Onworld, they stepped into a late spring climate in a southern hemisphere transition zone from temperate to subtropical on the west coast of Nashara. The local sun was shining in an impossibly clear blue sky. Naero smelled a sea breeze wafting over the extensive coral reef system they had spotted offshore, on their way down.

The expanded Mystic camp and settlement appeared to be only a few months old, built next to a much smaller, older camp of pop-up nanohuts and actual tents. This older camp had the looks of having been on Thanor-4 for perhaps a few years. It had been used by the Mystic explorers and researches who first discovered the strange world and then flocked there to examine its even stranger Cosmic energy fields–and whatever this other thing was.

Intel Marines from the 7th Division–the Intel Division that worked closely with the Mystics–stood guard almost everywhere around the perimeter. 7th Division Spacer Marines were known both as *The Ghost Knives* and *The Seven Deaths*. Their motto was short and simple: *Fury in Battle.*

The camp itself looked to have a wide open circle in the center. As it spread out, each High Master had a separate camp set at three equally spaced points along the inner circle. The three camps radiated out into their own wide circles and represented all Three Wisdoms of the Spacer Mystic Harmony:

The Spacer Mystics were big on geometrics.

Naero spotted all three banners.

Chaos, beneath a red banner.
Order, beneath a blue banner.
Change, beneath a gold banner.

Jan sighed nervously as they drew closer to the entry point.

Naero reached out and took his hand. "It's going to be all right, Jan. We'll find a way to convince them to help us. Both of us."

He shuddered and shook his head, rubbing his arms. "I still feel like broken glass all inside, N. Those bastards messed with me and my head so much. I might not ever be the same. But what is this thing on this planet? It's freaking me out."

Naero sighed herself. "Try to ignore it, Jan. I feel it, too. Whatever happens to us, we are never the same, Jan. But with effort and hard work, we can choose to change for the better, and become what we want to be. I know your heart, my brother. I know you are strong and brave. This is the blood we come from. I swear to you–we shall both find our way."

Two young female adepts strode up to greet them at the entry checkpoint to the camp. The heavily armed Intel Marines stepped to either side. All Mystic adepts wore tight-fitting, gray spacer togs, with a hood and mask worn only for ritual combat and on missions during wartime or for Spacer Intel.

These young women were twins, only a hand taller than Naero, but still. Long black hair in high Spacer ponytails, almond shaped eyes, amber in hue and bright–light golden skin tones. Hard Spacer bodies, agile and athletic as one might expect among Mystic adepts, from their intense martial training. She could almost sense their skill and power.

Naero guessed somehow that they fought best as a pair.

They kept their oval faces impassive but not harsh. Naero actually thought them very pretty, and had a sense that she might like them. What a relief, after the nightmare she had had with Hashiko.

"Greetings. I am High Adept Chang Fu-han," the first one on Naero's right stated calmly–most likely the older of the two.

"And I am High Adept Chang Lijuan," the other said, in the same exact voice and tone.

Chang Fu-han continued. "We have been sent to bring High Adept Naero Amashin Maeris, adept candidate Janner Maeris Ramsey, Shalaen Kinmal of the Yattai, and the visitor known as Gaviok before our Mystic High Masters."

"With regret," Chang Lijuan said. "Only these four may proceed beyond this point and enter within the circles of Mystic Wisdom."

Chang Fu-han motioned with a strong, slender hand to her right. "Please, the rest of you in this party are welcome to wait for word from your companions within the Spacer Marine mess tent nearby. You will be well cared for as our honored guests."

"If you so desire," Chang Lijuan added, "you are free to return to your ship and await word there. It is quite possible that the deliberation of the High Masters may take up a good portion of this day."

Naero turned to her friends, and hugged Zhen, Tarim, Enel, Surina, Eugene, and several more of her crew who closed in around her to wish her well.

They all knew what was at stake.

Naero grinned. "Don't worry. We'll find a way to work everything out. We'll send word when we know anything definite."

Their people stepped back, watching and waiting for them to go out of sight. Naero smiled and waved one final time.

She hoped to see her people again.

She turned to Jan, Shalaen, and Gaviok. "The Mystics have protocols about speaking and being spoken to, which none of you are going to know. I don't even fully understand them all myself. So until you three are instructed in such things, it might be best to let me do most of the initial talking. Be polite and speak to others only when you are directly spoken to. Keep in mind that Chaos masters and adepts can be abrupt and even rude; be prepared for that. Most likely, they will ignore us, if we are lucky."

Jan and the other two nodded. Gaviok seemed entirely out of his element, but he had also insisted on coming along to speak with the High Masters, and especially the Chaos practitioners.

Chang Fu-han motioned again with one graceful hand. "Follow, please, honored guests." She and Chang Lijuan slipped to the port side and then went forward down a path lined with colorful cloth barriers rising up on either side. The twin adepts strode forward side by side with calm ease, leading them on with a careful pace that was neither too fast nor too slow.

"High Adept Naero," Chang Lijuan noted, turning her head back on her graceful neck while she kept walking. "It is clear that your people honor you with great love and respect. I was greatly pleased to witness such a clear demonstration of ardent affection and devotion."

Naero bowed her eyes slightly. "Thank you, High Adept Lijuan. You honor me and my people."

"Not every adept wishes to be your nemesis, High Adept Naero," Chang Fu-han added. "Just as all adepts do not desire to be your friend. Yet you served the Clans with great honor and distinction during both the Annexation War and the High Crusade. For those reasons alone, many adepts personally feel, very strongly, that you should be given a fair chance, despite whatever failings and inherent dangers you bring with you."

"Again, my thanks," Naero told the twins. "I am glad there are at least some with such reasoned views among the Mystics."

Naero still felt the definite pull of whatever strange force was present on Thanor-4.

In fact, whatever this thing was, it was like a pillar of Cosmic Fire shooting out from the planet. No one with any abilities could fail to notice something as glaring and obvious as that. Naero pinpointed it to within less than two klicks of the Mystic camp itself, and from what she could tell-

It is guarded by layers of shields and barriers, and most of a full, armored Marine regiment beyond that.

Thanks for the update, Om. It doesn't look like they want anyone getting near that damn thing, whatever it is. And probably with good reason. This thing should scare anyone.

13

At the entrance to what appeared to be a large, round, colorful tent, Naero spotted two old acquaintances: Adept Makita Lii and Adept Iselle Donovan. Naero had nearly killed them and Intel Admiral Klyne during her first Mystic testing, which had gone very wrong as well.

Naero and they weren't exactly friends, therefore, and they both paled and grew wide-eyed–in not a little fear–when they spotted her approach.

"Hold, summoned guests," High Adept Makita said. "Others are still arriving and taking their places. It may yet be a few minutes longer until we can bring you all in before the High Masters."

"Very well, High Adept," Chang Lijuan said.

"What others?" Naero asked quietly.

Iselle shot her a look. "They will give the word, once the High Masters and their guests are ready."

Chang Fu-han raised one eyebrow. "There is no need to be abrupt, High Adept Iselle. No need for...rudeness. None of us present are Chaos adepts."

"If I was rude, it was because of *her*, High Adept Fu-han. She did not address me properly with her question, and you know it."

"Forgive me my rudeness, High Adept Iselle."

"Neither are we, or have we ever been, on familiar terms, High Adept Naero Amashin Maeris. You will therefore address me as High Adept Iselle Donovan, if at all, to my liking."

Naero held her tongue. She had been in the wrong, and had nearly killed people with her out-of-control abilities. That they could hold a grudge against her could be quite understandable.

Finally, she chose to voice a general question over the continued silence. "Can anyone present please tell me more about this strange planet, Thanor-4?" she asked.

It might help pass the awkward silence they were stuck in. She could listen without the burden of having to speak, and she really wanted to know something about this bizarre world.

Lijuan and Fu-han brightened and took turns immediately, talking quietly. But they spoke informally to Naero and her people, on purpose.

"My older sister and I were part of the Mystic exploration team that arrived here nearly two years ago. What do you wish to know?"

"Lijuan and I have been to all five continents, many times. We've even been part of the contact teams that deal with the local near-humans. The barbaric tribes from the deep interior are barely sentient and cannot be reasoned with. But in the Bay of Thanarra, there are four main city states of near-humans, where all of the four continents join together. They are very backwards and violent–especially the Vaedo."

14

Fu-han projected a holoscreen from her wristcom above them. "The four continents bunched together are Thanarra, Vaedor, Kallos, and Maedor, each with their own city state and culture. But according to our laws, we do our best not to interfere with them or their ways."

"What is this isolated continent called again?" Naero asked.

"We call it Nashara, after a fabled land the natives speak of in their legends," Lijuan said. "But the native Thanes don't even know that it exists, yet–just as they don't know of the monsters on the eastern half of Maedor in the deep interior. Which makes Nashara perfect for Mystic purposes."

"And what purposes are those?" Naero asked.

High Adept Iselle Donovan jumped in, commenting in general for all to hear.

"Well, after all, with the untimely destruction and the loss of *Janosha*," Iselle said, with stinging emphasis, "the High Masters are considering Thanor-4 as a possible replacement. This world could become the new Mystic Homeworld for the Order of Chaos Wisdom and its adepts."

"Oh," Naero said. "Very well then." Things grew quiet again.

Om, you are quite certain that I had nothing to do with the destruction of Janosha?

Naero, I keep trying to explain to you. Planet Janosha was not in any way destroyed. Whether you had anything to do with its disappearance or not, it simply ceased to exist. The planet was not there any longer. There was no destruction. If there had been, there would have been some trace of it left behind, in the wake of such destruction.

That still doesn't make any sense, Om. No planet has ever just vanished before.

Then it is a mystery that shall remain unsolved for the time being. Ask Shalaen, and Alala, and even Baeven. They will all tell you the same thing. We simply do not know what happened. No one does–and that includes the High Mystics.

Collective ignorance did not re-assure Naero that she would not be blamed for the planet being gone. She had been out of control at the time, wielding Cosmic powers neither she nor anyone else could fathom or understand. To anyone's mind, she remained the obvious suspect.

Jan nudged her, and Naero almost jumped.

"N...Naero...sib, they want us to go in now."

She shook herself.

15

Mason Elliott

High Adept Chang Fu-han kept her slightly golden face and her amber eyes impassive. "Honored guests, the three High Masters of the Spacer Mystics and their guests will speak with you now. Please enter within."

The twins parted the entrance curtains for them to pass inside.

Naero lifted her head again, gave Jan's hand a squeeze, and strode forward to face her fate with courage.

3

The large tent above them had programmable plasteel panels to let sunlight shine down inside, if that was desired. Only a few were pweaked clear. The ground beneath their feet was still covered in a carpet of soft, blue-green grass and aromatic, sandy soil beneath that.

Three risers and three small, separate sets of stands had been erected directly before them, at the far end of the enclosure.

Naero wondered why they had not used fixer clouds to construct more permanent structures for the Mystics.

Perhaps the High Masters had not yet made the final decision to remain on Thanor-4 permanently.

Naero walked forward slowly, taking a good look ahead of her at the assembly.

She spotted High Master Vane, seated on her left, with about ten other high level Chaos adepts sitting behind him. But his two Prime adepts flanked him on either side as his bodyguards.

Most Prime adepts were selected in male-female pairs, for reasons Naero still did not understand.

In fact, Naero had rescued both of Vane's current Prime adepts from the torment of the enemy's vile, Darkforce generators, just as she had Hashiko, Jan, and Shalaen for that matter.

But Chaos adepts were not known for their tact or gratitude. This pair had only stooped to thank her briefly, over a short comlink. She was probably lucky to have gotten that much from them.

Zhii Kim was the male, the adept of darkness, so dark he appeared to be a black hole shaped like a person. His counterpart, Fel Wilde, was his exact opposite. The adept of light, she was so dazzling that she shimmered with a bright white light, even when she veiled her Cosmic powers so as not to blind people with her brilliant glare.

Naero did her best not to look at High Master Vane directly, at his glowing red head, covered in roving eyes—glowing and pulsing with crimson anger within his deep, dark gray hood.

Since the tragic loss of his most favored adept, Mitsubishi Hashiko, Naero knew that Vane blamed and despised her, and openly sought any excuse to destroy her. She knew very well that his vote was already set against her.

The events on Janosha had only fueled that fire of hatred, despite the fact that Naero had also saved him from being taken prisoner by their foes. Vane was not only vindictive, but he was also convinced that she was a Cosmic monster, from a family that spawned such monsters.

Naero nearly missed Intel Strategist General Thadian Ingersol, another ideological foe, seated among Vane's people with a few other, sour-looking military officers. How appropriate that some of her enemies should side together.

Next, in the center of the assembly, stood High Master Tree of Order Wisdom, in long, sweeping blue robes of many hues. If Vane's Cosmic aura was openly scarlet, Tree's Cosmic aura was silver-blue.

High Master Tree was tall, and his face defied any description of age. Stable, serene, secure, and calm, as one might expect in the High Master of Order. Yet to Naero, his piercing eyes flashed blazing blue at times.

She needed to remember that all of the Three Wisdoms of The Mystic Harmony could be very dangerous, each in their own way.

Strange. High Master Tree only had one Prime adept present as his bodyguard. Naero wondered where the other one was—the male.

The female looked familiar somehow. Perhaps Naero had seen her in a dream in the past. Naero did not know her name, but the tall, slender young woman pulsed with bright blue energy, not unlike Shalaen. Everything about the Prime adept seemed to be a shade of blue, so it was difficult to determine skin, hair, or eye color.

High Master Tree stepped back slightly, and Naero was stunned to see—in place of the Prime male adept on the left—Admirals Klyne and Sleak, her aunt, who was very pregnant by now, and due within the next few weeks.

It bothered Naero that even steel-hearted Aunt Sleak looked nervous, and smiled at her niece only slightly. The same number of Order adepts, about twelve, sat behind High Master Tree and his guests.

The last group on the left represented Change Wisdom. High Master Jo grinned and laughed and could not seem to stand still. He looked to be a boy of about ten years old. Small, slender, golden-haired, fair skinned, with glowing, golden eyes. Naked, except for what looked to be a clean white loincloth of some fashion.

It wasn't surprising that his Cosmic aura was bright, shimmering gold. He joked and poked fun at his guests, and the dozen High Change adepts behind him. Most of his followers were much like him, small, energetic, and jovial. They seemed quick to laugh and spoke back and forth almost incessantly.

High Master Jo's female and male Prime adepts flanked him on either side, keeping watch all around them. They were on duty as bodyguards, a fact that had hit very close to home since the well-coordinated enemy attacks on all three Spacer Mystic Homeworlds.

Attacks that had nearly succeeded.

The female Prime adept was named Tessa Fae, and she had mastered shifting. Her Spacer form was that of a dark brunette of medium height, with jet black skin and dark brown eyes. Yet even as she stood on guard, she casually shifted form from one dangerous creature back to her own form, and then on to the next: an enormous, Durian purple tigress; a huge, sinuous Zhimori shockpython; a powerful Gythanian rockhulk. She shifted forms without effort.

Naero had heard about her counterpart as well, the male named Den Kurtz. He did not seem to have what most would call an actual physical body. Naero spotted red-violet eyes flickering within a hazy, indeterminate form, a shapeless miasma or haze of Cosmic energy that was almost completely amorphous.

Even Om noted it.

That one is very close to becoming an energy being, Naero. He is as close to being such as possible, and yet still be said to possess a physical form.

Very fascinating. I wonder what his Cosmic abilities are, Om?

I'm guessing he can manipulate various states of matter and energy almost at will. That would make him a very formidable opponent. Yet, the fact that he still retains a physical form would still make him vulnerable, and to energy attacks as well. Every strength and advantage has an inherent weakness and disadvantage.

Naero noted three or four elders from the Clans seated on either side of High Master Jo, who seemed to be carrying on several conversations all at once. Naero did not recognize any of the elders.

More plasteel panels in the tent dome above them were pweaked clear to open wide. A bell somewhere behind the assembly rang out clearly, chiming slow; the same tone sounded three times.

Naero, Jan, Shalaen, and Gaviok found themselves ringed with a circle of light before the Three High Masters.

High Master Tree rose up and spoke first.

"High Adept Naero Amashin Maeris," he said sternly. "You stand before us with our many grave concerns about you and your Cosmic abilities. Who are these others with you, and why have they come?"

Naero bowed her gaze slightly. "I greatly appreciate being able speak my case before the High Masters. This is my younger brother, Janner Maeris Ramsey, and these other two are my friends and allies. They can also use Cosmic energy, and seek your counsel and wisdom, and they are here on my behalf as well."

"This is very irregular, High Adept Maeris. It is not up to you, in your situation, to bring witnesses or others to support your case. The deliberation of the Mystics is not for outsiders."

Naero shifted her feet slightly. "My apologies. Impudence was not my intent. Please hear me out. There are important reasons why I brought each of them with me. May I explain?"

She could tell Master Tree was about to adhere to the rules–whatever they were–and refuse.

Master Jo jumped in. "Please, my fellow High Masters. These matters are already incredibly irregular. You cannot deny that all of us sense something important about each of these others. Let us bend the rules this once, at least, and listen briefly as to why they have come. We may yet hear things of great interest to us and the Three Wisdoms."

Thank you, Naero said silently.

That gave Master Vane a chance to bluster. "Why are we even bothering with this at all? Adept Maeris is guilty of many crimes; she is a clear threat that needs to be-"

Master Tree clearly resisted the strong urge to roll his eyes. "Very well, we will hear these brief reasons. Please do not leap ahead of us, High

Master Vane. We have not even begun to discuss the issues at hand that we come to discuss, let alone reached a point where we can pass a fair and reasoned verdict on them. We know your opinions all too well by now. You have been badgering us with them for many days. You, too, will have your turn, and your say."

Tree turned back to Naero. "Speak, High Adept Maeris."

"High Masters, first let me say this: I agree that there are many serious problems involved with my not being able to control my Mystic abilities yet. That is exactly why I came to the Mystics for testing and help. And instead, I was forced to survive a long, brutal training period with the most difficult of the High Masters, taking the most difficult Mystic path, learning Chaos Wisdom first, with trainers who were clearly hostile to me and my efforts. They did everything to cause me to fail. And now, High Master Vane has made it very clear that he still wants to see me destroyed."

Silence.

"She has a point," Master Jo said.

"Oh, please," Master Vane said. "What whining drivel. Of course she's going to say all that."

Master Jo raised both hands and blinked. "Yet, excuse me. I thought we were going to hear from you about why these other three persons are with you? Please proceed with that."

"Excuse me, High Masters. I was getting to that next, after my introductory statement. My brother Jan needs to be tested and trained by the Mystics as well. He was just rescued from the enemy, and is showing definite signs of developing his own Cosmic abilities, similar to mine—and with similar…difficulties."

All three High Masters briefly sucked in a breath, and took careful note of that.

"Great," Master Vane said, "Another Maeris monster. Why should we be surprised that they keep spawning?"

Aunt Sleak cleared her throat, shot the Chaos Master her battle smile of steel, and rested both hands on her swollen stomach.

Vane could only snort and look away.

"Let her speak," Master Tree said.

"Also," Naero said. "I'm sure that Intel has informed you all about our dangerous, outcast brother Danner, Janner's twin whom the enemy is using to produce great quantities of Darkforce energy for them. If Jan learned to defend himself and his mind, Danner would not be able to take over Jan's mind and body again. And let me tell you, from experience: Danner has more powers and abilities than Jan

21

and I put together. Plus, he is completely insane and amoral, and he can also absorb the Cosmic and Psyonic abilities of others. What if the enemy turned him loose as a weapon?"

The High Masters considered all that she said.

"Regardless of what you may think about me and my situation, my brother is a loyal Spacer who has committed no crime, and done nothing wrong. He deserves your help. Once he has been fully healed and trained, he might even be able to help the Mystics and Spacer Intel track down his twin and our enemies. And, as soon as he recovers from his ordeal, I'm certain he will have vital intel and insights to offer concerning his experience with the Darkforce generators and the secrets of the enemy research labs."

High Master Tree looked at Jan. "Janner Maeris Ramsey. Do you wish to be tested by the Spacer Mystics?"

"I do. But with one condition. I have been tortured by our enemies for a long while, and I will still need some time yet to recover from that. But I also need to learn to defend my mind against our foes. I would appreciate the help of the Mystics."

Master Vane rose to his feet. "I would be happy to be the first to train this Maeris whelp, just as I have all the others."

"No!" Naero and Jan said together.

"Perhaps that is where we went wrong with them," Master Jo suggested.

"Perhaps," Master Tree said. "But with the outcast, he trained completely with both of us, in the other two Wisdoms, before he was sent to High Master Vane."

Vane grunted. "You two fools know very well what went wrong. You let the outcast interact with the alien artifact located on Janosha, thinking that we could control what happened thereafter."

"Do not speak of that," Master Tree said sternly.

Vane ignored him. "I told you it was folly, and it blew up in all of our faces. It nearly destroyed us all, and unleashed the first of these Maeris abominations on our universe! And now you are prepared to repeat that disaster all over again on this world."

"Ridiculous," Master Tree said. "We have taken every precaution."

Master Jo added, "We have no intention of repeating anything. And you had a direct hand in those past events as well. Do not deny it."

"I did nothing," Master Vane said.

"If only that were so," Master Jo said. "Yet you are notorious for getting both wrong. You act when you should do nothing, and do nothing when you should act."

"Both of you fools can bite me."

Master Tree turned back to Naero. "Very well, High Adept. If your brother is willing to join us, we will assist him in any way that we can. In honor of Clan Maeris, I will personally begin his journey with training in Order Wisdom. As soon as he is able, he can begin with me and my adepts."

Naero bowed her eyes slightly again. "My Clan and I thank you, High Master. I could not ask for more consideration."

"And I thank you," Janner said. Then he stepped back.

"Very well. And these other two? Clearly, neither of them are Spacers, yet they remain very intriguing."

"High Masters, this is Shalaen Kinmal, daughter of Mining Consortium leader Nevano Kinmal–and now a fully evolved Yattai."

All three took note of this important new revelation.

"How is this possible?" Master Tree said.

Master Jo sounded confused. "We thought she was only half-Yattai?"

Shalaen stepped forward, shoulder to shoulder with Naero. "Greetings, High Masters. May I speak?"

"Please do," Tree told her.

"Intel had informed me before, that the Spacer Mystics have been attempting to contact the Yattai, for more than three centuries. Since the Spacer Mystics were formed, they have done so without success."

"That is true," Master Jo said. "The Yattai keep to themselves, in their own alternate reality, a universe adjacent to our own. Yet they have ignored every attempt by us and other interdimensional entities to contact or interact with them in any way."

Shalaen nodded. "I am currently in your dimension, yet I also seek to make contact with my people. I want you to know that I could not have fully evolved into a complete Yattai without the assistance and insight of my good friend, Naero Maeris. I owe her my life. Without her, I would be working for your enemies as one of their slaves. What's more, you should also know that she has the power to transfer, quicken, and increase the Cosmic and psyonic abilities of others. Not only that, but she still carries within her the Kexxian Data Matrix, whatever Intel may think. Those two things alone I think, would make it necessary to dispense with these foolish designs to eliminate her. As I've said, Naero and I are very good friends, and she is an honorable person who seeks to serve her people well. If any harm would come to her by the Mystics, then I and my people–once I contact them–would be greatly alarmed and offended."

"Is that a threat from the Yattai, or just yourself?" Master Vane asked.

Shalaen smiled sweetly. "Consider it a promise…from both. You are the ones who desire contact with us—not us with you."

Master Tree held her eye. "Shalaen Kinmal, you and your father are our honored allies. You are here only as our guest. We are happy to work with you in any capacity, but any issues between the Mystics and High Adept Maeris will be resolved without your assistance or interference. We ask you to respect us and our ways."

"I intend to, as long as they do not harm one who is as a sister to me."

Master Tree finally looked to Gaviok. "And who is this being, where has he come from, and why is he here?"

Master Jo looked extremely interested and intrigued. "I do not recognize his species of insectoid as any of the cataloged sentients that we have yet encountered."

Even Master Vane spoke up. "This creature's Chaos energies are nearly limitless. They rival my own. I insist that we must study him and his kind thoroughly. I've never seen anything like him!"

Naero ignored Vane. "This is my good friend and ally, Gaviok. He and his people are from the Unknown Regions of the Gamma Quadrant. They can use Cosmic power, mostly in the form of raw Chaos energy. We could learn much from them and the other races that they know. And they also happen to be the enemies of our current enemies, and might be willing to join our Alliance of free sentients, united against such threats."

Master Tree looked very pleased, so did Master Jo, both of them very eager. Even Master Vane looked enthralled. An entire race of Chaos Wisdom sentients? Vane could hardly control himself.

"Honored guest," Master Tree said. "We look forward to getting to know you better, and establishing good relations between us and our peoples, for our mutual benefit."

Gaviok bowed low and spoke with distinction. "As do I. I have great respect for Spacers and their allies. They are honorable people, and we all face terrible foes who mean us all great harm. That is clear. I want nothing but good will and the highest cooperation between my people, our allies, and you and yours."

"Splendid!" Master Jo said.

Gaviok suddenly swelled up with Chaos energy until he towered fifteen meters above them all.

Everyone was startled, and his voice boomed.

"Yet, let me say this. Naero is not only my friend and ally. She is, as you would say, my Clan—my family. As if we came from the same nest. I would defend her with my own life, and so would the many *zillions* of my species–against any threat. If any harm would ever come to her, we would consider it a very serious matter, indeed–akin to an *act of war*–against our race and our allies."

Gaviok had his say. He shrank back down to his regular size, shorter than Naero.

"And that is not a mere promise," he added. "Consider it a direct and very real threat."

High Master Tree clasped his hands calmly in front of himself and spoke with steady ease. "New friend and ally, Gaviok. We too wish for nothing but good will between us and any other sentients. Let us work together to resolve any troubling issues. But I repeat, the ways of the Spacer Mystics must remain our own, and will not be interfered with by outsiders, no matter who they are. Any who wish to be our allies and friends must accept and honor that."

"Then let us seek honor, wisdom, and cooperation together, as sentients of good will should do. Yet my words stand, High Masters."

Gaviok stepped back and spoke no more.

Tree finally turned to Naero. "It appears that you bring us both opportunities and further dilemmas and complications to deal with, High Adept Maeris. Will it always be thus with you?"

"Forgive me, High Masters," she said. "It seems as if my life…has never taken easy and uncomplicated paths. But I always mean well. I always strive to do my best, and what is best for my people, whom I love more than my life itself."

Vane simply snorted in derision.

"Well spoken," Master Jo said. "But do you really mean that, Naero Amashin Maeris? Would you stake your life upon it?"

Naero raised her chin. "High Masters, I thought that I had clearly done so, long ago. And is that not why I have been summoned here before you all? To decide my fate, after all that has happened?"

"High Adept Maeris," Master Tree said. "I look at you, and I foresee full measures of the greatest dangers and catastrophes, equally combined with the chances for amazing breakthroughs and stunning illuminations. I am at a loss–to either study you intensely, or to side with Master Vane, and eliminate the many threats you pose once and for all. My mind and heart are greatly and deeply torn. And I fear that either course of action could be a very grave mistake."

Master Jo jumped in. "Naero. What is it that you wish?"

She lowered her eyes for a moment. Then she turned to her companions. "Jan, Shalaen, Gaviok. I love you all, and would give my life for you. Now, in your love for me, I want you all to promise me–

25

however this turns out—it is my choice. I am filled with energies and powers I may not ever be able to control. If I am driven mad by them, or become a danger to others, or lose control beyond all hope—I want the High Masters and Intel to end my life and destroy me."

She touched each of them with both hands.

"I want to remain who I am, who I wish to be, in control of my faculties and abilities. If I should become a monster, as some fear. If I turn on those whom I love, with destruction and death—I could not bear that. If I become such a threat, I want that threat to be eliminated, even if that means I must be killed. Promise me, on your highest honors, that you would not oppose or seek to hold it against others, even after my passing. Promise me. Please. I beg of you."

She put her arms around her little brother. Jan sobbed. "I swear it, sib. And that all goes for me as well!" he exclaimed.

She hugged Shalaen next, who said, "Naero, my sister, you have my word."

Finally she put her arms around Gaviok and held the mighty warrior's head to her breast. She knew that the mantid could both smell and sense emotions—he knew her love and respect for him.

Gaviok turned pale pink in color—nearly white. Naero had never seen him take on such a hue. "My word is yours, Naero. You know what that means."

"I do—it is adamant. It is unbreakable—and you honor me greatly, *abani*."

"I thought I knew what honor was…until I met you, Naero."

Naero hugged him again, and placed a kiss on his insectoid brow.

Gaviok went pure white in her arms.

Naero turned back to the High Masters and strode forward before them, neither cowed nor defiant.

"You ask me what I wish. I want to remain myself—who I am—who I am meant to be. I wish to learn how to control these terrible powers within me, and use them all for the good of my people. Please, I beg of you, help me…please help me. I fully comprehend the dangers that lurk within me. I fight them each and every day with all that I am, and even I fear, too often, that will not be enough."

Master Jo stared down at her. "We can only promise you an extremely difficult path to trod, Naero Amashin Maeris. With no guarantee of success."

"So be it."

Master Tree folded his arms behind himself. "We shall take these burdens on together and explore them in great detail," he told her. "Be warned. We shall test you and your powers to every limit, to every breaking point. But you must tell us all that we ask of you, and obey us, even when it does not make sense to you. Can you do all of these things?"

"I will."

Tree turned to Vane. "The decision must be unanimous, High Master of Chaos Wisdom. And you have been strangely silent. What say you?"

Vane remained seated, and spoke calmly from under his hood.

"You both know I think this to be a grave mistake, and why. Yet I am prepared to prove it to you, once and for all. Go thy way, therefore. Waste your time on this creature, for it shall profit you little. You are on fire already and refuse to see that you are already burning. Your wasted curiosity and good will and opinions are irrelevant, and will mean nothing in the end. I shall bide my time, and when it is vital for me to act for the good of all, I will do so. And no hand shall prevent me. It will not take long for me to be proven right. I have spoken."

High Master Tree turned back to Naero. "Find your way among the adepts of my Order," he told her. "You and your brother shall be under my hand directly, but you will each be handled separately. You brother will be examined, healed if possible, and prepared for his own path of testing and training. Later today, Master Jo and I will have many questions for you to answer in great detail. And then, upon the morrow, your intense training shall begin, in every way that we can devise. Do you accept these terms and these challenges?"

Naero bowed her eyes. "I do, High Masters."

"With the severity of your training, you will also be given time to relax and heal, if need be. Your family and friends are welcome to come and go, and visit you as it is possible, according to our laws. If some of them wish to stay, a place will be made for them, nearby. You will need their support—greatly, I fear. We would not deny you that."

"Thank you," Naero said.

"Then, for now, I release you to get settled and prepare yourself, High Adept. Go your way, with your brother and your friends."

"Thank you, High Masters," Naero said. "Thank you all for giving me this chance."

Master Vane grunted in disgust.

27

4

The Thanoran sky above them was partly cloudy the next morning and presaged rain coming in from off the ocean. The sun struggled to shine down.

The Mystics had set up a sparring arena nearby, carved into the top of a low green hill. It measured nearly three kilometers in diameter, and was filled with a variety of terrain features, from grass, to rocky outcroppings, to sand, brush, and dense trees of several amazing varieties. There was even a small lake, deep feeder streams coming down from the nearby mountains, a small waterfall, and what would become a tributary to the nearest, large river basin, emptying out into an even larger, salt marsh river delta out to the coastal sea.

Naero had spoken with High Masters Tree and Jo long into the night before. They grilled her with every question they could think of concerning her powers and abilities, and to what degree she could use or control each of them.

They spoke with great length about the events on Janosha, and what she thought had happened to the planet.

As Om himself said, no one knew exactly or understood what had happened.

They reserved grilling her on her Dark Beast for another entire evening, and told her as much.

She met twelve Order adepts on the practice field right at dawn as she was instructed, under the watchful eye of Prime adept Von Ramirez, the blazing blue adept with the intense, Cosmic energy aura.

All twelve of the other High Adepts welcomed her with what she guessed to be an attempt at a sound thrashing.

They set upon her all together, without warning.

Naero used every ounce of skill and power that she possessed, and gave a good account of herself, even punishing them when and where she could. But even after extensively training with Baeven, it was still like fighting a dozen Hashikos all at once.

Each of the adepts had their own styles, combinations, and methods of fighting to deal with.

They came at her from all sides, and battered and kicked her around the sparring arena. Naero did her best to get away and separate some of them, but they continued to close in on her time and time again and pummel her.

Four or five of them at most, she might have been able to handle.

But twelve High Adepts all at once were simply too much–too overwhelming. In less than an hour of such intense sparring and chasing, she was already battered and exhausted.

"Hold," Prime adept Von finally called, having watched the lopsided contest intensely all the while.

The twins, Changs Fu-han and Lijuan, stopped kicking Naero and immediately helped her up, offering her their hands in the warrior's grip, all the way up to the elbow, as their steel forearms solidly locked and embraced.

"You are a formidable opponent, adept-Naero," Fu-han said, wiping the blood and dirt from her nose.

Lijuan smiled, rubbing her badly bruised neck from one of Naero's spinkicks. "They told us what a fighter you are, but we never expected anything like this. Welcome, to a place of honor among the Order adepts."

The other ten closed in eagerly, all good-hearted smiles, readily offering Naero their names and arms to shake.

Except for the twins, they all seemed to be in male-female pairs:

Raymon Cherokee and Miisha Aztec

Allon Nelson and Dojen Kothari
Rinaldo James and Karabella Vaughn
Jaedar Ahmed and Huan Lii
Sean Walker and Heron Alexander

"Do you always fall upon the new adepts with such a welcome?" Naero asked.

They grinned. "Such an initiation for a new adept is customary for all of the Three Orders when we train," adept Heron added.

Adept Raymon laughed. "Remember that when you train with the Change adepts tomorrow, and the Chaos adepts the next day. They all say they have big plans for you."

"I just bet they do." Naero could feel herself pale slightly. "Something to look forward to at least," she muttered.

Adept Jaedar put his hand briefly on her shoulder. "You should feel proud, adept Naero. Most adepts are forced to submit within the first five to ten minutes of the initiation–at best."

Adept Huan agreed emphatically. "Only one other adept lasted longer that you. He endured the initiation for well over an hour before he chose to submit."

"And who in the heck was that?" Naero asked. "One of you guys?"

Von Ramirez shook her head proudly. "He is my counterpart and the other Prime adept of Order Wisdom, but we shall not speak his name for now. He is currently on a far-off, secret mission for the Intel and the High Masters. And Mystic customs say that it is bad luck to speak adepts' names while they are on such a mission or at war. Hopefully, he shall return to us. And when he does, then you shall behold the Champion of all the Orders. He has advanced far beyond any of us, at great cost to himself, and knows no rival or equal upon the sparring field. Then you shall meet a true warrior, one who has surpassed us all."

Suddenly the three High Masters stood above them, looking down.

Von led the Order adepts and Naero to bow their eyes slightly, in respect for the High Masters.

Master Vane spoke first. "Well, Maeris. Why did you allow these others to beat on you like that? Why not just flip out, like you did on Janosha? You could have easily unleashed your monstrous side and crushed them all."

"You would like that, wouldn't you, High Master Vane?" Naero said. "We were just sparring here. There was no need to take such terrible risks. There wasn't a High Master that needed to be rescued."

Vane only sneered back at her.

"We have heard much about this vaunted Darkforce creature lurking within you, adept Maeris," Master Jo said.

The three High Masters positioned themselves all around her suddenly equidistant and the other adepts instinctively drew back.

High Master Tree looked at her sternly.

"Unleash this creature. We wish to see it firsthand and study it for ourselves. Unleash it. I command you to do so. Do it...now."

Terrified, Naero tried to pull away, but they were all around her.

"You don't know what you are asking me to do. Like I've told you, I can't control it, and it would have access to all of my energies and powers, and more beyond that. It will feed off this strange planet and everything on it. Everything, don't you understand? If I do so...I might not be able to regain control of it again. It could kill everyone, and then keep going–until someone or something stops it."

Master Vane smiled slightly. "Indeed."

"Do as we bid, adept!" Master Tree shouted. "You promised to obey our commands."

Even High Master Jo yelled at her. "Do it!"

Their three auras flared until they became pillars of scarlet, azure, and golden flame surrounding her, threatening to incinerate her with their raw might.

They each held both hands out against her.

"Very well," Naero told them. "It is you who demand that I do this thing. I will not be held responsible for whatever happens."

Naero spread her stance and clenched both fists, closing her eyes.

Somehow, she felt strange, as if there were great pressure or gravity, like that of several atmospheres, crushing down on her. And it seemed that even within her own mind, she was cut off from Om within her.

Perhaps she could find a way to unleash just a portion of her Dark Beast–the way Baeven could–so that she could show them–warn them how dangerous it could be.

Yet she had not even learned to do that much.

The instant she even considered unleashing the Darkforce creature trapped within her, it flung itself with all its weight and fierce might against the fickle barriers she had set up inside her.

Its raving, rampant lust for power and destruction shook Naero to her very core, as it always did.

And though it warred against every sane thought in her being, Naero did as she was commanded, and turned the vile thing within her loose.

31

She wrestled with it instantly, trying to regain control of its madness—madness that rushed and swept through her body and soul.

The ground withered and split beneath her very feet as her Dark Beast tried to tap into the direct energies of the planet.

Something blocked it from being able to do so.

Next, it sensed the strange, alien artifact nearby–the obelisk or whatever the hell it was. Naero saw the thing clearly for the first time in her mind, but it seemed to shift and change form in her vision, all the while calling to both her and her Dark Beast with its own fierce, seductive call.

The thing was like a statue at first, then a Cosmic flame, then it boiled and shifted. Then the vision and all sense of the artifact completely winked out, cut off as well. But how? What was doing all of this? Via what power?

Just as Naero's Dark Beast triumphantly seized control of her flesh to fall upon all that stood nearby in fury–Naero found that neither she nor her Dark Beast could actually move. Something kept them both frozen in place, as if they were locked where they stood.

Her Dark Beast snarled and howled in frustrated defiance, roaring up through her throat. Naero fought with all her might, trying to ram and tamp the thing back down inside of herself, compacting and pressing it. She tried to force it back into its hiding place.

Yet the more force and violence she applied, the stronger it seemed to grow, even though it was stopped now by the frozen prison of their body.

Finally, seeing no way to actually unleash its will, it exhausted itself and withdrew on its own, falling back in angry despair, slinking back into its dark hiding place, biding its time until it could truly break free once again.

It did not even bother trying to comprehend whatever had thwarted its efforts this time.

Naero gasped suddenly, realizing that she was even having trouble drawing breath.

She clamped her own barriers back down on her Dark Beast, as it slunk and slumbered inside of her.

Then she toppled down onto the shattered crater all about her, almost completely spent. She thought she might black out, and the sky above seemed to darken and spin.

High Master Tree touched Naero, and she could finally breathe properly at last, and weakly twitch.

"What…what did you do to me?" Naero asked.

Master Tree attempted to explain. "We used the power of all three Wisdoms and the ultimate Cosmic energy of the combined Harmony to suppress the Darkforce creature inside of you, and immobilize it."

"Even with all three of us focusing all of our energies," Master Vane said, "we were barely able to do that much…this time. Tell me. What do we do as she continues to grow even stronger and ever more powerful? Eventually, she will surpass even us–all three of us combined. What then?"

"Don't tell her that," Master Jo protested. "You will only give her Darkforce side hope. What she knows, it will know also. And now–thanks to you–it will know that such may be eventually possible. Each time we attempt to wrest control of it or study it further, the thing will struggle even harder to break free!"

"Oops," Master Vane said. "Fools. As if it will not have enough raw cunning to figure out all of that on its own."

"Be that as it may," Master Tree said. "We have finally gotten a good look at it up close, and we know that we can suppress its emergence–at least for the time being. We have also gained many valuable insights and perceived its energy flows and bindings, and how it attempts to use them all. We saw how it tried to feed on any energy flow available. We can contemplate all of this, and study the thing further, adding to our knowledge base. It has weaknesses that can be exploited; it is not all powerful."

Naero was still having trouble getting back to her feet.

The three High Masters ignored her and walked away, still heavily debating and arguing everything they had just witnessed and observed.

Von looked over Naero and placed a hand on her. "I think that's about enough for her first day; the High Masters did her in with all of that. She's completely drained for now, but they'll still want to grill her more tonight. And–of course–the Change adepts can't wait to have their fun with her tomorrow."

The Prime adept motioned to two others. "Allon, Dojen, take Naero back to her quarters and put her to rest. Then catch up to us by the sea cliffs north of here for our daily Cosmic energy meditations and drills."

Naero was still dizzy when Dojen and Allon hoisted her up and carried her back to her own quarters, nothing more than a small, pop-up nanocabin, the same type that were commonly used for impromptu shore leaves–easy set up and take down.

The pair of Order adepts were gentle and considerate. They made sure she had lix paks and food ration bars handy, and tucked her into her small nanobed in her cool, darkened cabin. But as soon as they

33

had her comfortable and settled, they told her goodbye and promptly went back out to return to their own regimens and duties.

She wished she had Jett, but Naero drank a standard lix pak and then drifted off.

At some point she started dreaming, and in the haze of her dreams, she saw herself naked and floating helplessly, spinning around, perhaps in the Astral Plane?

Then she saw the strange alien obelisk again, the artifact that somehow defied description. It seemed to be drawing her in toward it like a magnet. Then she even accelerated, racing toward the thing through the sky at impossible, hypersonic speed, as if from thousands of kilometers away. If she slammed into it at this velocity, she'd be impaled upon it.

Or worse.

She got the sense that it would explode, in a detonation unlike any that had ever been witnessed. But she could not prevent herself from being drawn toward it. And anything this powerful was like the most addictive substance in the universe to Naero and her mind. She craved and hungered for power just like this, deep within herself.

Somehow, she knew she couldn't allow herself to touch the artifact—not even in a dream, or on the Astral Plane, or wherever the hell she was.

She forced herself awake in sudden terror.

Naero snapped up in her small nanobed, sweating and gasping, just before impact.

Whatever the hell this damn thing was, it was very scary—powerful scary.

It had a will of its own, and it was somehow starting to focus more and more directly on her.

And Naero had no idea why, or how it was able to do so.

Not good. Not good at all.

5

The High Masters kept her up late again, asking her questions until her head was whirling like a spinning top. Naero told them everything she could explain about her Dark Beast, and her perceptions of Cosmic Energy, Chaos energy, and Darkforce energy.

Naero feigned exhaustion and begged off to go rest some more.

But, actually, she wasn't that tired at all, not after resting and recovering most of the day before.

Naero stayed up all that night, preparing the sparring arena for her session with the Change adepts the next day.

She showed at the appointed time. Iselle and Makita introduced the others–also in female-male pairs:

Oshara Wallace and Timan Ramsey–distant cousins!
Ilura Romanov and Danikan Konrad
Perra Valmont and Hanta Cheyenne
Linden Apache and Symon Patton
Zelana Bucci and Vaeshen Taylor

Master Jo's Prime adepts, Tess and Den, watched over the session.

Iselle smiled happily, almost eagerly. "Makita and I have been waiting for this day, Naero. Now that we're all friends, here—are you ready for your initiation match?"

Om...we ready?

Yep.

Naero smiled back at her new friends. "Are you?" Naero looked around. "All of you?" She transported and cloaked, just as they swarmed at her.

Immediately, thousands of Naero holoclones appeared, moving and babbling all over the sparring arena. The general murmur grew maddening.

"Stay together, and locate her. Now." Makita commanded. "She's just using basic tricks; she still can't defeat all twelve of us. Maybe five or six—but not a full dozen."

Naero went after her distant cousins first.

A remote Chaos energy construct erupted beneath the feet of Oshara Wallace, ensnaring her in hundreds of stinging, stun-energy tendrils and yanking her fifteen meters underground.

She disappeared, screaming and struggling.

Timan Ramsey attempted to pursue, and endured several shock charges that left him convulsing on the ground. Iselle checked him and turned to Makita.

"He's going to be out of action for at least several minutes to an hour."

Makita nodded. "Maeris is a worthy opponent; she's an experienced warrior as well as being a strategy savant. I'm guessing she's layered the sparring field with her various traps and surprises. Stay together. Be careful. Sense and scan for any energy signatures. Remember, she has only fully trained in Chaos Wisdom and energy—not Order or Change. Those are two major weaknesses. The rest of us have fully trained in all three."

As they proceeded with their search, a huge amoeba of Chaos energy sucked Makita down into it and tried to pull him underground, as well.

Nine Change adepts attacked with shimmering, blazing, golden energy attacks.

The Chaos amoeba winked out.

Every one of those nine attacks struck Makita, and took out their leader...by their own hands.

"She's toying with us!" Iselle said.

"Put Mak with Tim. They're just stunned. They'll come to...eventually, and find us."

Ilura looked back the way they came. "Tim's body's gone. He's gone, just like Osha. She's taken them somewhere."

Danikan Konrad stated the obvious. "She's taking us out, one by one. We have to locate her, and end this charade."

"Maybe we should split up-"

Iselle rolled her eyes. "No, Perra. That's exactly what she wants us to do—divide our numbers even further. Everyone in close, and listen up." For a few moments they whispered together and argued a bit more.

"What do we do with Mak?" Perra finally asked.

"He's no good to us now," Iselle said. "Leave him behind. Let's move out—just like we planned."

All nine of them cloaked, without warning, disappearing from view.

Several minutes passed.

A slight shimmering in the air swept over Makita's still form.

Then he vanished as well.

Several attacks struck that precise area, as the other nine Change adepts closed back in.

"Dammit!" Iselle said. "She must have transported, and taken Mak with her."

"Translocation uses a lot of energy," Ilura noted. "Even if she taps into the planet's flows, she drains herself a great deal every time she does so—especially when carrying someone else with her."

Danikan chuckled. "She can wait and re-charge. She's playing a stealth game. She won't attack us directly; there are still nine of us. She'll just keep trying to pick us off one at a time. Isn't that clear by now?"

"We have to find her. Everyone. Use every gift and ability you have, and locate her. Now. We take the fight directly to her."

Hundreds of wire-like Chaos filaments shot up from the ground and speared through Danikan. He gasped as the shock-charges disrupted his faculties and dropped him.

Naero appeared, balancing seventy meters up on top of a high tree. She used *the voice*.

"YOU GUYS LOOKING FOR ME?"

"Is it another holo?" Iselle asked.

"No," Ilura said. "It's really her."

"Attack!"

37

Naero laughed at them, encasing herself in a large Chaos mek. She rose up into the air, smacking one large fist into her other hand. "Bring it, morons."

She unleashed a torrent of Chaos energy blasts and scarlet lightning bolts straight at them.

The remaining eight Change adepts flashed into attack mode, weaving their way through to pounce on the mek, taking it apart and draining it in seconds. Energies flashed and several explosions detonated as they took the construct down.

It dissolved and faded.

Iselle looked around. "Where is she, Ilura? Where's Maeris? Don't let her escape!"

Then Iselle looked around for Ilura.

Then she looked back for Danikan's stunned body.

Nothing.

They were down to seven.

For the next half a standard hour, the remaining Change adepts proceeded with their search throughout the sparring arena. With each trap they triggered, they grew jumpier, more paranoid. They began snapping at each other more and more.

Hanta Cheyenne had to take a leak. They hadn't expected the initiation battle to last so long.

Six of them formed a protective circle around him as he did his business. They weren't taking any chances.

Naero–the real one–appeared among her holos, here and there. She taunted and teased them, luring them into further traps, drawing them into the deep woods.

Iselle turned to Hanta…three minutes later, just as *his* holo winked out.

They raced back to the sounds of a brief struggle behind them.

"Crap!" Iselle said. "She figured it out."

Now they were six.

A swarm of hundreds of glowing red Chaos hornets–each the size of a fist–exploded out of the tree canopy and swarmed on them, buzzing and droning.

The six adepts attempted to stand their ground, using wave attacks and shield waves to take out many of the bugs.

Yet dozens snuck in to sting them and explode with stunning energy attacks as they burst and released their power on contact through their painful stingers and jaws.

Perra shrieked and passed out, twitching, covered with bursting Chaos bugs zapping her.

Linden Apache led them to the nearby lake. They leaped into the deep water to escape. The remaining Chaos insect swarm disrupted on the lake's surface.

Iselle, Symon, Zelana, and Vaeshen swam to shore or rose up out of the lake.

Linden did not.

Perra's body had already vanished behind them.

They were down to four.

A number Naero could deal with.

She charged into them directly.

A scarlet beam from her third eye punched into Symon Patton and drove him back through several splintering trees.

A sonic blast from her screaming mouth sent Iselle skipping and bouncing across the surface of the lake before she could use her formidable telekinetic abilities.

Zelana and Vaeshen engaged her up close, energized punches, strikes, and kicks. Naero wheeled and fought as the three of them became a blur of punches, elbows, knees, and kick combinations.

She broke through Vaeshen's defenses and staggered him with a hurricane of whirling, whipping kicks, driving and battering him among the large rocky outcroppings nearby, deflecting or enduring Zelana's attacks. Rock and stone splintered and shattered, a cloud of dust choked and obscured the air around them.

Vaeshen went down hard, but he still went down.

Zelana shot up into the air and blasted the dust cloud with ranged energy attacks—golden bolts and blasts of golden Cosmic energy. She waited intently, scanning the area with her heightened senses, waiting for anything to move or show itself.

When the dust cleared, Vaeshen was gone.

In midair, Naero suddenly grappled with Zelana from behind.

Then Naero…exploded.

Zelana crashed into the ground, smoking and unconscious.

When Iselle crawled out of the lake again, Naero stepped up to the water's edge, a ball of scarlet Chaos lightning around her other raised hand.

She offered Iselle her free hand, all three of Naero's eyes glowing with blood-red Chaos energy.

"Are we done here, Iselle?"

Iselle bit her lip and nodded. "For now." She took Naero's hand, and rose up out of the water.

"Let's collect the others," Naero said. "I just had them tied up and stunned. Some of them are probably getting free on their own by now."

Ten minutes later, they had everyone gathered together again by the waterfall. Naero dragged up a netbag from the ice-cold stream, filled with borbbles of Jett and pods of juicy Spum, just waiting to be cracked open. She made sure to bring enough for all.

A few moments later, they were slugging down Jett and gorging themselves on the only blue mystery meat, gobbling it down in chunky bites, with the sweet, tangy blue sauce running over their sticky fingers.

They laughed and joked. Even somber Makita and snooty Iselle found some humor in their current situation. Everyone loosened up. Tess and Den even ceased observing and joined them.

"We'll have a real sparring session next time," Makita said.

"And not just a dog pile beat down at my expense," Naero added.

Iselle grinned. "You're going to have to take on all of us at some point," she said.

"And the word going around," Hanta noted, "is that the Chaos adepts have something very special of their own planned for you tomorrow, Maeris."

"Hmm…that is a concern."

"You're tricky enough on your own," Den said, absorbing another borbble of Jett and a pod of Spum. His shapeless form spit out the empty containers seconds later. "Hey, this junk food stuff is pretty good."

Naero smiled pleasantly, with her hands on her hips.

"I think we still have some time. Anyone like to work with knives or blades?"

6

Rain came in off the ocean again for a few hours. Naero listened to its gentle patter and spray while she rested, then went off after lunch with the Change adepts.

She had been up all night. After what turned out to be a long nap in the afternoon, she felt more than ready for another pick-her-brain-clean session with the High Masters that evening.

Naero had some questions for them this time. It couldn't remain a one-way street. More could be learned from an actual conversation or debate—not just an interrogation.

Every evening after sunset—somewhere between the ninth and tenth hour—the High Masters held their late evening dinner, by themselves, or with all or some of the adepts from all Three Orders. Whoever wanted to show up, showed up, including any guests that were on hand.

She was dying to know how Jan was doing. Naero thought about her friends and even Admirals Sleak and Klyne. Were they all still here, waiting to see her when she could?

Officially, she would not be given time to relax or go visit with anyone outside of the Orders until the end of the first week, and the end of each week thereafter.

From what the other adepts told her, they all worked and practiced hard six out of the seven days each week. Each day, Naero would train rigorously with one of the orders, and its High Master–Order, Change, Chaos–then repeat. Two full cycles each week. Each seventh day was a free day, where the adepts were off duty to do as they pleased.

Some adepts took it easy. Some went off on their own, wherever they wished, and others met in secret and kept training or sharing knowledge between the Orders.

Naero even got the very strong sense that there was some definite romance going on between several of the adepts–both within and outside of the pairings, and among the Three Orders as well. How interesting.

The High Mystic adepts were all consenting adults, of course–but the unspoken rule was that personal affairs and relationships were to be kept strictly private, and secondary–if not tertiary–to one's training. They could never to be allowed to interfere with the missions of the Mystics and the High Masters of the Three Orders, in any way.

If the Masters were forced to step in and comment on or take a hand in adept private matters, such an act would result in a severe loss of face for both parties.

All adepts were strongly advised about this by the Orders as a whole. They were fully expected to maintain their private lives quietly on their own.

The High Masters took their meal together every evening around the same time, and usually argued and debated something vigorously long into the night, until the early bells of the morning.

The late supper itself was usually prepared and served in large quantities, most likely by an Intel chef or one from the attached Marines. Each night was a banquet style meal for anywhere from three to sixty persons. Anyone not attending dinner was expected to make that known to the mess hall staff, in order for the proper planning to be made.

The fare was excellent and varied each day, according to a menu approved in advance by the High Masters. There was usually plenty and to spare. Naero wasn't that picky, and never went hungry. Adepts always had their own private stores of snacks and instant meals in their quarters, if they missed a meal or needed to snack on something.

Tonight they had a poultry, pasta, and veggie dish with a rich, creamy white sauce that was spiced perfectly and incredibly tasty. Dessert was some kind of tangy, orange berries and cream on a delicious sponge cake.

Naero was always pleased that she could have as much Jett as she could chug down. She never got tired of her fave.

Once she was finished eating, she watched and waited until the High Masters finished their desserts. Vane, in fact, had three huge helpings, the hog. She had never seen him eat before. He could be quite the glutton.

Naero went over to them all and did her best to direct the discussion for that evening from the very start.

"Good evening, High Masters."

"Maeris," Vane sneered at her, with a scowl.

"High Adept," Tree said calmly, with a slight bow of his head.

"Naero!" Jo exclaimed with excitement.

"I want to speak with you at length about something that continues to trouble me greatly. No one has yet to make mention of it."

All three of the High Masters stopped and looked straight at her, as if expecting something important.

"I think you know what I'm going to bring up. If I can sense it, I know all of you can. What is this frightening Cosmic power source on Thanor-4? It seems to have a will of its own, and it has been calling to me ever since I arrived. I've even started to see it in my nightmares. What is it, and what does it want with me?"

High Master Vane started laughing. "Ah, yes. And so the end begins once again. Did I not tell you that she would be drawn to it, and it to her? We stand even more upon the brink of total and complete disaster than ever before–just like we did years ago, back on Janosha. And, I might add, with another member of the accursed Maeris family! How fitting."

Master Tree spoke calmly. "High Master Vane, you always say too much when you should be silent, and not enough when you should tell all."

Vane laughed again. "Again–bite me, you pompous windbag. You know very well where this is heading. We've seen it all play out before. Do we repeat our mistakes yet again? That is the grossest folly and stupidity."

"We know much more now than we did back then," Tree said. "We have taken every possible precaution, and now we will be doubly vigilant. Our mistakes of the past shall not be repeated."

"Perhaps not in the same way," Vane added. "But your assurances have failed before."

"No plan is perfect," Master Jo said. "Nothing is ever certain except change, and we cannot always foresee or guide the direction of that change. If the universe wants its way, it shall have it, no matter what we do."

"We cannot speak of these things yet," Master Tree said. "It is only her third day among us. There is still so much for her to learn, and so much for us to learn about her. Now there is the brother to worry about as well...he does indeed show definitive signs of sharing...the same condition particular to their direct bloodline. And there is the additional concern of the missing brother–the insane one being used by our enemies."

"We should not withhold information from her," Master Jo protested. "Informing her fully may help her understand the situation better, and give her a better chance to her defend herself."

Tree shook his head slowly. "I disagree. Overwhelming her with too much information, at a difficult time such as this, might make her even more vulnerable to the artifact's considerable power–which even we do not fully understand. We should not speak of it, and she should not even think about it. The more she does so, the more it will imprint itself more strongly in her mind, until she cannot resist dwelling on it. Once she fixates on it, she will be lost."

Vane continued to laugh. "You two both think that you can prevent what is clearly going to happen in the end. And I will be there, ready and waiting to act. To do what we should have done from the very beginning. But no. You two idiots think that you can find a way to use Maeris for your own purposes, like a toy, a tool, or a your own private weapon of some kind. Wait until she turns on all of us–all of us, mind you–just as I have foretold. You think she will obey you? She will not even be able to hear your words. Then you will see that I was right all along, once it is far too late."

"Enough," Master Tree said, putting an end to the debate for the moment. "High Adept Naero Maeris. You will tell us everything that you know about this situation in brief, and explain what thoughts and dreams have come to you concerning it. After this, you shall only report directly to us, whenever you have any thought, vision, or dream concerning this situation. You are not to dwell on it, or continue to think about it in any other way. In fact, I want you to do all that you can to *not* think about this situation, and to keep it from taking hold of your mind. If you begin to obsess over it or cannot stop thinking about it, you need to tell us that, also."

Naero attempted to protest. "I agree more with Master Jo. Keeping me ignorant will not help me. Tell me what I'm up against. Why is this thing drawn to me, and me to it? Help me understand."

"You are not ready," Master Tree said. "And neither are we. You need to strengthen your body and mind, and balance out your abilities. There is so much for you to learn, still. And for us to learn about you. You need to achieve all three Wisdoms, but there is no time for little more than a crash course, in order to stabilize you as a Mystic adept and prevent you from losing control of yourself as your powers continue to increase."

"I do agree with Master Tree in this regard," Master Jo said in support. "He is right, Naero. Once we have time, you can train fully with the Order Master on Taeha, and finally with me on Oorrii. But we must stabilize you first, or you will never survive long enough to have a chance to complete your full training. Your growing powers will overwhelm and crush you long before then, I fear."

"Trust us," Master Tree said. "Trust our wisdom and the process, at least for a month or two. That is not so much to ask. Trust in our training and give us all the chances we need. You need time to explore and strengthen your abilities and your control of them. We need some time to study you further, and learn better how to guide and help you along this difficult path. Once we are better informed, and you are more confident, then we can begin to tackle other issues."

Master Vane still scoffed. "Do we even have one or two months? You fools really think any of this is going to wait that long? Each day she grows more and more powerful, closer and closer to going out of control."

Master Jo snapped at Vane suddenly. "We are her only chance, and we will all work diligently to provide her with the best chance that she will have to succeed and survive. And you will do your part as well, High Master."

Master Vane raised both eyebrows. "Yes, indeed. Certainly I will waste my time further on an obvious lost cause–just to prove my point all the more to both of you fools in the end."

Naero gave the High Masters a full account of every thought, dream, and interaction she had had with the mysterious artifact thus far.

She appreciated all that they were trying to do for her. But whatever they said, she and Om both agreed that they desperately needed further information.

On her free day that weekend, she could go back up to her ship.

45

Mason Elliott

If Baeven was still around, she had a lot of questions for him. The High Masters let slip that they had faced a situation such as this once before–with another member of Clan Maeris–and possibly with another one of these strange artifacts. How many of them were there? Where did they come from? And somehow, it had all ended in some kind of disaster once before.

Everything pointed to Baeven, and perhaps one of the main reasons that he had been banished, made an outcast, and sentenced to death in the first place.

Vane seemed to believe that Naero and the High Masters were going to somehow repeat that same mistake or series of mistakes–whatever they were.

More than ever now, Naero needed to know exactly what had happened in the past.

That night, she dreamed that the obelisk had finally stopped shifting its shape, and took on a completely new form.

Now the bizarre artifact looked like a statue, made out of some kind of unbreakable material.

Now it looked exactly like Naero herself.

7

The following morning was capped by a drenching rain and slight thunderstorms that rolled up from the south. At sparring practice Naero went to the arena, trying to expect anything–even a Chaos adept beatdown.

Many of her traps were still in place. She could attempt to play the same cat-and-mouse game she had used with the Change adepts.

Yet once she arrived, she saw only three persons, and one of them was Gaviok. Naero raced up to her friend and hugged him.

"How are you?" she asked him.

Gaviok grinned as only a mantid could. "Never better," he said cheerfully. He was his normal, cheery, dark blue color, but it lightened slightly when he came near to her. Gaviok had a great fondness for her, mostly because she was Baeven's niece.

Naero scanned the area with her various senses and abilities. Her sense of warning wasn't even flickering.

Mason Elliott

"I half expected the Chaos adepts to jump all over me the second I arrived," she said. "I thought for sure Master Vane would put them up to some deviltry involving me."

Gaviok laughed. "Who says he didn't? Don't you see, Naero? They're shunning you. It's a terrible affront, a direct insult to your honor, you, and your Clan."

Naero chuckled and rested her hands on her hips. "I'm so hurt I could cry. So, if I'm being shunned by the pak, what are you and these other two doing here?"

"You know I don't care what anyone thinks," Gaviok said. "And Daiyana Fae and Arnall Blooding here are contraries, so they're going to do just the opposite of whatever the rest of the group does. I find it both amusing and rather refreshing."

Contraries, huh? Naero had heard about such people among the Spacer Clans, but never among Mystics. How did that work?

She went up to them and offered her hand.

"Hello, I'm Naero Amashin Maeris, from Clan Maeris. Glad to meet you."

Both the male and the female smiled. Then they slipped around her to either side and turned their backs to her.

"Goodbye, Maeris Naero adept," the female said. "It is a great unpleasure to meet you. I am not Daiyana of Clan Fae. Isn't this weather wonderful?"

Lighting shattered a tree up on the heights, and they were all getting soaked out in the open.

"Farewell, Maeris Naero adept," the male added. "I take no happiness in our meeting. I am not Arnall of Clan Blooding. I have no intention whatsoever of sparring with you today, or pitting myself against you to learn any of your puny fighting secrets."

He came at her immediately, punches and kicks flashing. Naero gave ground, fighting off his combinations with effort.

"Hold, hold!" Naero shouted.

Arnall merely redoubled his attacks. He just missed her with a mind blast that Naero dodged.

"Lay on...continue!" Naero shouted. Arnall immediately stopped sparring and went over to sit down by Daiyana.

Gaviok came up to Naero. "See what I mean? Those two are fun."

"Yeah, fun and annoying. So, my friend. You're an adept now, I see. In Chaos Wisdom, no less. How did your initiation go the first day?"

"Brilliant," Gaviok said with great pleasure. "They attacked me with amazing skills and techniques I had never seen before. Then I chased them

48

all over the arena until I had throttled everyone of them into an unconscious state. It was great fun. It took them a full day to recover, and I was immensely disappointed when they didn't want to give it all another go."

Naero covered her mouth and struggled not to burst out laughing. She could just picture that.

"I do have one complaint," he said. "The food here is sufficient, but the taste is not quite to my liking."

Gaviok seemed to relish fish heads, pickled bug guts, and other nasty stuff that would make most species hurl from just glancing at it. Of course normal food would leave him wanting.

"Master Vane is very impressed with my innate Chaos abilities, Naero. He says I'm such a natural, that he can't wait to train me in every way possible. He said it is a terrible shame that I do not have the high enough capacity to develop a psyonic third eye."

Naero suddenly had a wild idea.

She hadn't used her biomancy quickening ability in a long while. What did they have to lose?

Arnall and Daiyana ignored them and started sparring among themselves.

Naero summoned her own third eye, linked with the psyonic centers in her mind. Then she mindlinked with Gaviok, studied his own psyonic source points, and let him experience what she could do with her third eye, through his mind and his abilities.

After a few hours of practice together with their minds linked, Naero felt certain that she could awaken the same psyonic ability in Gaviok's mind. She explained the modification process to him, and the slight risks involved.

"There may be some pain," Naero said. "It might take you a while to adapt to it and fully make use of its abilities. Beyond that, I think the worst thing that would happen is nothing. Are you still game?"

"Of course," Gaviok said. "I heal even faster than a couple of Spacers I know."

"All right. Here goes. Whatever you do, don't break the link until I do. I'm merely triggering the psyonic potential for the third eye to form within you. You will have to develop it on your own after that, if it does awaken. It will then act as a new gateway for your psyonic powers."

The connections failed the first four times she tried to make them.

On the fifth attempt, Gaviok's third insectoid eye–a psyonic insectoid eye of Chaos energy–popped open wide.

"Ohh!" Gaviok exclaimed.

A scarlet beam drove into Naero without warning from Gaviok's new eye and drilled her right into the rocks nearby, winding her.

"Naero! I'm sorry," Gaviok exclaimed. He rushed forward and helped her up with one dexterous claw, covering his new eye with the other.

She caught her breath, and quickly stood behind him. "Now, let's mindlink again and work on a little control, shall we?"

"Good idea. Thank you, N. This is amazing. Wait until I show Master Vane!"

"Oh, let's give it a day or so," Naero suggested. "And it might be best if you don't tell him how much I helped you develop your third eye. Just say I helped you bring it out. That would not be untrue."

"No, it would not."

By now, Daiyana and Arnall were watching their every move intently.

Both of them summoned their own third eyes and came up to Naero and Gaviok.

Daiyana spoke first. "Goodbye, enemies. We can completely control all the abilities of our third eyes. And we already know how to shoot that lame forcebeam out of ours, as well."

"So," Arnall added, "there would be absolutely no reason for you to teach that useless technique to us, so that we could learn how to not use it. Both of us would be very ungrateful if you did so. Shall we finish?"

Naero laughed. They were a hoot.

"Whatever you do," she told them. "Don't let me mindlink with you two, or teach you that lame technique that both of you already completely understand. I would be extremely unhappy and unwilling to help you. Because I think we must become the worst of enemies. Are you ready to stop? I will end with Arnall last."

Naero mindlinked with Arnall first.

In another hour, all four of them were having contests, blasting targets out of the sky with forcebeams from their third eyes. Naero also increased some of their other existing Cosmic abilities while she was at it.

After they finished, they all relaxed and shared some Jett.

"I hate this stuff," Daiyana said with a smile.

"No," Arnall added. "It is terrible. I don't want another." Gaviok handed him one.

Daiyana frowned. "I care a lot about what happened to Hashiko," she said. "She was always nice to me. Her death was completely your fault, Naero."

"I agree," Arnall said. "I think the other Chaos adepts were right for shunning you like they did today. Master Vane is always fair and nice, and has good reasons for hating you. He is such a great guy."

"I am certain the others will be very happy to experience the new technique you did not teach us today, Naero," Daiyana added.

"Yes," Arnall said. "We will be sure to be gentle with it, and not surprise the living shit out of them at all."

When it came time to break off, Gaviok and the contraries went back to their compound. The latter walked backwards, telling her hello, and to have an awful day.

Naero went back to her nanocabin.

Just three more days. All she had to do was make it through three more days of training, and then she could get back to her ship and try to get some answers.

In the afternoon, she actually trained with High Master Vane. That was very strange, to say the least.

As soon as they were together, he started to instruct her on the basics of the Harmony, and how each of the Three Wisdoms balanced each other out and led to a fleeting period of desired stability.

"It never lasts forever," he explained. "It can't. Nothing does. But there cannot simply be constant change and flux, either. There must be periods of relative stability, or nothing can ever be accomplished. That is why the wise strive to achieve and maintain Harmony—for the good of all."

Naero paused. "I'm considering how strange it is to hear those words, coming from a Chaos Master."

"Then you're still an idiot, Maeris. Just because Chaos Masters accept things as they are and as they will be, it does not mean that they desire each moment to be in a constant state of turmoil and destructive change. That would serve no purpose at all, and is just as unrealistic as wishing and hoping that things would somehow never change, when it is clear that they always have, always do, and always will do so."

He grunted in frustration.

"Do you actually think that we do not think of the future, and just dwell on the present? Even Chaos Masters desire time to pursue matters that they wish to pursue. Like others, they want time to have the ability to learn and enlighten, and comprehend all that they can in the time they have. And to pass that knowledge and wisdom on to others who can not only perceive its value, but actually pursue the *furtherance* and growth of that body of knowledge into the future.

We're just not as vocal or romantic about doing so as the other Orders are."

"I know you still hope to have a chance to kill me someday," Naero told him. "I just don't understand why you are still committed to helping me."

Vane hummed absently, puttering on a datapad. "I know you don't, Maeris. Your capacities for reason have always been quite dim and limited. That's just the way you are. I agree, helping you is indeed a waste of my time, but I must do so in order to honor the concept of fairness that is of such vital importance to the other two Orders. It's an even greater waste of time to argue that point, so there it is. I will do my duty to the letter, and not one jot less or more. And hope has nothing to do with me having to destroy you when the time comes. To me, it is an eventual fact."

"Forgive me if I fully intend to prove you wrong about me, Master Vane."

"Impossible, Maeris. And I have no interest whatsoever in any shade of the waste of time called forgiveness, either. Either you are responsible for something or you are not. And we all must take responsibility for our actions. I don't blame you for anything, Maeris. Not even Hashiko's death any longer, or whatever you did to Janosha. It was just a planet, after all. The universe is filled with them. What is past is past, and I've gotten over my own stupid personal problems with the entire mess."

Vane paused and shook his finger at her. "Yet you remain a ready and constant threat to all. Eventually, others will realize and accept that fact as well. And I will be there to end that threat. You said yourself that you would not want to lose yourself and become a wanton thing of mindless destruction. You should take comfort in the fact that I fully intend to be there to stop you, when that need arises. And it will."

Naero sighed and looked down.

How could she argue with all of that?

She hated it when even Vane started to make sense to her.

8

Naero survived three more days of sparring, practice, and instruction with the Three Orders. She continued to make friends among the other adepts. Not everyone cared for her, but that was as it always was.

The other Chaos adepts finally agreed to play with her, and their first real practice session was pretty fierce.

It more or less broke down into a free-for-all. But Gaviok and the contraries were on her side–usually–so that made a big difference. The others could not simply decide to swarm on her with impunity.

And the new third eye forcebeams that the four of them used evened many scores. The other Chaos adepts struggled to adapt, and began to mutter that they wished Naero would find a way to upgrade some of their abilities and techniques as well.

None of them possessed the ability to quicken others in quite the same way that she could. And as Naero shared her gifts freely with the other adepts of the other orders, the sulking Chaos adepts quickly found themselves to be at severe disadvantages when they sparred with the others.

She'd help them out eventually, but let them stew on that for a while and suffer being outmatched.

Naero trained and worked more and more with the High Masters each day she was assigned to one of them.

They carefully studied her every power and ability in great detail. They mindlinked with her as she performed certain actions and techniques, studying the flows of Cosmic energies through her brain, mind, and body. They tried to duplicate some of her feats and abilities. Some they could, to varying degrees. Many others they could not. Certain abilities remained unique to her in both kind and degree.

Surprisingly, Naero found Master Tree almost as difficult and unyielding to work with as Master Vane. In his own way, Tree was relentlessly demanding, exacting, and exhausting–almost brutally so.

Everything had to be perfect.

Everything had to be exact, precise, and complete.

Sessions with the Order Master were relentless tests of endurance bordering on physical torment and agony. It was a paradox that Tree was at once kind and understanding, and yet still a very harsh taskmaster. He used every moment of their time together efficiently and effectively.

Naero got used to needing a nap after their marathon sessions.

And, worst of all, Tree demanded to understand the minutiae of every, little, thing. Naero wasted almost an entire day with him trying to perceive and understand the KDM within her. Yet those efforts remained a complete bust in the end.

At least Naero felt more reassured, now that none of the High Masters would ever be able to sense Om within her mind–since he was part of the KDM.

Her sessions with Vane were, as he promised, kept to the bare minimum. No less, no more. But she did manage to learn things from him as well. The opportunities were always there if she looked hard enough. But she could never expect anything extra at all.

She actually began to appreciate their Cosmic sparring sessions together. Whatever stoic position he claimed, Vane still enjoyed beating on her, and he was, in fact, an opponent like no other. Vane remained a superior foe that she could endlessly strive to best and measure the overall progress of her skills against.

From her experience, that only made her better in the long run.

Truth be told, Naero enjoyed her sessions with Master Jo most of all. She seemed to learn the most from him, and Change wisdom made the most sense to her. It fit the most with her patterns and general view of things. To Naero's way of thinking, Enlightened Change made all things seem possible.

On top of that, High Master Jo was a hoot–the most delightful prankster–a true mercurial trickster after her own heart.

At the most unexpected moments–maddening moments–he would pull off some of the most astonishing gags with perfect timing, in ways that were masterful, inspiring, and scintillating.

Such as when he filled the cave they were practicing in with horrible-smelling gas, and laughing, holographic apparitions within the glowing vapors.

He stink bombed them all.

But what Naero cherished and learned most from Master Jo was a true sense of joy and sheer appreciation. He did everything with a sense of élan and even pure whimsy whenever he could manage to get away with it. The Eternal Wise Child–he could be both completely serious and infinitely playful at the same time.

Another truly wonderful paradox.

More than with any other power, Naero could sense High Master Jo's love and compassion for all things. They seemed boundless, infinite. Vane seemed incapable of such; his was a raw, harsh justice, stark and untempered by any mercy whatsoever. Tree was somewhere in the stoic middle between the two. Doddering, verbose, ponderous, slow to act–and more concerned with order in the end than fairness, as one might guess.

But it was Master Jo who truly seemed to have full empathy for things, and he was never afraid to change his mind, or look foolish, or do what needed to be done in order to accomplish the right and best thing. Truly Wisdom and Justice, tempered by Mercy and Compassion.

With the help of all three High Masters, each in their own way, Naero began to truly perceive the value and the wisdom of each Order, and how they all grudgingly cooperated and worked together to form a rational, consistent, working whole.

It was never perfect–it never could or would be–but it did manage to work. It could work, but only if everyone tried in good faith to make it work.

The overall objective: to create a Harmony of thought, principle, and idea that was the basis for an enlightened, forward-thinking path– a path for Spacers or any sentients who could see and accept the value of it.

Finally the first, seventh day came. The first free day for the adepts, including Naero, Jan, and Gaviok.

She met with them at midnight, as soon as their free day actually began. They all embraced, and Shalaen joined them as well. Shalaen had not tested to become an adept herself, but she had stayed to work with the High Masters and Intel very closely in an attempt to locate and contact her people, the Yattai.

Naero wanted to hear all of their stories, but first—more than anything—she wanted to get back onto *The Flying Dagger*, and pilot her own ship back up into orbit around Thanor-4.

To get away from the pressure, sleep in her own quarters, and sup in her own galley with all of her crew would be an indescribable luxury.

So much had changed within the space of a mere week.

Tarim and Zhen met her at the wide-open, rear-loading bay, the ship all prepped and ready.

They fell in behind her, and Naero walked through the start of a small, cheering, applauding gauntlet of her twenty-one other crew. They welcomed her back aboard as she made her way almost frantically toward her bridge:

Jima Ortega
Juan Keller
Fenton James
Prentiss Fox
Kayleen Flynn
Tommis Barrett

Naero passed through into the midship decks of her vessel.
More crew waited for her, lined up on either side in the galley.

Harra Ahmed
Spenser Gordon
Chandra Adams
Trudi Cheyenne
Lakara Donovan

Her cook, Tolen Kothari, had a special late meal of steaming, Hovari blue crab prepared and waiting for her. One of Naero's favorites. She could smell the unmistakable succulent aroma of the Hovari bay spices in the air.

She could almost taste the melted butter and sliced, white lemons waiting in small dishes, ready to drizzle and dip the long, thick, juicy tubes of crab meat in before devouring them.

"I can bring your supper to you as soon as you are ready, Captain."

Naero licked her lips eagerly.

The assistant cook, Eugene Blooding, called out from over at one of the stoves. "Captain Naero. I'm fixing up a nice pot of my special black gravy that you like so much. I've got fresh, medium-rare, Gynarian cattle steak, and Loshin sweet bread and butter to enjoy it with. We'll bring it all up with your big platter of blue crab."

Naero almost stopped and feasted right there, but she wanted to get up into orbit first, and then contact Baeven privately in her personal quarters.

After that, then she could relax and eat.

She passed through medical, and then the crew quarter deck.

Finally, she reached the open bulkhead leading to the bridge.

A final cheering gauntlet of her bridge crew, plus Rendar Nelson, her chief engineer, shouted their ecstatic welcomes at her.

Enel and Surina grinned at Naero, and spun her captain's command chair around for her to take her rightful place.

Then they all took their posts. Enel as pilot, next to cute co-pilot, Sying Lii. Enel's radiant lover, Surina, at her comstation. The other bridge crew were already waiting.

Naero settled in and almost cried. Even after just one week, it felt so good to be home.

Her home–the one she had made for herself and her people.

Her ship.

Her fingers touched her controls with the tenderness of a lover.

"Prepare to launch," she commanded, choking up.

They shot into the sky seconds later.

The freedom Naero felt.

In minutes, they were in high, geosynchronous orbit above the Spacer Mystic colony on Thanor-4. She could see Nashara below them.

Naero breathed a sigh of relief, and turned helm and command over to her pilot, her second.

"Enel, I...I need a few moments to freshen up."

She went into her private quarters to be alone for a short while. On a whim, she curled up on the soft, luxuriant black nanofloor.

It pweaked around her, form-fitting as if she were a small white and black jewel. It warmed to the perfect temperature. The way it was used to doing, whenever she chose to sleep naked and alone on her floor.

She got up and went to her comstation.

The call to Baeven went out. It had to.

Was he still nearby?

Was he still waiting to hear from her? She hoped so.

Naero took a few minutes, snuggled back down, closed her eyes, and breathed evenly. Even without pweaking up her oval nanobed, she could relax at last in her own space, and feel comfortable, secure, and safe.

But time passed, and no response came from Baeven or his ship.

She called Enel and Surina. "Hey, either of you have any word from *The Shadow Fox*? Are they gone?

"I have an update, Captain," Surina said. "Let me join you in your quarters."

It must be something important, then. Naero made sure all of her security was up and running properly. Security systems Baeven had helped her install.

Rina appeared at her entrance and chimed, a second later.

"Enter," Naero said. Her panel slid open, and Rina step within, allowing the panel to close behind her.

"Captain, *The Shadow Fox* departed two days ago. Something important came up."

"Did Baeven say anything? Did he provide any details?"

"He said that he was leaving a coded message for you on your private comstation–one that only you could decipher and listen to."

"Thanks, Rina. Rotate the duty shifts so that everyone can take a turn with me in the galley. They don't have to bother bringing anything up. I'll be down in less than a quarter hour. I expect a full report from you on the trade fleet's activities."

Surina smiled. "Ready and waiting, sir. Captain Max and the others are really raking it in. Did you hear that he just got engaged?"

Naero's heart fell only a little. "Who's the lucky gal?"

"Vanna Fae. Word is they got together somehow, and now they can't keep their hands off one another. Each of them is besotted with the other."

"Captain Vanna Fae, Piper's older sister? She always was a stunning beauty, all right." And she was almost as tall as Max, too, dammit. Curse the tall.

Naero smiled with good nature. "Well, good for them, Rina. Sounds like a great match. They're both great people–part of our family–and they deserve their happiness. I'll check in with them both at some point tomorrow. Let's make sure some greenhouse flowers reach them. Something radiant, fragrant, and pretty for young lovers."

"I'll take care of it, sir. See you down in the mess hall. Very glad to have you back, even if it is only for a day."

"Sure."

Surina left even as Naero decoded Baeven's message.

It was self-erasing, so she made a quick copy just in case there was something she needed to listen to again.

Baeven's voice spoke calmly.

Sorry I had to leave, Naero. Good to know they're not going to execute you right away, at least. I'm sure Master Vane is disappointed. My cloaked sensor drones picked up traces on the deep space borders of our long lost friends–those two alien vessels–the Dakkur hordeship and the G'lothc cruiser. They laid low for a while, hiding out since their attacks on the Mystic Homeworlds failed. But if they have returned to our quadrant, I'm guessing they're planning some new trouble for us all. I'd better check it out, for the sake of everyone.

It seems as if you'll be relatively safe for a while, as you continue your training. I've done what I can to study the alien obelisk on Thanor-4 from a safe distance. Trust me, that is the best way to do so. It is indeed one of those damn things, so whatever you do, don't go near it. Don't even look at it. Try not to even think about it–even in your dreams or especially on the Astral Plane. You don't want it to notice you, key on you, or focus on you and your mind as a target. It seems mostly dormant now, but such artifacts are completely unpredictable–and if it fully awakens, it will become dangerous and unstoppable. Stay away from it, at all costs.

We can have a long talk when I get back, and I'll tell you about my fateful encounter with a similar device back on Janosha. It involved your mother, too. And the resulting disaster was a major reason for my becoming an outcast and being sentenced to death by the Mystics.

Whatever you do, Naero, don't go near it. Take care of Jan and Gaviok. Don't let them near it, either.

The relatively brief message ended, and the original dissolved completely. Naero did not need to hear it again, and erased the temp copy.

She sighed deeply and left to join her crew in the galley, for a good meal and to catch up with Jan and everyone else.

By the next night at midnight, she'd need to be back onworld to continue her intensive training with the Three Orders.

Yet being kept in the dark always bothered her. She would rather know exactly what she was up against. It was unfortunate that Baeven had to leave.

Fear of the unknown was the worst.

9

Naero didn't mean to sleep in the next day, but she had stayed up very late the night before, celebrating with Jan, her crew, and friends. After hearing all of their mostly good news about how their weeks went, it seemed as if, for once, something might work out in their favor and possibly go their way. At least now there was an overall chance of it.

She dozed peacefully in her oval nanobed in her serene, darkened quarters, and listened to the watch chime nine bells.

She almost never slept that late, despite the fact that she had been up until nearly four.

It was actually Om who mildly startled her out of her sleep.

Naero. I love you. I can't help it. I have to tell you exactly how I feel about you.

She snapped awake, blinking and knitting her brows. Huh? Om–what?

I've figured out what's wrong with me. Why I've been dealing with all of these sweeping, crippling emotions. I know now. Like so many others...I'm falling in love with you.

Seriously, Om. I know you've been goofing around with your emotions and developing your own sense of humor and all, but this isn't funny. I've got waaay too much on my plate right now for anything like that–especially from you."

I...I'm sorry Naero. You're right, of course. But I just can't help myself. You're all I think about, and it's driving me batty.

You're inside my head. We can't do this. And any way, you're an AI. What do you know about love?

I feel everything you feel, Naero. I know everything you know about such things.

Yeah. That's helpful. I'm certainly an expert. She stretched under her zilken sheets and nanocoverlet.

Please. Just hear me out. I've given this a lot of thought. It's actually perfect. What could be more natural? We're always together. We're already as one mind, body, and soul. We're part of each other. You go out of your way and always find excuses not to have relationships. You don't have or make time for anyone else, and with our...condition, you worry about taking a lover and hurting him in his sleep. That could never happen with me. We can be happy together, if you just let me try to love you.

Whoa and triple whoa, Om! You're racing. Do you even hear yourself? This is completely crazy. We can't have a romance...the two of us...in my head!

No, listen. I've thought of everything. I know how frustrated–both physically and emotionally–you've been for a very long while. If you are worried about the sex–

Sex.

Sex? Holy Ka-rap, Om. Haisha! And double Haisha! What in the bloody hell are you talking about?

I've accessed all of your thoughts and memories on the subject of passionate fulfillment, Naero.

Oh, please. Kill me now. Om, snap out of it. Again–

Who could know what you want and like better than me? I feel and understand your every desire, things you keep only to yourself. Things you don't tell anyone else. Not even your closest family and friends. I know what you want...what you need.

Naero shook her head.

Please, please tell me this is just some terrible nightmare.

Our mind controls all of your pleasure centers, Naero. The brain is in fact, the largest sex organ in the body. I can meet your every aching need–your every desire for pleasure, satisfaction, and fulfillment–forever, my darling.

"Aauughh!" Naero groaned, clutching her temples. "Please stop talking, Om. You are killing me. I never thought I could feel so humiliated inside my own head. And I can't look away or get away from you, like I could with someone else with their own mind and body. This is too close, too intimate, too fast. You're scaring me. It's too much."

No. No! I would never hurt you, Naero. I only want to help you. Can't you see how perfect this could be, for both of us? I know how very much you need love. I know how much you ache to be loved. I do. And you deserve it. You're a beautiful person–when you aren't being a jerk.

Gee, thanks, Om. How romantic. Way to sweep me off my feet.

Remember, Naero. Part of my mind is patterned after yours. I have as much tact as you do.

Thanks for the reminder.

Maybe they were too much alike.

I've studied everything there is to know about sex, pleasure, and human relations.

Om, there's more to it all than what you find in the databanks. There has to be attraction, some kind of spark.

I've accessed the KDM on such matters as well. I am part Kexxian also. Did you know the Kexx were incredibly sensual and intimate as a race? They mated for life and would suffer greatly when a spouse died. And even though they were reptilian, they were capable of enjoying love-making for up to three days–in perpetual, mind-jarring ecstasy–until they passed out from dehydration and lack of food and sleep.

Good for them. Kexxian lizard love. Fascinating. Be that as it may, I'm not having psyonic sex with you, Om.

We share the same mind and feelings. Here is just a taste of what I can do for us...together.

No, Om. No. I forbid-

Waves of sudden, incredible pleasure rippled through her entire body.

Naero gasped, wide-eyed. Hey eyes rolled back up into her head until she thought she might black out. She couldn't talk, couldn't breathe, her entire body aflame with lust.

Mason Elliott

She shook violently and convulsed, her legs and arms stiffened and extended, twitching, and thrumming on her bed until she thought her hands and feet might explode from her body, along with her head.

She either rolled or flung herself off her bed to land on the soft floor, trying to crawl away. But she couldn't move any longer.

For a few brief seconds, Naero did pass out.

Only to come to gasping for air as if she were being asphyxiated, mind reeling, her heart coming to life on its own, as if using nanoexplosives to try to blast its way out of her thumping, heaving chest.

Om called to her eagerly.

See? We can give each other hours of such joy. Admit it, Naero. We love each other. Why should we not give in to our innermost desires? We can make each other happy. Why should we not do so?

Naero finally caught her breath.

Damn it, Om. You nearly killed me! Any more of that and my heart will go nova and my head explode like a blood-filled melon. Don't do anything like that to me–ever again. Is that clear? That is *not* what I want from you. Did it ever occur to you to take the time to ask me what I really want in a relationship? In a lover?

For once, Om was stricken and speechless.

She could sense how heartbroken he was, but at the moment, after what he had just put her through, Naero didn't really care.

Rejection and broken hearts were all part of love, too. Not every attempt at finding a lover worked out–Naero knew that. In fact, it seemed as if most did not, until a person found the right one for them, if they were lucky.

I'm...I'm sorry, Naero. I just thought we could be happy together. I was so excited. I thought I had the answers. I thought...I could make you happy.

Not like this, Om! This isn't what I want. You can't make another person love you that way. We're friends. We're partners. I've never thought of you as a potential lover.

I guess not.

Look, I know how hard it is for you to learn to control all of your emotions. They're still so new to you. I've been working at it my entire life, and I still can't get mine right at times. Keep working on it. You'll get the hang of it, eventually.

I'll keep trying, Naero. Emotions are truly a complex maze to navigate. Something else I wanted to discuss with you.

What's that, Om? I have kind of a busy day planned.

I also came across some interesting biomancy and teknomancy techniques in the KDM. I wanted to share them and their basic theories, principles, and techniques with you. We might want to try some of these.

Great, Om. That's more like it. I'd be happy to work with you on something new. What do we have?

The Kexx mastered techniques far beyond what you and I could even conceive of at our current levels of understanding. They eliminated disease from all of the races they guided. In the end, they could tap into the Cosmic energies of stars directly–the Powers of the universe itself–and transform themselves into several different types of energy beings. They could bend and manipulate matter and energy at will. Their powers were truly miraculous. They could leap the impossible distances between galaxies and into and across other dimensions by force of will. They wished and dreamed things into being. Ideas and possibilities that they focused and bent their thought on became real creations and the very substance of reality.

As he spoke, Naero closed her eyes and beheld several flashing visions from the KDM.

Visions so real, it was as if she and Om were witnessing them firsthand.

Near the end of their existence, the greatest among the Kexx were like...like gods. I can find no other description that comes anywhere close to depicting what they were and what they could accomplish with their limitless minds. The mightiest of the Kexx could replicate themselves in multiple forms–entire, sentient armies–created out of raw thought, matter, and energy to serve their will. Fleets of invincible warships with weapons that make yours look like feeble tin cans, clattering around, spitting at each other in the dark.

The Kexx and Drians would need all of their might and skill, for they and their Allies–the nearly equally amazing, humanoid Driuns– faced the most deadly and implacable foe the universe could ever conceive of: the destroying force of the G'lothc and their countless hordes and minions. Using the destructive power of the Darkforce, the great foe had emerged out of another dimension–an entire dimension where they and their kind had managed to destroy and lay waste to everything–even most of themselves.

Yet a remnant of that dark foe spilled into our universe, and began their own rise to power–a terrible power that demanded all things be crushed before it.

The G'lothc destroyed all life across three entire galaxies before they came up against the Drians, who fought them to a valiant standstill. But it was only the Kexx who were able to truly turn the grim tide and drive the G'lothc into total defeat and annihilation.

Anything less would never have stopped them.

That much became clear to all: it was kill or be killed.

Two other galaxies were nearly destroyed by the massive war–a terrifying war waged more than the course of a million years, and with great loss of life. For the destructive might of the enemy was very great, and nearly unstoppable.

The Kexx and their allies were not destructive by nature or bent upon any desire for power or conquest. They were wise and benevolent, and forced to defend themselves. Yet once driven to the task at hand, in the end they rose to the fierce challenge, and were undaunted. Out of their limitless imaginations, the allies created entire fleets of invincible warships at will. Forces with one driving purpose: to overwhelm the ruthless G'lothc, to wipe out their last homeworlds, and even obliterate their very stars during the course of those astounding, final battles.

And as they perished, the once undefeated G'lothc howled in vain, unable to believe that death came solely for them–and they comprehended what fear truly was–for the first time in their dark existence–only at the very last.

Naero shuddered at such amazing visions sweeping across the limitless vistas of her mind. She beheld so much in such a few amazing instants that it was completely overwhelming. It nearly stunned her.

She trembled.

It wasn't until the end that Naero realized that Om had been speaking to her in the Kexxian language, and that she had hung upon every word and followed them and the visions they evoked and conjured completely. She did so so naturally that it was effortless.

She did so without thought.

Naero trembled, sensing more and more the limitless potential that the secrets of the Kexxian Data Matrix held within her.

The concepts for biomancy and teknomancy that Om raced through her mind were breathtaking–nearly beyond belief.

And these were only the most basic, childlike concepts of them all.

To the neargods of the Kexx, these lesser concepts would have undeniably seemed trite, perhaps even silly or infantile.

How could she–a mere human woman–even begin to apply or implement any of these techniques and abilities, let alone all of the limitless, incomprehensible miracles that stretched out beyond them?

Such limitless power. Did she have a right to use any part of such power and knowledge? Did anyone?

Staggering. Utterly staggering.

Om laughed with her at how small and ignorant they were.

I'm just as overwhelmed, Naero. Trust me. But we can start exploring these basic concepts and possibilities a bit at a time, from the beginning. Let's try basic star-tapping and replication, for now, partner—abani. I think that will be more than enough for now.

Naero sighed and blinked. Tapping into the energy of stars. Khai had mentioned something like that once.

Replicating herself in various ways—separate, fully functioning, other versions of herself. How was such even possible? Yet in her mind, now—she knew that it was.

Om, we'll make time to work on these things. We might not ever be lovers, yet we are *abani*. But right now, I do have other matters to attend to.

I will faithfully pursue all of our goals, and keep you apprised of my progress. I like it when we speak Kexxian in your mind. It helps greatly, and keeps us on the same wavelength of thought with the KDM. Let us continue to do so.

Very well, Om. I agree with you; let's continue to do so. We will communicate and think in Kexxian. It seems only natural anyway. I'm going to go out shortly.

Naero took a mist shower, dressed, and left her quarters for a late breakfast and to see to the needs of her people and her fleet.

First she had to check on Jan. She checked his status. Jan slept in, too. He was still in his quarters.

Naero went there first and chimed his panel.

Jan snapped it open, but from what she could see, the guest room was completely torn apart. There was even damage to the walls and outer hull.

Naero nearly panicked. She called out over her wristcom.

"Tarim, security detail. Jan's room. ASAP!"

She stepped into the darkened room. "Jan? Where are you?"

She heard sounds of what appeared to be some kind of struggle within. Jan came hurtling at her. She had to fight him off, deflecting powerful kicks and punches.

"Jan, stop it. It's me!"

He grinned at her with a wild look in his eyes. "I know!" he shrieked eagerly, and attacked her again.

67

Mason Elliott

Jan shook his head, and his face blinked at her in fear and confusion. "Naero...help me...Danner's trying to take over again!"

10

Naero tackled Jan and wrestled with him with all her might.

She tried to mindlink with him. Perhaps she could help fight Dan off somehow.

She could tell when Danner flashed into Jan's mind briefly, because that insane laughter would start pouring out of Jan's babbling mouth.

Jan had had some basic training with the Mystics, fortunately. One of the first things adepts learned was how to shield their minds from others. But Jan was certainly not an expert at it yet, and Danner was a powerful, lifelong, psyonic savant, with a special link to Janner's mind from them being twins.

Jan clearly resisted and fought his insane brother off with everything he had.

If Danner won, who knew how much destruction he could cause using Jan's body?

Naero had seen Dan take out entire warships with nothing but his mind and his many Cosmic powers.

Mason Elliott

He could destroy a small merchant ship like *The Flying Dagger* easily, and kill everyone on board.

Naero finally held Jan down and achieved a mindlink.

She could sense the battle between the minds of the two brothers.

Get out of his head, you bastard!

Danner laughed relentlessly.

He used Jan's body to pummel her with several painful blows.

Naero endured them and tried to hold him back down, and maintain the mindlink.

Danner raved, as usual.

Going to kill you all. Going to take his body and go on a rampage. And he'll be stuck where I am, back in one of those damn Darkforce generators!

Naero closed her eyes, trying to picture herself grappling with Danner within Jan's mind.

He was still stronger than her.

Stronger than them both on this level.

Within the expanse of his mind, Jan tore a dark, yawning portal open with his bare hands, as Naero tried to fend off Danner.

N, shove him through here. It's the only way to shut him out of my mind. We have to drive him out by force!

Together, both of them fought Danner, kicking, punching, and shoving him into the dark portal.

All three of them battered and tore at each other, but together, Naero and Jan barely crammed Danner through the strange hole.

Jan finally sealed it off.

Naero and Jan gasped, and came to, out of the depths of their mindlink, still wrestling with each other.

Even as Tarim and the security team of five others jumped on them both to pull them apart.

Naero quickly explained what had happened.

They contacted the High Masters on Thanor-4's surface.

Master Tree had Jan shuttled down for an immediate crash course in further, psyonic mental defense.

No one could afford Danner taking Jan over again.

*

Naero stepped into sickbay.

Zhen smiled. "Glad you could join us."

"Us" was Aunt Sleak and her twin girls kicking around in her enormous belly while medtek Trudi Cheyenne assisted with the checkup.

Everything on the medbed readouts looked good.

Zhen smiled, using her healer's sight, not the readouts, to confirm her findings. "Mother and babies healthy and strong. I'd say they'll join us within two weeks–three, tops. Come here and check it out, N."

Naero did so, coming close, using her own sight to do the same thing. She rested both hands on Sleak's tummy.

"I'm glad you're here," Naero said. "Jan and I do appreciate the support. You can tell Klyne the same thing."

Sleak smiled, resting her strong hands on Naero's. "Klyne went back to work once he realized the High Masters weren't going to execute you."

"Yet," Naero said, "they still could. You heard about Jan?"

"I did. Just one more reason I'm sticking around. I can't do much else until I pop, anyway. Zal's on his way now. We both know it's going to be soon. This is a good, safe place to have our girls enter our universe. And the medical people at hand are all top notch. I ought to know–I had most of them educated and trained for years."

Zhen and Tru smiled and nodded.

Naero giggled, feeling the vital essence of her tiny nieces roaring like little flames of life, beneath her own strong, gentle hands.

The next batch of Maeris girls. It was a stirring feeling. One that she could not completely put into words, but that was not necessary. Some things could only be felt to fully experience them.

Aunt Sleak chuckled as well. "I had this weird dream the other night, Naero. Perhaps you'll get it; I sure couldn't."

Naero smiled. "What was it?"

Sleak shrugged. "It was weird, like I was sleepwalking or in a trance. You and Jan were there, too, and you were the same way–as if you were in a daze. We were standing in the middle of nowhere."

That piqued her attention. Naero looked up. "What were we all doing?"

Sleak shook her head. "Not much. Just staring at this weird statue."

Naero felt her blood freeze in her veins.

"What statue?"

"It was weird. It kept shifting shape. Sometimes it was kind of scary. Usually it didn't look like anything at all, but the way it moved was freaky. Once it looked just like Jan. Another time it looked just like me, and that was very strange. I felt like that statue of me was looking straight back at me. Then it would change again. But it took your form several times, Naero–in several different poses. Each time, it held its shape longer and longer. It kind of freaks me out now, just thinking about it."

Naero nodded. "It should. Let me explain why. You need to put that statue out of your mind, and do everything you can *not* to think about it."

She briefly explained why and what she knew about the enigmatic, alien artifact. She wondered if they should even be talking about it, and suggested that they not do so. What was its connection to her blood?

"Aunt Sleak, I think you'd better tell the High Masters, very briefly, about your dream. They'll want to know. And then you should try not to think about that artifact. That's probably for the best."

"Will do," Aunt Sleak nodded.

Naero shuddered, feeling just a twinge of her sense of warning flickering in the background of her mind.

11

Naero returned to her nanocabin on the surface of Thanor-4 after midnight, a long day of catching up behind her. She needed to sleep more, and that was just as well.

With her aunt's weird dream still fresh in her own troubled mind, Naero braced herself. She worried that she would start dreaming more and more about the obelisk—the alien artifact that seemed to keep taking her form.

But she did her best not to think about it, and pushed it completely out of her mind.

That was a great relief.

The nightmares she did have…were, oddly enough, about dragons.

Gigantic, long, sleek, glowing dragons of every color, some with horns and rippling tails and claws, a few with wings. There was an entire cloud of them, like monsters, writhing and breathing flame and lightning, and some even shooting bolts of Darkforce energy out of their eyes and gaping maws.

Massive destruction followed in their wake.

They laid waste to entire fleets.

They destroyed entire worlds, and both devoured the flesh and absorbed the life force energy of anything living.

What were these visions and where were they coming from?

Om suddenly came to her aid as she woke up, startled.

You are seeing visions of the Kahn-Dar. That is how they go to war and attack. They are Cosmic energy creatures, and very difficult to kill. They are more dangerous than most of the Dakkur in that they can fly, and move at great speed, both through an atmosphere and through space itself. Some of them can even shapechange, and take on humanoid or other forms.

Naero attempted to go back to sleep with all of that in her head.

At some point past four bells, Naero's sense of warning spiked off the charts, sending stabs of pain through her head. A second later, alarms and warning sirens went off all over the camp.

In the distance, Naero heard the unmistakable sounds of battle being unleashed. She knew those sounds very well.

The heavy Spacer Marine regiment guarding the obelisk was unleashing total hell on something.

Could the enemy be invading the planet?

Master Tree came straight for Naero and placed his arms protectively around her. Even his normal iron composure seemed shaken.

"What's happening?" she asked. He didn't answer her.

Then she smelled the charred smoky ozone scent of a Cosmic energy blast. And blood. Tree was wounded. Blood ran down both his arms and over his hands.

"You're hurt."

"Our smartblood will close off my minor injuries. The artifact is moving, and we must relocate to a secondary camp on the opposite side of this continent. You will come with me, Naero Maeris."

"Jan, Aunt Sleak, the others!"

"The other High Masters will get them to safety. You are my charge. Come. We must transport."

"Wait," Naero said. "Listen!"

They heard nothing.

Seconds before, a great battle was being unleashed.

Now there was no sound at all but the light wind.

Then the ground shook and rumbled, as if a great earthquake was splitting and cracking the planet wide open like an egg.

Coming right for them.

Master Tree teleported them in a flash of blue lightning.

They reappeared near a beach on the eastern side of the continent of Nashara. Sea cliffs stood nearby.

Thanor-4 had no moons, so the Marines at hand labored quickly and efficiently to finish expanding the outpost into a full camp, aided by clouds of construction fixers.

In the nearby woods, Mystics work with the construction teams to create another sparring field, similar to the other, but twice its diameter, to be ready for the next day.

Huge Marine troop transports stood ready, Naero guessed, in case a mass-evacuation was required.

Naero rose up on her gravwing briefly and surveyed the camp expanding rapidly before her eyes.

Another full division of Spacer Marines set up an extensive defensive perimeter all around the camp. Gunships, starfighters, and close support ships floated up in the air at the ready. Gravtanks, meks, and artillery units took up their positions.

Naero spotted several naval destroyers and a few cruisers higher up in the atmosphere.

When Naero returned to the ground level, she was relieved to see Jan with Master Jo, and Aunt Sleak with Master Vane. Naero hugged Jan and Sleak.

"High Masters," Aunt Sleak said, "as both a retired naval admiral and an adept, I demand to know what has happened. Did the enemy attack us again?"

"Come with us," Master Tree told her, his face grim. "We will explain all that we can."

They followed the Three High Masters into one of the private Mystic starships that the masters used for their needs. A small emergency starport existed, but it was being greatly expanded as well.

Along the way, the Prime adepts for each of the High Masters joined them. Makita and Iselle backed up Von.

Yet all five Prime adepts looked pale, bloody, scorched, and beaten up. They had clearly all been through the ringer.

Makita and Iselle looked even more spooked and terrified than they had been with Naero's little accident. The one that had nearly killed them. Yet even as they stood there, each of them began the process of healing themselves and regenerating. High Mystic adepts were a tough lot.

In a large conference room on the Mystic starship, the High Masters took places at a nanotable and seats they pweaked up from the nanofloor for their numbers.

The masters called up several large holoscreens above them to assess all that had transpired within the last standard half hour or less. Everyone still seemed stunned.

"Let us start from the beginning," Master Tree said. "A moment. Backup feeds from the Intel vidcams are still coming online."

They all studied a long, aerial shot of the west coast Mystic camp late that night, as it came into view in the dark. Time, around 4:13 in the morning.

In the null circle surrounding the alien obelisk, something ominous began to move. Multiple vidcams and scanning drones attempted to zoom in on it from every angle.

The closest ones disrupted and burned out immediately.

Long range zooms revealed the alien obelisk beginning to move, and spin, and shift shape as it often did, without warning.

Then it took the shape of a young, athletic spacer girl with long hair. Like a statue all in muted shades of dark gray

The heavy waves of layered shielding began to buckle and disrupt next, sending showers of sparks and bursts of explosions from destroyed shield pods and generators.

All along the defensive perimeter, the heavy Marine regiment stationed there activated, calling up all reserves to the line, as alarms and sirens sounded.

Tanks and heavy weapons heated up and began to glow, preparing to fire. They prepared to unleash enough firepower to destroy an entire army, or a large city.

The alien artifact, now in the form of a young woman, opened its blinding violet eyes.

A radiance that fleets in orbit suddenly noted down on the planet below, as energy scans spiked beyond known limits and destroyed entire sensor and scanning arrays on every ship.

The statue with the blinding eyes stepped down, and the surface of the planet yawned and split, fissuring out from it, as the bedrock of if Nashara heaved and groaned.

More strange energies and lights pulsed from the walking juggernaut, and all remaining shields in that area collapsed.

The Marines opened fire in that instant.

They poured blazing ordnance, beams, and explosive blasts at the statue, cratering the ground further all around it.

Nothing living–nothing known to exist–could have withstood such intense, destructive fire.

Yet the statue ignored every attack and kept walking, entirely invulnerable, oblivious. Nothing could harm whatever it was made of. Many of the attacks seem to deflect or bounce off.

Yet other attacks, the statue appeared to absorb directly.

Scans revealed that the statue was drawing in energy at a fantastic rate.

"What direction was the artifact moving in?" Aunt Sleak asked, her face, like most of the others in the room, pale showing shock at what they were watching.

"Yes," Master Vane, sneered. "Tell us, what was it heading for?"

Naero guessed, and blurted out quickly, "It was heading straight for me."

Everyone turned and glanced at her. Her analysis proved exactly correct.

"Watch what happens now," Master Jo said. They all swept back around to stare at the holoscreens.

As the Marines attempted to increase the ferocity of their attack, a blinding pulse of violet energy fanned out from the statue in the sweeping flash of an instant.

The energy ring's diameter widened faster than thought, and passed through the entire defensive perimeter instantaneously.

As it did so, gravtanks, meks, massive artillery pieces leveled straight at the statue, and heavy gun emplacements all flared for a brief instant and were swept away.

These advanced weapons did not explode.

They were all completely disintegrated in one blinding flash of total oblivion.

Naero thought she noticed something strange about the statue's face.

High Master Tree froze the vidfeeds for a moment to allow them all to take in what they had just witnessed.

"An entire heavy Spacer Marine armored regiment," Jan noted, nearly stammering, "completely annihilated in the space of a thought."

Master Jo was about to speak, but Gaviok interrupted him, his carapace solid black, in his extreme defensive mode.

"What power is this?" the mantid asked. Even he sounded as if he were at a loss.

Shalaen spoke up, clearly striving to remain calm on her own. "There is no power such as this," she said. "There is none like it that any of our peoples have witnessed or ever known to exist. Nor even among our enemies. Even removed from the scene and watching these vids replay, one can feel it. There should be no such power as this. It threatens my sanity. We should all take the time to be very afraid."

Master Vane spoke up, glaring casually in Naero's direction. "We have witnessed such a power—once before—with another of these alien artifacts, on what was then, Janosha. It behaved slightly differently, but it was much the same. We tried to study it, as we are attempting to study this new one now. Yet, much like the other, it is nearly beyond all comprehension, and any attempt to control it."

Vane hesitated. Shame was rife in his voice when he spoke again. "We attempted to do so, and were soundly punished."

Naero closed her eyes solemnly. "Did none of those thousands of brave Marines survive? Are we certain that they are all dead?

That very thought tore her heart out of her chest and stomped on it.

"I was going to say, before," Master Jo added, "as amazing as it it sounds, none of the Marines are dead. The strange energy wave stripped them of all weapons and armor—even their uniforms, somehow. It left them all smoking, stunned, and naked where they fell."

Naero covered her mouth with both hands, her relief was so great.

Master Tree continued. "When we are certain the danger has passed, we will send their brothers and sisters to collect them and see to their conditions. They still lie where they fell, unconscious."

"Let's watch the rest of the vids," Master Tree said. "The High Masters and I did make an attempt to contain the artifact, much the same as the way we suppressed your more violent abilities, High Adept Naero."

Master Vane rubbed his apparently aching head, his robes, like those of the other two High Masters, still blasted and scorched. "For all the good that did us," he muttered.

Tree started the vids again.

The three High Masters transported in and formed a triangle directly in the path of the approaching statue, with Master Vane, the strongest of them all, out in front.

Orbs of intense Cosmic energy, blazing scarlet, azure, and gold, encased each of them. And around all three, an even larger sphere of shining white energy protected them.

They attempted to form such an orb of light around the statue, and for a moment, the artifact halted, and appeared to be either confused, intrigued by, or studying the sphere's composition.

78

Then it lifted one hand.

A ray of intense violet energy punched out from that hand, expanded into a cone of the same might, and shattered all before it.

The spheres and energies of even the High Mystic Masters disrupted and shattered like glass, dissolving in mid-air.

The three masters were hurled off their feet and flung back, battered and set on fire, like mere children before a hurricane of violet flame.

They recovered their wits and retreated, transporting away.

The statue resumed its forward march, three-quarters of the way out of the crater and nearly at the stricken defensive perimeter.

Intel forces and the Prime adepts led a brave but futile attack from all directions, trying to slow the statue down.

The thing blasted and swatted them away like insects and kept walking. Nothing could stop it.

The naval destroyer *The Mikado* swept in close to the ground and strafed the statue, pinpointing the area around it with heavy, concentrated cannon fire.

The statue absorbed the attacks as before.

Dazzling rays from its glowing eyes disintegrated the entire warship in a blinding flare of naked power.

One hundred and eighty stunned crew slowly floated naked to the ground and lay still with the vanquished Marines.

Nothing known to Spacers or any other sentient race appeared capable of stopping this thing—or even slowing it down.

Finally, for no apparent reason, the statue mysteriously halted, shifted shape a few times, and then froze where it stood.

Master Tree cut the vidfeeds. "It has not moved or even flickered since, by all reports."

"Why did it stop moving?" Naero asked.

Tree turned to her. "I believe that was the exact moment that you and I transported from the west coast camp to the east coast camp here, Naero."

"I'm guessing," Master Jo said, "that once you were out of its sensory range, the very purpose for its actions was no longer present. It no longer had a reason to act."

Naero shrugged. "So, I am its reason to act. Why? I guess we could transport back in and see if starts advancing toward me again."

Even Master Vane's eyes widened. "Oh, hell, no, Maeris. None of us are getting spanked by that infernal thing again, just so that you can conduct a silly experiment."

"Are we certain that it is evil?" Naero said. "I did not detect any Darkforce energy, or any presence of alien tek, like that of our enemies, that makes you feel sick inside to be near it. And it appeared to go out of its way to avoid killing our people, when it clearly and easily could have done so. It selectively destroyed all weapons and gear, leaving our troops stunned and helpless–but still alive. How could it even do that? No weapon can do such a thing."

Shalaen placed a hand on Naero's shoulder. "The more important question to ask, my sister, is what does this thing want with you? Why is it so interested in you?"

Master Vane snorted. "Isn't it obvious? Why do any of these strange, elusive beings want to capture Maeris and make use of her for their purposes? She's a monster–a living, breathing, potential weapon of mass destruction–just waiting to be exploited and unleashed, and she also has the KDM within her. Isn't that all enough?"

Shalaen shook her head. "I do not think that is it. We have all witnessed but a fraction of this artifact's frightening power. None of us can even conceive of matching it in any way. I think that it could very easily wipe out this entire world in an instant, if it but chose to do so. Yet it is not bent upon destruction. It wants something, and it clearly is not about to let anything stand in its way when it is about to move."

Gaviok took up Shalaen's train of thought. "I think I follow you. Yet the artifact does appear to have some kind of limitations also. It stopped moving toward Naero once she was too far away for it to track and follow her exact location. Perhaps its sensory abilities are limited, in ways that we cannot understand."

"Yes, yes," Master Tree said. "It is specifically goal-oriented. Once the goal passed out of its range of perception, it stopped moving and went dormant once more."

"What does it want with me?" Naero said. "If it had been able to reach me…what would have happened? What would it have done to me?"

The three High Masters grew very silent suddenly.

All three of them were hiding something. Naero knew for a fact that her outcast uncle had directly encountered one of these things–a very similar alien obelisk or artifact, if not exactly alike. She didn't know the details, but she more or less guessed that the results had been catastrophic in some way. Baeven and many others had been very nearly destroyed, including Naero's mother, who had also been present at the time and somehow involved. Baeven had almost died as a result, and he had never been the same since that time.

The encounter and his involvement with that artifact had helped destroy his life among his people.

It was Aunt Sleak who spoke up.

"We need to know what happened with the other artifact like this one," she said. "You mentioned that there was another one. What happened to it? Perhaps that will shed some light on what we should do now with this one."

"We cannot speak of such," Master Tree said flatly.

"We will not speak of it ever again," Master Vane said flatly, "not upon pain of death."

"Cannot. Will not," Aunt Sleak said. "What rubbish. Tell us what happened or at least why you will not even broach the subject."

Master Jo spoke plainly. "Because we can't recall them. All traces of those events have been purged from our minds, by the power of the artifact itself."

Tree nodded. "To this day, all that we know are the events leading up to the...mysterious occurrence. And those that followed."

Vane continued for them. "We decided that when–*not if*–more of these immensely powerful devices were encountered, we would do our best to study and comprehend them, and seek to control any and all interaction with them. Also for the good of all."

Master Jo gave their conclusion. "Only one person living truly knows what occurred on that fateful day in that hour. And by all logic, he should have been slain by whatever resulted from that cataclysm. We had meant to destroy him ourselves, not only for his gross disobedience and defiance of our will, our laws, and our very ways– yet somehow, he managed to escape and elude us. He even found some way to stave off the terrible fate awaiting him. When he fled Janosha, he was filled with such terrible Cosmic energies, raging so out of control, that he was a threat to anyone or any living thing that he came near to."

Vane spoke once more. "We thought the outcast was merely running away somewhere to perish on his own. To our mind, no being could survive what he had endured–what was so unstable within himself."

Naero rose up defiantly, her blood up, her fists jammed on her hips.

She had heard enough.

Aunt Sleak sensed her mood and tried to pull her back.

Naero jerked her arm away out of her aunt's steel grip.

"You filthy hypocrites. My Uncle Kean suffered great and permanent loss and harm at the hands of one of these devices. So dangerous that you won't even let yourselves remember what it was, or what it did to him."

"He is an outcast," Vane roared. "He directly disobeyed us, and nearly destroyed all of Janosha—until you came along to finish the job! You of all your Clan have no right to speak his lost name ever again!"

Naero stood up to him. Let him strike her down, if he must. "I will speak his name, if I so choose. I will dare to shout it from the heavens if I must. This isn't about what Kean did at all. This is about all of you and your inadequacies. All of you failed, just as you are failing with this artifact. The high and mighty three Mystic High Masters, three frauds more like it—failed to control this device. And who bore the brunt of that failure? Surely not any of you, but my uncle did so—my blood!"

She stepped away, enraged, and then whirled upon them, extending an accusing finger. "You blamed him for your failures, for unleashing forces none of you could control. And then you made him your sacrificial lamb. Once you murdered him and took his life, the problem would be solved. The terrible forces contained within him would be extinguished with his life. Your guilt and your crimes would be covered up. Even if he escaped, you bastards fully expected him to suffer and die horribly, somewhere on his own where you wouldn't have to watch his torment. I'm glad he found a way to survive, and spite you hypocrites ever since!"

Naero crossed her arms in front of herself and whipped around, giving them her heaving back.

At that moment, she wished she could destroy them all. Perhaps she should transport herself to the artifact right now and fling her arms around the damn thing.

Master Jo tried to reason with her. "Naero, there is some truth to what you say. But there were many other things going on at that same time that also affected our actions, decisions, and what happened, as well. Your former uncle openly defied and disobeyed direct orders, not once, but repeatedly. And many persons died because of that. He nearly killed your own mother, his sister, whom he claimed to care about. He was out of control, with what you would call his own Dark Beast. We were barely able to suppress and contain him, just as we did with you. But despite our best efforts, he was going to explode at some point, and possibly take out all of Janosha. We had to destroy him before that took place, take him somewhere safe. But he broke free, and escaped before we could do so."

"And look at what happened," Vane said. "Not only did the outcast survive, he became a renegade, and an outlaw, reviled for his treachery and duplicity–responsible for countless deaths on all sides of nearly every conflict since that time."

"A life the Mystics drove him to," Naero noted.

"A life he chose," Aunt Sleak said, "but none of that can be changed. The question remains: What do we do now with this situation, and this artifact?"

"The only thing we can do. We keep Naero away from it at all costs, while we continue to study the artifact and learn more about its secrets." Master Tree said. "That way, we avoid repeating any of the mistakes from the past. Our only defense will be knowledge."

"And once again," Naero said, "I ask, what would happen if I did interact with this thing?"

"Theoretically," Master Tree noted, "some kind of merging or recombination. The device will either become part of you–or you will become part of it. We're not certain how much of either."

Master Vane snorted again. "I'm still not certain Maeris's mother wasn't infected by that first device as well, back then. Look at the trouble we're having with her three children–showing the same dangers as their former uncle."

"Those effects were triggered by their contact with the Kexxian Data Matrix," Aunt Sleak said.

Vane persisted. "Can we be certain of that? Danner never came into direct contact with the KDM for years."

Jan jumped in. "Danner came into contact with it through his connection with me, at the same time that Naero and I did. Yet it is true that by then, he was already a powerful psyonic genius."

While they still argued, Naero called up one of the holoscreens again and replayed some of the vid footage, zooming in on the artifact statue's face.

Master Jo looked over at her. "Did we miss something, Naero?"

Naero paused.

Suddenly she grew even more worried.

Om noticed it at the same time.

"Its mouth was moving. The statue was saying something," she said. "It was talking all the while."

Everyone stared at her.

"What was it saying?" Master Tree asked.

Naero started watching the vid close-ups from the very beginning.

"It was speaking something in Kexxian," Naero said.

No, Naero. It was singing…in Kexxian.

Naero felt frozen stilettos of ice slicing through her veins. "I...I recognize that tune. I know that song. I've heard it before. I've sung the words."

"Why would it be singing in Kexxian? What was it saying?"

Naero cleared her throat.

Yah-duu Ah Shah Lah! Shah hah lah shah-dae! Yah Jhah Vah Shah-Lae! Ae duu vah. Ae duu vah shah lah!

High Master Tree received an emergency com from Spacer Intel and the Marines back at the western camp. Tree brought it up on screen.

"Master Tree. The alien artifact has taken the statue form again and is on the move. It has turned due east, and is walking straight toward your coordinates on the east coast. Oh, no!"

"Captain Valmont, Valmont," Tree said. "What is happening? Report!"

"It...it just vanished, High Master. It must have transported. I say again, the artifact is gone–off all scans."

"Track it, from orbit if need be. Locate it. A Cosmic energy source that enormous cannot hide."

Tree turned to Naero. "Don't sing anymore, Naero. Pilot, launch immediately. Get us in orbit until this crisis is over."

Naero felt the Mystic starship lift off, fearing that they could be zapped by the strange artifact at any moment.

Was it Kexxian? Was it attracted by the KDM? Was that why this thing was after her?

12

High Master Tree came to Naero and her people an hour later, in orbit around Thanor-4, with the latest updates.

"The situation has stabilized. The artifact statue is making a precise, concerted search of the continent of Nashara–in overlapping spheres. It apparently scans each circle for about fifteen standard minutes. We don't know how it does so, but we've computed its sensory range to be about one hundred kilometers."

Naero nodded. "Does it know about the other continents? Does it even understand that it is on a planet?"

"Why would it not?" Master Tree said. "We must assume that it can do all of this and more. It has even transported into the ocean, to the exact center of its next search diameter, if that happens to be offshore. It could search the entire planet if it chose to do so. Nothing we know of could stop it. Yet, it does not seem to have the ability to fly or to leave the planet's surface. It can only move from one stationary position to the next–within its transport range."

"Then how did it get here?" Jan asked.

"That, we do not know. We assume now that they are Kexxian artifacts or devices, from what Naero has said. If that is true, they could be millions of years old. Who knows what their function is? But we will continue to attempt to study this one, and any others we locate."

"So," Naero said. "What do I do now?"

"Simple. Those of you who are adepts will resume your training—including you, High Adept," Tree told them. "We have yet another secret camp set up on Thanarra."

"Near the locals?" Shalaen asked. "The native near humans?"

"Close enough. And we are also close enough in species to pass as some of them. They think we are priests and priestesses of their sacred gods. Even in their violent societies, such religious orders are revered, respected, and almost never accosted or harmed. Most Thanorans consider it a great sin to harm a holy man or holy woman, and that affords us protection, respect, and freedom of movement among them. We can go almost anywhere unquestioned, and be welcomed and well-received. They value our wisdom and knowledge, especially as healers."

Naero was puzzled. "If I'm busy training, will I even have need to go among them?"

Tree smiled. "I am making this part of your training, High Adept. There is more to being a Mystic than martial training and Cosmic energy manipulation. The Thanorans present constant problems to be solved. They come to us for help, almost on a daily basis. Anything from lesser disputes and disagreements to other matters of great import. I want you to work with them. I and others will observe how you perform among them."

Naero was at a loss. This was an unexpected shift. It was just like the High Masters to catch her off guard and put her out of her element in order to test her under duress.

As Vane once said, everything was a test. Naero guessed that they wished to distract her also, to keep her mind busy and definitely not thinking about the unstoppable alien artifact that was hunting for her.

She still felt as if she needed to protest. "But I don't know anything about these peoples or their cultures. I don't know their language."

High Master Tree frowned slightly. "Use a translator like everyone else. Adepts Chang Fu-han and Chang Lijuan will accompany you, along with many others. They are experts among the Thanes, and have been here since the beginning. The Thanes know and highly respect them. Identical twins such as them—especially among the holy ones—are considered rare and powerful magic."

The Chang sisters arrived at that moment, smiling at Naero.

"Skim our many reports and research on Thanian culture and practices," Fu-han said. "We will catch you up and teach you how to act, and what to say, and how to dress among them."

Lijuan jumped right in, as she usually did. "We will teach you about the four main peoples and city states: Thanarra, Vaedor, Kallos, and Maedor. This is a time of great strife among the four city states, and we have been trying to negotiate a lasting peace between them, ever since we arrived."

Fu-han shook her head sadly. "To no avail. The city states are packed so close together in the same bay, only a few days away from each other. They are so warlike and competitive, they hardly have the concept of peace."

Naero stared back at Master Tree. "And you expect me to step in, and help solve these problems?"

Tree looked back at her. "I expect you to do your best and try hard. I did not say that I require you to succeed. The only stipulations I make, are the same ones we all operate under among backwards sentients. We cannot solve their problems for them. And we are not here to uplift them, or give them new tek before they are ready for it. We are not here to pick their leaders. They must do such things.

"But we can counsel, guide, and influence them, and help them learn to use reason and logic, to make the best decisions that they can make—for themselves. And this is very important: *Unless we are forced to defend ourselves, we must never use violence among them.* They expect us to be peaceful and refrain from doing so. It will discredit us greatly if we behave as violently as they do. They must learn from their mistakes."

Fu-han added. "Any tek we bring with us must be concealable. We have had cloaked fixers design translators, comunits, and other devices that are disguised as local adornments and jewelry. Even if they leave our persons or are stolen, any devices we carry are programmed to become inert and inoperative."

"That is enough for now," Tree said. "All of you get some rest. You will need it later today. After your morning training sessions on board, prepare yourselves and go down to Thanarra."

Naero went to her quarters.

The Changs sent her their many data files, prioritized in the order they thought she should scan them. Lijuan brought her three sets of Thanoran dress and gear, Naero's size. Two sets for daily wear, one set for court visits. The natives were a feudal society, complete with feudal hierarchies.

Naero tried one of the outfits on. It consisted of linen undergarments that were wrapped and tied. Then a linen shift–which doubled as a nightgown–and finally, a wool tunic that went down to the knee, and was usually dagged. The priests and priestesses of the local deities wore garments that were off-white or slightly gray, but always trimmed in blue, to denote their status. They also wore hoods, trimmed in the same color, and simple leather belts around their waists, usually with a useful leather pouch or purse to carry things in.

They wore soft leather boots, trimmed in fur, that rose to the knee. In the heat of the high summer, they wore leather or woven sandals.

Priests carried no weapons, unless you counted the small iron utility knife that all Thanorans carried, and a wooden spoon kept in one's pouch, used mostly for eating meals. If they traveled, the natives wore a small leather pack or shoulder bag, and carried a leather waterskin.

Only the warrior classes wore armor and carried weapons: iron mail shirts, coifs, mittens, and leggings, studded leather coats of plates, round and kite shields, and conical, iron and leather helms with nasal guards. The most common weapon was the iron axe, and then the spear, and various horse bows that fired iron-tipped arrows. However, the local mount was actually more of a domesticated elk or reindeer-type mammal, called a *gult*. The natives had no horses, and they used saddles and reins, but had not developed stirrups, yet.

There were various types of iron swords, but swords were expensive, and exclusive to the nobility or their bodyguards. Both males and females of the proper class, apparently, could become warriors. The development and use of steel was haphazard at best.

The mark of a warrior remained the axe and spear, and the long, iron-hilted fighting dagger or short sword, called the *karath*.

As a priestess of the local gods, Naero would wear an *ocalo,* a small circle of ornate, knotted and polished silver or brass on a leather cord or chain. This was the holy symbol that they used to pray and heal with, the eternal circle, a mandala of infinity.

Naero waved Lijuan off. "That's enough for now. I need some sleep. We can go over more later today. I don't usually wear clothes to bed, but I'll sleep in these to get used to them. Thanks, Lijuan."

Her friend nodded, and said good night.

Naero flopped down onto her sleeping panel and almost instantly dozed off, native garb and all.

13

After lunch, Naero was already tired. Her sparring sessions with the Order Adepts on board the Mystic vessel went well, but it was exhausting, especially after a night of short sleep. She wore her new clothing all that morning.

When she had the time, she could program her nanosuit to imitate the local style of clothing. That would be much more efficient in the long run.

She napped on the cloaked shuttle that transported them down to a secret mountain starport near the foremost city state of Thanarra. These were the natives who actually referred to themselves as Thanes.

From the hidden mountain starport, the adepts would transport into a much closer cave complex that posed as a sacred burial place and a shrine to the gods, guarded only by the Mystics. From there, Naero and her companions would make their forays down into the sprawling city state of Thanarra, and across the Bay of Thanarra to the other three city states beyond.

Thanarra was a walled city with three main walls, with towers and gatehouses guarding the access points from without. Soldiers manned and patrolled the walls. The city itself radiated out below them in concentric rings and spokes of streets, punctuated by larger stone and tile roof buildings of one to three stories tall, and even what looked to be walled estates near the coast and others strung up into the mountains in other directions.

Although it was a bright, sunny afternoon, the wide streets were still bustling after the midday meal. Pedestrians walked about on their business. Many used walking staffs of wood, plain, polished, carved, or even decorated. The staffs seemed to denote some sign of social status.

Wealthier citizens also rode various gults. Naero spotted patrols of soldiers, marching in ranks with shields and spears in groups of a dozen or larger–some patrols mounted on gults, moving from one city garrison to the next in their circuits. People made room for the patrols.

There were countless carts and wagons with solid wooden wheels. A few gult chariots, pulled by one to four gult. The city was punctuated by simple circles and squares with fountains or wells. From the little Naero had read, Thanarra was blessed with the richness of fresh aquifers running under it from the mountains.

This water-wealth also assisted the tilled, tiered farming among all the lower river valleys that spread out from the city state. Several broad, dirt main roads spread out from the city into the farming country and to the ports nearby on the coast. The roads were paved brick or cobblestone only within the city limits.

The large Bay of Thanarra was active with small wooden fishing boats with lateen sails, and larger merchant boats and barges with no more than two simple masts and square sails. Some of the vessels had oars. Each of the ships had eyes painted on the bows, or the carved wooden figurehead of a person or some kind of mythical creature.

Many of the locals wore conical straw hats with wide brims, called a *thon*. With summer waxing, Naero and her party intended to purchase their own thons in the open air markets. Naero found the straw hats quaint, with everyone below in the city bobbing and scurrying around in them, looking like archetypal wizards from one of her friend Ty's dopey vidgames.

There were only seven adepts on this mission with Naero: the Changs, from Order; Tenarra Fox and Kent Marshall, from Chaos; and Oshara Wallace and Timan Ramsey, from Change. They wore all of their gear, and carried plain, polished wooden staffs, slightly taller than their heads, as holy people often did.

Naero posed as a mediator, and that was how she would be presented. Her ocalo, or holy symbol, was shining silver, which was sacred to the natives. Other than the Vaedo, most did not use gold and silver as money, but for adornment. Their coins consisted of copper, bronze, and even iron. Each adept had a small amount of money for their needs.

As they made their way down into the city along the paths from the caves, the first thing Naero noticed was the stink sweeping up toward them on the winds from the sea.

"Does it always smell this bad?" Naero noted. All of them could not help making faces.

"It is indeed unpleasant," Chang Fu-han said. "But you will get used to it after a few hours."

"The lice and vermin are much worse than the smell," Chang Lijuan added.

Screw that.

Tenarra Fox spoke quietly. "The more people, the greater the stench and parasites. Thanarra has a near human population of about twenty-thousand."

"Vaedo has the largest, overall population—about forty-five thousand," Kent added. "Wait until you smell it—most of the Vaedo still think bathing is unhealthy."

Naero blinked, still wrinkling her sensitive nose. "Can't wait to go there."

Oshara laughed. "It can make your eyes water at times. But since my last visit, I came prepared this time. I have some scented nanonasal filters, enough for all, if anyone wants some." She held out her hand from her pocket, revealing what looked to be several pairs of clear, tiny elastic bands. Naero and the others quickly grabbed for them. Even the Chaos adepts thanked her for her foresight and generosity.

"How do they work?" Naero asked.

Oshara shoved them into her nostrils one at a time. "Stretch them around the tip of your small finger, and then up your nose. The nanomaterial is activated by mucous and will adhere to the inside naturally and last for about a standard day." The days and nights on Thanor-4 were roughly close to that.

Naero put hers in. Instantly, the air smelled much better. Not perfect, but much better.

"I have more if you need them. They won't keep out the worst smells," Oshara added, "but it is an improvement."

91

Mason Elliott

All six of them thanked her.

"We need to talk about our procedures with food," Chang Lijuan added. "The Thanes will offer to feed us on a regular basis, as is their custom with holy people. But their food can be both spoiled and diseased, and often contaminated with local parasites. Our Spacer metabolism will protect us most of the time, but to be sure, use the pouch of salt and spices we've provided each of you with. Just sprinkle at little on each meal that you eat. It is a practice and a custom that most Thanes follow, and will not be noticed. Nanoenzymes in the powder will neutralize anything harmful on the food."

Timan chuckled. "Too bad it doesn't help the taste much."

All of them but the somber Chaos adepts laughed.

Chang Fu-han picked up the instruction. "When you do eat, always try to eat something to please your host. If you really hate everything that is offered, simply state that you are fasting. The holy people do that on a regular basis, and it is also accepted, but be consistent to avoid offending. It is normal for us to drink wine or beer with a meal, but not strong liquor such as whiskey. It is a sin for a holy person to get drunk, and unless it is a high day or period of celebration, public drunkenness is frowned upon and, even punished by exposure in the stocks."

They met more and more of the locals as they descended into the city proper. Most people ignored them. A few honored them by lifting both hands palm out, and nodding briefly with their heads. In turn, they nodded, and kept moving.

Skin color could be anything from stark white to pure black, dark gray, and various shades of brown and gold. Hair color varied as well–black, brown, red, gold–even white and blue. Eye color seemed to be black, blue, green, hazel, amber, or purple. Eye shapes were anything from very round to slanted.

Fortunately, their disguised Spacer translators worked perfectly with the local tongue. Naero could make out several conversations and even a few arguments very clearly as they passed along.

The Changs kept theirs turned off, because they had already learned the native language–Thanorian–and spoke freely with any who engaged them.

Then without warning, an old woman came running out of a small stone house, her hair disheveled, tears and a frantic look on her pale, gray face. She shouted to them, almost in a panic. "Holy ones, bless you. Please help me, by the gods, please help me!"

The Changs placed their hands gently on the old woman's arms as she rushed up to them.

"Calm yourself, greatmother."

"How may we help?"

"My greatson, he is not even three summers. He is sick, and he is dying. Please help me." She pressed a small pouch of coins into Fu-han's palm. "All that I have is yours. Please, please heal him."

"Keep your money, greatmother," Fu-han said, giving her back the coins.

"Take us to the child," Lijuan said.

The panic-stricken woman turned and tried to run again, and nearly collapsed. The Changs supported her between the two of them.

When they came inside the small stone building, Naero saw a small boy with shaggy dark hair lying on a small bed off to one side. She strode forward. She alone among them had the healing sight.

Naero knelt and placed her hands on the child to examine what was wrong with him. He was sweating and chilled with a high fever, and he was very weak. He looked up at Naero, his veiled green eyes delirious.

The boy smiled up at her, and Naero ran her hands through his hair gently and smiled down at him. She tried to determine what was causing the fever, and found it right away.

Food poisoning. The child had eaten something contaminated. Left to itself, it would in fact take his life. He was also malnourished, dehydrated, riddled with worms, and had a slight skin infection on the insides of his dirty legs.

The little boy looked up at all the holy ones gathered around him and weakly laughed. "Look, gramma. The spirits have come. The spirits of light come for me."

The old woman covered her eyes. "Save him. He thinks you are here to take his spirit. Please, do not let him die!"

"Not this day," Naero said.

She carried the boy over to the chamber pot and stimulated his upper digestive tract with healing energy, causing him to vomit anything left in his system.

Naero handed him briefly to Lijuan.

"Fresh water," she said. The grandmother poured some out of a water jar into small bowl and brought it to her. Just to be sure, Naero sprinkled the general Spacer curative powder into the water. The all-purpose medicine, nutrients, and biotics would help the body heal naturally on its own, bolstering the immune system. It should also flush out the worms.

93

She made the boy drink it. He resisted weakly, but they got it all down him with a minimum of choking and spluttering.

The fast-acting medicine swept through the boy's system.

Naero knew he was going to poop, pulled up his nightshirt, and held him on the chamber pot as he did so. The grandmother came forward and helped Naero clean him off and wash him up. Naero also applied a healing salve that should clear up the skin infection.

At some point, the boy nodded off. They wrapped him in an old wool blanket and put him back in bed. His color looked better and he was breathing stronger and easier.

Naero checked him again with her sight. His fever was broken, and most of the toxins and the parasites were out of his system now. After some rest, he would probably wake up very hungry.

Naero instructed her friends to have the stealth fixers decontaminate everything throughout the dwelling.

"He's going to be all right," Naero finally told the grandmother.

The old woman went down on her knees and tried to kiss Naero's hands. Naero lifted her back up.

"I want you to listen to me, greatmother. The boy ate bad food and its poison nearly killed him. I want you to boil your drinking water on your stove, and bake, boil, or fry your food well from now on, but do not burn it. Use citrus in your cooking if you can. Feed the child more greens."

"I will, holy one. I will do my best, but we are poor."

"Are you here by yourselves?"

"No, thank the gods. My son and his wife live with us. This is their boy, and a little girl just born that my daughter-in-law carries with her. My son works with the fishers, and his wife washes clothes on the shore among the rocks, and does sewing, and helps mend nets. I help out here as I can. We are poor, but happy overall."

Naero examined their small kitchen in the one room home. Bread and cheese wrapped in old cloth. Some smelly fish, probably the source of the food poisoning. Naero sprinkled some nanospice powder on it, and some more in the water jar.

"We have done all that we can do and must go," Chang Fu-han said. She handed the woman a few coins.

"Get some fresh food for the boy from the markets. He will sleep for a time, and will be hungry when he wakes. Blessings to you and your kin, greatmother."

The old woman wept for joy and raised both palms, bowing her head in thanks. "Blessings to the gods and their holy ones. Thank you, thank you for helping us."

They made their way out into the street, where a small crowd of people had gathered.

Many paid homage to them as they passed on.

"Thank you, holy ones."

"Praise the gods."

"Thank you, for helping Ama and the boy."

They said nothing for a while.

Finally, Kent made a comment. "Was that all really necessary?" he said. "Look at the time we have wasted."

"We are not having this same, standard argument, Chaos adept," Oshara said, and then sighed.

"No, seriously," Kent said. "What real good did we do? You may feel better now, but the infant mortality rate among the natives is still sixty percent or more. The same thing could happen to that boy tomorrow, and he'll be just as dead, like others all over this city. What difference does it make anyway, if they live or die? We should not have interfered. Let things be as they will."

"No," Chang Fu-han said. "A holy one here on this world would try to help when asked to do so. That is part of their purpose. They would not simply let things be as they are."

Lijuan was quick to add, "And when we came here two years ago, the infant mortality rate was more than seventy percent. We have helped change things for the better."

"That's just it," Tenarra said. "We're fakes. We shouldn't even be here, and neither should our tek—our medicines. We're lying to these people and toying with them for our benefit, to make ourselves feel better about using their world for our purposes. Can't you see that? We should just leave them alone, and whatever happens to them, happens."

"I see your point and your line of reasoning," Naero said. "But I still disagree. If I see someone who needs help, or someone asks me for help, if I am able to give it, I'm going to do so."

"Agreed," all of the others said. The two out-voted Chaos adepts sighed and rolled their eyes.

The made their way through the city, bought their thon hats and some fresh dried meat, cheese, and fruit in the marketplace.

What Naero wouldn't give for a borbble of Jett and a pod of Spum.

It took them another hour to reach the palace at the highest point of the city, well-defended and set behind high walls. They approached

95

the massive, heavily guarded gatehouse, even though the ironbound gates
and doors stood wide open, with many troops lining the way.

The leader on duty hailed them, and soldiers came forward to search
them for weapons–male on male, female on female.

The veteran woman-warrior searching Naero got a bit grabby for
Naero's liking during the pat down.

"Must you handle me in such fashion?" Naero said, trying to catch the
flavor of the local speech in her protest.

The warrior woman chuckled. "Everyone entering the palace gets
searched," she said dryly. "No exceptions, even holy ones. The last group
of assassins that attacked the palace all posed as holy ones. Before that–
circus performers. Don't flatter yourself, chicky. You're a firm one, you
are. But ya don't have anything I want or need right now." She winked at
Naero. "Move along!"

They passed more soldiers, and squads of archers milling about. There
was a stable in the huge courtyard, where they heard gults stamping and
snorting. Guards were posted at regular intervals.

A male courtier or court official met them at the open palace gates.
The palace also looked to be a fortress, and had a hexagonal wall with six
high towers and battlements. The palace keep lay within, a four story
structure with stained glass windows starting on the third floor.

The keep was cleaner than any place Naero had seen thus far, but both
it and the people in it still smelled, nose filters or not.

The palace bustled with guards and nobles, and servants, all scurrying
about doing something.

They were led into an antechamber to the throne room and told to wait
there. After half an hour, a servant brought them watered wine, and bread
and cheese. Naero ate a little, but put her head down on the table and slept
some more when she could.

After another half hour, another courtier came for them, squeezing
through the door. He was a big, fat man with expensive looking robes and
thick legs. His belt was wide and plated with silver, and his long karath
dagger had jewels on the hilt.

The Changs brightened. They obviously knew this man. He also wore
a silver medallion on a thick silver chain, with the graven image of a bear
on it. He had a barrel chest, and an enormous belly to go with it.

"Lord Tholsen, our good friend," Fu-han said, taking his big hands.
Lijuan placed hers on theirs and smiled together with them."

"Sister Foon, Sister Lijoon. Wellmet. How are you and your brothers
and sisters this day? I see some new faces. Introduce me."

Fu-han did so quickly. "Sisters Tenarra, Oshara, and Naero. Brothers Kent and Timan."

Lord Tholsen shook hands with them all. "Wellmet, I say. Now, which of you is our new mediator?"

Everyone pointed to Naero.

"Bless me, she's so young and pretty, and so tiny. I would think her a minstrel or a dancer–but surely not a mediator."

Naero stepped forward and took both of his hands as if he were an old family friend.

"Wellmet, milord. I assure you, I will do my best in my situation."

"Indeed. Let us hope so. We are ever in need of wise heads and patient minds. In truth, I am glad you have come. Our Majesties are quite beside themselves."

"Say that it is not so," Fu-han said. "What is the situation?"

"What can be done?" Lijuan added.

Lord Tholsen let out a great sigh, as if he might deflate entirely. "Why, what has changed? No one wants to listen to anyone. Everyone seems to want to murder everyone else and rule everything. While we Thanes only want the constant warring and raiding to end–for the sake of trade, and for the sake of all. The Emperor of the Vaedo continues to play his bloody little games. He likes everyone at each others' throats. The Kall have learned to trust no one but themselves and their mastery of their ships, and so, therefore, no one can trust them, either. The Maedo are suffering more than anyone these bloody days. Their position and situation is the weakest, and so they remain defensive and silent, withdrawing at the least insult or sign of aggression. They've withdrawn into their mountain forts."

"So, as usual," Fu-han said, "the four city states remain divided and at each others' throats, constantly on the brink of open war."

Lord Tholsen nodded. "Yes, that about covers it. The endless raids continue, but no one will make a move openly, in fear of the other three banding together against them."

"A four-way standoff," Naero said. "That does not sound good for anyone."

"It most certainly is not," Lord Tholsen said. "The stalemate must be broken, but everyone is afraid to do so, and risk making themselves a target for the other three to dismember."

Naero considered the situation. She needed more time to learn the particulars if the High Masters wanted her to take a crack at negotiating a solution.

She also needed more time to read more of the reports.

"As mediator, I want to speak to the representatives of all four parties separately, before I meet with them all together," Naero insisted.

"I can arrange that, over the next few days," Tholsen told her. "In the afternoons, say around this time?"

"That will be fine. Who can I speak to today?"

Tholsen blinked. "Why…Their Majesties, of course."

"Of course."

"Just give me a moment, and we'll be ushered in shortly."

"Thank you, milord." He slipped out.

Naero immediately turned to the Changs.

"Quick, what do I need to know about the King and Queen of Thanarra?"

Fu-han spoke first. "King Arrok is a warrior king, but with a keen mind. He wants things to change, but is not in a place to change them. Most of all, he wants to protect his people from the sort of thing that is happening to the weaker, less numerous, Maedo. There are only about four or five thousand Maedo left, where there used to be twice that many. Queen Liita of Thanarra is a warrior queen, with a bad temper. And, while she is not as intelligent as her lord, yet his lady is more compassionate in some ways. They have two children: Prince Shondar, who is fourteen and very headstrong, and Princess Iiden, twelve, whom everyone dotes on, especially her parents."

Lijuan took over. "The king and queen secretly despise Emperor Vauk of the Vaedo, a vulgar, ruthless bully, but the Vaedo are currently in the strongest position of all the city states. There is mistrust between King Arrok and Haikoda, the Sea King. Haikoda trusts no one and will only meet with others on his ships. It is said that he will never set foot on land until there is peace. The sea people number about fifteen thousand, and control the bay with their warships. Everyone needs them to some degree. Queen Aijarri of the Maedo warrior women was betrayed by the Vaedo, and has suffered several crushing defeats in the past two years. The Maedo are in a bad way. If not for their mountain fortresses, they would have been wiped out by now."

Lord Tholsen returned to them at that very moment.

"Good sisters and brothers," Tholsen said. "Their Majesties will see you now."

14

The throne room was filled with guards and nobles of the Thanarran court, milling about on either side of a long, dusty purple carpet leading up to the two thrones. The vaulted stone ceiling, about fifteen meters up, was decorated with woven tapestries, just like the walls. Guttering torches of pitch and candle lanterns provided light in the large, drafty room.

To Naero's nose, all of the Thanarrans smelled bad. The constant odor was difficult to overcome or ignore. She could smell the king and queen—and the queen's nasty perfume—even as she approached the thrones.

She stopped at a safe distance, about ten meters, leaned on her staff, and bowed her head as she dipped one knee. The Thanarrans did not require people to actually kneel before them.

"Wellmet, holy sister," the King said. "I am King Arrok, ruler of Thanarra, with my beloved Queen Liita by my side. You are the mediator the priests sent to help us?"

Naero looked up at them, cast back her hood, and smiled. "I am. My name is Naero, and I am your mediator."

The queen became livid. The king burst out laughing.

"Why, you're nothing but a child," the queen protested. "The holy ones sent us a little girl to mediate for us? Outrageous. Emperor Vauk will dip her in sauce and devour her for breakfast like one of his dainties."

"Verily," the king said, still chuckling. "Is this some jest? Please, tell us, child."

Naero shrugged. She took the king's eye and held it with force of will. "Forgive me, Majesties. I am older, wiser, and much tougher than I look. Please do not judge me by appearances. I will do my best for you."

The king pondered for a moment, rubbing his beard. "The gods must have sent you to us for a reason, perhaps one we do not yet understand. The situation remains impossible–and in any case–I like what I see in your eyes, Sister Naero. We have nothing to lose here. Perhaps the others will underestimate you as well. You have our permission to act in our names, for the good of all."

Naero dipped her knee again and bowed her head. "Thank you, Your Majesties."

The Queen clapped her hands twice. "These holy ones will dine with us at our table tonight, in honor."

They were given leave to explore the palace, the gardens, and the palace grounds–as well as provide with a chamber to rest in until dinner was served that evening. After dinner, they would return to the Mystic caves in the mountains. Naero studied the layout of the palace.

They arrived early for dinner. Naero felt her sense of warning spike as they approached the dining hall. One of their cloaked spyfixers sounded a quiet alarm through the comdots in their ears.

Om. What is going on?

The cloaked spyfixers have scanned the food and the table setting for infection or disease. It appears that the actual cups and dishes for the royal family have been coated with an invisible glaze of a strong poisonous substance. Any food or drink served in those cups and dishes will become lethal if consumed.

Naero whispered the situation to the other adepts.

"The rest of you stay here and watch everything. The Changs and I are going to speak with Their Majesties. Don't let anyone touch or put anything on these dishes."

They went looking for Lord Tholsen, but could not find him.

A page put them in contact with the House Master, Gavan, who took them to the Captain of the Guard. The captain sent word to the royals, and went to the head cook and the royal taster. The king's loremaster, doctor, and apothecary were all sent for.

A full investigation began. Naero and the Changs each went with one of the three fact-finding teams, who began to question anyone involved with washing and storing the dishes and setting the table.

They came back to one of the meeting rooms in half an hour and disclosed their findings.

"So," Naero said. "Three people handled the place settings for the royals. A dishwasher, a serving girl who brought them out to the table, and the table-setter."

Turvar, the dashing Captain of the Palace Guard, jumped in. "We are questioning the dishwasher and the setter and we have searched their quarters and work areas. Nothing points to them."

Naero and the Changs and their fixers had confirmed that. No trace of the poison yet.

"Where is the serving girl?" Fu-han asked.

Gavan the House Master paled. "That is a problem, I'm afraid. Jannil lives near the palace with her family; you can see her home from the west wall. She asked if she could go home today–to tend some family who had taken ill. I sent her home right after she brought the place settings out. She's always been a good girl, a very sweet child."

"I know the girl," Turvar said. "She comes from a good family, very loyal. I can't believe she would have a hand in anything like this."

"It is always someone you would least suspect," Naero said. "Show me the girl's family home on our way down. Captain, get your people to that house as fast as you can."

On the west side of the palace, Turvar pointed down at the tidy house of the serving girl Jannil and her family.

"I have to get away by myself," Naero told the Changs. "You two go with the captain."

"I'm going to stay here," Naero announced. "Perhaps I can speak to Their Majesties at some point. Let me know what you find with the serving girl. Search her home well, and bring her back to the palace."

After they left, Naero ducked into an empty chamber.

She cloaked and activated her psyonic wings.

Once she was invisible, it was nothing to leap off the west wall and float down to Jannil's home. Naero landed toward the rear of the home and approached the back door and windows.

Immediately she heard tense voices within.

"I did as you asked," a young girl's voice sobbed. "Gods forgive me, it is done. Now keep your word, and let my family go free. Do whatever you wish with me. My life is forfeit, either way."

An oily voice spoke calmly. "We must wait until we have news from the palace," the man said. "Be at peace, little one. It will all be over, very soon."

Naero slipped in through an open window.

Jannil faced down five large men, all of them heavily cloaked and hooded, yet they bristled with weapons, and all but the leader held long, blackened daggers in their ready hands.

They only awaited orders.

"Tie her up. Gag her with the rest," said the oily-voiced man

The four thugs quickly overpowered Jannil. In seconds she was tossed in among the rest of her family in the meeting hall, crying and murmuring like them. Naero made out the girl's parents, a younger brother and a sister, even a small child of about three–all helpless.

One of the thugs glared at the captives and then spoke nervously. "Master, we should have heard something by now. Something may have gone wrong. We should flee."

Their leader thought a moment. "I agree. Make sure of them all. Slash their throats open. Don't get any of the blood on you. Then we slip out of the city."

Naero had heard enough. She zapped all five thugs with partial stun bursts to weaken and disorient them.

The thugs staggered and nearly fell over.

"What is happening to us?"

"Witchcraft! I can barely stand."

"All strength has left me!"

"Get out, you fools. We must get away from this place!"

They fell over each other to scramble out of the house.

The five thugs had barely staggered forty meters away, when Turvar and his guards fell on them and subdued them further, beating them senseless and tying them up.

Naero slipped back out the window and up to the palace. In less than an hour, the assassins and Jannil and her family were all hauled up to the palace guard tower for questioning. Naero and the Changs were present for most of that.

It was clear that Jannil and her family were helpless pawns. The thugs were clearly trained professional assassins, and revealed nothing, even when the palace guards beat and tortured them.

The king and queen entered quietly, wearing cloaks of disguise so that they could listen in.

"We're wasting our time," Turvar said, spitting in the face of the smiling leader. "We've seen their kind before. They won't tell us anything useful."

"The gods shall reveal the truth," Naero said. "Let me examine the leader." She quickly formed a mindlink with him.

This man's stench was even worse. He reeked of death.

"Who hired you, assassin?"

He tried to mock her. "Who else? The gods."

It was a small matter to search his unshielded thoughts.

"You were hired by Haikoda, the Sea King. He paid you and your guild three hundred talents in silver."

The leader paled. "Filthy witch. Unhand me! I did not say that. You couldn't know that. Sorcery!"

"The Sea King paid for your services, but you actually work for Emperor Vauk of the Vaedo. He blackmailed Haikoda into doing so, by kidnapping the Sea King's youngest brother, Jigan. But Jigan is already dead. You dipped the youth in whale blood and fed him to the sharks, feet first, while Emperor Vauk looked on and laughed at the sight."

The Master Assassin foamed at the mouth in rage. "Filthy, rutting, bloody witch!"

Turvar struck the wretch so hard with his heavy, gauntleted fist that broken teeth and blood sprayed out.

"Murdering bastard," Turvar shouted. "You and your vile kind are steeped in blood. The hangman's noose is too kind for you!"

Naero sighed. "This entire scheme was meant to bring the Thanes and the Kall to war–whether the royal family perished or not. Planted evidence would point to the Sea King. The poison is a lethal concoction made from the puffer fish. The assassins themselves have already boasted about how much Haikoda paid them for the deed."

The Master Assassin went mad, seething and fuming at her through his broken face.

"The final goal is clear," Naero continued. "Once Thanarra and Kallos weakened each other sufficiently through a senseless war, Vaedor would sweep in to conquer them both, and in the end, Emperor Vauk would rule all things."

Naero stepped further back in disgust. "That is the truth of things, as the gods reveal them to me."

The king and queen pulled their cowls down and revealed themselves. All present bowed to them.

"Stand with us, my good friends," King Arrok said, "in the face of this naked treachery. Errant knaves, you who sought our lives and the lives of our blameless children."

Warrior Queen Liita gritted her teeth and drew the long gleaming sword she kept at her side. "Hang them. Hang them now, before I run them through by my own hand. You meant to murder my children? You devils will harm no one ever again!"

The killers were ushered out to their fate.

The king came forward and took Naero's hands in wonder. "Forgive me for doubting you, holy sister. The gods have given you the gift to read men's hearts and discern the truth?"

"At times, my king. When they see fit to grant me that power."

He placed her hands on his face.

"Prove it to me. Something I have never told another, even my beloved. When I was a youth, I broke my arm. How did it really happen?"

Naero closed her eyes, and formed the mindlink.

"You told your parents it happened during sword practice, but earlier that morning, you rode you father's warhorse in the fog and fell hard when it threw you."

King Arrok gasped and turned away.

"Amazing. It is true then. Thank you, Sister Naero. Thank you for saving our lives, and the lives of our people. Whether anything happened to us or no–there would have been war, and Vaedor would have been the winner when all was done."

The king left them all, deep in thought at all that had transpired.

Queen Liita sheathed her sword, and also came to Naero.

"My sweet child, I, too, doubted you. Can you ever forgive me?"

Naero bowed her head. "There is naught to forgive, Your Majesty."

"You have saved my life, and the lives of my family. I can never repay you, You shall be welcome within our halls at any hour. You have but to name your wish, and if it is in our power, it shall be granted."

"Nothing but your good will, my queen."

"I am a woman, so I must ask. Did you truly read the heart of the king? Are you blessed which such power?"

"The king is a good man, and strong of heart and will, my queen. Yet as you know, he is beset with many troubles, and worries greatly about the future of his reign, his children, and his people."

The queen sighed. "Verily, it is all too true. The threats we face are clearly very grave and many."

Naero squeezed the queen's hand. "You are a brave people who face everything that comes with courage. You shall find a way. Your lord loves you, and your children, more than his own life. He would give his life for all of you–a thousand times over. Fortune favors the bold."

"Thank you, holy sister. I am fortunate that I do not need the gods to tell me all of that, but it is nice to have it confirmed. I must confer with my lord now. We will need to contact the Sea King and inform him about all these things, and his poor brother. I weep for my cousins."

"Cousins?" Naero said.

Queen Liita laughed. "Did you not know? The gods do not reveal all? My grandmother was a Kall; I am of Kallos blood in part. Haikoda and I are cousins. He will not take the news well, I'm afraid."

"I look forward to meeting with him."

"He is a grim man, who trusts no one. And seemingly with good reason, these troubled days."

"My queen, before you go. I must ask. What will happen to the young serving girl, Jannil?"

"Poor thing. Yet she did betray us. A trial will be held for her and her family to decide their fate."

"May I request mercy for them?" Naero asked. "The gods would wish it so."

"Yet we must live in the real world, not that of the gods, holy sister."

"You did say I could ask for anything, my queen."

"I did. They will be spared then, even the girl. But she must leave the city and join the holy ones. That shall be her punishment."

Naero bowed again. "Your Majesty is just and merciful."

The queen smirked. "Not when people try to kill my family. With all the uproar, my family and I will dine in private tonight in just a short while. Will you and your brothers and sisters be kind enough to join us? I'm sure my lord and I will have many questions for you by then."

Naero bowed her head. "You honor me, my queen. We shall be there, at the appointed time."

15

Dinner with the royals went long into the night. Their Majesties did have many questions. They wanted to know exactly how Naero was going to mediate with the other city states.

That made it difficult to answer, because as yet, Naero did not even know, herself. And even though they were not satisfied by her cagey answers, the royals did see the wisdom in her waiting to make up her mind, and form a final strategy, until after she had met with all the parties involved.

They did warn her greatly about the other leaders–especially Emperor Vauk of the Vaedo, who sounded more and more like a real piece of work.

Naero and the other adepts were so exhausted by the time they left the palace that night, they slipped into the darkness and transported straight to the Mystic stronghold in the fastness of the mountain caves.

She was too tired to file a report to the High Masters, and made a note on her comunit to do so, first thing in the morning.

And yet again, morning would come all too soon.

*

Om woke her up even earlier than expected. No warnings going off for a change, but it was right after five bells.

Sheesh, Om. Is something wrong?

No, nothing that I know of.

Then what the crap do you have against me sleeping?

Because I have good news for a change.

This better be good. I could have snoozed for another hour.

Hear me out. While you have been playing Mystic adept, I'm almost positive that I've figured out both Kexxian startapping and biomancy replication.

Seriously? Both of them?

Yep. I can let you go over the basic process and the energies involved, and then we can start practicing.

That's amazing, Om. Sure. Let me grab a mist shower, explain away, and then we can give them a go.

Om spoke to her very rapidly, in fluent, technical Kexxian. Both of their minds began racing back and forth, sharing data and information, faster than any normal mind could think.

By the time Naero sealed up her black togs, she had a good idea about what they were going to attempt. The dangers were increased, also, so they meant to go slowly and start small at first.

Om fed her information continually, even as she transported them out into the continent of Thanarra's unexplored interior, hundreds of kilometers away, on a fresh desert plain she had selected from the orbital mapping scans.

There was nothing around them that could be harmed, and from late at night till dawn, the desert itself was quite cold. Only the sand under the stars was still warm, and glowed light blue.

All things in the universe possess a degree of Cosmic energy all their own. Tapping into a star is in some ways similar to tapping into a planet, but the distances are of course far greater in certain ways, and yet solar radiation on a planet in a system is constant, and everywhere all at once. The rates of collection and the flow rate of intake are all on different scales entirely, and there are countless variables that must be experienced firsthand and gotten used to.

Naero took a few deep breaths, watching her footprints fill in with shifting sand behind her as she walked. She found a dark, outcropping of volcanic bedrock to stand upon for their first attempt.

All right, Om. I think I'm ready for our little test run.

Remember: it's only for an instant. Take in the smallest amount of Cosmic energy from the star possible, and then shut the process down. It doesn't matter how little you take in. The idea is to connect, and then disconnect. We can experiment with gradually expanding the length of the tapping connection and the amount of energy collected as we go along.

Naero still shook her head in disbelief.

I can't believe the mightiest of the Kexx could do this sort of thing, Om. It even sounds crazy, just in concept. The power seems like it could be limitless to me. No wonder they could accomplish so much.

They lived and breathed not only the powers of the stars, but of the infinite universe itself, Naero, and of all possibility. Such energies were like their life force–like their very air, and the blood coursing in their veins. They became true Cosmic beings, at one with the universe and all its powers and potentials. Yet they also respected and explored all of the inherent perils and dangers at each step along their journey. They made their mistakes, too, and grew in true wisdom with the exponential powers they gained.

So, what happened to them, Om? If they were so all powerful, after they had defeated this great threat to the universe, where did they go and why?

No one knows. Perhaps that is another mystery that we shall unravel one day, as we grow in wisdom, and perceive the secrets of the KDM. Perhaps when we are truly ready for that knowledge, it shall be revealed to us.

Maybe you're right, Om. I don't even fully know myself or what I'm capable of yet. And I've sure messed things up, over and over again. Sometimes I feel like a walking, talking disaster, just waiting to happen. There's so much I don't know yet.

Then let's try to learn a little bit more, while we still have the chance, Naero. To learn, we must dare to make every possible mistake and failure there is, and learn and grow from them.

I'm with you, Om. Here we go. Startapping experiment number one!

Naero closed her eyes, reached up to the heavens with her yearning fingers, and even farther out with her mind and with all of her Cosmic awareness and abilities open. She did everything as they had thought it out and planned.

So much happened within the flash–within the space of that single instant.

It happened so fast, she did not even have a chance to blink or gasp for air.

The sensation was both exhilarating and completely frightening.

For the barest fraction of a thought…she joined with the power of a star. There was a bright flash of light and energy.

Naero woke gasping and smoking the next instant, in pain.

She lay within a crater of hot, instantly fused black glass, thirty meters deep and a hundred meters wide, steaming up into the night air. Smoke and vapor roiled off of her.

Her hands tingled, and they were still glowing from within when she looked at them, but they faded even as she looked on.

By all the signs, they should be dead. They should have been vaporized, but they had survived the brief fusing or whatever it was.

Om. Talk to me. What happened?

We did it, Naero. For a fraction of an instant, it worked. But we couldn't sustain or control it. The flash effects of just the residual energies caused this crater to form in the local strata. We should locate somewhere else. Intel noticed the energy spike and is sending a team this way to investigate.

We shouldn't tell them?

What are we going to tell them, Naero? We don't even know anything, yet.

I guess you're right, Om.

They transported far away from that location, into a lowland meadow. Tiny insects began biting her exposed flesh, leaving small red bumps that itched. Naero pweaked her nanosuit to exude a working insect repellent. She spread it over her exposed areas.

What next, Om?

Replication. First, study something simple, like one of those insects, with biomancy.

Naero remembered her biomancy lessons with Master Vane back on Janosha. A sharp twinge of pain in her heart still stabbed her when she thought of her family, the gentle Tua.

She focused, and read everything about the small insect. She understood its basic form, function, and composition; its life cycle; why it behaved the way it did. She understood it completely. How it was born, lived, and died, and broke down back into raw components of energy and matter.

She perceived the tiny spark of the life force that existed in all things that were alive, whether plant or animal. Some called it the Lifespark. Others called it the soul. It was the essence of living energy, without which nothing could be said to be alive. A powerful form of Cosmic energy in itself, with a specialized purpose and function.

And in studying that tiny insect, Naero suddenly had an important insight, an illuminating epiphany.

Lifespark energy was the exact, polar opposite of the Darkforce in almost every way–like matter and anti-matter. The Lifespark burned fiercely with the yearning purpose that all things should live and thrive, and seek to be alive and pursue their functions and designs.

Whereas the Darkforce only sought to destroy…everything. Its driving purpose was to cause everything to cease to exist and stop living or doing anything. The static nothing of non-functioning matter. A simple, grim purpose: destroy all that is. The final death, from which nothing could return.

The goal of the Lifespark was everything. The goal of the Darkforce was nothing.

In both forces, she suddenly saw the three wisdoms: Chaos, Order, and Change. And between the ever-shifting balance between the two forces, she beheld the Great Mystery of the Harmony. The Harmony was not in fact a goal–it was a force, and a power, and a purpose within itself, in its own right.

It included and accepted the Lifespark and the Darkforce together, all that they were, and everything in between.

The Harmony would not be denied, and balanced the two forces of life and anti-life–so that all things could have their chance to strive and be, to change and grow, and fulfill their potential. It was neither black nor white, or right or wrong, or good or evil.

It was the universe. It was everything that was possible. It was everything that could and should be, all at the same time. It was the time given to everything. It was both the beginning, and the end, and the way that all things continued on.

Having fused with the power of a star. Having gained these Cosmic insights, Naero Amashin Maeris gave the matter no further, direct thought for the moment.

She lifted her hand and formed one of the tiny insects into being by thought–by force of will alone.

She wished it into being.

The raw components fused together in an instant before her very eyes. One instant it was not there. The next instant it was.

Naero. We've done it! You replicated a lifeform out of nothing but the building blocks of matter and energy all around us. You've replicated a living thing!

Not quite yet, Om.

She sensed something was still wrong. Her tiny creation did not move or function. It was like an automaton. A golem. It still lacked the Lifespark that would truly make it alive and cause it to go forth with its function and purpose.

Then she knew.

She was the creator.

The Lifespark must come from her.

The gift of life...was hers to bestow.

Without another thought, Naero pursed her lips and breathed softly upon the small thing.

She could feel the Lifespark flow and pass from out of her and into the tiny insect, by just a fraction. It quivered, thrummed its small wings, and took off.

Naero swooned and fainted as the ramifications of such power staggered her, just as tapping into the star had stunned her and left her prone and helpless on the ground.

In her mind, she gasped. She curled up in a knot and shuddered, convulsing with terror.

Om, I ask again. Should I...should we...should anyone have such power? How could the Kexx live with the weight of it? I've only created an insect, and yet I'm nearly being crushed by what I have done. What right do we have to do such things?

Think of it as a gift, Naero. As blessing that must not be allowed to become a curse. A responsibility that must be tempered and used with wisdom.

Naero wept, wiping the burning tears from her eyes.

And love, Om. Shalaen once told me that all power, of any kind, is best managed and tempered through love. Love is like the Harmony. Oh my gosh, Om. *Love is the Harmony.* And the Harmony is Love. True balance is the Three Wisdoms combined, and the result...is Love.

The crux, the balance point of Harmony between the Lifespark and the Darkforce...is Love! Holy blinking crap! I understand now. *That's* how Baeven is able to control part of his Dark Beast and make it work for him. He joked with me and said that he learned how to do so by accident–through love. I thought he was kidding me, just putting me off! Damn it, he was absolutely right!

Excellent, Naero! We've replicated an insect.

Okay. What next?

Now we work on reversing the process. You can replicate something, and you can negate it, or re-absorb it if it was once part of yourself.

Hmm…I can sense the insect somehow…about ten meters over there.

We can sense it because the Lifespark came from us, it is part of us as well.

Naero attempted to cup it in her hands. But the insect moved around, trying to get away, making it difficult to capture it.

I got it! Oh, no, Om. I smashed it. I didn't mean to.

Yep. It's dead all right. The Lifespark you put into it has fled.

Can I make it alive again? Breath more of the Lifespark into it?

I don't think so. There's nothing in the replication process that describes anything like that. It appears that once something is dead, death is not reversible. You could repair this insect's physical form, but once its Lifespark has become part of it and then left it, it will not return, nor will it accept another. Each lifeform–even replicants, apparently–are in some way unique, therefore, and can only exist under certain parameters. It appears that death is in fact, final.

I'm going to try anyway. Just to see what happens.

Naero did so.

Nothing.

She made the attempt several times. Each time, nothing happened.

See? Life is finite, somehow. Absorb or disperse the raw components and then try to make another replicant.

Naero took a breath and did so. She hadn't taken the raw components from herself, so she merely dispersed them.

Next, she concentrated, and formed another new replicant, just as she had before. She breathed a new portion of the Lifespark from herself into the tiny creature.

And like before, it buzzed its wings, and flew off.

This time, she caught it and reversed the process quickly, feeling the tiny slice of the Lifespark return to her and the raw components disperse.

Congratulations! Now we can replicate. We can't bring anything dead back to life, but we can quicken a replicant and cause it to function. In the days ahead, we will replicate larger and more complex lifeforms as we go along. The final test–will be to replicate yourself, Naero.

Sheesh, Om. The universe can barely handle one of me. What would it do with two or more?

Om laughed also. *I shudder to think, Naero. But we should still find out. Remember, you will be the primary being still, the original. Any of your replicants will answer to you and you will be able to control and command them. They are still just matter and energy, filled with whatever purpose, power, thoughts, or ability you give them. Imagine being able to summon an entire army of replicants at will. That's the kind of thing the greatest among the Kexx could do.*

I don't know if I'll ever be able to do any of that, Om. I don't know if I want to. But we'll see where it takes us, for now."

You will always have the power to re-absorb or negate their existence, Naero. Your replicants will not be able to do so to you.

That's a relief.

Her wristcom chimed. Uh-oh. Gotta get back for sparring practice. Oh, crap. I still haven't filed my report with the High Masters.

They transported back to the Mystic stronghold, after a good morning's progress.

16

Naero took on seven adepts at once in sparring and held her own against them.

She didn't win–but neither did they.

You're improving, Naero. Each day, your power and skills are increasing.

That's what I'm worried about, Om. Am I growing too fast? Will I be able to control it all? That's what the High Masters are concerned about as well.

After her workout with the Change adepts, Naero checked on the status of the artifact statue. Still methodically searching Nashara, by all reports.

Relentlessly.

Next, she filed a brief report on her first actions in Thanarra as Mediator, promising a more detailed report later. The Changs had probably covered everything in minute detail in their reports anyway. The twins would stay with the king and queen of the Thanes, on their own mission.

After lunch, Naero and six other adepts, a pair from all three orders, would go down into Thanarra, and take a ship out to sea for a meeting with King Haikoda of the Kall, the sea people.

Today her companions would be: Miisha Aztec and Allon Nelson, from Order; Lii Yin and Trevor Elkins, from Chaos; and Ilura Romanov and Danikan Konrad, from Change.

As they traveled, Naero had Om feed her the information on the sea people and their king from the Changs' reports.

Haikoda is in his late thirties, and a widower. His wife, Vaxxanna, was slain by an arrow from the Maedo during a raid. She died in his arms. They only had one daughter, Vaxxalla–wild, fierce, and beautiful, taking after both her parents. She is only thirteen years old, but she is destined to become a mighty Sea Queen after her father's reign.

Interesting. More, Om.

Haikoda also has an extended family of three younger brothers: Nokarro, Yeshida, and Jigan–the latter, as we know, was recently killed by Emperor Vauk of the Vaedo. All of Haikoda's brothers have been loyal to him...unto death.

As is his younger sister, Kutira.

They paid a trade barge at the docks to ferry them out into the Bay of Thanarra, to meet with Kutira, the king's sister. She would take them from there to meet with her brother. Kutira apparently enjoyed the company of holy people, unlike her brothers, who trusted no one outside of the Kall.

Princess Kutira's cutter, *The Blue Vixen,* swept in quickly, a mid-sized, fast-looking ship with a blue fox painted on black sails, and a figurehead of a leaping blue fox on the prow–above a wicked-looking iron ram, used in both war and raiding.

The vessel slipped up quietly and docked with the barge.

Naero spotted archers in *The Vixen's* rigging, as well as javeliners and other fighters poised to board on command. She could smell the burning braziers where crew with naphtha and pitch firebombs waited to hurl them against any sign of an attack or betrayal.

The Kall lived and moved in a treacherous world.

They took no chances.

Princess Kutira appeared at the port, midship rail–keen gray eyes, olive skin, curly, shoulder-length, dark brown hair. She wore form-fitting, blue and black leather armor with a blue scarf headwrap, and a silver filet set with black pearls. Several thin, silver rings hung in her ears, and one in her nose. Armored leather gloves and high boots completed her rakish look.

A fox-headed, silver-hilted cutlass hung on her left hip. Several matching silver fox-head daggers were sheathed all over her person.

She was short, and very pretty at twenty-one.

Naero's exact size and build, in fact. They could probably share clothes.

She admired the princess's style.

Kutira caught her eye. "You are the mediator?"

"I am. These are my brothers and sisters." Naero motioned to the other adepts.

The princess kicked a rope ladder with wooden rungs down to them with one foot and smiled.

"Welcome aboard."

Once they climbed up on deck, the Kall ship and its crew worked quickly to finish its trade with the barge. Goods in crates, barrels, and sacks were swapped in crane nets and swing winches, back and forth.

Once their deals were completed, any other terms and payment were completed. Kutira's second, a large, dangerous-looking brute of a man, rippling with muscles, saluted the barge master and shoved off.

Kutira raised both palms and bowed her head. "May the gods favor us all, holy sister. I am Kutira Asharra Nahavanel Ta'Kall. Wellmet."

She held out her hand. Naero took it, and matched her strength. "I am Sister Naero."

Kutira's eyes widened, and she grinned even wider. "Such steel in the eyes and arm of a priestess? I feel as if I'm looking into a magic mirror–at an image of myself, had I joined the holy ones."

Naero nodded. "We do seem much alike. I hope that we may be friends, Your Highness."

Kutira flung an arm around her and laughed. "Let it be so. Call me Kutira. Come, friend Naero. Allow me to show you *The Vixen*–my beloved ship. I helped build her. My brother, the Sea King, had her designed especially for me."

"A generous gift, indeed. It is a fine vessel."

The ship got under way and put up all its sail, making exceptional speed. Kutira took them on tour belowdecks, just before Naero and the other adepts could get their bearings in the bay. Perhaps that was on purpose.

The place they were meeting the Sea King was supposedly a cleverly guarded secret among the Kall.

Kutira offered them all excellent wine in her quarters. "I hear tell," she said, "that part of your gift as a mediator is a power from the gods to read people's hearts. Forgive me, if I must test this for myself. Can you tell me what is in my heart and mind?"

Naero nodded. "I will try. The ability comes and goes at the will of the gods. I cannot always summon it–like a trained bear."

The princess chuckled. "All good tricksters and fakirs say the same thing. If their powers should fail them, then it is the fickle will of the gods."

"Just so," Naero said. "If you wish me to attempt a demonstration, I will need to touch your face with my hands. It should not hurt. Permit me?"

Kutira set her feet and nodded.

Naero made the mindlink.

"You are mourning deeply for, your favorite older brother–the youngest of them–Jigan. He was always very kind to you. Your favorite."

Kutira stiffened, and for the briefest instant, tears came to the brink of her eyes.

She recovered and shook her head. "Ahh...anyone with such knowledge of recent events could guess such things."

"I can tell you the course we are taking to the hidden cove to meet with your king. I can show you on your charts where the cove is, even though the maps do not show it. I, myself, have never been there."

Kutira folder her arms in front of her. "Spies may still know of it; that is possible."

Naero paused, surprised herself at what she discovered. She leaned in close and whispered in the princess' ear. "You are deeply in love with a man–a great warrior–yet he is not of the Kall, your people. No one but yourself and he knew of this...until now. Shall I tell you his name?"

For the first time, Kutira paled and pulled away, staring at her in wonder, and a little fear.

"No, Sister Naero. Speak not. I do believe you now."

A horn signal sounded above them, and they went back on deck.

Five other warships moved in to escort them.

All began to put out smoke screens to hide their movements.

When the smoke cleared an hour later, they were at the hidden cove, while several clouds of smoke moved out across the waters of the bay.

The Blue Vixen pulled alongside a larger warship, its black sails decorated with a scarlet sea lion–half-fish, half-lion rampant. Some of the ship's rails were decorated with ornate silver engravings. The Sea King's ship bore a silver figurehead of a matching, rampant sea lion.

Boarding ramps were extended between the two ships. Naero and her party went over, with Kutira leading them.

They went down into the large vessel and into what Naero guessed was a large meeting room–or war room. It was decorated with tapestries and charts. There was a large, polished wooden table and chairs.

A powerful looking man sat in the shadows at the end of the table, Two other men similar to him stood on either side of him.

Naero saw the family resemblance with Kutira and guessed them to be the other princes, Nokarro and Yeshida. The ages seemed about right. Nokarro's symbol was the white sea eagle, Yeshida's the silver swordfish.

They wore garb similar to their sister, but tailored for men. They were armed with similar weapons. Yeshida appeared to be an archer. Nokarro bore a polearm weapon, similar to a naginata.

King Haikoda leaned into the lantern light, his sharp, intense face impassive. Black beard and moustache, shaped and oiled. His black eyes were withering, like drills. His skin was ruddy; even sitting, he was tall; and he had large, strong, dexterous hands.

The Sea King cut quite the dashing figure himself.

"Welcome, Mediator. I am Haikoda, Lord of the Kall."

"My name is Naero."

"An odd name, for an odd gull. Such violet eyes you have. They are indeed rare. Kuti, tell me what you have learned from this one?"

Kutira went and stood behind the king. "She indeed has the gift to read the heart and mind. Do not let her touch your face or head, brother. She cannot read you unless she touches you."

Haikoda narrowed his eyes. "Good to know. Tell me, *Mediator*. What is there to mediate these troubled days? What do the gods care if we all kill each other? They have never cared so much before."

"Would it not be better if there were less war, less slaughter on all sides, less disruption of trade? Population growth, instead of misery, plague, disease, and famine? Which do you enjoy more–the laughter and happiness of your people and your children–or their lamentation and despair?"

"And I want a a herd of unicorns from fabled Nashara to sing to my daughter," Haikoda laughed derisively.

"You mean a glory or a radiance of unicorns, milord...not a herd."

He stared at her and his mouth fell open slightly. "You speak like a fool, about childish things no one can bestow. When the angels go to war, and unicorns race across the beaches, sing to the stars, and call to our children–then the Kall will accept the dream–nay–the fairytale of peace. You ask ignorant questions, for a less unpredictable and bloody age. You speak of a time such as our world has never known. Are the gods even real? If they care about us all so very much, why do they not put an end to such things?"

Naero smiled. "This is not the world of the gods, milord. This is the imperfect world of people. Of us, we foolish mortals. In the end, the gods can only guide and advise, but it is we who must make things change–for the better or for worse. The responsibility for your world and your choices…remains yours."

"Well spoken. You are correct. Our evils are our own. We are indeed at fault, not the gods. Yet still, why have they not helped us?

Naero looked around at her comrades and then back to the king. "We are not unicorns, but are we not here, milord?"

"Then let me hear you speak. What is it that you advise?"

"What do all the four peoples want?"

The king laughed. "To vanquish the other three and wipe them out."

Naero shook her head. "I do not think that is so. If you really asked your people, most of them would want peace. All peoples live to thrive, not to merely murder and be murdered. People wish to be free, to live their lives, work the labor of their choice, and raise their families in peace. They would live in peace with each other, given the choice. Given the chance. We must work together to make such choices and chances real and possible."

Haikoda laughed. "Hah! You talk of angels and unicorns again. Holy ones always make everything sound so easy…if everyone just did the right thing, the world would be perfect, a paradise."

"It is not easy. It is never easy. Peace is the hardest thing in the world–to withhold the desire for vengeance. To not kill or ravage others, after they have done so to you. To not take what others have and make it your own, simply because you have the power to do so.

"Oh, great king, hearken to me. Once begun, the cycles of hate, killing, and retribution become like a prison of iron, and perpetuate violence in thought and deed throughout each generation. None of it shall end, until you all choose to make it end. That cycle of death and hate must be broken. It is so very easy and seductive to destroy anything. Building and sustaining anything is the infinitely harder task–especially peace."

The Sea King interrupted her. "Do you know your ancient history, good sister? There used to be seven city states, not four, if you recall. The three lost peoples were from Loxos, Pelenarra, and Shukai. At one time, all three had their golden age, where they were the mightiest and most populated. Now they are dust, their peoples slaughtered or absorbed as slaves. The Kall are partially descended from a remnant of the Shukai, those who took to the safety of their ships in order to survive."

Naero grinned slightly. The Kall survived and thrived, much like Spacers did. "You have but one choice, milord. To wallow in an age of murder that wears all down to naught in the end, or seek an age of wisdom and reason–an age of peace. The gods hope that you will choose the ways of life, not death. All of the senseless warring has sickened even them."

Haikoda frowned, and the sorrow in his deep eyes seemed very great for but a moment. "Indeed. I can well believe that. We are all sick of it. Yet how do we proceed? For myself, I trust no one but my kin and my closest people, and with good reason. That has kept me and my people alive through many betrayals and treacheries. How do I seek peace, when there is none?"

"Peace does not exist until it is made. Peace can only be made with one's enemies. Then, once it is made, it must be maintained."

"Again I ask, how do I begin, without making myself or my people vulnerable?"

"That is why I am here, milord. I have spoken with the king and queen of the Thanes. They feel much the same way, and they are also willing to try."

"They would take my head in an instant if I were in their power."

"Would you do the same to them?"

"Perhaps…but perhaps now, I would not. The Thanes are our strongest trading partners, at the present. They trade hard with us, but fairly. They can be trusted in most things, but not all. In the past, they have seized our ships and cargos without payment when the need arose. And they have held my people for high ransom."

"Just as you have raided their coasts, and taken who and what you would in your need–as all the lands do. Raiding, kidnapping, and ransom are nearly a profession in all the lands."

"I do not deny it. Fire is combated with fire, at times."

"Yet when will it end?"

"So, King Arrok and Queen Liita are of like mind. What of the others?"

"This is only my second day, milord. Arrangements are being made for me to speak with the others."

"I must withhold my judgment, and my hand, until you do so," King Haikoda said.

Naero grinned and crossed her arms in front of herself. "That is easy for you now, since you have just completed successful raids against both the Vaedo and the Maedo."

The Sea King smiled right back at her, knitting his fingers together. "In all things, timing is the essence of discretion."

Kutira suddenly leaned in and whispered something to him. Haikoda looked aside to her in surprise. "You are certain of this?"

Kutira nodded. "See for yourself, brother."

He turned back to Naero and held out both of his large hands. "Sister Naero, show me your hands, please. Come, I will not harm you."

Naero raised both eyebrows, but came forward and placed her hands in the king's. "This is a strange request, milord."

"No stranger than what I see with my own sharp eyes. Holy sister, these are not the soft hands of a priestess. These are the hands of a warrior. I thought there was something about the way you moved. Feel the strength in you! By the heavens, these hands have known skill with a blade, or I am a landwalker."

Naero allowed herself to blush slightly. "As a holy one, I do not like to speak of it. My greatfather was a Thane and a swordmaster, who instructed all the family in the swordarts. I learned from a young age, and was no exception."

Haikoda slapped the table and made it shake. "I knew it! I knew it to be so. Come, little sister. The Kall love the swordarts like the milk from our mummies' teats. We must have a demonstration of your skill. I demand it. The Kall love demonstrations of blade skill. It will make us think better of you—better than we already do."

Naero immediately tucked both hands within her sleeves. "I'm afraid that is not possible, milord. I took the vows of the holy ones. It is unfit now for me to make use of or even handle weapons of war."

Haikoda stood, rising up to his true height, and his face looked hard, as if he were about to become angry. "You refuse me? I'm not asking you to kill anyone or even shed blood for sport. Just a brief entertainment of your blade skill. Nothing more. It will amuse us. You ask much of me. I ask only a little thing from you."

Naero nodded in assent at last. "Very well, milord. A brief demonstration of skill, then. As long as I do not spill any blood, my vows are not broken."

Now Haikoda's eyes twinkled merrily. He was obviously just beginning to enjoy himself.

"Up on my table then! Square off with my sister Kutira. She is the poorest fighter among us." He glanced aside.

The princess flashed her brother a quick, dirty look, obviously offended.

More than likely, Kutira was exceptionally skilled.

"Give the priestess a cutlass! Have you ever handled one, Naero?"

Someone tossed one her way. Naero caught the spinning, flashing weapon, plucked it out of the air, and saluted with a flourish.

"I may have...on occasion."

The Kall began to laugh and chortled and placed eager wagers.

Even a few of the adepts calmly took odds.

On their first pass, Naero gave ground, measuring Kutira's skill. She was strong, fast, and tricky—an excellent fighter.

Kutira halted, they saluted, and matched blades again.

This time Naero pressed her attack, and the crowd roared even louder.

Kutira held her ground. They dueled back and forth. Naero could have drawn blood if she wished, but did not.

Naero sped up slightly, with a touch of Mystic quickness that Kutira could not match. She performed a powerful disarm on the princess, which knocked her silver fox sword free.

With a speedy flip, Naero passed over Kutira and landed behind her, reached out an extended hand for the streaking blade.

She grasped the hilt just in time, and caught it while still looking the other way.

The blade point halted not thirty millimeters away from the startled Sea King's face.

Even he gasped.

Naero held the two cutlasses up behind her, hilts and handguards thrust back out.

Kutira took them.

"You asked for a demonstration of skill, milord. Does that suffice?" Naero asked.

Haikoda stared, then rose up laughing and clapping. "By the gods, yes, holy sister. Your greatfather trained you well. What a Kall you would make. You're a very devil with a blade!"

"I will not be doing so again. I am a mediator, not a warrior."

"What a pity."

Kutira was shocked but obviously impressed as well. She was not angry, just surprised. The princess embraced her. "Now we are indeed friends, holy Sister Naero. I will indeed think much better of you after this."

"We all will," King Haikoda said, still clapping. "You may be a mediator, but at least now we know you possess the heart and soul of a warrior. You will understand all of us better."

Kutira used her fast cutter to return them to the docks of the Thanes later than night, after the celebration.

17

For once, Naero got back, filed her report on time, and got to sleep at a decent hour.

She had to wake early again for more secret training with Om, followed by her regular sparring session–this time with the Chaos adepts– and then another afternoon and evening with the locals–this time with the Maedo.

That would be a full day for anyone.

Om got her going at five bells.

They returned to the desert at another location, and Naero tried startapping into Thanor-4's sun again.

Better this time. She could read the flows slightly before they overwhelmed and stunned her briefly. No crater this time, just a ten meter circle of fused black glass. She even managed to hang on to a modicum of the energy she took in.

She used that energy to fuel her subsequent replication attempts in the uninhabited forest they transported back to. Naero replicated larger insects and reabsorbed them. Earthworms. On a whim, she tried plants. Plants were surprisingly complex and difficult in some ways. She tried to replicate a wildflower and nearly exhausted herself. Finally, she tried a tiny rodent, somewhere between a mouse and a vole. Why couldn't she get the tail right? There were quirks and complications to each and every lifeform. It was rather maddening.

She thought of the Kexx and their godlike mastery of such things, and couldn't imagine replicating herself, let alone doing so multiple times. All of her duplicates could have minds of their own, able to function according to her will and design, and do what she told them. She could form them out of energy, or make them actual flesh-and-blood duplicates.

It all seemed so impossible, but that was the kind of mastery they were working toward.

Sheesh, were the High Masters going to be surprised when she sprung that little trick on them. Part of her couldn't wait to see the looks on their faces. Part of her was afraid.

But for right now, she was still having trouble with flowers and mice.

A sudden idea struck her.

An energy form could be used as a weapon—like a microbomb.

She put the last of her Cosmic star energy into an energy mouse. Who cared if the bloody tail was too short?

She willed her little servant forward, imprinting a simple order on its mind, triggering it with Chaos energy.

Run under that small red maple tree and explode.

The glowing little energy mouse scurried over to obey.

The detonation obliterated the small tree, and left a smoking crater ten meters wide in the dark, rich soil. The blast knocked Naero back on her butt.

Whoa, she had to remember that little trick.

It's just a variation on the exploding Chaos construct, Naero. The theories and principles are very similar.

But if I do it with replicants, they become my little smartbombs. And if I use Cosmic star energy, Om, I don't have to channel it directly through me like Chaos energy from my reserves. It won't exhaust me the same way. That's going to be a huge improvement.

Her mind began to race. All different kinds of energy. Flashbomb bugs. Bugbombs. Mousebombs. Cosmic energy bubblebombs to take down shields.

A bird flew overhead.

Tomorrow, she'd try to replicate a bird. Cosmic energy construct birdbombs. And she could change the construct from energy to flesh and back to energy again, at will–once she became adept enough at the manipulation.

She would get better.

That's enough progress for today, Naero. We have to get to your sparring sessions back on Thanarra.

Aww...man!

What about your next free day? We could spend the entire day practicing replication and startapping.

Maybe. It's very tempting, Om. We can do a little of that, but not the whole day. I want to catch up with everyone. I can't wait to see Jan and all the others. And I miss my ship, my quarters."

All of the Chaos adepts were lined up waiting for her that day with strained looks on their faces–including the two stuck-up Prime adepts, Zhii and Fel.

Daiyana and Arnall, the contraries, were off to one side, ignoring them all.

"Goodbye, N!"

"Farewell, my enemy!"

Naero laughed. "Goodbye to you goofs, too!" She turned back to the others. "What the heck is all of this about now?"

Gaviok strode up, his powerful carapaced arms behind his midsection. He was light blue in color, usually meaning that he was amused or very pleased with himself. "The other adepts have something they wish to ask of you, N."

She glanced over at them. "All right, let's have it."

Fel Wilde spoke first. "If you would be willing," she began hesitantly. "Uhh...we know that you have helped all of the adepts from the other orders...increase the effectiveness of their Cosmic and psyonic abilities. What we wish to know, is...is-"

Zhii Kim took over impatiently, blurting the matter out bluntly. "Can you quicken our abilities in the same way–even teach us new ones, if possible? More than half of us cannot summon or use the techniques of the third psyonic eye. Would you be willing to assist us in this manner, for the good of our Order, and the advancement of the Mystic Orders as a whole? What makes one of us stronger, makes all of us stronger. It is only logical."

Naero held up both hands. "All right, all right. Enough of the hard sell. I can see it's difficult for you folks, and the word 'please' doesn't seem to exist for you. You want the same favor I've done all the other adepts, but it burns you guys to have to depend on someone else, or ask nice for something."

Pharrah Decker got angry and nearly stormed away. "See, I told you the tricky bitch was going to make us beg for her help! I won't do it. I won't beg!"

"Hey, hey, calm down, Pharrah," Naero told her. "I'd be glad to help you guys. Gaviok, talk her down."

"Listen to reason, Pharrah."

"She hates Chaos adepts, because of Master Vane. She doesn't like any of us. Why should she do anything to help us?"

"That's not it. You've got me all wrong. I try not to hate anyone," Naero said. "I'm not a Chaos adept. I don't know what else I am yet, but I know I'm not a follower of Chaos Wisdom. But I don't have to be. Look, all of you guys, I just want to come to an understanding. I can have respect for you. We can all have respect for each other and work together, whatever we choose to believe. Isn't that the point of the Harmony, that all three Wisdoms should compliment each other and work together?"

Pharrah looked confused. "What are you saying?"

"I'm saying nothing says that we have to hate each other. We can all get along. Gaviok and the contraries are Chaos adepts—we get along just fine. We're all stronger if we help each other, not constantly competing and trying to screw each other over!"

"But...Master Vane."

Naero rolled her eyes. "Screw Master Vane; to hell with him! Come on—admit it—we all know what a major assbag he can be."

"She's right," Gaviok said. "I respect his knowledge and wisdom regarding Chaos energy, but he is a major bag of ass."

Even a few of the Chaos adepts chuckled at that.

Naero clapped a hand on one of the mantid's broad shoulders. "Gaviok, you didn't quite get that right, my friend—but I like your spirit."

The contraries couldn't help adding their two creds.

"How dare you!" Arnall said. "Why, High Master Vane is the most wonderful man there is. He is good-natured and kind...like a big friendly bunny."

"Yes, I love him," Daiyana said in a robotic voice. "He is so nice, I wish I could marry him, and give him many bug-eyed children from my urgent loins."

Naero spluttered with explosive laughter and nearly choked on her own breath and mirth. Several of the other adepts were laughing so hard by that time, they could barely stand.

Poor Gaviok. He alone looked around in clueless confusion.

"I don't understand? Does she really wish to have Master Vane fertilize all of her eggs with his seed spray?"

Now everyone roared with laughter, faces turning red. They could not breathe.

"Yes, yes," Daiyana insisted. "I want his seed spray on my eggs more than the breath of life itself!"

"Oh," Gaviok said, with a characteristic dip of his head. "Very well, then."

Everyone roared again.

The mantid looked around at them all. "What is so hilarious?" he asked, in honest confusion.

Trevor waved his hands in surrender. "No more...please! My head hurts...my sides are splitting!"

Naero spent the rest of that day quickening and working with the other Chaos adepts, helping them improve their various abilities.

After lunch, Naero and her band made their way to the Thanarran docks again. A private trading vessel was contracted to take them to the cliffs of the Maedo, for Naero and her companions to meet with the strange and elusive Amazons. The lowland areas of Maedo on the coast were a no-man's land–literally–contested by Vaedo, the Kall, and the Thanes. All had fought over it. The Maedo could barely trade, and only inhabited the unassailable heights of their own city state.

But their lethal archers and blowgunners slipped down in the lower areas to snipe at any enemy invaders they could find, and make them pay a heavy toll.

On this day, Naero took six others with her: Pharrah and Kenden from Chaos, Rinaldo and Karabella from Order, and Perra and Hanta from Change. The winds were up and the waters of the bay looked rough.

More surprises. A strange warship and three heavily armored barges hugged the coast and pulled up to the docks.

They flew the rippling, golden dragon banners of Vaedor.

Bells rang out from the city walls. Then horns.

Ranks of warriors rushed to the dockside area, taking up defensive positions as if it were an invasion.

Maybe it was. Naero scanned the barges and saw them to be loaded with heavily armed Vaedo troops.

Trumpets sounded. Naero heard harps playing. A large, powerful-looking man came to the railing of the ship, surrounded by guards. He wore golden robes and his fists bristled with golden and jeweled rings. On his head he wore a golden dragon crown with four points.

His skin was very pale, white even. His eyes were sapphire blue, and his shoulder-length hair was golden. His golden beard was neatly trimmed and edged in actual, dazzling gold. His broad chest was bare beneath his gilded robes. About his waist, he wore a wide belt of what looked to be gold-plated skulls, a jeweled scimitar–and a golden codpiece that nearly reached to the deck of the ship.

Yet his eye was cruel and cold, his bearing proud and haughty, and his doughy face and thick pink lips sneered obscenely, like those of a man steeped in violence and debauchery.

The golden dragon god's trumpets blared.

The golden man lifted his muscled arms, and his slaves fell to their knees around him.

"I am the god of this world. I am the golden dragon of the Vaedo. I am Emperor Vauk, and I demand that you holy ones meet with me this day."

Naero bowed her head slightly. "Forgiveness, milord. But that is impossible. We are already scheduled to meet with the Maedo today."

"Impudence! You dare defy my will?"

"We serve the will of the gods, and they direct us to speak with the Maedo, milord."

"I am a god as well. And I command you to come away with me so that we may speak together. I must know what lies you have been told by all these others–these petty upstarts and mortal rulers who defy my divine authority."

"We have heard no lies, milord. Everywhere we hear only of your greatness. And thus we have reserved the true place of ultimate honor for you."

"The place of ultimate honor?" Vauk asked, looking suspicious.

"Yes, is it not customary among the gods to speak to the greatest last? On this world, you are the greatest potentate among all the city states. Your realm is the largest and most magnificent; your armies, the greatest and most numerous. We knew that you would be greatly offended if we did not give you your place of highest honor and come before you last, as is only right and proper."

"You are the mediator sent by the gods? The ones my spies have told me so much about?"

129

"Yes, milord. I am-"

He waved one hand in boredom. "As one of the celestials, I do not care for names, least of all yours. I will call you Mediator. That is enough. You and these so-called holy ones claim to have been sent by the gods?"

"Yes, milord."

"And why would my radiant kin fail to inform me of such a mission?"

"I'm certain they know how very busy you are, milord."

"Well said. You are polite enough, at least, Mediator. I give you that. But so young...and a pretty thing, too."

Naero did not enjoy the gleam in Emperor Vauk's eyes as he appraised her form and face.

"Mediator, it is said that you can read the hearts and minds of mere mortals. Surely you could not do so with a god."

"I would not dare to do so, lord. Lest I be overwhelmed by your great splendor and magnificence."

"Oh," he said with a grin. "Oh, yes. I do like your ways with words. But I warn you, Mediator. Many others have tried to flatter me. They now hang from my walls along its full length, and feed the crows and gulls— both the short-lived, and the dead. They die, singing to my name for forgiveness. Sometimes...I take mercy on a few of the wretches, and have them dropped into the sea or onto the rocks for a quick end. Other times, I give them water, and keep them singing and praising my name for weeks at a time—or until the birds strip them clean. The crows and gulls always go for the eyes. Eyeballs must be a delicacy."

Naero bowed. "It has been a pleasure speaking with you, milord. But our chartered ship awaits."

"Why don't you let my ships take you to the Cliffs of the Maedo, Mediator? We can dine and talk more along the way. I assure you. You will not gain audience with Warrior Queen Aijarri and her Amazons this day. I am certain of it."

Naero was curious. "And why is that, milord?"

"Because I have convinced them to go on...let us just say, a tiny errand for me. One that will benefit us both, greatly."

Om, get our cloaked spyfixers all over that area. I want to know what is afoot.

Will do, Naero.

"I thought the Vaedo and the Maedo were currently in a state of perpetual war, since the fall of the Maedo lowlands to your illustrious armies, milord?" Naero said.

Emperor Vauk grinned again. "I see that the gods do indeed keep you surprisingly well-informed, Mediator. Yes, we are still at war. But I happen to have the queen's second born–her young son, Tavul–as one of my guests. My agents just happened to capture him recently. He is currently still alive, but only at my whim. He hangs from a golden cage thrust out from my very own balcony. My guards keep the birds away from him…most of the time, for now. If the warrior queen serves my will well enough, I may even keep my own word…and let him go free. Or, since he is a shapechanger, perhaps I will see if the young prince can turn into a bird, and fly away."

"You must excuse us, great lord," Naero said. "But our word has been given, and we must keep it or be dishonored. If we cannot meet with the Maedo today, we will do so this evening. And then with you upon the morrow. This I promise."

"Very well, then. We shall return here to pick you up around this same time, tomorrow…Mediator." He gave her his back and walked out of sight. His guards closed in behind him.

Naero and her people reached the Maedo cliffs in less than two hours.

The Maedo lowered a message to them, saying that the queen had taken ill, and would need to meet with them another day.

Naero and her people had their ship move further down the coast, out of sight.

Word came to her from Om.

Naero, a mighty warrior matching the Maedo queen's description is leading a large band of warriors secretly through the dense trees along the coast.

Where are they heading?

The Kall have a secret shipyard less than three hours away, on the coast, near the backside of the Maedo mountain forts. The Maedo are carrying many crude incendiary bombs.

They mean to burn the shipyard and the partially constructed ships there.

And a large quantity of cured lumber which the Kall have been hiding and preparing there for years.

The Kall need ships to survive; one of their weaknesses. The Vaedo must have found them out somehow. Emperor Vauk's spy network seems to be very extensive. Why waste their forces on taking that shipyard out, when they can blackmail the Maedo into doing it for them? Om, do you have eyes on the captured Maedo prince, Tavul?

Yes. These coordinates–you can view the area directly through our spyfixer vidlinks.

Naero went belowdecks and made plans with the other adepts.

"Three of you cloak, transport, and use gravwings and stun needles as needed–but rescue Prince Tavul and bring him safely on board our ship."

Pharrah nodded. "Will do; leave it to us. See you back here…N."

Naero turned to the other three adepts. "You guys with me. We're going to stop that attack. We'll flash stun both sides if we have to."

"Why are we interfering?" Kenden asked. "Are you certain the High Masters would want us to do this?"

Naero shook her head. "They sent me here to attempt to negotiate a peace. I am acting as I see fit. How can I do anything if these people are constantly at war? If we rescue Prince Tavul, there is no reason for the Maedo to attack the Kall, and Vaedor's plot will be foiled."

Naero transported and placed herself directly in the path of the Maedo Queen, and her eleven hundred Amazon warriors. The vast majority of them were, in fact, women.

Why were there so few men among the Amazons? How could they possibly maintain a breeding population?

We have not had time to go over that, Naero. The Maedo are indeed near-human shapechangers. Some of them in mated pairs can change into male form, as needed, for purposes of procreation. Some few are actually born male and prefer to remain so. The vast majority of the population, however, is normally female.

Very…unusual.

The reptilian sentients on Shongo-5 have a similar ability, if males are needed. But they actually transform by shedding their old forms, like a husk.

Anything else I need to know?

The Maedo are extremely warlike, much like their other Thanoran cousins. They are acrobatic; they are expert climbers in trees or mountain rocks. They travel very quickly along swing and zip lines maintained throughout their forests and mountains. They use poison-tipped javelins, arrows, and blowgun darts, both to stun, and to kill. They have long fighting knives, and curved sabres with handguards that can be used one or two-handed. They move quietly and only wear light leather armor at most. Their laminate bows have the longest range of any bows on the planet–over a klick on a windless day.

Thanks, Om.

"Here they come," Hanta Cheyenne whispered.

Naero strode forward and raised both hands over her head. She openly called out, "I am the mediator, sent by the gods. I have come this day to speak with Aijarri, Warrior Queen of the Maedo!"

Numerous poison arrows and blowguns darts, firing right at you all!

"Shields up!" Naero cried.

18

Naero and the adepts deftly deflected arrows and javelins with their arms and hands.

The Maedo blowgun darts bounced off their personal shields.

Queen Aijarri stepped out of the shadows of the forest as her warriors quickly encircled the four adepts, training weapons on the four all the while.

Naero nearly gasped, seeing these people for the first time, instead of descriptions in reports.

The Maedo warriors were all breathtakingly beautiful. They were also tall–damn them–none under 1.83 meters. The queen herself was 1.91 meters, about the same height as Naero's good friend, Chaela.

They had finely chiseled features, and their skin was jet black–blacker even than the near-human Naivatch. Even the lips of the Maedo and their palms were black.

But their eyes were mostly golden and amber in color, like the eyes of lions–predator eyes. Their hair was various shades of blue, from pale blue to midnight blue, so dark it seemed blue-black, much like Naero's own hair.

They wore their long hair in low ponytails, with ornate wooden, metal, and lapis hair bands, set at the base of their neck in back, or in a knotted bun. The Maedo were long of limb, slender and athletic, with narrow hips and broad backs. Soft leather gloves and moccasins or sandals covered their hands and feet, which looked slightly larger, possibly from them being climbers.

Their clothing and armor consisted of a leather tunic, belted at the waist. They wore studded leather battle harnesses or baldrics for their gear and weapons—and what looked to be padded leather arming caps. They had small bedroll packs on their backs, and each carried several weapons. The laminate bow seemed to be the predominate weapon. Next came a slender bamboo spear, which was socketed and could be broken down into two equal pieces. One piece could double as a blowgun. Then came various javelins, saber, and numerous fighting blades—even what appeared to be a small tomahawk or fighting ax.

The Maedo's leather battle harness had numerous pouches and pockets. Their lightly plated, scaled, or studded armor covered their arms, legs, and feet, with additional padded armored caps at their elbows and knees. Each Maedo warrior carried what looked to be a long coil of black rope, and several iron climbing hooks and grapples.

"If they fire upon us again," Naero said quietly, "we stun the entire lot of them. Then we revive the queen."

Queen Aijarri approached them without weapons in her hands, her countenance roiling with emotions—anger mixed with surprise, and even fear. Her nostrils flared wildly. Dozens of warriors with drawn weapons waited only for her command to attack.

In fact, all of her people seemed to be expecting an attack at any moment.

"What are you doing out here?" the queen demanded. "How did you find us? By what right do you delay us?" Her golden eyes flashed as if on fire.

Naero met her gaze calmly and spoke. "As I have said—before you attacked us—I am the mediator of the holy ones. My name is Naero. I chose to keep my meeting with you this day, and persuade you to give up this errand, one that you have been tricked into by Emperor Vauk."

Upon hearing that name, the queen looked sickened, and spat on the ground in front of her. "You are in a war zone, Mediator Naero.

135

My warriors thought you to be some surprise trick or trap of our enemies to ambush and kill us all. The Vaedo have posed as holy ones before, in order to do such things. They are devoid of all honor, and the Darkheart—the Emperor of the Vaedo—is not a man, if he ever was one. That murdering bastard could not have been born of woman. We believe him to be a piece of some devil's bloody shit, animated by demon wizards, and sent to plague our world with his evils."

Naero grinned. "No one seems to like him very much."

Queen Aijarri blinked, and then laughed. Then her war face snapped up again. She folded her arms in front of her.

"If you know why Vauk sent us, you know where we are going, and why we must do this thing. I cannot let anyone stand in our way, Mediator. I cannot do so, even for the holy ones."

"Let us speak of these matters," Naero said.

"No. There is no time for such talk. The emperor holds my only son's life in his blood-soaked hands—curse that Vaedo devil!"

"I promise you," Naero said, "Tavul will not be harmed. He is under the protection of the gods and is safe, even now. My sisters and brothers and I shall return him to you this very night. You have my word."

Om, please get me confirmation of that from our spyfixers. Tell me that the others have rescued him.

Will do, Naero.

A look of pain and fear came over the queen's face, and she clenched both of her fists at her sides in frustration. "I do not even know you. We have not ever met before, you and I. Even the gods have abandoned me and my people. Why would they help us now? What is my son to them? How can I trust you when I cannot trust anyone? How can I believe you when you tell me that he is safe, and that he will live out this night?"

"Because I am asking you to do so. I will prove what I say."

"Oh, and that is supposed to be enough? When last I knew, my youngest was in the filthy hands of that bloody, golden, murderous bastard!"

"Great warrior queen, stay thy wrath. Only the power of the gods can save Tavul. But you must break off this attack and return home. I promise you, upon my life, your son will be waiting for you if you do so."

The queen paused to ponder her words.

Naero. The other adepts have the youth. He is safe and unharmed, although there were a few slight...complications.

I don't care about that, Om. Are they on board the ship again?

I'm afraid that's one of the complications. Agents of the Vaedo, posing as Kall, attacked the ship we hired with fire and sank it, killing everyone on board.

They meant to kill us as well. What else?

Prince Tavul was poisoned, and he was being given just enough antidote in his water to stave off death. It took a while for the other adepts to fully neutralize that poison. He is fine now."

That's good, because I just put my life on the line. Locate *The Blue Vixen*. Have Pharrah contact Princess Kutira for help. If she agrees, have her help them bring Prince Tavul to the Maedo cliffs tonight, when I signal them. Tell me when all is ready.

I will, Naero. Your friends think they are speaking with you when I contact them through the spyfixers.

They don't need to know otherwise, Om. You're my secret weapon.

You know I love you, Naero.

Om, don't start all that again. We don't have time. Please. Just help me.

"I don't know what to do," Queen Aijarri said. "If I do as I you say, if we do not do as the Vaedo emperor commands us–how will I know my boy will live?" The queen was obviously in torment.

"Your son is already safe," Naero said. "We have but to go to him at the Maedo Cliffs, overlooking the Bay of Thanarra."

"No, I will not trust you, or anyone with the life of my child. If you are truly from the gods, you will use that power to prove it to me. Right now. This very second. If you do not–if you cannot–then you are not of the gods, and this is some devil's trick. We will roll over you, and burn that Kall lumber mill and shipyard to the very ground, this very night!"

"Very well, my queen. Let me pray. You shall have your proof."

Naero knelt down, and went through the motions of praying.

Om, link me with Pharrah through the spyfixers. This is urgent.

The link snapped open, and Naero heard Pharrah's voice through the comdots in her ears.

Naero? This is Pharrah.

Pharrah, the queen is demanding proof of life. Project a holo of him to me here through our comlinks and I'll do the same, so that they can talk briefly. That should be enough.

Hololink will be open in five seconds, mark.

"My queen. The gods will give you a vision of your son, Tavul. You can speak to him yourself and see that he is well."

The holo of Tavul appeared instantly.

The Maedo gasped in wonder and drew back.

"Mother, mother!" Tavul cried.

"Tavul, my boy!" the queen nearly sobbed and reached out to her child.

Naero rose up quickly and shouted, "Do not touch the vision or it will vanish! I can only sustain it for a short time. Speak quickly!"

"Tavul, who are you with?"

"The holy ones, mother. They saved me somehow. I fell asleep, and the next thing I knew, I was here with them. Truly, it is a great miracle."

The queen's mouth fell open, and no words came out. She dropped to her knees. "Are you all right, my boy? Have you been hurt?"

"I was sick, but the holy ones gave me a potion that healed me. I'm fine now. They say they will bring me to the cliffs of our people. I can't wait to get home, mother. I can't wait to see you again."

"Forgive me, my son. But I must know if this is truly you, or merely some sorcery. What day is today?"

"The tenth day of the fifth month, mother."

The queen closed her eyes, obviously wanting to believe. "You have a scar on your right elbow, my boy. How did you get it?"

"Father grazed me with an arrow, when he shot an assassin trying to carry me off."

Aijarri gasped slightly again. "We will be together again shortly, Tavul. Tell the holy ones to take you to our cliffs. I will be waiting there."

The holo vanished.

The queen turned where she stood and called aloud to her fierce warriors, "There shall be no attack on the Kall this night, my people. We return to our cliffs, and the Darkheart can go rut himself to death!" She spat once more.

Aijarri offered Naero her hand. Naero took it and held it.

"You are quite strong, and very young for both a holy one and a mediator, holy sister."

Naero smiled and shrugged slightly. "I have always been full of surprises."

The queen laughed. "I'm guessing that. It is a long way back to the cliffs. Run with me, holy sister, and let us speak on many things."

Naero bowed her head. "That is why I have come, my queen. To speak with all the rulers of the city states, and attempt to mediate a peace among the lands."

Aijarri opened both eyes wide. "You have not spoken with Emperor Vauk yet?"

"Briefly. I will see him tomorrow."

"Beware, then. Your status will not protect you in the least with that devil. He is a sick, twisted fiend. If only the gods would see fit to remove his rotting head from his festering body."

Naero thought of the lives of everyone on that ship that they had hired. None of those people deserved to die.

Talking with the queen was a real eye-opener, to say the least, confirming much about the Maedo and the entire situation that Naero had read about in the reports.

None of the lands were blameless in the constant strife.

But it became very clear that the emperor of the Vaedo continually used his large armies and his extensive spy network to play all the lands against each other for his own gain and benefit.

In two cases that Naero knew about already, Emperor Vauk had kidnapped the children or kin of the other royals, and forced them to attack one another. And it did seem that the Maedo had suffered much more than the other three combined.

If something did not change, simply by attrition, there would soon be only three great city states, and not four. Anyone could see that the Vaedo were preparing to wipe out the Maedo, and then planned to focus their growing powers on the other two.

It was well after sunset when they reached the Maedo Cliffs.

As Naero planned, *The Blue Vixen* appeared out of the fog to return Prince Tavul.

Then two other Kall ships swept in out of the fog as well.

Naero! Those are the two ships that sank our chartered vessel. They are filled with enemy agents from Vaedor, only posing to be Kall. Now the princess is signaling them. They do not know the correct replies.

Stun blasts, Om. Have the adepts nail those vessels with Cosmic stun blasts before they can attack.

Already, Naero's keen eyes spotted the flaming braziers and oil bombs being readied and uncovered.

The three adepts on *The Blue Vixen* lifted their staffs and hands to the stars.

Bright flashes of light enveloped both enemy warships.

In a matter of instants, the false crews collapsed and sprawled stricken upon the decks of those two ships, above and below decks.

Several Kall ships–including the large warship of King Haikoda, himself–roared in at the very next moment, surrounding the two renegade ships.

There was no escape, and no battle, since the imposters were already stunned.

Naero rode a lift on chains and ropes down to the deck of *The Blue Vixen*. She embraced Kutira and her adept friends, thanking them.

Prince Tavul stood by nervously. He looked over at Naero with his large golden eyes, trying to be brave.

"You are the mediator?" he asked.

Naero offered him her hand. "I am, Prince Tavul. My name is Naero, and I am your friend."

Tavul looked around at the Kall, and sighed.

"So, I am to be ransomed, then?"

Naero laughed and shook her head. "No, my friend." She reached up and touched his young, handsome face. Sheesh, even at thirteen, the kid was taller than her. "There shall be no ransom."

Naero led Tavul to the lift and winked back at Kutira.

Now it was the princess who sighed. "You are right, Naero. Even if my brother doesn't like it. It is the right thing to do. If only you had come to us sooner. Perhaps we could have-" Kutira looked away.

Naero took Kutira's hands. "I'm sorry. I wish we could have saved your brother, Jigan."

A fierce light lit Kutira's fair face, which burned with tears, and the wind swept through her hair. "I know very well who is to blame. I shall never forget it, nor forgive."

Tavul smiled happily as he rose up into the air. He waved at them. "Farewell, Princess Kutira, my pretty friend. My good holy ones, thank you all and the gods themselves for rescuing me. I owe you my life."

Kutira smiled through her tears and waved up at the handsome boy. "Go in peace, my friend. Let us pledge never to harm each other."

"You have my word, Kutira."

"And you mine, Tavul. Let all witness it."

The Sea King and his two remaining brothers strode up quickly to join their sister.

A brief squabble concerning the loss of ransom was quickly settled.

"My lords," Naero pointed out, "you have just regained control of two of your lost warships, completely unharmed, undamaged, and fully loaded for war. You have captured two large units of villains posing as your people—and perpetrating murder, rapine, piracy, and war falsely in your name. I suggest you question these spies and assassins thoroughly before bringing them to justice. I'm certain you shall learn many interesting things."

Kutira knelt at her oldest brother's side and kissed his hand. "The mediator has done very well by us, my brother. By freeing Prince Tavul and returning him to his mother, Naero prevented an attack on our secret lumber mill and shipyard, a loss that would have set us back decades!"

King Haikoda asked for a seat to think in, and one was brought up on deck for him.

He listened to all that was said, and then looked at Naero in wonder. "Is all of this true? Why have you done all of these things to help us?"

"I am here to help all toward the ways of peace," she said. "For that is the will of the gods. There has been enough blood. Even the warrior gods grow sick and tired of seeing their beloved children constantly butcher each other for no reason. It is time to put an end to such folly and madness. Peace and reason will serve you all better."

Even the mighty Sea King was at a loss. "We have never known such. How do we even proceed?"

"The holy ones will advise and counsel you all, if you would only listen to us. Both the Maedo and the Kall have seen fit to make no war this night. It is a start. It is only a beginning, and must be continued, no matter how hard it becomes."

"I am listening, child. You force me to listen."

"I am listening as well," a mighty voice called down from another lift that had been lowered from the Maedo Cliffs. "Haikoda, mighty King of the Sea. Queen Aijarri of the Maedo thanks you for the freely returned life of her youngest child, Prince Tavul. And I thank the holy ones for his miraculous rescue from the clutches of Emperor Vauk."

Haikoda stared at Naero in wonder. "But how? How was this achieved? No one escapes with their life from the very teeth and claws of the blood-soaked golden dragon?"

Naero clasped her hands together. "The gods wished the boy to be spared and set free, and so he was. Yet they seek not to meddle in your affairs directly. That is not their way or wish. You world is your own for you to rule. If you count on them to do what you should do for yourselves, they will surely turn away. They but give you all these few chances to solve your problems on your own–between one another. For that is the way things should be. They placed you all in charge of your world. It is not theirs. You are all responsible for what comes of your world: peace and life, or death and destruction. The choice remains and always will remain yours to make. Make the right choices long enough, and you will have no need of the gods."

Queen Aijarri called down from her lift. "For too long, the Darkheart has set us all at each other's throats, Haikoda. Our peoples grow weaker, while he only grows stronger. This night I owe you the life of my son, and offer you safe passage. Will you not come up to us, great king, and let us speak of peace, with the mediator of the gods between us?"

"I wish that I could, great queen. But I swore a great oath–before the gods and all that exists–to never set foot on land, and to stay on the ships of my people until the Kall are safe and secure in their freedom. I cannot break such an oath."

"I understand. Keep your great oath. Then, if you swear my safety upon the lives of your blood and your people, great king, I shall come down to you, alone and weaponless. And we shall speak of such matters on any ship you name."

"How can I refuse such a brave offer, which I cannot make myself? Come down then, weapons or no, as you are, Queen Aijarri. Upon my life and my honor, you shall remain both safe and free among us."

The Queen signaled for the lift to be sent down, and she stepped out to take the hand of the Sea King in greeting.

"Ware! In the port rigging!" Kutira suddenly cried out.

A Kall archer bent her bow at the Maedo Queen. None could stop her from firing.

Haikoda himself stepped before the queen to take the shaft in his own breast, protecting her according to his vow.

But at the last instant, Naero leaped in. The arrow struck her in the back, and protruded out the front of her chest. She gasped in agony and felt her eyes roll up.

Haikoda caught her in his startled arms. "No...no, little sister. That shaft was not meant for you!"

The assassin crashed to the deck the very next instant–dead–riddled with arrows, javelins, and even a few well-thrown knives.

Kutira rushed forward to examine the body.

"Was she one of us?" Haikoda asked in disbelief.

Even Kutira stared in shock before she nodded. "She...was. Gevana and I were playmates. Yet see what I find in her pockets...Vaedo gold coins!"

The princess flung the bloody coins into the sea in fury.

Naero felt the adepts examining her. She trusted in her friends. They would heal her.

Naero. Poison. The arrow was poisoned, with the same blowfish venom meant for the Thanes!

I'm getting dizzy, Om. Help them neutralize it.

I'm trying.

"Poison," Naero muttered. "Blowfish...poison-"

The Sea King paled. "If that is true, I'm afraid...she is gone. There is no known cure for such poison."

"Lay her down," Pharrah insisted.

"Let us tend her!" Kenden said.

"Give us room!" Rinaldo said. All three adepts did their best to heal, neutralize, and regenerate her. First they removed the arrow very carefully.

"It...missed my heart, at least," Naero said, weak and choking for air.

"Lie still. Don't talk," Pharrah ordered.

The Sea King looked on and could not believe his eyes. "Amazing. The lethal wound is healing; I can see the flesh closing up."

"My friend," Queen Aijarri said, pulling him aside. "Let me send word to my people on the cliffs. They will be worried about what is happening down here."

"Please, do so, great queen." He turned to his brother. "Nokarro, her life is yours to watch over. Yeshida, Kutira, stay with me and our little mediator." The king shouted aloud in a fell voice, "Death to any who lift a hand against the royal family, or any of our honored guests. Allow no further treachery!"

Ahhh...at last, we've done it, Naero. We've neutralized the toxin. In a few moments, you will start to feel much better.

Thanks, Om.

After a few tense moments more, Naero felt her strength return, and spoke aloud for all to hear.

"I'm all right. Help me to my feet, my friends."

Naero rose up, and allowed a shimmering, blue-white aura of Cosmic energy to surround her entire form from head to foot.

The crews of all the ships present, even the king and queen themselves, gasped, backed away in awe, and fell to their knees.

"The child shines with the very light of the gods themselves!" Queen Aijarri proclaimed.

The Sea King shook his head as if he might go mad. "She lives. She should be dead, and yet she rises from such a wound, hale and unhurt. Truly, it is the will of the gods!"

"I was spared," Naero said, "from the brink of death by the will of the gods. For my task among you is not yet finished–to bring a lasting peace to all the children of the gods. To help you establish peace upon your world, for you and all of your children. Are you not all tired of war and senseless death and misery? Together, let us work to find and sustain a better way– the way of peace, and freedom for all."

Naero went to the king and queen, lifted them up, and embraced each of them, as her aura slowly faded.

Later that night, when all was done, not only a new treaty, but an alliance had actually been formed between the Maedo and the Kall. Trade would resume between the two former foes. Maedo forest and mountain warriors would help protect the secret shipyard, and the Kall would help protect what remained of the Maedo lands and the Maedo's access to the bay.

Naero filed her report to the High Masters, certain that they would find some fault with it, and threw herself on her bed to sleep. Of course, she thought she was doing a great job.

She dreamed of dragons again, including nightmares about a terrible golden wyrm drenched in human blood.

The time to meet with Emperor Vauk would come the very next day.

19

Naero had trouble replicating a tree the next day. Trees, as they turned out, were incredibly difficult to get right–just something about them. One of hers even turned all rubbery and floppy for some funky reason.

How. Embarrassing.

Frogs, even birds, a squirrel-type creature–even a kind of deer and a bear–she was able to replicate just fine after a few attempts. Mammals seemed easy. Mammals just came to her naturally. Maybe it was because she was one. Perhaps that gave her an edge. But trees? Even little trees, damn it. Even just saplings were nearly impossible.

Trees were tough. Maybe it had something to do with their lifespans being so long and stretched out. Naero wasn't quite sure.

Finally, they went to a place on one of the continents that had large primates–a baboon creature with gray fur, living on the edge of a savannah jungle.

Naero tried replicating one, and it seemed to go all right, but the attempt also gave her a massive headache.

That was something new.

The more sentient a species was, the more painful it was to attempt to replicate it. Go figure.

Naero, that's enough replication for today. I knew we shouldn't have skipped startapping, and gone with replication first.

Cool your drives, Om. So we mix it up a little? Let's hit the desert and try some startapping. We still have some time.

All right. Now today, we just want to focus on tapping a small amount of energy and being able to store it again, for a longer period of time.

Gotcha, buddy. Will do.

In the desert, once they startapped, Naero attempted to store the tiny amount of Cosmic energy within herself.

Instead, her Dark Beast broke free just enough to gobble it down.

Emboldened by the energy feed, it lashed out in fury, trying bust out completely and seize control.

For an instant, Naero forgot that what she had access to–her Dark Beast dis as well–and its lust and hunger for any type of energy was constant and ravening.

First she thought she could simply wrestle with it, and drain the energy it had seized back out from it. Yet anything it devoured, it transformed into destructive, Darkforce energy. If she absorbed such energy directly, she would be infused by its taint, leaving her open to her Dark Beast even more.

Naero…remember what we have learned about the Lifespark and the Darkforce–how they balance and even compliment each other to form the Harmony–the true balance of all energies Cosmic.

Dark and Light.

Life and Death.

Creation and Destruction.

I'll try to balance them out, Om.

She struggled to summon just enough of the Lifespark to balance with the Darkforce powering her monster within herself.

Naero gasped.

Almost instantly, her Dark Beast wailed, bereft of all its stolen power. It roared in fear–in terror, actually–and slipped away to hide.

The thing within her had never shown fear before.

The serenity of the Harmony suffused Naero. She hovered on the brink of becoming an energy being. She pulsed first with Scarlet Chaos energy, then Blue Order Energy, and finally a mix of the two, creating violet energy.

Violet energy…just like that of the artifact statue.

She swelled with energy until she towered ten meters over the spot she stood upon. Her hands and arms shifted into huge scarlet katanas. Red, blue, and purple blades emerged out of her energy form.

She looked like Baeven in his partial, Cosmic energy being form.

In a flash it occurred to her.

This was hers. This was what her partial energy being form looked like when it took shape.

She couldn't wait to try it out.

"What are you doing, Naero?" High Master Tree suddenly asked.

She felt all three of the High Masters suppressing her powers once more, siphoning them away.

She did not try to resist them–this time–but at some point, that was going to change. Naero shrank down to her normal form and size.

"Just trying out some new ideas that came to me."

"We and Intel have been monitoring some strange Cosmic energy spikes showing up on the planetary scans each day at about this time," Master Jo stated.

Naero tried a bluff. "What's the big deal? I've been trying to use balanced energy strategies to help control and contain my Dark Beast," Naero said. "Isn't that one of the goals I'm supposed to be working on?"

Master Tree looked uncertain for once. "In theory, yes. But it troubles us greatly that you have been going off on your own–and doing so–without our input, and without us there to safeguard you, should you lose control."

"See, we cannot trust her," Master Vane said. "What if she goes off on her own and loses it? She could wipe out an entire continent before we could arrive to contain and suppress her. It's the exact same situation on Janosha. What if the artifact statue should sense these Cosmic spikes and seek to investigate them? What if it takes her over, like the one on Janosha did with-"

Master Tree cut him off sternly. "She did not know that, and does not need to know the particulars of that event."

Naero, do not tell them about your replication abilities just yet.

Don't worry, Om. I'm not about to.

So, the artifact on Janosha took over Baeven somehow? What did it do to him? What did it do with him? Naero vehemently disagreed with the High Masters. They wanted to keep her ignorant, and saw safety in that strategy. Yet, more and more, she needed to know exactly what had happened back then to her uncle.

147

She needed to know in order to better control what just might happen to her as well.

"High Adept Maeris," Master Tree said, "we are deeply concerned and alarmed by this secretive, reckless behavior and frankly, with some of your choices and decisions that you have made in your role as Mediator."

"What have I done wrong? I have achieved a major treaty between the Maedo and the Kall."

Vane snorted. "What have you done wrong? Where do we begin? This was busy work. This was a lark, meant to keep you occupied so that you did not get into trouble. And here you are in the thick of it. You are only supposed to be negotiating these issues, not making them turn out the way you want them to–pretending to use godlike powers, duping the natives, and meddling directly in the affairs of the natives–far beyond any authority we ever thought to give you. You meddle too much, and you enlist the other adepts with you in doing so!"

Naero tried to ignore Master Vane. She knew exactly what he was going to say. "Look, you three gave me a mission, and I have taken the initiative to try to actually do something with it. And I have done real good. Tell me now, what was I supposed to do? Let the Thanarran royal family be murdered? Let Prince Tavul of the Maedo be killed, just like Prince Jigan of the Kall? Without my meddling, the Maedo and the Kall would be at war right now, to the detriment of both. Instead, they are at peace, and have formed a mutual alliance."

Finally, Master Jo came to her defense. "Brothers, she makes many good points. We did send her on this mission. What real harm has she done within the farce that we ourselves have established? She has brought about positive results, and avoided direct violence, whenever and wherever possible."

"I am not convinced," Master Tree said. "All of this could collapse and turn bad very quickly. And I am very uncomfortable with the element and level of deception being used, as far as manipulating the natives through their superstitions."

Naero couldn't believe it. She had to go ballistic on that one. "Seriously? You sent us among the natives, posing as 'the holy ones,' and yet we are not supposed to use that at all to our advantage, or to the furtherance of our mission? If the results are good, what do the methods matter?"

She had never witnessed Master Tree nearly go into a rage. "*That* opinion is dangerous and problematic almost in its entirety. I question it by its very nature. The ends cannot always justify the means. Can you not see the danger in that, High Adept Maeris?"

Master Jo shook his head. "I strongly disagree. No one is saying *always*. Yet, face the facts–sometimes the ends *do* justify the means. We should not fail to act just because we *might* do harm. Harm will be done anyway, even if we just stand by and let things happen the way Master Vane would. Why should we not try to modify things and make things better for all concerned?"

Vane jumped in. "That is not what we should be doing. Why are we even meddling at all? Who cares what the natives do to each other? We shouldn't even be here or be involved. Maeris is right in one thing: If you don't expect her to do what she does, in the way that we can guess she's going to do it, why in the hell should we give her the task anyway? I know very well what's going to happen. All of her attempts at peace are going to lead to the worst kind of war imaginable. Everything she touches ends in disaster and destruction. When has she not left destruction in her wake?"

"You all gave me a task," Naero said again, reminding them. "I have made it my own, and I am pursuing it to the best of my ability. It is far too late now to get cold feet, well after the point where I have committed so much time and effort, and the fates of so many are already at stake. You yourselves said that I would more than likely fail, as others before me have failed. At least give me some trust to make the best effort possible, using my own methods."

"I still question your methods in many ways," Master Tree said, folding his hands together. "But it seems that we are all both invested and fully committed to you seeing these matters through, whether we like it or not. Tell us, then, Naero. What do you think we should do?"

Naero spoke bluntly. "Easy, kill the sleazy emperor of the Vaedo and defeat the Vauk. We could do so in less than a day, and save tens of thousands of lives. The Vaedo are constantly fanning the flames of war, and playing everyone against the others for their benefit. They are without honor, and cannot be trusted. They are the obvious, greatest obstacle to peace between the city states."

Vane covered his face with his hands and shook his head in frustration and despair. "Now do you see the problem?" he howled.

"I do," High Master Tree said, his face very grave and troubled. "Naero Maeris, this is the exact reason why I commanded you expressly not to use violence. Is it not your go-to solution for everything? We cannot interfere in that way, and simply pick the leaders for the natives–and certainly not through assassination. That is not our role, or our place."

149

Mason Elliott

"Why in the hell not? You tell me...exactly how are the other city states supposed to negotiate peace with a diseased maniac like Emperor Vauk on the throne of the most powerful and numerous nation, with the largest army and active spy and assassin network? That is why Vauk keeps winning, and everyone else keeps losing. He is a genocidal maniac, a deluded tyrant, and a brutal, bloody thug of the worst sort. Why is his life so important, as opposed to all of the people he kills and tortures and maims on a daily basis?"

Master Jo looked at her pointedly. "Yet, the High Masters are still right. It is not our place to decide who lives and who dies; that is a slippery slope that we cannot go down. You must find another way. We do not work this way."

"Yes. We do," Naero told them. "What a load of crap. We face down tyrants all the time, and kill their sorry asses–cold, stone dead. We took out Triax Gigacorp in the Annexation War. We exterminated the Ejjai invasion during the High Crusade–and it was a very good thing that we did!"

Master Tree took up the argument. "High Adept Maeris, you are confusing what our people–the Spacers and our military–do, and what the Mystics do. You cannot confuse the two. The Mystics do everything they can *not* to directly interfere in primitive cultures and backwards worlds, for good or ill. It hardly ever turns out well in the long run. And we are very careful about what we do, and how we do it. That is why we have so many rules concerning such things."

"So, I can be used as an all-out weapon when we are at war, when serving attached to our military, but when I'm just an adept on my own, my hands are tied on undeveloped worlds? We can't do what we would normally do to protect others, the way that we in fact, protect ourselves and our people? You've read the reports. This guy is a major problem. If we can't deal with someone like him, what in the hell are we even here for?"

Vane finally lowered the boom.

"That's just it, Maeris. You don't even get it. We wouldn't be here at all, doing any of this, if the artifact wasn't here, if Thanor-4 was not the best current candidate for the new replacement Mystic Homeworld for Chaos Wisdom. Understand this: we would be ignoring the natives and their issues absolutely. They would be completely left on their own–as I personally think they should be. If they kill each other off completely, then so be it–that's their problem, and their business. My constant vote is for total, non-interference."

"I disagree," Naero said.

Vane rolled his eyes again. "We get that, Maeris, boy do we get that with you. Trust us; we know. Unfortunately, we have to deal with this kind

150

of crap, as you so rightly refer to it, because my two counterparts think that if we are using the world of these natives for our purposes, then somehow we owe them some kind of deal or guidance, or assistance–as long as we just happen to be here. While I contend that we owe them squat; all of this is nothing more than a needless irritation and distraction. I have no problem with lying to and deceiving these poor, backwards, ignorant boobs to get everything we need and want from this planet. But why should we interact with them at all? It is maddening."

"Undeveloped or not," Naero said, "they are still people who have worth, they are sentients, and they deserve to be free and live in the same security and freedom that our people demand for themselves."

Master Tree and Master Jo shook their heads.

Tree took up the argument. "But according to our rules–the rules of the Mystics–we cannot directly solve their problems for them, or hand-pick solutions for them that we like."

Jo backed him up. "They must learn to solve their problems for themselves. We can only advise and help them. They must make their own decisions."

Tree pointed his finger at her. "I forbid you, directly, to take the life of Emperor Vauk, or have a hand in his death. This is also a grave test for you, Naero Maeris. This is where your former uncle failed. He could not be obedient to the High Masters and serve our direct will. Especially when it became difficult for him to do so. What choice will you make?"

Naero lowered her eyes. "I am obedient to the will of the Mystic High Masters, even if I strongly disagree with them. Yet that does not and should not trump my free will as a Spacer in a free society. Nor does it change what I see to be right and wrong."

Master Jo took her hand. "We know this is a difficult trial for you, Naero. Yet, just as in the Spacer military, there are many good reasons why you cannot simply act unilaterally on your own and do whatever you wish. We are watching everything you do, and every decision you make, very carefully, in order for us to decide what is best to do with you, for you, and for the good of our people. The natives are not on trial, in our minds, Naero–*you are*. So make your choices, and choose wisely. This is the very reason why you are being tested in these ways: to see what you choose to do, and how you go about doing it."

Everything was a test…

Master Tree clasped his hands. "We also forbid you to conduct these Cosmic energy experiments on your own, High Adept. You will only do so with one or more of the High Masters present to study you."

We can still do that, Naero. It won't really make much of a difference if they observe us startapping or not at this point.

Fine. But I still want to keep the replication stuff secret for now. We need some kind of an ace up our sleeve, Om.

I agree. They don't need to know, for now. And replicating doesn't cause Cosmic energy spikes that they can track. We can pursue it whenever and wherever we like.

"Get going, Maeris," Master Vane ordered. "You're already late for your sparring session with the Order Adepts."

20

That afternoon, Naero anxiously awaited her scheduled meeting with Emperor Vauk of the Vaedo. What was she going to say to him now?

She brought another six adepts with her: Jaedar and Huan from Order, Zelana and Vaeshen from Change, and Mathron and Wing from Chaos.

She wasn't quite sure now who was observing who. She guessed that the other adepts were reporting back to the High Masters directly, concerning her actions. Let them do so.

Emperor Vauk just happened to be late that day. Naero felt certain it was an oversight on his part.

According to the reports from their spyfixers, a large force of Vaedo warriors heading toward the Kall shipyards had been repulsed in the mountains and in the coastal forests. Another similar force had made a push up into the Maedo highlands, to little avail.

Yet the golden dragon demonstrated that it could respond swiftly to setbacks. He kept his foes on the defensive, when he could not pit or play them against each other. And he had the resources to do so.

Naero guessed the new treaty and the alliance between the Kall and the Maedo came as a very rude awakening to the emperor.

His golden pleasure barge, protected by a screening fleet of Vaedo ships and military barges, finally pulled up to the docks.

As always, the Thanes were prepared for treachery or war at a moment's notice. Yet they did not balk at an opportunity to trade, either. Vaedor controlled many wealthy lands and resources.

The emperor did not meet the holy ones on deck this day, but summoned them to his presence down below.

Naero and her friends were escorted carefully into the lower levels of the vessel.

Many Vaedo guards and warriors lined the way.

That fact was made very clear to them all. But if it was meant to be intimidating or threatening, it did not work.

When they entered the floating palace, the opulence and debauchery were somewhat impressive, and nauseating, but Naero had witnessed much worse displays.

The Celestial One himself was busy emerging mostly naked from what looking to be a shallow, simmering, bubbling orgy pool, filled with concubines and pleasure slaves of various kinds, genders, and ages.

Naero was not surprised in the least–she even expected such a display of depravity. It did not shock her, as he intended. Emperor Vauk was just the kind of twisted freak that wanted to rub his dirty business in everyone's face and gloat on it.

Guards stood at hand, very close by, at the very edges of the pool, with gilded spears at the ready.

Three corpses floated in the pool, one strangled–apparent from the throat bruises–one stabbed and hacked up, and another with a throat simply cut wide open.

Since Vauk had been the only one in the pool with a dagger at his side on a gilded cord over the shoulder, it was very clear who the killer was. And that his sex surrogates apparently had to endure both mutilation and murder as well, as part of the emperor's sick pleasures.

Naero had never wanted to eliminate a tyrant so badly. The wretch cried out for it. Thanor-4 would be a much better place. Everyone would be better off without this disease of a creature in charge of one of the most powerful city states and armies.

And yet she could not harm him and had given her word not to. Just how was she supposed to work around such a lunatic?

The bloody, orgy bubble bath pool actually withdrew from the chamber into an adjoining area, most likely for cleaning and removal of the corpses.

Emperor Vauk's thick, pasty body remained unimpressive, and thankfully was quickly dried off, perfumed, and wrapped in golden robes.

The lengthy, golden codpiece was obviously a joke.

His slaves labored to lift his bulk up onto the pinnacle of a high, golden throne, shaped like a pouncing golden dragon. The motif was everywhere, of course.

He suddenly fixed his gaze upon Naero and began…to lecture her.

"Let us speak plainly, *Mediator*." He spoke her position with dripping sarcasm, as if it were some kind of insult.

Platters of expensive-looking food and drink suddenly surrounded the adepts, and smiling, fawning, half-naked slaves and servants invited them to partake.

Naero, the stealth fixers are telling everyone not to eat or drink anything. Everything you see before you is poisoned in some lethal way.

We guessed that going in, Om. We aren't here to eat or get drunk–or killed. We'll stun all these jerks or transport out if we have to. Then let the emperor suck on that.

"There are no gods," Vauk said plainly. "We all know it. You know that as well as I. And, I don't know how you freed Prince Tavul or learned the things you learned in order to irritate me. I don't care. It all ends now. You may be sorcerers, you may even be demons, but I am the closest thing to a god this world shall ever see, and *anyone* who opposes me ends up face down in their own guts and blood. I assure you of that. I will drown you all in your own piss, shit, and blood."

Naero was not dissuaded by his rant. She spoke evenly, when she had the chance.

"Everyone wants something, Emperor Vauk. I have asked all of the other rulers what they desire–what they would like to see happen for them and their people. Now I am asking you. What do you want, and what do you want to happen?"

Vauk giggled slightly to himself. "What do I desire? Why, 'tis simplicity itself. What else would a god yearn for? I want it all–all that there is. I want everything that exists and that will ever exist. All must bow before me and feel the weight of my feet upon their necks. Need you even ask?"

"Forgive me, lord. But you just said that there are no gods. By that reasoning alone…you are not a god."

Vauk waved a hand. "Of course I'm not. All illusion and fakery. That is why I killed off all of my holy ones or forced them to worship me instead. Religion is but tool–a useful lie to rule over fools. Were you not listening to my golden words? I said I was the closest thing to a god this world shall ever see."

"Yet you are mortal, milord. You will not live forever. What shall come after you?"

Vauk shrugged. "I don't really care. Let the world be consumed in flames after I am gone. It does not matter. It won't matter to me after I die. After death there is nothing any way. But while I am here, I intend to rule– to reign over all and force them to do my will or perish."

"What about your people, the Vaedo? What shall happen to them?"

"Don't care. Couldn't care less. What do slaves matter? They will die or become slaves to someone else."

"Why could they not be free as well?"

"Oh, please. What do slaves need with freedom?"

"The other city states will not bend to your will so easily. They too are proud, and they shall oppose you."

"I hope so. I hope they do. I'm counting on it. Then the game will be a challenge, at least."

"That's all this is to you, milord…a bloody game?"

"Yes, and intend to win it. None are my equal, including you, little girl. You think I fear you and your so-called holy ones, whom you use to spy on everyone and make them fear that you know something important? That is why I do not allow them in my lands. Your kind and your lies have no power over me."

Naero sighed, took a step forward, and clasped her hands calmly before herself.

"Emperor Vauk of the Vaedo, things are not always as they seem. They do not have to be like this, unless you make them so."

"That's just it, child. I am making them so. Deliberately. Because I want to."

"Yet it does not have to be this way, milord. With almost no effort, you could live in peace with your neighbors–trade with them, help one another. You could work together in friendship and cooperation, for the good of all. You could turn this troubled world into a paradise, not just for yourself, but everyone."

Vauk laughed openly. "And what would all that accomplish? How utterly tedious. The good of all? Phaugh! I took you for a charlatan and a scoundrel, Mediator. Yet I never thought you mad. Speak not to me of such things. I want war–a war of conquest and cataclysm–the likes of which no one has ever seen before."

"This is your will then, milord?"

"Indeed. You know, there were once other city states as well. Loxos fell to my grandfather. The fools thought that the knowledge contained within their scrolls and books would somehow serve them better than strong armies. They made a treaty with Vaedor and Pelenarra. They thought themselves so wise and smart, until the grand army of the Vaedo swept into their city, bent them all over, and buggered them–from the oldest to the youngest–with flesh and bloody iron. We burned all of their books and scrolls in the streets and hurled them into the flames. A scant few remain, as my concubines and whores for my pleasure."

He waved a hand absently, dismissing the brutal slaughter and destruction of an entire people.

"Then my father dealt with Pelenarra and the Shukai in similar fashion. I was young and got to help a bit with the Shukai, but sadly, too many of the latter escaped on their ships, and eventually became the Kall. Break the fools, pit them against each other, and then ravage them all. Their children will always be forfeit to our whims, and shall perish by fire and sword.

"But before we butcher them, I always make a point of having my armies rape everyone–strip them of all pretense and humanity– before we rip open their throats and bellies, and crush their heads. That is the way to truly destroy an adversary. Kill all of their children, and you kill them and all that they could ever be. There is no coming back from that. That is devastation; that is power!"

"So…you are bent upon on such a war?"

"I am. I have never been otherwise. Within the year, most likely. Definitely by next spring. I will march across the lands and crush all who defy me. And none can stop it–let alone the nonexistent gods. The other lands cannot stop me, nor can you. Go your way, therefore, and bide what time you have left…Mediator. Play your parlor tricks. Do as you will, for my plans are nearly ready, and all the known world shall scream, and shriek, and burn as I watch and smile."

"There is nothing, milord, that I can do or say to persuade you otherwise?"

"You cannot stop me. No one can. In fact, the more you sue for peace, the weaker and more desperate I assume you and the others to be. My victory is therefore assured."

"My friends and I must depart, milord. It appears that, by your own words, my mission to you is at an end."

Weapons suddenly bristled and barred their path in all directions.

"No," Vauk cried out in triumph. "Let them go. Let them run. Where can they hide? Use your time well…Mediator–the few scant days, weeks, or months left to you. When all is done according to my will, and my armies have burned, and hacked, and raped their way across the three city states. You shall be found and dragged to me for my personal pleasure and amusement. You…who thought to oppose me and my will."

"I shall inform the other rulers of your intent. They will stop you."

"You do just that. It is far too late for that. Tell them to fight as hard as they can. Even if all three band together now, they do not have enough numbers, or power to stop me. In the end, you shall see, I shall drag them all down, and torment, ravage, and butcher their children before their eyes– burn them alive and screaming–and slaughter them all…slowly."

Naero did not bow as she and the others turned their backs and left.

"Farewell, Emperor Vauk. You were right. You are not a god."

Vauk's echoing laughter followed after her.

"You will be sent for…Mediator. I will take my time slowly with you when you come to me!"

They emerged from the depths of the emperor's hellish barge, and the Vaedo pulled away.

Naero already knew that she had failed. The High Masters had said that the task was impossible from the very start. How could anyone mediate peace with such a monster at loose upon the known world?

Apparently, Naero had her answer. The other leaders most likely expected as much as well. All seemed poised for war.

She went immediately to see the Changs and arrange an emergency meeting with King Arrok and Queen Liita of the Thanes.

Fu-han and Lijuan led her and the others into the queen's parlor, where the royal family was playing table and parlor games with some of the other nobles and their families.

The pretty queen proudly introduced her children. Crown Prince Shondar was taller than Naero herself. The red-haired lad was fourteen, strong and hale, playing a game of some kind of chess against his noble father, and winning, much to the monarch's mixture of pride and chagrin.

The youth beamed when Naero was introduced. "Mediator Naero, wellmet," he said, taking her hand in his. "My parents have told me so much about you, and I have heard so much more. I hope we get a chance to talk. I have so many questions."

"After our game is done," his father growled.

The boy grinned. "That shouldn't take too long."

Both of them laughed at that, but the king still looked worried.

"Iiden, my daughter," the queen called. "Come and meet the mediator I told you so much about."

The princess had been reading a tale of high adventure to a wide circle of young friends from an open scroll in her white hands. Her radiant gray eyes flashed as she acted out the parts and did the voices.

When her mother called out to her, Princess Iiden stopped what she was doing, put down the scroll, and hiked up her sky-blue dress to run over to Naero and her mother.

With her long golden hair and slender form, at the age of twelve, the princess looked like every young princess should–bright and beautiful. She was overly excited and blushed and could barely speak at first.

But that changed very quickly.

"Wonders, mother. Is this her? Is this the mediator of the gods who saved us all from the assassins?"

"Yes, it is she, my child. Sister Naero of the holy ones, meet my radiant daughter, Iiden."

"Indeed," Naero said. "She is a star, sent down from the heavens themselves."

Iiden showed no pretense and hugged Naero instantly. "You're so tiny," she said with a laugh. Yes, even the twelve-year-old was taller than Naero. Dang these people.

Iiden kept rambling. "I want to know so much. I want to know all about the gods. Have you seen them? What do they all look like? Describe them to me in complete detail. What do they wear? How do they fashion their clothing? Where do they live? Have you seen it–the realm of wonder and legends? What's it like? Do they have unicorns from the fabled land of Nashara there? Is Nashara real? What do the unicorns eat? Do unicorns poop in the heavenly lands? Do the angels have to clean it up? I would dearly love to meet an angel–or a unicorn, for that matter. Have you ever met one of either, Naero? Please, please tell me."

Naero's mouth fell open.

Queen Liita laughed. "Don't worry. My daughter can have that affect on many. Leave off, my daughter. Give the mediator time to speak with your father and I."

"Yes," her brother called out from his chess game. "Don't exhaust the mediator with all of your silly questions. Unicorn manure, indeed!"

Iiden stuck her tongue out at her sneering brother. "And that for you, brother. My questions are not silly."

Naero shook her head. "I'm sorry, princess. I am still in this life. I have not had any visions of the Beyond, nor have I been called there. The gods make their will known to the holy ones in our minds and hearts. We do what they wish of us, and go where they send us."

Iiden frowned somewhat. "That is no help at all."

"Go, child," her mother said. "Return to your friends and be merry."

Iiden went back to her crowd, and was soon laughing and rambling again with her friends. She was indeed a child of light.

Once the king admitted defeat, he and the queen drew off into a council chamber nearby to talk with Naero and all the adepts present.

"I'm afraid," Naero said, "that the news in the end is not good. I have failed. I'm afraid there will not be peace. In fact, I fear that there will be war instead. A terrible war to decide the fate of your world."

Naero explained all that she could tell them. They had learned about the treaty and alliance between the Maedo and the Kall. Word apparently traveled fast.

Then she told them about everything that Emperor Vauk had said.

The king and queen stared at the stones on the floor with grim faces.

"Within the year, next spring at best, the emperor intends to unleash total war upon all of you," Naero informed them. "If he wins, it will go hard upon everyone, from the least to the greatest."

The king let out a deep, heavy sigh. "Just as we feared all along."

The queen clenched her fists. "They will ravage and burn everything in their path. Even if we defeat them in the bitter end, and take Vauk's head, the world as we know it will be destroyed in the process."

"I'm sorry," Naero said.

The king put one of his big hands on her shoulder. "None of this is of your making, holy sister. We knew it was coming."

Queen Liita joined in. "The emperor has been preparing for this day for years—and his sires before him. The Vaedo lust for conquest has been evident for generations. And their spies and assassins seem to be everywhere."

"All the lands have not been idle," King Arrok stated. "All of us have been preparing against such a thing. But it still goes hard, knowing what will come."

"You must band together," Naero said. "That is your only chance. You must join the alliance with the Maedo and the Kall."

"Even so, we are still outnumbered," King Arrok said. "The Vaedo have been experts at playing all sides against each other. I think that has been their greatest power."

"Then strip it from them," Naero said. "Deny it to them. Only together can you survive. Once Vaedor has been defeated, and the golden dragon emperors are no more, then you can live in peace. This war must be fought; nothing can be held back. If not for your sakes, then for the sake of all your peoples and your children. You know very well what the golden dragon will do to them."

A fire suddenly awoke in the eyes of the King and Queen.

It was the warrior queen who spoke first and fiercely drew her sword. "By the gods and all light, we shall fight them. They will need to cut every drop of blood from my body before I let those murderous wretches lay their bloody hands upon my fair ones!"

The king rose up and kissed her, wrapping her up in his big arms.

"My beloved, warrior maid. You won my heart that day long ago, when we fought back-to-back against the foe until we two alone stood victorious. So we shall stand once more! They will not have us, nor our babes. We shall fight to the last!"

When their blood had cooled, they sat down at the table.

"What help can the gods give us?" the king asked. "Is there anything they can do?"

Fu-han knitted her fingers and spoke. "Forgive us, Your Majesties. The gods sent the mediator to attempt to broker a peace. Unfortunately, there is none to negotiate. The Vaedo are bent upon war. The gods do not interfere in such human matters."

"Unfortunate, but true," the queen said. "These are mortal troubles that mortals must resolve. This is our world, and we must make of it what we can. We must fight for it. We thank the holy ones and the gods for what they have attempted."

Naero spoke, staring hard at the Changs. "No good will be served, however, if the Vaedo crush everyone else. The emperor even means to kill off all the holy ones. If the gods allow us to do so, the holy ones might be able to provide information that might be of use to the allies."

The king nodded. "That is something, at least. We would be grateful, for any help or advice."

Fu-han and Lijuan stared back at her impassively at first.

Then they nodded their assent.

A Vaedo victory would not be good for anyone involved.

King Arrok rose and put one hand to his sword and the other to his broad belt. "Let word go forth then, for the final preparations to be made, for as long as we have to make ready. War is coming. These grim matters will be decided within a short period of time—one or two years at best. The fate of our world and all or our peoples now rests within our hands. That is perhaps as it should be."

Later that night, Princess Iiden went out alone to the great shore of stars. First she wept bitterly in great anguish. Next, Iiden sang to the stars. Then she turned and sang to the forest, like a small jewel in the night.

Naero watched over and protected her. Fixers kept watch all around.

No harm would come to that child, even if the Vaedo brought forth an entire army.

Shetanna stood ready in the night to make certain of that.

At last, Sister Naero came forward.

"Whom do you call to in the trees, Princess?" Naero asked her.

Fair Iiden started at first, and then ran to embrace her.

"It is from a legend of far off Nashara, where the queen of the unicorns is said to rule in harmony and wisdom. In those legends, our world was threatened by war, and monsters, and demons—much as it is now, I suppose. A young human queen—no older than I am—sang to the forests, and called forth the unicorn queen. Together, by their wisdom an courage they helped their peoples rise above every threat, every challenge and peril, to make their land a paradise."

Iiden sighed. "I know…I'm just a silly little girl, wishing for something to exist that does not." She sighed so deeply.

"But I'm old enough to know what is really coming—our own demons, that we have made, are coming for us all, and they shall do their worst. I fear war and its terrors. I'm afraid, Sister Naero. I have no wish to be raped, or burned alive, or murdered, along with all that I love. I just wish that the other parts of the legends were true as well, and that the forces of light would come to help us, and give us their courage."

Naero took Iiden's hands and held them. "Iiden, you and your people have that courage. You are a force of light for your world and your people. You are a living, breathing angel of your people. If anyone ever deserved the unicorns of Nashara—from your age of legends—to come to them, it is you. Be brave, young princess. You and yours and your deeds of valor shall write the legends of tomorrow–legends that shall live on and inspire others, far into the futures of your peoples. This is the blood you come from; I have seen it. These troubles that lie ahead are not the end. They cannot be. Fight! Don't let them triumph."

Iiden bit her lip. "I'm still just a girl. If I am to face all of these terrible things, I wish that I could see a real live unicorn...or an angel. Just one. Just once."

Naero stroked Iiden's shining hair under the starlight. "May your heart's wish be truly fulfilled one day, child of light. Keep the wonder that is in your kind and gentle heart. Let it burn bright. Defend it! When all is done, many will have great need of your beauty and wonder, to guide them out of the darkness and terror that lies before you all."

21

Naero returned and made her final report to the High Masters.

It was necessary for her to stand before them and discuss her failure at being a mediator.

Master Jo was the only one who seemed to come away with a positive take on the entire situation.

"High Adept Maeris...there was not much chance of you succeeding at your mission going in. This war was probably inevitable. Yet thanks to you, the other three city states will go into it allied together, and not just picked off one at a time or used against each other."

Naero shook her head. "It is still going to be a very terrible war for the locals. I wish I could have prevented it."

Master Vane, of course, burst out laughing. "I can't believe I'm saying this, Maeris, but you surprised me. I thought for certain that you were going to lose it and just start killing and slaughtering people left and right. What happened? Why didn't you?"

Naero felt her anger rise. "I still might do just that!" she added.

Master Tree raised both hands. "Let us hear no such talk. Do not bait her, High Master Vane. And High Adept Naero Maeris, do not allow yourself to be baited. In fact, I must commend you, Naero Maeris, on controlling what you think you should do with being obedient to our will. You have eschewed violence, when it would have been both tempting and expedient to rely upon it. You passed the tests we set for you."

Vane grunted.

"For the most part," Tree continued, "you refrained from killing anyone. That was good progress, as we see it."

A cold chill shot through Naero. Was Master Tree right in a way? Was fighting, violence, and killing her natural solution to everything?

Om...am I really like that? Am I a killer, someone who only seeks to solve my problems by killing?

No. You are an honorable warrior, Naero. One who has been forced to defend yourself and you people against threats that would terrify the mightiest. Yes, you have killed. Most of your enemies required killing.

Most, Om? Just most?

Can we ever speak in absolutes either way, Naero? The universe is such a messy place.

Naero bowed her head. It is indeed, Om.

"Well, that is all finished and done with," Tree said. "There's no need for you to go among the natives any longer. Now we can concentrate on studying your expanding powers and the other matter at hand."

Tree wouldn't mention the artifact statue directly.

Naero still felt the need to protest.

"But...I want to find out what happens to them all. I don't just want to abandon them."

Tree raised a disapproving eyebrow. "Why not? What does it matter? Read the reports after the fact. Adepts Fu-han and Lijuan will see to them. The natives are their little project, not yours. Come now, a few weeks ago, you didn't even know anything about these natives. Do not let sentiment distract you from the very important matters at hand. Are you really going to sacrifice all of your goals and your people for a few backward savages on some nameless mud hole?"

Naero knew Master Tree very well by now. Order above all else, even fairness and justice. In his own way, Master Tree was just as cold and heartless as Master Vane. Vane was simply more brutally honest and open about his callousness. Or maybe she was the one that

165

was unenlightened. In his own way, Master Tree was also right. Naero couldn't really change things either way for the Thanorans. Why worry about it? What was happening here that wasn't happening across countless worlds among all the possible universes and realities? Struggle, war, aggression–competition for resources–life and death.

Perhaps she merely had to have more stoic faith in those outcomes, tending more toward Order than destructive Chaos.

Yeah, who was she kidding. Like she could do that?

They dismissed her. It was getting late, but Master Jo pulled her aside at the last moment.

"Naero. I've been having very troubling Cosmic dreams and visions of late. Have you as well?"

She went on a hunch. "Let me guess–about dragons?"

Master Jo grinned. "I had a feeling we might be on the same wavelength. What have you been experiencing?"

"I keep seeing these enormous dragon creatures–an entire army of them–attacking our worlds, systems, and fleets. They seem almost unstoppable. There aren't any reports of anything like that anywhere?"

Master Jo shook his head. Naero was always relieved that he was the one High Master who was shorter than her.

"No yet. If we had any reports like that, Naero, we would be at war with the creatures by now."

"Are we seeing a vision then? Something that might happen in the distant future?"

Master Jo stroked his dry lips as he stretched them. "It doesn't feel like that–more urgent–like a looming threat. The High Masters and I can't put our fingers on it. You and I and a few others are all seeing something similar–including your brother and your aunt. We are seeing these things for a reason."

That surprised Naero. Aunt Sleak was having the dragon visions as well?

"I agree, High Master," Naero said. "It seems to be some kind of growing warning–the sense of urgency is increasing–but we don't understand what form it is taking, or what it means. What are these visions trying to tell us about these creatures? Are they literal beings, or representative of something?"

You need to tell them the little that we know, Naero.

I agree, Om. I just have to figure out how to word it.

Naero cleared her throat. "The Kexx fought such Cosmic monsters long ago. They were called the Kahn-Dar. Like their allies, the G'lothc, the Kahn-Dar were Cosmic shapechangers, and could assume various forms–

including the huge, Cosmic energy dragon-forms they used in war. The Kahn-Dar were not only from another galaxy–but came from many other dimensions as well. They could gate, or travel between gates, other planes, galaxies, and dimensions–almost at will."

Master Jo's face suddenly grew slightly pale and concerned. "You have access to the lore of the Kexx? Why have you not spoken of this before? This could prove vital."

Naero held up both hands in defense. "I have only just begun to learn the complex Kexxian language, High Master. The vast majority of the KDM by far remains a mystery to me and my limited mind. But I have seen glimpses of many things. In the great war with the formidable G'lothc, the Kexx and the Drians also fought and defeated the Kahn-Dar. Now it seems that we will need to fight these creatures at some point as well–perhaps sooner than we think.

"We have already fought the Dakkur. They were allies with the Kahn-Dar. My guess is that a remnant of both races survived that ancient war, and are now attempting to increase their numbers, utilizing G'lothc Darkforce tek to become the new masters. Minion races like the Ejjai are mere slaves compared to them. The Ejjai already refer to them as their masters."

Master Jo shook his head. "And here we had our new Mystic Enforcer out scouring our systems for any sign of these creatures. Perhaps we should call him back here, if we think an attack is imminent. The Mystics created him and the first of his Cosmic Swords to help stand before such threats as this."

Was Master Jo talking about Khai? A sudden thrill rushed through her at the prospect of seeing her old friend.

Master Jo continued thinking out loud, as he often did. "His powers would be a great help, in fact. And who knows how the ancient artifact statue will fit in with all of this, if it is indeed Kexxian? There remains far too much that we do not know or understand."

Naero lifted both of her arms in frustration and let them flop back to her sides. "I know. I constantly feel that way. I've even had a few visions where the Kahn-Dar are attacking the statue directly, like they are trying to devour it, or absorb its powers, somehow. None of it makes any sense!"

Master Jo's mouth fell open and his face grew very pale. "Naero," he said. "No one else has reported such a thing."

"What?"

"No one else has had a vision of the dragon creatures and the artifact statue together in the same dream, fighting each other at the same time. You are the only one."

The ramifications of that began to soak in. "Oh...crap," Naero muttered.

"Naero, I want to try something in order to gain more information. Allow me to mindlink with you, and let's take a quick little journey."

"Where are we going?" For a minute, she was afraid he was going to suggest they go visit the artifact statue.

"Let me explain briefly. Of all the High Masters, I am the Traveler—the one who can see and pass into the other planes, dimensions, and realities—almost at will. I can key on your mind and your visions, and use them to attempt to pinpoint where they came from."

"You can...trace them back to where they came from?"

"I can try, but it takes enormous quantities of Cosmic energy to do so, even for a few moments. I will set us on a loop, but I may very well pass out from the stress, and the extreme exertion. Don't worry. If I do black out, we will automatically sweep back and return here, to our own place and time. We might see nothing at all. Yet, we might see something elsewhere that will give us clues as to what we might expect. But just because something happens one way in one possible dimension, does not mean that it will happen that way exactly in another, or at all. There are so many variations and variables possible. So much that we Mystics still do not know."

Naero smiled. "And here I thought the High Mystics knew it all."

Master Jo shook his head vehemently. "Oh, Naero. There is so very much to know in even one universe such as ours—let alone an infinite number of possible realities and universes. The sheer magnitude of it all is beyond all words and all the known systems of thought. To speak the truth, all three of us High Masters are like ignorant children, laughing, crawling, and muttering in the grass at night, trying to comprehend the mysteries of the stars above us. Even arrogant Master Vane is stupefied by the immensity of it all; it is truly humbling. I cannot tell you how numb with fear we are at times, frightened by all that we do not know—and perhaps never shall know."

Naero chuckled. "Ignorance recognized is the beginning of wisdom," Naero said.

"Wisdom from the Clans?" Master Jo asked.

"A Kexxian proverb, I'm pretty sure," Naero said.

Master Jo blinked. "Then the ancients won't mind if I borrow it from them. I like that very much. Are you ready for our mindlink and the dimensional sweep attempt? It won't take long. We'll just see brief glimpses here and there, if anything."

Naero took a few deep breaths and centered herself, not knowing what else to expect. "I'm ready," she said at last."

Master Jo's third eye opened, blazing with golden power.

Naero's third eye–shifting red, blue, and violet–sprang open wide as soon as he laid hands upon her face. Naero shuddered as his power rippled through her body, mind, and soul.

To her surprise, the both of them instantly transformed into either energy beings, or spirit forms on the Astral Plane.

To Naero, it seemed as if they rose up high into the air suddenly, as everything else–including the stars–flashed and whirled around them.

Then they reached a point or spot where they did not seem to move any further, and stayed in one place, while everything shifted and flashed around them.

Realities and dimensions pulsed past them, and all they could do was look on and try to see what they could see.

Master Jo was correct in part. Much of the time they saw nothing.

Yet at other times they glimpsed the world of Thanor-4, in many variants.

One was scorched and blackened, all life blasted and ripped off the entire surface.

Somehow, Master Jo's Mystic focus zoomed in.

In another variant, the artifact statue was completely gone. Deep craters of glowing Cosmic ruin, gouged thousands of kilometers into the shattered, broken planet.

In another dimension, the alien statue lay toppled and lifeless, face down, blasted and scorched–completely drained of whatever vast powers it had once contained.

Yet another showed the aftermath of a great battle. Nothing survived. Dead Kahn-Dar lay everywhere–along with burning wrecks of starships, entire Spacer Marine regiments wiped out. Not even the Mystics had been spared.

They all lay dead to the last.

Master Jo and Naero both saw their own twisted, broken bodies lying slain among what had become an enormous, open grave in the grim aftermath of such a conflagration.

Other visions simply showed the artifact statue, inert and eternal, standing like a slumbering sentinel in its original location throughout the passing eons.

Master Jo did black out, and they began to sweep back toward their origin point. Naero clung to the High Master, afraid about what would happen to her if they became separated. Would she be lost in some kind of interdimensional limbo, forever?

On the return trip, Naero saw variations of the same visions, increasing in number and severity.

The Kahn-Dar were definitely coming for them all–cutting across all Space-Time and various dimensions and possibilities to get at them.

To Naero, their purpose became very clear.

They meant to destroy the Mystics once and for all, and seize the power of the Cosmic artifact for their own.

22

Unfortunately for Naero, Master Jo was still unconscious upon their return. Naero carried him to the other High Masters.

"What did you do to him?" Master Vane shrieked. "Maeris must have lost control and attacked him. I told you we couldn't trust her!"

"Calm yourself, High Master. I'm sure it is nothing so diabolical as that. Why then would she bring him to us? High Adept Maeris, explain."

"Before he passed out, Master Jo said that you should summon the Mystic Enforcer back to Thanor-4. I agree. You should do so now, please. We are in grave danger."

Vane looked startled for an instant. "Yeah...from you!"

Naero told him. "When–not if–the Kahn-Dar attack, you will wish you had a thousand of me."

Master Tree calmly closed his eyes, surprisingly without hesitation. Naero felt the power surge forth from his mind.

Tree opened his eyes. "There. It is done. The summons to the Enforcer has gone out. Now, give us the details, High Adept Maeris."

"What has happened?" Vane insisted. "Not that damn artifact statue again."

"Let her speak," Tree insisted.

Naero quickly told them about her and Master Jo's little dimensional sweep and what they witnessed.

"Ridiculous," Vane fumed. "None of that is certain. It could mean anything. There are countless possibilities."

Naero became insistent. "Master Jo passed out. He did not see what I beheld on the way back. The Kahn-Dar are allied with our enemies; we know that much. And they are most definitely coming for us all–for me, the Mystics, the artifact statue–they want it all, and they mean to have it. Cosmic energy is food to them."

"Then why is there no warning of their approach?" Tree asked.

Naero pointed at the ground. "This is it. This is the warning, these dreams and visions so many of us are having about these dragon creatures. I saw us fighting and even in many cases, *dying* in the course of direct combat with the Kahn-Dar, in other similar or adjacent dimensions. So, what I want to know, is ours one where we win–or where we all die?"

"Only we can decide that," Master Tree said. "Did you see how or when they will strike, Naero? How will they come at us? Why is there no other warning of their approach?"

"We will not see them coming through our regular Space-Time by any normal means. You've been looking and scanning in the wrong ways. Their onset will be sudden and incredibly destructive," Naero said. "They are gating through many dimensions and possibilities in order to secretly get at us here–in this one particular reality. Their attack could come at any moment, all at once, and without warning. They will attempt total, overwhelming surprise and destruction."

Om, tell me how the Kahn-Dar attack and fight again. I forgot.

Various Cosmic blasts and attacks, from their mouths, eyes, claws, and even their tails–energy in various forms, including the Darkforce. They can feed upon and absorb any energy. Some can breathe poisonous smoke or acid. Others can shoot or fling poisonous or exploding spikes or spines. They can still attack physically, and with their great size and might, they are very formidable.

Tree and Vane worked on reviving Jo.

Naero tried to contact Jan. Nothing. Probably still training.

Aunt Sleak. She and the twins had time to get safely away, somewhere else.

No response.

Naero tried her ship. All links. Even her secret frequencies.

Some kind of sophisticated jamming.

All communications were down.

The perfect prelude to any attack.

She activated the proper codes and sent out spyfixer relay distress calls: Intel, the Alliance, Spacer Navy, Spacer Marines, her own fleet, and *The Dark Star*...even Baeven.

Anyone who might help them against what was coming.

She quickly returned to the High Masters, who were locked in debate.

Master Jo was conscious again. That much was a relief.

"What about activating a planetary shield?" Vane said. "Will that hold these monsters off?"

Master Jo shook his head. "Not in the least. You heard Adept Maeris. They're travelling dimensionally. When they fall upon us, they'll come out of nowhere."

Master Tree tried his comunit. "I can't reach my ship," he said.

"We're being jammed," Naero said. "I can't tell how this is being done, but it is everywhere across the planet's surface. I can't reach the adepts on Thanarra, either. We're cut off. All communications are down."

"The artifact statue, perhaps?" Master Vane said, trying to reach out with his abilities.

Naero shook her head. "Who knows? I can't tell. Yet, why? It has not done so before. Why would it do this now, of all times?"

"It is more likely," Master Jo said, "that this is an effect caused by the coming of our enemies–a distortion brought on by their various wild, Cosmic energies. Perhaps it presages their invasion."

Master Tree spoke calmly. "We have sent messengers on foot and by vehicle to all of our forces, to gather together and prepare for combat. We will not risk launching any of our ships outside the planet until that is done."

"What about Nashara?" Naero asked. "Even with the planet's energies, the artifact statue is like a flaming beacon of Cosmic power. Surely the enemy will attack it first on that continent."

Master Vane laughed. "We have the vast majority of our forces there still. That damn statue is better protected than we are here."

"And, as we have seen first hand," Master Tree said, "the artifact statue isn't exactly defenseless on its own."

"That's it!" Master Jo said. "I can forge a telepathic link with my Prime adepts–Tess and Den. They're on Nashara. We can check in with them; see what's happening there."

Jo focused, making the psyonic link.

Waves of Cosmic power rippled through them all without warning, staggering and disorienting them.

Naero and everyone present gasped, shaking and struggling to stay on their feet.

"What in the hell was that?" Master Vane said.

Master Jo snapped out of his trance, gulping for air.

"Is it the Kahn-Dar?" Naero asked. "What's happening there?"

"What is the status of the artifact?" Master Tree demanded. "Where is it?"

A heavy, bass pulsing sound–a sensation of throbbing, Cosmic energy–erupted right behind Naero.

Master Vane's eyes widened in terror. The first time Naero had ever seen him afraid.

Naero whirled around, snapping up her defenses, third eye and all.

The artifact statue stood directly behind her, humming and throbbing, pulsing with waves of intense, Cosmic power rippling right off of it.

It was shaped like her, and lifted its hands to take her.

Naero's defenses melted and vanished before its naked might.

The three High Masters flashed around it in a perfect triangle, glowing with their own energies–attempting to contain the artifact.

Naero heard Master Jo in her mind.

Flee! Get out of here, Naero. It cannot touch you!

In one instant the statue emitted a violet pulse wave that blasted all three High Masters away, and dissolved the nanostructure entirely.

But Naero got the chance to transport away.

She went to the desert.

Startap, Naero. Startap!

On it, Om.

Naero filled herself with Cosmic power, shutting out her Dark Beast this time.

The artifact statue appeared ten meters away, still keying on her, arms still outstretched to grab her. It began speaking to her in Kexxian.

"Time...no time. They are coming."

Naero nailed the thing full on with everything she had. Tremendous Cosmic blasts poured out of from both hands.

Her heaviest assault didn't even slow the thing down.

It absorbed every bit of energy and kept coming.

Naero transported again, this time to the forest where they did their best replicating.

The artifact statue followed her one second later, stalking straight for her, dissolving and disrupting anything in its path—rocks, trees. Greenery withered and turned to white and gray, lifeless dust in a wide swath all around the thing.

"We...must merge. You are the one. The others will be—inferior selections—at best."

What others? What is it babbling about, Om?

No idea.

She startapped and transported into the mountains overlooking the Bay of Thanarra.

It followed her there just as fast, coming for her. Relentless.

"Merge with me. The others are inferior selections. They will not survive. You know this."

"I don't know anything!" Naero shouted. She prepared to transport again.

Even as she did, the statue stared back at her—

With her own eyes!

23

Naero appeared, shaking and gasping in her private quarters on her flagship, ready to fight or flee again. Her state room recognized her and lit up instantly.

She drew her scarlet energy katanas and waited, whirling around for a few seconds, making sure nothing snuck up behind her or popped in.

Nothing. The statue did not follow after all. Perhaps there were limits to its powers.

Perhaps it was out of time, as it said.

Scan for it, Om. Where is the statue?

Om hesitated only a moment. *The artifact statue has returned to Nashara. All scans and visuals still disrupted. Spyfixers en route to scene. We should have something within minutes.*

Naero called over her com to her crew. "This is Captain Naero to all crew. Battle stations. Cloak and prepare for battle. A major attack is imminent from enormous, Cosmic dragon aliens known as the Kahn-Dar. Cloak, assess the situation, and pick the best battle options. Advise any other ships in the vicinity to do the same, if possible. Com through spyfixers if all other coms continue to be jammed. Enel and Surina, command this vessel and stay alive. Wait for further orders. I'll be on the surface, and I may need you to effect a rescue. I love you, my *abani*. Luck to us all!"

What are we going back down there for, Naero? That thing is there. Nothing can stop it!

So are my friends and family, Om. We go check on the High Masters first—then Jan and Aunt Sleak. All of this feels worse every second. I can't say why. It just does. Let's go.

She transported back to Mystic camp in the Thanarran mountains.

Intel troops, Spacers, Marines, and adepts scattered everywhere, trying to don combat armor and check weapons, preparing for war.

Naero stopped Allon Nelson. "Where are the High Masters? Are they all right?"

He looked frightened. "Something big's happening, N. They say something's going down on Nashara. The artifact statue's out of control—even worse than before. All personnel planet wide have been ordered to either dig in or evacuate. Intel and the High Masters are preparing to nuke the area all around the artifact statue from orbit."

"What? They'll contaminate half the planet! Take me to them. Now."

They found the High Masters at the starport, preparing to retreat from the planet. They looked startled and surprised to see her back among them.

"Maeris," High Master Tree snapped at her. "We thought you were safe back up on your ship!"

"I was. I barely got away from the artifact statue. I thought I should report back here and see if I could help. And I still haven't located Jan and Aunt Sleak. I'm not leaving until I know they're safe."

High Master Vane grew livid and started shouting. "Shut those vid feeds down, you fools. Leave the equipment behind. Everyone board the first available ships and let's go. Get back up to your flagship, Maeris. Your brother and your aunt are being evacuated on one of the other ships."

"Which ship are they on? I'll go up in that one. Why aren't their com units working? I want to talk to them."

"How the hell should I know which ship? Most coms are down. Obey your orders and get out of here. It was you who was endangering everyone. That thing was after you. Now get the hell off this planet. That is a direct order."

Something wasn't right. The other two High Masters weren't meeting her eyes.

"What's wrong?" she said. "What aren't you telling me?"

Naero. Vid feeds from the spyfixers. You need to see this.

Naero called up a holoscreen of her own, and gasped.

There was the artifact statue—with Jan and pregnant Aunt Sleak unconscious, floating, and suspended in two separate, glowing violet spheres of Cosmic energy.

They were helpless and being drawn toward it.

Naero's mouth fell open and she covered it with both hands.

The artifact seemed to be analyzing them, in some apparent attempt to choose between the two.

Her blood turned glacier cold as she recalled the artifact statue's cryptic words to her in Kexxian.

The others are inferior selections. They will not survive.

"No!" Naero screamed.

The three High Masters surrounded her.

She already felt them suppressing her abilities, draining her energies.

"You can't help them now, Naero—no one can," Master Jo said. "You'll only make things worse. Trust us."

"No! You knew it had taken them. You lied to me. Let me go to them. I won't leave them there to die. They're my family—all that I have left!"

Naero struggled to break free. They increased their efforts to contain and neutralize her. "We know this is difficult for you, Naero." Master Tree said. "You must obey us and do what we say!"

"Not this time."

Tree persisted. "Hold her, brothers. Our Enforcer will arrive shortly. He will help us."

"We might not have that long," Master Jo said. "I'm sensing an immense, interdimensional distortion. It can only be the Kahn-Dar. They are coming for us all."

All three of the High Masters continued to struggle with Naero.

"No good!" Master Vane cried. "She's only getting stronger."

"Naero, listen to us," Master Jo said, trying to reason with her. "You will all be destroyed. It doesn't want them. It wants you. You cannot give it what it wants."

Master Tree shouted. "Drain all her energies. Do it. Now! Maeris, it's manipulating you. You cannot go to it. That is exactly what it wants. If it absorbs you and all of your abilities, it will have a host that it can go

178

anywhere and do anything with. There will be no going back! Such power cannot be contained. It will destroy you and transform you into the very monster of destruction that you fear!"

"Then I will die trying to save them!" Naero screamed.

She withdrew into herself for a moment.

Startapping, Om. Break us free. Don't kill them, but we are getting out of here to save Jan and Aunt Sleak. Make it so.

Defensive protocols locked and set. Responses defined.

Now, Om!

"Her power's spiking rapidly!" Master Jo said.

"She's startapping and breaking free of us!" Master Tree said.

"Destroy her. Destroy her now while we still can!" Vane roared.

Naero saw Vane's main eye pulsing bright red.

Naero clenched her fists, opened her third eye wide, and screamed.

Waves of raw Cosmic force rapidly expanded out from her in all directions, cratering the buckling ground as she floated in mid-air.

Ribbons of dark and light energy lashed out and flung the High Masters away from her as if they were toys. The pulses of force rocked the starships sitting nearby and shoved them aside, crumpling and damaging their hulls.

Naero focused on the pillar of Cosmic flame flaring in her consciousness nearby. Power that would terrify anyone.

She transported directly into the heart of the artifact statue's black glass crater.

24

Naero squared off with the artifact statue.

The thing became more and more like herself all the while. It stared back at her through her own eyes, her own face, which looked to be living flesh and blood.

It even formed a third eye similar to her own, which pulsed with violet energy like the other two.

How and why was it mimicking her?

She startapped again, filling herself with as much power as she could control, and not pass out or give in to her Dark Beast.

Jan and Aunt Sleak still floated in their violet energy spheres, contained and helpless.

Somehow, Naero sensed that they were still alive, at least for the time being.

Violent winds of force swept in all around them, whipping dust, debris, and ichor that rippled off the artifact statue into a maelstrom of Cosmic energy that quickly enveloped them.

Naero struggled against it to try to reach Aunt Sleak, who was the closest to her.

Then suddenly, all within a certain radius around the artifact statue went calm, as if within a typhoon's eye.

The artifact statue reached out a hand to her and spoke plainly. "Merge with me. Do so quickly, before all is lost."

"What are you?" Naero demanded.

"Merge with me…and all shall be revealed."

Naero shook her head, remembering the warning of the High Masters not to touch it.

The thing focused on Jan and began drawing him to it.

"No!" Naero shouted, wrestling with it in her mind, putting forth all her power. "Not Jan. I won't let you have him!"

The thing released Jan and began drawing Aunt Sleak in.

"No! You can't have either of them. I will fight you with every breath I have. With all that I am!" Naero thought of her unborn nieces.

Om attempted to warn her. *Naero, you cannot fight this entity–whatever it is–its powers are beyond imagination. Incomprehensible!*

"Silence, automaton; you are not real, yet," the thing said, and effortlessly turned Om off in Naero's mind like flipping a switch. The thing glared at her, engulfed in Cosmic power, finally pointing at her brother and aunt. "These others are genetically similar, but they will not suffice. They are are inferior. They are not-"

"Us," Naero said, beginning to perceive the real truth. "They are not us. That's it, isn't it? You are me, or like me, or a version of me…somehow. How is any of this possible? How can any of this be real? What are you?"

Shaking with terror to her core, Naero almost added, *What are we? What am I?*

The statue's hands became flesh and blood, just like her own, and reached out to her.

"Merge with me…with us…while there is still time. We have answers to things you wish to know…and others that you do not. Knowledge always comes with a price."

That frightened her even more.

"I won't make my decision until the others are away from here and safe. Those are my conditions."

It lifted one hand.

"No!" Naero shouted, interrupting its actions. "Let me do so. Then I will know they are safe."

Naero focused. Transporting others alone was much more difficult when she did not accompany them.

The thing released Jan and Aunt Sleak, letting them float gently to the ground.

First Jan.

Then her aunt and the twins. They were all safely on board her flagship, and would appear on the bridge. Naero's crew would take care of them.

Naero turned around, and the artifact statue stood directly in front of her. It made no effort to touch her, and except for the glowing violet eyes and the inconceivable sense of power, it became entirely flesh and blood. Once naked, it now donned clothing and gear exactly like her own to veil itself with.

Like looking into a mirror image.

If it was her, or some copy or version of herself, how could it be so powerful? And even more importantly, what could it in turn be so afraid of? What material was it made of that it could duplicate her so perfectly as it continued to key on her?

"The time has come," it told her. "You must choose. Many more dangers and difficulties await, but it shall go easier on us all if you choose to go on this journey willingly. And likewise, it shall go harder on all of us—if we must force you to do so against your will."

Naero nodded. "What's going to happen?" she asked.

The thing smiled at her with her own mischievous half-smile.

"None of us ever know that. Make your choice. Do you accept what is to come—willingly—or not?" The Naero-Thing held up both hands palm out, fingers slightly extended, yearning.

It was that slight yearning that tipped the scales for Naero, despite all the warnings and misgivings.

Naero raised both of her hands.

"I do so…willingly," she said.

Her fingertips touched the fingertips of the artifact statue.

There was either a flash or an explosion. Naero could not tell which.

Either she was absorbed by and became part of the artifact statue, or it became part of her.

They were no longer on the surface of Thanor-4. They floated and flipped and drifted, but Naero felt paralyzed. She could not move or even twitch or blink. She was not breathing. At first she thought that she was in the Astral Plane. Yet no, there were stars all about her, not the obscuring haze of the astral aether.

"Where are we?" Naero asked. Her lips and mouth did not move, but her voice seemed to come out all the same.

The others responded through her voice, but like a chorus of voices all her own. "The Nexus of Reality. The gateway to all shifting possibilities of all known, actual, and potential universes. The beginning and the ending of all things."

"Why did you bring us here?" Naero asked, still trying to take the enormity of it all in.

"To prove to you that it exists. To prove that we all exist. To prove that all the many threats we face are far too real."

"What...what are we?" Naero asked.

The answers came thick and fast, nearly overwhelming. Their raving threatened to drive her over the brink of madness.

"We are a Spacer!...a Destroyer...a warrior...a monster...a fool...a creator...a lover...a friend...a killer...a healer..."

The chorus voice cut them all off before her mind exploded with them all shouting at once.

"We are the sum total of our existence and awareness from across all known reality and possibility, from every universe and dimension that we can and will exist in. Some versions of our self have even sent warnings back to us, from parts of us that exist up to three millennia into the future."

"I don't understand," Naero said. "Why? Why is all of this even necessary?"

"For this reason: a great threat to all that exists and ever will exist shall arise. Both as individuals and collectively, we shall play an important role in whether this threat causes all things to cease to be, or it is defeated. Our Mystics and many other interdimensional beings have long foreseen and known of this coming threat. They are trying to prepare for it as best they may, but all involved must play their roles."

"What roles?"

"That is what all of us must choose–to aid the Great Destruction that is coming, or seek to defeat it. The G'lothc began it long ago, creating and spreading the imbalance of Cosmic forces throughout every reality, dimension, and universe that they could poison with their destruction and their very existence.

"Even after the vast majority of them were defeated and destroyed, this Cosmic poison continued to spread throughout all reality. Eventually, it will grow even stronger, and even take shape and form a will of its own, driven by the power of Darkforce energy to wipe out and annihilate everything that exists—all that is possible. We speak of the Cosmic Prophecies, and the Great Destroyer. Not even those evil beings known as the G'lothc could fully foresee what it was that they had unleashed upon all that could ever be."

Naero recalled her reoccurring nightmares and visions about a vast, overpowering Darkforce, completely out of control and unstoppable. A true oblivion that absorbed and destroyed everything and everyone that it engulfed—reducing all to literally nothing. She knew very well that if such a power were to expand out of control, all things would cease to be. The limitless possibilities of all that could ever be would be completely wiped out, and might not ever be capable of being renewed or restarted—ever again. A final reduction to *Absolute Nothing*, for all eternity.

"What must we do?" Naero asked. "How do we fight such a thing if it cannot be defeated?"

"For good or ill," their chorus voice sounded, "we are part of this thing, and it is part of us. In that truth, there are many strengths and weaknesses. Yet even so, the way must be found. Progress has been made. Two of the three Guardians have been selected and chosen. Two of the three great obelisks have been discovered and merged with their Guardians. One of the two great Cosmic Swords has been forged, as well as the Swordmaster—he who shall wield them. We will have a direct hand in the forging of the second Cosmic Blade, even it costs us our lives. Without the two Cosmic Swords, there is no chance of victory. Even with both blades, the chances of defeating the Great Destroyer across all realities is scant at best. Only the Guardians have any chance to tip the scales. Even they might not be enough."

"Wait," Naero said. "I'm trying to follow all of this. You're saying that my uncle and I were chosen to be these Guardians? Chosen by whom? By what? How? We didn't ask for this. Why us?"

Naero couldn't believe it. She was arguing with all of her possible selves throughout the universes.

"Why is anyone ever chosen for anything? The first Guardian found the first obelisk on Janosha, and there was little or no communication or understanding between them. Even worse, that was the most painful and difficult obelisk to encounter, because it was fashioned from both G'lothc and Drian tek. *It had to be.* The first Guardian did not choose to merge willingly with all of his possibilities at the beginning, and so it went worse for them all. He was nearly destroyed by the process. Yet he also started all of us on our path to find and merge with the second obelisk, waiting for us here on Thanor-4."

"What do you mean by all of that? He put all of this into motion?" Naero asked.

"Our mother was present before the first merging, and was touched by the obelisk's energies. All her children shared in the many potentials of that open path as well. A path that brought you and others of your blood later to Thanor-4, to merge with the next obelisk and be revealed as the Second Guardian."

"So...two Guardians have been chosen."

"Aye, and the third and final Guardian has yet to be revealed."

"But it will be someone from our bloodline, who has been exposed to the power of the obelisks? That has to be Jan. Jan must be the third Guardian."

"That is not certain. We have another sibling."

Oh, gosh. Insane Danner; she'd forgotten about him. What if he found or was drawn to the last remaining obelisk somehow? The very thought of him merging with that kind of power chilled Naero to her marrow.

"We are forgetting still others," their Chorus noted. "Our aunt and her offspring have also been exposed to the power of the obelisks now. The third Guardian could be any one of them. And be warned, any of the three Guardians can choose at any time to aid the Great Destroyer—or seek to thwart it."

Great, now Aunt Sleak and her daughters were all sucked into this hell as well. What if one of them developed their own, Dark Beast? Would they be able to control it?

"Where is the third obelisk? "Naero asked.

"On a lost world called Xanathar, whose location in this galaxy has not yet been revealed to us."

Great. Only one quarter of their galaxy was roughly explored. This Xanathar could be anywhere, just waiting for anyone—friend or foe—to stumble upon its immense secrets.

"Wait," Naero paused. "You said the first obelisk was extra dangerous because it was fashioned out of G'lothc and Drian tek?"

"Yes, its focus was Chaos energy and the Darkforce."

"Then, what was our obelisk made of and focused on?"

"A mixture of Drian and mostly Kexxian tek, focused on Change energy, but utilizing all of the known forms of Cosmic energy."

"And the third obelisk?"

"Said to be mostly Drian and some Kexxian tek, based mostly on Order energy."

"Okay," Naero said. "I think I got a handle on this. My uncle is the Chaos Guardian. I'm the Change Guardian. And the third Guardian–whomever that turns out to be–will be the Guardian of Order. We all represent the Three Wisdoms–and the three main Cosmic energies that comprise the Harmony. And the Lifespark of the Harmony is the polar opposite of the Darkforce. So, how does this Great Destroyer arise, and what do we all have to do to defeat him or her or it? And you also mentioned the Swordmaster, and his two Cosmic Swords? That has to be Khai, the Mystic Enforcer. But he only has one sword right now."

Their chorus spoke again. "Yes, but the second sword must be forged before the final guardian is selected, or very shortly thereafter."

"Why?"

"Because, the Great Destroyer will be revealed shortly thereafter and must be defeated."

"And how do we know all of this?"

"Because the wise and the Mystics throughout all of the realities and all of the possible universes have foreseen and foretold it."

"Oh, okay. Then I guess we'd better make sure that the second sword gets forged. I think Khai said something about it being made from a special type of metal."

"Ur-metal–leftover material from the last universe, prior to this one. Nearly impossible to find, almost impossible to fashion, the rarest, most powerful and precious material known to exist."

"Well, the Mystics must have had some to make the first sword."

"They did. They used all that they possessed. There is no more at this time."

"Then where did they find what they had?"

"They scraped together every amount that was known to exist, and they barely had enough. The last portion came from the first obelisk itself."

"The first obelisk?"

"The obelisks were fashioned by the ancients from all the Ur-metal that was known to exist at that time. The first Guardian took away a small quantity of the Ur-metal for his own use as well, which his obelisk fashioned into two glowing green battle blades."

Baeven's twin disruptor blades–they were Ur-metal? No wonder they were so powerful.

"What about the Ur-metal from the second obelisk?" Naero asked.

"Most will be needed for the forging of the second Cosmic Sword, as will that of third. But there are other sources of this rare material out there. A great quantity of the hyper-dense material must be collected. The Mystics know how much is needed."

"So, we are the second Guardian. Do we get some kind of weapon made of this Ur-metal?"

"Yes. There is enough material for a short sword, or two fighting blades, like those for the first Guardian. They will be part of us, and we can absorb them into our bodies, and summon them at will. They will adjust and key to our abilities. But we will need to get used to controlling and training with them. That will take time."

"I'm superb with knives. I'll take the two battle blades."

"We need you to picture the form of such weapons in our minds, in order for us to form them."

Naero closed her eyes and focused, concentrating hard on picturing two perfect fighting blades in her hands.

She could picture them in her mind, but they would not form in her frozen hands.

"Why won't the blades appear when I try to summon them?"

"We are between all of the realities right now. They will not appear until you return to your own dimension, and learn to summon them there."

"Oh, how do we do that?"

"Patience. Once you return to your reality, there will be an intense energy wave detonation, and then the Kahn-Dar attack will commence seconds after that."

"Oh. That all sounds...fun."

"It is not. There is greater chance that many of us will perish in that battle. That is but one of the many reasons we try to assist each other."

"I don't understand. Why do any of this? Why is it so important?"

"Because all of us share in the collective strengths and weaknesses of the others. If one of us perishes, we all grow weaker overall. If one of us survives and grows wiser and stronger, then we all grow wiser and stronger. The might of all of our existences are stronger together than each one on its own. This is a great part of the near limitless power that we can tap into inside of ourselves and call upon in times of great need. Part of the gift of being one of the Three Guardians."

"Well, then, what if I don't want to go back? What happens if I just stay here in this null region, and I don't go back to Thanor-4 at all?"

"You must return to your place of origin eventually–where we first merged–but if you truly delay too long, the Kahn-Dar will still attack. Without us there to help fight them, all life on that world will surely be completely wiped out, and the planet sucked dry of its energies. None of us want that."

"I guess we don't. Well then, now that we put it that way, I'd better get back, if we have a fight to win. So, I'll be able to fight with all the strength, speed, and power of all of my other selves? This should be easy, then. Bring on those Cosmic dragons!"

"Hold," their Chorus said. "You do not understand. We have just merged, and there will be many trials and complications when you return that you must first overcome. It will still take many long years of difficult training and sacrifice before you can call upon the full range and extent of all of your powers and abilities."

"Great. So, I'm going back to this big battle, and I won't be able to just zap everything to blazes?"

"Hardly. Our powers in your dimension will only be slightly greater now than before the merge–which were still quite formidable on their own, mind you. And you might even be able to summon your Ur-blades…if you have time to focus enough to do so in the heat of battle."

"Might? I might be able to do so? Is there anything else about this that can actually help me in this battle that I'm walking into?"

"No, not really. Oh, yes–the other complications–you will start suffering the wasting Cosmic sickness from the feedback of the merge also. The first Guardian went through much the same thing, but without this knowledge. You will need to find a cure for it on your own pretty fast, before it dissolves your physical body, or causes you to explode if you channel too much Cosmic energy all at once. That may take some time, as well. But don't take too long. The Cosmic disease brought on by the merge progresses at different rates for all of us, depending on our situation."

"Wait…I've also been given a Cosmic disease that's going to kill me, if I don't find a cure on my own? Wahoo, this deal keeps sounding better and better. None of us thought to explain this part of the deal before we made the choice?"

"We should take heart. Each one of us that accepts the merge and survives makes all of us both smarter and stronger…eventually. And you joined in the knowledge of all of this willingly, so it should go much easier for you in the long run than it did for our uncle. You know what to expect now, so you won't be trying to fight it or resist it, and you also know what you can expect and do to help yourself."

"Great. If I survive all of this crap, everything's going to be all orgasms and rainbows."

"That's the spirit…although we didn't use those words, exactly."

"I was being sarcastic. All right, get me back. I'm so pissed off now, I can't wait to fight something. Those damn dragons better watch out!"

"Huzzah, we all say to us. Fortune favors the bold!"

"Is there any way to shut ourselves up? Haisha! I can't take this much more of us. Get me the hell out of this crazy-ass place!"

25

After the flash of her return from the Cosmic Nexus, Naero stood in the black glass crater back on the planet. The artifact statue was gone, and at the exact center of the crater, the only thing that remained of it was a small, round puddle of flat, gray Ur-metal. So odd and dull that it made lead somehow look shiny.

The air seemed to pop or implode all around her. Waves of Cosmic force rippled out from her and seemed to sweep over the planet at impossible speeds, flattening trees and any structures at random, flipping entire starships nearby over on top of each other.

Next thing she knew, Naero lay flat on her back with an aching head, staring up at a swirling, cloudy Thanoran sky.

She had a sick feeling in the pit of her stomach, and sensed the first rumors of her own Cosmic sickness, the backlash of her merging with all of her possible selves, scattered throughout all the known possibilities and universes.

Yet, as imperceptible as it almost was, she did in fact feel slightly stronger, slightly smarter, slightly better and more secure than her former self had been all on her own. And she had been right. Now she knew many things, and had answers to questions that she hadn't known or understood before.

She flipped Om back on like hitting a switch. She never knew that she could do that before, or how. Now she did it without hesitation.

I wasn't inert, Naero. I experienced everything you did in the Null regions. Our communication link was simply interrupted. You couldn't hear me.

She'd definitely need to remember that trick.

Naero shot to her feet, looking around urgently. A large swath of thunderstorms was about to cut loose. "Om, contact the spyfixer network and tell our people to get ready for a fight."

Done.

She closed her eyes and pictured her new Ur-blades.

It took a few moments, but at last she felt the blades form in her hands. The metal was strange and unearthly, unnatural to the touch, flat gray. Even light did not seem to fall upon them properly. Very weird. But they were also a part of her and her abilities now.

She did not dispel them, under the circumstances, in order to test her theory, but she felt certain that she could summon them at will, just like her Chaos energy katanas.

Just thinking about her Chaos swords brought them blazing to life in her hands like torches in the gloom, forming over and channeling energy right through her Ur-blades.

Haisha! She could feel the energies pulsing through her entire body. Channeling her abilities through her new Ur-blades increased their effectiveness by several orders of magnitude from the sensation of it. And when she startapped even slightly, she could barely hold onto them.

The skies split and the first of the Kahn-Dar penetrated the dimensional veil. A blue, dragon-like creature seventy meters in length, and wreathed in azure lightning and energy came forth.

Naero guessed that she was going to need all the extra might and help that she could muster in the fight coming her way.

Then she gasped, noticing something else strange.

The Cosmic power levels of Thanor-4 were way down, almost completely reduced. Now, the planet was just like any other.

When the artifact statue vanished, apparently, so had all the planet's hyped up Cosmic energy levels.

191

In some ways that might be good. At least her enemies would not be able to feed on either one and grow stronger. The Kahn-Dar were energy-absorbers. Let them try their tricks now.

Three more dragons gated through the dimensional rent in the sky. A larger green, a shorter but thicker red, and another blue. Then four more of various colors. Then a dozen.

For their size, the Kahn-Dar zipped through the sky at incredible speeds. All of them turned and focused their blazing eyes on Naero, and dove down for the kill.

"Oh, shit!" Naero yelled. The enemy ate Cosmic energy, and she was filled with it.

Numerous Cosmic attacks rained down from the shattered sky, and fell ruinous upon the land all about her position. The black glass crater erupted and dissolved in a whirlwind of glass shards and fire, lightning, and destructive energies of every color and hue.

Naero transported up into the air, using her gravwing, and slashed with her energy swords at the throat of the first blue.

Cutting into the Kahn-Dar was like slashing through metal, or the armored hull of a starship. Even with all of her enhanced strength, it was that tough.

The creature shrieked in pain, its voice piercing and painful like a psyonic or sonic attack. The cry rattled Naero's skull. Blood trickled from her ears and nose.

At first she thought blood streamed from the creature's wounds–then some kind of aether, or energized ichor. But finally Naero realized. The Kahn-Dar were, at the very least, partial Cosmic energy beings, with not exactly physical bodies.

When injured, Kahn-Dar leaked or bled pure Cosmic power.

The monster whipped around so fast and attacked. Naero barely had time to transport out of the path of its blinding blue lightning assault shooting out from its jaws.

She transfixed the creature on scores of thick spears of Chaos energy. Then she exploded them.

The detonation triggered an even larger, secondary Cosmic explosion.

Naero instinctively curled up and shielded herself in overlapping spheres of dense, defensive force.

The blast tore through them like they were paper, and Naero plummeted out of the sky, scorched and smoking like a burning stone.

She blinked and gasped, struggling to breathe. She had even blacked out for a few seconds. Now she fell with the charred, burning pieces of the Kahn-Dar that she had just slain.

The head of the creature seemed to be at least partially alive, and still spat lightning. The dismembered thing slowly dissolved.

Other Kahn-Dar–those not stunned or flung back by the massive explosion–dove straight for them at top speed.

Naero was forced to transport again to another part of the sky.

The Kahn-Dar devoured and absorbed the pieces of the dying one, cannibalizing it right before her eyes. She recalled that it was normally very natural for these creatures to kill and devour each other.

More of the Kahn-Dar continued to pour through the rent in the dimensional veil.

How could they fight so many of the things? There were dozens of them already, and more slipping through each second.

Torrents of heavy artillery from the Marine batteries and warships ripped up into the invaders.

Cosmic fire from the latter slashed into the warships, disrupting shields and doing heavy damage. Other attacks cut through the unit shielding and blasted glowing gouts through the Marine positions.

The fight was going to quickly turn into a bloodbath.

Om, I've seen glimpses of this battle. We need to plug that hole. That's the only way we can win; otherwise, they'll pour through and overwhelm us. I'm going to close that dimensional gate.

How? From the energy levels, it will take a gigablast to disrupt it. That could possibly wipe out everything within sixty to a hundred kilometers!

Not if I pinpoint the center of the blast in the upper atmosphere, so that the blast range envelopes only the dimensional rent. Damage on the ground will be greatly reduced. We ignited such a blast once before, Om. Back on Janosha.

Yes, and we destroyed a third of a continent. And how do you know the Kahn-Dar can't just open it again, or another one in a another place?

We don't, Om. But I have a strategy in mind.

Now I'm really scared. Incoming!

Naero cloaked and transported. Several Kahn-Dar crashed into each other over her former position.

She discovered that cloaking didn't keep them from eventually locating her, but it did confuse and slow them down.

Here we go, Om. Tell our people to button up and keep their heads down. Retreat or flee, any way they can.

Naero, the High Masters are demanding that you to stand down. They want you to turn yourself over to them…immediately.

I can't, Om. Not in the middle of a battle of this magnitude. Ignore that order like we never heard it. Now let's fight!

I'm with you, Naero. I'll help you direct the blast away from the ground, but our forces are still going to take a pounding.

Can't be helped at this point. Roughed up is better than dead.

She selected the safest vantage point she could find. Air-zero, directly behind the dimensional rent, with dragons still pouring through it on the other side.

Naero startapped until she transformed, then she bloated herself until she nearly blacked out, and her Dark Beast threatened to break free.

Naero formed a cloud of hundreds of floating Cosmic energy bubbles around the rent, each the size of a bowling ball.

Then she transfixed the three Kahn-Dar slipping through, exploding them at the same time she set off the bubble cloud.

Om transported them thirty kilometers away.

Still not far enough.

The blast wave hit them seconds later, and drilled them into some forested hills. Naero barely buttoned up.

She quickly startapped, ignoring their pain, and transported them back to the High Masters.

Up in the sky, the dimensional rent was gone—completely disrupted. The remaining Kahn-Dar were still alive, but stunned and floating in the sky. Dead Kahn-Dar couldn't remain airborne and would dissolve, unable to sustain their Cosmic energy forms. Or their fellow dragons would feast upon their energies.

On the ground, things weren't much better for the defenders.

Order a full retreat, Om. On my direct authority. Abandon equipment and weapons. The enemy has no use for them. Get everyone out, on anything that can fly.

On it. It won't take much. Most of our forces have already withdrawn, and are already reeling in full retreat.

Naero found the High Masters, battered and bloody, being healed and tended to by their Prime adepts.

"You are under arrest," High Master Tree said.

Naero nodded. "I am. When all are safe after this battle, I will confine myself to my quarters on my flagship and await your investigation and judgment. But not until then."

"Destroy her!" Vane shouted from where he lay on a medbed, his face and head bandaged and bloody. "She's even more of a threat to us all now—more than ever before!"

Naero shouted to the other adepts. "Get everyone out. Transport the High Masters to the safety of their ships in orbit. The invaders can't fight us if there's no one on the planet to fight."

"Naero," Master Jo muttered, half his body still badly scorched. "What are you doing?"

"The artifact is gone. So are the planetary energy levels. If the Mystics leave this world, there is no reason for the remaining Kahn-Dar to be here. Nothing left for them to fight, no Cosmic energy for them to devour or absorb. They came here expecting an easy feast. I'm guessing they were lied to."

Master Jo grinned. "Brilliant. I agree. Get the others out. Get everyone out. I support your denial strategy, but you are still in serious trouble."

"When am I not? Everyone hear that?" Naero shouted. "Master Jo agrees with me. Let's move."

"What do we hear from the east coast and Thanarra?"

The Mystic Enforcer is helping the east coast base hold their own. He has slain thirty to forty of the Kahn-Dar—

Naero spluttered, choking on her own breath in startled awe. He's killed thirty or forty of those things, Om? By himself?

It appears so. He closed off the dimensional gate as well…in a similar fashion to our own. He is currently leading our forces in a fighting retreat out of the atmosphere.

Admiral Klyne suddenly cut in over the spyfixer link. "All units, all units, continue retreat from the planet surface behind the defensive grids set up around the planet. If the invaders attack us up in the black, we stand more than ready for them this time."

Dozens of Spacer and Alliance naval fleets surrounded the planet in interlocking firing profiles from many heavy warships.

Naero smiled and transported up to her own private quarters. She'd check on Jan and Aunt Sleak in a minute. The cavalry arrived quickly. Even the Kahn-Dar would be fools to attack straight into the teeth of such massed firepower.

You were correct, Naero. With nothing left to fight or absorb, the Kahn-Dar are gating out, leaving this world and dimension completely. They can sense the forces arrayed against them out in space. Their surprise attack has collapsed, and failed completely.

We took away all of their objectives. What about the locals, Om? Are the natives all right?

Damage is minimal in their isolated area, although they probably witnessed a very frightening light show in the sky, and the ground shaking at times. Without any tek or Cosmic energy to speak of, the Kahn-Dar ignored them completely–as if they were insects.

Great. We couldn't hope for much better than that. Now, we wait, Om.

For what?

To face the music, for what we've done.

26

Jan and Aunt Sleak were still weak from their ordeal, but recovering. She briefly told them what she could about what had happened between her and the artifact statue–and the serious trouble she was in with the High Masters for disobeying them.

Within the hour, Aunt Sleak delivered her twins; as expected, two healthy girls with red hair and gray eyes: Anyazhel Shiina Maeris and Nuviarra Lythe Maeris.

Her tough-as-nails aunt was up and around shortly after giving birth, laughing and smiling. Naero got to hold both babies and smile at the pretty little things–hands and feet so delightfully tiny. She gave each of them a token of a small, ceremonial Maeris fighting knife.

She could tell them apart by their ears. Anya's were slightly more pointed than Nuvi's.

Naero warned Jan and Aunt Sleak about the last alien obelisk still out there on a lost, ancient world of the Kexx called Xanathar. Most likely, either one of them or the twins would turn out to be the Order Guardian, for all that meant to the four of them today.

She did not bring up Danner, for now.

Naero waited nervously on edge, for half that same day, for word from the High Masters to present herself to them for their evaluation and judgment.

The Changs contacted her instead.

"We wanted to warn you," Chang Fu-han said. "The High Masters are discussing your situation at this very moment."

Naero was startled. "Why wasn't I informed? Why was I not summoned?"

"The three of them are still recovering from their injuries," Chang Lijuan added. "They and their Prime adepts are discussing the matter on the Astral Plane, while their bodies continue to heal on their medbeds."

"Thank you, both of you. I appreciate you guys telling me this."

Fu-han added. "Good luck, Naero. Many of the other adepts were also gravely injured during the battle with the invaders, but most still remain on your side. They want things to work out for the best for you."

"Yes, good luck, Naero."

"You two will continue to take care of the Thanorans, right?"

Both of the bowed their heads, looking very sad.

"No," Fu-han sobbed. "With Thanor-4's heightened energy levels gone, the Mystics are abandoning the planet entirely. The natives will be left entirely to their own fates. After all that has happened, perhaps that is for the best."

"You two don't really believe that, do you?"

Lijuan had tears in her eyes. "We must. We have no choice. The decision has been made, and remains final. We can do nothing."

Naero signed off and informed Jan, Aunt Sleak, Tarim, Zhen, Shalaen, and the rest of her crew what was going on.

Tarim would stand guard, while Zhen and Shalaen monitored her body on a medbed in the infirmary. She would take a short nap, drift off into the Astral Plane and find the High Masters, in an attempt to defend herself and her actions.

Naero hadn't done it much, but going into a trance to enter the Astral Plane shouldn't be all that difficult from what she recalled. Master Vane had specifically shown her how once. And she had gone there lots of times in her sleep, in her mind, to speak with Khai, using their astral crystals. But that was on their own little private wavelength.

Back then, her friend Khai had also vanished without a trace, while she was still training on Janosha. Now he turned up again as the Mystic Enforcer, and wielded one of the Cosmic blades. And it sounded like he was quite the badass.

Naero herself had never been completely trained in astral travel, and didn't know much about exploring or moving around. Master Vane had taken her there once, just to teach her the basics and give her his marker, and many other times later to spar with her in areas he isolated for them. She never went there on her own.

If all else failed, she could probably focus on Vane's marker to locate him.

Zhen and Shalaen smiled and tried to be reassuring, standing by her side while she relaxed and went into the astral trance.

Naero focused her mind and abilities, controlling her breathing. She struggled to recall the little she had learned.

Within several minutes of focused meditation, she opened her eyes and found herself floating in the Astral Miasma, the nebulae of energy. Naero hugged her knees to her chest.

Om spoke to her, even more easily here than in her own mind before.

I have accessed some of the Kexxian Matrix's data files on the Astral Plane. Like everything else, they explored it quite extensively.

Om, I'm naked here. I'm not complaining, But how do I put astral clothing on again?

You control everything here by imagination and force of will, Naero. Concentrate on your favorite clothing and gear, and they should appear.

That was easy enough.

She looked down and saw her favorite Nytex flight togs and gear, programmed just the way she liked them.

Naero blinked, spinning and twirling in one spot in the aether, turning upside down. But she was still stuck in one spot.

Why can't I move more than a meter at a time in front of us?

You're not used to this reality. So it's not clear to you.

The aether around her looked opaque. Not mist. Not smoke or vapor. And it glowed slightly with its own bluish-gray light.

In the twilight, she glowed softly blue-violet-white with her own light from within.

"I once heard rumors that the Mystics could travel and send messages this way, but I thought it was all just a myth."

Since the other planes are entire universes within themselves, it is said they are all nearly infinite. Thus it is difficult to pinpoint any kind of location or person unless you already know them.

Naero instinctively tried to stand up, but there was nothing to stand on.

Then she recalled Master Vane's marker, and bingo! There it was; it appeared right before her.

Where she found him, she would find the other High Masters.

At least she deserved a chance to be heard by them all. To try to explain herself and her actions.

Naero could not simply stand by and let them decide her fate without her being present.

She focused on the crimson and black star more and swept forward, seemingly at great speed.

She came to an abrupt halt, like a starship coming out of jump at its destination.

The opacity around them partially melted back. They proceeded forward, opening her visual field far wider. She made out the area around them as the miasma peeled back.

Slightly below them, she saw spheres within glowing spheres, all spinning within greater spheres.

Her own sphere, glowing white-blue, suddenly surrounded her like a glittering soap bubble.

Yet it did not pop when she poked at it.

One sphere in particular, the largest, glowed and pulsed blood red, containing a withered old man with a long beard, pacing and fidgeting impatiently.

Burning eyes vanished and reappeared at random all over his bald head. The red sphere absorbed Master Vane's marker.

Was this Vane's true form? What he really looked like?

His scarlet sphere was also flanked by two smaller spheres with figures inside them.

Om made a calculated guess.

His current guardian adepts, no doubt. The ones you rescued from the enemy Darkforce generators.

I think so, Om.

So, this was what Zhii and Fel looked like on the Astral Plane.

She suddenly wondered what she looked like.

At most times, every High Master had at least two champion adepts protecting him or her, each of them very close to mastery themselves. Like Hashiko had been.

Naero studied Vane's new guardians for the very first time on the Astral Plane, and tried to see into their strange spheres.

Their appearance here was different, but some things about them remained familiar.

One of Vane's Prime adepts, the swirling, smoky male, appeared to be so deep dark black, he could be a singularity. This adept's sphere was flat black on the surface and barely transparent. She could barely make Zhii out inside of it.

If Naero had been able to breathe, she would have gasped.

Instead she simply raised her hand to her mouth.

She recalled now that she had seen many of these adepts long before–in her dreams, nightmares, and crazed visions. That was how they appeared to her. Perhaps she had even been on the Astral Plane somehow when she saw them in these forms.

Fel, Vane's other Prime adept, was obviously the blazing white, feathery female, the exact opposite of the other. So brilliant and blindingly radiant, she could be a pulsar. Her orb was like a high intensity bulb, blinding and almost completely crystal clear–with her lighting it from within. No veil here.

It occurred to Naero that during her initial testing, Klyne had had male and female assistants as well. She still couldn't guess what the significance of that pattern was all about.

Why, then, weren't any of the High Masters female?

Everyone seemed to ignore her where she floated.

The next larger sphere, farther away, glowed silver-blue.

If she focused intently on it, she discovered she could zoom in with her third eye–her mind's eye.

Within a silver man sat serenely, neither young nor old. Master Tree, in his purest form of Order.

Two smaller guardian spheres flanked him.

Master Tree's wispy female adept, Von, glowed with intense blue energy in a deep blue sphere.

The male likewise glowed with vibrant green force within a green sphere, a shining sword sheathed down his broad athletic back. He seemed very familiar somehow.

She did a double-take. Long blond hair. Green skin. Big glowing sword.

Yep. In the flesh. Or…his astral form at least.

It was Khai! She was sure of it. Here he was at last, alive and well.

Khai had actually succeeded in his great task of forging the first Cosmic Sword sword in the heart of a gigantic pulsar. That was it, on his back.

Naero gasped again. Now that she knew what he sort of looked like, Khai had also been the dreamy green hunk from many of her past, pent-up nightmares. The one who kept sticking his sword through her head.

What did it all mean? She wasn't nuts enough yet?

Now she knew for certain she needed serious help.

And to do some actual dating at some point, once and for all.

If the Mystics continued to let her live.

Khai must have sensed her inner turmoil, or thoughts, or maybe just her concentration on him.

Mr. Green god even glanced her way for a second, looking just as confused and puzzled by her sudden appearance.

Neither of them had ever met the other in person.

Naero covered her face with one hand and looked aside, withdrawing her sphere suddenly further away.

How fricking embarrassing.

She crept forward again…slowly.

The third and final sphere glowed golden, and contained an equally golden child within, energetic and bristling with lightning. He bounced back and forth inside like a gigantic electron.

Master Jo, of course.

Two flanking spheres.

One of his adepts had no clear form, eyes gleaming within a shifting, flickering miasma like the Astral Plane itself–Den. His female counterpart shifted shape from one fantastic creature to another–Tess.

When Naero made out their voices, she could sense that an intense debate had been going on. One that still continued.

"We cannot be certain in this matter," the golden child insisted. "We do not dare act in any rash way."

"Agreed, High Master Jo," the serene silver man added. "She might yet be another Trickster, from what I can tell."

"Yes. Quite possible, High Master Tree."

The old man in the bloodred sphere blustered impatiently. "Fools! Always conspiring against me. Taking positions opposite of mine for no reason but to anger me. I've been telling you all along, this child is clearly the Great Destroyer–long foretold. Our duty is clear. She is a threat to all existence. To multiple dimensions. She must be eliminated, at once, before she can grow even more powerful."

"High Master Vane," Tree said. "None of us can be sure of that fact. Including you."

"I am."

"You are always certain when it comes to destroying someone," Jo added. "Your pure Chaos answer to everything. Destruction or Creation."

"It works."

"No. It doesn't. It only delays and worsens the inevitable," Tree said. "The Universe shall have its way. We all know this. You were mistaken with the last savant when he appeared, and now he remains at large–a renegade beyond even our control."

Baeven? Were they referring to her uncle?

Vane rolled his eyes. "Idiots! The renegade is the Trickster, I say. This child must in fact be the Great Destroyer. Just look at the powers roiling within her. They will surely corrupt and overwhelm her entirely and drive her mad in the end. She will go berserk on a scale that makes her recent outbursts feeble and puny by comparison. She must perish now, while we have a chance to put an end to her. While the only crime she has committed is destroying a single planet!"

"We've repeatedly studied the mysterious disappearance of Janosha," Master Jo said, "and we still cannot be certain that she had anything to do with it."

"Really? Who else could it be then? Planets like Janosha aren't in the habit of just obliterating themselves suddenly for no reason at all!"

I cannot allow this.

Quiet, Om. Don't do anything. I'm trying to listen.

Naero...they're discussing our destruction. The Chaos Master means to destroy us.

Master Jo continued to protest. "You can't just kill off every entity that manifests Cosmic Abilities such as these. Our universe is peppered with them. We must continue to locate and guide them–not find excuses to execute them. Like the Others have told us. Tricksters often appear to oppose Great Destroyers. Without the former, final victory is never possible. "

"High Masters," Tree said. "This young woman also possesses the Kexxian Data Matrix. We cannot destroy her without destroying it. Intel and the Spacer Council value our wisdom, but even they would not agree to such action."

"Regrettable," Vane said. "Yet I cannot take the risk. I have decided this matter on my own."

"You have no such authority on your own," Tree insisted.

"I cannot stand by and allow our galaxy–perhaps our entire universe–to be destroyed just to satisfy your foolish philosophical and theoretical whims."

Master Vane turned to his adepts. "My finest students, obey me. Delay these fools. Keep them occupied whilst I act for the good of all existence."

203

More rapid than thought, the male ensnared the blue sphere and its satellites in coils and tendrils of darkness. The female enveloped the golden sphere and its companions in waves of of pure light.

Naero tried to pull away, but in her panic she did not know where to go.

High Master Vane sped straight at her with impossible speed.

I must act, Naero.

No, Om. Please, this is already bad enough. Don't do anything.

I cannot comply. I must defend us!

Naero went down on her hands and knees before Master Vane. She called out, her voice projecting. "Please, do not attack me. I only wish to be trained to control my abilities. I have struggled hard to do so."

Vane bore down on her, arcs of pure scarlet energy bristling around him.

"Far too late for that, monster. You must perish for the good of all. I told you this hour would come."

Instinctively, Naero drew back again, trying to evade his attack. She rose up within her receding sphere.

Vane closed in once more, gathering his powers.

"Don't do this," Naero begged. "Please. Help me. I know I can't fully control all of my abilities yet. I'm trying as hard as I can."

"Yes, and look at the results? Countless lives crushed and eradicated. Janosha vaporized–an entire planet. You must never be allowed to reach your full potential. Now hold still and embrace your fate."

Naero put her hands out before her, holding her palms out defensively–pleading.

"No. Don't. I can't be responsible for what–"

"I know. You can't help yourself. You are an abomination!"

Vane smashed into her, piercing all of her defenses as if they were shattering glass. Here in the Astral Plane, he had the mastery.

In the distance, she sensed that Master Jo and Master Tree had finally broken free.

Too late.

Master Vane attacked, trying to overwhelm her with raw power.

He pummeled her with impossible blows.

In the end, he beat her up badly, but only succeeded in knocking her around once more.

Om roared in their mind.

Kexxian defense protocols unlocked and on line.

Energized glowing armor of some advanced origin formed around her like a hi-tek battle suit.

Naero saw out of her third eye as it awoke and burst into radiance like a blue-violet-white star.

Master Vane came at her once more, all of his powers focused through his primary scarlet, burning eye centered in his forehead.

All of his other flaming eyes closed as he concentrated, his skull wreathed in weird Cosmic flames like a mane of Cosmic fire.

"See how powerful you have already become? No adept could have withstood those lethal attacks. We must finish this now, before the others can interfere."

"Please, Master Vane. Please, don't do this."

"You will fall before the greatest of all Cosmic attack techniques. I am one of the few who have ever learned to master it–the Eye of Annihilation!"

The same Chaos technique that had destroyed Hashiko. Even she couldn't control it properly.

A massive, bloodred beam of destroying Cosmic force shot straight at her.

It all happened so fast. Naero heard Om screaming.

Reflection defense. Analyze incoming Cosmic assault. Duplicate and reflect attack tenfold!

Just before the incoming blast vaporized her, a blue-violet beam shot out of her own third eye to war against Master Vane's powers.

The Cosmic flows flared intensely.

Naero screamed as if her body and soul were being sucked through the eye of a black hole's needle.

The wide, violet-blue beam quickly drove back the red beam to its source.

At the last instant, High Master Vane cried out in terror.

"Impossible! There can be no such–"

The destroying energies ignited on contact.

A massive detonation on the Astral Plane blinded the area within a few light years.

High Masters Jo and Tree barely managed to withdraw and shield the others. All of their spheres shattered.

Pure Cosmic energy punched into High Master Vane right before Naero's eyes.

Driving him back like a white hot comet.

He struggled against it with all his might, obliterated to glowing ash and dust, screaming in the wake of his own annihilation.

High Master Vane's dying force of will echoed off into the universe.

Naero would have caught her breath if she had any.

The outcome left her completely stunned for a shuddering instant.

Om…what did we just do?

We had no choice. My sole purpose is to defend our current form.

Naero stared down at her hands in terror. Tendrils of Cosmic energy rippled and still curled off of her body and her sphere like smoke.

Om…Haisha!

We just killed a High Master of the Spacer Mystics!

27

Naero did not have much time before the Mystics and Spacer Intel came to apprehend her.

The first person she called was Baeven. No answer.

She left a desperate, secret distress call for him.

Then another for Captain Tyber and *The Dark Star*.

Next Jan, Aunt Sleak, and her crew. She made it quick. As of this moment, she was a criminal and an outlaw–a wanted murderer. She didn't exactly see a way around or out of that fact, but she needed to get some time to sort it all out, and consider just what were her options.

Her head was already spinning and aching.

Her life–the life she knew and loved–was over. Naero was still in shock and had not yet begun to mourn that loss.

She could speak with her family, friends, and crew more later, through covert means. But right now, she needed to escape and find a place to hide and regroup.

The galaxy was a very big place.

Baeven had eluded capture and execution for years.

That thought suddenly staggered Naero in her tracks. She nearly went into convulsions.

Was she only repeating the mistakes of the past?

Would she be made an outcast, losing her name and identity, completely dishonored–just like him? Would they order her terminated on sight?

She knew her own people wanted to help her. She couldn't allow that. She couldn't implicate them in her crimes.

Naero gathered some gear she needed, launched in her private, super-modified, Ghost Dragon F59L…and vanished.

Her last order to her fleet spread them out, in a wide-dispersed search pattern as if they were looking for her.

If the authorities wanted to take the time to board and search each of her ships–that was going to take them a while.

Meanwhile, Naero made five rapid jumps over the next multiple hours. She could not sleep, and spent a good deal of her time covering her tracks and passively monitoring the spyfixer network through Om, so as to be untraceable. When she wasn't glued to that, she was checking Baeven's secret channels.

Still nothing.

When it became clear that the search for her expanded outward in all directions–finally–she circled back and returned to Thanor-4 early the next day.

True to their word, the Mystics and Intel had completely abandoned the undeveloped world, now that it was no longer of any further use to them. All of the fleets and starships were completely gone, as if they had never been there at all.

She had several hours before her rendezvous with *The Dark Star*, and hopefully *The Star Fox* as well. Naero programmed her nanosuit to mimic her native Thanoran clothing, and transported down to the surface to have a final word with the leaders of the Thanes.

Overall, the natives were clearly terrified by the little they had seen of the Kahn-Dar attack. Naero went to Thanarra. King Arrok and Queen Liita were ecstatic to receive her, and brought her before them.

They sprang from their thrones and embraced her in the throne room, before the entire court.

"Holy sister," Queen Liita said, with tears in her eyes. "We feared that you and so many of the other holy ones had abandoned us in our hour of need. What has happened? Tell us this is not so?"

Even the Changs had not been allowed to explain anything.

Naero already knew what she was going to tell them. She had it all prepared.

She might not ever make it back to their world, nor might any of the other adepts. She knew the Changs would, if they were ever given the freedom to do so.

"I'M SORRY," she announced, using *the voice* so that all could hear her. Her words echoed throughout the chamber.

"THE GODS HAVE SUMMONED MANY OF THE HOLY ONES TO JOIN THEM IN THE HIGH HEAVENS. WE HAVE NO CHOICE. WE MUST OBEY. THOSE WHO HAVE BEEN CHOSEN ARE ALREADY GONE."

"But why?" the king asked. "And what were these fearful portents in the sky? And why did all of creation rumble beneath our feet? The people are terrified, and rightly so."

"YOUR MAJESTIES, THERE IS LITTLE TIME, AND I MUST ALSO LEAVE SOON. PLEASE, LET ME EXPLAIN AS BEST I CAN."

"Leave?" Queen Liita said, looking stricken. "You've only just come back to us, and you already speak of leaving?"

"I'M SORRY, BUT I MUST. THERE IS NO OTHER WAY. THE TRUTH IS ALWAYS HARD TO HEAR. THE AGE OF LEGENDS HAS RETURNED. NOW WE ALL HAVE OUR BATTLES TO FIGHT. JUST AS YOUR WORLD PREPARES FOR WAR, SO DO THE HIGH HEAVENS. DANGEROUS DEMONS AND MONSTERS FROM THE BEYOND, FROM THE DARK ABYSS AND THE VOID THEMSELVES—THREATEN TO BREAK FREE AND DESTROY ALL OF CREATION. THEIR NUMBERS ARE LIKE THE STARS IN THE SKY—SO GREAT, IN FACT, THAT EVEN THE GODS CANNOT FIGHT THEM ALONE.

"HEAR ME. WE HAVE ALL BEEN CALLED TO BATTLE. WE HAVE BEEN CHOSEN TO FIGHT BESIDE THE GODS, TO DO OUR UTMOST TO DRIVE OUR TERRIBLE FOES BACK INTO THE ABYSS. THE MESSENGERS OF THE GODS, THE HOLY ONES WHOM YOU KNOW AS GENTLE MORTALS AND HEALERS AMONG YOU, ARE IN FACT WARRIORS AND SOLDIERS OF GREAT RENOWN IN THE REALMS OF THE SPIRITS, ON THE OTHER SIDE OF THE VEIL.

"THERE THEY TAKE UP THEIR SECRET NAMES AND TITLES, AND DRAW THEIR SHINING WEAPONS OF LIGHT TO DEFEAT THE ALL-CONSUMING DARKNESS. WITHOUT SUCH EFFORTS, THE ENEMIES OF LIGHT WOULD QUICKLY REDUCE MORTAL WORLDS SUCH AS YOURS TO NOTHING BUT LIFELESS ROCK. THIS BATTLE MUST BE FOUGHT IN THE SPIRIT REALMS. MORTAL WORLDS WOULD HAVE NO DEFENSE AGAINST SUCH TERRIBLE FOES. THAT IS WHY WE MUST GO WHEN WE

ARE SUMMONED, AND IT MAY BE THAT WE SHALL NEVER RETURN TO THIS
WORLD, EVER AGAIN."

The king drew his sword and saluted her.

"Then go, good friend and sister. Fight for the light in the Spirit
Realms, and we shall do the same in the mortal climes. As you have said,
we all have our battles to wage. And ours will most assuredly be here. This
much we do understand."

Naero returned his salute and ceased using *the voice*. "You have all
grown so much. Yet my heart foretells that you will need to grow even
further, and become even wiser. Do not let your wars change or destroy
what is best in you–honor, freedom, justice. These and your children are
those things that are truly worth fighting, and if need be, dying for. Yet it is
even harder to find a way to live for them, and bring them into a better age
for all."

"We shall fight to the last sword, the last breath," the queen said. "Yet
before we part, is there nothing you can do to aid us?"

"I can only give you this." Naero brought out a scroll she had the
fixers prepare. She handed it to the king and queen. She knew they could
read and make use of it.

Their Majesties opened it up and began to peruse it. Their eyes went
wide.

"How…how could you gather such information?"

Naero smiled and shook her head. "That is unimportant. Make good
use of it while you can. Emperor Vauk's forces are detailed there, but they
are already moving, and will not remain in their current locations for long."

"What is the purpose of this great and terrible war he plans against us
all?" Queen Liita asked.

"He's going to murder all of your children," Naero said. "Wipe out an
entire generation, so that none of your lands or people shall ever recover.
The Vaedo will dominate and enslave all who remain thereafter. That is
why you must stop him."

"How do we fight him and protect our children at the same time?" the
king asked. "Even with the other two city states, the Vaedo armies still
outnumber our forces almost two to one. We know what he will do–engage
and bottle up our forces in one place–and then attack our homes."

"Don't let him trap you. Fight him only where he is weak, not where
his is strong, until you have worn him down. Always choose the time and
place of your battles. Stay mobile. Move fast. Bleed him as he chases you.
And one other thing."

"What is that?" the queen asked.

"Find the safest place for your children that you can make or devise, and defend it to the last. You know he will seek to take it, at all costs."

Naero suggested the mountain defenses of the Maedo, but left such decisions up to them. The Thanorans were all still working out their crucial alliances.

"I'm sorry," Naero told them "I must leave you now. If it is at all possible for me to return to you all at some point in the future, I will do so. But look to yourselves, for I cannot promise it."

Their Majesties nodded.

"We understand," the king said.

Queen Liita hugged and kissed her. "May the gods watch over us all."

"Good sister," King Arrok asked. "Will you but grant us one boon. If we should fall, what is thy secret name in the Spirit Realms? If all are so changed upon the other side of the veil as you say–how should we know you, if we should pass on and look for you there?"

Prince Shondar and Princess Iiden looked at her eagerly.

Naero walked out onto the starlit balcony of the palace keep, and reached her hands to the stars.

She transformed before their eyes and took on her accustomed role of the warrior woman dressed and masked all in black, her twin blazing scarlet katanas crackling with force and lightning in her hands, her dark psyonic wings unfurling in the mountain winds, lifting her in the air above them. She used *the voice* once more.

"In the Spirit Realms, I am known as Shetanna, the Dark Angel of Death, and I have never known defeat in combat. Fight on for your world and your children, and fare you well. My heart is with you."

She slowly cloaked, and faded away into the night upon the shadowy whispers of the wind. Iiden clung to her older brother and wept.

Naero left them staring in awe and transported back to her small, hidden ship in the high mountains. She still had hours before *The Dark Star* would arrive.

Naero…I wouldn't normally bother you with something like this, but I'm detecting a rather strange anomaly.

What do you mean? What kind of an anomaly, Om?

Cosmic in nature, but very faint. I was barely able to detect it. I could only do so through our combined sensory abilities. It is that weak.

Let's check it out.

They tracked the anomaly to the east cost of Nashara. Naero was amazed at the destruction, even in the wake of the Mystic's departure. She had heard that the Kahn-Dar gated in there as well, and many of them had fallen. Their bodies were Cosmic in nature and dissolved upon death, leaving nothing behind.

What was this thing, then? Om was right, it was Cosmic energy in nature, but its signature was very faint. She kept losing it, and found it difficult to pinpoint.

Finally she spotted something.

Good thing the night was so dark.

It zipped around like a flickering lightning bug. Even using her gravwing, they couldn't catch up to it.

Finally, Naero transported, and captured it in her cupped hands.

She tried to peer in at it.

A blinding flash and a puff of smoke. The pop of the small explosion surprised and startled her more than it did any injury.

Whatever the hell it was, the chase was now on.

Even spot transporting, Naero couldn't capture it again.

Naero remembered something she learned from sparring with Master Vane, of all people.

She encircled the thing in a net of Chaos energy and slowly closed the encapsulating sphere all around it. Then she made the sphere transparent.

The creature inside made her gasp and blink.

A tiny, blue-violet Kahn-Dar, the size of a small seahorse, like a tiny, flickering wyrm. But now she had it fairly trapped.

Then she felt it. The creature was trying to mindlink with her.

What do you think, Om? Should we try to communicate with it? It seems pretty harmless in this state.

Yes, it is near death, in fact. The Kahn-Dar can change their size at will. And when they perish, they can go in a flash, fade away, or shrink smaller and smaller as they die.

It's dying? Should we try to help it?

It is an enemy. It came here with the rest to destroy us all. Remember that.

All right, I will. But I hate to watch anything die needlessly.

Even Ejjai?

Point taken.

Naero cautiously opened her end of the mindlink. I am Naero Amashin Maeris, of Spacer Clan Maeris. Who are you?

The tiny creature bobbed in front of her face.

Womi, of the Kahn-Dar. Have you come to kill me?

I will if you force me to, but I don't have any great desire to do so. I do not kill without reason. Don't give me a reason, and we can talk.

Very well, Spacer Naero. We can speak before I perish. I wish I had never listened to the others. I wish I had never come to this terrible place. Now my life is forfeit. The others promised us all a great Cosmic feast of powerful energies, and all we found here instead was death.

Why are you dying, Womi? Is there anything we can do to help you? And why should we, since you came here to attack and kill us?

All good questions. I know all you see in me is an enemy, yet many of my race wish only to live fierce and free. Bestow upon me enough Cosmic energy to sustain my life, such as it is, and I will speak plainly of what I know.

Naero startapped and fed the tiny, flickering wyrm a small amount of energy. It glowed brighter, but did not change size. And it did not flicker as much.

There, Womi. Is that enough?

The creature sighed. *Yes, for now. Thank you. Enough to stave off death, at least. You are fearful beings indeed, if you can sip from the power Cosmic so readily. We were not told the truth about you all by half, and for our folly, we have paid a heavy price. We should have learned that we could never again trust the others, especially when they promised us an easy triumph over your kind. Are all of your people as mighty as you?*

Oh, heavens, no. Lots of my people are much stronger than I am. Like the guy with that sword, for example. In fact, I'm considered somewhat below average–a weakling, really.

Womi glared at her with an uncertain look. A weakling, eh? Well, I suppose it matters not. Perhaps the others betrayed us completely and sent us here to be slaughtered. Curse them. What is there that I can tell one such as yourself, Naero?

Who sent you to attack us, and why? Tell me what you know, and I will do my best to see that you live. You can even go back to your own dimension if you wish. I will not stop you.

If only I could. And if I did so, others of my kind would quickly sense my condition and rush in to finish me. I would be an easy conquest for them, and my power would quickly become part of another.

Naero had almost forgotten about the Kahn-Dar being cannibalistic, attacking and feeding on others of their own kind. She had seen it.

What is wrong with you, Womi? How are you injured? Can you be healed?

I cannot say. I may be able to be regenerated somehow, but not healed. I was struck very hard during the battle in the neck, close to the head. Now only my head can move and function. I cannot feel my body, and it hangs useless below me. It will not respond. Can you not tell that?

Naero looked, trying to study him with her sight. Womi was so small, and so very odd, it was difficult to tell what was natural for his kind. But now that she studied him carefully, his body and limbs did in fact droop slack and lifeless beneath his head.

We can look into improving your condition, Womi, but right now I want an explanation as to why your people attacked us.

Many of us served the Dark Ones long ago, but we no longer desire any master but ourselves. Now the others, former servants such as ourselves, are striving to become a power in their own right. The Kahn-Dar only seek the chance to feed on concentrated sources of the power Cosmic, and to grow stronger and live free. The others deceived us completely, as they always have. My race is still tainted by the Darkforce, and susceptible to its allure. We crave power far too much and can be easily tempted by it.

Who are these others, and how have they deceived you into attacking us?

They said it would be easy–mere hatchling's play for our greater powers. Yet so many of us died. You were all very much capable of defending yourselves and shutting down our gateways. Not weaklings and fools at all, like they said you would be. And that devil of yours with his devil's sword! We were clearly no match for such fury. The others did not warn us about that threat at all, curse them!

What others? Speak plainly. Are we talking about the Dakkur? You both used to be allied with the G'lothc.

Yes, indeed. We thought ourselves rid of them for all time, but now they have gained a foothold in this galaxy. Now they seek to conquer, and crush, and subjugate all before them–just as they and their former masters ruined their own galaxies, and drained them of all life in their insatiable lust for power. They are the pupils of the Dark Ones, and will not be stopped. They can only be destroyed. That is the only way to defeat them.

Naero really wasn't that surprised. She had heard rumors and mention of Baeven and Gaviok fighting the Dakkur. And clearly, they had not left the galaxy.

Their enemies were out there this moment, lurking, plotting, gaining strength.

Womi, you're telling me that the Dakkur have gained a strong foothold in this galaxy? Our galaxy? Where? Where are they expanding their control and dominion?

Far off, in what you call the Gamma Quadrant. You have not explored it yet. Far away from your skies, they have established six new Dakkur homeworlds: Maggoth, Shokk, Kolothon, Xoggoth, Churrok-Kul, and dark Nakkra-Kron. Xalkar I, the Shadow King of the Dakkur, has spread destruction and death to every nearby system via his slaves. The new Dakkur Empire has crushed several important, powerful races, and wiped out their worlds, stripping them of all life. Now they only breed more armies of their slaves.

That had to be where the Ejjai were being bred in vast numbers, at the high expense of other interstellar races unfortunate enough to be near them.

The Dakkur were following in the true footsteps of their Dark Masters. If they ever got their hands on enough of the Darkforce, unlocked the true secrets of G'lothc tek, and began to apply its destructive capabilities wholesale–they might never be defeated.

Womi, I need you to show my people and I where the Dakkur are in the Gamma Quadrant. Can you do that?

I can tell you where it is best to look for them in general. My people ride the Cosmic and dimensional winds by instinct. We do not bother much with maps and such things. But I have a price of my own for divulging such knowledge, if it is so vital to you.

And what is that?

Find a way to restore me to my former self and grant me safe passage. Do that, or I will not tell you anything more, or aid you any further. That is the bargain that I make with you and your kind.

If we do so, Womi, then you must promise in turn never to attack my people or their worlds again. And, to try to dissuade others of your race from doing so.

You won't have any more trouble from me. But I cannot speak for others of my kind. They're notoriously independent and unpredictable. But I don't see many wishing to repeat our recent folly. Is our bargain struck, then?

Done. I will begin studying you when I have the chance, to see if I can figure out how to regenerate your crippling injuries. I don't have a great deal of experience dealing with Cosmic beings and energy creatures of your advanced nature, but I will do my best.

215

Very well. Just find me a nice quiet place to rest in the meantime, and I will do my best to recuperate as much as I can on my own–if I can find a way to do so.

I'm going to keep you with me, then. Do you mind if I place you in one of my pouches?

Fine with me. I can use the rest. Just don't crush me.

We'll try to avoid any crushing.

Naero tucked him away.

Even as she did so, a Cosmic energy spasm racked its way suddenly through her body. That wince of pain only served to remind her that she needed to find a cure for her own Cosmic sickness, before it burned her up, melted her, or caused her to explode.

Merging with the artifact statue had cursed her with a growing Cosmic sickness, which would eventually consume her, one way or another, unless she devised or discovered some kind of cure.

Once she located Baeven, she felt certain that the two of them could have a long talk and attempt to figure out something.

If he had found a way to avoid such a fate, then so could she.

Naero drifted off, concealed within the cloaked, darkened cockpit of her small, advanced craft, still hiding out on the surface of Thanor-4.

Unfortunately, in her troubled state, she had bad dreams and visions about fighting various monsters, Darkforce generators, and the grim, overwhelming tide of the Darkforce itself.

Om had to wake her for the rendezvous when the time came.

Naero. The Dark Star has arrived.

Much to her surprise, Tyber and Zhen rushed to embrace her when she landed in one of the launching bays.

Zhen must have transferred over to Ty's ship at some point.

"Greetings, Naero," Alala sounded out over the ship's com. "Welcome back. It is very good to have you with us again."

"Thanks, Alala." She hugged her friends in great relief. It did in fact feel good to be in a relatively safe place, and with good friends beside her in her time of need.

Naero sensed Om and Alala sharing a rapid back and forth of information and greetings as well. They were talking all about upgrades and the KDM, and Om tried to explain their situation to Naero's prodigal AI offspring. Alala was the core of the hybrid ship that allowed it to be such a self-aware miracle–a living starship. While teknomancing to save her life, Naero inadvertently created Alala, patterned after her own mind.

Om and Alala, both being AIs, could communicate on a level and with a rapidity that Naero did not bother to intrude upon.

Now that she could breathe at last, Naero sat down to a fine meal with her friends, and while they ate, spoke at length about her situation, and what she needed to pursue.

She didn't even know how to get around to explaining Womi to anyone, so she kept that little secret to herself, just for the time being.

As usual, Naero had far too much on her plate.

Yet, now that she was in good company, Naero could let her guard down slightly and relax a bit. She even allowed herself the pleasure to drink a few borbbles of Jett with her meal, and found them both satisfying and re-assuring.

She belched, rubbed her full tummy, and turned to Ty. "So, T. When are we meeting up with *The Star Fox*?"

His face fell slightly. "I can't say, N. We haven't had any word from Baeven, his ship, or his crew yet."

Alala cut in. "We are proceeding to search the area near Baeven's last reported position. That is all the information that we have to proceed upon."

Naero knew that they had already jumped away from Thanor-4, but she hadn't known where they were heading yet.

"Well, I suppose that's better than nothing."

With time to kill, Naero and Om continued their startapping and replication efforts.

Yet that proved frustrating as well.

The worst thing was still trying to replicate herself.

Naero could create a lifeless duplicate of herself–which would pass as a dead body, but that was it. Try as she might, she could not perfect the ability to breathe the Lifespark into the thing, and have it live or move around, even for a little while.

She couldn't get it.

We're missing something, Naero.

Naero slapped her hands on her thighs in frustration.

Then tell me what it is, Om. Because I don't have a clue what's wrong. We're doing everything the way we should, and it's not working. So you tell me.

I just don't know. Some insight eludes us. Perhaps if we explore the full life cycle, that will tell us something.

They kept going until Naero almost passed out again.

After five hours of solid slumber, Naero was summoned to the bridge. An actual distress call finally reached them on one of Baeven's private channels–secret channels that only he could use.

Ty's com officer opened the link and looked to him and Naero. "Ready, sir."

Ty motioned for Naero to go ahead.

"Baeven, this is Naero. Good to hear from you. We have a lot to talk about. What's up with the distress call?"

Usually it was Baeven coming to her rescue, not the other way around.

A female voice came over the link instead.

Naero recognized it as the voice of either Baeven's strange ship, or one of his equally strange crew that she had not met in person yet.

"Naero, this is Jia. I'm glad we've found you. We desperately need your assistance."

"What is it, Jia? What's happened? Where's Baeven?"

"That's what we need your help with, Naero. He went off on a mission to investigate something very suspicious involving the enemy, and we have not heard from him since that time."

Naero felt her own concern spike, as Jia continued.

"Baeven has been missing for many days–as if he vanished."

28

"You don't understand," Jia attempted to explain.

Talking to her was like talking to Alala. Naero still didn't quite understand exactly who or what Jia was. But Jia was making an attempt to describe her deep connection to Baeven.

The Shadow Fox and *The Dark Star* were both docked together, hurtling through jump space to their next search destination.

"Baeven and I are linked together very closely, in ways I cannot explain. Normally, I can locate him or determine where he is very quickly. But he disappeared days ago. I suddenly couldn't sense him any longer. Something very serious has happened to him, and I cannot tell what–or where he is."

Naero had to ask. "Jia…who are you? What are you? How could you have such a connection with Baeven?"

Jia hesitated. "Naero, to answer your questions requires long, complicated explanations, which I am not comfortable with providing at this time–without Baeven present. Once we locate him, then we can pursue such discussions further. But I ask you to trust me. What I have told you is true."

"I'm not questioning your veracity, Jia. I just want to understand things better. I hate to ask this, but what if…what if Baeven were killed or destroyed? Would that account for your lack of a connection with him? Would you two be cut off?"

"No, that's not it," Jia said. "Baeven isn't dead, or disintegrated. If he was, I would know that as well. But something bizarre has definitely happened to him. We're cut off, and he is in danger. I can sense that he is in great distress, but not exactly where or how. He is incredibly strong, but if we do not find a way to reach and rescue him—he will eventually die."

They continued searching for Baeven in every way that they could possibly think of. Naero even tried dreaming about him at night, to see if she could pick up anything about him on the Astral Plane. But she clearly had no idea what she was doing.

She was actually afraid to go there herself again directly, without being completely trained. She somehow felt certain that the Mystics would be watching for her there, and might be able to trace her back to her physical body. She just didn't know what was possible and what wasn't.

As the hours passed into the next day, they continued to jump in several directions, to several possible locations, all further and further out into the Unknown Sectors beyond the border.

Closer and closer, it would seem, to the unexplored mysteries of the Gamma Quadrant. Closer to their mysterious alien foes.

Naero continued to work with Om on startapping and replicating each day. They had reached another plateau, and it was far more difficult without having access to a zoo, or a continent full of real animals and lifeforms. The few cats, birds, rodents, lizards, insects, and fish that Ty's crew had on board as pets really didn't count for very much.

Plus, their owners were extremely reluctant to allow their precious pets to be used as test subjects, no matter how much Naero promised that they would not be harmed.

She was reduced to petting and handling the various creatures in order to get genetic samples to work with, and that proved very inefficient.

Perhaps an attempt at a smaller version of herself might work better.

She replicated one that was only about half her own size, at 0.76 meters.

No dice. Same as before. The Lifespark would simply not take hold and animate the replicant naturally from within.

She reabsorbed her latest failed attempt.

Why? Why didn't any of it work?

Perhaps it has something to do with the increased levels of brain activity of a sentient being. The body cannot live if the brain and the mind are not also alive and in proper sync with the body.

You might have something there, Om. I'll take those parameters into consideration. But you also said something before about studying the life cycle. When I was with Master Vane on Janosha, he taught me many lessons just like that. It was the only true way to fully understand the complete development and function of any lifeform.

On a whim, she replicated a squawking island sea bird–from raw memory. It started out as a fertilized egg in her hand, hatched, and rapidly matured into an adult, and then quickly died.

Naero reabsorbed it.

Next, she replicated a marine reptile, also from memory, and passed it quickly through its life cycle before it died. She studied precisely when the Lifespark took hold and grew, and when it left the body.

She was even startled to see a small glowing orb of the Lifespark itself, which returned to her, its source.

She replicated another one. And this time, she cut off the reptile's senses and kept it in a deep coma, so that it did not suffer during the process.

There was no reason to cause the replicants undue pain.

At last, Naero felt she had gained enough important insights to try something completely different.

Naero formed a Cosmic egg or artificial womb in her hands, an incubator of life. She replicated herself slowly, from fertilized egg to infant–and infused the Lifespark gradually as needed, until the infant could emerge and survive independently.

So that was what she looked like as an infant and toddler. It did match the pics and vids of herself that she had seen.

She kept her replicant in its protective coma, passing it through the entire life cycle and forcing it to age, studying the brain, mind, and the intricate life force energy levels and flows in the replicant all the while. Om helped her keep notes.

It was kind of freaky to watch a version of herself age so rapidly.

And when her replicant breathed its last breath, she nearly sobbed.

Again, she saw the same little glowing orb of life force energy that had come out of her, and now returned, melding back with herself effortlessly.

Naero reabsorbed her replicant.

She had witnessed something like that once before back on Janosha, with the elderly Tua who surrendered their lives. Had it been their souls that she had seen, wending their way free of their bodies, going on to their next journeys?

Then Naero realized–she'd been so focused on the attempt that she forgot about what she had actually accomplished.

She had done it.

She had succeeded in bringing her her own, full-sized replicant to life. It had been born, lived, and died, all in the span of a few brief moments.

Now she understood the full range of life.

Next, she played with the size of the replicant, creating and absorbing them within seconds. Full-size, half-size, one-quarter size–one-tenth. She could make them any size she wanted. With adjustments, she could have made a giant version of herself, if she so desired.

At least then she would be taller.

Without warning, she pitched forward onto her face, nearly blacking out.

Om barely caught them, rushing sustaining energy back into them.

Great progress, Naero, but that's more than enough for today. Let's get you some rest again. You need it. Stop driving yourself to the point of exhaustion.

I did it, Om. I understand what to do now. I can do it.

Om put her to bed. No arguments.

Tyber was having about the same degree of luck and frustration with a tek project that Baeven and Naero had given him. The concept was for a new type of stardrive. Not a jump drive–but a *leap drive*. A drive that would propel starships over far greater distances in shorter periods of time. The next great paradigm shift in star travel.

Naero and Om had stumbled upon some of the concepts that they gleaned from the KDM, yet the concepts were far from complete. However tantalizing the leap drive tek was, it remained a long way from being useable in any way.

She wished that they could crack the KDM, or even learn the wormhole-forming tek of the enemy, or the gating abilities of the Kahn-Dar. All seemed beyond them and their current knowledge and understanding.

Ty continued to work with Alala and Om. Her *abani* Ty was one of the few Spacers outside of the Mystics who could teknomance–an ability Naero had quickened in him. And through Alala, he could speak with Om about the KDM and various tek ideas. Om could even do so while Naero slept.

222

Naero finally leveled with Zhen, Jia, and Alala about her little crippled Kahn-Dar friend, Womi.

Together, they studied the diminutive dragon and attempted to come up with a plan to regenerate his stricken condition.

"I know this much," Zhen told Naero. "He, she, or it is a Cosmic energy being of the first order. It's as bad as trying to study Shalaen—or your own unique weirdness, for that matter, N. I'm pretty sure that you can only regenerate this creature on the same level of existence as it. You will have to transform yourself at the same time in order to even have a chance."

"Interesting. Are you also telling me that Womi doesn't have a gender?"

"Not specifically, from what I can tell, even as an energy creature. Plus, their race are shapeshifters. They could be whatever they wanted to be at a given moment, if it served their needs."

Naero went on referring to Womi as "him." That was easier for her.

Sometimes they had to go into adjoining rooms to discuss things. Womi was not only quite the wit, but his raw intelligence was off the charts. Plus, he remembered everything that he saw or heard perfectly.

And they still were not convinced that he would not betray them somehow in the end, after they did heal him.

Womi tried to heal himself, but that did not work well, either. He only stabilized his energies in his condition, and grew slightly larger.

He took to locking his jaws onto his tail like a tiny Ouroboros. Naero wore him like a pretty sapphire bracelet on her right wrist. He liked sleeping that way, finding the close proximity of Naero's own Cosmic abilities comforting and invigorating.

At times he lightly snored in his teeny voice, but even Naero's sensitive ears barely picked it up, and only when things were deathly quiet around her, like at night.

Naero tried three times to transform into an energy being on a similar wavelength and combination of energies as Womi.

All three times, her efforts failed.

Yet on the fourth try, she sustained it, biomanced, and tried to open some of the Kahn-Dar's broken energy pathways down his spine from his head, focusing on the point of injury.

She gasped and paused. Becoming an energy being for long periods of time magnified all of her feelings and emotions to a very high degree. Everything she experienced became incredibly deep and intense. Every sensation became difficult to control. That was a new complication to deal with, as if she didn't have enough control issues.

The attempt was especially exhausting, and Naero quickly felt drained after only several minutes.

She had to startap again just to keep from passing out.

Oh! Oh! Womi exclaimed. *I feel...something!*

Zhen and Naero looked.

Clear for all to see, the tip of Womi's tail began to twitch, then wave back and forth slightly, rather that hanging still and limp, as usual.

Finally, they had another breakthrough on a different front, within the hour.

Baeven's spy probes signaled that the unique energy signatures of the enemy G'lothc cruiser had passed in and out of a certain area of deep space–and more than once.

Jia instantly changed course and headed in that direction. It was the only new clue that they had.

They barely discovered the first Ejjai freeze world as they passed on through that way.

This was obviously an enemy holding and staging area for Ejjai freeze troops, lying in frozen stasis, just waiting to awake and receive their masters' commands to attack.

Several billion Ejjai, sleeping on that one nameless world, complete with all of their fleets and equipment. Ready-made for an invasion.

Naero instantly considered destroying them. Her fists clenched, her temper peaked and burned hot, whenever she thought of the ruthless, murderous Ejjai.

Alala, Jia, and Om all cautioned her.

"We cannot harm them," Jia said.

"She is right," Alala added. "Then the enemy will be alerted to our position, and that we have passed by this way. We can mark the location on our charts, and arrange for allies to destroy them later, when the time is right."

Naero shook her head and scowled. "I remember the High Crusade. I know very well what that number of Ejjai can do–the wanton destruction and butchery they can inflict on helpless populations. It will haunt me forever. All of the Ejjai need to die. We must wipe them all out."

Ty waved a hand before her face. "Easy, killer. Take it easy. We can't tip our hand, just yet."

But the secret base also alerted them to the fact that they were entering enemy territory. Even Jia felt that they were on the right trail this time.

Baeven had slipped off alone in an insertion pod. After his second jump in this direction, his crew had heard nothing back from him since that time.

Out of the black, Naero went to Womi and asked him, "Have you ever heard of a world called Xanathar?"

"No," he replied. "I can't say that I have. Is it important?"

"No, just a weird legend. I was just curious, what with the Kahn-Dar being so far-traveled and all."

"Sorry. I am very grateful for our progress. I want you to know that I do intend to keep my end of our bargain, if you can fully restore me. I never thought I would say this, Spacer Naero, but I'm actually starting to enjoy myself with you. It would be a pity if your Cosmic illness destroyed you in the end. You must not let that happen."

"What do you know of such things, Womi?"

"Not much; just that I can sense the Cosmic disease growing within you. You must find a way to stabilize your messed-up internal energies, or they will most definitely destroy you. Such things are a very serious concern."

"Anything you can tell me? Any serious advice, something I might try?"

"Not in the least. I have no idea what type of creature you are, or how the power Cosmic affects you. I'd be of little help. I can't even regenerate myself."

"How long do you think I have?"

"Hmm…depending on how tough you are, and how much pain you can stand. I'd say a few months at least, before the agony becomes unbearable. But I'm clearly guessing."

More than ever, Naero needed to locate and rescue Baeven. She needed his counsel greatly. He was the only other person besides herself who had gone through something like this—and beaten it.

29

The very next day, they were in jump again, searching the vicinity.

They located another Ejjai freezeworld, with a similar number of billions of frozen enemy shock troops, just waiting to awaken and go to war.

It boggled the mind. How many such hidden bases could there be?

Then they came across something even more ominous, on the borders of known space.

They came across a vast debris field of asteroids and planetoids, stretching out over a great distance.

Concealed on those countless rocks, they detected even more countless batteries of robotic missile launchers and automated mass drivers.

"An impressive offensive or defensive battle screen," Jia announced.

Naero ran a few projections with Om.

These weapon emplacements are many decades old, Naero. They are still fully functional, but they have been waiting here for a very long time. I sense that they are, in fact, Dakkur tek.

Naero covered her mouth nervously, rubbing her lips with one hand. "So many. Any attack from here would take time to reach us," Naero said, "but the enemy could still rain death on our worlds from far away with such weapons."

"It might not even take so long," Alala added. "Look at the possible variations on these missile payload delivery systems. These smartmissiles can jump, multiple times, as needed. They can cloak, and even phaze if need be, and they can carry any kind of payload packed into them–atomics, nerve agents, biochem warfare–even gigabombs."

Naero grew even more concerned. "Not just a rain of death–a storm of total destruction. After we get Baeven back, Intel will need to send some spyfixer nebulae out here to take these systems over. We can pweak them and convert them for our purposes, against our industrious foes. Who knew that they've been working out this way for so long?"

Everything they continued to find was increasingly chilling. Their determined enemies seemed to be way ahead of them, as far as the planning phases were concerned.

At their next startapping session, Naero and Om made a huge mistake.

Cosmic power rushed into them.

They took in too much, and it still kept coming.

Om, this is just like before–but a thousand times worse. What the hell do we do? How do we stop it?

I don't know. I'm trying.

Even worse, her Cosmic disease latched onto the excess wild power raging through her, and accelerated completely out of control.

Intensely painful, glowing sores erupted all over her body.

Naero was forced to transform into an energy being to keep the Cosmic sores from melting her physical body into greasy slag on the spot.

She pulsed with Cosmic force, glowing brighter and brighter, beginning to shimmer.

Haisha, Om. I can't see straight. We'd better transport out into space. If we detonate, we could vaporize the entire ship.

Hold on. I'm going to try something.

Om, it's too late. I'm going to explode!

Even worse, her Dark Beast wrestled with her to break free, feeding on all of the excess power. Yet the raging contagion of her

Cosmic illness sapped its strength and caused it just as much agony as it did her. It suffered as she suffered.

Hold on, Naero. Hang on!

I can't, Om. I'm going to burst. Help me!

In desperation, Om took control. It felt as if he were shredding them.

A bright flash–pain–as if they were being ripped to even smaller pieces.

Both of them shrieked in agony, but they finally broke the startapping link, and closed the floodgates at last.

They were alive.

They had survived...somehow.

Yet Naero instantly sensed that something was very, very wrong.

Naero shook herself, sat up, and stared.

Impossible.

She blinked and looked into the blinking eyes of an exact duplicate of herself, both of them slightly shorter.

Shorter.

Shorter? Damn that all to hell.

Somehow...she was even shorter now?

Haisha! She might as well blow up all over again.

Nobody warned her about *this* possibility.

Naero II–the Sequel–grinned back at her like some flipped-out dope.

"Haisha! Hey, at least we didn't blow up, right?"

"Naero..." another voice gasped.

Both of them glanced over and blinked at a very strange humanoid being, and covered their mouths.

This being was male, obviously naked, and he was pure black. Not just black–black, black. Black like a singularity itself, literally smoking with wisps of Cosmic ichor, vapor, and coruscating energies.

Even when he opened his mouth, inside of him was all black.

Only his eyes were a different color.

Deep violet eyes, just like those of the two Naeros he gawked at.

"Om?"

"Yes. It is I. What the hell, eh? At last, I've got my own body!"

This was all too crazy. Waaay too whacked out. Naero checked deep within herself quickly–and panicked.

"The KDM. Om, it's gone. I don't have it inside me anymore." She almost panicked, then turned to the other Naero.

"Is it in you?"

"Hey, don't look at me. I don't even know what you're talking about."

"It's in me, N," Om said. "Don't worry, I still have it."

"Om, what happened? What the hell did we do?"

"I'm sorry. It was the only thing I could think of to keep us from being destroyed. I used all of that energy to fragment us into three parts. Myself and the other you are replicants…if you will. Copies of you. I just happened to pweak myself and make me male–at the last instant–to match my personality."

"Well, good job. Haisha. We're not dead. Now frickin' change us back."

"Screw that," Naero II protested, crossing her arms in front of herself defiantly. "I wanna live a little. This throcks."

"Uh…sorry, N. I…kind of don't know how to do that."

"Say again, Om? Now get with it. Just…reverse the process, like re-absorbing a replicant."

"Very well. Tell me how. I don't even fully understand how I did it. I just guessed. I haven't a clue how to reverse it all."

This was bad. For once, Naero was speechless.

Om had done this–replicating–even transferring his own mind and personality, and giving Naero II her own, independent, conscious thought.

For right now, it appeared that Om had done all of this, and he would need to find a way to undo it.

Naero shook her head.

Damnation.

Naero II looked around, feeling her stomach. "What is this sensation? Oh, I know. Wow. I'm really hungry and thirsty all of the sudden. I've never felt that way before. You guys got anything to eat or drink?"

Naero didn't know what else to do, so she startapped briefly, and transported them back to her quarters.

She certainly didn't want anyone to see her new…additions. How would she possibly explain them?

She and Om had gotten themselves into this mess.

Just maybe, they could all find a way to fix it.

She gave Naero II a borbble of Jett and a pod of Spum from her junk food stash.

"Hey," Om said. "I've never actually tasted food on my own before, either. Let me at some of that action."

Naero absently handed him the same meal deal, opening the borbble and the pod to show them how it was done.

Om and Naero II guzzled and ate with their fingers like starving people. When they were finished, they tossed the empties on the floor and took turns belching and laughing back and forth.

"That was great!" Om said. "Give us some more."

Naero II pushed past Naero and started raiding the junk food stash all on her own.

Naero II looked back at Om over her shoulder.

"I've got all the good stuff here. What'll you give me in trade?"

Om grinned like a goof.

Naero's mouth hung down.

Were her two replicants actually starting to flirt with each other–right in front of her? Uh-oh. That would not do at all.

Okay, she had to do something–try anything to slow things down. She needed time to think.

Tap. Focus. Biomancy.

First she needed to completely understand them, these replicants that were, in theory, part of her.

While they focused on eating more, Naero placed her hands on them and examined them all the way down to their genetics.

No surprises.

"Hold still now," she told them.

"For what?" Om said.

Naero II giggled again. "That tickles."

They were her. Both of them.

Genetic copies. Exact Replicants.

Like he said, Om had just pweaked himself to be male–a slight variation.

But unlike her, mentally they were, in part, still like children. Short attentions spans–selfish–easily distracted. They were experiencing so much of the real world on their own for the first time. They had almost no frame of reference, other than some of her basic instincts and raw memories. They had her mind, or at least its patterns and neural net–and at least some of her ideas and common experience.

Yet neither of them had ever had their own body before, or were used to dealing with all of the stimuli around them. To them, existence was a total rush of power and stimulation. They were drunk–on reality.

Just as she could be made tipsy by heady rushes of massive Cosmic power.

Naero placed her hands on their heads gently, one at a time.

Being used to reality, she could modify their reactions and behavior. But at the moment, she needed time.

Time without having to babysit them so that she could figure out how to reabsorb them and get them back inside of her.

Otherwise, this had all the makings of a total disaster.

Sleep. She had to put them to sleep for the time being, and triggered those needs in them.

"Wow, I need to lie down," Om said. "Is this what a food coma is like?"

Naero II stumbled and yawned, stretching in true, catlike Naero fashion. "I'm sleepy too. Must be all this great chow."

Naero kept them from clunking heads and calmly helped them snuggle down on the nanobed in her quarters. She darkened the room.

A new, terrifying thought occurred to her.

These two replicants had every potential ability she had.

And, perhaps…every flaw, as well.

More frightening possibilities. What if they had the same out-of-control powers, and startapped into the Cosmic flows, and got stuck in them, just like she did? What if they went insane like Danner?

What if they lost it and exploded?

Two Cosmic quantabombs detonating. Twice the bang. Twice the fun.

And not only that–if they were both like her–what if each of them had their own Dark Beast?

Things kept getting more interesting, and more terrifying, each second.

And she could still barely control herself.

Naero didn't know where to begin.

Tek. She needed tek. A medbed would help her analyze herself and them.

She transported to the medical bay, a part that was not being used currently.

It took only a moment to procure a medbed. She lay down upon it and analyzed herself first, using biomancy and teknomancy to determine the slightest changes in herself–including the deplorable loss of an entire three millimeters of height.

Her complete self-analysis took more than a standard hour.

Should she bring her replicants here, or bring the medbed back to her quarters? There was room in her quarters for the medbed, and with her greater need for secrecy, perhaps the latter would be best.

But when she transported back to her quarters, they were still dark within. Yet immediately, she detected something very wrong. Her sensitive nose twitched.

231

What was that damn musky scent in the air?

Her blood went cold.

Oh, no…

Holy crap. Bloody hell!

Naero II sat astride Om, both of them going at it like Bundian weasels on fire.

Naero could not speak. She could not breathe. Her mouth gaped open like a trap door.

Her replicants began to pulse with Cosmic energy at their…exertions, lit from within. Ribbons of light and darkness, actual sparks and little lightning bolts shot out from both of them as their excitement peaked.

They laughed and smiled, completely absorbed in their sexual efforts, taut naked bodies sweating, mouths gulping joyously for air.

Both of them seemed very close to a mutual fulfillment.

Haisha! What if they actually cooked off and blew up?

Naero II looked over. "Hey, N. You're back. Why didn't you tell us this was so much fun?"

Om popped his head up, giddy, laughing and wide-eyed. "You gotta try this, N! Now I know what you mean by the exclamation 'Wahoooo!'"

Om howled like a Zandarian coyote.

It was both exultant…and quite off-putting.

Naero was quite certain that she was going into some kind of shock.

Her face had to be as red as an old-fashioned Terran tomato. She covered her eyes with her hands and turned away as they continued to jerk, moan, convulse, and thankfully, finish their task at hand.

Her replicants didn't know any better. And that was the problem. They had no prior knowledge or any inhibitions.

She had literally just watched herselves pleasure themselves. How utterly mortifying.

Once they fell back breathless she slipped in and sent them back to sleepy land. But she couldn't wipe their stupid grins off their faces as they snoozed.

After their exertions, putting them to sleep was pretty easy.

It took her a while longer to swap them out on the medbed, studying each of them carefully.

Hours later—with the help of five new, adapted medical fixers, and several biomancy experiments—she thought she had the answer at last.

She ignored calls from her friends, insisting she needed more rest.

Sleep was something she actually did not get, but she did find an answer to her dilemma—at least in theory.

As usual, it was all about Cosmic energy and energy manipulation. She was starting to see a pattern there.

Combination and balance were often the key, just like Master Vane–or herself–rushing a bird from egg to death. Patterns, no patterns, and patterns that did not at first seem to be patterns.

More and more, she began to understand how so much of life was comprised of intricate patterns and flowing waves of blended, converted, Cosmic energy, and ever-shifting, manipulated energy.

All so very mercurial and complex. Staggering. Staggering and astonishing in its terrible beauty and utter majesty.

She could not see very much of it before, but now she could, as she grew in both experience and wisdom. Om had manipulated them when they were infused–no, bloated with Cosmic power–and cut them off from the Cosmic energy flows of their universe that threatened to destroy them.

In the end, he saved them by splitting them off into three parts, and releasing most of the excess energy back to the Cosmic source. That knowledge and insight was helpful as well.

They had emerged, therefore, in three versions: herself–the original–and two replicants–one female and one male. But the process of pulling together the needed resources had not been perfect, and it reduced her slightly, which was why they were all shorter than she had been, originally.

Screw that!

She just needed to reverse the process, reabsorb them into herself, and expend any excess energies that resulted, to return everything back to normal.

Easy-peasy now, to her mind.

Who was she kidding?

Hell, while she was at it, maybe she could finally make herself a little taller.

But first, she had to experiment with the basic process. From what she had learned, theory was often very different than the actual application. There were variables that could only be experienced firsthand, in the course of actual execution.

She would create a small, basic replicant in the same, exact way that Om had, and then reabsorb it.

As she did so, she completely controlled its mental state and did her best to keep it docile and obedient.

As docile and obedient as a fierce little ten-millimeter, doll-like version of herself could be—with even a portion of her defiant mind and temperament.

MicroNaero.

She looked like a fairy with her tiny gravwings. An exact copy, down to its equally tiny Nytex flight togs, Spacer weapons, and teeny wristcom suicide device. If her micro-copy set off the miniaturized device, it would still blow up, and most likely destroy the entire medbed.

The only thing she could not replicate was Womi. He remained far too complex, and continued sleeping on her wrist.

MicroNaero stood there and crossed her arms, tapping her foot and talking up at her creator with a tiny, squeaking voice.

Naero barely made out the words.

"So, what now, Giganta?"

Interesting. Would all of her replicants have her scintillating attitude?

Naero took a deep breath.

With a wave of her hand she put her little copy into a deep sleep, just in case there could be pain.

She never wanted to be cruel or indifferent.

Then she transformed and reduced it—not to raw materials, but a step further, to pure energy. Finally, she reabsorbed that energy—as if it were the simplest thing.

There was some pain on her part. She let the energy rush up through her arms too quickly.

That could be compensated for.

On a whim, she gathered more energy and created several more of the same tiny replicants.

Soon they flitted around her, hands on hips, scolding her, giving her tiny pieces of their tiny little minds.

She'd work on behavior modification later, to make them more cooperative. That would come along.

Suddenly, Naero felt weak again, to the point of passing out.

She quickly reduced her sprites back to glowing pods of proto-energy, and drew their essences back into herself.

The spell of fatigue quickly passed.

That was also a good lesson. She had to remember to startap. If she expended too much of her own, primary internal energies, it would drain her and knock her out.

But her two, life-sized replicants had been formed out of a dangerous excess of energy. That meant, in theory, that when she re-joined them with herself, she would also experience an exponential excess of Cosmic power once again.

Managing all of that at once was going to be tricky.

She started with Naero II.

She paused and smiled, patting her replicant on the shoulder.

"Sorry, sweetie." Naero sighed. "Hope you enjoyed yourself."

Haisha, she was starting to sound like Saemar.

For some reason, she suddenly missed the rest of her family and friends horribly.

Reabsorbing Naero II went surprisingly fast. Yet within an instant, she was bloated with dangerous, near-lethal levels of wild Cosmic energy.

But this time, she was ready for it.

This time, she reversed the startapping process. If she could take Cosmic energy from the universe, she could give it back, siphoning the excess power back into the nearest star and the Cosmic flows that naturally existed around it, her, and everything else in their dimension.

That was the trick. She didn't have to keep it all inside of herself and risk exploding. The difficult part was finding a proper outlet, and then surrendering the energy with the right matching flow level, to give it back without sucking herself dry or blowing up.

That little triumph left her so confident, that she immediately turned to reabsorbing Om. Get the task done.

Almost immediately, Naero realized that she was horrifyingly wrong.

Ribbons, tendrils, and tentacles of incredibly complex, Kexxian-infused Cosmic flows, blended biomancy, and teknomancy ripples rose up to defend him.

She warred with the KDM defensive protocols dangerously over her head again, without a clue.

The only thing she could think to do was reabsorb Om instantly, make him a part of herself once more. Then there would be nothing to defend against.

Om awoke inside of her mind, disoriented and confused, but part of her once more–and so was the KDM.

Then she gasped, fighting against a sudden swell of tremendous Cosmic energy–a hundredfold greater than before.

Om nearly shrieked in her mind.

Naero! Imperative that we shield our current form in every way possible. A massive explosion and something even worse is imminent.

We've unleashed it from the protocols and now it is beyond our control. Hurry!

I'm trying, Om.

Try harder. Don't let up. Otherwise, we will not survive.

The ship, Om. We can't destroy the ship.

That can no longer be avoided. Destruction cannot be avoided.

Everyone was about to perish, and it was entirely her fault.

Naero used all of the energy she had left, and startapped for even more, covering herself in layered waves of protective force.

Next, she attempted to transport them out into space, as far away from *The Dark Star* as she could.

It won't work, Naero. Still too close.

Then the air around them went opaque and sparkling blue.

Naero tried to gasp, but could not.

The explosion detonated out from them—yet worse than the explosion, something else erupted from within her—a thing even more terrifying.

The raw energy of the blast transformed and actually came to life on its own, a ravenous, uncontrollable entity of jet-black Darkforce energy and utter malevolence.

This was her Dark Beast set free on its own, yet still linked with her mind. Chaos itself and annihilation personified, exactly like the destroying amoeba-like monster of her repeating nightmares, which absorbed and penetrated her very flesh and devoured and crushed her completely: body, will, and soul.

That's exactly what it was.

She looked on, petrified with horror as it came to life before her staring eyes and went on a rampage.

But it struggled, flipped, and whirled in place.

It couldn't maneuver properly, and there was nothing close by to destroy.

Where were they?

Then she heard Womi's voice.

My, you are incredibly fascinating—especially for a weakling of your kind. Since we were preparing to explode…I thought it best to remove both us and our Cosmic energies to the Astral Plane.

Her Dark Beast whirled about suddenly, and looked straight into her.

Its ragged maw grinned with knowing recognition.

Then, even worse, it rushed at her, faded from sight, and melded back with her—once again.

For a few brief seconds, she had nearly been free of the vile thing, and wasn't even aware of it. The massive blast had simply let it spring free for a few moments.

Naero realized fully, therefore, that her Dark Beast wasn't just part of her.

It was her.

And she was it, too.

Much more than Om, she and that terrible, sickening, delightfully wicked, and deliciously seductive force of total, gleeful destruction and abject evil...

Were all one and the same. Another terrifying paradox.

The very real monster lurking deep within her was both *Other*, and also herself–somehow all at once.

Whatever she did, she would never be free of it.

Naero shuddered and convulsed, instantly curling up into a tight, opaque sphere of Cosmic energy. She hugged her knees at what she was and wept.

She *was* a monster. No way to deny it now.

Om attempted to reach her.

Naero, it's all right. Our physical form is still waiting for us back on the ship. No one else was hurt; we survived the blast.

Had they? Had Om seen and perceived what she had just realized? Could he see it? Or had it all just been another of her mad delusions?

She shook her head and sobbed.

I'm not so sure about anything anymore, Om.

Womi tried to cut in. *Are you speaking to someone else telepathically? I keep hearing this buzzing sound and these echoes when I try to link with you. The explosion is past. Should I take us back, now?*

30

Naero actually struggled to rest after her intense ordeal, tossing and turning–experiencing further nightmares, fears, and many, very unpleasant visions.

Jia, Alala, and Om woke her four hours later, calling to her in her quarters.

Om, what is it now?

They think they've found where Baeven might be.

Naero reported to *The Dark Star* bridge minutes later.

"Looks like another secret enemy base of some kind," Alala informed them. *The Star Fox* was still docked and linked with them. Both ships took up orbit around a strange new planet.

Jia jumped right in. "Now that we're this close, I have a good feeling that Baeven is in fact down there, somewhere. And whatever has happened to him–I was right. He is definitely in trouble. We must find him and extract him, as soon as possible."

Om cautioned her, *Naero, the enemy has gone to much greater lengths to mask and cloak this facility than any of the others we have found thus far. It has advanced tek that my scans can not penetrate. You will need to be extremely careful.*

My middle name, Om.

No. It most definitely is not. I'm serious about this, Naero. This place shrieks trouble, and we'll be walking right into it. There is tek here that we've never encountered before.

Then let's learn what we can, before we go in.

Together, Naero and her comrades performed a quick survey of the new planet, and especially the secret base. Jia provided them with a full report.

"We think it is some kind of weapons lab or R&D development base; it must be important. Our enemies have invested a lot into this one location. The facilities are extensive; much of them underground, armored, well-shielded, and even cloaked. We barely stumbled upon it because of the G'lothc ship signatures out this way. It must have stopped here, and more than once, according to the traces. We remain very lucky that the enemy still thinks that it can pop around with impunity. They don't believe that we can track them in any way."

"Where's Baeven?" Naero asked. "What kind of tek and defenses are we up against?"

"I was getting to all that," Jia added. "Be patient. We have a lot of ground to cover. The defenses are hi-tek and layered. Here are the specs. Use your teknomancy to absorb them."

Naero connected fluidly with Alala and did so.

Haisha! These were incredibly intricate defenses.

"There are also full battle groups of *active* Ejjai, hidden in mountain bases, backed up by hunter-killer teams of Dakkur–led by Dakkur champions."

Naero envisioned her battle royal with Oth, back on Janosha. Where she had taken her revenge on the creature that had slain her best friend, Gallan.

"The enemy also has dozens of fleets just waiting to swoop out from hidden planetary bases scattered throughout the system and attack, if the planet should ever come under siege. We don't want to kick over this hornet's nest. With any luck, we can sneak in, get Baeven, and get out without attracting any attention. That's the plan."

"Do we know where Baeven is?" Naero asked directly.

"That's the problem," Jia said. "We don't. We can't actually see into the base, either. Some kind of shielding or tek defense is keeping our penetration scans from getting through. It is heavily defended in every way. On the outer layers we can detect various hi-tek sensor

239

arrays and robotic gun emplacements. This installation could withstand multiple heavy attacks, and defend itself very well against attackers–and, most likely, careful infiltrators as well."

Naero let out a sigh. "Copy that. That's where I come in. I'll slip in all stealth mode and locate Baeven. I just wish we knew what to look for, or where."

She did feel somewhat better having *The Shadow Fox* along with them for the ride. They could get into deep trouble very quickly this time.

Naero hadn't even thought of a way to tell them that she was both slowly dying from a growing Cosmic infection she couldn't stop, and that she might also explode and kill them all at any moment.

There was not good way to spin all that.

Nor did they have any backup.

All flags stood against them. No friends any longer, ever since she killed High Master Vane. Anywhere they turned, everyone who had been their greatest allies would now be on the hunt to take them down.

It hurt Naero deeply that her own people–her own beloved Clans– would view her as an enemy, now. She was a wanted, heinous criminal–a murderer.

The Spacer authorities would have to formally capture her and bring her to trial before they could ostracize her, making her an outcast like her uncle.

Only then could they strip her of her name and all she was.

Time to check out the planet surface in stealth mode.

Immediately, something wasn't right. Naero's small cloud of spyfixers sounded silent warnings.

For starters, the region all around the enemy base was highly toxic– unnaturally so. Good thing she was already buttoned up in her stealth armor.

She had her spyfixers scatter and perform a toxicological survey.

Naero carefully gathered some samples from the poisoned streams and pools, now a real-life contaminated dead zone. Nothing lived there. Not even bugs. The trees and plants–even the grass–were either all dead or carefully replicated fakes–all camouflage.

Once they shunted those samples back to Zhen for analysis, they might have a better idea about what kind of bio-weapons program the enemy was operating. The research base maintained a disciplined, very low profile operation–within striking distance of their foes.

At least thus far, anyway.

And even if someone did look for enemy activity, the searchers would have to stumble upon the Intel base in the middle of nowhere to even have a clue. They wouldn't have access to Baeven or his sensor drones and passive and active probes. And even then, nothing around or on the surface of the planet gave off any sign that serious tek was at work there, unless you got right up close to it.

The level of security and secrecy began to scare Naero.

Even Intel did not operate on any kind of a level like this.

What in the hell were their foes up to? They were definitely planning something, and as usual, it was going to be both big and nasty once they unleashed it.

And that begged even more questions. What had happened to Baeven? Baeven never got stuck like this. What had he run afoul of that *he* couldn't handle?

Maybe there was a first time for everything. But every second on this bio-weapons world raised more troubling questions.

Word from Jia on their secure channel.

Still no sign of any signal from Baeven.

Naero and the two ships sent specially coded signals out on all of their special frequencies and channels. Calls and signals that only Baeven would recognize.

No response.

He was either separated from his own formidable tek–again–rare if not impossible. Or he was captured, or hurt badly enough that he could not respond…or worse.

Naero had a very real sudden fear.

What if the enemy had somehow captured Baeven…and had him prisoner in one of those nightmarish Darkforce generators? That would certainly explain a lot.

"Jia, we've searched all day. Other than attempting to infiltrate the base itself, I don't see how we're going to find him. I've got to make an attempt at getting inside."

Silence.

"There is another way," Jia said. "Something difficult that we haven't tried yet. A special kind of telepathy that only I can perform."

"Then let's do it. What are we waiting for?"

"It's…problematic."

"How so?"

"To make it work, Naero–I need a host body to temporarily place my mind and essence in."

"Huh? Your mind runs the ship? You don't have a body, Jia?"

Welcome to my existence.

Quiet, Om.

"No," Jia said. "I do in fact have a physical body...but for many good reasons, it isn't really here with us right now. I kind of had to leave it behind."

Naero wasn't going to ask, at least for now, just how Jia had her mind and soul separated from her physical body–or what that physical body happened to look like.

Her head was already spinning.

Jia went on. "For my special type of telepathy to work, I must have a physical body to work through."

Naero did not hesitate.

"If it will find Baeven, then use mine."

"Be warned, Naero. It's not as easy as it sounds, taking someone's mind and soul inside of you. Being a host to another sentient's consciousness...even for a short time, can be difficult, dangerous, and incredibly painful."

"Yeah, yeah. Bring on the pain, then. What else you got?"

"All right. Let's rendezvous at the Delta-3 landing zone and take it from there. I'll instruct you what to do."

"Jia, I just naturally assumed you were a person–of some kind. Am I correct?"

She laughed. "I am a person, Naero. I just don't have my body right now. It's ...a little complicated."

Everything with Baeven and his weird ass crew usually was. Where did any of them come from? They were all individual members of their species. Where were their homeworlds?

"Sooo...if you don't have your body with you, Jia–what exactly are you?"

"For now, I am *The Shadow Fox*–Baeven's sentient, self-aware ship–a living ship, much like Alala and *The Dark Star*. I function as a large part of its mind–its intellect. I bolster its raw computing power. But the ship can also function very well without me when necessary."

"Okay. Question answered. See you soon. Tell S'krin and Danjen to keep their togs on."

"I don't understand, Naero. Neither of them wear togs."

"Just an expression."

What in the hell was she getting herself into now? Becoming a host body for yet another personality?

Om couldn't help commenting. *Could be fun. A self-aware intellect working in conjunction with a complex machine? With Jia and Alala around, I could be in love, Naero...again.*

Haisha, not Om in love again. Please, anything but that.

Whatever there was between Jia and Baeven, Naero was pretty sure it was love–and not the platonic kind either. Naero would bet the fleet that if they ever did see Jia's body, it would be a definite eye-opener.

Keep your togs on, too, this time, Om. I can't speak for Alala, but I got a serious hunch that Jia is already taken.

Dang. They say the good ones usually are.

Who are "they?" You don't even know any "theys," so don't get cocky, Om. Sheesh, I should have never let you develop a sense of humor.

"Ah, but I have. Too late now."

Naero sighed, continuing to worry about whether they could slip into that enemy facility without being detected or captured themselves.

If Baeven couldn't find a way out, how would she?

31

They made it to the rendezvous point, and Naero crossed over to *The Shadow Fox.* Both of their ships remained docked together and cloaked.

Naero used the special sensors of her spyfixers to locate the vessel and place both of her hands on the hull.

Weird. With her teknomancer abilities, she could sense the living ship's energies, and even Jia's superior intellect, just a part of this amazing craft.

She linked with Jia again.

"I'm here, Jia. How do we do this? Through our teknomancing, or our mindlink?"

"I'm afraid it's a little more complex than that, Naero. I will need to split my soul off from the ship, and join it with you directly. You must take my soul inside of your existence, and provide it both a safe place and access to your bodily functions."

Didn't that sound inviting. "So, I have to swallow or ingest your soul somehow?"

"You do not actually devour or consume as such. Absorbing it and keeping it whole and intact within you is perhaps a better description. I will become part of you for a brief time."

"Sounds like a fun ride. And once you have access to a physical body, you think you can locate Baeven?"

"Yes. If he is here, my abilities will locate him."

"How can you be so sure?"

"Because, Baeven is a part of me, and I am a part of him. The two of us became as one a long time ago."

Naero really needed to hear that story, too.

Again, who and what was Jia?

"Then let's do this," Naero said. "Tell me what to do."

Now I'm questioning whether this is a good idea or not, Naero. We do not fully know this entity called Jia, or her motives. Is it wise to give her access to our minds, our current form, our abilities, and the KDM?

I'm sure you'll be able to keep our secrets safe from her, Om. Right now, it is vital that we do this, to locate Baeven.

Very well. I will protect our secrets and monitor the situation very carefully.

You do that, Om. I know you will.

"I am ready," Jia said.

A medbed emerged from the floor of *The Shadow Fox's* open landing bay. Naero climbed up and lay down on it.

She gasped somewhat as the neural sensors and connections writhed like a nest of snakes over her face and head, zapping her slightly at times with impulse tests to neural net links and connections as they formed.

"Hey, that stings," she finally complained.

Our minds are being linked with and accessed. Is this an attack?

Wait, Om. Don't do anything.

"My apologies for any discomfort," Jia said, "but the links must be made quickly and precisely. The transfer from machine mode back to a bio-mechanical mode is much more difficult than a simple transfer from one bioform to another."

Now Naero was curious. The process was easier with bioforms…in what way?

Naero observed, studying and recording the dizzying array of techniques at work with both her teknomancy and biomancy skills. "So, transferring or absorbing a soul essence from another bioform would be a lot simpler?"

"Indeed. Going back the other way, from bioform to machine mode, is also much more difficult. The interface the essence must travel through is twice as complex, between two completely different modes. Yet any such transfer becomes much easier after the initial process."

"Yeah, I get that. The first time for anything can often be a pain. This is all extremely fascinating, Jia."

"Links established. I will begin the transfer. As I warned you, there will be surges of pain as I transfer my essence within you. Focus on making a safe place for me within your mind. Inform the Kexxian neural defense entity within you–the one calling himself Om–that I am joining you as a guest, not as an attacking invader. I am very curious to meet with him on this level and discuss many matters–including the KDM."

"I'm sure he feels the same way about you, Jia. It should be a very interesting meeting of the minds."

"Try to relax, Naero. I'm restraining you somewhat as the transfer begins, keeping your motor functions in stasis. You must remain still."

Naero's eyes went wide and her mouth gasped in breathless torment as the first rush of pain rippled through her.

Haisha! Someone was pulverizing her bones.

"Hold still. I feel it through you as well. Transfer nearly complete. Almost there."

Naero ground her teeth and swallowed another scream. She was sweating hard by now.

Now it was like plasma borers shooting up through her body and out her head.

Then the pain of the transfer suddenly ceased.

Naero blinked, sweating and trembling on the medbed as it sank back into the landing bay floor.

She staggered back up to her feet.

Naero looked around her.

"Jia?" she called out.

I'm here, Naero. Transfer complete. I'm in your mind; my essence is part of you for now. Thank you for trusting me.

Om called out to her the next instant.

Welcome, Jia. Amazing. You are...a Driathan, in fact. I see it clearly now. Accessing all Kexxian data on Driathan, and their creators, the Drians. Now I know that we shall have much to discuss, you and I.

Agreed, Om. I cannot hide my nature in this form any more than you can being Kexxian. Both of our creators were once mighty allies, and did great things together. May we do so as well. Yet, they were also mysteries to each other, just as we remain.

Naero spoke to them both directly through their internal link, sitting cross-legged on the loading bay, closing her eyes to concentrate and keep their intellects separate.

So, absorbing a soul from another physical lifeform is much easier than this was, Jia? I sure hope so. That was supposed to be a little pain?

I'm sorry, Naero. You can never say how it will be on the first attempt. The soul and mind are astral and physical reflections of each other—two halves of the same coin, as humans used to say. Together they form our basic essence. What makes us who and what we are.

What is a coin again?

Naero laughed. Om, a coin was a physical form of money used in ancient times. Much like we use digital credits now for trade. Small disks of various semi-precious metals, often stamped with images or words on either side. Hence the expression Jia used—two sides of the same coin.

From her place within their mind, they experienced Jia's presence as a warm, glowing light within them—a bright star.

For several long minutes they discussed the ramifications of minds and souls. How to absorb, protect, and control them, once merged with them.

But Jia also warned them: *There have been and most likely will always be beings who are able to mount mind and soul attacks on other entities. Such attacks are both psyonic and astral in nature, allowing the attacker to take over the mind and soul of another and inflict their will over the other entity—even to the point of controlling their physical body, or even damaging or destroying a person's own essence in the process.*

Naero shared her contest with Danner, how he had been able to take over Janner, and even switch minds and souls with him somehow.

In their ancient war with the G'lothc, both the Kexx and the Drians learned all too well how the great enemy were both shape-shifters and soul killers. The G'lothc used such abilities and attacks with ruthless impunity, to inflict great damage.

Om added quickly, *Yes, and those were among many reasons that their foul kind were all hunted down and eradicated.*

Naero thought of Danner again. What would or could she do if he took over Janner again, or even herself?

I'm curious. The Spacer Mystics taught us how to shield our minds, but how would you defend against such a direct attack? What if another entity did force itself into your mind and try to take control?

Jia answered. *Usually a strong mindshield is sufficient, Naero. Always remember that within your own mind, your will is supreme. You can do anything. If you discipline your mind and force of will enough, no outside power–no matter how strong–can force you to do anything against your will. The trick is not to let fear defeat you. Fear and strong emotions weaken your force of will and your ability to resist, or even control yourself. Try it with me. I will lift your right hand up.*

Jia did so. Naero's hand rose up, but Naero did not do it.

That felt…weird, Jia. I couldn't stop you.

You were not prepared to, nor actively trying stop me. You were unfocused. Now, concentrate. I will try to lift the same arm again. Don't allow me to do so this time.

Naero felt the intense pressure between them. Yet this time, she easily shielded herself from Jia's thoughts, and incredible force of will.

Her hand did not even twitch.

See? I can do nothing if you do not allow me the freedom to do so. And if another entity tries to attack or invade your mind, you could use your own force of will to punish and even harm them.

Look out, Danner. Knowing that made her feel a little better now.

Naero had another insight. Could this work to help her control her Dark Beast? Or would it not, because the creepy thing was in fact a part of her already? How could you defend yourself against yourself?

Did that even make any sense?

Both Naero and Jia could sense Om's burning curiosity.

Yet how was this possible, Jia?. My access files from the KDM state that the G'lothc could not only tear souls out of others, but also feed on soul energies–even devour and destroy them.

Jia sighed very deeply. *That is true; the G'lothc wielded a very great and terrible power over those whose minds they conquered and overcame– but they did so first through fear or strong emotion. It is an inherently evil thing to destroy and nourish oneself on the souls and essences of others. Doing so stains, taints, and poisons the devourer, and twists their own existence for all time. Another reason, among many, why the voracious and opportunistic G'lothc had to be eliminated. Yet in the end, the cost of winning such a horrific war led both the Kexx and the Drians to question greatly, how much they themselves had been tainted and corrupted by the extent of such a long, terrible conflict.*

Naero put in: I know only a little about the Kexx, and I have only heard mention of their allies, the Drians. The Drians created the Driathans, did they not? And you are a Driathan, Jia. What, then, are the Drians to you? Something akin to gods?

For a moment Jia let her own guard down, just for an instant.

In that bright flash of insight, Naero and Om sensed the overwhelming grief, loss, and despair that all Driathans endured—even millions of years later—at their sundering from their beloved creators.

My kind can barely speak of what the Drians meant to us, Naero. To us—their beloved children—they were indeed part gods, part beloved parents, part guides and mentors. We adored them, for they would not let us worship them, nor would they let the destruction of their great war touch us. They did their best to protect us—for one of the things the G'lothc desired above all else was to take us over and control us. It was said that our fate was at the heart of the war—the very cause of it. And like any parent, the Drians fought with all their might and wisdom to protect their beloved children from being subjugated, tormented, and enslaved by such hideous and foul beings as the G'lothc—who corrupted and destroyed all that they touched.

Yet in the end, we all paid a great price for that conflict as well—even in victory.

With Jia's soul inside her, Naero was moved to great sadness, and felt herself weeping. Just the memory of such loss was an intense burden, and Jia and her people had felt the full force of such grief for a very long time.

At the Great Sundering—when the Drians said farewell and left us to stand upon our own—our sorrow at losing the shining light of their love and wisdom was nearly more than we could bear. All of this universe still mourns the loss of their light and knowledge, and their immense beauty and wisdom. The Driathans remain a pale reflection of the Drians, made in their radiant image to leave some fragment of them behind as a gift to all of Creation. We are but pale shadows of their inspiring awe and wonder.

Naero did not really have much of a concept of what a real god must be like, but she knew that her friend Tarim still worshipped one with great reverence. Some remnants of the Old Earth religions survived among the miners and others who were once downtrodden in various corners of the known systems. But just from sensing Jia's deep, heart-wracking emotions, Naero had a new insight into what having and believing in gods and creators had to be like.

She thought of the poor Thanes on Thanor-4 with renewed respect.

She felt great remorse and sorrow for Jia and her people. To have had such very real entities be an every day part of life—whom all had loved and adored—and then to lose them—nay, even worse, to suddenly be abandoned by them—had to be a very terrible ordeal indeed.

Within moments, Jia's strong emotions had Naero sobbing and weeping even harder.

Naero struggled to regain control over herself and wiped her eyes.

Hey. Jia. Om. I'm sorry I distracted us. We can talk ancient history and compare notes a lot later. Right now, we have a job to do. Let's get to it. Jia, do what you need to do and go where you need to go to find Baeven.

Jia agreed, and concentrated her force of will and her considerable psyonic abilities through both Naero and Om.

Within seconds, Jia in fact located Baeven somewhat, as if zeroing in on a part of herself that had been torn away from her and was missing.

And in that instant of relief and joy, Naero sensed the furious and passionate love and longing that existed between Jia and the mysterious outcast who called himself Baeven.

Jia was right. The two of them were one with each other in many intimate ways, which Naero could only in part sense, glimpse, and still feel slightly embarrassed about. Such feelings were far too strong–and intimate.

Somehow, Jia and Baeven were, in fact, two halves of the same actual coin. They had become one together.

He's alive, Naero, but he's growing weaker. I don't understand this. He's trapped within the actual Intel base somehow. He merged with it while trying to phaze through its walls to investigate. Some kind of strange feedback energy trapped him within those walls. He can't get out on his own, and if he doesn't, his physical form will eventually perish. We must get inside to free him.

Naero activated her gravwing, still in stealth mode.

Lead on, Jia. Take us to him. We'll get him out, somehow. But we can't allow ourselves to get trapped in the same way he did. Then we'll be stuck, too.

They approached the enemy base from within a series of ancient volcanic lava tubes and caves, some of them now submerged by dangerously contaminated mountain streams and aquifers that pooled and then ran off from within to the lower elevations below.

With her gravwing, Naero flitted above the toxic pools and past a few underground security check points guarded by heavily armored Ejjai and Dakkur troops, either in sealed armor or lab suits.

At last they reached a hidden landing and loading bay, filled with several factory and processing ships, humming along and working at full capacity production mode.

They passed further within several separate, sealed areas. Naero took a moment to have her fixer cloud decontaminate her, to help avoid detection.

Naero worried about what kind of lethal military grade agents their enemies could be producing in such vast quantities in this bio-weapons facility. And to what end?

Clearly their foes were preparing to wage a large scale biological war. Against Spacers? The Gigacorps? All of humanity?

Loaders and movers sent guards, teks, and researchers into and out of the main facility. Hundreds of Ejjai worked like fiends just within this one area. To Naero, it looked more like a hive of very determined, industrious insects.

Panels and doors opened and closed routinely, admitting and taking in the flowing traffic of more personnel.

Naero zipped into a big storage area or warehouse with plenty of maneuver room. She didn't want to bump into anyone. To be even safer, she hovered above and moved about up in the air, virtually invisible, but not quite immaterial.

She wasn't about to attempt to phaze through any of the strange walls yet.

Especially not after whatever had happened to Baeven.

They followed several section leaders around, trying to learn the layout of the facility, until they managed to secrete themselves into some kind of immense launching bay.

No starships, however. Just thousands more of those mobile launching tubes for some kind of missile, probe, or strike drone. Very similar to, but slightly more advanced than the enemy batteries they had located in that immense planetoid field.

Then Naero noted that there were in fact starships. These launchers were packed in cluster units, and were definitely mobile. They had AI's of their own, and could even jump and operate independently.

I'm registering that these dispersal drones can perform jump-7, Naero.

Equal to our best warships, Om. Not good.

Hundreds and thousands of these compact launcher vessels, with each launching tube in each cluster about the size of a normal person. Each delivery vessel bristled with almost a hundred such launch tubes.

The enemy was mass-producing these weapons and delivery systems on a daily basis.

Jia and Om spoke up at the same time.

This is a massive bio-weapons program, Jia observed.

Analysis: These drones will deliver replicating bio-toxins over a wide interstellar area, N. They are designed for planet-wide assaults—to destroy entire populations quickly with fast-acting biowar agents.

Even Naero was aghast at the scope of it all.

The enemy never did anything in a small way.

251

Om went on. *No mistake, Naero. Most of these devices are already filled with the actual toxins. Only a small percentage remain empty. Estimate project completion in less than one standard week.*

Jia joined in. *From scanning their navigation, I've learned that fleets of these droneships will be towed or transported in bulk ships to their launch areas under the cover of common mining and merchant vessels, already cleared and waiting for these false shipments. The coordinates and their dispersal patterns are already pre-programmed.*

What are their target destinations, Jia?

Mass attacks on every known populated world in the Gigacorps Sector. Based on these estimates, more than ninety-seven percent of the human race and other sentients could be wiped out within a few standard months. Spacers in a few months more.

Naero herself despised the Corps, who still clung to their empires of hundreds of systems.

Yet all of those countless, innocent people did not have a choice. Even the duped landers of the Gigacorps did not deserve to be slaughtered like this.

Jia gasped suddenly.

Baeven has finally sensed my presence. He's coming to meet us at that section of wall over there.

They floated over to the spot she indicated. Naero examined it.

I don't see anything, Jia.

He's here, Naero. He's trapped within the walls themselves, partially merged with their basic structure and the strange energy fields permeating this place–they are based on Darkforce energy. It's very difficult and exhausting for him to try to move around or emerge.

Before their eyes, transparent fingertips and then a transparent portion of Baeven's face struggled to push out from the wall, like a tormented phantom. He looked to be in pretty bad shape.

Bae! My beloved, Bae. Stay strong–reserve your strength. We'll find a way to separate you again.

The urgency in Jia's thoughts struck Naero with how deeply Jia cared for Baeven.

Meanwhile, Om focused all of his powers on trying to analyze the walls themselves. *These walls are incredibly strange, Naero. They were fused with advanced nano-vibronic particles that maintain an interior energized field at the particle level. This tainted field resists phazed, near-astral projected entities, and any object or person that is cloaked. It is specifically designed to block the passage of any such unknown particles or entities.*

The enemy has done their homework, Om. They were among the first to attempt to use phaze suits and phaze armor. They know that Spacer Intel captured and has been experimenting with such tek on their own for a long while. Some people with psyonic abilities can even phaze through normal barriers and materials. And Spacer Mystics or other psyonic users in astral form can penetrate any physical structure to spy on things visually. Baeven managed to do so for years. But at last, the enemy has developed a counter-barrier that resists such efforts, and even sets up a feedback trap for any such users. They'll get stuck inside and slowly perish.

What do you think, Om? It seems like we've come across something similar to this before, haven't we?

Yes, when we attempted to learn the secrets of The Dark Star's ion cannons. The walls came to life with tentacles similar to those of the Darkforce generators. They tried to draw us into the walls and absorb us physically. Many of the energy signatures and components are very similar. But this defense is more advanced in every way–passive, active, and subtle–in order to protect the enemy secrets here. And the personnel. They couldn't be under constant attack by the very walls themselves.

The enemy knows there's someone like Baeven around. I bet they fashioned this defense and this trap with him in mind. They know he's out there searching for them.

He is unique, Jia said. *There are no others like him, as all shall see one day.*

Copy that. Yet our current problem remains, Naero told them. How do we extract Baeven–alive–once he has been merged with such hi-tek materials as these?

Naero and Om used teknomancy to study the wall. Nothing.

Jia was just as stumped. *He will eventually perish if we don't find a way to extract him. In fact, he cannot survive in there for much longer– we're talking hours–a day or two at most.*

Om quickly noted, *And we're under the gun in other ways, as Spacers say. A full-scale biological war is about to be launched against all of humanity. It may take only several weeks or months to transport these dispersal drones from this site and get them all into optimal position.*

Perhaps even less, Om. What if the enemy uses their wormhole tek to gate them all into position? That would get them into place even faster.

But before they could tackle the coming biowar, they had to spring Baeven free from his current prison.

A sudden possibility occurred to her.

Om, what if we look at this like a replication problem?

Naero touched the walls and tested something.

I'm right. I know it. These walls aren't just tek–*they're alive*–living machines on a very basic level of raw cunning, bordering on sentience, yet still slaves to the will of their dark masters. Just like the Darkforce generators.

Jia and Om started following her train of thought.

Om hadn't experienced or explored such replication and absorbing methods as deeply as she had. She pieced together her concepts from several ranges of experience, including fighting the actual Darkforce generators. More from Om, Alala, and even Jia herself. Insights of combined biomancy and teknomancy origin flashed into her mind from all of her past experimentation.

And somehow, she was even pulling concepts out of the KDM.

Teknomancy concepts flowed into her mind faster than even she could follow, to the point of being painful.

See? The principles and theories are all parallel, if not completely transferable. I think we can do this. Follow my lead. I want to try something.

Naero fed them entire races of data even as she prepared herself.

I'm going to treat Baeven as replicant matter and energy, emerging from these vibronically energized walls. Jia, your link with him is the strongest. I'm going to use your intimate knowledge of him to draw him out and separate him from these living machine wall particles that are holding him.

And they're not just trapping him.

They're slowly absorbing and devouring him. That's just one of the reasons why he can't get out on his own.

Link with him, Jia. No matter what happens. Keep the link with him open, strong, and focused. You are his lifeline.

I will perish before I break it.

Naero felt the incredible force of Jia's mighty will. Who was Jia? What was she?

They began.

Naero placed her hands on the wall. Through Jia's intense link, she could sense precisely what was Baeven, and what wasn't.

And with that knowledge, she could separate them.

Speaking of intense, this was the first time she had a chance to really see Baeven for what he was. The readings…the energies on, around, and within him were all off any scale imaginable. If Jia was amazing–Baeven was beyond scary. Not just a monster–*a behemoth!* Baeven was a force of the Universe itself–a living, breathing, walking Power that could not be denied.

Naero felt the glacier-like chill crackle up her spine.

There were many parallels between herself and Baeven, as well.

Was this what people were afraid of when they looked deep into her?

Clearly, any other normal person or Spacer would have been slain and absorbed by these walls long ago—in a matter of minutes or hours. Baeven had withstood them and held them off—*for weeks*.

She used teknomancy to separate the wall particles and spread them back—like peeling off the layers of an onion—and biomancy to draw Baeven back out.

His hands emerged first.

Naero knitted her fingers with his and pulled.

His face emerged again, silently screaming in agony. It took all of her strength to keep him from pulverizing her hands.

We're hurting him terribly.

He can take it, Jia. And so can I.

Pain is better than death, Om added.

Naero kept pulling, using her abilities to separate his body from being fused within the wall.

But the process taxed her as well, nor did she possess unlimited flows of Cosmic energy. And she could not keep going and startap again at the same time. If she stopped, they would need to start all over.

Before Naero blacked out, she focused all of her strength and heaved backward, dizzy and drained.

He toppled out from the wall, his huge form flattening Naero's small weakened frame to the ground. Baeven was a huge guy, dense like duranadium. With him unconscious, his overwhelming deadweight crushed her to the floor.

32

Naero could feel Jia become so overwhelmed with emotion that she instinctively took charge of her own body in its exhausted stupor, and dragged herself out from underneath Baeven's bulk.

Jia regained control and rolled him over onto his back, and was about to cover his face with kisses.

Naero just barely recovered enough strength to restrain her.

Uh, Control to Jia. I get how you're feeling and all–I'm glad to see him, too–but he's still kind of…my uncle. It is going to get beyond creepy if you start swooching him and slip him the old mouth serpent–especially using my mouth. Please don't.

Jia laughed and pulled back, relinquishing control.

Of course. I'm sorry, Naero. You're so funny at times.

Yeah. That's me, all right. A laugh riot each and every minute.

Actually, Jia, she's not all that much fun sometimes.

Stuff a sock in it, Om. I'm on a roll here.

What in the world is a sock, N? And where would I stuff it if I had one?

I'll tell you exactly where, Om.

Oh, I see now. But I do not have either an oral or anal cavity.

That's been a problem all along, Om.

Baeven began to stir.

Then Naero took notice. Jia was healing him, using Naero's fading energies to replace and mend some of the cumulative damage and trauma Baeven had endured while being trapped in his merge with the machine particle walls.

Naero still felt woozy, and Jia's efforts weren't helping.

Naero. You must both startap and intake biomechanical fuel and lix.

She was already way ahead of him on the startapping front. After that, she tore open some concentrated food bars out of her belt pouches, and sucked on her armor's lix tube. The nutrient-rich rations and fluids rushed into her as she choked them down as quickly as she could.

Over several minutes, she wolfed down nearly three days' worth of rations and lix. All the while, Jia kept siphoning energies from her and transferring them directly to Baeven's body and bloodstream through biomancy.

This direct healing transfer is the only way, Naero. Even on a medbed, Baeven would not be able to eat for a day or two at best. This way, we can regenerate and revitalize his systems, and boost his own amazing abilities. But I think we just barely caught him in time. Even Baeven could not have regenerated himself on his own in such a weakened state as this.

Now he can, Jia?

Naero had to study that, and learn his advanced techniques if possible.

Yes. Just another of his amazing abilities. There, his own powers are kicking in now. He should be able to recover enough to complete the healing process, given time.

Baeven regained consciousness a few moments later.

"Naero? You came here alone? How did you figure out a way to get me out? I sure couldn't."

Naero rested a hand on his arm as he sat up, still staring and shaking his head. "It wasn't easy, Baeven. But I'm not alone. Jia's soul is in me, too; I borrowed her from your ship at her insistence. I couldn't have located you or done any of this without her help. Come on, we have to get you out of here."

"No, you don't understand. There's no time. Uh...still so weak. Just let me sit here for a while. I'm starving. Anything to eat or drink?"

Naero gave him the rest of her combat rations.

"Maybe you should take these slow."

257

"I'll have a stomach ache, but I can keep them down." Baeven inhaled them. She gave him all of her lix.

He doubled over with cramps suddenly and groaned, but he did not throw up. In fact, he seemed to grow stronger by the minute. Baeven was tougher than, and recovered faster than, anyone she had ever known.

He nodded at the drones assembled for launch all around them.

"I take it you've figured out what's going on here?"

Naero nodded.

"We have. Bio-weapons and lots of them. Enough to take out all of the tens of thousands of Gigacorps worlds–or at least their populations."

Baeven sagged and let out a long, ragged breath. "And Spacers, too. The enemy fast-action, bio-toxin plagues have been specifically designed to be incredibly lethal and virulent, Naero. To Spacers, humans, most near-humans, and all of the known species–everyone except the Ejjai, of course."

"All in one." Naero sneered. "Bastards."

"I agree. We can't let them get away with this, Naero."

"Don't worry, Baeven. They won't."

Om, the Kexx must have had some knowledge of this kind of advanced biological warfare back in their day. Come up with some way to counter this.

They did. I've been searching all this time for counteragents and neutralizers.

Jia added her information through Naero's voice so that Baeven could hear.

"The Drians fought this madness as well. While we freed Bae, our crews have analyzed the toxin samples we sent back to our ships with the spyfixers. Your friend Zhentisa is quite the genius when it comes to bio-medical and biowarfare research."

Zhen had gained lots of firsthand experience during the Annexation War with the enemy's Cosmicide devices. She had been directly involved in countering several similar agents–yet nothing as advanced as this.

Naero, Jia, and Om discussed the situation internally, and then informed Baeven about their preliminary plan after he had rested for a short while. It could not be avoided.

"We think we have the beginning of counter strategy," Naero said. "We'll leave a nebula of our spyfixers behind us, modified specifically to biomed mode. They'll replicate as needed and adjust or neutralize the toxins to our specifications–even the units that haven't been constructed or filled yet. They'll fuse themselves with every launcher and begin the counter-modification process."

"What do you mean by modification?" Baeven asked.

"Thanks to Zhen, we'll modify the toxins on a level that won't be detectable. We'll attempt to reverse the process, given enough time. If the fixers succeed, these agents will only take out Ejjai clones, and they won't harm humans, Spacers, or any of the other sentient or near-sentient races."

"But what's to stop these goons, or anyone else who gets their hands on this tek, from changing that back around, or sending out a totally new batch of whatever against our people, Naero?"

She shook her head, and Jia spoke through her. "We can't foresee or prevent every attack or threat, Bae. One thing at a time. But we should be able to use this opportunity to inoculate our populations and our worlds against these known agents, and any variations. And through that, any future Ejjai invasions at the same time. Once modified to our specs, these toxins will take out the Ejjai in seconds, if they ever come around again."

"Exactly," Naero added. "And now, thanks to the KDM, anyone who wants to try to counter us would have to be on the same level as the Kexx, to defeat all the safeguards and little tricks and traps that we're going to put in place with the modification. And there aren't too many advanced intellects like them floating around anymore."

"Okay, you've convinced me. I like it." Baeven struggled back up to his feet.

Naero frowned. Haisha. Why was everybody besides her so fricking tall? Even her own blood.

"When do we start?" Baeven said.

"Already in motion," Naero told him.

Right, Om? We are going forward as planned, correct?

Affirmative. As planned.

"Like I said, our modified spyfixers are implementing our counterstrategy even as we speak. All they need is time. Let's get you out of here."

Baeven smiled. "Excellent. Now that I'm free and feeling better, as long as we're here, why don't we just peek in on the enemy leaders and scoop some more intel? Perhaps we can figure out where they're coming from, or where the Dakkur and G'lothc ships are based?"

Naero fingered the shiny blue bracelet on her right wrist. Perhaps not the best time to awaken her little friend, Womi. The little guy could sleep for days.

"All right," Naero said. "I'm game. Just don't try to phaze through any more walls, Uncle. I don't know if we could extract you again."

Baeven grinned. "Don't worry. If you haven't noticed, in my line of work, I very seldom make the same mistake twice."

259

They passed through several security checkpoints like ghosts, following after, or floating past or over Ejjai and Dakkur.

The command post was deep within the facility's bowels. Surprisingly enough, the facility leader was neither an Ejjai or Dakkur–he was human or near-human, disguised in some kind of armor from head to foot.

Who was this mystery man…or woman? A renegade Triaxian high official? A Hevangian overlord? Someone from one of the other Corps?

"I am weary," he complained to his aides and guards. "I will retire to my private quarters for a short repose. Do not disturb me."

The other foes bowed obediently, and filed out quickly, even the Dakkur champion.

Naero and Baeven shuffled out of the way as they did so.

After lying down on his large, pop-up nanobed, the mystery man somehow deftly phazed his hand into his chest and pulled out a small black pulsating cube–ten millimeters square–and pressed one glowing side.

"Unless I'm either mistaken or completely insane, *that* is an advanced G'lothc primary emulator," Baeven said, obviously very intrigued. "In fact, it appears to be a meta-frequency, *interdimensional* emulator–based partially on stolen fragments of Drian and even Kexxian tek–an end product of the ancient war."

"I take it Intel doesn't have one of those?" Naero said.

"Nobody has one of those. Not even me. Jia and I have only heard tell about them…in theory, and in legend."

Om chimed in.

Both the Kexx and the Drians understood such advanced tek and made considerable use of very similar devices toward the end of their Great War.

"So, what? Now this jerk is going to sleep? That device must not do much if he's only using it to take a nap."

"Naero, I think he's doing far more than that."

Both of them could sense something going on.

Om. Use biomancy and teknomancy to modulate the parameters of our senses to operate on these strange dimensional wavelengths. Then we can really see what is happening.

Got it. Adjusting to this mode. Almost there…

"Just as I suspected," Baeven noted.

All of the colors in that room shifted to shimmering, transparent gleaming shades of smoky gray, silver, brown, and black. All other colors were reduced to muted pastels or completely washed out–but the contrasts were incredibly sharpened.

Some kind of three-dimensional, holographic shell of the mystery man appeared to be snoozing in his bed. It was, in fact, more than that. It had substance–but that one wasn't real. Naero guessed that if it were poked, it might even react and wake up, giving the actual, real-time entity a chance to re-merge with his shell–his decoy.

Any physical vidcams and recording tek security in the chamber would, however, be completely fooled.

The real enemy entity stood across the chamber in an open pocket dimension of some kind, opening a swirling vortex of Darkforce energy– not unlike a small galaxy or hurricane of dark Cosmic power–a meter or so above and before his upturned face mask.

The entity himself became smoky and transparent. Yet within him, something alien and amorphous writhed; tendrils and veins of Darkforce energy snaked and shifted through his body and up into his mind and back. Despite his outward, humanoid form, within, he was more like a weird jellyfish–an invertebrate man 'O' war of some malignant and sinister nature.

The very sight of it unnerved and frightened Naero beyond reason.

It made her feel sick just to watch this mad thing ooze and shiver.

Even worse, some kind of wyrm–a disgusting Darkforce parasite–hid within a small shielded egg, lurking and invisible within the Spacer's right lung.

Naero gasped. This person was a Spacer, and the enemy both controlled him and had implanted some kind of Darkforce parasite inside of him–in order to control him when it needed to, and much, much more.

Naero focused on the sickening parasite. It gave off very strange Darkforce readings.

It was a soul essence hiding within that wyrm.

And it was vile and destructive beyond belief.

"What in the burning fuck is that disgusting and horrifying thing?" Naero demanded. Just being near it creeped her out to no end.

Even Jia gasped. *No. Impossible. They were all slain...to the very last of their number.*

"It cannot be," Baeven said.

Kexxian data confirms it, Om informed them. *That...is a G'lothc spirit. Or more precisely–the lost and fallen soul and essence of a G'lothc– now in control of this person and an arsenal of deadly weapons.*

Even Baeven could not believe it. "How is this possible? How could their souls survive–millions of years after their demise?"

Jia broke in.

261

They...would need special places to linger in, perhaps another dimension, even. A universe where their immense, negative Darkforce energies could be sustained. Either that, or else they would need physical hosts–yet their energies would wear down any normal physical form very quickly and destroy it. Few hosts would last for very long against such power.

Naero though of something Danner once said–about having his mind put into other bodies and burning them out. This kind of possession, or whatever it was, must be something very similar. And a technique that was equally as vile and pernicious.

Jia was very afraid, and in great distress. Naero had never felt her react in such a way. She was nearly in a panic. *This thing–or spirit, or creature–whatever it is–must be destroyed, Bae. At all costs.*

Agreed. Om noted. *The threat is far too immense. Yet it stands to reason: If there is one of these abominations...will there not be others?*

"Let's watch and listen first," Baeven said. "It's preparing to communicate somehow–perhaps with others of its kind. We might learn something very important here."

"It can't see or hear us, can it?" Naero asked Jia.

I don't think so. Our cloaking devices are astral phazing units in nature, theory, and application. A completely different tek. We're modulating to be able to spy in on his interdimensional sub-reality, but I think we're still undetectable within our own.

Naero hoped Baeven was right. To their horror, the vortex opened, and a flurry of G'lothc spirits, raving and writhing, tried to boil out of the open portal.

Yet some kind of barrier or power held them back and prevented them from flooding out.

Their harsh, rasping voices boomed psyonically, almost causing pain.

"Has the time of our great deliverance arrived? Is it now at hand?"

"Patience, siblings. We must be patient yet a while longer. All is nearly ready. We will set these inferior beings of this galaxy to lay waste to one another. After all sides have been sufficiently weakened, then our deliverance shall come at last."

The barely restrained Darkforce entities shrieked and convulsed in furious, all-consuming lust and rage. Naero could sense it.

So could Naero's Dark Beast–just as hungry for power and destruction as these terrible things were.

As if they all sang different verses of the same horrific song of dark desire. Such was the lure of the Darkforce, which yearned only for oblivion and desolation.

"So easy for you to say," the disembodied, lost souls howled. "We cannot endure our torment any longer. We demand to be free. Now. Provide us with hosts to enslave to our will!"

"You know full well that we cannot–not yet. Our hosting process still has not been perfected. Once the wyrms are set free, the host bodies deteriorate far too rapidly. They decay and become useless after a only few days or weeks."

"Do something. Make them–force them to last longer. Use more power!"

"Don't eradicate all of the vermin, siblings. We shall have need of their bodies as our veils–our vessels to contain us–once the hosting process is perfected. Continue to pursue and increase the extent of our experiments."

"Not to worry; yet the breakthrough we seek still eludes us. Countless slaves from this entire galaxy perish each day in our secret labs, as will countless more until the exact solution is found. We shall always keep the strongest and the best hosts for ourselves–for our purposes."

"As always. And the remnants as breeding populations–cattle to feed our clone hordes, as well as our, needs and demands. Our colonies in this galaxy still remain vulnerable. We must continue to grow in power and strength."

"We shall enslave them all in good time. These vermin who manage to trouble us and set back our plans in this quadrant shall fall to our dominion very soon. They are ignorant of us, for none of any true worth or might shall rise up to oppose us before all is too late."

"As for other matters, have we tracked down the Yattai or the others of the hunted?"

Shalaen, Naero gasped silently. Shalaen was of the Yattai.

"We grow closer to all of our goals. But like the Oden, the Yattai are even more wary and elusive. Yet we shall bring them all to heel, under the weight of our power, and grind them to our purpose."

"Have we located and captured the Driathan, so that we might break him yet?"

What? Jia exclaimed.

"We are closing in on him with each day. He is out there. It is only a matter of time before we pinpoint his secret location. He will be a formidable foe, but soon we shall capture and crush him. Then at last, the great goal shall begin to be achieved at last, and all of his secrets and the mysteries of his kind shall be ours to seize, to study, to do with as we will."

Bae, do you hear that? Jia said. *They're close to finding and capturing one of my people. One of my guardians, somewhere out there. We must find and rescue him first–before they can reach him–before it is all too late. If the G'lothc learn the secrets of my people–if they should locate and seize the hidden sanctuary–they will have the power they have always craved. This time, they shall make themselves unstoppable and immortal. This time, they will become invincible. The Kexx and the Drians are gone. No one will be able to defeat them!*

"I agree with you, Jia. But first we must finish our work here, my heart. All of these machinations are part of their dark design for this galaxy."

The creatures continued to chortle, gloat, and plot together. "Who gets the Driathan's precious body after we shred its soul and feed upon its energies and secrets?"

"By our rights, Admiral Korleth-Tulkas claims the indestructible body and will make it his very own. This victory shall be his. His claim and his place is first in line to receive such a boon."

Thousands of voices begged and demanded the same prize instead, arguing and laying out their claims, moaning and screaming their futile protests.

"Patience, siblings. Soon we shall have our choice of mighty hosts and vessels to pick and choose from. Then we alone shall control the Power Cosmic. And no filthy spack conjurers nor any of these upstart races or beings shall ever gain the power to oppose us once we perfect our goals and roam free. Countless galaxies shall fall once more to our dominion."

"Our triumphs made all the sweeter because we shall master the cherished spawn of our great foes from of long ago. Those who dared to defeat us in the past."

"All past insults shall be avenged. Proceed on all fronts and on all schedules with Admiral Korleth-Tulkas and our other spawn: *The Servants of the Cosmic Wyrm*. This relay portal will be closing now, and we shall be cut off from you all once again–until the galactic portals are opened for the final, grand invasions."

"Very well. Only for a little while. Then we shall all be unleashed full force, free to devour and subjugate all of existence at will. All things move in the inevitable direction of our ultimate favor and triumph! We shall feast upon them all!"

The vortex gate winked out without warning.

Then a glowing whorl of shadow, shot with scarlet lighting, appeared out of nowhere, about a meter in diameter in the other portal's place.

The enemy Thing appeared surprised.

An amorphous voice spoke through the whorl.

"Beware, Ullogk–"

"Korleth? Why do you waste the precious Darkforce? What could be so urgent?"

"Through you and the others, I sensed something amiss during the great summoning that we all just held together. With my new growing Cosmic abilities and awareness, I sensed a grave threat to us. At first I could not make it out, but now I have pinpointed it in my expanding senses for a moment. One of our ancient enemies spies upon us–upon you yourself–right where you are. I sense the fleeting soul essence of a very powerful Driathan. Perhaps even one of the High Ones. It is there among you, Ullogk, hiding within a pocket existence very close to you. Who knows how much it has already heard and witnessed?"

"Impossible, Korleth. Driathans are tek-based. They cannot project themselves or their soul essences, into the Astral Plane or any other. They are not capable of such feats. How and why would they ever leave their immortal bodies behind? It makes no sense."

"They might risk doing so, if they could find a way to spy upon us. Hear me and obey, Ullogk. I do not know how this is possible, but such has been done and the Driathan entity is there somehow. My enhanced Cosmic abilities confirm it. We have learned new tricks; perhaps they have, also."

"How do I locate and destroy it if it is spying on me? It could be listening to us right now. We can't be sure."

"Focus all your abilities into a psyonic neural detonation pulse."

"So be it. If I can capture its soul essence, it may lead us back to its precious, immortal body. I must pursue this. Even if I am destroyed in this form, Korleth, that is of no consequence…all here has been set into motion, and shall go forward, even without me. All of us must continue to proceed exactly as has been planned."

"Shield yourself as best you may and attack. Learn what you can about this development. If our foes can spy upon us with such ease, we must take further precautions. To our eternal victory, then."

The Darkforce, instant-communication whorl collapsed and vanished.

Om, don't worry about me. Expect a heavy Cosmic or psyonic attack of some kind. Shield Jia's essence as much as you possibly can.

Doing so now, N.

Naero put up all of her own defenses. Baeven and Jia did the same.

They did not have long to wait. What seemed like a deafening shockwave of gray, Darkforce-fed, pulsing psyonics sliced through all of their minds.

Everyone screamed, as if their minds, their very souls were being shredded and immolated.

265

Naero came to, gasping, on the floor, still cloaked, but struggling for breath and sanity.

It wasn't every day that she felt her mind being minced up and scorched to cinders.

Warning, Naero. That massive Cosmic psyonic attack was not set for us, but targeted specifically at intricate Driathan neural patterns. Even with our shields, Jia took the brunt of that attack. She's dying. And when her soul dies, all that she is will perish.

Naero looked around in panic.

"Baeven? We've got a major problem."

She stepped back.

Baeven was not himself.

Definitely not himself.

His eyes blazed with bloodred light. His form swelled up even larger, black-black, deep jet like unlight itself. And the red light of rage snarled out from deep within him, causing even his teeth to glow with the same destroying, Darkforce energy.

Coils of darkness like lashing whips or tentacles snaked out around him, as he transformed into an energy being and fell upon the Ullogk-Thing.

Every part of Baeven suddenly bristled with razor-sharp, energized green disruptor blades.

This was definitely a terrifying side of her uncle that she had never witnessed before.

This was his own Dark Beast as the monster began to fully emerge.

Just like herself, and perhaps even Jan and Dan.

Did they all have a Dark Beast within them?

Why didn't everyone?

The damaged G'lothc spirit coiled within its astral form like some evil jellyfish, poisoning an egg from within, snarling and cackling as Baeven's multi-bladed hands tore into it, ripping and scything into the evil thing lurking within.

Ullogk laughed even more.

"So, another filthy spack vermin who has dabbled in the Power Cosmic? We shall deal with your kind soon enough, upstart. Go ahead and slay this form. Do what you will. It is too late. Both myself and your Driathan whore are already doomed."

Now it was Baeven who began to laugh, as one gone mad. He grappled with the vile thing and hammered it to the ground, smashing and mutilating it.

"You're not going to die, you filthy, wretched thing. I know how to deal with your kind, scum. Slay you? Don't make me laugh. If she dies, you're only going to *wish* that I had killed you."

Baeven's blades–his entire body covered with them–flashed and sliced in blinding motions.

Naero could hardly believe it.

Baeven tore the G'lothc spirit out of its host's dissolving astral form, and somehow, he either absorbed or consumed it.

Within himself.

Then, even more terrifying, Naero thought that she could detect the faint psyonic screams of the G'lothc–as Baeven tormented and tortured it unmercifully within the fierce depths of his own indomitable mind.

Baeven unleashed and enraged could be a pretty terrifying force of nature to witness.

Meanwhile, Om struggled to save Jia somehow.

Naero. I don't know how to heal a dying Driathan astral form–a soul essence. The complex structure of her mind is nothing like ours. I don't know what to do to fend off this level of attack. Help me.

Om's urgency brought her back to one of their other, current predicaments.

Jia was still nurtured within Naero's own mind and soul essence that she shared with her, and yet Jia still faded and continued to wither and perish. Her great force of will and strength of power, Jia's very essence had been severely damaged and failed so rapidly, despite Om's best efforts to bolster her in every way.

What had the G'lothc done to them all? Some kind of psyonic and Cosmic attack and soul-poisoning, all rolled up in one.

Very scary, that such things could even exist.

Jia. Save Jia. Just as something else continued to go very wrong with Baeven. As Jia faded, he seemed to lose control more and more.

He once said that Jia joining with him had saved him from his own self-destruction. Possibly from his own Cosmic disease from the ancient artifact that he encountered?

Yet now, with Jia dying, Baeven was losing control of himself all over again. His Dark Beast continued to struggle to break free.

Bae...no, my beloved...do not give in to the Darkforce. Whatever happens to me...find a way to help him, Naero. He struggles with the same affliction to the Power Cosmic as you. He must retain control. I can't help calm him any longer. I am so weak.

Her instincts had been correct.

Naero, the attack was, in fact, some kind of actual psyonic poison. We must isolate and neutralize it.

How, Om? I can barely detect it. How in the hell do we do counteract something like this?

Concentrate with me, Naero. I will show you.

Naero closed her eyes. With Om's guidance, she saw Jia's soul, again like a small shining star or will-o'-the wisp. But it was as if an amoeba of shifting darkness attacked and tore away at Jia's soul essence, trying to absorb and destroy it, all the while feeding on its energies and growing stronger, while Jia grew weaker.

This was a Darkforce psyonic poison, virulent, active, and malignant.

Naero recognized that shifting darkness almost instantly–a psyonic, astral form of Darkforce. The devouring thing from her nightmares. Did it exist on every level or reality? Was there no escape from it forceful devastation?

Initial analysis complete. This is a psyonic form of negative energy Darkforce venom. Expel Jia's soul, but keep it contained within an astral shield sphere. Then incinerate the psyonic Darkforce poison attacking her Burn it away before it destroys her.

With what, Om? The Darkforce is almost invulnerable to direct attack. It instinctively absorbs and takes over other forms of energy.

I thought you discovered a way to either balance or cancel it out?

Only in part. It's not perfect.

Yes, the combined positive force of the Harmony and the Lifespark– the Cosmic polar opposite of the Darkforce

Naero pictured her efforts in her imagination in order to shape them.

Jia was still in her mind. All of this was taking place in her mind.

Her mind.

Naero remembered something both Jia and Baeven had told her.

In your mind–you are god. Your imagination and your force of will is absolute. You control everything. Anything there, is at your mercy.

The energies sparked and spluttered in her hands at first, but after several attempts, at last she drew Jia's soul out of her open mouth, just as she pictured it.

She could see that Jia was still under assault by the hideous, Darkforce poison, designed specifically to obliterate her kind.

Jia's soul tried to escape, but Naero's protective Cosmic sphere contained it.

Actually, it was *exactly* like the glowing soul orbs she had witnessed after the Tua burials back on Janosha.

Were all souls the same?

No time. Use the Lifespark.

Bright flashes of harmless, harmonious Cosmic energy blasted the shadowy amoeba within, burning it away from Jia's soul, which fortunately did not seem to sustain any permanent harm.

In fact, the harmonious energy healed and regenerated several slight burns on Naero's hands.

Naero was the absolute master of her own mind.

Very good, Naero. She's stopped dying at least. Now, implant Jia's soul within Baeven, in order to renew their special, symbiotic link and re-stabilize his...unique condition.

Naero rushed over and shoved Jia's essence into Baeven's bizarre and dangerous new shifting form while he still wrestled with Ullogk.

He whirled and raised one of his bladed hands to lash out at her.

No, Bae. Stop! She is your blood, the daughter of your beloved sister. You will not harm her!

Baeven hesitated and strained at the last second, shuddering where he stood. He blinked, his eyes shifting back and forth from red flame and their normal, dark, steel-gray color.

He staggered back upon his heels and shook himself, shrinking back down to his normal form.

Jia and he were one again.

33

Baeven pitched forward onto his face.

Naero rushed forward and barely caught him.

He and Jia were both drained and barely conscious.

Naero even sensed the trapped spirit of the G'lothc called Ullogk. It cowered in the recesses of Baeven's mind, torn to shreds and barely existing. The thing was terrified, and frozen in stunned stasis, blind and dumb, stripped of nearly all its senses and energies.

Baeven had nearly destroyed it, yet it still clung to its un-life—just barely.

They'd definitely need to figure out what to do with that vile thing later, once Baeven and Jia fully recovered.

Naero barely had the strength to haul Baeven out of the facility, but his huge size also made doing so awkward for her small frame.

She didn't want to risk trying to either startap or transport in her own weakened state. No exploding, please.

Finally, once they were clear of the facility, there was still the contamination all around the area to guard against. She shielded Baeven and used some of their spyfixers to teknomance a cloaked and shielded medbed. Then she used that to tow Baeven back to the ship with her gravwing.

Baeven and Jia were barely coming to outside of the hidden Intel base by the time they reached their ships. Their cloaked crews stood guard on their perimeter

Warning. Massive enemy assault preparing to strike this area in less than two standard minutes.

Naero called over her com to their ships and the guards outside.

"Bring it in people. Prepare to launch. We need to bug out of here."

She thought of the words the G'lothc entities had exchanged.

Ty called back. "What's up, N?"

"We've got what we came for. I'm guessing that several Ejjai strike forces are going to pulverize this area any minute."

The enemy would eventually discover that their secrets on this world had been compromised. But to what degree, they still would not know.

She strode forward a few more steps before the poisoned ground itself, back around the base, erupted and opened up.

Wave upon wave of thousands upon thousands of jump drones shot into the sky and beyond, leaving the planet in sheets of launching fire.

Naero gasped.

A massive assault on humanity and all sentient life had just been launched.

Even at jump-7, the bio-weapon drones would take many weeks and possibly months to reach their coordinated targeting positions among the Corps, the Alliance, and the Spacer Extents. But eventually, they would take up their coordinated positions and launch their lethal payloads

The Spacer spyfixers were now part of them. The question remained: Would the fixers be able to complete their vital mission? Only time would tell.

Either way, there now existed no other way of preventing the attacks from taking place.

Their only hope was to neutralize and or modifying the fast-acting alien bio-toxins, waiting to be dispensed on board.

A blazing green sphere like a comet zipped down through the atmosphere and hovered just above the ground, opposite their combined starships.

Danjen and S'krin rushed up to Naero, armed for battle but looking very worried.

"It's him." Danjen said. "The new Mystic Enforcer. I don't know how he's tracked us down, but he's here."

271

He's come after us, Naero.

I know that, Om.

"From everything that we've heard–Baeven's the only one who could possibly stand up to him," S'krin added, looking over at Baeven lying on the medbed. "And he sure isn't in any condition now for that kind of fight."

"Split the ships up. Load him and Jia in and get away. We'll signal you and meet back up at one of the rendezvous points."

Danjen's eyes widened. "Naero. You can't face this guy. We can't let him near Baeven or you."

"Now that he has that damn sword, even Gaviok and Baeven couldn't take him down," S'krin said. "He's indestructible. The best they might be able to do is fight the Enforcer to a draw."

"The Mystics still have a standing order to capture or kill Baeven," Danjen said.

"I'll slow him down, at least," Naero told her friends. "You guys get away. I want to have little talk with the Enforcer, and then we'll bug out afterwards."

Danjen stared at S'krin for a moment. They both broke and fled back toward *The Star Fox*, with Baeven and Jia in tow.

The bright green sphere shrank down and then dissolved, leaving a tall, powerful-looking, green-skinned warrior standing on the ground. He rippled with athletic muscle, his chiseled face set. Stern golden eyes. Long, flowing golden hair.

A radiant sword slung over one shoulder.

Khai towered over Naero as he strode toward her–like a fierce, angry, green god of vengeance.

He kept his arms moving easily at his sides, and merely glared at her.

Naero grinned her best, characteristic half-smile, and placed her hands on her slender hips defiantly.

"Good to finally meet you in person, Khai. I still need to thank you for the friendship we shared, back while I was on Janosha."

Khai nodded stoically. Naero took in a breath. He was definitely an impressive specimen. Tall, of course–about 1.98 meters. Almost the same height as Baeven.

"I thank you for yours, as well, Naero. I would not be here today without the assistance and insight you gave me, and your camaraderie. Yet, unfortunately, that is all behind us, now."

Khai's face remained impassive.

"Before we do this, tell me one thing, Khai. What happened? I tried reaching you for months–every night. I missed you. I was worried about you. What the heck happened?"

Khai did look away slightly at that. "My apologies for that, Naero. It was but a stupid accident on my part. While recovering from some injuries at one point, I broke my mind crystal–crushed it to dust and fragments. The Oden create and grow them out of the same master crystals. Once one of the mind crystals is broken, the link cannot be reformed. I greatly regretted that as well."

"Oh...okay."

He looked at her sternly. "Come. Enough chatter. You know very well why I am here. Why the Mystics watched the Astral Plane and traced you through it, and sent me here in direct pursuit. My business is with you this day." He fixed his eyes solely upon her.

Naero lifted her head high and steeled herself. "Say what you have come to say to me, then."

"Very well. High Adept Naero Amashin Maeris, of Clan Maeris. For your crimes against the Spacer Mystics, you are to be brought to justice to stand trial and judgment for the crime of murder–the murder of a High Master. Please come along quietly, with what honor you have left, and face the fate you have brought down upon yourself. From our past association, I bear you no ill will. I have no wish to harm you, so I warn you: do not attempt to resist."

Naero struggled to grin weakly. "And if I do...what then, big guy?"

Khai spoke plainly, showing no emotion or reaction.

"Then I shall use force to return you to justice. Naero, I warn you again. Do not provoke my hand. You will regret it."

Naero chuckled. "What...you're gonna beat up on a poor little helpless girl like me?"

"You are far from helpless, Naero. Just like your outcast uncle, you disobeyed your superiors and absorbed part of an impossibly dangerous alien artifact. Then you used the powers you gained from it to murder a High Master. And you admitted to already being unstable and dangerous even before all of that."

Naero lost her composure for moment and looked down in shame.

"I–I didn't mean to, Khai. You need to understand that. Vane was trying to destroy me. I acted instinctively, only trying to defend myself. I did not mean to kill him. I merely reflected his own attack back at him. I didn't want that to happen. He left me no choice. All of the High Masters knew that I couldn't control my abilities yet."

273

"All the more reason to return. You were thought to be very honorable once, Naero. Return with me now, and prove it to be so. Face justice for your actions. Nor do all hold Master Vane blameless in this affair. Yet the life of a High Master was taken–by you–a very grave crime that must be answered for. Return with me and make your defense; your case is not beyond hope."

"I can't, Khai. I can't go back right now. I have pending threats from our enemies to pursue that will not wait."

Naero plucked a spyfixer out of the air and tossed it to Khai, who deftly caught it.

"Relay the data in that spyfixer to Intel and the Mystics. The proof of what I say is contained therein. Renegade or not, I still pursue the foes of our people. There are grave new enemy threats out there and on this world and others, that we're only just learning about. I can't go back with you, Khai. Not now, not yet."

Khai sighed heavily and looked down. "That is not your choice to make. I regret this, Naero. You are forcing my hand against you."

She chuckled a little. "So, what are you going to do, Khai? Kill me right here in cold blood?"

He shuddered slightly. "Only if I must. You are wanted to face justice. I am the Mystic Enforcer. All use of force–including and up to lethal force–in apprehending you has been granted."

Several ion cannon attacks from *The Dark Star* struck Khai all at once, driving him back.

Naero's people poured direct fire at him with the ion guns.

"Don't kill him!" Naero shrieked.

She could not be the cause of another Mystic's death–not even to save herself.

Tarim shouted over their open link. "Don't worry about that, N. We've hit him with everything we've got. Nothing's touching him!"

It was true. Khai regained his feet, his green shield around him once more. He walked through their intense barrage as if it were but wind. Beams and blasts glanced off of him.

Haisha! He's even immune to the ion cannons, Om!

Enemy assault units converging on us as well, Naero.

The Dark Star kept up its intense fire, all to no effect.

"Retreat!" Naero shouted.

They fell back out of range just as an Ejjai battle group swept in, blasting the entire area, backed up by a Dakkur hunter-killer unit.

Dust and smoke quickly obscured the scene of the erupting battle.

"What's happening in there, Om?

Then she felt it. An intense Cosmic energy spike–like a pillar of Cosmic flame–a beacon.

He has drawn that sword of his, Naero. Astonishing...he's moving swiftly among them. Khai's slaughtering them each second.

Even from a distance, obscured by the haze of battle, Naero detected the cries of the dying, the energies being unleashed, and the multiple explosions of warships and vehicles.

A slaughter took place.

Khai took on an entire army and annihilated it–in a matter of seconds.

Naero had not heard the Dakkur shriek like that since the time she saw Baeven and Gaviok fall upon them.

The Ejjai battle group has been completely wiped out, Naero. The Dakkur attempted to flee. All of them have been crushed or blasted to death. Khai just beheaded the last Dakkur champion.

In the flash of an instant, Khai's verdant, protective sphere shot over to where they were and faded. Khai emerged, stalking slowly toward Naero, his glowing sword in his right hand–warping the very air and every field and flow around him.

Yii, one of the fabled Cosmic Swords of the Spacer Mystics, forged in the heart of a hyper-dense, massive star. It was fashioned from a great quantity of equally hyper-dense Ur-metal. Its powers? Nearly limitless, as it just demonstrated.

"So, Naero," Khai remarked "you have not lost all of your honor, I see. You still choose to face me alone, so that no others of your crew are needlessly injured, or worse. Quite admirable; even brave–but futile."

Naero bowed. "I retain all of my honor. And I thank you, Khai, for not taking their lives outright. I know that you could. Their allegiance and great friendship is mine; they would gladly give their lives for me. But I will not let them do so needlessly."

"My business is not with them. You were correct to restrain them, Naero. You just witnessed a small demonstration of what I am capable of. They are no match for me. I am fully in control of all of my abilities. I neither kill nor destroy by accident or instinct, or without cause or reason. Your friends are not at fault here, Naero Maeris. You are."

He paused and took a single breath.

"Surrender, Naero. It is over. You are no match for me, either."

Naero smiled. "We shall see."

She charged him, circling for an opening.

He moved his feet effortlessly. The superb footwork of a master swordsman.

When she attacked, his defense–every move–was perfect.

Khai was a consummate master with his blade.

He sliced her energy cutlass out of her hand and disrupted it.

She knew he would. That gave her time to get in closer, using all of her advanced speed.

Naero plunged her energized battle blade at his chest, with all of her weight and strength.

She would not kill him, but she fully intended to wound him badly enough so that he could not fight, or follow her for a long while.

The unbreakable metal splintered and shattered against Khai's breast as if her battle blade were ice.

Naero blinked and staggered back from him, her hands and forearms stinging and partially numb.

Impossible. Khai wore no armor—barely a nanotunic down to his knees and high boots.

Khai was invulnerable? How was he shielded?

His spinkick swept at her so blinding fast, and hit with such raw power, that he knocked her off her feet and flung her away. Naero barely caught herself and flipped back up to a crouching fighting stance.

Once again, her experience sparring with Baeven had saved her.

No one but Baeven and Danner had ever struck her with such force.

Not Gaviok—not even Master Vane.

Khai was clearly in their league. Perhaps even beyond it in some ways. Nothing seemed to touch him. He was unstoppable.

Naero needed to play for time.

Just a little longer.

They circled each other.

"You're stalling, Naero. I won't let your friends scoop you up as you are planning. I'll disable their ship on this enemy world, if I must. Then they won't be able to get away. You will doom them and you will still end up my prisoner."

She drifted back with her gravwing.

He floated up into the air at will and came at her without effort.

Naero tried taunting him. "Hah, you're a lot of big talk, Khai—as long as you have that crazy sword of yours. Is that the source of your powers? Your focus for your Cosmic abilities? Is that what makes you so indestructible? What are you without it?"

Khai casually flung his sword into the ground, where the long gleaming blade buried itself effortlessly up to the hilt.

"My sword Yii is without equal—yet it is only part of me—not a crutch. We are one, and our powers are as one."

Naero paused and touched down again, resuming her fighting stance.

276

Now at least, he fought on her level.

She hoped.

"Sword or no," he told her. "I have never met my equal in single combat."

Naero knew that to be true. They clashed. He struck her twice and nearly winded her. Superb technique. Fast and powerful. Baeven could not have done better.

She feinted and then surprised him with a blinding fast flipkick of her own, knocking him off his feet.

Khai flipped over and came up to a similar fighting stance.

Naero shook her hair and grinned. "Nor have I," she told him. "But I suppose there is a first time for everything."

Khai smiled. "I think not."

They circled some more.

Naero led him away, always retreating.

"You can't run forever, Naero. I can track you now. Even if you manage to get away for a time, I can find you...anywhere."

Khai closed with her, impossibly fast–speed to rival her own.

He blasted her with a single, massive punch that almost knocked her out. Her face, mouth, and nose bled.

Khai nearly took her down with one blow.

She staggered and fell back again, startapping and regenerating.

Right into the heavy defensive batteries of the secret alien base perimeter.

Naero dodged, as their enemy's weapons cut loose. They batted Khai around for a few seconds. Their barrage just barely missed her as she cloaked and transported.

Khai summoned Yii to his hand, and the destruction began.

Three more enemy battle groups swept in to join the attack. Khai would make short work of them, and he would destroy the enemy base, but doing so would still delay him.

In the resulting confusion, Naero transported and slipped on board *The Dark Star*. She immediately ordered Ty and Alala to get them all well away from that place.

34

For days they swung around, retreating back through the Gigacorps' Unknown Regions. They evaded and changed course multiple times.

Finally, after leaving behind a dizzying campaign of numerous false trails and clues to confuse any pursuit, they made their rendezvous with Baeven, Jia, and the crew of *The Shadow Fox.*

Baeven's ship was still faster, and would tow them the rest of the way back toward Corps Space proper, while Ty conducted some further experiments on the new leap drive tek they were stymied with.

Jia's soul re-merged with her ship at some point. Yet Baeven was still recovering from his ordeal. He finally revealed just how close to death he had been.

Naero understood now that it was his link to Jia that helped him maintain control of himself and his sanity. For him, Jia's love for him and their link was a calming, stabilizing force.

Jia was Baeven's harmony—the positive energy in his life—that kept his own Darkforce demon at bay.

It frightened Naero what her uncle might become without such a positive force in his life. Just as she terrified herself with her own fears, of Dark Beasts, and lethal Cosmic diseases.

Naero knew that she must find, for or within herself, such a stabilizing force of her own to heal and sustain her. Otherwise, all of her Cosmic powers would eventually conspire to destroy her—one way or another.

And if she faced these problems at some point, she still feared what might become of her siblings, Jan and Dan.

But first, before she could save anyone else, she had to save herself. Naero had some recovering of her own to accomplish.

As soon as there was time, she would take counsel with Baeven and Jia, and try to decide what their next course of action should be. Could Khai really track her now, as he claimed? If so, how? He let slip that the Mystics had tracked her through the Astral Plane somehow.

So much to learn and do.

She needed to speak with Womi as well, and find a way to heal him further. The Kahn-Dar were experts at traveling through various dimensions. Perhaps he could advise her and instruct her further on how to manage exposure to the Astral Plane and any others. How to avoid detection.

"Zoa," Jia said, when they sat down to make plans. "That should be our next destination. It is the nearest possible Driathan Sentry world—my world. Yet the enemy is searching much further out into the unknown. From what they said, they were closing in on another of my people. We can't know which one."

"But they have not found it yet," Baeven noted. "If they had, the Driathan alarm beacons would have sounded. The enemy could be lying, or simply mistaken. We cannot panic and lead them straight to you all by rushing around in haste. That will only make things worse, Jia, and put your people even more at risk."

Naero had so many questions of her own. They spoke freely of things she had so little knowledge of. "Guys, I think the G'lothc spirit called Korleth-Tulkas mentioned something about the imminent capture of another Driathan, like Jia."

"Naero," Baeven said, "you need to know: Jia is not just another Driathan...she is *The* Driathan. More than a leader. Jia is...sacred to her people, in many ways that cannot be described or easily put into words."

"Baeven, how many Driathans did the Drians create, and where are they? Why must they all hide or sleep, or whatever it is that they are doing? The enemy seems to want them more than anything else. If they were the cause of the Great War, what did the enemy want with them?

Korleth spoke of capturing and torturing, taking them apart somehow to learn their many secrets. What secrets? What could such a captive reveal to the enemy?"

"Too much," Jia said. "The secrets of the Drians are contained within each of us, just as mighty as those of the KDM within you. The Drians and the Kexx were very different, but in spirit, they were like brothers and sisters. Both advanced races controlled and protected many secrets. Advanced tek were just part of them. Their knowledge and wisdom were their greatest achievements."

Naero paused a moment. "The enemy wants something specific from the Driathans."

"The enemy desires all things. But my people are very strong. Our miraculous android bodies are the pinnacle of artificial life and creation– virtually indestructible. We could resist such efforts to torment and break us for a very long time. Yet in the end, the G'lothc were the peerless masters of the Darkforce, and of pain and destruction. No doubt they would be able to devise a way to break even the Driathans, to destroy our minds and souls, and take over our bodies for their own purposes once and for all."

"Is that their primary goal, then?" Zhen asked. "To conquer and take over the Driathans to make use of their immortal bodies?"

"That indeed would be a major victory for them. But the goals of the G'lothc and their allies have always been numerous and complex. They made mention that their attempts to take over and possess the minds and bodies of other sentients have fallen far short of their expectations. Under their control, their hosts burn out and break down after a short time and become unreliable. The Darkforce destroys all that it touches. Yet they still continue to conduct such foul experiments, on a wide scale, from their own words."

Naero shuddered to think of that.

"That's only one reason they want the Driathans, then, Jia? To use their bodies as indestructible, undying hosts for their dark and vile spirits?" But I sensed it–they instinctively hate all other sentients and see them as their foes–their prey. And they are actively seeking to capture, enslave, or destroy any of the remaining advanced races: they specifically mentioned the Yattai, the Oden, and our Mystics. They tried to capture all three of the Mystic High Masters. All are at risk."

"Khai is half-Oden and half-Spacer, from Clan Williams," Baeven said flatly. "He is a formidable foe. The Champion of the Oden, wielder of the Cosmic Blade Yii. He shall come to be known as the Great Swordmaster, an important part of the Cosmic Prophecies. I never put much stock in them, but the first Cosmic Sword of legends actually exists now. That much cannot be denied."

"Baeven, I've heard mention of such things–as if they were fairy tales, but I don't have any idea what most of that means."

"First, a little history, Naero." Baeven smiled and stared straight up, still resting and recovering on his nanobed

"The High Mystics sent Nerrek, Khai's father after me before he disappeared. He was the Enforcer back then. Nerrek and I clashed and fought each other to a draw several times, until the Mystics realized that if they kept after me, all they'd accomplish would be to drive me into becoming the very monster they feared. Vane still ranted that I would become one of those anyway–the fabled Great Destroyers that they always mutter about in the same breath with the Cosmic Prophecies. Mystics everywhere are said to be obsessed with all of these dusty old Cosmic legends–legends older than even the Kexx and the Drians."

Naero rested her chin on her hand and placed her other hand under her elbow as she paced. "I knew Khai before. I knew he was an Oden, or least half Oden. What are they, in fact? I keep hearing about them, but I can't find any more specific information."

"The Oden are an enigma within themselves–unique, like all the Cosmic races," Jia said through *The Dark Star*. "Their homeworlds are also hidden. Most of the advanced races keep to themselves, concealed to a high degree. The Oden are extremely ancient. It is said that they even existed at the end of the last universe before this one. And, as such, they are by their very nature invulnerable to virtually anything from ours."

"I've noticed that ability in Khai. Very handy, I'd say."

"Yet they are still mortal; they can be overwhelmed and destroyed by raw force and power." Baeven noted. "For that matter, they live only slightly longer than Spacers. They are not immortal like the Yattai. We briefly discussed the substance called Ur-metal, Naero. It exists only in very small quantities throughout existence, and is very rare–like some kind of super-alloy."

Naero nodded. "Khai and others told me that Ur-metal is the cumulative remnants–the fragments from all of the universes before ours. And that besides its raw Cosmic might, it is the only substance that is capable of doing direct physical harm to an Oden or other higher-functioning Cosmic entities. The Mystics used all that they had acquired to produce Yii."

Tyber scoffed a little in uncertain disbelief. "I agree with N. It all sounds like fables and fairytales, if you ask me. I would not believe any of them, had I not witnessed firsthand what that sword and its wielder did to those enemy fleets and armies. The Enforcer obliterated them all–in mere moments."

"They are not fables," Baeven said. "Naero is correct. Khai's sword, Yii, was fashioned from nearly all of the Ur-metal that was known to exist. And its forging has been foretold for eons."

Naero stopped pacing and put her hands on her hips. "What if we get the sword away from Khai? Can we use it to defend ourselves against him?"

Baeven shook his head. "No. It doesn't work that way. He and the sword are one. He can merge with it. He can even conceal it within himself at will, if need be. It would never harm him. But if you were able to harm him, you harm the sword, and vice versa."

Naero sighed.

"A lot of good that does anyone, when we can't harm either one," S'krin said. "From what we've seen, they're both indestructible."

Baeven smiled his grim smile. "Yes indeed, and hence our problem. Together, he and that sword are nearly invincible."

"He boasted that he could track me on the Astral Plane," Naero said. "So, what do we do, just scurry about and wait for him to bag us all?"

Zhen shook her head. "We have to warn everyone about these new enemies and what they're up to. Not just the biowar attack, but these terrible beings that can take over the minds of others–even Spacers from what you said, N. Obviously, they've already infected and influenced all of the Gigacorps. How much further does it go? What about the Alliance? Joshua Tech? What if they infiltrate Spacer Intel, the High Command, the Elders–even the Mystics? What if they've already done so?

Naero, the G'lothc were masters at shapeshifting and destroying their foes from within. They taint and poison all that they touch.

So, how do we detect and fight them, Om?

As yet, none of us know the answer to that.

Naero snorted out loud. "And Intel and the Mystics are going to listen to us? To me? To Baeven? They're going to believe the ravings of a bunch of renegades and outcasts like us? Not until it's too late, I'd say."

"We still have to make the attempt," Jia said.

Baeven announced, "I'm preparing several secret messaging drones and sending them to those whom we know that we can still trust. Anything you want to tell your aunt and uncle, Naero?"

Naero's mouth dropped open for an instant.

"Nothing comes to mind. So much has happened, I had nearly forgotten. Oh, Baeven, at least I got to see and hold the twins. They were so beautiful."

Baeven looked truly sad for an instant at her words.

Naero hoped she'd live to see them all again someday–all her family and friends. "So I ask again," she said, "what is our enemy up to? We know they have long-term plans to subjugate and destroy any other advanced sentients–anyone with the power to oppose them in any way."

"Shalaen," Zhen said, turning pale. "She's Yattai. She is in as much danger as you all are. The enemy tried to capture her once before." Z looked at Tyber and her lower lip trembled.

Baeven looked at Zhen, and his face softened for just an instant.

Perhaps like Ty and Zhen, he had been young and in love and afraid once as well.

"We are all in danger," Baeven said. "And we shall all face such threats together, united. The G'lothc are very thorough and relentless. They will crush and exploit anyone to serve their ends."

Zhen spoke up again. "I know. They really planned to use that advanced bio-toxin to destroy most of the Gigacorps and their human populations, the Spacer Clans, and all the known races. Just think, what if we hadn't stumbled upon it?"

"That plan is still in effect," Naero said. "And if our spyfixers do not complete the task given to them, some of that original plague might still break out. Our foes plan on crushing and dominating everyone, eventually."

"That is why we must go to Zoa," Jia said. "From there, I can link with all of the other Driathan sentry worlds throughout the galaxy, and we can learn all the information that they have gathered and observed. It must be one of our sentinels that our foes are closing in upon. We must learn who their quarry is, and go to his or her rescue."

"I'm not arguing against that," Naero said. "But I'm just trying to understand. Where are the Driathans? Why don't they fight? What are these sentry worlds, and what are they protecting? How can they be in such terrible danger, if they are all hidden away where no one can find them?"

"That's just it," Jia said. "If they capture one Driathan and break him or her, they can use the information they gain to expose all the rest of us and hunt us down, one by one. Each of the sentinels controls only part of the truth."

"And what is that truth?" Naero said.

Baeven cleared his throat. "That the vast population of immortal Driathans are currently helpless–and ripe for the picking. They sleep in a self-induced stasis, hidden within their lost homeworld, the sacred world of Ur-Jahal. If the enemy takes them all over, our foes will become immortal."

"Okay," Naero said. "Very well. To Zoa it is, then. So, you are telling me, that there are millions of helpless, immortal, indestructible Driathans asleep on some lost world somewhere–just ripe for the picking by our worst enemies, who plan on destroying and possessing them?"

Naero clenched her fists. "Well, I tell you what, all of you. We aren't are about to let that happen. Not on our watch. The enemy is moving with all of these sinister plans of theirs. I say we keep on exposing, uncovering, and disrupting them as best we may. Who's with me?"

All present shouted in the affirmative.

35

When the others had all gone, Naero sat beside Baeven.

"Uncle, the time has come. Tell me what happened on Janosha with your alien artifact statue. Tell me why you were declared an outcast and sentenced to death by our Mystics."

Baeven frowned and sighed. "Oh, Naero. That seems so long ago now. I had so little free will in the matter."

"I know," Naero said, taking his hand. "A very similar pattern of events ensnared me, I'm guessing."

"I told you not to go near that, thing, Naero."

Naero smiled sadly. "Like you, Uncle, I'm afraid I was given very little choice."

"I haven't had time to ask you very much about your ordeal, Naero."

"We haven't had much time for anything, but now we do."

"Did you really kill High Master Vane?" he asked.

She looked down. "I did. I'm not proud of it. It was an accident, really."

"Good. Vane needed killing. That vicious old bastard. He'd lived too long as it was. That was his problem. Life meant nothing to him. Did you know that he stole the body of one of his adepts who died accidently? The jerk did it to replace his own. That's how he lived so long. Too convenient, I always said."

Naero thought she might be shocked, but found that she wasn't. Vane had mentioned some such, once.

But then…how did Vane take over the body of another without it wasting away on him? Even the G'lothc had not been able to perfect that trick, not even over millions of years of trying–at the expense of other sentients.

"Tell me what happened with you and the artifact on Thanor-4," Baeven said.

Naero thought her eyes might pop out of her head and fly around.

"Haisha! No way in hell, Uncle! You are going to sit right there and tell me your story first–every bit of it–and then and only then will I tell you mine. You owe me that much!"

Baeven laughed. "I guess you're right."

Naero, you need to remember that I was a Mystic prodigy. I left to train on Janosha before the age of ten. Master Vane did not like me much, and he was very hard on me. Like you, he was fearful of me and my abilities. Yet there could be no denying that my powers were very strong, even from the very beginning. No one understood the alien artifact on Janosha, and until I came along, it had remained dormant.

Each year I trained hard and my power grew.

Eventually, the artifact began giving off more and more strange Cosmic energy readings from time to time–readings that were very frightening in nature. No one understood what was happening, least of all myself.

Even for the strange world of Janosha, with all of its bizarre energy flows, the energy readings on that artifact were terrifying to all who attempted to study it.

Several Mystics and adepts who tried to examine the artifact were slain, or maimed, or driven mad in terrible ways.

Even the High Masters were at a loss.

The situation grew worse all the time, and there was no apparent connection yet to me or to my rapidly maturing abilities. I was assisting Master Vane with retrieving the bodies of two such casualties when I somehow grew disoriented and dizzy.

I somehow touched the artifact to steady myself.

My transport powers went out of control. I thought I was going to explode. I started popping all over the planet, so rapidly that I could not stop or control it.

Then, even more frightening, the statue came to life and came after me, transporting right behind me. Even worse, it was disrupting all of the energy flows of Janosha, causing fierce Cosmic storms and dangerous energy vortices. If the process continued, the entire planet might be torn apart.

Next thing I knew, I ended up out in space, far beyond the planet itself. I barely had enough air to survive. One of the Intel naval vessels guarding Janosha rescued me in time.

Down on Janosha, the artifact statue went inert again, and appeared back in its original place and position. It was around that time that the High Masters determined that it was comprised completely of pure Ur-metal–the very material needed to forge the Cosmic Swords of legend.

After my strange incident, I was strictly forbidden to go near the artifact again. Vane said that I was clearly the catalyst causing it to malfunction. He said that it was caused by some growing evil within me.

The High Masters built a fortress around the artifact in an attempt to isolate and contain it. That seemed to work. More years passed.

When I came of age at twenty, your mother, my beloved little sister, Lythe Ivala Maeris was almost seventeen. She had just completed her two years of naval service training, and elected to join the Mystics. She did Change Wisdom first, and then Order Wisdom, leaving her training in Chaos Wisdom for the last. My training was nearly finished, but I was so unique that I was kept on as a Prime adept while she went through her final training.

Things quickly seemed to go wrong near the end of that time.

First, the time dilation protection that the High Masters had worked so hard to put into place, suddenly collapsed and went down without warning.

Then one day, the protective fortress around the artifact imploded. All of the careful defenses completely shattered or dissolved.

Vane rushed to me and told me that the artifact statue was starting to melt down or do something very strange. It was feared that if the thing dropped through the planet to the core, it might even become a singularity and engulf all of Janosha.

The artifact had come to life somehow, and was suffused with Darkforce and Chaos energy. Tendrils and tentacles of Darkforce had slain many of the guards, and even destroyed several warships sent to attack it.

If the artifact reached critical mass, it might destroy the planet in a variety of ways.

High Master Vane ordered me to depart from Janosha. He gave me direct orders to do so.

I said that I would not–not until I found Lythe and made sure that she was safe. I couldn't find her. Vane would not tell me where she was. He kept lying. First he said she could not be found. Then he tried to tell me that she had been slain–that she was already dead.

I didn't believe any of it. I knew in my heart that my little sister still lived, even though she must be in great peril.

There was something Vane was hiding–something involving Lythe that he wasn't telling me.

I went to the site of the implosion, a scene of tremendous devastation.

Lythe was there. I could see her, floating unconscious in the air, trapped within some kind of Cosmic energy sphere.

Tendrils or tentacles from the artifact were holding onto her sphere, trying to drag it in through the rubble of the destroyed fortress.

"She's still alive. I have to save her!" I said.

Vane interposed himself between myself and Lythe.

"You can't help her, you fool. She's as good as dead. You'll be drawn in as well, adding your power to the artifact. It will reach critical mass and destroy us all!"

"Get out of my way!"

I fought Master Vane to a desperate standstill over the next few seconds. He held me off, but our battle drew us closer and closer to the artifact. It dragged us and the sphere holding my sister nearer and nearer to itself.

When I sensed that the artifact was trying to zap me, I transported at the last instant. It nailed Master Vane instead, captured him, and began drawing him in also.

I thought to use Cosmic energy absorption against the artifact. I had become an expert in that technique, but this was a level of power beyond anything I had ever encountered.

I transported around the artifact statue to a different point at random, each second, taunting it.

"You don't want them. You want me," I told it. "Let them go. Fight me. I'm the one you want!"

The thing warped and shifted shape. It stopped drawing the others in toward it.

In an instant, it transformed and looked just like me. It even started turning from Ur-metal into flesh. It looked at me with my own eyes and spoke to me with my own voice.

"You are correct," it told me. "You are the proper match."

It focused all of its attention on me. The energy spheres containing Lythe and Vane rolled away downhill.

It charged me and we locked together. It tried to overwhelm me. I tried to drain away its energies. The fight escalated, beginning to melt and break down the wreckage all around us.

It was reaching critical mass, just as Vane warned.

A Cosmic detonation like what was coming could destroy the entire continent. It would definitely kill us all.

Then I sensed it. The Darkforce monster lurking within my mind and soul. It was ravenous for power.

Instantly, I funneled those great quantities of Cosmic energy into my dark monster in an effort to avoid the approaching blast. But that only made my monster stronger. It struggled to break free. I began to transform into an energy creature, bent only on destruction.

If that hyper-violent thing broke free, it would be just as devastating as the blast itself.

I grappled with the artifact statue again. It redoubled its efforts to overwhelm me, fighting against the dark thing trying to emerge from me. Both powers tried to overwhelm my force of will. I struggled to pit their might against each other, but I was still between them. They were tearing me and each other apart.

It wasn't enough. I felt the detonation coming, and did the only thing I could think of. I let the monster within me engulf the artifact statue, swallowing it whole. It gulped it down, biting off the arms that fell away.

Then I took my monster back within me and trapped it within my mind, in the prison where it had been locked away.

When the blast came, I tried to direct it out from me. I funneled it straight up into the sky and out into space. I became not just an energy being, but some kind of conduit for all of that Cosmic power.

I remembered screaming and doubling over, curling up in a knot.

The force of the blast ripped through the artifact, my monster, and myself, fusing us all together as one.

The shock wave and blast effects damaged and disrupted everything within six hundred kilometers. It knocked out all electronics, and all the Mystics within range suffered psonic blast trauma, and bled psyonic ichor from their mouths, noses, eyes, and ears.

I came to, and at first I was deaf. I was still smoking and the upper portions of my body were badly scorched and burned. I felt half-dead. I hurt everywhere, especially when I tried to move.

When I did look up, I blinked at the circle of blazing sky far above me. I was in a steaming hot, black glass, crystalline tube that appeared to have been bored nearly forty meters into the solid bedrock. The diameter was about half that.

When my senses returned, I realized that I wasn't alone.

Somehow I had found my little sister, Lythe, and curled myself around her protectively. She was so small and I was always so big.

Somehow, my last act, my last thought before I thought we were all about to die–was to find her and protect her–to shield her, even with my own body if I must.

And she seemed to be fine. Except for some vapor rising off her, she was unharmed, not even burned like I was. Her breathing, heart rate–all strong. She was merely stunned.

I was so glad that I ignored my own pain, and picked her up in my arms and wept.

When I had it together enough, I transported us up out of the tube.

The devastation around us was…incredible. Everyone within the Mystic compound was injured and in shock. All tek was disrupted. I found Master Vane in some rubble, barely alive, burned worse than I was. I did my best to stabilize both of our injuries. Then I carried him and Lythe to the nearest structure still partially standing–the nearby starport.

All the starships there had been tossed about and disrupted as well.

I was injured and growing weaker. I couldn't transport any longer. I barely made it to the starport. Some Intel guards and several adepts recovered enough to start doing triage. Then the naval ships on patrol in orbit came down to assist. Their tek still worked, and a naval cruiser was set up as an emergency field hospital.

I know it was only minutes, but it seemed like hours before someone came by to help us.

With proper treatment, I regenerated rapidly over the next few hours. But I didn't feel right inside. Something was still very wrong, deep within me. I was sick somehow. I could feel it. I didn't know what to do. At times I would experience these spikes of intense agony, and for an instant, it felt as if I was going to explode all over again.

I feared what I had seen within myself. I could never let that thing out, ever again.

And then there was something like a voice, trying to speak to me from deep within, yet it was too far away for me to hear what it was trying to tell me. None of it made sense. Half of the time, I thought I was going insane.

So did others. Most thought me mad.

Master Vane recovered quickly also, and immediately began his campaign with the other High Masters to have me executed.

The only good thing was that Lythe came back around. She was the only one who seemed healthy and unhurt, and she hardly left my side from that moment on. She grew worried, and had the other adepts keep us informed on what was going on around us.

All three of the High Masters studied me and came to the same conclusion. From my ordeal of interacting with the artifact, I had contracted some kind of rare, ancient Cosmic sickness. The energies surging through me were unlike anything that anyone had ever seen before. I was clearly going to waste away or explode at some point, and no one knew exactly when–within a standard year, or the next few seconds.

That was all part of the problem that demanded an urgent decision to be made.

In that climate of fear, terror, and ignorance after the incident, no one knew anything. And therefore, they did not know what to think.

The artifact was no more. Completely destroyed, except for the arms, which had twisted and frozen into two indefinite shapes of precious Ur-metal. Yet compared to the artifact, they now seemed completely inert.

The artifact had affected the High Masters as well, and burned out part of their memories concerning the event. All they knew was the little I chose to tell them.

Regardless, Vane insisted that I had grossly disobeyed him by saving my sister Lythe. If I had listened to him, and left the planet, the incident would not have occurred. Even if something did happen, Lythe might have lived or died in any case–but that did not matter to Vane. He claimed that he was trying to protect everyone, and could not fail to do so at the cost of the life of one adept.

I knew I had made the right choice.

I did make the mistake of trusting the other two High Masters. I told them about the monster I had within myself, how it had emerged during the struggle, and how it nearly escaped during the incident.

All three High Masters seemed to grow incredibly paranoid about this information. It seemed to go along with one of the old Cosmic Prophecies somehow. Vane started ranting that I was clearly revealed to be a Destroyer, a legendary force of destruction feared by many astral and interdimensional beings that the Mystics had congress with.

Destroyers were doomed to grow mad, and could be consumed by the Darkforce. Ancient legends said that they could devour entire galaxies–even collapse and disrupt entire universes–if that could be believed. But the legends insisted that such events had all happened before in the past, and could very well happen again at some point in the future of every possible universe.

These Destroyers could only be checked or stopped by other legends, such as Cosmic Tricksters, various types of Champions–even other Destroyers like themselves–whether they slew each other or canceled each other out somehow. Many times, the Destroyers could not be stopped, and that universe ceased to exist–completely negated.

All three of the High Masters quickly turned against me.

The fact remained that I had disobeyed them and had gone against their will in several serious instances. They said they had no choice when they sentenced me to death. I could perish any moment, and take half the planet with me. For the good of all, my life needed to end.

They made me swear to them, on my honor as a Spacer and a Prime adept, that I would not resist, and would accept my punishment willingly.

My sister Lythe was my only defender.

She alone stood up for me before all of them, utterly fearless, and pleaded my case with all of her passion and devotion.

Her pleas for me fell upon deaf ears–even when she insisted that I could be exiled somewhere, on a world where I could not hurt anyone else but myself. They would not listen. They were still afraid.

So in the end, I did not fight. I calmly gave them my word.

But from that moment forward, I never had any intention of keeping it.

Lythe offered to go with me–willingly into lawlessness. I could not allow her to do so. I swore a promise to her, and made her swear a promise to me, that she would pursue her own life of honor, and forget me if need be. I did all of that for her sake.

She could not be a part of what I was going to become–what I already was. And I did not want her to see that. Her Mystic training was nearly complete any way. She could move on to better things. I had no wish to poison her life the way mine was going to be.

Two days before my execution, I broke out and made good my escape in a fast Intel courier. I injured many, but I strove not to kill anyone. I was slightly wounded initially, but I would recover.

From that point I was an outlaw–a renegade–with a high price and a death sentence on my head. Anyone could kill me, no questions asked. I became one of the most sought-after criminals in known space.

Every hand was against me, and many sought my life.

I survived under many names and guises. I used every ounce of skill and power to survive and remain free, descending into the criminal elements everywhere.

I learned that everywhere, there were secrets, and secrets meant power and wealth to those who could manipulate and control them. I became a rogue agent, dealing in the direct commodity of information and secrets, playing all sides against each other.

Our universe remained a dangerous place. I exposed plots and things that even cost many Spacers their lives. But had I let them go on unexposed, they would have cost far more. Everyone on both sides just assumed I was a traitor, so I used that to my advantage. Even when it appeared that I was betraying my own people, I made sure that in the long run, things worked out to benefit them.

I hid out a lot on the fringes, and in the Unknown Regions. They became my havens. I had several specialized ships I used. When things got too hot for me, I would go exploring for a while into the Unknown. I strove to have the latest tek. I always tried to have a way out set up—or several, if I could manage them. I had aliases and disguises in many places.

But it wasn't enough. The Mystics and Intel sent a special ten adept kill team after me. They tracked me down relentlessly through the Astral Plane. They came not to capture—but to slay me outright. I barely escaped, badly wounded.

Yet during our battle, I had been forced to kill three of the ten adepts on that kill team. Your friend, Admiral Klyne, was one of those who survived. All of them had been former friends and comrades of mine.

Several Intel fleets closed in on me. My ship was damaged. My jump drive crapped out just as I made it to the Gytoran Wormhole. My ship was being cut to pieces, even as I plunged into the vortex.

And, as everyone knows, the Gytoran Wormhole is completely unstable. It can spit you out anywhere in the galaxy—three quarters of which is unexplored. No one had ever come back from it yet—although a few, like me, have managed to do so since that time. But back then, for me it was either a one-way trip into the unknown—or death.

When I emerged from the other end of the wormhole, completely at random, I had no idea where I was. I still don't know where I came out exactly to this day. I couldn't get back there if I tried.

My ship was severely damaged, I was badly wounded—dying really. My Cosmic disease had grown so bad that I was close to exploding again, or unleashing the monster inside of me.

I barely managed to crash land on a strange world that seemed to be the nearest earthlike. Boy, was I both wrong and fortunate at the same time.

I was on Zoa, Jia's gateway world to Ur-Jahal, the secret Driathan homeworld hidden by their masters, the ancient Drians. Jia still won't tell me or anyone else what quadrant of our galaxy Ur-Jahal is hidden in.

293

Jia extracted my broken, diseased body from the wreck of my ship, took pity on and saved me. To this day, I do not know what it was that she could possibly see in me.

She healed me–and from what she says, that was no simple task. In order to do so, she had to become part of me, and I had to become part of her, in ways that I still do not understand. But it was as if the two of us became, in fact, part of each other.

We also we fell in deeply love with each other, in so many ways too marvelous and fantastic to imagine or explain–the most magnificent thing that has ever happened to me in my entire life. I am devoted to her, and she to me–for all time. We are everything to one another.

Jia gave me so many gifts. *The Shadow Fox* is, in fact, a Drian ship. It is a living ship–with or without Jia's soul essence imbued within it; the most advanced starship I have ever seen. I have learned many of its secrets, but not all. I have learned to use Drian tek to aid my various efforts.

Jia came with me, because we could not be parted. For reasons she keeps to herself, she insisted on leaving her miraculous, immortal body behind.

Baeven paused and shook his head and gasped, obviously in fond memory.

I cannot speak to you in the words of any known language and tell you how beautiful my Jia is to me. It is something that a person could only witness and experience for themselves. But know this: Jia was the pinnacle of the Drian powers of creation. The Drians *specifically* created her to be as much like they were as possible, in order to guide, protect, and lead her people. If the Driathans have a goddess…it can only be Jia.

Naero, I hope that you will be so fortunate, one day, to behold my beloved completely, in all her splendor and majesty–as she truly is.

The Driathan legends say that they were meant to be the gift of the Drians to all the galaxy–to the entire universe after the horrors and devastation of the Great War. That was why the Drians protected their creations so much–some say even at the cost of the Drians' own existence. And in the Cosmic Prophecies of all the sentients, the Driathans are specifically mentioned multiple times–as having their own important roles to play in the fate of the universe.

To escape from Zoa, Jia had to seal away the Cosmic gateway to Ur-Jahal. She had our ship locate other naturally occurring wormholes that would return us on a one-way trip to the Alpha Quadrant. We have returned to Zoa on two other occasions since that time, but I still have no idea where it is located.

When I returned, I could control my monster within–at least partially, after the fashion that you have seen. And that has served me well, indeed. But I also learned that I had been made an outcast. I was no longer a Spacer. I had no name. No honor whatsoever any longer. I was seen as a rabid animal, who only needed to be put down.

*

Baeven leaned back and knitted his hands behind his head.

"There, now you know what happened to me and the alien artifact I interacted with, Naero. How I became an outcast, and how I met Jia and gained my ship. Now, I need to hear your story. All of it."

"But wait," Naero said. "I want to hear more about Jia, and you, and your Drian ship, and the Drian tek you use. And what about your crew? Where did they all come from?"

Baeven now crossed his arms in front of himself. Apparently a characteristic Maeris Clan thing to do. "Naero, I've told you quite enough for the time being. Now, I insist that you tell me what I want to know, or you and I are going to have a very interesting sparring match."

Naero laughed. "Hey, you're still recovering."

He glared at her as only he could. "Try me. I'm feeling much better every instant. Now talk."

Naero laughed. "All right, all right, but first I need a-"

Baeven sat up, and telekinetically yanked a frosty cold four-pak of Jett out of a hidden lix cooler. Naero barely caught it, and went back a bit to keep it from smacking her in the head.

She cracked the first borbble open before telling him about her own ordeal.

36

As if they didn't have enough major problems, Jia informed them that even at jump-7, a journey to Zoa and back would take almost two standard weeks.

No one knew what kind of time they had to work with, and there were no known wormholes out their way that could get them any closer.

The enemy certainly held a major strategic and tactical advantage over them with that ancient wormhole tek of theirs. The G'lothc cruiser and the Dakkur hordeship could travel back and forth at will over great distances.

Naero had another healing session planned with Womi later that day. If things went well enough, perhaps he would tell them where in the Gamma Quadrant they could find the new enemy homeworlds that had been established there.

While both ships remained docked together, Baeven worked with Naero, Om, Ty, Alala, and Jia to teknomance and pweak the drives on *The Dark Star* to make them even faster and more efficient.

Yet, sadly, Baeven's miraculous Drian ship was still far more advanced. He tried to explain some of the differences.

"We'd need advanced materials that we just don't have access to, in order to top out Alala's specs to come to anything close to *The Shadow Fox*."

Naero sighed. "We've learned so much already from you and Jia and your ship. I keep working with Alala and Om and our fixers, trying to fabricate the advanced materials we require. We have the specs you gave us, but I never thought just synthesizing materials could be so complex— and exhausting. And there are tons of basic things just like that in the KDM that are simply way over our capabilities right now."

Baeven laughed. "Don't beat yourself up too much, Naero. If it's still beyond Jia and Om, it's going to take a little while for us and them to catch up. But we have to continue to advance, working on overcoming our weaknesses, building upon our strengths."

Naero nodded. "Our people have always known that. While our enemies still seem to have knowledge far beyond our own. That keeps us us at a serious disadvantage."

"We're lucky they can't seem to duplicate those ships they have, or all of their advanced weapon systems."

"Baeven, we can't afford to give them time to do so. Ty, what about that new leap drive, the one we cobbled together from those KDM concepts that Om gave us? Any luck on getting that working?"

"We've assembled a prototype projector generator, but it would still take a massive amount of raw Cosmic energy just to test it."

Cosmic energy.

She turned to Baeven. "You and I can generate Cosmic energy. Perhaps we could power it. If we could get that prototype working, jump drive tek would become obsolete. Our foes would no longer have the advantage over us. We could leap across half the galaxy or farther in an instant."

They walked back over to Ty and his tek crew, who brought out the experimental device on grav lifts and, with Jia's kind assistance, popped the device up from the floor. It was even more compact than a jump drive.

"I wouldn't advise a full test right now," Tyber warned. "There are still too many variables. We don't know what any of the effects could be for certain. It might torch any ship trying to use that thing—including this one. We might reach our destination all right...as a burned-out cinder."

"There's currently a fifty-seven percent chance that the device would function properly," Jia said.

"I say fifty-six," Om projected."

"Buma-luma," Naero said. "Or potato-potata, take your pick."

What in the heck is a potata?

297

Naero ignored Om before giving her opinion.

"So–in principle–we're basically talking Space-Time travel here, right? If this Kexxian leap tek works, we could get places faster than anyone. Maybe even faster than our enemies. That would be a huge advantage. I don't think we can ignore the chance at such a possibility."

"But we can't help anyone if we're all dead, either." Baeven said. "I'm up for taking risks as much as anyone, but let's pweak our chances of success a little more than fifty-fifty before we do an actual test run."

"Om, Jia, Alala," Naero said, "keep working with Ty and the über-geek squad here. "Let us know what our chances would be by the end of this standard day. If they're high enough, we'll give it a shot. Keep working with Baeven, too, if he feels up to it."

"Will do," Alala said, noting. "These Kexxian schematics are amazing. Even this Drian ship is not as complex as this one Kexxian device, and that's saying something. Om and I are probably the only ones who can even understand the concepts of just parts of it. Some of them are even beyond us."

For now, at least. I continue to study them and make progress.

Baeven clapped a hand on Naero's shoulder.

"In the meantime, you and I have some work of our own to do. If we're going to be fighting G'lothc-possessed foes, Mystic Enforcers, Dakkur, and who the hell knows what else–haisha–we'd both better be in top form. You've had further training with the Mystics, Naero."

And she might not get any more.

"That's good progress," he went on. "And you now possess many abilities that I do not. But I trained with Master Vane and the other two High Masters completely for many years. There's still much for you to learn about raw fighting, increasing your speed and strength, working in the Astral Plane and other dimensions, and honing all of your Mystic skills. As well as the ones that are unique to you since your encounter with the artifact."

Naero nodded and looked up at him.

Baeven was telling her, once again, that they were going back to training hard together.

And that he was going to do his level best to beat the hell out of her while doing so.

But Naero knew for a fact that she could take it, and give back plenty of her own. Baeven would learn things from her, too. It was always that way with talented opponents.

"I'm up for all of that. And let's be honest about something else," she said. "We both have similar problems controlling our Cosmic abilities. We both have our own Dark Beast within us that yearns only to break free, rampage, and destroy."

Baeven looked at her and nodded. "You know now that it is Jia, in part, who helps me control myself and the monster within. Without her–without her love and compassion for me–I would have ended up a mindless monster, or worse, long ago. Just as the High Masters feared, they would have been forced to take me out."

"Thank goodness for Jia, then."

He looked into Naero's eyes. "You have held her soul within you. You sense what she is–her great dignity and honor. Her goodness. She is my angel, my savior. I cannot put into words what Jia is to me, and the depths of my feelings for her, Naero. Sometimes I would give up the entire struggle and everything–all that I am–if only to have her in my arms for one entire day. Nay...for one mere hour of bliss and peace, alone with her."

"I have never seen a Driathan," Naero said. "Are they really as beautiful as the legends say, Baeven? Or did you just tell me that because of your love for Jia?"

Baeven sighed. "One day, Naero, you will tell me if I have spoken the truth or not. Each of the Driathans was a miracle, fashioned lovingly by the hands of the Drians in their enduring image and imagination. Perfection, immortal, indestructible, self-regenerating. And Jia was created to be their paragon–the closest thing to being an actual Drian, without them actually re-creating themselves entirely in her mirific android form.

"In the absence of their beloved masters, when the Driathans awake and come into their power, she will be more than a mere queen to all her kind–she will be the nearest thing they have to a goddess."

"Is she that beautiful, then?"

Even Baeven took in a deep breath.

"I have been many places in this universe, Naero, and I have seen many wonders. Yet nothing has come close to her. When we first found each other, I was broken, dying, diseased, and accursed. At that point I yearned to die. Jia healed me, slowly and tenderly in her embrace, and brought me back from the brink of my own dark abyss.

"She looked upon and within me and I her for months at time, speaking only to each other with our eyes as I slowly regenerated, bathed, and healed within the grace of her all-encompassing light. For all that time, I was unable to speak. Not a word. But we forged our great bond, and the powerful link between us was formed on levels that even we cannot describe. Without her I would be a terrible wretch–beyond nothing. A witless, destroying beast that would need to be killed."

"Where are the Driathans? What are they doing?"

"That is difficult to explain, Naero. Even I do not fully understand it all, and I am closer to Jia than anyone. Perhaps she could attempt to explain it to you. They adored their creators so very much, their beloved masters, the Drians. It pained them greatly that the Drians suffered so much and even felt corrupted from the Great War with the G'lothc and their formidable allies.

"When the Drians bade their beloved children all farewell and vanished, it came as a huge shock to the Driathans. Just imagine what that would be like. If you had amazing gods living and working and teaching among you—an enormously enriching and endlessly rewarding part of your entire life—and then one day, all of them were suddenly gone. Millions of Driathans mourned, and the grief that came out of what they call The Great Sundering left them stricken with loss and despair.

"To assuage this pain, the Driathans hid themselves away on their miraculous living homeworld of Ur-Jahal. A marvel in itself, constructed lovingly for them by their creators. The Driathans hid their entire planet and put themselves into a deep slumber in order to contemplate and heal from their immense loss. The Cosmic legends say that they shall only awaken when the fate of all the Universe—of all Existence—is to be decided. If they should fall prey to Darkforce before that time, then all of that shall be lost."

"So what are these sentinels Jia speaks of?" Naero said.

"Jia is their leader, the leader of all her kind. To protect Ur-Jahal and all of their slumbering people, the sentinels keep watch from numerous hidden locations for any sign of the Darkforce growing or being used. The guardians only take measures and actions, if need be, to keep Ur-Jahal safe and secret. Its location is one of the true mysteries of our galaxy. Each sentinel is in touch with Ur-Jahal, for their living homeworld has a will all its own. Yet no one sentry bears the knowledge of the complete location, and only has a clue. Only Jia can go there at will, for she is one with it. But she goes there by instinct. Even she could not point to a map and tell you its coordinates.

"But our fear is that if the enemy captures one Driathan sentry, they can break that one and use its knowledge to deceive, track down, and break all the others. Then they can put the pieces of the puzzle together."

Naero gasped slightly and covered her mouth. "That's exactly what the enemy has always wanted. If the lost G'lothc spirits found the Driathans all sleeping, they could conquer them, possess them all with their vile spirits, and take over their immortal android bodies with ease."

Baeven nodded. "They'll seize power and dominion over these galaxies. And the Kexx and the Drians are no longer here to stop them. The great enemy would indeed become unstoppable–virtually the new gods–by fiat."

"Where is she, then?" Naero asked. "Where is Jia's body? Why can't the two of you be together?"

For the first time since she had known him, Baeven's composure nearly broke. He almost sobbed. Then, as she looked on, he steeled himself the very next instant.

"That is a long tale for another time. Some griefs and sacrifices are too difficult to speak of, Naero, even for a brutal outcast such as I."

Naero laughed. "Well, you can keep playing the slimy villain to the rest of the universe all you want, and I know that role serves you and the rest of the galaxy well. But if someone as great and good and beautiful as Jia can love you, Uncle–as she so clearly does–with all of her heart and soul–then you could not be so totally evil."

He shook his head and his countenance clouded. "We all still have many choices to make, Naero. Both you and I. Who can see what the end of all things shall be? We both need to be fearful of that."

301

37

Naero, Zhen, Jia, and even Baeven prepared for another attempt at healing Womi further. Nearly everyone would be in on it this time.

She had finally taken the time to explain the situation with the currently tiny Kahn-Dar to them all.

They almost didn't believe her about her little dragon bracelet, until Zhen backed her up.

What could she say? She took in strays.

Their problem at this time was that Womi had regained some degree of feeling in his extremities. But that was it. He was still crippled, and had lost much of his free range of motion.

They performed the regeneration techniques the same way as before.

Yet this time, there was almost no further progress.

"Maybe that's the problem," Naero said. "We need to do something different–something we haven't thought of or tried yet."

The introductions had all been made. Womi jumped right in. "Humor me, Naero. I've been thinking this over for days. Try healing me...this time, on the Astral Plane."

Naero shook her head. "Not a good idea. Every time I go there, the Mystics have some way of tracking me down."

Womi shook his head. "It's not the location. They've clearly already placed an Astral marker on you somehow. I can't see it here on the Prime Material Plane, but I can smell it. Perhaps they even did this long ago. They can eventually get a lock on you and find your body, anywhere you go, as long as you have that Astral marker on you."

"Then how in the hell do I get rid of it?"

"I can find it on you in the Astral Plane and get rid of it."

"How do you do that?"

"Easy. I go inside you and eat it. Once I consume the marker and its sealing energy, the marker will dissolve, and it won't work anymore. Of course, they'll know their marker is gone, but they won't be able to track you anymore, or do anything about it."

"Will it hurt?"

"Sure...like crazy. But only while you're in the Astral Plane."

"How can I prevent someone from doing this to me again?"

Womi smirked. "I'll show you. You don't seem to know much about this stuff for being a Mystic."

"I'm a weakling among my kind, remember?"

"Hah! Yeah, right...you...a weakling. That one gets funnier every time you float it out."

"Look, I hadn't gotten around to Astral training, all right? Then all of this crap exploded in my face. After I blew away one of the three High Mystic Masters–I don't think they're going to give me a refresher!"

"All right...don't get mad, N. If you haven't been trained yet, you haven't been trained. That's not your fault."

"I didn't say it was. You're the one who made an issue out of it, you little goofball!"

"Issue? What issue? Hey, stick with me, my sweet. You wanna know stuff about dimensional travel? I know stuff that would curl your so-called Mystic Masters' ears and light their bums on fire."

"If you know so much, then why don't you train me?"

"Well, get me back up to snuff and I just might...if you're nice to me."

"Okay, deal. Take us to the Astral Plane and removed my tracker, and I'll give your healing a shot there."

"Good. I think we're onto something here. Hold onto me, and don't let go, Naero."

She gasped as they flashed into the aether of the Astral Plane miasma, racing through it at impossible speeds.

This time, Womi was as big as a naval battleship, but still as crippled as he was. Naero barely clung to Womi's horns on his head.

Naero tried to picture something that would help her hold on—a saddle of some kind, with reins and stirrups.

She felt like a total idiot doing so, but imagination and force of will were everything on the Astral Plane. The items actually appeared in an instant from her imagination, under her and in both hands and feet.

They really did help.

"Okay, N," Womi's voice boomed and echoed, "get with the healing. Make it quick, before one of my kind senses us and comes to munch on us."

When Naero got down to it, it was actually easier. She was already linked with Womi, and could see the parts of him that were damaged.

All she had to do was heal and regenerate those portions of him.

She startapped and focused positive, healing energy on them.

At the same time, she instinctively learned something vitally important about Kahn-Dar.

They were indeed interdimensional creatures by their very nature. The reason they could flow and gate into all the other dimensions at will—was because a small portion of their existence seemed to exist in many of those dimensions—all at the same time.

Thus, they could really only be slain in the Prime Material Plane.

If they perished there, every part of them perished in all of the others.

Womi let out a resplendent cry, feeling even more of his range of function returning to him.

"Yesss!"

His long body waved a little more, undulating and whipping back and forth in his speed. His front and rear, big hand-like claws opened and closed slowly, instead of sagging limp. His head twisted around more.

"Naero, do you know what this means?"

"Not a clue, so tell me flat out."

"You just have to heal me in each of the nexus anchor dimensions, and I can finish regenerating from that point on. We've done it!"

"We have?"

"I mean...you will finish healing me, right?"

"Sure," Naero said. "We had a deal, correct?"

"We sure did. Let's go."

"Hey, Womi. Why don't you take care of my little Astral marker situation, if you can?"

"Sure thing. Hold out your right forearm. That's where it is."

"How can you tell?"

"I can smell it. I can see it. Here let me show you how."

In a flash, they came to a complete stop, floating in the aether. Womi was tiny again, and wrapped himself around Naero's head like a small, glowing blue circlet.

"Open your mind's eye–your third eye. I'm going to show you how to look into things the way the Kahn-Dar are able to do. You can see right into anything that exists, and see its essence–as well as any flaws, weaknesses, illnesses, or imperfections in its structures and flows."

Naero focused through Womi, and looked at things the way the Kahn-Dar could see them.

She saw it immediately. The Astral marker, what looked like a small, pulsing orb of swirling red, blue, and gold energy, pulsating and flashing within her transparent right forearm.

Their bodies were both clear like crystal, with an aura of flickering, Cosmic energy on the outside–as if the outer surface of their bodies hardly existed.

"Hold still," Womi said. "Let me take care of that annoying marker."

She winced as he used his tiny, sharp teeth to gnaw and burrow into her clear astral forearm.

She blinked and gaped. She almost grabbed him by the tail and yanked him out, it hurt that bad.

He wiggled his way into her forearm and wrapped his jaws around the marker. Then he gobbled it down, and absorbed its energies.

After Womi wiggled his way back out–Naero wincing all the while– he bent around in the aether and patted his swollen tummy. He actually licked his chops.

"Mmm...very tasty."

Naero studied herself, seeing the twisted, sickening energies coursing through herself. Her Cosmic disease–and the tainted threat of the Darkforce.

Powers that were slowly destroying her each day–each second.

"How do I make my own marker, again? How can I track things, like what was done to me?"

Womi bobbed and nodded. "Simple, especially here. Your marker is part of you. Picture *what* you want it to be. Picture *where* you want it to be. You can place it inside of something, or someone, as long as they don't resist or actively guard against it. If they can sense it, like we can, it can be destroyed. For example, place a marker inside of me, Naero. Go ahead. I will allow it."

Naero closed her eyes and tried to concentrate.

"No, no," Womi said. "Keep all of your eyes open when you focus your power here on the Astral Plane. Things you create and cause to appear will do so, where you imagine them."

She formed her marker–a small, brilliant pinpoint of intense, blue-violet light. Then she pictured it inside of Womi, just behind his head.

Womi grinned. "Now you can track me, and locate me, and come to me in an instant, anywhere on the Astral Plane."

"Really?"

"Try it out. I'm going to flash over to the far side of the Astral Plane, the farthest point away from where we are. Focus on your marker, and come to me there."

Womi vanished the next instant.

Naero recalled doing this same thing with Master Vane's marker. She pictured her marker inside of Womi. Then she picture herself with her marker.

The aether shot around her in the flash of another instant.

She came face to face with Womi, looking her right in the eye.

"Excellent. For a weakling of your kind…you are a natural. Now, I'm going to try to place a marker in or on you. I want you to set your energies to not allow that."

"How?"

"You will sense my marker. Use your force of will to destroy or absorb its energies on contact with yours. No one will ever be able to mark you again–without your direct permission."

On the third try, she managed to get all of her defenses and energies set completely right.

"See?" Womi said. "You can do it. Now, let's finish my healing, if you don't mind."

"Okay. Where to now?"

Womi grinned his toothy grin, becoming enormous once again.

Naero's saddle, reins, and stirrups were back also. She was already using them.

"Hang on. We are going to take a little tour of all the dimensional nexes. And you are going to repeat similar healing processes in each of them. Then I will be free, and very close to whole again. I can take my convalescence over from that point on."

Their journey turned out to be a grand tour.

"This is the Opposite Dimension," Womi explained. "Adjust your thoughts and patterns. It is tougher than you might guess. Everything here is backwards."

For the first time in her life, Naero felt sickened by flying, weak, frightened, and very disoriented.

Womi was flying and talking backwards. Everything took direct thought to adjust to. Why did she feel so afraid? It was mind-numbing. Naero looked at her badly shaking left hand. Everything seemed reversed. Color. Motion.

"Everything is structurally opposite here," Womi assured her. "I know gender is important to your kind. So...don't panic at suddenly being male."

Naero screamed. "Get us out of here, Womi. I don't like this. Everything feels...wrong. I'm so scared."

"Because everywhere else, you are so brave."

"This is really creepy. I don't like being a guy. It's...too weird."

"We won't stay long. The Opposite Dimension is the opposite of everything you are used to. Deal with it. The faster you focus on healing me, the faster we can move on. Just remember, reverse the healing process that you used in the Prime Material Plane. I know that doesn't make sense, but trust me, that's the only way that it will work here."

"I...I don't know if I can." What was wrong with her?

"Naero, listen to me. You are still you. Maintain that and focus. I know this is difficult. You want to leave this place, right?"

"I sure as hell do. I don't feel right. Get me out of here!"

"Then do what you need to do to escape, before you think about things too much."

Healing. Reverse the process.

Almost numb with terror, Naero did everything backwards, ending with reverse startapping, draining Cosmic energy from herself and giving it back to the universe.

She suddenly noticed–here her disease was a stabilizing force, healing and making her slowly stronger.

And her Dark Beast? It was filled with the shining, radiant light of the Lifespark and the pure Harmony...and it was sickening.

Why did that all make her so angry?

Then Naero gaped and realized.

Here, in this dimension, he was bitter, petty, cowardly–and evil.

No. It wasn't right. He had to end this nightmare. Get out of here. Escape!

"Excellent," Womi said. "Say goodbye."

Naero couldn't take it all any longer. He started screaming.

Womi flashed into another dimension.

Naero looked at and felt herself. She gasped, still shaken. Thankfully, she seemed all back to being her normal self. Even her Cosmic disease and her Dark Beast were back to being the ominous threats that they were.

That wasn't exactly comforting, but it was better than the disorienting madness of the Opposite Dimension.

She wondered if the contraries would even be able to deal with that place. There, they'd probably make sense.

"I don't think I ever want to go there again," Naero said. "Where are we now?" Now that she had her act back together again, she looked around.

There was aether, but everything was suffused with light. The very air seemed to glow with particles of radiance. A shining aura lit both her and Womi.

"This is the Dimension of Light. It is a glorious place."

They soared through towering, endless clouds of light; nebulae of brilliant stars. Floating, liquid-like seas and oceans of light awaited.

After Naero healed Womi there with her glowing hands, she didn't want to leave. But Womi told her they had to.

Next, stop: The Dark Dimension.

Here everything was shades of darkness and the power of raw unlight. Vision seemed completely reversed. It was still possible to see somewhat, and sense things, but everything was shadows.

"I thought it would be evil," Naero said. "Why doesn't it feel evil?"

Womi laughed. "Dark, Light–Black, White–Good and Evil. Such distinctions do exist everywhere, but not in the ways you think. Things are what you make of them. All things can exist in all dimensions. They are the myriad possibilities that do not come from a place–they come from sentient minds blessed or cursed with free will, depending on how you look at them.

"You can still commit every evil act at the zenith of the realms of light. Just as you can still do all good things in the nadir of the realms of darkness. *And everything in between, Naero.* The choice is always yours. Only the planes of the Lifespark and the Darkforce are absolute–positive and negative realms. Life and Death. Existence and Non-Existence."

"What are the Kahn-Dar?"

Womi grinned. "Whatever we wish to be, when we wish to be it. We are opportunists, yet we have our own rigid code of honor. We will devour each other if we can, but at the same time, we can also be incredibly loyal and loving. Haven't you figured us out yet?"

Naero covered her mouth with both hands. "Haisha," she exclaimed. "You're pure Chaos–always as you are–as you choose to be."

"That's how we are always free. Ready to go?"

"Surprise me."

"I will."

Naero shrieked.

They passed through a dimension that was all flame and fire. Thankfully, in their energy forms, they weren't burning up.

"We'll pass through the elemental energy planes and their borderlands. The Plane or Dimension of Fire is actually where the borders of the dimensions of Heat and Air come together. Just as the Plane of Ice is the border between the dimensions of Cold and Water. There's a Plane of Lava between the planes of Earth and Heat. There's even a Plane of Mud."

Naero nodded. "Between Earth and Water–I think I see the pattern, Womi. All the elements stand on their own and interact with each other at some point where they combine. Do I have to heal you in every one of them?"

"No. Just the primary nexes: earth, air, fire, and water."

One by one, they did so. Each time, Womi regenerated a little more, regaining a bit more of himself.

They passed into the Dimension of Dreams and Possibilities, next to the Spirit Realms, on the borders with Light and Darkness, and the Lifespark and the Darkforce.

"All of the Spirit Realms can be perilous places, even more so than the other dimensions. Each realm has its dangers. All sentients have a complex spirit or soul. Our choices cause our spirits to be drawn either toward the Harmony, or the Darkforce, and thus send our souls on a journey toward one or the other."

"Your people knew the G'lothc and served them for a time. Where are the G'lothc souls in the Realm of the Dark Spirits?"

"So close to the border with the Darkforce that they are nearly indistinguishable. That would be a fearful place indeed. I have never been there, and have no wish to go to it. Thankfully, we do not have to. And the Spirits of Light can be just as perilous, trust me. We will remain at the borders of each plane, long enough for you to heal me. That should be enough."

Naero continued to heal her friend at each stop they made.

Next they reached the Galactic Nexes. Here, each galaxy in their universe was like an open window, waiting for the traveler to go through it. They spread on in every direction, as if from the center of a great sphere, layered on and on into infinity.

"Do not go that way," Womi warned. "Unless you are an experienced traveler, it is far too easy to lose yourself, and never find your way back."

Naero healed him again. "There, is that it?"

"Yes, thank you, Naero. I am nearly complete again. There's just one more place I want to show you."

They appeared in a realm–of nothing.

It was stifling. Petrifying.

"Womi. What is this awful place? I don't like it."

"This is an alternate dimension where the Darkforce has had its way and won–destroying everything–even itself in the end. Nothing remains. No possibilities whatsoever."

"The Darkforce did all of this?"

"Not just the Darkforce. The Great Destroyer awoke in this dimension. The Great Destroyer is an entity that suffuses all existence in the power of the Darkforce, where all is annihilated, leaving nothing behind. The Cosmic Prophecies are real, Naero. It is possible for this devastation and oblivion to occur in every universe that has existed, does exist, and will exist."

"I don't want to see this anymore, Womi. Please, get us out of here."

The next instant, they were back on board *The Shadow Fox*, in the medical bay.

Womi seemed almost completely healed. His range of motion back to normal. He flitted about in joy and popped around at will, obviously pleased with his recovery.

"Now keep your word to us, Womi. Tell us where the Dakkur have established their new homeworlds in the Gamma Quadrant."

"I will," Womi said. "I can't show you on a map, but I can take you there and show you. Once you get some bearings, I'm sure you can eventually figure it out, with all of your tek. Hold onto me again."

Naero checked and suited up her togs again, and turned to her friends. "Gotta pop out one more time. Back shortly."

With that, they were gone.

Womi was huge once more, and Naero rode on his neck, just behind his head, with her saddle and reins. They were flying through space, somewhere in the Gamma Quadrant.

Om, you're getting all of this, right? Can I put you in charge of recording all of the galactic navigational scans?

Doing so now. Will compute them all with the KDM once our full scans are complete.

Thanks.

"Womi, can you give us even a rough idea where we are, here?"

"Somewhere near the edge of your galaxy, in an outermost spiral arm."

"But you're sure it's in the Gamma Quadrant, right? And yet–maps and star charts mean nothing to you?"

"My mind has trouble thinking in those ways. I see energies and locations, not the greater whole."

Naero considered the possibilities. "Hmm...two spiral arms are at the edges of the Gamma Quadrant. The Sagittarius Arm and the Scutum-Crux Arm. We have to be in one of those. It will take time, but we'll figure it out."

"The new Dakkur Homeworlds are six in number."

Womi showed her each system, flashing through the galaxy at will, gating over vast distances.

"Maggoth, Shokk, Kolothon, Xoggoth, Churrok-Kul, and Nakkra-Kron–each has been completely subjugated and taken over, with thriving, Dakkur breeding populations."

Each of the Dakkur worlds was stretched out in a line, great swaths of distance separating each one.

But in each location, the Dakkur and their Ejjai slaves brought havoc and destruction to all of their sentient neighbors, fighting six separate interstellar wars, each within a diameter of several hundred light-years around every established Dakkur homeworld.

Naero gasped.

The enemy had invaded their galaxy at these far distant points, in a quadrant her people had yet to explore.

And from what she saw...their enemies were winning and gaining strength throughout all six of those areas of influence.

When they had seen enough, Womi took her back to her friends.

"You have kept your word to me," Naero said. "I honor you for that. I suppose you'll be going now, Womi, my friend?"

Womi made himself about her size, and whipped his tail through the air in excitement.

"Almost immediately, Naero. I have important things I must see to. Yes, we are friends, now. As strange a friendship as there has ever been. But I shall always be in your debt. I have your marker still. You can come to me any time, if you like. Perhaps I can help train you further in dimensional traveling."

Naero smiled. "I'd like that. My people and I would also like to remain on good terms with you and your people, Womi. Is that at all possible? We know who our enemies are now. Let's work together."

Womi shook his head. "I can only speak for myself, Naero. My people are not at all communal. We can't agree on anything very often, unless it is to swarm and feed–or mate. We wish now only to be free, and after this latest disaster, I doubt if the Dakkur will be able to persuade any of us to do their bidding ever again. I will come visit you, when I feel like it. Do the same with me. Good fortune to you and your kind. If you intend to fight the Dakkur and these dark G'lothc spirits, then I think you will need that and much more. Try not to get killed, and please do something about that nasty Cosmic energy infection of yours."

Naero grinned. "Death is to be avoided."

Womi smiled. "It most certainly is. Farewell for now."

The next instant, Womi vanished.

Naero was going to miss him.

Her right wrist felt naked without the little blue dragon wrapped around it.

38

Naero attacked Baeven again, deflecting off the heavily reinforced and shielded practice room walls and ceiling. They fought in a blur of speed and strength.

She attempted to sweep his legs.

Her leg rebounded painfully, as if Baeven were made of Ur-metal.

She countered with a springflip kick to his face to daze him.

She spun and flipped away.

Baeven just missed grabbing one of her ankles.

She grinned. Not this time.

"Hold," he called out.

They had been sparring and practicing and trying out several techniques and combinations for almost three standard hours.

Both of them perspired and breathed hard.

Baeven had a bloody lip and one bloody ear.

Naero had taken more damage than that, bruised and bleeding in several places that she strove to ignore and regenerate.

"I'm still seeing a problem with developing your skills, Naero. You're focusing too much on everything at once: speed, power, technique, strategy, precision."

"So, what do we do?"

"Let's go back to basics. Focus on developing one element at a time. You're incredibly fast, Naero–just like your mother–and she was faster than anyone I ever knew."

Since they were on a breather, Naero rested her hands on her hips and looked around. She snatched up a lix pak and chugged it down.

"So, what do I do?"

"Stop worrying about all the rest of it. Focus on speed. Pour all of your focus and your energies into moving faster. Concentrate solely on that. That is how I increased my speed. Power and all the rest can come later."

"So, I become faster. But if my attacks don't do any damage, then they won't even matter?"

Baeven shook his head. "You'll never get it, then. You can't think about your progress that way. Like I said, don't worry about anything else. Speed. Focus on speed. If you can keep me from striking you, that is a victory. If you can slip in and even touch me, without me hitting you, that counts as another victory for you–just for now."

"Okay. I trust you."

"Don't go that far. I'm still your opponent. Give me your hands, Naero."

She did so. "What for?"

Baeven modified her Nytex gloves to where they glowed bright green. He did the same thing to her feet, knees, and elbows.

"There. Now if you can touch me, you'll leave behind a glowing green nanomarker stain on contact to prove it. We can reset each time we go again."

She grinned her fighting smile through her bloody nose and lips.

"Good. I don't just fight with my hands."

They squared off and sparred heavily for yet another hour.

At first she had the same problem penetrating Baeven's formidable defenses.

She manage to slip in a few grazing touches.

But Baeven clobbered her good another time, not letting up on her at all. In fact, the fury of his attacks seemed to increase.

Then, slowly, within the last half hour, things began to shift. First she began to evade his combinations with greater and greater ease.

Then she slipped in under his guard and tapped him right on the nose. The glowing imprint of her fist gleaming right between his eyes.

By the time the hour had ended, Baeven struggled more and more to connect with her, and several of her glowing touches showed themselves bright on his body–half of them in vital areas.

Naero got so excited she giggled.

"It's working. I'm really starting to get it. Thank you for showing me how to train this way, again." She leaped up and hugged him.

"You're most welcome," he said, always a little startled by her affectionate displays and outbursts.

Especially after the pounding he had just administered.

"Now...I want you to help me work on something, Naero. Something personal, that you alone know to be my own special weakness. Something that I desperately need help with, perhaps as equally difficult and definitely more dangerous."

Naero gave him her puzzled look.

"Okay. I'll try." What was there that she could teach him?

Baeven almost looked embarrassed.

"Both of us know full well that our energies also feed and empower what you refer to as our Dark Beast, the Darkforce shadowthing that exists within us. This demon, beast, monster, or whatever you want to call it, is part of us and our imagination. Yet we know that it only yearns to break out and destroy everything in its path."

Naero hung her head in shame and nodded. "Yes. I have been the victim to my own Dark Beast as well, too many times, it seems."

"As in killing Master Vane. That is why Khai is after you."

Naero grimaced.

She didn't have the heart to tell her uncle that killing Master Vane had been her fault alone. On that occasion, her Dark Beast had nothing to do with it.

"Don't torture yourself so much, Naero. I believe everything happens for a reason. At one point, Vane was convinced that I was the Great Destroyer as well. The Chaos Master's solution to everything was the same: kill it. If it might be a threat, destroy it."

Naero had a sudden flash of insight.

"Vane was your master, too. And like with me, he tried to kill you."

Baeven nodded.

Naero rested a hand on his strong arm.

Baeven placed his hand over hers.

"I know you did not want to kill him, Naero. And I know for a fact that he gave you no choice but to defend yourself. Everything that lives has that right. Even the Mystics cannot take that away from us—whatever they say. We are not obligated by any right, law, or duty to allow anyone to force us to stand by while they murder us."

Naero bowed her head. "Still, I wish with all my heart and soul that it had not happened—that his blood was not on my hands. I will always regret that."

"I guess that's the difference between us, Naero. Because I wouldn't have. Perhaps that is why I need your help and advice so badly. I'm more ruthless and brutal than you are. My life has twisted me in that direction. I know it."

"What can I do, Uncle? I don't know how to help either of us."

"You're doing it right now. You seem to be able to directly control your Dark Beast, as we call it. And you can do so, all on your own, it appears, without someone like Jia to constantly calm you down and block out the madness. Something I cannot do on my own...yet."

Baeven paced away from her, throwing up his hands in frustration. "Is it something I lack within? Is part of me truly evil or mad? Why did your artifact statue speak directly to you? It explained so much to you. I never got any of that information. Why not? I always felt that the artifact I merged with was trying to say something to me, but I could never hear it."

Naero Shrugged, "I don't know, Uncle. I could have never conversed with mine, had I not learned Kexxian from the KDM."

Baeven's eyes widened. "Perhaps that's it. Tell me again, what your artifact told you about the three ancient artifacts in general?"

Naero sighed. "Not much, really. The last of the three has yet to be found, on the lost world of Xanathar. Jan, Dan, Aunt Sleak, or one of her two daughters will somehow be destined to locate it, and become selected as the Guardian of that artifact and its wisdom. The remaining artifact represents Order. Its tek is supposedly almost pure Drian." She licked her dry lips.

"Go on," Baeven said.

"My artifact represented Change Wisdom. I am supposedly the Guardian of Change—hopefully Enlightened Change. The tek of my artifact was almost pure Kexxian—a fitting match for the KDM."

"So the tek of my artifact was based on that from the G'lothc?"

"Yes, you are supposedly the Chaos Guardian—and that includes the Darkforce as well. Together, the three Guardians of the Three Wisdoms control the power of the Harmony, the only power that can balance out the Destroying nature of the Darkforce. The so-called Great Destroyer is the embodiment of the Darkforce itself."

Baeven waved his hands. "I don't care about the Cosmic Prophecies right now. If your artifact spoke to you in Kexxian, then does that mean that I have to learn G'lothc in order to speak to mine?"

"I don't know. Perhaps. But where are you going to learn G'lothc?"

A vicious grin spread across Baeven's face. It was more than a little unnerving. "Perhaps our friend Ullogk can tutor me."

"The G'lothc spirit that tried to attack your mind? I thought you were going to destroy it."

"There hasn't been time. It's still whimpering in the prison I constructed for the vile thing. I will see how cooperative it can be, given the right encouragement."

"Be careful, Baeven. Don't let it know anything we don't want it to know. If the G'lothc were anything like the Dakkur, it's possible that what one of them knows, all of them will know after a while. We don't know how their minds work, or their souls. They've managed to survive even death somehow, and still remain a threat."

"We'll see. I'll keep you updated on my progress with the thing's interrogation. I've broken its mind, so learning its language shouldn't be too difficult, given time. Now, back to the present. I need you to teach me how to control my Dark Beast without Jia. It is vital that I learn that."

Naero sighed. "I'm not even completely sure how I control mine. And I can't always do so. I completely lost it back on Janosha. I destroyed the enemy, there, but it was only a fluke that I didn't annihilate everyone else on our side."

"But you didn't," Baeven said. "If it had been me, I couldn't have stopped myself at all. That's too big a risk."

"Om helped me, perhaps in some of the same ways Jia helps you. He found a way to cut me off from the Cosmic flows so that my Dark Beast could not feed on those energies. Of course, that was much easier once the planet was gone. He cut off my oxygen as well. As I grew weaker, so did my Dark Beast."

Jia intruded on their discussion.

"Naero, I've been comparing data with Om. We've been meaning to tell you this for some time, but we waited until our analysis was complete. You did not vaporize the planet of Janosha."

"I didn't? Then what happened to it? How could it just disappear? Planets just don't do that."

"Not usually. Yet somehow this one did. It is not entirely impossible. Baeven has told you about Ur-Jahal, the homeworld of my people, the Driathans. It is an entire planet that is cloaked and hidden, as if it has never existed. What few know is that even its location can be changed, if need

317

be, in order to keep it safe. But doing so would require a vast amount of Cosmic energy, almost staggering beyond belief. Only the Kexx and Drians had the tek to even attempt such things. Not even the G'lothc could perform such a feat, for their energies were always devoted toward destruction and the subjugation of others."

Naero sighed again and held up her hands. "I remain stunned and confused by what happened, but at least it's good to know that I wasn't responsible for wiping out an entire planet and all of its lifeforms."

First of all, the energy levels were all wrong, Naero. Analysis proves that you simply could not have destroyed or transported an entire planet. Even the amazing energies you unleashed at that time could not have accomplished such a feat

Naero smiled. "Well, then wherever Janosha is now, I hope it is safe and free."

"We cannot affect that either way. Back to the matter at hand," Baeven said. "I would like to train with you, in whatever way we need to. We both need to learn to better control these Dark Beasts within us. I want to be able do so on my own, without depending so much on Jia. She can't keep propping me up. She will need to take up her own body once again at some point, and serve her people as she was destined to."

Naero shook her head. "I can explain everything that I've figured out, but I need just as much help as you do, Baeven. But you're right. We both need to find a way. We have to try, for the sake of everyone."

"I agree."

"Baeven, all of those years that you trained with the Mystics, didn't they address stuff like this? What did they teach you?"

He nodded. "The condition we share is unique and has not been encountered before we two. Advanced meditation, mental and psyonic discipline, deep personal introspection and therapy sessions have the potential to help. Yet none of that has worked for me; I've tried. Once in combat, with my life threatened, the bloodthirsty monster inside me ignores any attempt to control it, and puts forth all of his efforts to break free and assume total control. I have fought it all my life, and only Jia has been able to help me control it."

"Well, those control techniques might not have helped you, but they might help me or give me some insights. Can you teach them to me?"

"I will. Perhaps you're just a better person than I am, Naero. Perhaps I am simply more evil and chaotic inside than you are."

Naero frowned and paced slightly. "You are the Guardian of Chaos Wisdom and the Darkforce, so that might entail special problems for you that the Change and Order Guardians won't face. We also have to consider that."

She paced some more, sifting through her thoughts, concepts, and ideas on the matter. "I don't think we've found the right angle to approach all of this. There's something we still don't know. Something we're missing. Something in my intuition is telling me this, but I don't know exactly where to look or turn for the complete answers. Right now, we just have parts of the puzzle and its answers. How about this? We need to share our insights. Why don't we both try letting our Dark Beasts out just a little bit in our partial forms and study them? Perhaps then we can find a way to manage them better."

"Their very nature seems to be devoid or all rationality and reason. How can we use that against them?"

"We don't know yet, but both of us have developed strategies for controlling them and keeping them tamped down inside of us. Why do those ways work? We must first build on our successes, and understand them."

"Then I suggest we wait until we train in the Astral Plane or wait until we arrive on Zoa to make such attempts. Things could end very badly if something goes wrong and one or both of us lose control in the close quarters of a starship in space. We can't afford to destroy one of our ships accidently, or kill any of our friends, while conducting such tests."

"Agreed," Naero said. "Speaking of crew, I still want to hear about all of your people and how you came across them. They seem so devoted to you. I remain very curious."

A chime on both their coms went off, summoning them back to engineering for the first leap drive test that evening.

"All long stories for yet another time, Naero. Come, we are needed at the testing."

They arrived at engineering on board *The Dark Star* to find Tyber and Zhen present.

Dr. Zhentisa already had two medbeds set up there.

Captain Ty spoke first.

"Glad you two could join us. This is just a preliminary test for the leap drive to see if we can generate enough Cosmic energy to power and activate it–even for a few seconds."

While the teks prepared for the test, Zhen started treating Naero's practice injuries, while Ty kept explaining.

"Even this process is going to be dangerous. Haisha, both of you look as if you've been in a fight already."

Naero grinned, lifting her battered head up like a proud child. "Sparring practice."

Zhen pushed her back down. "We're not joking here, N. No one has ever done this kind of thing before. This tek is dangerous and experimental. If you and Baeven are going to be our Cosmic power sources, you are going to need all of your strength. You can't just waltz in here all worn out or beaten down."

"There are many important reasons why we must train hard together," Baeven said. "They are just as important as these other matters, and we don't have much time. Proceed, Doctor. Don't scold us. Tell us what to do."

Tyber jumped in at that point. "We hook you two up to the leap drive according to the specs, and you two basically become our batteries. Without a steady and very significant source of Cosmic energy to draw from, there's no way in heaven or hell that such a device like this will ever work."

Naero looked at Baeven and they nodded.

"Let's give it a whirl," she said.

They stretched out on the medbeds. It took several frustrating minutes just to hook up all of the connections.

"All right," Tyber told them. "I'm throwing the switch. Both of you try to give us a trickle of Cosmic energy."

Naero startapped and did so. Immediately she felt the Cosmic energies within her being siphoned off, passing into the collectors of the device. It felt like a yawning maw ready to drain her dry. That frightened her slightly, reminding her too much of the Darkforce energy generators of the enemy.

She nearly panicked. Looking over at Baeven, he appeared to be straining as well.

"No, no," Ty said. "Don't fight it, and don't let up now, of all times. In fact, I need you to increase the flow of Cosmic energy slightly. Dial it up and give us more–imagine about ten times what you've put out so far, if you can."

"Just nod or shake you head," Zhen said. "Stay focused. You're readings are elevated but stable for now. Don't try to talk. As the intensity of the drain increases, you're probably going to experience some discomfort."

Yeah, no shit–like burning icy pain shooting through her body like nanofibers of pure agony. No problem.

But as both of them increased the Cosmic energy feed, the leap drive prototype sputtered and emitted flickering, glowing pulses and flashes of light as it struggled to fully activate and come on line.

"More, give it more," Ty said. "About a hundred times more. Imagine it. Let it flow into the device as you steadily increase the energy levels."

Naero startapped again and redoubled her efforts to comply.

Suddenly the device shuddered and emitted a bright, blinding flash.

Naero and Baeven convulsed on their medbeds and cried out.

For an instant, the device sucked Naero dry and left her gasping, close to blacking out. Baeven seemed to be in the same bad way.

Then the prototype disrupted and lurched to one side, smoking.

Zhen hovered over her patients, checking their scans and examining them with her healing sight.

"Dammit," Ty said, going over the ruined device with several fixers and teks looking on. "Burned out the interface completely. That will take hours to refit and bolster the parameters for that factor alone. We just don't know enough about what we're doing here. It's all experimental. This tek is so complex and strange that most of the time, I'm still guessing."

"We almost powered it up," Alala told them. "Don't be discouraged."

Om added over his link with the ship. *This is good progress. Alala, Jia, and I will crunch the numbers on the various data analyses and compare them to the Kexxian theoretical design spec simulations. From what we learn here, our next attempt will take us forward even more.*

Ty laughed. "Or blow us to kingdom come."

"Uh..." Naero said. She looked over at Baeven.

He just drank a bunch of nutrient-rich lix and promptly went to sleep. Naero saw his eyes roll up and felt hers about ready to do the same.

"Z, that little ride sucked both of us dry. Do what you can to replenish our energies. Like Baeven, I'm going night-night here."

Zhen kept one hand on Naero's forehead and the other clutching her pale hand. "Go ahead and rest, N. You'll be all right. I've got you." Z smiled down at her.

Tyber's voice trailed off. "Perhaps if we recalibrate the energy collectors and beef up the inducer parameters and shielding, it won't even require half as much Cosmic power–just for a raw start-up."

39

While she rested, Naero experienced visions and nightmares again.

She saw Khai, patient and determined, resting in meditation within his green transport sphere, projecting himself rapidly through jump space in swift pursuit.

Now that the Astral marker placed within her was gone, she figured the Enforcer didn't have a precise lock on her, but who knew what other tricks he or the Mystics had up their sleeves? She had no doubt that she and her comrades would run into him at some point, and that she would have to face him again.

Neither she nor Baeven knew of any way to prevent that, except to keep moving and jumping. Proceeding toward Zoa would take them further away from any pursuit.

Baeven explained that the Mystics had grudgingly accepted a mutual stand off with him. Unless he became a direct Cosmic threat, they would no longer pursue him actively or directly.

Naero was another matter entirely, especially since her situation involved her killing a High Master.

Khai would never stop pursuing her until he either captured or killed her–and he was among the most formidable opponents she had ever encountered.

She knew that on her own, even in her best shape, she was no match for the Mystic Enforcer one-on-one.

But that could eventually change. She and Baeven were training hard each day. Given enough time, she might learn to defend herself better.

As the days and the jumps passed on their way toward Zoa, she and Baeven made good progress on reducing their weaknesses and increasing their strengths. All of this, despite the required beatdown sessions.

Gradually Naero grew not only faster, but also more powerful and accurate, in tune more with both her physical prowess, and all of her growing abilities.

Not only that, but more and more, she developed the ability to mimic or learn the psyonic abilities of others. And once she had a working understanding of them, she continued developing her power to use biomancing to bolster and increase the effectiveness of those innate psyonic abilities in others.

"This could be a huge source of income," Naero remarked to Zhen and the rest of her friends. "If I'm not locked up or executed, Spacers will line up to have me augment their psyonic abilities and make them more powerful and effective."

"I wonder if that is wise," Zhen said. "Can our people handle the increase in such powers? Could it go to their heads and corrupt them? Look at what your powers have done to you, and what you struggle with, N."

Naero nodded. "We'll have to consider all that. Just one more reason why I wish I could talk to the Mystics. They could help me decide the wisdom of such things. My outlaw status puts a damper on me conducting any kind of business."

"I know, N. You joke, but I know all of this puts you in a very tough spot. I know how important your honor is to you. I know you're hurting."

Zhentisa took Naero's hands in hers and smiled at her, looking into her eyes. "My dear friend–as much as a pain in the ass as you can be, I wish that you could see, for once, the way others see you. So many people love and admire you, N. They really look up to you. You're a good person, with good instincts–just like your parents. You don't want to hurt anyone, unless you have to."

"But the fact remains: I have hurt people, and I'm still a killer on the run, Z. I'm a renegade on the lam, who has dishonored herself and her Clan."

Zhen patted her hands. "And some day in the future we'll find a way out of that. But for right now, I still believe in you, and so do all of your family, friends, and crew. We will stand with you, Naero–to the bitter end, if need be, and we'll all go down together if it comes to that."

Under her running circumstances, Naero had all but given up any thought to ever having a life that anyone might even attempt to call normal.

But that was the place she found herself in.

Nor would she begrudge Zhen and Ty or anyone else among her friends, Clan, or crew from going off to have lives of their own at any point. She hoped that they could, in fact, and that they all didn't end up dead somehow because of her and her transport full of problems.

Before they could reach Zoa-4, they conducted further tests of the leap drive in the observation chamber adjacent to the medlab.

The latest version of the device was slightly larger and more durable– and the interface much improved–thanks to all that they had learned from the failure of the first prototype.

Tyber announced proudly, "We think that it will only take one of you to power it up this time. And this time it should be easier to modulate one energy source than two variable sources. That might have even been part of the problem last time."

Naero climbed up onto the medbed. "All right. I'll volunteer. Baeven, you standby in case I pass out, or something else goes wrong."

"Will do."

"Very well," Zhen said. "Here we go."

The links and connections went faster and smoother this time.

"Start feeding the device Cosmic energy," Ty said. "Give it a steady flow. It can take it this time."

Naero startapped and produced a large surge of Cosmic energy. She gasped slightly.

The energy collectors on the device latched on to the energy flow, automatically attuned to it, and actually began drawing it out from her– almost by force.

She resisted the drain instinctively at first, feeling a bit dizzy at the sudden demand.

"Don't let up now," Tyber said.

Naero steeled herself to relax and not fight it, despite the feeling that she was being slowly bled dry. Again, it was too much like the energy leeching of the Darkforce generators. Dizziness and even waves of nausea followed and slowly increased, but she keep the flow of Cosmic energy strong and constant.

Despite the discomfort, she could keep the power up at this level, at least for a while.

"It's working," Jia exclaimed. "The device is powering up, cycling, and storing energy in preparation for functioning."

Tyber clapped his hands.

"As soon as the generation sequence is primed, we can try to project and retrieve a tracking probe. There are some minor glitches and modulation fluctuations beyond the design parameters, but I think we'll be good to go on the probe test."

"Guys, I'm going to start feeling pretty weak here–I might black out very soon." Naero blinked and swallowed with great effort.

Tyber looked over at Zhen, somewhat worried. "Can she hold on for about two more standard minutes? That's about all the juice we'll need to send the probe and retrieve it."

Zhen looked at the readings. "I'm not sure. N's right; she's fading. The process is taxing her system close to its limits."

Naero gasped and then nodded, her face red and sweating. "T, it's all right. I can hold out that long."

Help me, Om. Help me hold out.

She focused on keeping the Cosmic energy flowing through her steady.

Two agonizing standard minutes passed.

"Got it!" Tyber said. "Launching probe."

A soundless blinding flash erupted.

Ty watched the scanners.

"Powering down. Probe retrieval in six seconds. One...two..."

"Abort! Abort!" Jia warned. "Feedback levels on retrieval increasing exponentially. This will cause a massive detonation of the probe!"

"Too late!" Ty shrieked.

"Focus all emergency shielding around the probe itself!" Baeven shouted, stepping in front of them all.

His emulators shot out in front of their ships to intercept the returning probe.

Naero still felt so weak, she couldn't even lift herself up.

Zhen drew them and Ty back behind the medical bay shields and brought down heavy blast screens.

That left Baeven in the observation chamber with the device and the returning probe out beyond them, blazing like a comet right toward them.

Then it detonated.

The blast vaporized every one of Baeven's emulators and then crumpled both ships, causing major damage.

Their deflector shields disrupted and the heavy blast screens ruptured. The hulls of both vessels decompressed and struggled to seal themselves.

Clouds of fixers raced to the affected areas and immediately began repairing the damage at all levels.

Naero and her friends picked themselves up and stared through the gaping hole in the blast shields and the blasted observation chamber. The leap drive device lay heavily damaged and burned out once again, smashed or blasted into the far wall, off its ruined gravlifts.

Baeven lay to the other side in a scorched, bloody heap.

"Hurry," Jia said. "Bae's hurt badly. He needs rapid medical attention."

Naero staggered to her feet. She and Zhen rushed into the ruined chamber and went to work on him immediately where he lay gasping.

He passed out, going into traumatic shock.

His chest was torn open, shrapnel penetrating close to his heart.

Naero moved in and carefully used teknomancing to draw out all of the pieces of foreign material from his wounds, while Zhen kept oxygen flowing to the brain, closed the injuries off, and re-knit the various tissues and organs to continue their functions.

Once the major damage was mended, they continued using their biomancing abilities to strengthen Baeven and bolster his life force energies back up to optimal levels. Then they brought him back around.

Without their miraculous efforts, even he would have bled out and perished within the space of a few minutes.

"Thank you," Jia told them. "Thank you for saving his life."

Any normal man would have been killed outright, yet Baeven had used both his considerable tek and Cosmic abilities to shield himself and all of them from as much of the destruction as he could take on.

He had saved them all–again–at great risk and cost to himself.

What a gigablast. All from a streamlined tracking probe no more than a meter in length.

That mishap was most unfortunate, Om said. *Yet we are theoretically much closer now to getting this extremely complex and dangerous device operating properly.*

Naero felt her eyes widen. "We nearly died," she noted. "I'm starting to question if all of this risk is worth it."

Baeven nodded. "It will be. How close are we now, Jia?"

"We can compensate for all of the problems we've had thus far and eliminate them. We'll still need more tests before we can attempt to transport an entire ship. Yet time grows short."

"Just let us know when you need us. Update us on any progress."

"Will do. In the meantime, it is imperative that I attempt to contact the other sentinels on our secret channels. It may take some time for a response due to the extreme ranges. But it could also focus our search and possibly save us a needless trip. If any of the sentinels are missing or do not respond, I should be able to determine who, and where."

The two ships separated when they finally reached Zoa-4. *The Dark Star* would remain in orbit, keeping watch and conducting its continuing tests on the leap drive.

The Shadow Fox would proceed down to the planet's surface.

Zoa-4 was a proto-world. Life-bearing, but all the lifeforms were simple. Basic plants and simple animals.

Close-up scans barely revealed an old crash site, decades old. The site was now almost completely overtaken by mosses, molds, lichens and algae. The moist, humid atmosphere proved very conducive to such growth. Zoa was nearly a swamp world.

Jia effortlessly passed her soul into Baeven, with Naero and Zhen monitoring the process with their healing sight. Both gained further insight into the procedure, and discussed the ramifications back and forth for a few minutes. Both of them noticed different things.

For Zhen, it was her first viewing of such a transfer with her biomancer skills.

"That was…incredible," was all that she could finally conclude. Part of her seemed to be in shock.

Routine scans confirmed Jia's information on the atmosphere of Zoa-4 being safe and breathable. The landing party disembarked and made their way first to the nearby crash site.

There really wasn't anything else visible to head to.

Yet once they reached the site itself, Jia emitted a single, clear lilting note out of Baeven's throat.

Om informed Naero that the note was a coded vibronic signal, filled with complex Driathan activation frequencies—and the earth itself opened up before them.

Naero felt Om gasp.

This world is a marvel, N. Everything looks as natural as could be— but it is all synthetic.

Are you certain, Om? Even the bio-scans read everything as completely natural.

The complex lattice structures are so perfect that they are nearly indistinguishable from biological life. But make no mistake. Zoa is an entire living, biomechanical world. It functions as a single, hyper-complex

327

android entity–right down to the nano levels that Jia's presence has activated.

Baeven himself moved quickly, despite two recoveries from recent severe injuries. His rate of regeneration was still staggering to Naero's mind. Yet now that they were on Zoa-4, he was obviously eager to reach something.

The planet seemed to be coming more and more to life as they passed through it. The world seemed to sense Jia's presence and respond to it.

Finally, just in front of them, an intricate series of heavily armored blast hatches opened in rippling sequence.

Carefully concealed beneath the surface, as one of the Driathan Sentinel Worlds, Zoa was an impregnable, biotek fortress.

As they went forward into the hidden structure beneath the surface, Naero spotted tatters of a dusty, old-fashioned Spacer nanosuit–first generation–before the improved invention of Nytex. They were covered with old, faded brown blood stains. Then a shattered Spacer helmet, still lying in the dust.

Naero gasped a little and snapped her head back to look at Baeven.

For one of the first times since she'd known him, he truly smiled with what could only be happiness.

"This is where you crashed," Naero said. "Where you met Jia."

"Zoa-4 is her private sentinel world. It more than belongs to Jia–it is part of her. It is her–her precise creation–the very first test of her powers that the Drians gave her. It is all that and much more. Only Ur-Jahal is far more amazing, according to her."

A well-defended pod opened up before them like an enormous, delicate flower–yet one bristling with hi-tek weaponry. The weaving of biomancy and teknomancy was so carefully woven together that both Naero and Om found it staggering.

Zoa was a living organism, and a living machine, all at the same time.

Naero had a pretty good idea where they were going, and why Baeven was so eager to get there.

They made their way down in the bower of the sleeping goddess of the Driathans.

Baeven led the way. The yearning look on his face grew more intense with each step.

Waves of light washed over them. Naero sensed and drank in the Power Cosmic, heavy upon the very air. It was woven and stuffed into the atomic level of everything around them.

The Power of the Cosmic Lifespark and the Harmony.

It flowed out from the center of the flower's pod or core, glowing with a scintillating, glorious radiance that spread throughout every atom and molecule of the planet.

You could breathe it in.

Both Naero and Om comprehended it all suddenly and understood.

Jia controlled and directed every atom of this living world.

She was its heart and soul–its Lifespark. Jia infused all of its forward evolution with infinite purpose and design.

She was its creator.

Just as her creators had been the godlike Drians before her.

Baeven knelt and caressed the core of the closed pod with his bare fingertips. It flashed with radiance at his touch and immediately yielded, unsealing, opening, and slipping back to either side.

They could enter within now, into an inner sanctum suffused with the pure light of the Harmony.

A goddess really did lie sleeping within.

A female entity of light–of beauty beyond imagination and comparison.

If Jia was but a shadow of the glory of the Drians, then their beauty and perfection must have indeed been unbearable to behold.

She lay curled to one side, wearing a soft, shimmering gown of some seamless, silken cloth that looked as if it were made of liquid light itself. Her glittering white-gold hair looked beyond holographic. Her skin itself– somehow a hue of both shimmering chrome and radiant white alabaster.

Baeven climbed into the bower without hesitation, wrapped himself lovingly around her, and curled up beside her tantalizing form in pure bliss.

As if that was his place–as if doing so were the most natural thing in the world.

For the first time in her life, Naero witnessed Baeven weep, and his tears fell freely upon his beloved's motionless, perfect face and hair like an awakening rain.

Naero gasped and covered her mouth with both hands as she herself wept. All present fell to their knees, stricken dumb.

The way Baeven looked upon Jia–the way he touched her–were the very personifications of love.

He turned Jia's perfectly sculpted face up to his and kissed her with passion, full upon the lips.

Jia's soul swept back into her miraculous form.

Jia stirred and came to life, every motion, each movement of her form flowing perfection–like watching art and beauty themselves move. And the more she awoke, the more the aura of light around her grew.

Enchanting.

Enthralling.

Her first act was to open her mouth and give herself fully to her beloved–kissing Baeven in return–just as passionate and yearning.

His hands went to her face, caressing every line.

And when she opened her shining, radiant green eyes to his, Baeven shuddered and was completely overcome. He sobbed and bowed his head above her breast, as her perfectly sculpted hands pulled him closer to her heart.

Naero wiped her own tear-stained face, unable to look away.

If just once in her life, she could have someone look upon her that way.

She wished that she could turn back and give Baeven and Jia even a few precious hours together. The two of them more than deserved it.

Yet this was not a time for lovers. They were at war with implacable, ruthless foes. All of them had risked much to come to Zoa-4 on urgent business. The fate of the entire galaxy might be at stake.

Jia smiled like the dawn of the Zoan sun itself, and lifted Baeven's face down up to hers, and kissed him deeply once again.

Then she pulled away, grinning as happily as any lover would.

"Later, my love. Now that I have returned, let me check with all of the other sentinels. You will also be happy to know that the gateway to Ur-Jahal has finally been sealed. I am the key, and I can go forward with you from now on."

"Do as you will; you will not leave my arms."

Jia nodded happily. "Hold me, then. I wish for no miracle other than the touch of your hands upon me."

She lay back down in Baeven's arms, and light pulsed out from her bower and flickered back and forth throughout the complex.

"Have a seat, everyone," Baeven called out. "This may take a while."

Several minutes passed.

Finally Jia gasped and startled them all. She sat up in a near panic.

"Govae. It is Govae that they have located. Even now, they assail him upon his own sentinel world of Dotar-2."

"Where is that, Jia?" Naero said.

"Dotar-2 is very far from us, I am afraid." She fed them the coordinates.

"Damn it!" Baeven said, reading his wristcomp. "In an inner section of the Cygnus arm–another part of the Gamma Quadrant–virtually unexplored by any of the current sentient races. Even with our current tek, it would take us decades to reach Dotar-2 and get back."

"Not with our new leap drive," Naero suggested.

"It doesn't even work yet," Baeven said. "The last preliminary test nearly killed us all."

"Then we'd better get to work," Naero said. "How come the enemy knows about all of this? How can they navigate so readily across such vast distances? I'm sick of them having every advantage over us."

"They don't always have to travel," Baeven said. "From studying Ullogk, I've learned that G'lothc minds can be completely linked with each other under certain conditions, sharing everything they know and experience."

"Like a hive mind?" Naero suggested. "Like the hive minds of the Dakkur?"

Baeven waved one hand. "Far more complex than that and over greater distances–even between galaxies, it would appear–and that is stunning. I have learned that each G'lothc soul operates as an independent, separate individual. Yet, once they are linked properly, each knows and comprehends what all the others know and experience. It is believed that the Yattai share a similar affinity with each other on their plane of existence."

"That would be another distinct advantage," Naero pointed out. "Instant awareness, communication, and coordination of their activities across vast distances."

"Yet even their abilities are not limitless," Baeven said. "The conditions allowing them to communicate and share information in this manner require vast amounts of Darkforce energy, the basis for all of their tek. Such transmissions are arranged over very short bursts of time. Naero and I witnessed one such exchange inside the enemy biowar facility."

"That also worries me," Naero said. "What about the Ullogk? Can it spy on us through you and alert the others to our plans?"

"Not unless it took over my mind," Baeven said. "And that isn't about to happen. Inside my mind, I am in complete control. As you know, Naero, the G'lothc mind and soul essence that I have imprisoned within me is cowering and quivering in stasis–entirely cut off from the others of his foul kind. I probably should simply destroy it, but I'm still studying it, trying to learn its language and weaknesses. I can't help thinking such information might prove useful to us one day."

"Just be careful," Naero said. "Those foul spirits of theirs reek with Darkforce energy, evil, and malice. I wish we could wipe them all out."

Baeven turned to Jia and took her hand. "What of your comrade, Jia? If we can reach him, what can we do?"

"Each sentinel world is well-defended. Yet any static defense can be eventually overwhelmed, given time and enough firepower. The alarms and warnings have gone out, to me here and to each of the other thirty-four sentinels and their worlds. Our brother Govae is under direct assault on Dotar-2. Our enemies of old move against us. We and all the Driathan people stand in grave danger."

"What's our plan of attack?" Baeven said.

"First, we must reach Dotar-2 in time. We must break the siege and rescue Govae before our foes can capture him and destroy and sift through his mind, his thoughts, and his knowledge as they tear him apart. They seek the location of the other thirty-five sentinel worlds, and of Ur-Jahal itself."

"How long can Govae hold out?" Naero asked.

"Quite a while. If things go against him, he will attempt to destroy himself before he can be taken. Yet he would only do so at the last need."

"What if the worst happens?" Baeven asked. "What if our foes overwhelm his defenses and capture him? What then?"

Terror washed over Jia's normally serene features. "Then I fear the worst. After they strip his mind, they could erase and eradicate his spirit essence. Destroying Govae's soul would revert his empty shell–his body–back to its proto-form. With the right tek and research, the enemy could use that proto-form as an open vessel. They could implant it with a new mind and spirit–one from the G'lothc. That would indeed be a very great evil."

"How so?" Naero asked.

"Then the evil G'lothc would be truly reborn into an immortal body with all of our hi-tek secrets, and many of those of our Makers. Just as the Makers feared. That is why they protected us from the Great War. Imagine the abomination of G'lothc souls possessing the ultimate hosts–the immortal bodies of my beloved people, that will never fail or wear out? There would be no end to the damage they could inflict upon the universe.

"First they would use the knowledge they gained to go on the hunt for the other Driathan sentinels, taking over more host bodies to use in their vile plots and exploiting our tek. Eventually, they would locate Ur-Jahal, and all of our people, locked in their healing sleep. Millions of perfect, immortal, self-healing hosts, ripe for the conquest."

Baeven rose up and clenched his fists. "We will not allow that."

"We must find a way to reach Govae, then." Jia shuddered. "I sense his pain and distress. I dare not alert him, for fear that they might detect our efforts and locate Zoa also. My poor brother stands alone against the full might of our dark foes!"

"Govae is your brother?" Naero asked, suddenly thinking of her siblings.

Jia smiled sadly. "So we were all created. All Driathans are brothers and sisters," she said.

"Do Driathans marry? Can they reproduce?"

"Not normally." Jia looked at Baeven briefly. "Yet love makes all things possible. Until I met Bae, there were many things that I thought were impossible. He has opened my eyes to so many things in this universe–love and pleasure not the least of them. Who knows then, what can be?"

Jia touched his face. Baeven leaned into her caress and kissed her open palm.

That was it. It was painfully obvious how these two felt about each other.

Naero had to give them them some privacy.

"We'll keep expanding work on the leap drive," she said. "That's going to take some time. Why don't the two of you take a break and get reacquainted, while we keep things going here on our end?"

40

Naero spoke with their crews while Baeven and Jia took their private time together on board *The Shadow Fox* in their quarters.

Naero arrived in the planning room first, prepared to update everyone on every status of their various projects and missions. With so many people stuffed into it from their ships, the room was a hodgepodge of scents to Naero's sensitive nose.

She could pick out each person's scent, their various colognes or perfumes, the wiring and plas smell of tek. She noted various forms of lix or food they had on them, or that they had recently snacked on.

After the briefing, they all returned to their posts and duties. Ty and his teks redoubled their efforts on the leap drive, scheduling a battery of progressive tests throughout the next few days.

They would continue to use Naero and Baeven as their Cosmic batteries to accomplish these feats–to continually power the latest variations of the new device. Jia could help a little with her control of nearby Zoa, feeding them pure flows of Cosmic energy.

But it all remained exhausting.

They had no choice.

Get the damn tek working and reach Govae, or allow him and all of his vast secrets to fall to their enemies.

Naero had to rest and refuel continually if she was going to keep up the schedule they required.

Batteries needed to recharge.

She reached out briefly into the Astral Plane during one of her rest sessions, attempting to reach Womi.

To her surprise, Khai was waiting for her to appear there and pounced on her almost immediately, swooping in to attack her. He got out a few garbled words before Naero broke off her connection.

The Mystic Enforcer stalked them relentlessly because of her–coming closer every second–just as she suspected.

And when he found them, they had no way to stop him.

Especially once he reached Zoa-4.

There weren't any enemy forces there to throw in his way. Even she and Baeven would be hard-pressed to fight him and that damn Cosmic Sword of his. Especially while they were both constantly being drained and kept so weak.

But they couldn't let anything stop them, either. They were the only ones who knew anything about these dire enemy threats, or who had a ghost of a chance of doing anything about them.

And even they remained ignorant–still in the dark about so much, constantly playing catch-up with their foes.

After more fitful rest, Naero went to check on the non-stop leap drive experiments.

Ty and his teks looked tired, bleary-eyed, and discouraged.

"Any luck with the probes?" she asked.

They shook their heads.

"Let's face it, N–we're making scant progress," Ty said, half-heartedly.

"Yeah…by constantly failing," Zhen noted. "By learning what not to do. Good thing you're here, N. We're out of juice. Time to feed the kitty again."

"Ugh…" She rolled her eyes. The device continued to suck her and Baeven dry of their Cosmic energies to power itself. And with Baeven still recovering from his injuries, and catching up with Jia, Naero was the only game in town at the moment.

"Okay. Just don't make me pass out this time, Z."

Dr. Zhentisa smirked. "No promises. Just lie down on the medbed, N."

"Genius. Where's my head?"

More of the same jolly time.

After they were done, and she had some lix and food, Naero finally felt like she could stand up and walk.

Good news. We sent out another leap probe and finally brought one back...without it imploding.

"Great, Om. Imploding–bad."

Alala cut in. "We've got something coming in from our scanning and comstation, Captain. Cloaked and approaching fast."

"What is it?" Ty asked. "Khai? The enemy?"

"The Enforcer doesn't cloak," Naero said. "He just charges in and kicks ass."

"Right."

"Even with the new sensor arrays Baeven gave us, we're still having a problem pinpointing or defining it. But whatever it is, it's coming straight at us like it knows exactly where we are. Arrival...within just a few hours."

"Track it as best you can and keep us posted."

They were running out of time.

With Khai also closing in–Naero could feel it on the back of her neck.

Now this unknown phantom coming straight for them.

Jia and Baeven finally joined them in the tek lab, both looking radiant and particularly pleased.

Over the next two hours, they ran one experiment after another.

"We've done it," Jia said at last. "We sent out a probe, even further than it would take to reach Dotar-2, and retrieved it safely. All we need to do now is refit the device to our ships, program our destination, and get going."

"Refitting now," Tyber said. "All fixers working toward that goal. I'll use teknomancing to speed up the reconfiguration. Just let me focus."

Naero shook her head in frustration. She and Om went over the data and had bad news for them all.

"Haisha. I'm sorry, my friends, but it's still not going to work. Even with all we've done, were still days away from hitting the go button on this device. Khai and this other thing are closing in on us too fast. They'll be all over us long before then."

"I have a radical suggestion," Alala announced to both ships. "Om and I have finished decoding more fragments of the KDM referring both to to leap tek–and its similarities to the enemy wormhole generators. The Kexx knew all about them. With simple modifications, we can also use a variant of this tek to open a temporary wormhole to Dotar-2. It's a one-shot deal with an unstable wormhole, and it will only last a few minutes, but it's our only chance of getting us there quickly. We can still continue to perfect our primary goals with the leap drive for future use."

"But the question remains, how fast can we make it all work?"

"Estimates with the fixers are between one and two hours," Alala said.

"That's more like it. Let's throck on that," Naero said. "Give the fixers the specs and I'll absorb the data from Om."

"Let's move, people," Baeven said. "We'll dock the ships again, and go through this one-shot wormhole together."

"One problem I'm seeing..." Naero said, absorbing the tek data flowing through the fixers.

"I see it, too," Jia said. She turned to Baeven. "The Cosmic energy requirements. They're off the charts. Powering the wormhole will not only burn out the device completely—there's a chance that it could kill you both."

Baeven smiled. He didn't even glance back at Naero. "What's a little risk among friends and family?"

Less than two hours later, they ignited an unstable wormhole aimed toward Dotar-2.

Naero couldn't even lift her head off her medbed.

She kept drifting in and out.

Baeven had fallen into a coma. Jia lay wrapped around him—only her advanced Driathan healing abilities keeping him alive as his body struggled to regenerate.

"Proceed through the wormhole," Om advised. "We have eighty-seven standard seconds."

Warning alarms went off.

"What is it?" Naero asked. She forced herself to sit up.

"It's Khai," Tyber said. "Coming in hot. He's trying ram right into us. We can't go through a wormhole cloaked. All shields up. Max acceleration."

"He'll try to damage and disable us," Naero said. "Or he'll phaze right through our hull and immediately go on the attack to subdue the ship and crew. He'll stun everyone with his sword, and neither Baeven or I can fight him right now."

"Another ship uncloaking," Alala said. "Naero, it's *The Flying Dagger*. It's firing all batteries on the Enforcer. No effect; they're just batting him around."

"At least they're delaying him," Naero yelled. "Get us through that wormhole!"

"Entering now," Ty said. "Both of our new friends are attempting to pursue."

"Don't let them!" Naero screamed. "Shut the wormhole down. Negate it and leave them behind us!"

"We can't. It's already unstable and collapsing at its own rate of decay. We can't disrupt it without killing everyone."

All of them sped through the wormhole's tunnel and radiant light show. The effects seemed to mesmerize all who stared out at them.

With nobody paying direct attention, Naero rolled off her medbed and crawled on her hands and knees over to an open scanning station.

In seconds, the wormhole spit them out the other side.

They emerged into a far distant arc of the Cygnus arm in the Gamma Quadrant.

Now they were on their enemy's turf, in unexplored space.

Then everything went dark on board.

All of their ships lost power, dead and drifting through space at hypervelocity.

They struggled even to maintain life support.

They experienced a total energy drain and power loss. Even their advanced fixers clattered lifeless to the floor, becoming useless balls of scrap metal.

This was something they certainly didn't expect from generating and utilizing an unstable Cosmic wormhole.

Minutes turned into desperate hours.

Without power, they were all forced to get into EV suits and use emergency lights and battery packs.

In less than two days, they would all suffocate, freeze, and die.

Naero finally got some of their hundreds of burned out fixers working. She sent a few out into space to try to locate either *The Flying Dagger* or Khai, if they were close by.

Only Jia's miraculous android body did not require life support.

More and more, Naero could see why the G'lothc would hunger for such indestructible, immortal, self-repairing synthetic bodies to use as their hosts.

At least Naero and her friends were still generally speeding in the direction of Dotar-2.

Too bad most of them would be dead, frozen popsicles by the time they shot past it.

Getting a weak telepathic message from Baeven.

Focus on it, Om.

Naero. Dotar's star. Tap its Cosmic energy. Use its flows and your teknomancy to restart our drives. Have our pilots sling us around the star and juice us up. I can't move yet. You must do this.

Baeven, like you, I can't walk yet, after powering our wormhole. I can't even stand up.

At least you're still conscious. Find a way, or all of us and our crews are all dead. Don't let that happen.

Okay. I won't. I'll find a way. Where'd you get such a crazy idea?

Baeven laughed weakly. *Khai just told me–telepathically. He's out there, somewhere, trying to do the same thing. Even that sword of his has temporarily lost all its power. He said that you alone would understand the concepts involved.*

She did. So, going through that strange wormhole had disrupted almost everything, it seemed–even Yii.

The stars. Of course. The stars were the answer. Always.

Energy. Raw Cosmic energy.

She had less that two standard days to figure out a way to startap and convert that power into a form they could use directly, before they were all dead.

They maintained contact with both *The Dark Star* and *The Flying Dagger* through the reviving fixers.

Tyber's crew relayed that they were limping along, still docked with them.

Om was somehow protected by being inside of Naero. But both Jia and especially Alala were also damaged from being part of their vessels. The crews struggled to put up old-style solar collectors and restart their failed drives.

A truly inspired idea, but it wouldn't work fully enough on its own. Yet it did give them emergency power and buy them more time.

Naero ordered the same. Solar collectors all around.

No sign of Khai. If they located him, they would assist him. Naero still did not want to be responsible for his death or that of any Mystic. Part of her hoped that he'd find a way to survive as well. She didn't hate Khai. They had been friends once and helped each other greatly. In fact, she admired and respected him.

But she couldn't let him capture her. She couldn't go back yet to take responsibility for her actions. Not until the current enemy threats were eliminated and she discovered a way to cure her own Cosmic disease.

Khai was simply doing his duty as the Mystic Enforcer, and she was a wanted criminal on the run. She couldn't fault him for any of that.

Technically, she remained both an outlaw and a murderer.

The solar collectors gathered power–enough to get some of their systems back up, even life support. Yay!

At last, their basic sublight propulsion restarted.

Naero also regenerated. She startapped a bit, and could finally sit up without passing out.

"All ships," she commanded. "Get us closer to Dotar's star. Throw up what deflector shields we can. *Dagger,* this is Naero. You might want to dock with us. We're going to go into a safe but close orbit around the star, and prepare to slingshot us all around it. It's going to be tricky, but I'll try to siphon off and convert the energy we need to restart our power cores and our drives as we pass. Run diagnostics and fixer repairs on all systems. Whatever you do, don't let us get sucked in to the star's gravity well."

Enel laughed over the link. "You got it, boss. Want us to make you a sandwich, too, while we're at it?"

"That would be very nice, smartass. Tell Eugene thick slices of Spum on Govanian pumpernickel, please. And a borbble of cold Jett…while you're at it."

"Fresh out at the moment, Captain. Good to hear your voice, sir."

"Damnation. Take us in, then, as close as we need to."

They danced upon the edge of oblivion, all three crippled starships docked together, lost in the unexplored Gamma Quadrant and spinning dangerously close to the nearest sun.

In Naero's current condition, startapping might yet prove fatal. And the additional distraction of a sudden flare-up of her Cosmic sickness did not help matters, either. Pulsating sores of disrupting, infected Cosmic energy, fed by the Darkforce, erupted all over her flesh, causing her intense pain.

The air was suddenly rank with psyonic ichor, fetid ozone, and putrefaction.

Naero attempted to use her weakened abilities to lick at the star as if it were an immense lollipop of Cosmic energy. Power–both she and their ships all needed power to restart their cores and save themselves.

To pull that off, they had to get in dangerously close to the star.

Too close and they'd all be reduced to a puff of atoms on the solar winds.

If she were in better shape, the process might prove easier, and safer. Yet she and Baeven were both still drained and beaten up from getting them there–spending all of their Cosmic energies to power the unstable wormhole that brought them out that way, on their dire mission.

Naero reached out tentatively with another tiny feeder ribbon, struggling not to open herself up to too much power. She and Om both knew what would happen then. A runaway, out-of-control power surge, building to a huge gigablast.

She struggled to avoid such a fate, almost too late.

Even the small feedback rush that shot into her smallest feeder tendril was nearly overwhelming in her reduced state.

The rush of pure Cosmic force raced through her sick and damaged body, transfixing her, consuming her last defenses.

Such power. Raw Cosmic energy beyond description. Naero gasped and tried to swallow.

That power nearly destroyed and incinerated her.

If she allowed it to suck them in, they would all be disintegrated.

Instant flaming death.

Om screamed in her head, but she could not make out his words.

Waves of Kexxian defensive protocols lashed out and melted and vaporized in the face of such naked might.

They struggled against a star itself–to war with and absorb those destructive energies and make use of them.

Om attempted to save them. More Kexxian defenses erupted and ramped up exponentially in expanding bubbles and spheres.

Naero screamed. Her veins, her heart, her brain–every atom of her brimmed with Cosmic force. Her Cosmic disease was both fed by such energies, and destroyed by them.

Even her Dark Beast fell back in sudden shock, bloated and blitzed on energy in a sudden, besotted coma like a drunkard.

Her friends and crew...her family.

They were all that Naero could think of and recall.

With one wave of her hand, she spent most of her power to fling their ships back from the impending destruction, restarting all three fusion cores at the last instant–even *The Star Fox*.

Naero finally understood, too late, as she barely managed to transform into an energy being.

She had managed to save the others even as the star pulled her into its gravity vortex.

Yet somehow, for the moment, the Kexxian fields around her stabilized.

She swam or soared through the intensely hot, expanding energies of the star's surface, as if it were an immense sea of energy.

Then she caught sight of Khai, the Mystic Enforcer, moving under his own power and force of will.

Bright green and glowing in his own energy form, he swung himself around, far outside the fierce core of the star, recharging his sword Yii within the might of the sun itself. Just as Yii had been created in a similar fashion.

Naero struggled to move toward him, still unable to keep herself from slowly being drawn in further, in her weakened state.

He looked her way, sensing her approach. Khai called out to her telepathically.

You're moving too fast, Naero. You'll be drawn into the core. You won't survive there long. I know that fact, better than anyone.

I can't stop myself; I'm sick and damaged. Please, catch me. Help me, Khai. I'm dying!

Khai strained and strove for her, the look on his face suddenly frantic.

He just missed her fingertips as she continued to spiral in.

I can't reach you in time! he said.

Naero smiled sadly, as an extreme calmness and serenity washed over her.

Like all Spacers, Naero knew that one day she would return to the stars.

She just had not expected it to be this soon—not while she still had so much to do. So much she still yearned to accomplish.

Naero took no further thought to herself. Her worries and fears were all for those she loved—for those who would remain without her.

A scant few months before, through all the many perils that she had faced, up to this critical moment, no one could have told her that she would stare such a stark fate as this directly in the eye. The most recent events of her life flashed rapidly through her mind as if they were vids.

Instants seemed to dilate into days.

She nearly swept past Khai again.

He lunged forward—expending his own energies, finally grasping her outstretched hand and pulling her back close to him, controlling their movement.

Khai telepathically shouted above the constant roar of the solar flows, trying to explain their situation.

Relax and listen, Naero. You're safe for the moment, but we both must focus our energies on continuing to circle the core without letting it pull us in. The only way to escape the star's gravity is to increase our velocity and ride the expanding solar flows back up toward the surface, and shoot out, kind of like a solar flare. Do you understand? We'll need to work together, if you want to break free.

Naero clung to him at first, gasping breathless in her energy form, that did not need to breathe. She calmed herself against the comforting luxury of his broad chest—so seductive. With Khai in his energy form, having his powerful arms wrapped around her was a little too enjoyable. Khai was normally a huge, muscular, hunky guy in either form, and she was so small in his arms.

In their energy forms, she suddenly realized that everything was beyond intense. All was light and every sensation. Everything was heightened a thousandfold–including all of her feelings, pent-up needs, and emotions. Normal minds weren't used to such hyper-stimulation.

When she looked up into Khai's impossibly golden eyes, she nearly lost it. He had just saved her life–for the moment, at least–and she felt both close and extremely grateful to her old friend.

Naero felt an overwhelming urge to kiss Khai, and much, much more after that.

But she was just barely able to pull herself back from the brink.

Such thoughts were insanity. It was just their situation and the heightened rush of stimuli making her feel all of that and more. It was too much. She needed to get control of herself.

Let's call a truce, she called back telepathically, her mental voice also roaring to be heard over the constant din. I'm not here to fight you, Khai.

Then come back with me quietly, Naero–as my prisoner. If you give me your word, I will not restrain you.

She shook her head. I can't, Khai. You know I can't–or do you? Do you know what our enemies are up to? What they are planning, way out here in the Gamma Quadrant? They've implemented a full-scale invasion of our galaxy, where we can't even see or fight them. And they're winning, Khai. They're crushing, and destroying, and killing anyone or anything that tries to stand before them. Hundreds of defenseless worlds have already fallen. Numerous sentient races and cultures already wiped out. And our foes will grow in power until they are ready to attack and overwhelm our quadrant in the same exact way. There's too much at stake out here, Khai, and you don't even know the half of what they're plotting.

Khai looked at her sadly. *I have my duty, Naero. When our truce is over, you will need to fight me.*

Naero lifted her head and returned his fierce glance. Did you hear anything of what I just told you? I will do what I must. I will fight you with every ounce of power I have, if need be. But I do not do so simply to avoid capture. This is bigger than any of us or our petty squabbles. Please, listen to me. It doesn't have to be this way. Just let me tell you where we are and why we are out here. What happens out here will decided the fate of all of our peoples–of many peoples.

More of your tricks to deceive me, Naero? To make me care about what you say? You would make up anything to–

What about the enemy biowar missile attack, heading for our quadrant, Khai? Right this moment, as we speak?

Preliminary scans revealed no such pending attack, Naero.

These are hi-tek enemy smartweapons. They can cloak and avoid all normal forms of detection in order to slip through our defenses. The attack is coming. We can prove it.

How convenient. An invisible alien attack that no one can detect or prevent. And instead of chasing after you, everyone's supposed to scurry around, chasing our tails, while you get away.

Naero smirked and pushed away from him. Are you always this dense, Khai? Would you just shut up and listen for once? So, you think we'd risk our lives to go all the way out here in the middle of nowhere in the Gamma Quadrant–just to avoid you? This isn't about either of us, or the Mystics. Please, for once, give me a chance and listen to what I have to say.

Khai frowned. *We need to focus on increasing our velocity and riding the solar flows back toward the surface. If we're lucky, we'll spot a solar flare about to discharge. We can ride it out, but this is going to take a while. While we do so–go ahead, if you wish–tell me about these so-called enemy threats of yours. I will do my best to try to listen.*

She looked up into his eyes and felt herself going all to pieces again.

You will? Was it just her, or was it him, too?

If he even felt a tenth of what was racing through her, they were in serious trouble.

The Enforcer looked back into her eyes very intently.

Of course, Naero. I'm not just some mindless, robotic goon. I care deeply about our people, just as you do.

Whoever started it, they were instantly kissing the next second, wildly and passionately, their Cosmic energies merging and mixing and flowing freely between them, nearly beyond control.

In their energy forms, neither of them wore any clothing or gear.

How convenient.

Inside the star itself, they were literally on fire with desire, glowing hands and mouths slipping and spinning and yearning all over each other.

Their mouths locked back onto each other and fused together, face to face, burning eyes to burning eyes.

Naero leaped upon Khai, wrapping her shining arms and legs tightly around him as he surged up into her. Both of their psyonic voices shrieked in blinding joy. They were spinning and driving together in near-mindless delight, riding the crest of a sirocco of passion on the solar energy waves.

Both of them pulsated with Cosmic power in total synergistic unison, waxing as they filled to overflowing with energy and joy. They swept up toward the surface, whirling faster and faster, gaining energy and speed.

They lost track of time, caught up in their Cosmic-induced madness, building and building until the powers and emotions within them reached critical mass and detonated.

They screamed again, and even in their energy forms, it seemed as if they suddenly both became not only transparent as glass, but insubstantial.

Cosmic and solar energy flowed between them, into them, out of them, and through them.

For an instant, they were as completely as one as two separate entities could be. All of their forces and energies combined into one.

Khai healed Naero, revitalized her, and gave her her strength back, and she did the same for him. They gave each other back to themselves, yet they were each still a part of the other now.

That secret would always remain between them.

Khai took hold of her Cosmic sickness and incinerated it.

He burned it right out of her with but a thought.

Naero strengthened weaknesses Khai had yet to uncover within himself. She did so automatically. They made each other better, stronger.

They parted abruptly, so much so that it was like a sudden agony that brought them both nearly to their knees in anguish.

They strove to become two separate entities once more.

It was torment to be separated from such a perfect state of ecstasy and bliss. Yet both of them recognized that, at least now, they could focus once again on being themselves.

Being so completely joined together was far too intoxicating.

Far too beautiful.

Way too terrifying.

The danger lay in never wanting to depart from that perfect state, and becoming lost within its tempting ecstasy–forever–to the abandonment and exclusion of all else.

Much too tempting.

Naero averted her gaze, trying not to look into his eyes again.

It took all of her force of will, suddenly, just to do that much.

Khai, what just happened was…amazing. Too amazing, in fact. I can't take it. We're not used to anything like this–neither of us.

Yes. You are right, Naero. I agree.

We're not used to doing stuff like that in our energy forms. It made me want to…give up everything and just stay like that, forever. I can't do that, not even for you."

He tried to touch her again, and Naero shied away from him.

She barely saw Khai avert his gaze the same way she did.

For an instant he looked completely shattered and grief-stricken.

You're right, Naero. I felt the same. Neither of us can control such heightened, extreme feelings and emotions in these forms. Although it pains me to my very core, I know you are correct. We can't risk losing ourselves to this...this madness of desire.

I agree, Khai. This is neither the time nor the place for such folly. Things are...far too complicated between us. Too much hangs in the balance.

Very well, Naero. Let's set this all aside and focus on getting you out of here, and back to your physical form. I think we need to be apart from each other for a time. You rejoin your ships. I will continue recharging Yii. Then these heightened feelings between us will fade.

Naero almost covered her mouth with both hands.

Part of her didn't want all of those special, dazzling feelings to fade.

But she couldn't dwell on that, now—or she'd go crazy with lust again.

First, they both propelled themselves as rapidly as they could, back up toward the star's surface. Thankfully, it took most of their abilities and their concentration to accomplish that much.

Before we got...distracted, Naero. You were going to update me. I think you'd better talk before one of us gets too...distracted, again. I don't know about you, but I'm having some serious trouble staying rational here.

She felt it, too. Likewise, Khai.

As quickly and as briefly as she could, Naero caught Khai up on everything that was going on with the enemy and their current mission.

See? We must stop these plots of our enemies. They are your enemies too, Khai. They were the ones behind the attacks on the High Masters. The G'lothc and their allies were trying to capture or destroy them. Just as they intend to do to the Driathans, the Yattai—even your people, the Oden, if they can find them. That's what the enemy does. They mean to subjugate or destroy us all. We must join forces to oppose and defeat them. If we don't, whether I am brought to justice for my crimes or not won't even matter. Me. You. Everything we care about will be dead or enslaved. The surviving remnants of our people will be reduced to mere slaves and hosts for our new, eternal masters to torment or use as they see fit.

Khai tried not to stare at her.

Naero realized now that there had always been something so sad in his eyes whenever he looked at her, before. They had been friends, once. What did Khai actually feel towards her, outside of their energy-form-induced craziness?

Naero just hoped it wasn't pity. She couldn't stand that.

I'm sorry, Naero. You speak well and make a very convincing argument, but under the circumstances, you know that I cannot fully trust you.

Naero looked down and away from him in shame, frustration, and anger.

I want to trust you, Naero...but I can't.

Naero uttered a deep sigh and shuddered. Khai was right. She had tricked him and many others before, time and time again. That was her nature. Why should anyone trust her any longer–especially after what she had done?

Yet, I shall tell you what I can and will do, Naero. I will withhold judgment until we return to our stars in the Alpha Quadrant, and our truce ends. Until that time, I will look into what you say is happening to the Driathans on Dotar-2. If what you say is, in fact, true-

She glared at him. It is. As the Mystic Enforcer, you will be forced to take action against our brutal foes. You must join with us in this fight. We need you, Khai.

He glared back at her suddenly, his force of will just as strong as her own. *I will decide what I must do, Naero. Not you.*

Come with me then. Let me prove it all to you.

Khai hesitated. *It will take me a while longer to fully recharge Yii, and myself within this star. Then I shall join you and your brave friends. My powers are not like yours, Naero. We are both very different, in many ways. I hope that the day comes, when we can speak together as true friends. I would relish that.*

We can still be friends, Khai. No matter what happens to either of us. I never stopped being yours. Remember that. You're right. I must return to the others. They probably think I'm dead by now. I've never been inside a star before–or escaped from a star like the way you are proposing. Please, can you help me do so?

I've helped heal and regenerate you somewhat, Naero. But you still have a virulent condition. One that I have never encountered; I fear that it will only return stronger. But how did you damage yourself in such a fashion in the first place?

Naero explained what she needed to about the bizarre wormhole they had generated in order to propel them all to their current positions.

If you do not find a way to heal the Cosmic sickness that is slowly growing inside of you, Naero–it will eventually consume you.

Naero shrugged. So, what else is new? But we kind of have a lot on our plate already, Khai. Don't you think? My condition isn't going to kill me just yet. But our enemies might. I choose to deal with them first, and all other concerns later.

When there is time, please allow me to examine you, Naero. During my own ordeal, I experienced just about every kind of Cosmic illness and injury that was possible–and learned how to survive and over come them.

Part of her wanted to play doctor with Khai very much.

She stopped herself right there.

Naero recalled how Khai had explored his energy form, more than anyone she knew, in order to forge his Cosmic Sword. And he had endured and overcome many terrible injuries and near-lethal effects in the course of doing so. His direct knowledge could prove invaluable to her and her lethal disease.

Perhaps my own experiences and insights can be helpful to you, Khai noted.

Naero nodded and smiled up at him. Great minds.

See, our truce could be good for both of us, Khai. Now, show me how to get out of this damn star.

Khai traveled beside her, both of them stepping up their velocity.

They spotted a bursting solar flare nearby and raced up into it.

Khai used his own energies to hurl Naero into the flows of the expanding, erupting solar flare, racing out from the surface.

Naero shot away from him, still gaining speed.

I liked what happened between us, Khai.

Me, too, Naero. Too much. That's the problem.

It was still beautiful. Naero laughed.

First she exploded out from the star. Then she burst forth from the solar flare itself.

Finally, the thought came to her.

Free from the star, she was brimming with Cosmic power, like a small, speeding pulsar in her own right.

In an instant, with barely a thought, she translocated herself back on board the tek bay of *The Dark Star.*

Tyber blinked and gaped at her as she suddenly flashed in next to him. "Hey Ty...everyone."

Tyber flung his arms around her. Zhen did so an instant later. "N-Naero? Jia and Alala said you–that you just died in that star!"

Naero grinned back at them. "Do I look like a ghost? You know me, Ty. Haisha, would I let a little thing like a star kill me? Heck, no!"

She hugged her friends back and cried a little.

Tyber gasped. Zhen shivered and cried with her.

"Naero!" the ship's voice called out.

"Greetings, Alala. I sense that many of your systems are still damaged from passing through the unstable wormhole." Naero placed her hands upon the hull of the ship, and instantly became one with it through her teknomancing powers.

"Let me refit your damages, and give you a few more upgrades while I'm at it. Part of me is sorry that you got pulled into this with us. The other part is very glad you're still here. We're going to need you and your ion guns in this fight that's coming up. Things are going to get very rough."

"If you go into danger, then I cannot remain behind. I know my great friend, Captain Tyber, and his entire crew will agree with me. We shall fight at your side, at all costs."

"There," Naero said, removing her hands from the hull. "Don't let Ty meddle with that leap drive again until we have it working right. All of your other systems have been optimized with everything I've learned from the KDM and *The Shadow Fox*. Now your ion guns will fire twice as fast."

"Naero. Wait," Ty said. "I've got some new ideas about bypassing that heavy alien security around Alala's ion cannons. Baeven and Jia helped me figure it out."

"I've had similar thoughts. No time like the present."

While she was up to snuff and still chock-full of Cosmic energy.

"If that alien tek is based upon the Darkforce, like I'm almost positive it is, then I think I know how we can defeat it. I've had some further experience since then on countering that kind of tek and negating its power sources. If we do this right, the rest of our ships could sure use some further upgrades of their own. But first I have to go over and rejoin my crew on *The Dagger*. I don't want them to think I'm dead, either. I'll return in about an hour."

Naero transported over to the somber deck of *The Flying Dagger*.

Enel and Surina were in the process of still comforting the rest of the crew.

When she spoke up, the pair screamed in joy and knocked her to the ground.

"Naero! You're alive," Surina shouted.

"Haisha! The captain's back!" Enel yelled. "Alert the entire crew. The captain's back. She's alive. Those other reports were all wrong!"

Naero gathered that she had been gone for a little more than three standard hours.

Gaviok blasted out of the lift to the bridge and picked his way rapidly through the other crew, pulling them to either side in his joy. He glowed bright pink.

He picked Naero up and repeatedly tossed her up into the air as if she were a toy. The mantid was the strongest being she had ever met, besides Baeven and Khai.

"Naero!" he shouted. "They said you had perished in a star. I'm so happy to see you alive!"

Naero laughed. "Gaviok! Good...to see...you, too. Put me down, you crazy bug...Before you...rattle...my teeth loose!"

The reunion with her crew was the happiest Naero had been in many days. She spent the first half of the hour going through her flagship, personally hugging and talking to everyone.

But the facts remained–they were all about to go into great peril once again.

The last half hour, she held a planning session with her officers and department heads. Everyone needed to understand what they were getting into.

At the end of that hour, Naero transported directly back onto *The Dark Star* to save time, even though by then, all three ships were docked together.

When everything was set, Alala opened the hatches leading to the ion cannon control systems.

Naero led her pacification team in.

This time, Naero was ready. She and Ty were armed to the teeth, and they brought Baeven, Jia, Gaviok, Danjen, S'krin, Zhen, and Tarim with them. All of them ready to do battle.

Black tentacles and tendrils exploded out of the walls.

Gaviok and Baeven simply ripped them apart. Behind their might, the others fought and blasted their way within.

In less than a minute, Naero, Ty, Jia, and Zhen reached the main controls, while the others fought off the alien defenses.

Jia attacked the security system directly, backed up by Naero and Tyber, penetrating the defenses with teknomancy.

"I'm keeping the security system from resorting to a self-destruction sequence," Jia said. "I can't hold it off forever. You two get in there and shut it down. Disable that security system."

Alala cut in. "The alien system is trying to take over the rest of the ship and cause it to explode."

We're fighting it off, N, Om said. *This system is powerful and insidious. Destroy it!*

Naero and Ty struggled to shut it down. Every time they thought they had a lock on it, it seemed to regenerate and emerge from another place they did not expect.

Ty tore back the shielding on the very core.

Just as Naero suspected, the security device was completely powered by what appeared to be a small Darkforce generator, the size of a person's skull.

Positive energy. They needed to use positive energy directly against this lethal entity. But Jia, Om, and Alala were all too busy holding the device's attack abilities off.

"Zhen!" Naero called out. "Attack this thing with biomancy."

Zhen hit it with everything she had.

"No good, N. I can't harm it. This thing absorbs anything I throw at it."

"No, Z. Don't try to hurt it. Heal it. That's the only way to damage this damn thing."

Zhen could heal with the best of them now—even Shalaen, and that was saying something.

She put the whammy on the Darkforce core and the entire section bucked and shuddered. She gritted her teeth and poured it on.

The alien defenses started to collapse as the core broke down and dissolved.

Finally, the generator imploded, just as Zhen passed out.

Naero caught her as she fell back, and checked on Z's condition. Her *abani* was spent, but all right. She had won the day for them.

Jia waded into the core herself, fearless now, dismantling the system all around her as she did, utterly crushing it in waves of teknomancy force, shutting the systems down.

She eradicated any part of the alien defensive tek that remained.

"It's done," Jia announced. "Alala, you and all of your tek are now completely free."

"Many thanks," Alala said.

Naero carried Zhen out as she started to come to.

Ty and Tarim both looked a bit concerned.

"Oh, don't worry, guys," Naero told them. "Our great hero here will be all right, as soon as she wakes up. She just needs a nap. Come on, Ty. We've got a lot of work to do. Get all your tek monkeys hopping."

41

When they reached Dotar-2 to begin their assault, Jia linked with the burning, ravaged sentinel world and cried out in pain.

"We have to hurry; the enemy has already overwhelmed and penetrated the planetary defenses. I can't reach Govae. They may have already taken him. Get us down there, Bae."

"Naero," Baeven said. "Let's start the excitement."

"Roger that," Naero said, signaling commands over her wristcom. "We're sending in *The Dagger* to draw the enemy's fleets off and keep them busy. *The Dark Star* will sweep in and back them up. Next, Baeven, Jia, myself, and all of our available fighters will assault the surface to find and secure Govae, and take him back from the enemy."

Tyber called over their secure link. "Beginning our attacks. Keep 'Tisa safe for me, will you, N?"

"I'll do my best, Ty. Like all of us, she can handle herself in a fight."

Khai still hadn't rejoined them, but they could not wait for him.

Even at the start of a huge battle, Naero chuckled to herself as they sped toward their objective, packed into the hold of *The Shadow Fox*.

What she wouldn't give if her only problem was just some smitten guy chasing her tail–for obvious carnal reasons. That should be the least of her worries.

Hell, she might even give a hunk like Khai a shot at the gold ring–if only things were simpler and different. But they weren't, and nothing seemed simple for her anymore. So much complicated, messed up crap in her life. And, like usual, she hardly had enough time to catch her breath, let alone attempt to figure it all out.

She would unleash her partial Dark Beast in battle for the first time, if she must. But she needed to stay in control, and she had not exactly been herself lately. Too much had changed.

Or perhaps she simply had.

She kept trying to tell herself that her Dark Beast was her–part of her. No matter how many times she tried to accept it, it just didn't seem real. All of that darkness and evil, lurking deep down inside herself.

It was all her.

It was her.

Herself.

Maybe that was the key to it all somehow, but Naero just couldn't see it yet, or know exactly what to do with all of that Gordian knot of self-knowledge.

The complete solution eluded her. Not that there was always a solution. As with being forced to kill Master Vane, things did not always work out for the best.

Just the opposite, in fact.

Warning, Naero, Om said. *An intense ship-to-ship battle has just erupted among the enemy fleets above Dotar-2.*

As planned. How are our crews doing?

Right in the thick of things. Arming them and all of our fighters with the new ion cannons was a stroke of genius. They're devastating the enemy ships, leaving them floating powerless, and then cloaking again.

Sounds about right. Ty said they were going to draw them off and keep them busy.

The Dark Star and The Flying Dagger now have the full attention of the enemy fleets.

Two ships? Just our two ships and several fighters against hundreds of enemy warships?

That was the plan. Yet our ships possess the crucial element of surprise–as well as the new, improved ion cannons–and all of our current advanced tek. Both of our forces are zipping in and out, firing rapidly while fully cloaked, systematically neutralizing ship after ship. They're causing so much confusion that the enemy are panicking, firing in all directions—even zapping each other. The chaos and confusion are nearly complete.

Naero nodded. Yet that was all just a diversion. "Jia, any luck locating Govae yet?"

She shook her head. "No, but I've realized that something is jamming my senses, somehow."

Got him. Below the surface at these coordinates. Lead our best fighters down there, Naero. Take the battle straight to the enemy. Jia's right. There is a strange interference pattern, but I'm scanning another Driathan mind signature besides Jia. Unlike her, all of his life signs are weaker. He must be either damaged or injured. Relaying all of this to the team via their stealth fixers.

Jia paused. "Adjusting my senses to compensate. Yes. That is Govae. We all have a lock on him now. He's hurt. Lead us down there, Naero. Bae, Gaviok, protect our flanks. Give us time. Keep them off of us."

Cloaked and on gravwings, they swept forward into the aftermath of a hellish war zone.

Waves and piles of wrecked Ejjai gravtanks, gunships, meks, and dead shock troops littered the ground as far as the eye could see.

The attack appears to have been planet-wide over the last week. The enemy has spent nearly an entire Ejjai freezeworld of forces to overwhelm the planet's formidable defenses.

Another enemy attack wave swept in before them up ahead, pounding the last defenses and some kind of vast, underground complex that the enemy had penetrated.

All of the enemy units focused around an open complex in the planet, similar to Jia's back on Zoa. But this one was being blasted, ripped open, and crushed by force.

The Shadow Fox took charge of the landing field and used fixers to set up defensive rings of cloaked auto-gun emplacements. The guns tore up the hapless enemy ships landed there, and held the area against all who turned to attack them.

And the enemy kept coming, from all directions, against any type of resistance.

Next, Jia used her abilities and their nebula of spyfixers to refit and bring back online all of the Driathan planetary defenses within ten kilometers of the base. Hi-tek defenses that had taken the enemy days to chew through, at great cost.

She snarled and opened up on the invaders swarming all around them with considerable fire power from the synthetic planet's re-activated defenses. The base literally bristled once again with automated, advanced Driathan weaponry and ordnance.

I'm scanning hundreds of Dakkur up ahead.

Enemy assault waves redoubled their efforts against the stiff, renewed defenses, probing and falling upon them to tear open shields, destroy gun emplacements, and pummel the area once again.

"Whatever's going on down in that base," Naero said, "the enemy's not about to give up without one hellish fight."

"Then lets give it to them. Attack!" Baeven commanded. "Let's take these bastards down!"

Jia sent in a wave of floating autoguns to clear a path before them.

Her attack wave got blasted to hell, but the drones did their job.

The attack got them down into the complex.

Gaviok and Baeven flashed slightly ahead, tearing apart any Dakkur or enemy stragglers.

No doubt more foes awaited them up ahead, and more still would eventually pour in behind them.

Naero and her assault team remained cloaked, sweeping in on gravwings, blasting right through enemy units as they passed overhead. They left death and destruction in their wake as they penetrated Govae's stricken base.

Om and their fixers assisted by optimizing target acquisition and fire control.

Naero led them forward and held back nothing. She unleashed the full advanced arsenal of her improved combat armor all at once. Multiple weapons and independent AI beam pods. Full spreads of microbombs. Layered waves of target-seeking, predator smartmines. The assault team's heavy weapons people unleashed close-support, rapid-fire, phalanx pulse guns.

In a matter of seconds, they pulverized the enemy's penetration teams to incinerated tek, meat, bone, and dust.

Naero sped through the air, focusing all of her senses through the enhanced abilities of her third eye.

With her advanced awareness, she could see up ahead of them.

They'd push forward, only to get stuck in one heavy firefight after another, as the staggered enemy positions stubbornly turned at bay and gave ground slowly against the assault team's onslaught.

They battled within an immense underground complex that might very well run under the entire planet's surface. Naero could sense no end to it.

Heavily shielded Ejjai shock troops had pillboxes and gun emplacements set up at key junctures nearby, backed up by full squads of enemy meks, poised to pour a hail of destroying fire at anything that came at them down the wide corridors of the complex.

The Ejjai were being backed up by hunter-killer units of Dakkur soldier drones, led by Dakkur champions.

Are we safe here for a bit, Om?

No enemy forces in range. I will alert you if any approach.

"Hold up," Naero announced. Their assault team gathered in, and she continued.

"I've analyzed the region around us. This is no good. This entire area is too huge. We'll be fighting in this underground complex for days this way. The enemy has infiltrated the underground base with large numbers of troops. They will eventually wear us down if we keep fighting them head on."

"What do you advise?" Baeven asked.

"The enemy's strategy is both obvious and effective, and we no longer possess the element of surprise. They know we're here now. But they're not focused on defeating or destroy us. If they take us down, so be it, but their strategy is purely a delaying tactic. They're trying to keep us from reaching and rescuing Govae."

This close, Naero used Om and her third eye again to precisely locate the other weaker Driathan signal.

"I've located Govae again at these coordinates," she said, relaying them to her friends. "Our foes have moved him three separate times to evade us. Everybody gather in close. I'm going transport us all into the nearest open juncture to our target, between two enemy holding forces. We'll surprise them and punch through before the enemy can move Govae again. Then, I'll transport right in on top of them to delay them, and the rest of you fight your way in to effect the rescue."

"We'll be with you shortly, then." Jia said. "Help Govae at all costs. We can escape straight up through the complex to the surface if we have to. I can clear the way for us."

Naero nodded. "I think we will have to do just that. Be ready, everyone. There's something else. The enemy has Govae trapped in something I've never sensed before. Some kind of horrific device that they're torturing him in."

Jia looked alarmed. "They're trying to break him, to tear his secrets from his mind and destroy him."

Naero added, "Whatever this thing is, its Darkforce energies are far beyond anything I've ever detected before."

It made the scary Darkforce generators look like bugs.

"Naero," Baeven said, "be careful. The enemy still has tek we've never encountered yet. Don't let them trap you in it like they have Govae."

"Don't worry about that. Now, let's hit them hard and rescue Jia's brother. Ready? We're all going in hot."

Naero steeled herself, startapped, and flashed them in.

42

Waves of strange Cosmic energy thrummed into Naero as she tried to reach Govae.

Yet these waves scorched her with stinging agony when she tried to tap into them. She gasped and drew back in terror and pain.

The enemy had somehow tainted and poisoned the Cosmic flows nearby, transforming them into living rushes of Darkforce torment.

Naero did her best to shield herself and charged forward through the barrier.

At last she broke through.

But doing so stripped her cloaking away. For the moment, she floated up toward the ceiling, unseen.

Dozens of enemy troops barred her way forward–into the chamber where the enemy was torturing the Driathan sentinel, Govae.

But these forces were far from normal.

Ejjai, a few Dakkur, even some humanoids and a smattering of other alien creatures. Yet each of them looked impossibly weird and twisted.

They glowed and pulsed from within with strange energies, yellow, orange, red, and green. Their flesh had become transparent, like some kind of shifting gelatin or plasma. Some of their veins and bones within them had turned black. They shambled about on patrol, their ruined faces drooping slack—open mouths moved and worked and twitched insanely—as if directed by another will.

Naero gasped.

She had fought against something like this before, at the end of the Annexation War. Back when she faced down the thing that Hevangian Admiral Maximillian Dreth had transformed into. Some kind of energy creature just like these. It had nearly been indestructible.

Then her heightened senses told her what was going on. All of these creatures were possessed by the Darkforce and something else—something oozing with malice. Their physical bodies would only hold up for so long before breaking down and being utterly consumed by the Darkforce. Long enough for the enemy to effect their will and complete their mission.

A G'lothc possession wyrm had activated inside each one of these creatures. This transformation was the result.

It did not matter to the enemy if these host bodies were consumed and destroyed in the course of their efforts. These foul abominations were the very source of the bizarre, poisoned Cosmic energies suffusing them, sustaining them for a short time, and permeating the entire area.

A ravaging G'lothc spirit controlled each host. Naero could sense them. She was sure of it.

Om, alert the others what we're up against.

The next instant, several of the things locked on her presence and came straight for her.

They fought with the same incredible speed and tenacity she had witnessed before, attempting to overwhelm her with their numbers.

The sheer weight and ferocity of their attack drove Naero back at their onset.

Naero gave ground, and at the last instant before they overwhelmed her, she unleashed a massive Cosmic energy blast to fling them back and obliterate a few of them. She was not so defenseless against these things now.

Yet there were so many. She could not face down an insane horde of this many of the things, unless her friends finally broke through to back her up.

Naero transported to the next section adjacent to that area.

Right among a full platoon of Ejjai meks guarding that location.

Her sudden appearance startled them.

359

Good.

Enemy fire erupted as she zipped among them and between their legs, fleeing further down a wide corridor, back toward the area where Govae was being tormented.

Being small and fast had its advantages…sometimes.

Naero took cover behind an immense, load-bearing support beam, while the blaster cannons of the advancing enemy meks chewed away at the structure to get at her.

Naero slowed them down with another Cosmic blast, but that would not hold them back for long. Their numbers were far too many.

She could retreat again, but that would not solve anything. As the meks gathered for another charge, their masters could be making good their escape with Govae and all of his secrets.

Naero could not allow that.

Time for something drastic; she could not let the enemy delay and beat them.

Gathering all her strength and focus, she startapped and even dipped deep into her own flows of stored Cosmic energy.

She created dozens of tiny replicants of herself.

They hovered around her, little gravwings humming like sprites, tiny fists clenched, little faces all determined. Little voices eager to please.

"What do we do, boss?"

Naero drew her advanced blaster machine pistol and sprayed the advancing enemy with fire.

It barely slowed them down.

As she ducked back, another intense enemy barrage chewed away at the huge support.

Naero turned to her sprites and jerked a thumb back at their advancing foes.

"Go get those meks, guys. Get in there and take them down. Each one of you pick your targets and set off a Cosmic explosion!

"Will do!"

"You got it, boss!"

"Let's get 'em!"

"Hey…I don't wanna explode!"

"C'mon, guys!"

Naero sent them all in. "No arguments, guys. Just get in there and blast the living hell out of those bastards. I have to get past them."

Her sprites shot away, determined looks on their little faces.

They streaked straight toward the enemy meks.

Naero flattened herself on the ground and threw up the strongest protective shields she had around her.

Within the corridor and the chamber beyond, the immense blasts and detonations went off, rocking the entire area and nearly collapsing it.

So much for all of those enemy meks.

The support pillar buckled and crumbled. Naero herself was flung back down the corridor by the intensity of the resulting blast waves.

Once she gathered her wits, she translocated past the enemy into the enormous, open launching bay beyond.

The attack was getting too hot for their foes, apparently.

The enemy scurried in panic, preparing to depart in the waiting G'lothc cruiser. The damn thing still looked like some kind of mutant, ginormous black squid. More than three quarters of its length was a mass of large, writhing black tentacles and appendages, each ending in a hi-tek weapon.

Naero had seen that enemy ship unleash a barrage before, and recalled the devastation it could unleash.

No doubt this ship proved invaluable in overwhelming the sentinel world's significant planetary defenses.

Several heavily armored Dakkur soldier drones, in the same black-black combat armor that their ship seemed to be made out of, hurriedly floated some kind of valuable cargo toward the enemy vessel, under heavy guard.

She zipped in closer and noted the form of a tall, glowing silver male Driathan, strapped down within the center of a heavy cargo gravpad, with energized restraining bands locking him down.

She counted not one, but six Darkforce generators fastened to his body, feeding off of his energies, tearing at him, and trying to rip out his secrets. They swarmed and writhed all over him like hungry, feasting demons.

This close to him, Naero could sense Govae's energies and life force fading. He writhed and shrieked and screamed within a pulsating mass of determined foes–slowly tearing him to pieces.

Naero's blood went to jagged ice in her veins.

One of the generators was twice the size of the other normal ones that she had fought before. This larger one seemed to be directing the others. Even worse.

Just as the enemy turned a corner, heading for the G'lothc cruiser's loading ramp, she spotted Danner looking out the faceport of the big generator.

361

At a glance, she could tell that her insane former brother was completely conscious, and controlling the generator he was in willingly—suffused within waves and layers of Darkforce energy.

She experienced so much Darkforce power that she could see Danner's skull and his twisted, crippled bones, black to the marrow with flickering energies and dark lightning. Control rods penetrated his head and flesh.

This much larger device was even more horrifying, and kept Danner and his inner Dark Beast at near critical mass, feeding and siphoning off him at a much high rate.

Danner had become the enemy's puppet, tool, and weapon all in one—their primary Darkforce power source.

They were using him to power their horrific devices and break Govae down into scrap.

The very air and reality around Danner seemed poisoned and twisted.

Naero's rage swelled to the point that her Dark Beast nearly broke free once again.

She shifted from energy being into a partial Dark Beast form, this one still her normal size, but packed with Cosmic force.

Her Ur-metal battle blades formed in both hands, and her scarlet katanas over them. Blue-violet energy blades jutted out of her armored form.

Naero enveloped herself in a wreath of Cosmic flame as she fell upon the enemy, spinning and buzzing through their packed ranks at impossible speed. She sliced, kicked, and wheeled through them like an energized buzz saw.

Shredded piece of enemy troops and fighting vehicles burst and exploded, scattered and sprayed all about the landing area and the enemy vessel.

Dozens of the Dakkur commandos converged on Naero like seeker missiles, attempting to hold her off and drag her down by their sheer numbers.

At the last instant, she translocated right beside Govae.

Her attackers smashed into the deck and each other. Others bounced off the ship or were absorbed by its activated defensive fields and destroyed.

Naero swatted Danner aside and focused a Cosmic blast around him that would have obliterated a battleship. She leaped in his place and ripped Govae's capture pod away from the other five G'lothc generators. She fought with all five of them at once, wheeling and kicking, trying to break free and escape. She nailed the generators with mindforce blasts, disruptor beams from her third eye, sonic blast screams from her mouth, punching and kicking and tearing at the writhing things in her battle fury.

She broke free and leaped away with Govae's body, and centered another Cosmic detonation on the foes directly behind them.

Her explosion flung her and Govae into the far wall of the hangar, smoking and on fire. The destruction was so intense that it severely damaged the five generators, Danner as he raced back in, and the G'lothc ship itself, tearing a great gaping, burning wound out of the side of the enormous living ship.

The vessel reeled and writhed. Naero thought she even heard it shriek psyonically in rage and pain as it absorbed the wound she had inflicted upon it.

A mass of writhing tendrils and tentacles seized Danner and the other damaged generators, drawing them inside the strange ship itself.

Within seconds, the huge G'lothc cruiser came fully alive, tearing itself free, calling up shielding, and preparing to shoot away. It hovered about the open maw of the hanger. It didn't even attempted to swing around so that it could level its guns at them.

Let them run. Naero remained with Govae, fighting and tearing at the rest of the enemy capture pod, trying to free the Driathan from the enemy's insidious tek even as it continued to cling to him.

The pod itself fought her until she sliced it away from Govae with her blades and flung it aside.

Naero finally pulled Govae free. He lay unconscious and nearly dead, from what she could sense, or heavily stunned.

The remaining enemy forces in that area poured into the open hangar from all directions, now that the gigantic squid prepared to depart.

The Dakkur and legions of Ejjai closed in around Naero and Govae.

A holo of the enemy leader–a Dakkur champion–appeared in front of the enemy hordes.

"There is no escape. Give us the Driathan and surrender, or else you die, spack bitch."

Naero spat on the ground before her. "No way in hell. Just try to take him, and I will butcher you all!"

The leader smiled his wide smile of crushing teeth and hissed.

"Death it is then."

Naero smiled her battle smile. "For all of you."

Their leader held up a claw and forestalled the attack for an instant. "I am Admiral Korleth-Tulkas. One day, I shall see you added to my master's trophy collection with all the rest of your pitiful kind. You stinking, spack weaklings, who dare to think and pretend that you are so mighty."

She recalled his voice, the one speaking to Ullogk and the others.

Korleth was just another Dakkur toady as far as she was concerned. But he was also possessed by a G'lothc spirit wyrm that had yet to transform, and that made him even more formidable–once it did.

"In and take her, my servants, yet keep her alive. We need more of her ignorant kind to power our generators."

Hundreds of foes rushed her.

At first Naero held them off.

Then she impaled every attacker within ten meters on multiple rods of Cosmic force, spearing out in all directions.

She detonated the rods, slaying, crippling, punishing, and wounding foes in expanding waves beyond them.

Naero plucked up Govae and leaped away.

Baeven and her friends burst through the complex walls, and fought their way toward her position the next moment.

The remaining enemy forces spread out and rushed to cut them all off.

A green glowing comet blasted through the G'lothc ship severing a handful of the tentacle cannons. It smashed into the Dakkur, scattering them like tenpins.

Khai rose up from the resulting crater unscathed, and went straight at the enemy ranks.

Units of Dakkur unleashed a torrent of fire from their advanced weapons, and charged at Khai to mow him down.

Khai ignored their concentrated blasts, completely invulnerable to their heaviest weapons. He waded right through them, his sword, Yii, absorbing energy and flashing faster than thought.

Yii sizzled as Khai flashed through them, blinding energies hewed and sliced the enemy and their tek to bloody, twitching pieces, and disrupting explosions.

"Unleash the horde!" Korleth-Tulkas's holo commanded.

A big troop carrier dropped down quickly.

Hundreds of hatches crashed open, dispensing waves of Dakkur troops. They swarmed toward the attackers, even as they pulled together to defend themselves.

Even Khai could not destroy them fast enough. He wisely flanked Naero and her friends on the right.

Naero shielded their position briefly, but she knew it could not hold.

Admiral Korleth's holo swelled to gigantic proportions and drove them on, his amplified voice booming. "Take the three Cosmic spacks and the other Driathan prisoner. Slaughter all the rest!"

The holo winked out.

Jia took Govae in her arms; his form began to shift as if it were melting. "My poor brother. They've murdered him. He's dying!"

Baeven shouted. "We're all going to get murdered here if we don't do something radical, Naero. Come, my battle brother. It is time for us to teach these scum another lesson—as we once did."

Baeven began to swell with a mix of both Chaos and Darkforce energy. Burning green disruptor blades emerged all over him. In an instant, he stood ten meters high.

"You cannot do this," Naero screamed. "I know! Baeven, if you fully unleash it—you cannot control it. You'll destroy us all."

He smiled down at her and Jia. "Then you two must bring me back before I do—before all is lost, including myself."

He turned his face toward their foes and snarled. They were about to break through.

"Prince Gaviok. Fight beside me!"

"Ever ready, my brother. We will make them recall the sack of Koguloth, and the fall and ruin of its dark king and his fierce queens."

Gaviok swelled up into his own gigantic mantid battle form, larger than Baeven. He turned jet black in his rage, and smoldered with deep scarlet Chaos flames.

The two of them strode before their comrades and bent to the attack.

Even as the shield collapsed, the Dakkur appeared to recognize them.

The entire horde drew back in stunned terror, shrieking and screaming.

"The Great Slayers! Fall back to the hordeship. The Destroyers Slayers have come upon us!"

The Dakkur hissed in abject fear. Hundreds of them soiled themselves in terror.

"They destroyed and ravaged an entire homeworld. How can we stand before them and prevail?"

"You cannot," Gaviok roared. "Let the vengeance of the Shai fall upon you!"

He and Baeven charged right into them. And in the tumult and carnage that followed, the Dakkur armies struggled and battled, not to kill—but to flee.

Even Naero had trouble following their swift movements. Baeven and Gaviok fought like enraged behemoths, crushing and mutilating the packed masses of their foes to either side.

They slew them by the score in blurs and flashes within the space of each second—until the enemy broke, completely terrified and routed.

Gaviok and Baeven ran them down and continued killing them wholesale, destroying everything in their rampage—even attacking the huge troop carrier.

Naero felt her sense of warning flare. Something was wrong.

The severely damaged complex buckled, shuddered, and collapsed— tens of kilometers all around them.

The enemy sprang their trap.

"We have to get out of here," Naero said. "They're going to destroy this entire complex, and bury us along with it!"

She led them back toward their only possible escape route—straight up.

Jia carried Govae in her arms. All of them activated their gravwings and fled the total chaos and destruction taking place behind, below, and all around them.

Anything living back down there wasn't going to stay living for very long.

The G'lothc ships rose up and opened multiple wormholes. Many more Dakkur rained down, cutting them off and dragging down into the collapsing structure.

Naero lashed out at several that fell on her, slaying several before they all slammed back into the unstable structure.

Khai sliced his way through several dozen more swarming on him.

A Dakkur champion blasted Jia point-blank with some type of shoulder-mounted energy cannon.

Jia screamed, throwing herself in front of her helpless brother Govae, trying to shield them both.

Naero shattered the thick skull of her last foe with a single rocking kick. She flung back the lifeless, crushed, and broken corpse with the force of the impact.

She turned at bay and launched herself right into Jia's attacker. She drove him straight through the thick walls of the complex and into the next section. All while the many levels all continued to cave in.

The champion commando swatted her back through the breach with an energized tail lash.

Only Naero's own shields and Cosmic protections kept her from being sliced in half. A flare of sparks spattered between them.

Khai broke free and struggled to keep the enemy horde from seizing the stricken Driathans. He slew many with Yii as they piled at him.

Naero's allies rallied around Khai, fighting back to back. They seized Jia and Govae and attempted to fly out.

The champion exploded out of the breach and grappled with Naero, dragging her down, crushing her to the ground. She struggled to break free, strength against raw strength.

Her Dakkur opponent pulsed with his own dark, tainted energies.

And transformed right before her, while she still wrestled with it.

She had not expected it to shift shape, but there was more than one of the foul presences contained within its rippling form.

Black tentacles and extra snapping heads and raking claws and constricting limbs exploded out from the thing. They grappled and shot out and enveloped Naero, dragging her down by surprise and wrapping around Naero's throat and face. The things throttled and strangled her, tearing at her and scorching her with Darkforce energy as they tried to absorb and devour her.

The multiple howling maws of the thing raved.

"This spack bitch is far more dangerous to us now than we ever guessed. Should we destroy her now? Yes, indeed. Yes, let us kill her, now. Tear her apart! Devour her energies. Kill her, and consume her flesh!"

Naero struggled to keep fighting. She struggled to even breathe.

She fired Cosmic lightning right through the Darkforce-infused abomination, but it stayed on top of her, crushing, constricting, and twisting her to death each second. More of the things continued to boil out of the one.

A bright flash.

Yii's shining blade scorched its way through everything it touched.

Her attacker shrieked in rage and pain and drew back, releasing her.

Khai severed all of the dark tentacles choking her in one bright, expert stroke. Yii missed Naero by a millimeter as it sliced through a ravenous enemy skull trying to rip at her face with its jaws.

Khai sliced the vile things away from her like a surgeon, and the roiling, twisting abominations vanished in bright flashes of shrieking Cosmic energy. Naero gasped and choked down air as she fell free, struggling to recover.

Khai glanced down at her in brief concern, and then strode toward their foes, undaunted.

"The G'lothc were wisely exterminated from the universe once before," Khai told them. "Their immense evils shall not be allowed to return. Go back to your Void of death, foul spirits. Your vile kind shall not be allowed to prevail here–now or ever!"

A dozen of them boiled together and tried to shift and combine with each other, swelling to huge proportions to fall upon the Enforcer.

Yii flared and incinerated an entire ring of the fell things all about them. They crumbled into ash and fell away.

The possessed Dakkur yielded and gave way before such might. They pulled back slightly and gave ground, avoiding Khai and his amazing sword directly. They fended off Khai's probing feints and thrusts with bursts and blasts of Darkforce energy. Even those energies disrupted each time Khai's sword came against them.

Yii could negate the Darkforce itself.

More foes transported in and sought to overtake him from behind.

Naero flashed back in, wheeling and kicking, battering them away.

She nailed them with blue-violet lightning from her blades and gutted them.

Naero and Khai fought side by side and back to back with their glowing blades as the shifting things cut them off and sought to drag them down again by sheer weight of numbers.

In less than a standard minute, the circle of death about Naero and Khai grew over their heads, as the two of them cut down and shredded any foe that came within their reach

Ruined, blasted enemy faces and severed heads and limbs writhed and snapped, and twisted among the quivering mass of the enemy fallen.

The fell G'lothc spirits animating the violated mass of flesh chortled, still manipulating their broken hosts, grim voices speaking in unison.

"Ahhh…the Swordmaster of the Cosmic Prophecies, doomed to fail and die alone. The preening Oden half-breed and his little Ur-metal stick that he prizes so much. We have long planned how to deal with you and your meddlesome race, wretch. Yes, indeed. We shall deal with your upstart kind—once and for all! You shall become our slaves. All shall feel the weight of our yoke."

"Wrong, you vile demons. You will perish before the light of my blade. You have no weapons that can harm me!"

The monsters laughed. "Servants, drag this fool down and kill him before our eyes. Seize the female. We command it to be so!"

Most of the remaining possessed Dakkur broke off fighting with the others. All of them rushed in and fell upon Khai and Naero, dragging both heroes back down with them into the depths of the collapsing abyss.

Several of the monsters swept at Naero as they all fought in mid-air, shifting form, shrieking and grinning.

"We'll finish with you, spack whore—after we've slain this green fool."

Naero used her gravwing to try to rise back up. Khai tried to fight free as well, but the enemy was bent upon pulling them down, and ripped at them and piled on to bury them.

As more of the possessed boiled over Khai, a mass of the things broke off, combined, and shifted shape right before their eyes, into something huge, hulking, bipedal, and menacing–towering over the Enforcer.

This new creature wielded two long, molten-looking blades in its claws as it advanced.

Naero immediately sensed something strange about both those blades.

They were also forged out of Ur-metal–the same precious substance that Khai's sword was made of.

"Khai, look out!" Naero race in and deflected several attacks at Khai's back as he fought with the others. Sparks and Darkforce lightning shot forth where Naero's own blades clashed with the blades of this new foe.

They spiraled down, continually dragged ever down into the collapsing sink hole. Naero voiced a battle cry and rushed her foe with her own flashing blades, driving the monster back. Huge chunks of rubble began to topple in at them from above.

The Enforcer emitted another green blast sphere, obliterating the lesser creatures all about them.

"Khai! Get out. I'm right behind-"

Yet the monsters she still battled with laughed and translocated in that exact instant.

Naero just missed running the vile things through with both of her Ur-metal battle blades.

Khai cried out before Naero could turn and reach him, even as he whirled and blocked the first cut of one of the enemy's blades.

Part of it tore free and transported.

The shapeshifter appeared directly behind Khai and Naero, the other strange dagger stabbed up to the hilt in the Enforcer's back. The point jutted out the front of the Enforcer's broad chest.

Khai gasped in shock and agony as the enemy sneered.

"Ahh, what a pity, mighty champion of the Oden. How we shall enjoy devouring your skull."

Khai thrust back and buried Yii into the shapeshifter's face in defiance, with the last of his might.

The creatures shrieked and snarled. "Even that will not save you, wretched half-breed! With you dead–all of your people are next!"

It reached around with its remaining Ur-metal blade to slash Khai's throat open and take off his head.

"Get away from him!" Naero screamed, fighting through the others.

Naero slammed into the monster with a flurry of wheeling, spinning kicks. She hewed off its limbs and thrust it away from Khai as he fell.

She flipped and drove the force of both her feet into the thing's ruined main head, crushing against and driving it through three thick support beams, drilling it into a thick wall that crumpled around the impact.

She grabbed it by one leg and arm, spinning around rapidly, swinging it into walls and supports as she battered it–raw power vs. raw power.

Finally the thing attempted to stab her with its remaining Ur-metal blade. Naero delighted in a Cosmic knife fight, and pressed the battle against her foe, rapidly carving and ripping the thing to shreds.

As it quickly became clear that she held the upper hand, it flashed away.

Naero wheeled to make certain it was not trying to backstab her as well, but this time, the thing had clearly made good its escape.

The next instant, the G'lothc ship far above them launched, rattling the air, and sped away.

"Gutless cowards!" she shouted.

Naero flashed down to scoop of Khai as the rubble closed in over them.

She transported back up to one of the rally points. The Enforcer lay on his side, gasping and bleeding Cosmic energy like blood from a vicious mortal wound, still clutching weakly at the weapon that impaled him. He started going into shock and convulsed.

Naero tried to reassure him.

"It's all right, Khai. Hang on. We're going to get out of here. We'll help you. I will not abandon you."

Khai nodded and then passed out.

The entire complex continued to began to break down across the surface and explode even further, collapsing under its own weight. Just as they enemy planned. They were all about to be crushed under several kilometers of wreckage.

"Get everyone out," Naero said. "We make it out of here or we're all dead!"

They maneuvered away from the ruined complex, bobbing and weaving as it caved in further and exploded beneath and all around them.

Baeven and Gaviok emerged from the wreckage, still fighting with the remaining enemy up top.

A handful of enemy warships launched from the surface and fled. They came about and fired a massive parting barrage, directly at Baeven.

At the last instant, Gaviok leaped in and endured the brunt of the attack full on and went down, scorched, smoking, and completely drained.

370

He shrank down as his energies ebbed away.

Baeven swelled up in size even greater, lashing out in his own full-on Dark Beast mode, erupting with destructive power. He raced up into the sky and blasted enemy battleships and a cruisers to dust. Then he leaped upon and dragged down an enemy destroyer single-handed, tearing and blasting at it until he drove the vessel straight into the buckling ground, causing the warship to explode.

The Baeven-thing rose up from the burning wreckage laughing and unhurt. It rampaged in random directions where their enemies still moved, crushing, trampling, and destroying anything that attacked him or blocked his way.

Naero was horrified, knowing full well what she had been like in that state.

Jia shook herself and came to among the injured.

"Jia," Naero called out, rushing over to her. "Baeven's lost it! We have to stop him before he comes back this way and turns on all of us!"

Startled and confused, Jia looked around.

"Govae? Where is he? I must help him first."

"He's not about to destroy us all."

Jia ignored her, crawled over, and knelt down beside Govae's still form where she spotted it.

"My poor brother. What have they done to you?"

Govae barely opened his eyes, and spoke with great effort.

"Jia…sister." He smiled up at her happily. "How good it is to see you, fairest. I am broken, I am finished. I shall be no more."

"No, do not speak so. You are in my hands now. I will see you healed." Naero could see the healing force go out from Jia in great waves and flow into Govae.

He shook his head and pushed her hands away with the last of his strength. "No, bright sister. I put this in motion myself–the only way that I could keep them from breaking me. I stayed ahead of them and their efforts. I had to…erase myself and all that I am, in order to protect you and the others."

"No, brother. No. What have you done? Even I won't be able to stop this."

He smiled sadly and strained to reach up to touch her face. "I know. It was the only way. Our people are safe, my dear sister. Ur-Jahal is safe. For now at least. Know then…that I told the vile ones…nothing."

Jia took his hand and kissed it. "My great heart."

"I am glad, that it is your blessed face that I look upon–*our sacred Kashahalla*–as I go on."

371

Govae faded away, and his form shifted back into into something neutral–a proto-Driathan form, neither male nor female–now devoid of any touch of the Lifespark.

Jia sobbed. "My brother is gone. Forever. We will never get him or his beauty and wisdom back. All that remains now is an empty blank."

"We can bury him," Naero suggested.

Jia slowly shook her head. "No. You still do not understand. We cannot risk letting the enemy have his body. That is what they crave. They could take it over still and make it their own. Nothing would stop them."

"Look out!" Zhen yelled, still trying to examine Khai's terrible wound. "Baeven's headed back this way, and he's still enraged. Do something!"

All of them fled and scattered to hide, except for Jia and Naero.

Jia took her hand. "Come. We will make him listen to us. His love for us both will still sing to him. We must calm him and bring him back to himself from the destroying darkness–back to us."

"So...you've done this before? It's easy, then?"

Jia looked worried and shook her head.

"No, it is never easy, and I am still weak. I will need your help very badly, Naero. Bae has never been this out of control before."

They used their gravwings to fly up toward him like insects.

As Baeven's Dark Beast rampaged straight toward them.

43

Jia held her hands out straight before her, trying to renew her direct link with her beloved. "Bae, stay this madness! Listen to me. Hear my voice!"

Baeven roared and backhanded her out of the sky, driving Jia into the shattered ground like a bullet.

Then he paused suddenly, shook himself, and hesitated. He looked confused, uncertain, and hesitant. He reached down and pawed at the ground, all the while shrinking down ever so slightly with each passing second.

Baeven dug up Jia and cleared the dirt and debris off of her still form, holding her cupped in his hands and shaking as he stared down at her.

Naero flew in and lifted Jia up to him in her arms, using *the voice*.

"BAEVEN…IT'S ME…NAERO. YOU'VE ALREADY HURT JIA. I KNOW YOU DIDN'T MEAN TO. BUT YOU DID. I KNOW YOU DON'T WANT TO HURT HER ANYMORE. I KNOW YOU DON'T WANT TO HURT ME. IT'S NAERO, LYTHE'S DAUGHTER. YOU LOVED MY MOTHER—YOUR LITTLE SISTER. YOU LOVE ME—HER ONLY DAUGHTER—YOUR NIECE. YOU LOVE JIA. KEEP

LISTENING TO MY VOICE. THINK ABOUT JIA. THINK ABOUT ME AND HOW
YOU FEEL ABOUT US. CALM DOWN. RELAX. GET A HOLD OF YOURSELF.
COME BACK TO US!"

Baeven continued to shrink down toward his normal size again.

He set them down on the ground and shook himself as if he were
drunk. Naero used her gravwing to keep them directly in his range of
vision. His eyes struggled to stay focused directly on them.

He still looked bewildered and confused.

Something out of nowhere seemed to upset or distract him.

He raised his fists, bristling with Cosmic disruptor blades again, to
smash them both.

"NO, BAEVEN. NO!"

One heavy blow fell, driving them back into the ground.

Naero barely shielded them from its raw power.

She could not withstand another such attack.

He blinked, shook himself, and drew back, uncertain again.

"THAT'S IT, BAEVEN. JUST RELAX. IT'S JIA AND NAERO. YOU DON'T
WANT TO HURT US ANYMORE."

Jia came around.

She flew directly over and wrapped her arms around Baeven's thick
neck, calling to him. She called him back to her.

He reduced down until Jia had her arms around him, and his around
her.

He fell to his knees, and dropped his gasping face into his hands.

"I'm sorry," he muttered.

Jia laughed. "Good thing I'm nearly indestructible. For a fleeting
moment there, Bae–I thought we had lost you for good."

"It's no a joke," he said. "You nearly did. I could have…killed you
all."

"But you didn't," Naero said normally, recalling someone who said
the same thing to her. "And you and Gaviok helped save us from that
Dakkur horde, when no one else could. Even with Khai helping us, we
could have never fought off that many of these things. The two of you
terrified them."

Baeven's head shot up. "Find him. Find Gaviok. They stunned him."

"Don't worry. I will." Naero swept back over the battlefield.

Finally she located the stricken mantid with her third eye, by his
fleeting Chaos energy signature.

Gaviok had shrunk down again to a very compact size, his life force
and other energies very low.

Naero tried to scoop him up, but he was also hyper dense–impossibly heavy–and nearly unconscious, moving weakly. Now he was pale white, green, and blue. He seemed to flicker, unable to change back to his normal dark blue color. Naero had never seen him this weak.

It would take all her own fading strength to transform, lift, and carry him back.

First Naero startapped, linked with him, and used biomancing to fully comprehend his lifeform and slowly feed him healing energies. What she saw was astonishing. Gaviok was unlike any lifeform she had ever studied or experienced.

"You're going to be all right, mighty Prince of the Shai. Thank you, for saving us. I saw what you did. You were very brave, enduring the brunt of that enemy barrage in Baeven's place."

Gaviok turned his face to her, his large eyes and his mandibles somehow off-putting, completely alien, and yet very expressive and intelligent as he clicked and spoke with effort.

"He is…my brother…and you are his kin. That makes you my family, Naero. I have watched you for a long while. My people and I owe Baeven many debts that we can never repay. You remind me of him, in so many ways."

Naero chuckled. "I'll take that as a compliment. Not everyone would. Yet this is the blood I come from, and I am proud of that."

"I know. I have never understood those who hate him."

"They cannot see him as we do. Come on. Let's rejoin the others."

"I think I can walk now. Thank you for your healing energies, N."

Gaviok swelled up until he was just a little shorter than her and turned from a shifting blue color to a deeper red-violet. He strode along, very regal and majestic. Each of his movements bespoke agility and power.

In battle, Prince Gaviok had been terrifying. The Dakkur fled before him and Baeven, and slew one another in order to escape the wrath of the two Destroyers.

That she was taller than anyone in their normal form always earned him points in Naero's pad.

Despite him being a mantid, she continually sensed a growing affinity for him. Gaviok remained someone she could trust and depend upon, even if he was very, very different from her.

"Where did you and your people gain the ability to use the Power Cosmic?" she asked him.

Truth be told, she realized now that she actually spoke with a prince of the lost Shai–one of the most mysterious, feared, and hated races in all the galaxy.

Naero had many of questions for him.

"I was born with these abilities, but I had no way to develop them until Baeven came along. He has helped me explore many of my powers and expand them and my mind, just as you have. But we are all still novices, with much to learn, I am afraid."

"How did you and Baeven meet?"

"He was in the process of rescuing me on a mission. Our ship was shot down, and we ended up on Lethe-6, one of the thirteen remaining Dakkur homeworlds at the time. The Dakkur called that world Koguloth. I had been captured by our enemies. Lethe-6 was a terrible place, where the Dakkur spawn and grow violent and wild in great numbers, until they gain sentience and join the collection on board their horde ships.

"Our foes from the Corps made the mistake of pursuing us and our allies down to the surface in an attempt to finish us off."

Gaviok shook his head. "They all died. Everyone died, friend or foe, except for myself and Baeven. We fought, and hid deep underground, and fought again every day. The two of us made war against millions of Dakkur each day–for months. The war continued until we slew them all to the last and turned the seas of Lethe-6 black with their vile blood dust– which also poisons nearly everything it touches. Together my battle-brother and I exterminated them. And when the next enemy ship came to collect the spawn, we killed all of them as well, and made good our escape.

"Yet the Dakkur devour their own dead and gain all their memories by eating the brains, even if they are rotting or desiccated. Thus the other troopships that came to their lost homeworld learned of our feats of battle on Lethe-6 against their kind, and fear us deeply as legends now.

"To them we are the Destroyers, near-mythical creatures who haunt their dreams and nightmares. The Dakkur cannot wipe those fear-soaked visions and memories of their slain multitudes out of their minds. They have never known foes such as Baeven and I–foes who will never be beaten–who will never give in and never surrender, but fight on until the last foe is struck down."

Danjen and Tarim came looking for them.

"Jia has taken Baeven on board *The Shadow Fox* to help him recover further," Danjen said.

Naero smiled. "You are a Ku, Danjen." The Ku were the forest people who had a symbiotic relationships with the Shai. They were feared greatly as well.

"I am a Ku," Danjen said, "and proud of it. Naero, will Baeven be all right?"

"I think he will now." Jia knew what medicine best to give him. Yet none of them had ever seen Baeven so shaken. Perhaps losing control was one of his greatest fears as well, similar to her own.

The fear of murdering those she loved, of becoming a mindless monster.

Tarim looked to Gaviok, not a little afraid of him, and then to Naero.

"Zhen wants you to help her with that green Oden guy with the sword, Naero."

"You are the great shootist," Gaviok said, turning and bowing to Tarim. "You are a fine marksman; even Baeven speaks of you with great praise. I'm sorry that we have not spoken before. I am pleased to meet any friend and acquaintance of Captain Naero. You are her crew by your uniform, and a Ramoran-human strain by your scent."

Tarim bowed low in return. "I am Tarim Martan, an Alliance miner by birth. Danjen tells me that you are a great prince among your people. And that I should show you high honor, my lord."

"The last, I'm afraid. I am Gaviok Sildion Hevokk-Zhattal, Last Lord of the Royal Shai, Heir to the Scarlet Star."

Tarim did something strange. He knelt and removed his weapons and placed them before Gaviok's feet.

"Among Ramoran fighters, it is our honor to recognize great prowess in battle. I watched you and Baeven fight this day, and witnessed what a true gift for battle really is. I lay down my arms before you in a token of my great respect."

Gaviok smiled. "I accept these tokens of respect with great gladness, Tarim Martan. We honor each other by fighting our foes however we are gifted. Take up your arms, warrior of the Ramorans. Walk beside us in honor, and let our foes fear where our feet tread. Let us all be friends and comrades here, from this moment on."

"I relish that," Tarim said, retrieving his weapons and standing up, joining them as they headed back toward the ships.

Then he seemed to remember something and turned to Naero.

"Oh, yeah. Did I tell you that Zhen wants you to join her in the medical bay on *The Dagger* Naero? She wants you to help her with that green guy. She said he's pretty bad off."

"I'd better go on ahead," she told them.

In Medical, she found Zhen ready to operate on Khai, who was still barely conscious, yet Zhen hadn't removed the Ur-metal dagger from his back yet. Naero prepped and joined them.

Medtek Ensign Trudi Cheyenne was the closest thing they had to a surgical nurse and did her best to assist.

"Zhen, what's going on?" Naero asked. "You don't have that weird dagger out of him yet? What are you waiting for?"

Zee almost rounded on her. "You know, after all of us nearly dying, I'm giving up being with Ty right now, trying to help this big green galoot—who frankly up to now has been hell-bent on capturing or killing you. But he just happens to be the first Oden—scratch that—the first Oden-Spacer hybrid that I've ever operated on, and I thought it best not to kill him outright. How's that for starters?"

Naero held up her hands. "All right, Z. I came as quickly as I could. I'm here, and I don't know anything, either. So, how can I help?"

"You're a biomancer, too. Obviously. And you've been doing it a lot longer than I have. So give me a hand. I know you understand Cosmic energies more than I do. What the hell is this stupid dagger made of? Every time I try to remove it, he hemorrhages something fierce and starts to die. Before he passed out again, Khai told me that Oden do not bleed exactly. They are normally indestructible and self-regenerating, as close to true energy beings as physical bodies can get and still remain physical. But this dagger defies all logic and makes him bleed pure energy."

Naero studied the wound and scanned the weird dagger while Zhen continued to vent.

"N, explain to me how I am supposed to operate with these artifacts that defy all logic and science? I don't see how to extract this dagger, with its even stranger energy signatures, without apparently harming him. I don't know what the hell this freaky material is. It does not even seem to exist, but here it is. My scanners go crazy every time I try to analyze it. Almost as bad as that bizarre sword of his. My scanners disrupt if I try to scan that.

"For example—among other things—that dagger appears to be both psyonic and somehow self-aware. It is clearly not an AI or any kind of a biomechanical entity. Yet it gives off tons of powerful psyonic readings; it even seems to have a will of its own. I'm worried it's going to start talking to me at some point. How will I respond? How is any of this even possible? How can an such inanimate object be psyonic?"

"Calm down, Z. I don't know what to do, either. But I'm pretty sure we have to take that dagger out of him, before it kills him."

She looked to Khai, not a little bewildered herself. "Right? We have to find a way to take the dagger out without killing you?"

Khai nodded. He looked weak and covered in sweat. Did Oden even sweat? Yet Khai was half-Spacer. How did that affect things?

Naero took a breath and tried to calm herself.

First she place her hands on him and tried to understand his physiology with biomancy.

She gasped. Pretty amazing, really. So much detail. So many levels of complexity. Very similar in some ways to when she tried to read and comprehend Shalaen with her sight. The sheer amount of detail and information was staggering and threatened to overwhelm her mind.

She had to pull away and lean against the hull for a moment.

"Now you begin to see the problem," Zhen said, folding her arms in front of herself. "When I use my sight, it overwhelms me, too. It's giving me a migraine. There's simply too much to attempt to comprehend."

Naero looked at Khai. Somehow he seemed to be getting weaker. She could sense that. His energies continued to fade.

And like him–Yii–his soulsword, had even lost its sheen and faded to a dull gray. Usually the damn thing was blinding.

Now just a little bit of brilliance glittered around its edges.

She knelt down by Khai and put her hand on his where he clutched Yii close to him. She felt his forehead with her other hand.

She remembered their time inside the star together and smiled sadly.

He felt like he was still in shock and going colder.

Then she touched the tip of the Ur-metal dagger, still protruding from his chest.

Naero gasped and felt the pain he was feeling, as the dagger severed his hold on all of his energies and everything that made him Khai. The dagger was filled with a fierce malice, driven by a single purpose. The Darkforce tainted that dagger and strove to destroy and drain everything of will and life force.

The dagger attacked Khai on every level.

Not just the physical.

The strange blade pierced her palm and would have gone all the way through if she let it.

When at last she pulled away and tried to seal off and heal the small wound, it actually resisted her Spacer smartblood, and direct biomancy healing.

In fact, that small puncture threatened to grow larger and spread.

Somehow it even linked with the stubborn remnants of her Cosmic disease, causing it to flare up again.

Naero clutched her wrist. "Help me, Zhen. Help me heal this cut before it takes off my entire hand!"

Almost in a panic, they both bent all of their biomancing skill to close the wound and heal the tissues around it.

But even together, they could barely keep it from spreading.

379

Naero finally perceived the Cosmic natures of the injury and bathed it in a rush of positive Cosmic force–Harmony and the Lifespark.

She fought the wound as if she would fight off the Dark Beast that lurked within herself.

They were all akin somehow, requiring the same equation to be balanced and restored.

Destruction–negative energy incarnate.

That was it. The dagger wasn't just Ur-metal. If Yii was charged with positive energies and dazzling Cosmic light forces, this dagger was just the opposite.

This dagger was charged with negative forces of annihilation. It contained Darkforce energies, like the ones the G'lothc and their hellish devices generated, which always seem tainted and poisoned.

The enemy dagger warred against Khai directly on several levels. It fought with anyone who touched it. It warred with the universe and all things, and any will that sought to control it.

She looked Khai right in the eye.

The Enforcer actually had pretty nice golden eyes to tell the truth. Despite the fact that he was currently being slowly drained and killed.

"Khai. This dagger is just the opposite of Yii. Isn't it? The enemy made this weapon to use against you specifically–or anyone like you."

He nodded, and tried to open his mouth to speak, with great effort.

"Shhh…don't try to talk. Conserve your strength. I know you're fighting it. But it's slowly killing you, isn't it?"

He nodded again.

"We have to find a way of taking the dagger out without killing him. But look at all the trouble we had with that little scratch I took from it?"

Zhen nodded. "You see my problem. A terrible wound like this? Will we even be able to seal it off in time? Let alone rid him of it before it kills him."

Om cut in.

This dagger is a very complex device, just like Khai's sword. He is the master of Yii, and it is part of him and shares his life force and does his will. To keep this dagger from killing him, Naero, you must take control of it and force it to do your will. Make it a part of you. Then it will cease to harm him. There is no other way. And there is not much time left.

Naero turned back to Zhen.

"I have to take control of the dagger and make its will my own. Then we can remove the dagger, close the wound, and heal him. If I'm not mistaken, Khai and Yii will be able to regenerate and heal themselves faster than we can, given time."

"And how do you come to know all of this?"

"I just kind of figured it out, through a combination of teknomancy and biomancy." She was fibbing somewhat, but at the moment, she didn't want to have to explain all about Om.

"Then you'd better get to it. Do your voodoo or whatever it is you need to do. Let's just get this damn thing out of our green patient here."

"Okay. I'm not sure how easy this is going to be."

"Not at all, I'm guessing. But as with most other things, I'm also guessing that if anyone can pull this off…it's going to be you, N."

Naero placed both of her hands on the dagger.

She gasped again.

The Darkforce within the dagger itself, the negative energy imperative to destroy everything living, lashed out at her and struck her full force within the battlefield of her mind.

Naero closed her eyes, summoned her third eye, and closed that, also.

Within the depths of her mind she saw Khai, wounded in many places and trying to fight the Darkforce as it slowly drained and wore him down.

Naero placed herself directly in front of Khai, interceding between him and the Darkforce.

She felt the agony as it rushed through her, cutting and ripping at her from within the destroying dagger.

It sliced her open until it uncovered her own Dark Beast, lurking within the shadowy recesses of herself.

And it bargained with her with eager hunger and surety.

"Ahhh…you are like us. You are strong. Let us join our strength together and kill and destroy. Everything around us. Serve us. Give yourself to us and serve our will and purpose. All must be destroyed!"

In answer her own Dark Beast rose up. And Naero bent the force of her will through it.

"My will is my own," she snarled through her beast. "I will never serve that of another. None shall ever make me their slave. You shall do my bidding. I command you not to harm this one any further. Release him!"

Light and darkness swirled within her mind, warring together.

A flash and she pulled back, the Ur-metal dagger clutched in her hand as she yanked it out of Khai.

She blinked and gazed at it, feeling the sting of its touch fading, and the strength returning to her hand that held it.

Deep within her mind, the will of the Darkforce within it wailed and faded as her own beast devoured it and made it part of itself–part of her and them together–conquering the weapon completely.

To her surprise, the flat gray metal shifted to being jet black and seemingly filled with bright stars. Strange and eerie–wholly unnatural. A frightening, maddening thing to behold. No such blade or weapon should rationally exist.

Yet it was part of her now. And more importantly–she and her Dark Beast were a part of it.

She quickly teknomanced a scabbard for it on her Nytex togs and sheathed it at her right side, along with her other battle blades.

But she felt its unnerving, Cosmic energies pulsing and shifting.

Then she realized and thought of Master Vane for an instant.

Chaos. The dagger was raw Chaos itself, and Chaos was always linked to the Darkforce.

All of that understanding swept through her awareness.

Meanwhile, Khai woke up, gasped, and threw himself out of the medbed, screaming. Even Z was shocked and taken aback.

"Are you insane?" Zhen yelled. She sprang upon Khai and struggled to heal him with biomancy. "What did you do, N? The wound won't close. I can't get it to close."

Naero pulled her aside.

"Let me do it. The wound will obey me. I'll make it go away."

"What? That doesn't make any sense, N. How can you do that?"

Naero calmly hoisted Khai up and placed him back on the medbed.

Yes. For the moment, he was unconscious once more and fading toward death.

Naero placed her hands upon the wound, feeling his energies and life force leaking out of him.

Then she simply stopped it, balancing the equation with the Lifespark and the Harmony. She took control of the wound just as she had with the alien blade.

The wound closed in an instant and even vanished, leaving Khai weak and spent, but alive.

Yii slowly began to regain its light, still clutched in Khai's hands where Naero placed it.

"He'll be all right now. We just have to give him time to regenerate."

Zhen gaped and stammered, "W-what did you just do? That was a mortal wound. Even biomancy wouldn't heal it. And suddenly, you just touch him…and it's gone? Am I going completely nuts?"

Naero grinned, forced to sit down herself by the energies she had spent. She put her head between her legs and caught her breath.

"No more than usual, you quack. Can't heal a simple little scratch like this, huh? Don't worry–I took care of it for you. Maybe you should get some rest, have your eyes checked or something."

"Have my eyes…" Zhen went pale and shot her fists down at her sides.

"My eyes are just fine. I know what I just saw. I just want to understand it, that's all."

Naero yawned and stretched and lay down on an empty medbed. "Sleepy. That was all very taxing. Gotta take a nap now. Hey, quackers, Don't do any unnecessary surgery on me while I'm out."

The blood drained from Zhen's face. "Why, you infuriating… You'll be lucky if you don't wake up with several new boobs of all shapes and sizes covering your front and back, damn you! That's what I oughta-"

Naero chuckled, dozing off already. "That should make me popular with the guys. They'll sure notice me coming and going. Keep me abreast of any such new developments, Z."

Zhen laughed and tore at her long brown hair. "Aaughh! After all we've been through today? And you still find a way to drive me crazy!"

44

Naero woke up later that evening.

She woke to Khai staring at her, looking extremely torn and troubled—the way he did when he thought she wasn't looking.

This time she blinked and stared back.

Why did he look at her that way?

Khai was apparently a very complex guy. She sensed that from her very first interactions with him—not to mention their canoodling inside a star.

There was that, of course.

Naero felt certain that he probably had a lot on his mind right now. And no small part of it was probably wrapped up around her.

Most likely, he was dwelling on what he should do about his duty to capture her and bring her back.

On one hand, they had dangerous enemies on the loose, plotting who knew whatever terrible things against just about everyone in their galaxy.

No one was safe. No one.

Yet on the other hand, Khai was still honor bound to either bring her in as his prisoner…or kill her outright.

Knowing Khai, she was pretty sure what he would eventually decide.

Once he fully realized that she was looking back, his troubled face returned to its impassive mask.

"You could have let me die or killed me outright," he said.

Naero knitted her brow.

"What?"

"It never occurred to you, did it? Even your doctor friend wouldn't have known. You could have let the dagger kill me slowly, or finished me off yourself. Nobody would have ever been the wiser. Yet instead, you saved me, Naero. You saved my life."

Naero pursed her lips.

"It doesn't matter if anyone else knew or not. I would have known. You fought bravely beside us, Khai—as any comrade would."

He shook his head. "Yet, we are not comrades, Naero. You know very well what my primary mission is. With me dead, I wouldn't be hunting you and attacking you any longer, trying to capture…or slay you."

"Nor would we have you here to help us. We need you to fight beside us against these foes, Khai. Everything else can wait. I've tried to make you see that. You know what we're up against. Our foes nearly killed all of us. They don't care about our petty squabbles."

She looked over at the Driathan Blank lying on the medbed. That which used to be Jia's brother Govae. "They murdered a nearly indestructible, immortal Driathan. Something none of us would have ever thought possible."

"They could not destroy his self-regenerating body."

"No, they wanted to keep that for themselves, simply to use as a host. But the miraculous being that was Govae is now gone forever—a terrible loss that we will never even comprehend. They destroyed his mind, his essence, his very soul—everything that he was and ever would be."

"At least we kept them from using his incredible android body as one of their accursed hosts. We could be fighting that now, as well."

"Yeah, that's true." Naero sat up and struck the edge of her medbed with her fist in frustration. "I've fought these devils, their lackeys, and their self-aware, Darkforce energy generators. Those things by themselves are horrific weapons."

Naero took a deep breath. "Khai, the G'lothc fought both the Kexx and the Drians to a standstill. Who knows what advanced tek they have to hurl against us? And I saw Janner's twin—my own former brother Danner— that insane freak. He was actually working *with* them willingly, inside a larger version of one of those vile generator machines. He's generating Darkforce energy for them, and they used that power to help destroy Govae. They got Danner from their allies in the Gigacorps. They tormented my brother Jan the same way, in one of those generators. I won't stop hunting these evil bastards until I find them and take them all out. After that, you and the Mystics can do whatever you want with me."

Khai knitted his brows.

"I'm truly sorry about what happened to your brothers, Naero. But justice among the Clans and our Mystics does not work that way. You don't get a pass on crime and murder so that you can pursue your own personal vendettas—even if they are against our mutual enemies."

"I'm not going to surrender myself to the authorities while these enemies of ours are on the loose, Khai. They will answer to me and my vengeance, by the weight of my hands, my allies, and all that I can do."

"Like Baeven, you cannot control your Cosmic powers, Naero. Look at what nearly happened. You two are as great a threat to everyone as the G'lothc in your current state. You simply won't admit that."

"I'll admit some of that, in part. But that's still not going to stop me from completing my objectives, whatever happens to me."

Khai tried to sit up. Yii flickered weakly, still in his hands.

With great effort and gritting her teeth herself, stiff and incredibly sore, Naero slipped off her medbed and pushed him back down with both hands.

But she did so, as gently as she could.

"Hey…hey. Let's stop arguing. Lie back down. Both of us just barely survived a major battle against impossible odds and impossible foes. Both of us need to heal and get back up to speed before we do anything."

"I hate to admit it, Naero. But at least you are right about that."

Naero held out her hand to him. "Keep our original truce going, then? At least until we're both not flat on our backs? I respect you Khai. I know you have to do what you have to do for your own reasons. I am the same way."

Khai took her hand, and measured her strength and determination.

"Our truce remains intact, until we both have healed, or we return to the Alpha Quadrant."

They both let go.

Khai sighed. "You know, in the meantime, I could teach you some further breathing and meditation techniques. They will aid in healing, and perhaps they will assist in helping you learn to control your negative energy side."

Naero snorted.

"What do you know about such? You've never had to struggle against anything like this."

Khai raised his eyebrows. "That is not true. All Mystics struggle against the negative energies within themselves, even if they don't have actual Dark Beasts inside of them. The greater our powers, the greater the struggle. We face that struggle each day of our existence. That is why we must either continue to grow in enlightenment or destroy ourselves. Didn't you know that? Even the High Masters face these choices and struggles, every second of each day."

Naero gaped and then covered her mouth with one hand.

"I didn't know that. I just thought Baeven and I were the only ones cursed like this."

"That is the great danger of Mystic Training. Some destroy themselves. Others end up needing to be destroyed."

"So, Master Vane wasn't joking about all that? I thought he was just being an ass."

Khai smiled sadly. "He was a major ass. Most Masters of Chaos Wisdom usually are...difficult to be around on a personal level. They're also the most likely to destroy themselves. Yet someone must focus on and teach others how to comprehend Chaos forces and energies, and how to understand and utilize them. Most of our Mystic abilities would not even be possible without the Chaos elements of the equation."

"I always found that fascinating," Naero said. "While I trained with him on Janosha, Vane was always trying to beat that fact into my head. He expounded all the time on how important Chaos was to everything–even to the Great Harmony of the universe itself."

Khai tried to make his own philosophy known. "Chaos is a great engine, a constant driving force behind both Creation and Change. Entropy and Destruction also create opportunities for new things to develop in response to change. But power and change without rational limit or control only destroys without logic or reason or purpose. For anything to be sustained, there must also be Order and Enlightened Change–guided by purpose and direction of all energies and potentials. Therein we find balance and Harmony, wisdom and enlightenment."

Naero knitted her hands together and stared at him. "The very reasons that the Spacer Mystics exist: to study and gain mastery and understanding over all of these forces–for the good of all."

Khai chuckled. "Chaos is indeed vital. Yet it must be properly understood and kept in constant balance by the forces of Order and Change. The Harmony of the Universe is sustained by the balance of the Three Powers."

"And the three acts of wisdom," Naero added, thinking suddenly of Shalaen. "Compassion, Justice, and Mercy."

"They comprise what we know and think of…as Love," Khai said.

The Enforcer gazed into her eyes a little too long, then turned away.

Naero smiled. Let him fall for her a little bit. What if he did?

She could do worse than a thick-headed champion like Khai.

And a little affection for her on his part just might help her cause, if push came to shove.

Haisha, was she turning into Hashiko, now?

In the days that followed, they continued to hunt for and pursue the enemy. But the trail went cold.

No one knew what the enemy's next move was, and in any case, they were all stuck out in the middle of nowhere still, until they could get the leap drives operating properly.

Generating another unstable, Cosmic wormhole would be a last resort, considering the first attempt that nearly killed them all.

And the potential for popping back in to their space completely disrupted and dead in the water, among potential enemies, would leave them desperate, and far too vulnerable.

Not a good plan at all.

All of them healed up from their injuries. Zhen and Ty seemed about as happy as Jia and Baeven, getting sufficiently besotted with themselves.

Naero and Baeven continued to train every day together, both as individuals and in teams with other members of all three crews, exploring all of their strengths and weaknesses.

Baeven and Khai avoided each other for the most part, and with good reason. They were like oil and water and did not mix, did not get along. They remained complete opposites. Baeven was Chaos, whether he liked it or admitted it or not. Khai, of course, was Order.

But Naero went back and forth between the two of them, training with both and learning as much as she could. Each of them had vital insights and knowledge to share that the other did not. And that was incredibly useful to Naero, who always felt torn and stuck in the middle of everything anyway.

Khai seemed to have his act together and never needed much help. Hell, the guy was pretty much just a step below being a High Master himself, without the title. That was why he held the position as the Mystic Enforcer.

But much of what Naero learned from Khai on several important levels was very vital to her in many other ways, and she passed on as much of that wisdom as she could back to Baeven. She did so in ways that he could grasp and make use of it for himself. Whether he admitted it or not, her uncle needed to learn many of those things himself–some of them even more than her.

Running with Khai during their truce turned out to be very valuable for both of the renegades. Naero and Baeven achieved several breakthroughs, and gained greater control over themselves and further understanding of their abilities and powers, almost daily.

They still couldn't enter their full, Dark Beast modes without losing all sanity and self-control, but they could keep them on better leashes and begin to understand them further. And their partial Beast modes grew more and more powerful.

Perhaps that would lead to greater overall control at some point in the future.

Naero herself seemed driven beyond obsession to one day gain total mastery of herself and all of her abilities.

It frustrated her to no end that she could not grasp or attain such control simply by force of will alone.

Khai shook his head and tried to counsel her during one of their sparring sessions. The guy was a brick–as bad as Baeven. They beat on each other relentlessly and he never seemed to take a scratch. But she felt battered and sore, and secretly had to heal herself and regenerate every chance she got.

"Do you always try to force your way through everything?" Khai asked her.

"Works for me."

"You're too hard-headed and straight forward, Naero. You're never going to balance everything out that way."

"Never's a long time. Who said I have to get it right? It just has to work."

Khai laughed. "Too bad you never got the chance to finish training with the other High Masters. They could have really helped you, I think."

"You trained with them. And you're helping me. You're passing their wisdom on to me. I say it does help."

Khai shook his head. "But I'm a better warrior than I am a teacher. They are the true experts at *teaching* their Wisdoms, and have done so for many years. I could never match them."

"You might one day, Khai. You might have to. No one lives forever–not even the High Masters."

He smirked at her. "Like you, I still have a lot to learn."

He suddenly pulled out a frosty borbble of Jett and held it out to her. Naero's eyes widened.

"Where in the hell did you–"

"Jia said Baeven still had a few of these hidden somewhere…for special occasions. I asked her for one. I hear it's your favorite lix."

"What's the special occasion?"

He shrugged and looked away. "We've been training hard. I thought you deserved a reward. I wanted to do something nice, while our truce still holds. I don't really enjoy being your enemy very much, Naero. I can't do anything about that, but I just wanted you to know how I felt."

"Thanks, Khai. Now give me that." She snatched the Jett out of his hands and started chugging it.

"None for you, buddy."

"That's all right. As a true Mystic, all I drink is rain water. I only eat nuts and twigs."

Naero almost snorted Jett out her nose. "Huh?"

He grinned. "I'm kidding, of course."

"Oh…okay. You're so serious all the time. I'm not used to you attempting to have…a sense of humor."

Khai took offense. "What do you mean, 'attempting?' I do happen to have one, you know."

"Okay. I'm sure you're great at parties–a laugh riot. But you still ain't getting any of my Jett."

"No loss. I've never really had any before. I don't usually imbibe soft drinks of any kind."

Her eyes widened. "Really? Seriously? You're not kidding this time, right? Well hey, then you just gotta try this stuff."

"No. I got it for you. Please enjoy."

"No, I insist. You have to taste this stuff. It's the best lix in all the universe. Just a sip, though."

Khai hesitated. Then he took a small sip.

Then he blinked.

"See?" Naero said. "What'd I tell you. Great, huh? Am I right?"

She'd never seen Khai astonished before. He was kinda cute, flabbergasted.

"Amazing," he said. "I've never tasted anything that good."

Naero had an idea.

She guzzled half of the borbble and smacked her lips.

Then she placed the rest of her Jett safely off to one side.

"There's half of it left…how about I fight you for it?"

He shot to his feet. "You're on. Let's go. You're going down!"

Naero grinned.

This time, just for once, she'd let him win.

But at least she had to make it look good.

The next day, they finally had the leap drives up and running again. With all three ships docked together, there wouldn't be a chance of losing each other.

But if they cooked off or imploded, they'd all die together as well.

Tyber and Rendar engaged the device while their crews stood by their stations.

In the flash of an instant, they went from the middle of the unknown Gamma Quadrant, to within 0.0032 light years of their target coordinates. They were back on the edge of known space near the Alpha quadrant, on the border with the expansion of the Alliance Systems and the Gigacorps.

They finally made it back.

But they still had no way to fully locate their enemies, or discern what their foes were going to do next.

For the time being, it seemed that the enemy had given up on trying to locate other Driathan sentinels and their hidden homeworld.

But they still had Danner, and they were still invading the galaxy. Naero wasn't about to let any of that stand.

Strangely enough, it was Khai who picked up the traces of the enemy.

As part Oden, he seemed to have an uncanny knack for tracking Cosmic signatures that no one else possessed. Not Om. Not even Jia.

"That Darkforce energy of theirs is faint," he said, using their sensor arrays to ferret it out. "But there's not much else that is like it. From everything I can see, they're somewhere in the Corps colony extents around the Hezzen System."

"That's right on the border with the Alliance colonies, in the areas everyone's scrambling to explore."

"Only a few mining probes have gone out that far," Ty said. "A quiet area without many dangers, from what is known."

Naero raised an eyebrow.

"Looks can be deceiving," Baeven said. "We'd better get out there to check it out. After we resupply at Takeda-3, it'll be a short hop. Then it's off to find our new friends and put an end to whatever it is they're planning now–and them. Permanently."

He suddenly looked directly at Naero.

"What about your Enforcer boyfriend? Have you convinced him to join our cause?"

She lowered her eyes and shook her head.

"I thought not." Baeven sighed. "He's a stubborn one. We'll have to rid ourselves of him, if he's going to try to take you in again–one way or another."

"He's helped us immensely," Naero pointed out. "Khai's given us both valuable insights into our...situations that we never had before. He's made us stronger. Not to mention he fought beside us on Zoa-4—with great skill and courage."

"Because he had to in order to survive," Baeven said. "Not because he wanted to."

"I think he wanted to. None of us would have made it out of that complex without his valor. I could not betray him like that."

"Naero, you're starting to like that stiff too much. He remains a serious threat to everything we're trying to accomplish. The truce you have with him is ending. He remains sworn to bring you back to face the tender justice of the Mystics—and myself included, if he can manage that as well. What if he kills one of us in the attempt? Either you do something to resolve this—or I will."

"No, Uncle. Don't do anything. Please. Don't make all of this worse. Let me try once more to persuade him. We have today. I'll speak to him again. Khai's reasonable, given the chance."

Baeven narrowed his eyes. "That time is passing all too quickly. We launch at dawn, if not sooner. You know we've spoken about this matter before."

"I'll handle it."

Baeven glared at her. "You'd better."

45

Naero, Khai, Zhen, Tyber, Enel, and Passaendra went to the open market at the Takeda-3 starport to purchase goods and supplies.

Several fixers bobbed along with them.

The new slap-together colonial starport was modular in nature, and could flex and change each day with the merchants at hand.

Naero bartered quickly and efficiently for what they needed, getting the best prices she could manage, almost without effort.

She'd been cutting deals since she could float and talk.

Naero loved being a Spacer.

She grew so quiet and so preoccupied that after a while, she even lost track of Khai and her friends, as they all wandered off on their own through the open market.

On a whim, Naero saw a blurt board ad and even went over to a local Galactic Zoo franchise to see a certain rare creature that was being advertised:

THE UNICORNS OF LARELLON-7

Naero thought of Princess Iiden and Thanor-4.

At the zoo, crowds of landers flocked around a shielded, circular, shining silver pen filled with a herd of actual unicorns.

There were about three dozen of them, somewhere between the size of a pony and a deer, and a little like both of those creatures as well. But there they were, pretty and delicate, and most of them even had blue eyes. They were pure white, with silken manes and tails, and ivory horns set in the middle of their foreheads. They ate special feed out of peoples' hands that was for sale, and people could even pet the skittish, hungry things and marvel at them.

And yes, they pooped unicorn turds at will, with no angels on hand to clean up after them. She laughed with joy.

Naero took her turn and even went back through the line again, studying the physiology and genetics of the creatures expertly with her biomancy. They were in fact, a true wonder.

She thought again of her friends back on Thanor-4 and the bloody, brutal war they were all probably up to their necks in by this time.

She thought of young Princess Iiden and her innocent wish on the brink of that bloody conflict, and hoped that her friends were all still alive.

If she ever survived her own ordeal, Naero would return to Thanor-4 one day, and do her best to grant the young princess her wish.

Suddenly Naero felt very homesick for her trade fleet, traveling from stop to stop in the new expansion booms, trading, negotiating, making money for her and her people–the people she loved. Her goofy, talented, quirky trading partners from all the Clans.

What a trade team they made.

If only.

What she wouldn't give to go back to what she could not.

Truth be told, Naero hated being an outlaw.

Naero returned to the market and finished shipping the last of their supplies back to the three ships. Then she called Zhen.

"This is N. Shopping for supplies is completed. We have the rest of the afternoon to ourselves. Where are you guys?"

Zhen laughed, goofing off with Ty as they bantered back and forth. "Clothing store, N. Here's the coordinates. Come over and join us. Once we're done here, we'll get some chow somewhere local."

"Clothing? You don't wear lander stuff, Z. And we can program any clothing or food we want on board the ships, any time we want."

Zhen rolled her eyes. "Live a little; get over here and figure it out. You're not saving up for your first ship anymore, cheapskate. Splurge for once."

"Okay. I'm coming. Khai with you guys?"

"Nope. Call him if you want."

"I'll catch up to you guys first."

She walked into the shop; quite an upscale local place, really. She asked about her friends, and the clerks led her to where else–the bridal area.

Zhentisa stood up on a 3-D holo pedestal in a sheer slip over her slender form.

She tried on holographic designs for wedding dresses.

Tyber drooled and cooed over each one.

Naero was somewhat stunned. Not really a slave to any kind of fashion herself, stepping out in any way wasn't really her thing. Not very often at least. Nytex togs were fine for her.

As far as she was concerned, she could live and die in her togs. And, maybe her dress uniform, once in a while.

The clerks waved their glowing design gloves over Zhen's delicate body, switching and swapping holo pieces and patterns.

Naero laughed.

"White, Zhen? You're wearing white?"

Zhen stuck her tongue out at her. "It is tradition."

"Which one?"

"Off-white," she admitted.

"Spring ivory," the smiling clerk said. The lander woman actually never really stopped smiling ear-to-ear. It was kinda creepy.

"Ooh...ooh. I like that one," Ty said.

"Better than the first thirty?" Zhen asked.

They quickly flipped back through their first three saves.

"You know," Khai said suddenly, making Naero jump. He was right next to her as if by magic.

She punched him lightly. He was carrying a big trunk of something on his back. It looked very odd, even for him, but the guy was a hoss. "Don't sneak up on me like that. You know, you can have that stuff delivered to the ship. You don't have to lug it around."

Khai laughed, setting his heavy shipping trunk down. Khai was incredibly strong, just like her and Baeven.

"Sorry. I was just going to say, if I recall what my mother told me once, a long time ago, it was considered bad luck for the groom to see the bride in her wedding dress before their wedding day."

Ty and Z knitted their brows. "That sounds really dumb," Ty said.

"Yeah," Zhen added. "I want him here with me to help pick out our outfits."

Ty suddenly paled. "Outfits? I was just going to wear my dress blacks."

Zhen gaped. "No, no–you have to match me. We're a pair. A couple."

Ty laughed. "A couple of what? Lander fools? Oh, sorry, ladies. No offense."

"None taken, sir." Same creepy smile.

"I'm just wearing my blacks," Ty insisted with a lazy sigh.

Zhen pursed her lips and glared. "Only if you want me to shoot you in them. Tell him, N. The entire wedding party is going to be color-coordinated. It'll be glacier."

"You'd better listen to the doctor, T."

"All right." Ty kissed her cheek. "For you, we'll wear any kind of stupid crap you want us to."

Naero shielded her eyes.

Oh, Ty. You're such, an idiot. Maybe Khai was right. Maybe it was bad luck. Or just maybe, Ty was a stupid goof.

Furious, Zhen pulled away and stormed out in tears.

Even the still-smiling clerks looked unsure about what to do.

Ty chased after her. "Hey. Sweetness? Come back. I said we'd wear whatever you want."

Naero turned and stared uncomfortably at Khai. What to talk about?

"Khai–there's something I want to know–did you really take on all thirty-six High Adepts and beat them?"

"No..."

Naero breathed a sigh of relief.

Khai both glared and smiled at her. "I took on all thirty-six High Adepts–*and* the five other Prime adepts, and kicked all of their butts. All at the same time."

He kept looking at her, completely serious. Then he pointed to the holo pedestal.

Out of the black Khai said, "You should get up there and try one on."

Naero scoffed. "Yeah. Right."

He grinned. "I dare you."

"Seriously?"

"You'd look great in one of those...things. Your mom did when she married your dad."

"What do you know about my parents?"

"I was a big fan of the galactic fights. I followed their careers like everybody else. They were celebrities." He bowed his head. "I'm sorry about their loss. They were great people, Naero. They meant a lot to everyone."

"I just thought about them as my parents. All that celebrity stuff was behind them after they got married. They started chasing other dreams."

Khai nodded. "You really do look a lot like your mom."

"Thanks. I always take that as a compliment. She was beautiful. And smart–and tough like you couldn't believe. And funny. She always made people laugh."

"Also like you. Please. We both know that I don't get out much. Do a little fashion show for a poor, deprived Enforcer?"

"It wasn't enough seeing my friend Zhen in her underwear?"

Khai smiled. "Please. Your friend's very pretty, but she's not exactly my type."

"Ooh, the Mystic Enforcer has a type, huh? Like Hashiko?"

"Hey, I'm not a bot. I'm still a man, just like any other."

"I'm not so sure about that." Naero raised an eyebrow. "It's okay if you do, but I was just hoping you didn't have a thing for guys."

Khai laughed out loud. "Seriously? After everything that–no. I'm pretty sure I've always liked gals."

"Couldn't find any of those hot green girls to keep you busy?"

Khai actually blushed a little and shook his head.

"No. To tell you the truth, training from birth with the Mystics as one of their prodigies didn't leave much time for dating or romance. The Mystics aren't very big on romance and that kind of stuff, if you hadn't noticed."

"Master Vane didn't seem to have much trouble sating his baser needs among the Tua females."

Khai's face darkened. "Chaos Masters are…notoriously amoral and unpredictable. And we all knew what an assbag he could be."

That proved it. She was an idiot. Probably not a good plan to mention the High Master she was forced to kill to the Enforcer who was supposed to be hunting her down for the crime. Especially now that they were on the edge of the Alpha Quadrant.

Naero wished they were flirting again, if that's what had been going on.

She sought a way to recover, stepped up onto the pedestal, and offered herself up to the fashion gods.

"All right. I'll play along. Ladies, give me the full bride treatment. Do me right."

The clerks perked up and smiled even wider, lifting their glowing design gloves. Then they hesitated.

"Pardon, miss. You're flight togs. Your…uh…hardware."

Naero recalled that she was still armed to the teeth.

"Oh. Sorry. I'll set my togs' programming to somewhere between sheer…and opaque." She removed her pistol belt, cutlass, and pouches. Then her gravwing, battle blades, bandoliers of microgrenades, mines, microbomblets, and energized throwing knives.

Heaped all together it actually made quite a pile.

Reduced just to her skintight Nytex, she winked at Khai and hit one of her presets. Her nanosuit shrank to more of a light gray tank suit, accentuating her superbly toned, athletic form.

The Mystic Enforcer looked appropriately enthralled.

His breath seemed to catch at her every cat-like move.

Naero was far from nude, but the skimpy suit still showed off all of her charms.

Then Naero unclipped and let down her shining mass of blue-black geisha hair. She veiled her big, bright violet eyes at Khai and shook her hair loose.

Khai's face turned red. He looked transfixed.

Let the poor sap suffer.

The clerks went to work.

"Such nice curves."

"Athletic toning. Perfect proportions."

"Your face and hair are exquisite."

After several attempts and near misses, they had *the* dress.

Naero caught her own breath.

She did look pretty great. From every angle. She could suddenly see what Zhen saw in all of this.

"What do you think?" she asked Khai.

His mouth fell open. He couldn't speak.

All he could do was nod like a bobblehead doll.

"Where are you two planning your honeymoon?" the eternally smiling main clerk brazenly inquired.

And with that, the spell was broken and crashed and burned right there.

No one said anything for a long moment.

Khai struggled to recover. "Huh–what? I guess…I'd better get this stuff sent back to the ships." He stood up, grabbed his crate, and left–a very dark, stricken look on his face.

"In a star…" Naero muttered sadly, watching him go.

The clerk looked completely confused by her words, and then shrugged and went back to her work.

On a whim, Naero purchased the design–at no small price–and stored it away. She set her togs back to normal, put her weapons back on, and sat down quietly beside the Enforcer's empty chair.

Just as the doors flew open again.

Ty brought Zhen back, everything smoothed over between them finally.

They went back to picking out their outfits, and those for their wedding party. Khai returned without his burden, and quietly sat back down, but not for long.

Naero and Khai were pressed into awkward service and acted as models.

Khai's green skin clashed and looked a little odd with a color scheme that was based on sea foam.

He still looked very quiet and extremely troubled.

"What's wrong?" Naero finally asked.

"This isn't right, Naero. I'm pretending we're friends. But we're not. I still have a duty to perform, one that there is no way I can avoid or deny. I cannot betray my Masters, my calling. I cannot betray myself and all that I am–not even for you."

What did he mean by that? Naero bit her lip. She placed a hand over one of his.

"Please, if you were ever my friend. Don't do anything here. Not now."

"All right. For you...I won't."

Naero turned to her friends, her mind racing. "We're starving. We're going to hit that sitdown place down the street. Can you join us there when you guys get done?"

Zhen smiled at her slyly, completely misunderstanding her.

"You two run along and have fun. We'll join you in a little while."

Like the complete dope he was, Ty rose up. "I could go with them. I'm hungry, too."

Z yanked the fool back down, gritting her teeth and clamping hard onto his arm. "You're always hungry. You're staying with me, tek-monkey."

"Ow, why are you hurting my arm?"

Naero led the way down the street to the outdoor café of the local restaurant.

They sat down quietly under a beautiful blue lander sky. They quietly ordered food. Then both of them picked at it as they sat there.

Khai spoke first.

"I'm truly sorry, Naero. But my duty is clear. I'm completely healed now, and we're on the border. I can't avoid it or put it off any more. I'm bringing you in. Don't involve your friends. When tomorrow comes, you must face me in single combat. This is a formal challenge. We can pick a place far away from here so that no one gets hurt. But you must fight me–for real this time."

"I can't convince you to come with us, Khai? You know the enemy is real. You know what we're up against."

"Will you not surrender yourself to me? Perhaps there is a way that we can still save you. Nothing has been decided yet."

"You mean after the Mystics decide to destroy me for killing one of their High Masters?"

"As I said, that judgment is not certain."

"But it is a distinct possibility. Right?"

"Yes. I'm afraid so. I will not lie to you about that."

"I can't do it, Khai. Not while our enemies are out there, planning to destroy us."

"You will face me then? I need your promise, Naero. On your honor. Otherwise, I will be forced to render all three of your vessels inoperative for a time, until our issue is decided in the morning."

"Don't do that. Part of me will fight you, Khai–to the death if need be. But the better part of me wishes we didn't have to do things this way."

Khai shook his head. "I just want to capture you, Naero. I will try not to kill or hurt you permanently."

Naero suddenly glared at him, her ire up. "Well, then–I guess I should be glad that the mighty Mystic Enforcer is doing me a great favor."

"I'm sorry about that, Naero."

"So am I. I don't want to be forced to fight someone honorable like you–who'd I'd much rather have as a…"

Khai looked at her pointedly. "As a what, Naero?"

"I-I was going to say, as a friend and ally." Naero could not meet his eyes.

Khai sighed once. "Tomorrow then?"

"Tomorrow, Khai. I'll pick a place and send you the coordinates."

Khai rose up and bowed.

"I'll be ready. At dawn."

He left his food uneaten. Naero paid for their meal and went back to the ships without calling her friends. She had a lot to prepare.

Khai had an entire cooler of Jett delivered to *The Flying Dagger*

Baeven and Jia were also waiting for her.

"We have a lock on the enemy. It is definitely Hezzen-5," Jia said.
Baeven showed her the scans.

"They already have several fleets concealed around that system. And the Cosmic energy readings are off the charts, even worse than before. They're getting ready to do something. Something big and dramatic."

"We have to get out there," Jia said.

"Have we tried bringing in help from our other allies?" Naero asked.

"We're spreading the word, but we're the only ones who can get there fast enough to do any good, for now. We need to be the vanguard in this fight, and disrupt their plans enough so that others can pour through the breach, pile on, and mop up."

Naero shook her head. "I just made a promise to Khai, on my honor, to meet him in single combat tomorrow outside the city. To decide our issue."

"Then let's go," Baeven said. "It's just words. What is that to the threats of the enemy? Big deal. So you break your word to someone who wants to imprison you, or worse? We need you in this fight, Naero. Our enemies are using powers and tek we've never seen before. We don't know what we're walking into."

"I can't go back on my word," Naero said.

"Then you'd better find a way, Naero. Haisha! Grow up."

"I don't see a way out of this, Baeven."

"Then you're just a stupid little fool. We'll have to leave you behind, and face the enemy without you backing us up and making sure we all don't get killed. How many of us will die for the sake of your sacred honor?"

Gaviok alone defended her. "Please, leave her alone in this, my brother."

"Yeah, I know. When it comes to being a fool for honor...you're as bad as she is."

Naero sat down in anguish, and buried her face in her hands. "I am a fool."

She had great difficulty sleeping that night.

She lay in her bunk, tossing and turning.

As the bells increased toward morning, she rose up to prepare.

Just before dawn, the part of her that wanted to fight Khai arrived at the coordinates.

Khai was already standing there, sword at the ready.

As the sun began to rise, Naero drew her energy cutlass. The two of them charged together and clashed.

Naero gasped and fell back, Yii impaled through her breast.

401

"No!" Khai cried. "What have you done?"

Naero smiled weakly. She sagged to the ground.

Khai held her in his arms. His hands went to her face. "No. No! I never wanted this!"

"I've kept my word," she said. "I met you in combat. But I'm sorry Khai. The enemy is moving against us all...I still had to trick you, one last time."

She could even see and speak through her astral link with it, but Naero's replicant turned transparent, and slowly dissolved.

"The enemy is planning something big on Hezzen-5," Naero warned him. "Even you and the Mystics should be able to sense it by now. If you want to bring me in, you'll need to track me there, and fight them as well. Captain Tyber and *The Dark Star* are waiting to bring you to us."

Khai snarled and tore his sword free of her replicant messenger as it continued to fade.

"Naero!" Khai roared.

Naero awoke from her sending trance with a gasping start, rubbing her chest. The astral link she had with her replicant dissolved with it.

The Shadow Fox and *The Flying Dagger* already orbited Hezzen-5, gathering vital intelligence on the enemy's activities.

They had jumped in the night before, as soon as Naero left behind her replicant on *The Dark Star*, and went into her sending trance to maintain her astral link through it.

Naero rose up and stretched. She left her quarters and went to the ready room.

"What do we know?" she asked.

"It's bad," Baeven said. "Main viewscreen."

Jia took over. "The enemy is using an improved version of the Cosmic wormhole tek, apparently without the energy-draining effects that we suffered."

Naero gaped, and covered her mouth.

On the main screen, a new stable wormhole stood wide open. Several Ejjai fleets poured through. Then the Dakkur hordeship they'd seen before.

"This is a staging area for a major invasion," Naero realized. "This is very bold–even for the enemy. How are they keeping that big wormhole stable for so long? It would take energy like that of Janosha to keep something like that open."

"Scanners are almost useless on the surface," Jia said. "But we're guessing they have several Darkforce energy generators working for them in tandem to accomplish this."

It must be more than several, Om noted. *From what we've seen of their capacities, even a dozen of those foul machines could not accomplish such a feat.*

Naero nodded. "Good. At least we have them where we can strike against them. Let's take them all down."

"Hold on," Baeven said. "I'm all for taking the offensive, but we have to be smart about this. They could vaporize us all–easily–with that much power at their command."

"But think," Naero said. "It's taking all of that power just to keep that enormous wormhole up while they bring their fleets through. If we can disrupt those Darkforce generator devices while they're using them at full capacity–bye-bye wormhole. So long, bad guys."

"And all of us right along with them," Jia said. "We have no idea what the full effects might be. A quanta-blast this huge might destroy us all, perhaps even the entire system."

Naero grinned at Baeven, checking her combat gear and weapons. "I love this plan more every second. Let's go. Every one saddle up."

Om asked, *What the heck is a saddle again?*

46

Naero went down to the surface with Baeven, Jia, and Gaviok to scout the situation on the ground.

Their primary mission: shut down the enemy Darkforce generators.

If that disrupted the enemy wormhole and cut off or damaged the enemy invasion fleets pouring into the Alpha Quadrant, then so be it.

But something wasn't right. Naero could sense that almost from the start. Her sense of warning was going nuts.

With this much Darkforce being manipulated, the Cosmic energy levels alone were on the brink of going out of control. They made absolutely no sense.

Naero hoped that Khai and the rest of their allies were going to arrive at some point. But she didn't have complete faith in that.

And even though their small scouting part was completely cloaked, they should have at least spotted some kind of enemy patrols or defenses by now. Something.

Why was the enemy leaving itself so wide open? This was too easy.

Then she felt the Darkforce energy close in around them in collapsing spheres and rings, sealing around them. It drew them ever forward. It slowly pulled them within like a living thing—like the force of gravity itself.

Naero, the enemy knew we would sense these intense energy signatures and used them as bait to lure us in.

"We're being pulled into a trap," Naero announced.

"Of course we are," Baeven said. "With these foes, we're always walking into a trap. We merely have to defeat and slay them all. Then we can go home."

"You have no home, Baeven. You're an outcast and a renegade, wanted dead or alive by just about everyone."

He scoffed at her. "And your point is? As long as I have Jia, she and our ship are our home. And no one is going to take that away from me without a fight to death. No one."

"What are you—"

"The enemy wants it all, Naero. Everything and everyone. You. Me. Jia. Our ships. Our friends. Our foes are the ultimate opportunists and exploiters. They will take everything they can get their hands on and use it all to their ultimate advantage. Right now they're probably gloating. They think they have us all right where they want us."

"Then…let's give them a belly full and more, Uncle. Let's ruin their party, as only we can."

"I agree."

They attempted to penetrate the enemy's layered Darkforce shield spheres containing them, drawing them closer to the enemy base or landing site.

Their initial attacks were merely disrupted or simply absorbed. They swept even faster toward the epicenter of the enemy position. The darkened, semi-opaque shield spheres made it difficult to make out anything within.

Their cloaking fields collapsed, and they became visible to the enemy's scans, hidden defenses, and myriad minions below as the exposed scouting team passed on overhead.

They drew intense weapons fire until Jia and Om could get the cloaking back up.

"They can't see us again," Jia said, "but they know we're still contained within their concentric defenses. Let's bore into that mountain range that is full of heavy metals. We'll be better off going in after the waves pass. They might think our ship was vaporized, and we'll still have it hidden as a way out."

"Great. Let's do it," Gaviok said eagerly.

"Either that or the energy waves will kill us all," Baeven noted.

Naero raised her hand. "Yeah, let's all vote against that outcome."

Their plan kind of worked.

They ordered their nearby ship concealed in the mountain range, so that it wasn't destroyed.

But the energy waves swept the four of them along, even when they tried to use their gravwings. Like a gigantic cyclone, it sucked them in to the center of the Cosmic vortex.

Naero sensed him as they drew closer.

"I've got a lock on Danner. I'm going in."

Baeven shook his head and tried to grab her.

"Don't just charge ahead alone. That didn't work before. We need to go in together, smart and united."

"Trust me. I'll break Danner free and be the distraction. The rest of you fall upon them with the element of surprise and finish them off while they're all focused on me."

Even Jia yelled at her. "No, Naero, don't. Wait!"

They were out of time. Naero translocated as close to Danner's position as possible sensing high level foes nearby as well.

The larger and more improved Darkforce energy generators were like Cosmic beacons. The enemy was sucking their hosts dry in order to help them increase and expand their energies, and summon their new invasion force through the enormous wormhole, all at the same time. Perfect coordination.

With all of the energy flows near critical, Naero couldn't spot or pinpoint their locations precisely.

But she did spot Admiral Korleth-Tulkas, bloated with Darkforce energy and warped by it, right as he smashed into her.

Korleth laughed as he smacked her around, glancing about and checking the area as he did so.

"Just the spack runt? Really, a stealth mission? And here we were fully prepared to capture your entire strike force for use in our generators."

Naero stopped him in his tracks with a mindforce blast. Then she drove him into the side of the gigantic Dakkur hordeship with a sonic roar.

"Sorry to disappoint you!" she yelled.

Korleth recovered and rose into the air once again. "This is going to be simple. Seize her, my siblings. Keep her alive. Cram her into the new generator specially prepared for her. Activate it immediately, and her power shall become part of our own."

He grinned, baring all of his great teeth. "We'll use her to bait the others, and seize them when they come to rescue her."

Hundreds of G'lothc-possessed Dakkur phazed in all around them from being cloaked.

They tried to ensnare her in energy chains and nets of Darkforce power.

They herded her toward an advanced, Darkforce generator capture pod. Just like the ones they had custom-made for Danner and someone else, who was trapped within another one on the other side of the device yawning open to receive her as its new power source.

Darkforce energy tentacles ending in weapons writhed toward her and fired.

They would take her in a matter of seconds.

She had no choice.

Naero filled the air around them all with orbs and bubbles stuffed with startapped Cosmic energy. She stuffed all of the available space with them until they covered and obscured everything within view.

Then she detonated them all in one massive air burst, transporting away at the last instant

She had hoped to use such a gigablast to tear Danner free.

Now she was forced to use up her best new trick in a last-ditch attempt to save herself, before they overwhelmed her.

And she did so…at the very beginning of their all-out battle.

Her gigablast obliterated the inert device meant for her, and severely damaged the ones containing Dan and the other mystery host.

The blast waves flung her back, and scattered her foes far and wide, or crushed and splattered them against the hull of the Dakkur hordeship, that nearly flipped over, and now lay on its side with its keel exposed.

Naero could barely get back up to her feet. She activated her gravwing. She raced in and used her swords to hack the mystery host free from its ruined generator.

It had a glowing blue energy form—exactly like Shalaen.

Holy Ka-rap. It was a Yattai!

This Yattai looked to be in very bad shape; close to death, even. She pulled him or it free and carried him away, her own reserves fading fast.

Her brief, massive assault left her almost completely drained.

Admiral Korleth and his surviving minions recovered and closed in on her again. Until she regenerated, Naero had no way to fight them off. She struggled to keep going, just to not black out.

The Yattai placed his hands on her, filling her with Cosmic Power.

Thank you… she heard him say within her mind.

Then he vanished, most likely back into his own dimension

Wait until she told Shalaen she had met another Yattai–and even rescued him. It. Whatever. She'd tell Shalaen just that–if she lived long enough to have the chance.

The enemy fiends began to shift form, merge, combine, twist together, and tried to fall upon her.

Naero whirled and kicked and fought, wreathed in blue-violet lightning. The daughter of The Invincible Cyclone, unleashed within a sea of lethal foes.

They fell upon her in waves, again and again.

Om poured out a fury of last-ditch KDM defensive measures that slammed into the foe, driving them back.

Om's final energy pulse negated and disrupted all Cosmic energy in a short radius–including the Darkforce. Korleth's possessed minions dropped out of the air and in their tracks like dying birds, convulsing as if stunned, sapped of all their might.

That's all I have, Naero. That last wave of mine couldn't hurt us, because we were already on empty. Now we're both completely drained.

Yet somehow, the enemy admiral was the only one who could pop back up, ready to fight.

Even the damaged megagenerator containing Danner twitched, sparked, and withdrew, limping back through a hatch and into the Dakkur hordeship, dragging with it the pieces of the empty machines Naero had shattered and destroyed.

Korleth stalked toward her.

Naero backed away like a breathless crab, scrabbling to get away.

The other possessed Dakkur continued to shake themselves, attempting to come around and rise back up.

Korleth hissed, "My master said that you could be troublesome, spack runt. Inconvenient indeed, but the megagenerators can be recharged and reconstructed. You've only succeeded in delaying our plans–not stopping them–and now, we still have you. No force or power remains that can save you. You friends are already retreating; they are not going to come to your rescue this time. Surrender."

"Never!" Naero screamed.

The Flying Dagger uncloaked and roared in.

Her flagship rammed into Admiral Korleth and his goons, crushing and scattering them.

The rear loading bay snapped open.

Zhen and Tyber stood there with Naero's crew, bristling with autoguns and heavy weapons–ready to repel all comers.

Naero desperately crawled toward them, screaming. "Get the hell out of here. It's all a trap!"

"Not without you!" Tyber yelled. Zhen and Ty zipped out with their gravwings to rescue her.

Naero met them and together they floated back with her toward the cargo bay. "Baeven and the others were cut off," Zhen said. "Now they're retreating, blasting a way out of the enemy shield spheres with Alala's help. They sent us in to get you. We'll only have seconds to shoot through before those barriers close up on us again for good."

"You guys have to get out of here!"

"Shut up," Ty said. "We're getting you out, or nothing."

Her crew unleashed hell from the starship and their packed weapons in the bay. The intense volley of fire drove the enemy hordes back once more.

"Time to go!" Tyber yelled, "Nothing will hold these things back for long. Hold her, Z. Don't drop her!" He fired right into the swarming hordes swelling up from below.

"I'm spent. I can barely move," Naero moaned.

Zhen held her back up. "Don't worry, I've got you, N."

She shot up toward the loading bay, turning and blasting foes licking at their heels.

Zhen flung Naero over her shoulder with surprising strength.

Naero drew her blaster pistol and tried to help cover their retreat.

"Stop squirming!" Zhen screamed. "Let me rescue your dumb ass!"

"Get ready to punch it, Enel," Ty shouted. "We've got her!"

"This is gonna be close," Tarim said, pouring fire into the foe.

Zhen flew into the loading bay, dumping Naero into the arms of the waiting crew.

Then she screamed.

Korleth flashed up into the loading bay from below, stunning and flinging the others back with the force of his massive, hyperdense body.

His razor-sharp tail impaled Zhen, wide-eyed and gasping on its glowing length.

"Aww...too bad," Korleth rasped. "So very close."

"No!" Naero screamed.

She tapped without thinking and ripped herself open trying to unleash her Dark Beast and keep control of it.

Moving faster than thought, she severed the long tail with her blades.

Concussive beams from all three of her eyes punctured Korleth. A mindblast crushed and deformed one side of his hyperdense skull. Her sonic scream slammed into the huge Dakkur. The force punched Korleth out of the open loading bay as the dock as the doors closed and the starship swept away.

Paralyzed and grief-stricken, even Naero's Dark Beast failed and shrank back in weakness, brought on by her intense, overwhelming grief.

Naero fought off blacking out, Cosmic glowing ichor and blood streaming from her orifices.

She somehow crawled over to Zhen and placed her hands on her dying friend.

No power in the known universe could heal such a horrible mortal wound.

"No, no," she muttered over and over again, sobbing. "I've got you, Z. I'll save you. I'll make it right somehow."

Zhen stared up at her, her eyes starting to glaze over. With the last of her strength, she reached into a pouch and pulled out a small, shielded metal cryo case, pressing it into Naero's hand.

"My babies…N. Ty…protect-"

Zhen was gone.

Naero pulled Zhen's body off the gigantic Dakkur tail blade.

A torrent of blood rushed out everywhere. Zhen's small torso was nothing but a gaping hole.

Naero still struggled with biomancy to heal such an impossible wound, even though doing so remained utterly hopeless. Not even Shalaen could do so.

Naero still struggled and fought against the undeniable with her weak, feeble efforts–awash and drenched with her *abani's* gore. Her hands and forearms were stained dark red.

Zhen's long, light brown hair lay spread out, soaked in her own blood.

Naero nearly went mad herself, sobbing and babbling.

"No, stay with me, Zhen! I've got you. You're not going anywhere, you quack. I swear to you. I'll find some way to make this right!"

The others of her crew began to come around and pick themselves up.

When Ty saw what had happened, he really did go insane.

It took six crew to hold him down.

Finally, Naero curled up together with him around Zhen's slender, still form, until the two of them wept and passed out.

47

Naero remained in the still, sterile silence of the medical bay.

She stayed with Ty as he mourned over Zhen's lifeless body.

Ty wept for the longest time.

Naero wept with him.

Ty took his beloved in his arms time and time again, and sobbed and convulsed with gut-ripping sorrow.

And like him, Naero felt she might go mad with grief. So helpless.

Losing her parents had been horrible beyond belief. At times, when she thought about it all too much, it still was. All the loss everyone suffered during the Annexation War, and ever since.

And yet somehow, all of that, and even losing Gallan–had not been this bad. And Naero did not know why.

She and Z had been like sisters, but they were completely different people.

Perhaps she felt responsible for Zhen's death.

For being too weak to protect her.

Maybe it was just the last straw.

Perhaps seeing the horrific effects on Ty made things even worse.

Then Naero spotted it clearly. A small, bright point of light.

She knew what it was: Zhen's soul–her essence–dispersed from her ruined body and about to escape.

Forever.

She was the only one who could see it. Ty had passed out again.

Naero lunged and reached out. She barely caught it, cupping the glowing soul orb in her hands. Then she sealed it within a small globe of pure Harmony.

Just as she had done with Jia's essence, Naero kissed the soul orb and breathed it deep within herself, in order to keep it safe.

Oh, Z. My sister…I have you.

She even heard Zhen's voice deep inside her, calling out in fear and confusion. "Where am I? What is this place?"

With her force of will, Naero put Zhen's soul into a deep sleep, to comfort and protect her, in the safest place she could find. It was very similar to controlling one of her replicants.

Naero kept her vigil of mourning with Ty, unsure of what to do next. She was always stumbling into unknown territory. She needed time to think.

Baeven and Jia, everyone from the rest of the crew–even Gaviok–filed in to pay their condolences as the hours passed, and tried to comfort them both.

"We need to speak to you, Naero," Baeven said. "We sent out a distress call. All of your former allies are coming to help. But they won't be here for days. The enemy hasn't fled. We hurt them, but we haven't beaten them. They've regrouped and are entrenched in their position. Their energy fortress seems impregnable for the time being. It's like they're waiting for something else to happen."

Something tried to click in Naero's mind, but she could not tell what it was. Her thoughts were still too broken and distracted.

Baeven went on. "We're researching another way to negate the enemy's defenses and get at them to shut down the rest of those Darkforce generators. Come to us when you're ready, Naero. We need you."

Danner. Her family, and the rest of her friends, would have to deal with Danner. And Admiral Korleth–with or without his deadly tail.

And anything else their vile enemies threw at them.

Naero's eyes felt as if they were on fire again.

More of the people she cared about could die–very quickly and easily–if she did not rise up and fight the enemy again, with all her heart and soul.

It was at that moment that Naero suddenly realized how sick of fighting she truly was.

What were their foes waiting for?

Baeven was right. It didn't make any sense. Naero knew that she should somehow know the answer, but everything in her head was clouded, both by grief and a growing desire–for vengeance.

She struggled to come out of her fog and think rationally. Her people needed her at her best.

Naero stepped out of the medical bay and called to Baeven. "I'll be there. Count me in. How soon do we move?"

Baeven looked back and smiled. "Week to ten days. Plenty of time to plan and prepare. We'll time our assault to begin as soon as help arrives and starts to pour in. That way, we can do what we need to do, and bug out when we have to, to make good our escape. We can crack their defenses without being destroyed. And by then, we'll have plenty of help, despite all of the enemy's current forces."

Jia tried to find something positive. "At least we shut that big wormhole down when we disrupted the generators on the planet surface. The enemy can't bring any more of their fleets through."

"For now," Naero said. "Admiral Korleth let slip that their generators could repair themselves, given time. We already knew they could regenerate. Then they'll open the wormhole again, and their invasion hordes will continue to pour through."

"You said we took out the megagenerator they had a Yattai in," Jia said. "We've relayed that knowledge to Shalaen. Maybe we can take the other generators down before they can find any more hosts."

"Maybe this, maybe that," Baeven said. "That's too many maybes."

Ty snarled suddenly from back inside Medical. "My 'Tisa's still dead, and she's not coming back!"

Nobody knew what to say when he lashed out like that.

Ty was still like a madman. So they just let him work through his sorrow and loss.

"Jia," Naero whispered. "Please, stay behind with me after the others go. I...I need to speak with you, about a matter of great importance. Privately."

Jia looked at her curiously, but did so.

They went off into a corner of the hallway and spoke together quietly.

"I have Zhen's soul, Jia."

"What?"

"I was barely able to capture it as it fled her body. But I have it. It sleeps inside of me, but I can feel it. It's her. I…just don't know what to do with it now."

"Naero. There's nothing you can do. You must release her and let her go on. To take the next journey, as Spacers say."

"No, I won't give up that easily. We have her genetics. We can biomance. What about a clone?"

Jia slowly shook her head. "Naero, no."

"Why not? We make a clone. We put her soul back into it. She's alive again."

Jia sadly shook her head again. "It won't work."

"A replicant, then–an exact copy, even down to the neural net. I've made them myself. I can do it."

Jia took her hands. "You can only make replicants while the original is still alive. That won't work once the person is already dead."

"Then it's back to the clone idea."

"No. That won't work either. No one can do so, Naero. Not you. Not anyone. Not even the Kexx or the Drians could conquer death."

"What?"

"Why do you think the G'lothc are having so much trouble with their hosts rejecting their spirit possessions? The Cosmic energies of the host eventually rejects the soul essence. Even if you made the best clone or replicant possible for Zhen, it would never be an exact, perfect copy of her original body. You could put her soul into another body, but she would merely die again, and suffer greatly."

"Is there nothing we can do?"

"There is…something. A procedure the Drians gained from their allies the Kexx. With your help, we could make it work, since you already have her soul. But I warn you, Naero. It is limited in scope and far from perfect."

"How limited? What will it do?"

"I will not bring Zhen back permanently, but only revive her for a short time, in order for her to settle her affairs, say her goodbyes. The way she never had a chance to."

"How short, Jia?"

"Hours. Not even a full, standard day. Every case is different. At first she'll be all right, but eventually, she'll start to weaken. Then she'll die again, in about an hour. No pain. She'll just go to sleep and not wake up. Would that be worth it, Naero? To see your friend die all over again?"

"Yes," Naero said, without hesitation.

She knew what Ty would say.

What Zhen would say. What Naero herself wouldn't give to have even another few minutes with any of her loved ones that she had lost.

"What do we do, Jia?"

"This is only going to work once. We'll have to repair her physical form with your biomancing."

"We can close the wounds and repair the flesh. What good will that do? She'll still be lifeless. I know that much from my replication experiments."

"Then your insights will help greatly. You can directly control and manipulate Cosmic energies, Naero. Using the techniques I'll teach you, we can bring her back to life–but only for a short while. You'll need to speak to Tyber once he's cogent enough to–"

"I know what Ty will say. He'd give his own life just to have even a few more seconds with Zhen–not to mention a few hours. But I'll talk to him, when the time is right."

"We don't have long. We'll need to prepare the body and keep it frozen until we're ready for the procedure. And then you'll have to put Zhen's soul back inside her."

"It will have to wait until after we deal with this enemy threat."

Jia hesitated, and then nodded.

*

The enemy chose not to let the week to ten days or so pass quietly.

The very next day, nearby Spacer Marine units from General Walker's Bravo Command and all the other Marine divisions began to pour in across Hezzen-5. Most of these forces were ship's troops, or troops stationed on nearby systems.

Now that they were fully exposed, large units of Ejjai, backed up by Dakkur and the possessed, had scattered all across the Gigacorps border world and were causing untold havoc and death.

The locals, about a billion total, were no match for the invaders.

Easy meat.

The Marines hunted the enemy down in good order, but even they had trouble with the possessed.

Naero and Gaviok joined the hunt, ready at a moment's notice to pop in and help deal with any greater threats.

Then something worse happened.

Within a single day, almost everyone on the planet became violently ill.

Landers, Spacers, the enemy–everyone who wasn't in a sealed suit.

Naero, the enemy plague has finally struck, he informed them. *The biowar missiles.*

415

She gasped inside her helmet. That's what she should have remembered. *What about our countermeasures, Om? Did they fail? Is everyone going to die?*

Too early to tell. The enemy strain is virulent, still attempting to mutate and fulfill its original objectives. Our countermeasures are trying to fulfill theirs.

What can we do?

Don't come out of that combat suit until it's resolved. I don't want us suddenly transformed into a puddle of biomatter.

That would be inconvenient.

She got on her link to Baeven. "This is what the enemy was waiting for all along, just as we warned. This attack will saturate the entire Alpha Quadrant. That's what they were waiting for—our enemies expected over ninety percent of us to die."

"And instead," Baeven said, "for the time being, everyone's just too sick to stand or function. Good thing the enemy is also affected."

"Not the Dakkur," Naero warned. "They're still immune. And the Ejjai that remain in sealed suits or vehicles can still fight if that changes. That's going to be a problem. We're rallying all the Marines on our side who can take them on, but we're still way outnumbered. Damn that wormhole!"

"Naero, a small percentage of the locals and our people are immune…including me, Jia, and Danjen. S'krin wasn't so lucky."

"Interesting. How small a percentage are unaffected?"

"Two, maybe three percent at most. That's all."

"Better than none."

"But it's random. And they are already overwhelmed, dealing with the sick—and the enemy attacks."

Naero fumed. They really missed Zhen's expertise with bio-weapons now. "Coordinate all data with the Intel bio-weapon teams. Maybe they can come up with something to help tip the scales. If someone has an immunity, that needs to be studied."

"I'll have your people take care of that," Baeven said. "Intel and I still don't play well together."

Naero received an urgent alert on her wristcom.

"Gotta fly. Literally. Something's gone hot, Baeven. Keep me posted."

"Give 'em hell, Naero. I'll join you when I can."

Naero's battle smile snapped up. "You know I will."

The remaining enemies who could still act decided to go for broke. Abandoning their own stricken forces, they regrouped and attacked the largest gigacity onworld–Delevor–home to over eighty million people, packed into an urban area of about four hundred square kilometers.

It was a bloody mess. The enemy raiders scattered everywhere, causing death and more death among the sick and the helpless locals.

Naero despised Ejjai–and the Dakkur were even greater killing machines.

Om, send our fixers in. I want every enemy out there pinpointed. Tell the Marines to bring in ground and air support. Coordinate all firing profiles to reducing the enemy as quickly and as efficiently as possible.

Naero, to modify one of your metaphors, those are an awful lot of needles to find in countless haystacks.

Lots of people are dying right now, Om. Let's get in there and do what we can.

The Spacer Marines and other personnel who could still fight performed beyond their best.

Everywhere they located the foe, fierce firefights erupted and took the enemy down hard. In the face of such horror, even Baeven and Khai went on the hunt, in the areas Naero and the other units couldn't reach yet.

They went in and took on the largest pockets of foes the fixers could locate, and single-handedly taught the enemy the true meaning of fear and terror.

But the battlefield was too spread out, and the defenders simply didn't have enough personnel on the ground.

The battle raged over three terrible days and nights. More Marine companies trickled in, but the defenders still could not contain the mindless, spreading destruction.

Three days of intense fighting, and they had cleared and secured only one quarter of the battle zone.

Losses among the stricken civilians became sickening. Most of the landers remained helpless from the plague, unable to flee or even hide.

Naero kept hunting, fighting, and killing, exhausting herself several times over. The advancing Marines and a few local defenders marched in right behind them in rotating shifts every four hours.

Whenever she collapsed from utter fatigue, Gaviok slung Naero onto his back as if she were an infant, secured her in a fixer-modified nanorig, and kept tracking the foe.

The mantid prince became Naero's dauntless champion.

Gaviok alone could match Baeven's ferocity in combat. And where the Destroyer went, the enemy soiled themselves, fled, and died. The mantid moved with incredible speed, churning and smashing through their foes. He shielded himself and Naero with Chaos energy, and not even

417

individual starship batteries could touch him. Ejjai, Dakkur–the possessed–
Gaviok moved through them efficiently in a blur of death. He left them
eviscerated or pulverized and crushed.

His hyperdense mandibles, claws, and legs tore through gravtanks,
gunships, and armor as if they were paper. Scarlet beams of destroying
energy lanced out from his three eyes, sliced through warships, and cut
down entire swaths of attackers. He trampled the enemy and kept fighting.

For the enemy, Gaviok became a nightmare unleashed.

While Naero repeatedly drained herself and was forced to periodically
rest and regenerate, Gaviok had the endurance to stay on task and continue
hunting and killing the enemy raiders.

No rest. No let up.

She often came to amid the cries of dying foes, took up her weapons,
and rejoined the fight.

Another two days of grueling, close-in combat, and they had secured
half of the battle zone. They got a break of sorts at the start of day six.

*Naero, Intel bio-weapons labs found a way to boost our
countermeasures. The plague will subside for us, and start to kill the Ejjai.
The labteks haven't been able to make it work against the Dakkur yet.*

The Dakkur are far fewer in number anyway. Taking down the Ejjai
will eliminate their numbers, and inoculate our worlds against further
invasions.

But other reports flooded in from every area.

Now that the locals started feeling better, they were fleeing in abject
terror. They fled by the millions, scattering in all directions, sometimes
right into the bloody claws of the enemy.

The chaos and madness were near total, and that was only going to
make things much worse.

We need to organize these landers, Om. Have Intel use our fixers to
spread the word. Tell the noncombatants to find a safe place to hide, with
enough food and water for three days. Bunkers, basements, mines,
underground strongholds. More help is arriving each hour, and this
madness will end. Anyone who can and wants to fight, have the fixers
make weapons and grenades for them. Intel will instruct them how to
organize themselves into fighting units. The fixers are our lifeline to the
local population. These people can fight back, and we can help each other
turn the tide.

Their efforts had limited success throughout the next day. The
population as a whole was still weak and demoralized from the effects of
the plague, malnourished and dehydrated. And they were terrified of the
enemy–with good reason.

The humanitarian effort of dealing with such an explosion of refugees quickly became overwhelming, and while the main battle was still being prosecuted, it had to be left to the landers.

Only the fixer clouds could help with logistics, but that was considerable.

Another priority alert reached Naero and Gaviok. What now, Om?

Naero, a large battle group of the enemy is forming up around one of the largest remaining population centers that our forces have yet to reach. Our foes have encircled it with thirty thousand troops and are closing the circle, killing all that they find.

How many landers in that circle, Om?

Almost twenty million, packed into domes and pyramid complexes. And we have no one to send.

Send us, Om. How many Marines do we have attached to us?

Nearly a thousand.

Thirty to one odds. Less than a full battalion, but they had to get in there. Naero got on the horn to her Marines.

"Leftenant Colonel Steiner, this is Strike Fleet Captain Maeris. You and your Marines and reserves feel like jumping into an all-out firestorm today?"

"Well, when you put it that way, N, how can we resist?"

She shunted the SitRep to him via Om, so that Steiner and his team could start planning up front.

"You weren't kidding, N. That's going to be one helluva shitstorm to drop into," Steiner admitted.

"We go in hot, and it only gets hotter. We're pulling in what ground and air support we can cobble together. But we're the only hope that any of those people have of surviving the next standard day."

"N, it's still going to be a blood bath for everyone involved. You know that, right?"

"That has never stopped."

Steiner nodded. "But I agree. It will be unbelievable if we don't go in. Damn it! We'll have all the help we need in just another day."

"Heinrich, my friend...none of us have an extra day."

"Ooh-Rah! We own the black; it is our domain. When do we hit these slashers, N?

"Now. We hit the bitches, now–and we ram them into the dirt as hard as we can, with everything we've got."

48

The enemy shelled the enormous local domes and pyramids of the gigacity with scattered artillery fire as they tightened the noose and swept in on the trapped population.

Marine air support began knocking out the enemy fighters and gunships, while others strafed exposed enemy armor and artillery units in coordinated attacks. Close assault ships took up defensive positions over the population centers, blanketing main approaches in interlocking waves of withering fire. But the foe was still too numerous, and too spread out for the defenders to contain them all.

The defenders could slow them down and punish them—but not stop them.

Gaviok went out into the teeth of the fighting, taking on the possessed wherever they reared up.

Naero made an attempt to rally the terrified locals.

The night before, she startapped and made two dozen replicants of herself, in full-on Shetanna mode: blazing red katanas and stealth armor, bristling with weapons and ordnance, like some futuristic, warrior goddess.

Each of her replicants went out among the local population to speak with them and their leaders. A heavy rifle team of fierce Marines and a fixer cloud accompanied each replicant. They were all linked to the original, and they could converse, but they would also echo her words if need be.

And each of Naero's reps could fight with her battle prowess, weapons, and basic skill–just not all of her full array of Cosmic abilities. Those only Naero herself could unleash.

Wherever they went, the story was the same. The locals and their leaders looked stricken, and cowered in abject fear before the might of the advancing foes.

Naero and her replicants chose key vantage points where tens of thousands could see and hear their words. They used *the voice*. The locals put her up on every vid and holoscreen nearby.

"PEOPLE OF DELEVOR, CITIZENS OF HEZZEN-5. THIS IS IT. YOUR MOMENT OF TRUTH. YOUR CALL TO ARMS. YOU MUST STAND TOGETHER, RISE UP, AND FIGHT!"

Many protested. "We're not soldiers. We're not warriors. We're just normal people! How can we fight these monstrous invaders?"

Others asked, "Who are you to tell us what to do?"

Then a murmuring began in the crowds as people began to recognize the legend that stood before them. It spread like fire through a dry forest.

"That's Shetanna. Shetanna has come! It's her, I tell you. I saw vids about her from the High Crusade. No one can fight like her. The enemy are terrified of her. She'll help us!"

They cried out to her.

"Shetanna! Shetanna! Shetanna!" And as they shouted her name, hope began to grow and sweep out from those locations, while the battle raged and pounded all around the outskirts of the enemy ring of death.

Naero lifted her hands to speak, and they all grew silent.

In other corners of the battle zone, Naero's replicants took their cues from her before similar crowds.

"GOOD PEOPLE, MY FORCES AND I WILL FIGHT TO DEFEND YOU TO THE LAST WARRIOR, TO THE LAST DROP OF BLOOD, BUT WE CANNOT PREVAIL ALONE. ANY OF YOU WHO ARE ABLE TO FIGHT MUST ARISE, TAKE UP ARMS, AND HELP US. YOU MUST FIGHT BESIDE US!"

The crowd still resisted.

Naero shook her head. "ALAS, OUR NUMBERS ARE STILL TOO FEW. WE ARE OUTNUMBERED THIRTY TO ONE. FEARFUL ODDS, YET WE STILL FIGHT ON. THE ENEMY ARE THIRTY-THOUSAND STRONG, YET YOU ARE MILLIONS. IF YOU WANT TO FIGHT, STEP FORWARD. WE WILL GIVE YOU

WEAPONS. YOUR NUMBERS CAN TURN THE TIDE BEFORE WE ARE ALL
SWEPT AWAY. DON'T JUST LURK HERE, WAITING FOR THE ENEMY TO
BURST IN AND KILL YOU ALL. STAND BY US! FIGHT BESIDE US!

"WHO WILL DEFEND YOUR PRECIOUS CHILDREN AND YOUR HELPLESS
ONES AGAINST THE INVADER, IF NOT YOU? YOU HAVE ALL HEARD THE
TERRIBLE ACCOUNTS. YOU ALL KNOW VERY WELL WHAT THE ENEMY WILL
DO TO THEM. THIS DAY WILL DECIDE IF YOU ALL LIVE OR DIE. IF YOU ARE
TO DIE, IS IT NOT BETTER TO GO DOWN FIGHTING? I SAY IT IS!

"STAND WITH US. FIGHT BESIDE US, AND YOUR NUMBERS CAN TURN
THE TIDE. YOUR NUMBERS CAN DEFEAT THIS FOE AND CRUSH THEM, IF
YOU WILL ONLY FIGHT BESIDE US. WHAT SAY YOU ALL?"

"Fight! Fight! Fight!"

The throng took up the chant, and brave men and women, teens and
the middle-aged, came to the fore, ready to be armed for battle. Naero
could still see the fear in their eyes.

The fixers quickly broke down nearby items and equipment from
shops, dwellings, and restaurants into raw components, and began passing
up blaster rifles and grenades in large quantities to be distributed.

"I AM SHETANNA, THE DARK ANGEL OF DEATH, AND I SHALL LEAD
YOU INTO BATTLE. TOGETHER WE SHALL TEACH OUR ENEMIES TO RUE ANY
DAY THAT THEY SEEK TO INVADE OUR WORLDS AND BUTCHER OUR
CHILDREN! RISE UP WITH YOUR NUMBERS AND CRUSH THE INVADERS. RISE
UP GOOD PEOPLE, AND FIND THE GREAT STRENGTH WITHIN YOU ALL. LET
US FIGHT TOGETHER. DEATH TO THE INVADERS!"

"Death! Death! Death!"

"Shetanna! Shetanna! Shetanna!"

Within six hours, nearly three million landers armed themselves and
swept out to overwhelm the advancing enemy forces.

The enemy was caught completely off guard and swept away in a tide
of intense blaster fire and grenades. The unleashed ferocity of the pent-up
locals finally ignited an incredible firestorm in the hearts of the defenders.
Led by Shetanna and the Marines, they could not be withstood by any
force. Nor one ten times as great.

Naero, Gaviok, and the Marines barely had time to rush here and
there, to take out the remaining Dakkur and a few of the remaining
possessed. They fought as bravely as ever, but it was the fighting people of
Delevor who won the day.

By the time the Allied forces began to pour in the next day, the locals
were in charge of their own defenses, and the Marines and Intel only acted
as advisors to them, helping them mop up and hunt down enemy stragglers.

*

Alliance, Spacer, and even Mystic forces continued to converge on Hezzen-5.

About the same time that enemy reinforcements arrived.

Above the planet, a furious naval battle erupted two days later.

Onworld, the final assault on the enemy stronghold got underway.

Naero acted as the distraction once again, her favorite role.

Bust in, cause maximum damage and mayhem.

Something she excelled at.

She had prepared herself for this assault for an entire day, building up her reserves; honing her skills with Baeven, Gaviok, and Khai; discussing strategy.

The enemy's dense, living shields still barred their way. A lethal, active barrier, immune to most weapons.

Naero could feel the waves of Darkforce energy lashing at her like the whips of a billion devils from hell itself.

First she transformed into an energy form. Then she went into her partial Dark Beast mode. That was the key to the process.

She wasn't just Chaos energy, not just Darkforce.

Naero became every form of Cosmic Energy there was—in perfect harmony.

She stood twelve meters high and was unstoppable.

She hit the enemy's barriers running. She strode through their strongest, most lethal defenses, and they melted before her.

Not without strain or effort—or even suffering—but she penetrated them with sheer determination and defiant force of will.

At this level of Cosmic awareness, she could vaguely make out Danner nearby, like a bonfire of Darkforce power. He shrieked, twisted, and laughed maniacally in his prison restraints, trapped in the private hell of one of the enemy's megagenerators, which continually tormented their hosts and sucked them dry.

Danner's bottomless sources of Cosmic force were beyond scary.

Naero hated to admit it, but Danner had always been strong—even stronger than she.

Danner was pure destruction. Madness. He thrived because he fed the Darkforce on endless hate—something they both shared and understood intimately and extremely well.

At times she pitied Danner and all that his life of agony, fear, and malice had twisted him into. He had never known the love that she and Jan had known. Unlike her and Jan, Danner had never known a moment of true happiness as a real, fully-functioning person. Naero cursed all of their hated foes rolled up into one. No person should ever be forced to endure such a life, especially her brother's twin—her former blood.

The enemy transformed all of Danner's hate and might into the Darkforce, in order to power their efforts and hurl those forces against Naero and everyone else.

Baeven agreed with her.

Danner served the enemy far too well, both as a power source and a potential weapon.

One way or another—that needed to end.

Naero clenched her fists and crossed her forearms in front of her, leaning into the vortex of Darkforce annihilation as she punched straight through it.

Her third eye burst into blue-violet flame.

Wings of light and darkness flared and feathered out from her back, beating like her thundering heart, sweeping her forward against the Cosmic hurricane of destroying force that the enemy unleashed against her.

She perceived and sprung their trap—on purpose.

As long as she was crashing through the front door anyway, she might as well announce her arrival for all to see and hear.

The enemy counterattacked.

She endured the brunt of it in her fury, keeping the enemy fixed upon her, making no attempt to deflect it. That alone kept those destroying forces from laying waste to the planet surface for hundreds of kilometers in all directions, and from incinerating whoever survived among her companions.

Some of the energy, she absorbed. Some she shunted into her Dark Beast to sate its ever-burning hunger. Even more she reversed and sent straight back into the universe itself.

But no matter what it cost her—no force in all the universe was going to keep her from penetrating that enemy stronghold.

Even if doing so tore her to atoms.

Finally, she reached the other side. She launched herself at Danner as soon as she spotted him.

Her blinding, all-out attack smashed into him, and she shredded the megagenerator with her weapons as they tumbled and wrestled, and fought.

Danner stared at her with his burning eyes, and laughed and laughed.

The enemy retaliated again.

Multiple weapons slammed into Naero, batting her around.

But the damage was done.

Without Danner boosting their Darkforce energies, the enemy defenses around their stronghold collapsed.

Solid stone near Danner and the Dakkur hordeship erupted–bursting and exploding in glowing shards like a volcano.

Baeven and Gaviok led the strike force up from where they waited for Naero's signal. They had tunneled right through the planet's bedrock.

They and the strike team punched into the enemy hordes, right behind the Mystic Enforcer.

Naero recovered and shrank back down to make herself less of a target. She swept toward Danner to rip him free of the remains of the shattered megagenerator.

She was ready to either fight him to the death, or take him prisoner– whichever way it went.

But a wormhole appeared behind Danner and sucked him away, into the Dakkur hordeship or somewhere else. Naero couldn't even sense his presence any longer.

What was going on?

Baeven and Gaviok pressed their attacks on either flank, and the strike force rallied behind them.

Even as the enemy ship prepared to launch.

Naero had a bad feeling suddenly, that they were all being played.

She tried to contact their ships.

"Jia, report."

The response came back garbled.

"Naero…Bae…help…enemy…swarming all over us. We…can't break free!"

The link went dead.

The Dakkur hordeship blasted off.

It was all a decoy, a clever diversion.

Naero wondered why Admiral Korleth Tulkas had not shown himself.

Korleth was up in orbit already, going after the enemy's real objective–Jia and Govae's immortal bodies. They would stop at nothing to obtain them.

They would torment Jia, and strip her mind of all of her secrets, and destroy her for all time, just as they had done to Govae. G'lothc spirits would then have two perfect hosts in such immortal, android bodies. Then they could lay waste to Ur-Jahal, and all else thereafter.

Naero transported up to *The Star Fox.*

Admiral Korleth Tulkas and a score of G'lothc-possessed Dakkur champions swarmed all over the Drian ship, tearing it apart from the outside.

Jia and S'krin attempted to defend themselves and their ship, but they were outnumbered.

425

And with the naval battle up in the black still anyone's game, no one was going to come to the aid of a small, unknown vessel.

"Jia, I'm here," Naero announced from the hold. The ship continued to rock and take damage. "I'm going out to knock them off the ship. Get out of here the second you can break free. Don't worry about me–they're after you and Govae's body!"

"Understood!"

Om, get Alala and *The Dark Star* up here to help. *The Dagger* can still cover and pick up Baeven and the rest.

On it.

Naero transported out into space, adjusting her energy form to not need air.

She smashed into the possessed Dakkur in her partial Dark Beast mode, knocking and ripping them spinning off into the black.

Destroying them didn't matter. All she had to do was get Jia free so that she could run.

She fought the foe beneath the vessel and spotted Admiral Korleth-Tulkas, also glowing with possessed, G'lothc Darkforce power.

He had transformed and swollen up to twice the size of the others, a huge monstrosity crammed with destructive power. He tore a gaping hole right through the hull and reached in, fishing around.

Korleth locked eyes with her and snarled over the open comlink. "You filthy, rutting, spack sow! Will we ever be rid of you? No one up here to save you now. I will peel the hide from your guts and devour your entrails and heart, before I grind your skull between my jaws!"

Naero set her stance to do battle, gathering all her might and abilities.

She gripped her Ur-metal blades and clenched her teeth. "Bring your worst, monster!"

"I will personally exterminate your troublesome kind from this universe!" Korleth came at her impossibly fast.

Naero matched him. Speed for speed. Blow for blow. They thrashed forward and back, fighting bitterly.

Korleth ripped at her with his claws. He snapped at her with his great crushing maw.

Naero shattered one of his thick legs with a single blow.

He grunted and whipped around, nearly cutting her in half with his regenerated tail.

She barely flipped over the attack to dodge it.

He leaped high into the vacuum at her and they wrestled, both of them crashing and spinning back down into the vessel, fighting and trying to crush each other.

Naero cried out and flipkicked Korleth three times, blinding fast, shattering his front jaw and many teeth, knocking him back end over end.

Korleth grappled with her, and smashed her repeatedly into the ship, doing considerable damage to both but he also knocked more of his minions loose, hurling them into the black.

Naero startapped and swelled with renewed energy, feeling her own consciousness slipping away, winking in and out for an instant.

She plunged her blades into Korleth multiple times, hewing him wide open.

The last four of the possessed Dakkur champions stopped attacking the ship and rushed to their stricken master's aid, trying to overwhelm Naero.

They bowled her over while Korleth regenerated.

One by one, Naero focused on each of the possessed and slew them, crushed them, and disrupted their energies.

When all was done, Naero cackled softly as one half-mad.

She could feel it, just like before. She was losing it.

She still had wits enough to try to protect the ship, although *why* became fuzzy and increasingly unclear.

By this time, Korleth had reached into the breached hull of the starship and pulled out his prizes: Jia in one massive, clawed hand and Govae's inert protoform in the other. The admiral laughed at Naero, still spewing taunts and threats, bristling with new shifting horrors rippling out from his writhing flesh.

"At last, our victory begins. And you're still too stupid to perceive what all of this means. All of you shall fall before us!"

Naero sensed it too late. A terrible Darkforce blast shot out of Korleth's maw, channeled right through him. Power enough to incinerate her. Korleth held this attack ready just for her.

A green sphere swept in. Khai suddenly interposed himself and Yii between the two combatants. He took the brunt of the energy attack at the last instant. His defensive sphere shattered.

Khai and Yii were blasted, and left floating out in space, dead or dying.

Naero kept laughing and saw her opening to strike. She shot straight at her foe, even when Korleth snapped his crushing jaws onto her extended right sword arm.

That actually hurt.

The soaring pain awoke her lust to kill.

Destroying everything around her became an irresistible desire.

She swelled up even larger.

In an instant, Naero whipped to one side and snapped the creature's thick neck against the crumpled hull of the starship, as if Korleth's spine had been a dry stick. She pulled her arm free from its twitching jaws.

"That was for Zhen!" she snarled.

It still thrashed and boiled with Darkforce transformations trying to attack her. Naero tore off its primary head in a feat of raw power.

She incinerated the abomination with white-hot beams from her eyes, roasting it to death in her hands.

Korleth's molten, acidic blood boiled into the vacuum of space.

Naero barely remembered to retrieve Khai and the Driathans. She stuffed them all back into *The Star Fox.*

She giggled and kicked Korleth's thrashing, charred, headless body away from her. The thing went spinning off into the void.

Rational thought became more difficult each second. Her name.

If only she could recall her own name. Who she was.

Then everything would be fine.

But the headless body of her defeated foe shook itself and surged back toward her, glowing with strange energies. Had she gone completely crazy?

The raw, ragged wounds of the corpse itself seemed to be chortling at her with grim, eerie voices. The voices even linked with her mind and used telepathy to communicate.

A new dark, shifting blob-like head pushed and stretched its way out of the ragged, ichor-steaming wound, wreathed in Darkforce power.

Red eyes and a grinning red maw tore open like a deep, jagged slash.

"Fool. Even now, you cannot control your powers. They are slowly destroying you. Submit! Bend to our will and serve us. Come closer so that you might become our next vessel!"

Some impossible force dragged her forward against her will.

A voice roared in her mind.

Somehow she remembered.

Om?

This cannot be. It is becoming a G'lothc, or at least the shapeshifting form of one. Naero. Join with me. Regain yourself. We must destroy it— before it takes us over. If it gains command of us and our powers, it will destroy everyone we care about!

Naero. She was Naero Amashin Maeris, and everything that meant. That was it.

That was enough.

Nothing was going to take control of her.

A G'lothc? They were actually fighting one in the flesh?

The Star Fox shot away and cloaked.

The horrible thing fell upon her in the black. She sensed its power and its hungry desire to gain control of her mind and abilities. It was filled with Darkforce might. It tried to absorb her, just like in her nightmares.

Naero fought back and acted instinctively. She shouted back at the abomination in her mind with defiance.

GET OFF ME!

A thick blue-violet beam of energy from her third eye punched into the thing, impaling and obliterating its core from yawning maw to tail.

In an instant the horrific thing broke apart. First it exploded as its powers disrupted. Then it collapsed like a small singularity and imploded, consuming even itself.

It collapsed into a small, dark pinpoint that threatened to pull Naero inside of it.

The white-hot beam from her third eye struck the phenomena one final time.

The pinhole drained nearly all of her energies from her in an instant. They cancelled each other out.

Then the phenomena winked out of all existence, without warning.

At last, Naero's battle and all of her frightening madness came to a crashing halt, leaving her completely limp and exhausted. Yet she still remained herself.

That by itself was a major victory, and the Driathans were still safe. Hopefully, Khai wasn't dead.

It was a good thing that she floated in space. She couldn't have stood up if she wanted to. Splitting pain erupted in her skull, as if invisible foes tried to pull her head apart with red-hot, metal hooks. She felt her growing Cosmic sickness make her want to vomit.

The Dark Star raced back in to gather her up.

49

Naero waited patiently while Acting Medical Officer Trudi Cheyenne checked over Khai with her healing sight. Her skilled hands and senses rapidly studied the Oden Champion's internal functions and energy levels.

Naero was very fond of Tru–but she still missed Zhen greatly.

Trudi shook her head and then turned to Naero with an impressed grin.

"I don't know which of you is more fascinating to examine–you with all of your growing, weird abilities and energies, or this stunning green, indestructible god and all of his powers. Both of you are equally amazing healers and unique specimens–of I don't know what."

"I don't understand," Naero said. She knelt at Khai's side and did what she had secretly longed to do again. She ran her hand through his long, flowing golden hair, brushing it aside from his handsome face with her fingers. His broad chest rose and fell beneath her other hand.

For an instant, it seemed as if his great heart thundered in time with her own.

"He was hurt in my place. Khai stepped in and endured that brunt of that terrible blast that the enemy unleashed on me, there at the end. They meant to destroy me. But Khai saved me; he saved us all. I saw them strike him down and leave him for dead. How could anyone have survived such an attack? I didn't think anyone could."

Trudi stopped smiling. "Yes, he was dying, and it has taken him several hours to slowly regenerate. He's still in some kind of self-induced healing stasis, but I think he will revive soon. Haisha, N. He sure is a hunk."

Naero sighed right along with her. "He is that."

Trudi sighed. "You know, N, it's still not too late to get out of here. Why don't you get away with Baeven and his crew? They've avoided the Mystics and their hunters before. You can still get away with them and stay free."

Naero pulled her hands away from Khai and shook her head.

"No. I gave the Enforcer my word. I swore to him that if he aided us, that I would return with him, willingly and without any resistance, and face whatever judgment or sentence the Mystics pass down."

"Naero...you murdered a Mystic High Master. Even Baeven never did anything close to that, and they still have a death sentence on him."

Naero sucked in a deep breath before she could speak again. "I know, but Khai kept his word, and his honor. He even went beyond them and sacrificed himself in my place, when all looked lost. Even if they do order my execution, they can just go ahead and kill me. I refuse to break my word and dishonor my Clan any further than I already have. I will stand and face justice for my choices and my actions."

Naero picked up Yii, feeling its immense power, nearly a match for her own. She caressed it, feeling it respond to her touch.

She handed it to Trudi.

"This sword and Khai are one. I have a feeling that once you place it in his hands, he'll revive pretty quickly. I need to go explain things to my crew and get them ready to depart. Tell Khai not to worry. He can find me in my quarters, awaiting his orders. We can depart for any destination he chooses. Just tell him to give Enel the coordinates."

"Naero. We're all going with you this time, to help you plead your case before the Mystic High Council. They must know what you and Baeven and all of us have done here. We foiled the enemy biowar attack. We beat back another enemy invasion. And we couldn't have done it without you, and Baeven, and everyone. We all fought them together. That all has to count for something."

431

Naero nearly broke down all of the sudden. "I never meant to kill Master Vane. He attacked me, tried to destroy me. He said I was the greatest threat to this universe that could ever exist. I never meant it to go that far."

Naero fell to her knees and stared at her empty fingers.

"And then Master Vane died–by my hands. It happened so fast. So easy. I can still hear him screaming in my mind as I took his life."

She looked up at Trudi. She felt her eyes pleading. The terror still filled her.

"What if…what if Vane was right? What if I am such a threat? Perhaps they *should* kill me now, before all of my abilities come out. Before I go mad like my former brother Danner. Take me out before I get all sick and twisted…by these strange powers I might not ever been able to control. Destroy me…before I can't be stopped."

Trudi hugged her, wrapping both arms around her.

"You could never do that. We all know you, N. You're our captain, and our friend–our family. Captain Maeris, you are one of the smartest, best people I've ever known. Look at all that you have already done for us, for our people, for the entire galaxy."

Naero sobbed and clung to her, shaking her head. "You don't know, Trudi. How much it all scares the living shit right out of me. When I'm suffused with all of that power, it's…like the most potent drug in the world. It's so easy to lose sight of everything–everyone real–to even lose yourself. Do you know what a frightening thing it is to feel like you can do anything?

"Just consider the ramifications of that. *ANYTHING*–good or evil. And nothing matters any more. It doesn't matter which you choose to do, because there's no one to stop you…but you. And you don't know if you can, or even if you want to. It's really, really scary."

Trudi pulled away and thought for a moment.

"I think I do see, Captain. I understand a little bit better now. So, what stops you then? What keeps you from whacking out and just slaughtering everyone around you–friend or foe?"

Naero blinked. She sobbed and buried her face in her hands. "I-I don't know. I guess I think of something Shalaen once told me, how all power is best utilized through love and wisdom, through harmony. I think of my parents, Jan, you, and all of my friends. Everyone who has ever cared about me, our people, our allies. I never want to hurt them. Even more, I don't want to let them down. Whoever and whatever I become, I want to find a way to do some kind of good, and leave the universe a better place after I'm gone."

432

Trudi pointed one finger at Naero.

"That's what you should tell Khai. And that's what you need to tell the High Masters. Stand up for yourself, Naero. Like you said, you don't know what you are capable of. You can't even control it all, yet. But that doesn't mean that you won't. Don't stand aside and let them execute you for not knowing. You might still find a way."

Naero turned away and nodded, heading toward her private quarters on *The Dagger*. "I won't give up. I won't. Thanks, Tru. You're a good friend...abani."

Trudy smiled. "All of us would be more than lost without you, N. I owe you my life and more. I can never repay you for all that you have done for me."

"You be happy, Tru. Whatever happens to me. Give Khai his sword, and tell him where to find me."

*

Naero sensed Khai's presence outside of the door to her captain's quarters a short while later.

She rose from her seat and smoothed her hands down the sides of her captain's togs.

"Enter."

He came in calmly, his chiseled face as impassive and serene as ever.

Then he even smiled slightly.

That really worried her.

"Despite our many differences, Naero Amashin Maeris, I have always thought you to be a person of high character and honor."

She arched one eyebrow.

Khai smiled slyly. "You just do so in your own way, after your own fashion. It pleases me greatly that you have kept up your end of our bargain–eventually–even under such great duress."

Naero folded her hands in front of her.

"Khai, I thank you, for saving my life–all of our lives, really. Did you...know that you would survive that massive energy attack?"

"In truth, I did not. But I felt certain that given the chance, you would find a way to achieve victory where even I could not. I gave you that chance, for the good of all. And thankfully, both the facts and the results have proven me quite correct."

She chuckled a little. "You've plotted our destination?"

He nodded. "Kalathar, the new secret, Mystic Homeworld of Chaos Wisdom. It was just selected. Few are they who know its true location. Once there, you shall stand and face your final judgment. I can do nothing to prevent that."

She took a deep breath.

"I am ready to do so. How long is the journey?"

"Several jumps I fear even with your amazing craft. I'm guessing at least a month, perhaps two."

"I suppose that will allow me a stay of execution in transit. Would you mind if we made a few brief stops along the way? They won't delay us long, and you have my word that I will not try to escape."

Khai sighed. "If we must."

Naero grinned. "In the meanwhile, I…I hope that you will dine with me and my crew, to get to know us all better along the way."

He suddenly looked into her eyes. "I would greatly enjoy that, Naero."

Naero kept her hands clasped in front of her and chuckled again. "Better than us always on the run, and you stalking us down and attacking us constantly."

"Yes. Much better, I agree. You cannot know how sorry I am, for all of that, Naero. Yet starting this night, it begins. We must communicate with the High Council via the Astral Plane and prepare for your trial."

Naero looked away briefly and sighed. "So soon? For months I have mostly avoided contact with the Astral Plane, obviously in order to prevent detection and pursuit…and any contact."

"Forgive me again, but that cannot be avoided now. The High Masters will want to begin your initial questioning, and get to know you more. They were just starting to when all of this happened. You know, they are more fair-minded and enlightened than you or others might think."

Naero felt the cold blood drain from her face.

She absently motioned for Khai to take a seat across from her as she slowly sat back down at her own little nanotable.

The demands of honor were indeed heavy at times.

Naero had given her word…unto death.

She knitted her hands and leaned forward with her elbows and forearms resting on her thighs to the knees.

"Just promise me this, Khai," she began.

He looked at her curiously. "If I can."

"I had hoped for a…stay of execution, to avoid all of this. Even for a few lousy days, or weeks. But when it comes down to it. When they sentence me to die I hope that it is you who will make an end of my life. I know that you and Yii will make it quick…and relatively painless. Please, promise me that."

Now Khai turned very pale, even for one who was green. His glance softened. His eyes tightened, and he seemed deeply troubled.

He spoke with effort.

"On my honor, on the lives of my people, Naero–you have my word. Yet if it helps, I heard all that you said to your friend, Trudi. She is right. You must defend yourself and your actions, even before the High Council. Do not fail to do so."

She wrung her hands until they turned purple. "For all the good that will do."

"Nothing is certain. As I said before, Master Vane was not entirely in the right to act as he did, in such a–unilateral fashion. You were not without cause."

"Yet his death at my hands only proved his argument about me even further. I'm too dangerous. I can't control my abilities. I'm a threat to everyone."

"All true. But there are many serious threats in the universe. Look at your former uncle, your former brother. Our many foes and their powers. Yet there is always hope."

Khai touched her hand. Naero jumped slightly and looked at him in amazement. What was he doing? What did it mean?

She kept her eyes averted.

"I have seen into your soul, Naero. And I tell you this. You are not a monster, as you fear."

Her eyes shot up and stared into his. Her voice shook. "What if I…become one?"

Khai swallowed hard. "Then we shall deal with that, should it come to pass. Perhaps you can still avoid such a fate, by your own choices and force of will, even."

She knitted her fingers again. "Why should they let me live after what I've done? I wouldn't. I wouldn't take such a chance."

"Do not panic, or lose hope, Naero. A way still may be found."

Naero shook her head again. "I can't see one. I don't think I have anyone among the Mystics who will take my side. Who will see me as anything but a murderer in this matter, now? I'm a monster. No one will believe in me."

"You are wrong," Khai said.

He knelt down and drew his sword. Yii blazed to life with all of its fierce energies, nearly blinding.

Khai placed the Cosmic blade at her feet.

"I have come to know you, Naero Amashin Maeris. I believe in and respect you. You have my allegiance and more, such as I have never offered to any other in all the known worlds. You have stood by me, even when it was my duty to kill you. You kept my life safe, when it was in your best interest to let it end–or finish the deed by your own hands–with none to stay you or be the wiser."

She lifted his sword, rose to her feet, and handed Yii back to him.

"You honor me, Khai. I fully understand just how noble you truly are. Much like Prince Gaviok, honor, truth, and steadfast, faithful service to others are everything to you." She hung her head.

"But I am…not worthy of such loyalty."

"Others shall be the judge of that. Do not mistake me, Naero. I have pledged myself to you, and not lightly. I will stand beside you until the end. I will speak on your behalf of your many brave deeds, and in your defense, doing all that I can."

Naero chuckled again and shook her head.

"I am your prisoner, Khai. By rights, you should have me shackled in restraints, or put in stasis for secure shipment to my trial."

"Who is whose prisoner?" Khai chuckled. "And here I thought I was dense."

She glanced at him, feeling puzzled.

"There shall be no chains between us, Naero. Only those bonds that we have already forged–some within the heat of a star."

He suddenly took both of her hands in his.

"By my heart and all that I will ever be, by the Powers, we shall find a way for you to live–and fully know what it is that you can be."

He kissed both her hands, still upon his knee.

Bolts of what felt like lightning shot up her arms. Naero gasped.

Khai rose up and touched her face with one gentle hand, thrilling her again with the jolt of energy at his very touch. How she had secretly longed for his hands upon her again–star or no star. She gasped for air.

She stared up into his shining face and could not look away.

His golden eyes looked deep into hers. She suddenly felt as if all gravity ceased and the universe itself stood still. She could not breathe.

"I love you, Naero," Khai told her. "I can't help it anymore. I have never felt this way for another. Can you feel the same for me?"

In answer, Naero sprang into the mighty arms of the Champion of the Oden. She knocked him flat back upon the nanofloor in another instant of ecstatic surprise.

Her hands knitted into his golden hair and brought their eager, gasping mouths together in searing ecstasy.

Together their mutual passions flared like twin blinding quasars of coruscating desire.

Whether she faced death or no would not matter for a time.

And maybe…just maybe…their current journey to far off Kalathar might just prove infinitely more pleasant and intriguing than Naero had originally assumed.

50

Naero plotted a course for Gairos-3, summoned her fleet and many others, and set all the proper plans into motion.

She found the right time.

After Ty broke down again when she told him about what was possible–and what was not–he immediately agreed to the process, just as Jia had proposed.

Just like Naero knew he would.

Like her, he had a lot of questions. *The Star Fox* still shadowed them. Naero just didn't let Khai in on that little fact.

Withholding information wasn't lying. Not exactly.

Jia crossed over.

"How should we work this?" Ty asked, getting very serious. "Do we tell 'Tisa what happened straight up? Do we let her know she's going to die again, in less than a day?"

"You tell us, Ty. How do you want to play this? We can explain the whole thing to her up front. Or you can just enjoy the time you have with her and then let her drift off, without her ever knowing. You tell me what you think is best."

"Will she...be in a lot of pain at the end?"

"No," Jia reassured him. "She'll just start to get tired, and drift off."

"It's my decision, then?"

"Yes."

"Well, if it was up to me, I'd just pretend the entire time and not upset her. Just enjoy my last moments with her." Ty's voice cracked and he came near to sobbing again.

He sniffed and wiped his face.

"But that's not what she would want. My 'Tisa was always about the truth. She'd hate my guts if I lied to her about something like this–if I just pretended that everything was okay. I have to tell her. But actually, I don't think I'll be able to get it out. It would be better if I took some time and wrote it all out. I could explain it to her in a letter without breaking down and getting all emotional. She can read it quickly, and grasp what's going on. Then she'll probably want to just say goodbye and spend time together...before the end."

Naero sighed and rested her hand on Ty's arm. "A lot of people don't get even this much, Ty. My parents never did. Neither did Gallan and so many others during the wars."

Ty pursed his lips and nodded. "No, I understand that, and so will she. I'm grateful for this much. I really am. Thank you both for this chance. It's...just a lot to deal with, and I know up front that I'm going to have to lose her all over again. But it will still be worth it, and she'll think so, too."

It took them another day to actually reach Gairos-3 and get everything organized, set up, and ready.

At the beginning of the next day, during the early bells, they started the procedure.

Jia, Baeven, Trudi, and a newly arrived Shalaen all assisted, preparing everything for the process.

Naero cupped her friend's face in her hands and breathed Zhen's soul back in her thawed, repaired body, while Trudi and Shalaen got her heart pumping and lungs breathing again.

The Lifespark from Zhen's soul filled her brain and mind, and at last her pretty hazel eyes fluttered open.

She looked up at her friends standing about her, and at first, she was scared and confused.

"What happened? Where am I?"

"You were badly wounded, Z." Naero said.

"Am I going to be okay? Where's Ty?"

Ty took her hands in his. "Hey, 'Tisa. I'm right here."

"You're scaring me, Ty." She sat up and felt herself.

"I'm not trying to scare you. But I do have something you need to read."

"Huh?…Read?"

Ty put his arms around her and placed a reading pad in her hands. "This'll save us lots of time."

Zhen read it all the way through.

She swallowed hard a couple of times.

Then she let the pad slip to the floor of the medical bay.

The rest of their friends and crew came in.

"Okay, so I don't have much time. So, we'll just have to make the most of things. I hope you will all understand that I want to spend every second that I can with Ty. Please, help me do that."

"We can put you on a medbed toward the end as you start to weaken," Jia said. "That will…give you a little more time."

Zhen hugged Naero. "Thanks for giving me this much, N. All of you. I might not have even had all of this, without you all. I know you, N. Don't blame yourself for what happened to me. You've been a good friend, even if you are a jerk sometimes."

"Oh, Z. I'm so sorry."

"I still don't want you to let me go," Zhen said, shaking her hard. "I want to live. When I drift off this time, take my soul again. Promise me. Naero Amashin Maeris, you promise me—right here and now—on your life and your honor, on the honor of Clan Maeris. You'll try to find a way…some way for me to come back. Just keep me inside of you for a while and try. Please, I'm begging you!"

Naero nodded. They clung to one another and sobbed. "I will, Z. You have my word." She reached into an armored, shielded pouch and pulled out the small, battered cryo case that Zhen had pressed into her hand for safekeeping that fateful day.

She place it back into Zhen's hands. Zhen shoved it right back at her.

"No, you keep that, N. I've given you my family. You must protect them and keep them safe. Help Ty find a way to have them born, and raise them all, and keep them free. They're the only part of me that will go on. If anyone can make it happen—you can. Tell my babies about me, N. Please… Let them know what I was like."

Naero stammered. "I…I don't know what to say. I will, Zhen. I'll see it all done. You…you could still be a part of all that, you know. There is a small way."

Zhen's mouth fell open. "I don't…how? What do you mean?"

"Well, after the wedding, and you and Ty have your brief little honeymoon, how would you like to give birth...to your son, Gallan?"

Z stared at her in wonder. "N, you can do that for me? How is that even possible?"

"It's your choice. Shalaen and I talked it over. We can use biomancy to speed up the development process. You can safely give birth to your firstborn, and you and Ty can hold him together in your arms, before...before the end. But if you think it's all too much-"

"No, no, I want to. Oh, N, yes, let's make it happen. I don't want to waste any time."

They reimplanted the child in Zhen's womb and made sure everything was ready...for later. Chaela and Saemar arrived just in time for the wedding.

Fleet Captain Naero Amashin Maeris performed the brief ceremony for Tyber and Zhen beneath the mountain waterfall valley of Gairos-3. The spectacular rainforest and the iridescent rainbows made for a perfect setting, just as Zhen had planned.

Zhen made for a beautiful bride in her spring ivory dress, beaming in happiness next to her beloved Ty in his sea foam tux, matching the bridal party. Everyone present wept for joy.

After the short ceremony and a brief reception, Zhen and Ty launched back up into orbit for a honeymoon on a small yacht that lasted only a handful of hours.

Then it was back to the medical bay on board *The Dagger*. Trudi was so emotional, she could hardly assist, but with Naero and Shalaen and Jia present, there wasn't that much to do.

Naero carefully progressed little Gallan through his gestation, while Zhen watch him grow with her healing sight, tears racing down her face as he did so. The birth was made quick and relatively painless—as much as any live birth could be.

In less than a standard hour, Ty and Z sat together holding each other and their new son, beneath the vista of the stars overhead through the wide, open viewport on board *The Dark Star*. That ship was larger and the view better. It was easier for other ships to dock with it, and people to come and go.

Friends and crew filed past to greet the little newcomer and congratulate the parents.

Just after dinner, Zhen's head sagged and her strength began to leave her.

My friends," Z called out, with effort. "It appears...that I don't have much time, now. Thank you all...so much...for what you have given to me this day. It's been an honor serving with you all and getting to know you. I love you all. But now…if you don't mind, I want to spend every second I have left with my Ty and my little Gallan–alone–if you can forgive me. Thank you all once again. If I do not see you again, farewell. Safe journey, my Clan, my friends."

They put her on a medbed and returned her to Tyber's private quarters immediately.

Everyone waited, somber and still, as the minutes ticked by.

Two hours later, they got the call.

Less than a half hour after that, with Ty cradling her and their son in his loving arms, a smiling Dr. Zhentisa Maeris gently drifted away again.

And true to her word and promise, Naero took her abani's soul back into her gentle keeping.

51

Days later, Naero transported alone down to the surface of lo-tek, backwater Thanor-4, overlooking the Bay of Thanarra.

It was late at night, and even from up in the sky on her gravwing, the four city states all seemed to be on fire.

She teknomanced and gathered data feeds from the spyfixer network she had left behind.

The city states had prosecuted their war against each other ruthlessly and with great cunning on all sides.

The massive armies of the Vaedo began it. It started with them. Months of grinding battle swept over the lands, destroying towns, burning crops.

But starting a war was not the same thing as sustaining a war or finishing one.

The Thanes, the Kall, and the Maedo joined together, fighting their enemies on land, on sea, in the desert, the forests, and the mountains. The allies brilliantly ground the Vaedo down hard, over weapons of iron and steel and wooden ships, and drove them back over their own high walls. Then the allies broke through those walls and tore them down.

Yet as the city state of the Vaedo burned—razed to the ground and their people were set free, the allies were yet in danger of losing the brutal war.

For Emperor Vauk, the golden dragon godking, had still managed to outmaneuver them all in the end. While the allies liberated his slaves and burned his golden city, putting it to torch and flame, Emperor Vauk and another army of five thousand elite warriors stormed the mountain fastness of the Maedo.

This fortress overlooked the great desert on the opposite side of the high passes.

Vauk lost more than three thousand troops reducing the mountain fortress, yet in the end, the stubborn Maedo defenses fell.

Naero went down to that area, cloaked and prepared to observe whatever she found.

The Vaedo had indeed broken through and slain the defenders—a mix of Thanes, Kall, and Maedo—all who fought bravely.

They gave their charges precious hours to escape down into the desert and flee toward the coast of the bay.

Emperor Vauk and his sixteen hundred soldiers left even their own wounded behind and now raced to overtake the nearly five thousand children from all the allies—between the ages of six and sixteen—fleeing in terror before them.

Naero infiltrated the Vaedo host, to spy upon Emperor Vauk.

Surrounded by his bloodguard of hundreds, the godking was being raced along in a great golden wagon with six gilded wheels, pulled by a dozen, sweating, foaming draft gult in their glittering harnesses. Each of the wagon's wheels and their spinning anti-personnel blades were already stained with human blood.

Vauk shouted, jostled around among his servants and concubines. "Run the vermin down. How can they be so far ahead of us, still? We've only been able to bloody my wheels with stragglers—the weak and the crippled left scattered behind. Catch them all out in the open. I want to slice through hundreds of them and mow them down! Leave a gory trail of the little wretches chopped to pieces and screaming behind us!"

His troops fanned out to either side, forming two wings or arcs out on the edges. Hundreds of Vaedo light skirmishers and cavalry spearheaded the charge.

The fleeing children were burdened by having the older kids forced to carry the younger ones, all of them exhausted. Their faces strained in terror. They struggled to reach a dried-up river canyon gorge that would lead them down to the delta salt marshes of the bay.

The children might reach it before the enemy overtook and encircled them.

Vauk stood up and gripped his golden railing, continuing to rave.

"After we capture the bulk of them, we will drive them to the beaches. I will reward my valiant troops by allowing them to ravage the spawn of our foes all night long in a great, drunken, bloody orgy. Do as you will with them! Then in the morning we shall impale all the brats—living and dead—all along the shore and leave them rotting in the sun for their parents to find. Then our triumph shall be complete, and the final destiny of our world decided. There shall be no further generations of our enemies—no more fools who dare to challenge a god!"

Even more important, from what Naero saw, the rocky gorge was very narrow in several places, and would greatly delay troops, giving the children—at least some of them—the best chance at getting away.

The deadly race continued along the ridges and up and down the dunes.

Naero blipped over to check on the children.

They weren't going to make it.

They were being led by Princess Laikalla of the Maedo, age fifteen, and Prince Shondar of the Thanes, age fourteen. They were backed up by Maedo Prince Tavul; thirteen, Kall Princess Vaxxalla; also thirteen, and finally, Thane Princess Iiden, age twelve.

Laikalla called out to all the others, "We need to hold them off. Five hundred of us—the biggest and best fighters, ages fourteen to sixteen—will hold the narrows for as long as we can last. That will allow the others to make it through and look for the ships. Tavul, Vaxxalla, and Iiden will lead the retreat from this point on. The rest of us, take up your position in the rear guard. We must hold with whatever weapons we have. Pick up every rock and stone that you can gather. We fight to the last the breath!"

Prince Shondar hugged his weeping sister goodbye. Then he drew his sword. "Go, Iiden! You and the others must lead the little ones to safety as best you can. Come, my friends. Prepare for battle!"

Naero had seen more than enough.

She took up a position on the top of the last dune crest leading down into the gorge that the children just started to rush through.

Naero clenched her fists and her teeth.

445

To hell with nonintervention. No one gave a damn what happened here any longer. These brave kids weren't going to be cut to pieces and the others weren't going to be butchered, raped, and mutilated that night.

Not under her watch.

The Spacer Mystics had abandoned Thanor-4 to its fate.

Naero no longer agreed with that premise. In that case, she was now free to act.

The Vaedo swept up the rise to run down their quarry.

Time for some theatrics.

Every second would buy the kids time.

A scarlet bolt of lightning crashed down, and Naero uncloaked in full-on Shetanna mode. Her violet eyes blazed, and the winds of night from the mountains swept through her dark hair and cloak.

The Vaedo halted for a moment, staring up at her in fear and wonder. From her vantage point, she could hear their words.

Emperor Vauk's golden wagon trundled up. "Why have you stopped? Forward. In and take them! Run them down!"

"But Emperor," one of his captains said, pointing up at Naero. "That woman appeared in a flash of blood-red lightning. She is either a goddess, or perhaps even–a demon!"

Vauk went into a rage. He flung his full golden wine cup and smashed the captain in the face with it, the red liquid splashing everywhere. "A woman? You halted my advance for a single bitch? I don't care who or what that whore is. You are led by a god! Attack, my champions. On to victory! We are thousands! What can one woman do?"

Naero smiled and used *the voice*.

"SHETANNA, THE DARK ANGEL OF DEATH, IS UPON YOU ALL. NOT ONE OF YOU SHALL ESCAPE."

She formed her Ur-metal blades in her hands and the earth split around her. Then she summoned her scarlet katanas over them.

Naero startapped all the Cosmic energy that she could muster.

With her battle cry ringing upon her lips, she sprang down and fell upon the rampaging Vaedo in vengeance and fury.

The children of Thanarra paused and shrank in fear within the adjacent gorge, stricken with horror by the fell blasts of scarlet lightning that erupted just over the next rise. Strange waves and bursts of light and power flared–amid the wailing and shrieking of the Vaedo army as it perished. The ground all about that area trembled and shook.

When all went deathly quiet, Princess Laikalla and Prince Shondar led a sortie back up that rise to stare down at the fate of the Vaedo forces that had pursued them all with rapacious and murderous intent.

Some of the enemy had been incinerated into piles of ash where they stood or swept forward. Yet the vast majority hung impaled, scorched to ash, and their skeletons still burning–upon glowing red, twisted blades of hot glass.

Death came so swiftly that most perished while they still charged forward. Few had time to turn and run.

The hot, glowing, hissing blades of thick, jagged glass had ripped out of the sand itself, and punctured and burned most of them alive– hundreds upon hundreds.

The deep trough had been transformed into an eerie, razor-sharp, glass orchard of red death, set within a smoldering black glass crater– a cauldron of glowing oblivion.

Naero dragged a stunned and muttering Emperor Vauk up to the crest of the rise and flung him down at their feet.

They drew back from her in fear, as if she were some apparition.

"His power is broken forever," Naero told them. "He meant to violate and murder you all, but now he is fallen in complete disgrace. He will not kill anyone…ever again."

Naero pulled down her mask to show them her face.

Princess Laikalla and Prince Shondar blinked and recognized her.

"Sister Naero!"

"Shetanna!"

They wept with great relief and joy, and rushed to embrace her.

Dammit, all of these kids were taller than her.

The vanguard of the ships of the Kall met them on the beaches within hours. Princess Kutira and *The Blue Vixen* led the fleet in the twilight.

She drew her blue-steel cutlass and her eyes blazed with rage and vengeance as she glared at Emperor Vauk, lying helpless in a filthy heap, under guard.

Her voice trembled. "Why does that scum still live!"

Naero stepped forward and stayed her hand. "It is for the Kings and Queens of your world to decide his fate, Kutira. He will meet his end."

She snarled and visibly shook with rage, barely able to restrain herself. "I must turn away then. I can not be near the Darkheart without taking his life."

While they awaited for the arrival of the other royals, the Kall saw to the rescue of the children. Several thousand of them in one spot quickly became increasingly messy and smelly, badly in need of aid.

The mariners dug hasty pit and trench latrines for them in the sand along the beach, and the children washed themselves clean down in the warm surf.

Food and kegs of water were opened and doled out.

Then the ships with the royals pulled up.

The Sea King, Haikoda, set foot upon the shore for the first time since he had been born, leading the others behind him to decide the fate of Emperor Vauk.

Naero greeted them, and turned to lead them. Cries erupted just ahead.

As they rushed up, Emperor Vauk held a little girl, threatening to cut her throat open with a small blade he had managed to conceal from them. "I want a ship! Get away from me, all of you. Stay back!"

He looked like the madman he was.

Before even Naero could act, Kutira swooped in, swinging on a line. She sprang upon the emperor, booting him aside.

She stabbed and slashed him with her karath and cutlass, screaming in ferocity.

Naero lunged forward and caught the child before the little girl hit the ground.

Vauk fell onto his back like the sniveling coward he was, whimpering and pleading, sliding down into one of the nearby catch-pit latrines on his shiny, slippery, golden silk robes.

Kutira rode him down into the pit, continuing to ram her weapons into his face, throat, and chest until both her blades chipped, shattered, and broke.

The thing that had been Emperor Vauk, the godking, slipped head first into a pit of human waste, gurgling, gasping, and spluttering, until the bubbles stopped, and his twisted, twitching, blood-soaked fingers and limbs froze.

Kutira rose up and still spat on him.

"Scum! Blackheart! You who have butchered so many. You killed my beloved brother, Jigan. For nothing! Burn in all the hells at once–and may the devils feast upon your stinking flesh and your putrid soul–if even they can choke you down their flaming gullets!"

Kutira held up her broken hilts. "Bear witness, all. My steel shattered upon his black heart. We always knew the scum had a black rock in his chest in place of a human heart. Here is the proof of it!"

She cast her broken weapons away in disgust. "My lords, we be at peace. I have slain the Emperor of the Vaedo. I have done this thing for the good of all. The long, terrible war of our world…is now ended."

King Haikoda strode forward and took his little sister in his arms. "If you had not done so, beloved sister, any of the rest of us would have. You are the bravest of us all." He kissed her on top of her head and held her close.

"Jigan's blood is now avenged." He motioned to their brothers, the remaining princes. "Nokarro, Yeshida. Drag that piece of filth and shit out to the deepest part of the sea, weigh it down with stone and iron chain, and feed it to the sharks–if they can stomach such corruption."

King Arrok held up his empty hands. "So passes the false god of our world. Let there be no others. I hereby proclaim peace over all our lands, my brothers and sisters. Our children shall no longer live in fear or want, and together–side by side–we shall make our world a paradise!"

"YOU HAVE GROWN BOTH WISE AND STRONG," Naero said to them using *the voice*. "KEEP THIS HARD-WON PEACE, THEREFORE. YOU HAVE ALL PROVEN YOURSELVES FIT TO RULE OVER YOUR PEOPLES WITH COURAGE, JUSTICE, AND MERCY. YOU NO LONGER HAVE ANY NEED OF ANYTHING FROM THE GODS. YOU ARE WORTHY TO RULE YOURSELVES. DO SO, WITH THE GREATEST WISDOM."

Naero chose that moment to vanish from among them.

Yet she still had work to do. A promise yet to keep.

Deep in a nearby forest, the fallow gult lived in great herds, like ghosts who ran beneath the trees.

With her biomancy powers, it took very little for Naero to manipulate that breed of mammals genetically, in order to produce and replicate a breeding population of a unique variation–similar to those species found on other worlds–such as Larellon-7.

She bestowed upon them much more–both intelligence and basic wisdom, and a peaceful disposition, as well as telepathy and even speech. On a whim, she taught them Kexxian as well, and the beautiful songs of the Tua, imprinted on their minds and hearts.

They all encircled her by the hundreds, bowing their regal heads.

"You are our creator and you have made us as we are. What is your will? Command us."

"Name yourselves in the language I have given you. Become the symbol of the beauty and wonder of this world," Naero commanded them. "Come with me."

Naero went to Princess Iiden late at night and woke her.

"Sister Naero? They said you were gone again. What is it?"

"Your dream has come true, princess. Follow me."

449

Naero took her hand and transported them onto the forest beach beneath the clear sky and stars.

"Ahh! This is magic!"

"You have been chosen, Iiden. You must lead all your peoples and the next generations into an age of peace, wisdom, and freedom."

"Me? But I am only a silly, foolish child. Why would they follow me?"

Naero handed her a carefully prepared scroll, filled with plain wisdom and knowledge, geared to their lo-tek level.

"Your hands have not been stained by blood. Use the powerful knowledge contained within this scroll. It is my gift to you and your world, to become a place of reason, wisdom, and peace. And here is the sign that you and your children shall be the chosen ones."

Naero sang a few words in Kexxian.

And the new unicorns of Thanarra came forth and emerged from the dark forests, singing and glowing in all their beauty and majesty, beneath the stars in exultation.

Princess Iiden fell to her knees, covered her face with her hands, and wept for all joy.

"I must leave you now," Naero told her.

"No," Iiden said. "Nay, say it is not so. We need you still."

Naero shook her head. "No. You do not. You have all that you require."

She lifted Princess Iiden up and sat her upon the strong, slender back of the unicorn queen. "The two of you shall become fast friends. Go forth to lead your people. Teach them these laws and wisdoms that I have bestowed upon you. Show them the wonders of your world that have been awakened. Farewell."

Iiden looked back. "Shall we ever see you again, Naero?"

Naero grinned sadly. "I cannot say. Perhaps. Go now, and be wise and fearless."

Princess Iiden rode off leading the herd, adding her voice to theirs, as they thundered off, singing toward the city.

"You can uncloak now," Naero said.

Naero turned to her replicant, the one she had specially prepared to remain on the backwater world of Thanor-4, and help guide and protect all the peoples she had come to love and cherish. She could disguise herself as needed.

"You have all of my basic knowledge and wisdom, Naero II, and my Spacer fighting skill, but not the KDM, nor my higher Cosmic abilities."

Naero II lowered her violet eyes in respect. "They and the problems that come with them will not be needed or desired. Thank you. I feel the same love for all of our friends that you feel. I will do my best to help serve and guide them. They are brave. They will come into their own. One day in the far future, when they are ready, their children shall join ours in the stars."

"I believe they shall, one day. I have no doubt. I've left a few stealth fixers with you. You can contact me if you need to, and even if I cannot come, I will try to send help in some form."

"It would be nice if the Changs could come back here at some point. They adore this world even more than we do."

"Right now, I don't know what is possible. But I will look into it, if I can. Good luck, Naero II; may fortune favor the bold."

They hugged each other, and for a moment, Naero felt what it might have been like to have a twin herself, or a blood sister. At least in this way, if something did happen to her, a good portion of her would live on somewhere, and still attempt to make a small part of the universe a better place.

"Safe journey, Naero I."

Naero sighed, and transported back to her ship.

Thanor-4 would become a place of wonder. In her heart of hearts, Naero did hope to return to it one day. They too, were her family now.

*

Later the next night, they made for Kalathar again. After a huge party on board *The Dark Star*, Naero awoke at four bells in her private quarters there.

She smiled and left Khai snoozing in their oval nanobed, transporting to the enormous viewport to stare up at the stars.

"Hey sweetie," a voice from the shadows called out.

"Saemar!" Naero exclaimed, opening her arms to embrace her stunning and voluptuous old friend.

At least they were the same height.

They laughed together. But Naero was puzzled. "What the heck are you still doing here, Saemar? By now, I thought you'd be…"

Saemar sighed, fanning herself with one manicured hand. "Ya know, sweetie, even I need to take a breather once in a while. So, I thought I might just look at the stars for a bit myself."

"Me too." Naero hugged her once more.

"Great minds, N."

Saemar could only endure quiet for so many seconds.

451

"So...the Mystic Enforcer, eh? They say he's like a super man or something. I'm just a little curious, N. So, the guy is green, right?"

Here we go.

"Yep. Green, Saemar. He's half-Spacer, and half-Oden. The Oden are all green."

"Everywhere...everything green, huh?"

"Yep. Green. Everywhere. More or less."

"Intriguing. So, you know I gotta ask. How is that big green galoot in the sack? Is he any good? I just gotta know."

"Saemar, let me tell you. Loving Khai is...beyond all the words in all the languages that have existed and ever will exist. Literally, like a Cosmic explosion. I've never experienced anything like it, and I've never felt this way about any man I've ever met. I am crazy in love with this guy–I would give my life for him."

Saemar grinned from ear to ear and shook her curly head. "Sounds like you got it bad, kiddo. Well, it's about damn time, if you ask me. Sooo, where did you two...first get lovey-dovey, eh? Was it a romantic location for your first time together? I bet it wuzzz."

"Saemar...abani...you won't believe it. *We made love inside a star.*"

"Huh? Say what?" Saemar stared and blinked in violent shock.

"A star. I turned into an energy being and I was dying. I got sucked into a star. Khai came after me; he helped find a way to save me, and together we just...lost all control. We kind of became one."

Saemar turned pale white and held up both hands. "Let me get this straight, sweetie. You and him. Ya made sweet, tender bonking music...inside a frickin' star?"

"Yeah, like I said, we just–"

Saemar sniffed. "I don't want to hear any more. I can't take it. Can't. Take. It. I don't even know if we can be friends anymore! I'll have to think about it, and let you know." Saemar waved her hands wildly.

She got up and staggered away. She teetered a little bit this way, then that–perhaps she had been drinking heavily from the party. She wobbled a bit. Her knees looked weak, but she kept going.

Saemar left the observation deck shaking her head and muttering to herself as if still in shock.

Naero smiled and chuckled to herself. She finally decided to return to her own quarters, and every good thing waiting for her there.

Khai could just wake his tight little green butt up and she'd make him glad for it. It wasn't exactly inside a star, but it was still pretty damn amazing what the two of them could accomplish together.

But best of all–Naero knew that she no longer needed to be alone. Khai loved her and told her so every chance he got. She finally had someone–someone noble and her equal to share her life with, whom she loved and respected.

And whatever came their way, the stars would always be out there for her, for them.

For everyone.

THE END

Please Post a Book Review Right Now

Please post a review of this book if you enjoyed it. Twenty little words are all that is required. Twenty words that say what you liked about this book while it is still fresh in your heart, mind, and soul. Please do so now before something else makes you forget.

Here is the link for Naero's Fury, if you purchased it on Amazon:

http://amzn.to/1hLrPpO

Please click on the link and post your review now.

Done? The author would personally like to thank you very much.

In this busy world, everyone is pressed for time. Our time is so important, no doubt. It has reached the point now where authors of nearly every stripe compete not only for sales, but to garner reviews from their readers. Some authors even stoop to "purchasing" reviews in social media that some services now offer in bulk.

In the publish or perish work of competitive fiction, book reviews from readers are golden, they have now become a commodity even.

Many in the business even consider book reviews as important, or even more important than book sales in some ways. As crazy as that sounds.

So therefore, trust us in this. If you have authors whom you adore, and you want to read more of their books in the future, please post as many reviews for them as you can in all of the forms of social media that you use.

Doing so will help your favorite authors in numerous ways that you cannot even possibly imagine. Never forget that fact. Book reviews matter a great deal.

And if by chance, if you find that there is something about this book that you don't like, and you really do want to help authors, before you slam them with bad reviews, try briefly contacting them instead with your concerns through their contact info that is always readily provided, or through their publisher. Most authors, especially new ones, are usually happy to get constructive criticism that will make their books better. Only hating, online trolls slam authors with bad reviews without giving them a chance. Real pros and fen contact authors directly with any valid concerns. That is the current, accepted etiquette. Please don't be a troll.

Amazon Kindle Review Link for Naero's Fury:

http://amzn.to/1hLrPpO

Barnes & Noble Review Link for Naero's Fury:

http://bit.ly/1GBEvdl

Smashwords Review Link for Naero's Run:

http://bit.ly/1enMh9G

<u>Other Review Sites</u>

Good Reads

Google

Pinterest

Reddit

Please post one or more reviews for Mason for each of his books, everywhere that you can.

Thank you once again.

Cheers,

Mason Elliott

About the Author

Mason Elliott grew up loving Science Fiction and Fantasy in all of their myriad forms. That love has transferred into his dedicated writing. Like most writers, he lives a spartan lifestyle and yearns to devote his life even more to his writing, and someday retire on the Pacific coast. So be a fan, buy his stuff, and enjoy!

Mason's Amazon Author Page:

http://amzn.to/1tXR7XK

Friend Mason on FB at this link:

http://on.fb.me/1qnBfJd

Like Mason on his FB fan site where he does most of his blogging:

http://on.fb.me/1ogFGcT

Follow Mason on Twitter at:

http://bit.ly/1nsqOSs

Visit Mason Elliott's website at

http://masonelliott.authorcontacts.com

ACKNOWLEDGEMENTS

First I would like to dedicate this book to my daughters. And as always, to the readers who have supported and believed in me for so long and on into the future. As I have said before, I will do my best to provide you with more great stories, for as long as I draw the breath of life.

Once more, none of this could be possible without the tireless efforts of my fabulous editor, Jennifer Cummings, the publishing board, and publicist Josh Marten. Special thanks again to all of my Beta readers, especially Lois, Paul, Doyle, Katherine, and many others. And eternal, constant thanks to my online writing group, my fellow toilers in the salt mines. I know we will always back each other up.

Please enjoy the following teaser from the first Spacer Clans Adventure, Book One:

NAERO'S RUN

A SPACER CLANS ADVENTURE

NAERO'S RUN

MASON ELLIOTT

NAERO'S RUN

by Mason Elliott

"We've got more than enough to consider here," Aunt Sleak said. "We'll post our final decisions on the Spacer ClanNet. All crew, take a breather. We're out of jump in less that two standard hours. Everyone on duty needs to be at their ready stations. Dismissed."

Naero went back to her quarters to do some laundry and a little more reading before they emerged. With regular effort, her quarters were less of a disaster than usual. She'd kept her bunk and her floor more or less cleared off, and slept in her bunk regularly now, instead of on the floor or in zero-G or a float bag.

And definitely not in her flex chair, as she had for years because she either couldn't get her bunk panel out or it was too piled up with crap.

Being small had its advantages. She could curl up like a cat and get comfortable almost anywhere for a snooze.

But keeping her quarters in better shape was a promise she made and kept–to herself–and her parents.

They emerged from jump with the customary shuddering of the ship. The fleet spread out into is standard formation, emerging back into real SpaceTime.

Naero punched up their positions on one of her screens, even though she didn't have bridge duty for several hours.

The Shinai flanked *The Dromon* on the port side, with *The Slipper* posted starboard. Their two smaller ships, *The Nevada* and *The Ardala*, brought up the rear this time.

A red hot scarlet particle beam, 60mm in diameter, lanced through Naero's walls like they were paper, disrupting her wallscreens.

A direct hit from a big gun.

At the very least, from a heavy destroyer.

Warning lights flashed immediately.

The rupture in the hull led to an immediate explosive decompression.

Naero held on tight to her bunk and went flat on the floor as the hull sealed itself.

All ships were vulnerable coming out of jump. They couldn't activate their shields until right after they emerged.

Someone had been waiting for them.

The Dromon continued getting rocked by multiple hits from what felt like several spinal guns and secondary batteries.

But the big planetoid could take it and give back plenty, her quad main guns humming and whining to life, coming online.

Naero hit her wristcom. All her screens down.

"Bridge. Status?"

"We stepped into it. They were waiting for us. We're under heavy fire. Multiple bogeys."

The general alert sounded.

"Battle Stations. Battle Stations."

Aunt Sleak cut over the com. "All hands. All hands, to your stations. Prepare for battle. All ships, all batteries, return fire. Launch all fighters."

Naero suited up and raced to the drop bay of her fighter. She met Jan along the way.

More intense fire. *Dromon* reeled and fired back.

She and Jan almost got rocked off their feet again.

A security team intercepted them at the launching bays.

Their fighters had already dropped with their backup pilots.

"The fleet captain wants you two at your secondary defense stations, not out in the mix."

Jan started to protest.

"Orders are orders. Get to your stations."

They ran to their remote gunnery stations, small secured cubicles with a chair and a console, operating triple pulse turrets on the hardpoints above them.

Naero brought up her autotargeting displays, weapons already powered up and humming.

The secondary battery gunnery stations operated independently and were well-protected. They were also fully automated, but they still functioned more effectively with a human interface.

Coordinated targeting profiles came online as she watched.

Jan operated a torp turret nearby.

Directly ahead of the fleet. Twelve elite Matayan destroyers, each with a dozen escort fighters.

Half of their number pursued and attacked a convoy of two dozen independent mining freighters.

Aunt Sleak's fleet scrambled, launched, and deployed a total of threescore fighters in a standard Alpha-Charlie-1 defensive screen.

They were outnumbered two to one.

"All batteries make ready. Incoming torps," the bridge com sounded.

Countermeasures took out half of the blips heading their way.

Spacer fighters and the forward defensive batteries blasted the rest.

"That attack's a diversion," Naero muttered.

Shinai's fire control and com computers fixed on and monitored all channels–including those between the hapless freighters and the corsairs.

"Mayday, mayday, we are under intense corsair attack. All ships. Assistance, assistance. Heavy damage and casualties."

"What do you want?" another panic-stricken voice cried out. "We'll surrender. You can board us. We have no goods and few supplies. Please, stop firing. Our ships are full of workers–full of people. You're killing civilians. We're on fire!"

Scanners displayed an awful, one-sided battle among the transports.

Most of the old bulk freighters didn't even have weapons.

Each of the heavily armed Matayan destroyers was more than a match for them or most of the ships in Aunt Sleak's fleet.

Except for the 6m quad spinal guns of *The Dromon.*

One crippled freighter broke apart and exploded under concentrated fire from three destroyers. It didn't have any shields, and only minimal armor. Its two turrets either didn't work or had been taken out already.

Static and Matayan battle language rang out in triumph.

Dromon's four primary guns cut loose, lighting up the entire sector. Its blue-white blasts ripped into the lead corsair flagship and its wingships, disrupting their shields.

The starboard wingship took two hits and listed to one side. Its aft section exploded.

"This is Captain Sleak Maeris of Clan Maeris. Enemy vessels, be advised: Cease hostilities and vacate this system or be destroyed."

Matayan curses and laughter her only reply.

"Clan Maeris," one of the freighter captains cut in. "This is Captain Philsen of *The Botaru.* Help us! Our situation is desperate. The corsairs are trying to destroy us. We don't know why."

"Acknowledged. We're coming in. Disperse if you can. You're still too bunched up. Scatter and concentrate on defensive actions. Jump if you're able. We'll try to draw them off. We're boosting your distress call."

Three more corsairs turned on the fleet, with all twelve dozen fighters full front on intercept.

The other trio of Matayan attackers kept after the freighters.

Naero heard the pleading and the screams on the open channel, just before another freighter got blasted to oblivion.

Naero realized she had tears on her face.

Was that how her parents went? Blasted to death by Matayan guns?

The rage she felt nearly overwhelmed her reason.

She checked her systems, gripped the controls of her gunnery station, and forced her emotions to go cold.

Against superior numbers, Naero and her Clan Fleet closed for battle.

Amazon Link to Naero's Run: *http://amzn.to/1eRKCOb*

Please enjoy the following teaser…an excerpt, from the next Spacer Clans Adventure, Book 2:

NAERO'S
GAMBIT

A SPACER CLANS ADVENTURE

NAERO'S
GAMBIT

MASON ELLIOTT

NAERO'S GAMBIT

Naero's Gambit Amazon Link: *http://amzn.to/1lx5Tyy*

by Mason Elliott

Klyne set the huge Mystic testing room on board *The Kathmandu* to muted gray. Smartwalls, floor, and ceiling, Naero saw no equipment, no padding.

The lights were set low.

From experience, Naero knew that in a training room, just about anything could pop up out of anywhere.

She wore nothing but her black Nytex flight togs.

To her surprise, Klyne and his two adepts wore dark gray Nytex togs also, but with hoods and masks pulled up over their heads. Only their keen eyes showed.

All three of the Mystics appeared to be in top physical condition, including Klyne.

One of the adepts was female, with huge green eyes and light freckles across her nose. The other was male, with the black slanted eyes of the Lii-Kim Clans.

If black was the color of Spacers, the Mystics traditionally wore gray.

They all sat with their legs crossed in lotus fashion, focusing their abilities through meditation, and mental discipline. They formed a triangle, each side about three meters apart, with them at the points.

"Follow our instructions," Klyne said. "Take your place among us. Sit in the center; sit as we do. Face the instructor."

A circle of white light appeared at the center of the triangle. Naero walked over and sat down in it, facing Klyne. Her skin barely began to tingle.

A wider ring of similar light appeared, including the instructor and his two adepts.

Every hair on Naero's body went stiff with electric force.

"You have chosen to come before the circle of Spacer Mystics to be tested for Mystic training. Speak your name."

"Naero Amashin Maeris."

"You agree to be tested?"

"I do."

"I am Klyne, the instructor. My assistants are Adept Iselle, and Adept Makita. We shall refer to you as Adept Candidate Naero. Follow our instructions. Respond only if asked to respond. If you require any medical attention, it will be administered at the end of the testing. Until then, you are expected to endure and continue to do your best. If you understand, say yes."

"Yes."

"The training will begin. Defend yourself."

Without warning, Makita's attack smashed into her.

She blocked one or two out every four or five blows.

A snapwheel kick sent her flying twenty meters, nearly winding her.

The only things that saved her at all, once again, were the experience and knowledge she gained from her training sessions with Baeven.

Makita proved stronger and faster than her, but he still paled in comparison to the outcast's terrifying prowess.

Makita charged her.

Naero met him part way.

She took several punishing strikes, but flipped him hard to the ground.

He swept her legs.

They tangled on the ground, wrestling, slipping out of holds, twisting like snakes. They pummeled each other all the while.

They broke, crouched low, and launched themselves at each other again, like Telurian fighting blue cranes.

Naero landed a whipkick on the side of Makita's head.

He clipped her under the chin, grabbed her leg and ankle and swung her hard into the floor, stunning her.

She struggled to get up.

For a few dizzy moments, she couldn't.

She rose up and staggered back into her fighting stance.

She half-smiled,

"Come on."

Makita bowed his head, just slightly, and drew back.

"Defend yourself, "Klyne said again.

Naero whirled to face Iselle.

Too late.

An invisible force slammed into her arms and torso, flinging her back.

She rolled with the strike and came back up into her stance.

Iselle fought her from a distance, punching and striking with her hands in rapid combinations.

Naero struggled to advance, to close the distance between them, while heavy, unseen blows rained down on her from every direction, knocking her one way, and then the other.

"Telekinetic combat," Klyne called out. "Try to sense and block the blows. You cannot see them. Reach out with your battle senses, with your mind. Feel them coming. Counter and deflect them. True masters can fight thus, without even moving, simply by concentrating."

At least Iselle still had to physically move in order to project her attacks. That was some help.

Closer. Get closer.

Iselle thrust both hands forward violently.

A wall of force drove Naero slowly back. She pushed against it, slowing it even more.

"Resist. Focus on the energy before you," Klyne told her, "before it smashes you into the far wall. Fight back. Defeat it."

She rolled to one side and then the other. The barrier felt solid.

Naero leaped up four meters, felt the top, and flipped herself over it.

Iselle withdrew a step, cupping both hands loosely on the sides of her face.

Spinning orbs of pure telekinetic force shot out, rapid-fire.

Naero barely perceived them where they warped through the air; they made explosive popping sounds.

She tried to dodge them. One whirred past her head like an invisible ball at high speed.

The next clipped her left shoulder, spinning her aside.

Another knocked one leg out from under her.

She kept her feet and ducked, weaving to either side in turns.

Iselle directed her attack at Naero's feet.

Naero lost her footing, slipping and sliding on what felt like a bunch of invisible ball bearings cast beneath her.

She tried to roll back to her feet, but panes of force battered her from all sides, keeping her off balance.

It felt like being a rubber ball, bouncing around in a box that someone shook.

The sides of the box rapidly closed in.

They tightened all around her, threatening to crush her.

She couldn't breathe.

Iselle released her without warning.

Naero sprawled, gasping, face down on the floor.

"I'm somewhat surprised," Klyne noted. "Preliminary tests demonstrate no psyonic aptitude or innate talent to my trained senses whatsoever. That in itself is very rare. After your battle with the former

Danner entity, we simply assumed that you would exhibit some kind of psyonic ability."

"I burned myself out dealing with the entity. I burned both of us out. I'm a nud once more." She admitted it openly. "None of my former abilities have returned."

So she wasn't psyonic anymore. Not even a teknomancer. Disappointing, but not the end of the universe.

"Yet I sense something incredibly strange within you," Klyne said. "What could it be?"

Was it Om? He was still inside her somewhere. He had not emerged again either.

"Take your place at the center of us once more. Face me again."

Naero did so, resisting an urge to massage several bruises.

Klyne positioned himself directly in front of her, sitting lotus fashion just like her and the others.

"I'm going to attempt to merge directly with your mind telepathically, one of my gifts. I'm also an Auralcognitor. Once I link with your mind, I can sense any type of psyonic energy field you might have, active, passive, or latent. I might even be able to trigger or bring them out to the surface. There might be some discomfort. Shall we proceed?"

"Sure."

"Do as I do. I will show you how to place your hands to effect the mind merge."

Klyne cupped his left hand firmly behind the base of her skull. Naero followed his lead.

He placed the fingers of his right hand on precise spots on her face.

Thumb on her forehead, directly between her eyes.

Index finger on her left temple.

The next two fingers curled slightly in front of her left ear. His smallest finger hooked at the point of her ear and jaw.

As soon as Naero placed her right hand the same way, she gasped slightly.

Thin hairs of what felt like burning hot energy threaded their way slowly through the layers of her awareness.

She could feel Klyne connecting with her thoughts, joining their two minds.

The dull ache continued to grow.

"You should be feeling the initial discomfort. Hold still. Keep focusing. Almost there. Almost..."

A spike of pure agony exploded within her skull.

Naero screamed, transfixed as if by lightning.

Through the torment, a voice awoke in her mind full-force.

Protocols unlocked and engaged. We...are.

Interface...partial.

Om awoke, reacting instinctively with fear and vast power.

Threat detected...Protect all access.

Neural net...INTRUSION. UNWARRANTED.

LEVEL 1.359 DEFENSIVE RESPONSE.

An intense blast wave of white-hot psyonic energy fanned out rapidly from the epicenter of her immolated mind.

Naero continued to scream.

As if far away in the distance, Klyne and his two adepts also shrieked.

*

Naero blinked, her eyes and mouth frozen open.

She lay with her head to one side, in a puddle of her own mixed blood and spittle.

More pain struck her when she attempted to move.

Blood continued to stream from her eyes, ears, nose, and mouth–a bloody mess.

It felt as if a fusion grenade had blown her head open.

She reached up with her hands, to make sure her skull was still intact.

Some kind of noise.

Warning alarms sounded.

A ship. Yes, they were on a ship. The Spacer Intel Ship *The Kathmandu*. She was...being tested, for the Mystics.

Something had gone terribly wrong.

Naero focused, getting to her hands and knees.

She heard other voices, groaning and whimpering.

Makita lay sprawled in a broken tangle, blasted across the room. His gray clothing had been shredded and scorched into tatters. He choked and coughed.

To the other side, Iselle fared little better. She lay convulsing, blasted, scorched, a yellow-white bone of her forearm sticking out of her wrenched flesh. One side of her face was blistered, her red hair burned, some of it still smoking. She trembled and shuddered in pain and terror.

Naero looked around for Klyne, and found the instructor in a burned, bloody heap, lying beneath a dark red smear on the far wall. His hands were charred black, and he was missing fingers.

Naero could not walk. She couldn't even stand. She crawled to Klyne as quickly as she could.

He still lived, just barely.

Then she noticed the intense effects of the blast, all around the room, less than a meter up.

A massive expanding ring of Cosmic force had sliced into the duranadium hull of the smartwalls, punching a deep crease right through them where they buckled, all along its full diameter.

The force of the strike disrupted all systems. The entire training room was compacted, crushed, and heavily damaged.

Rescuers struggled to force their way through the various ruined doors and access panels.

Naero's Gambit Amazon Link: *http://amzn.to/1lx5Tyy*

Enjoy this teaser to the Fantasy novel Mergeworld 1, by Mason Elliott and Garan R. R. Faraday.
Amazon Link:
http://amzn.to/1uboBDC

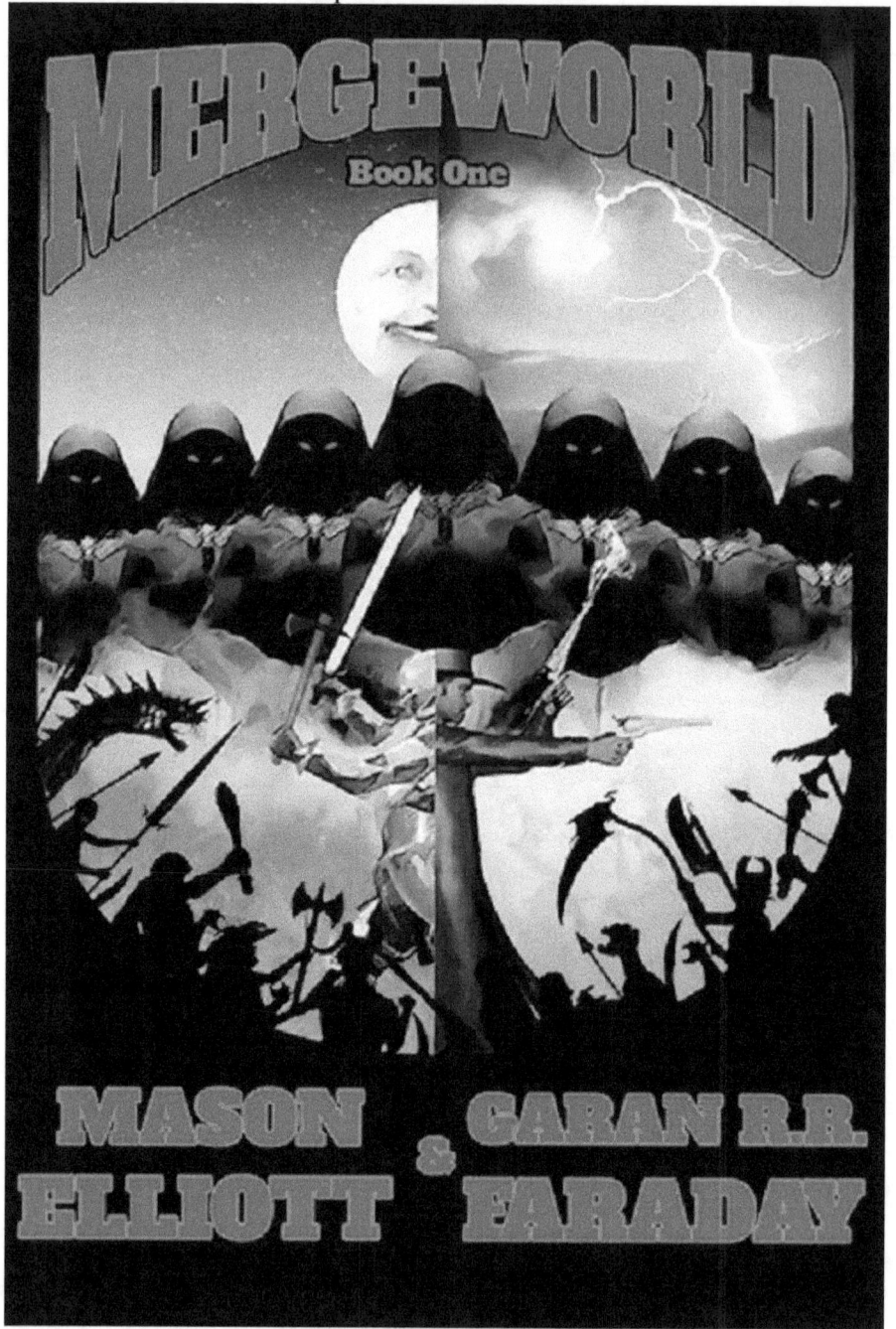

Mergeworld

Book One

by Mason Elliott & Garan R. R. Faraday

David Pritchard woke up gasping from one nightmare and went straight into another. A terrible agony tore through him as if the universe twisted him inside out.

Then he snapped back again.

What in damnation had just happened? Something...was very wrong.

Startled, groggy, it only took an instant for his bleary mind to figure it out.

Flames engulfed the front of his college apartment building. The stench of smoke, and the sounds of screams and breaking glass outside, only confirmed it.

He felt dazed, and blinked his scratchy eyes. The first thing he instinctively reached out for was the framed picture of his dead parents.

That was the last picture he had of them, taken a few years back, right after he started college in South Bend.

They hugged and smiled at each other in medieval garb at the Bristol Renaissance Faire up in Wisconsin. The picture froze both of them happily in time, retired in their forties. Unlike many parents that age, they weren't divorced and they still loved one another. One of their Ren-Faire pals had taken that picture for them on their digital camera.

The same camera retrieved from the car accident on the Illinois highway on their way back home from Bristol. A tractor-trailer jackknifed in the heavy rain and took them away.

The same weekend David begged off going with them.

He had blown that picture up in Photoshop, printed out an 8 x 10, and bought a nice oak frame for it. He kept it with him wherever he went. He'd die before he'd part with it, fire or no.

All that history and pain flashed through David as he clutched their picture close to him in the dark. He didn't even have to see it, just cling to it in his hands. That picture always sat prominently behind his small alarm clock on his night stand with his smart phone and wallet while he slept. That was how he found it, even in the semi-dark. He also grabbed his phone and wallet.

His clock normally flashed bright green. Power outage, probably from the fire. And the backup battery must have gone dead. Light switches? Nothing, of course, due to the fire.

The growing reek of smoke triggered his desire for self-preservation. Once he got out, he could call his friend Mason Tyler, who lived in a duplex over on Allen Street. His buddy Mace would help him.

Somewhat more awake now, David struggled not to panic. He staggered out of his room like a robot. His lanky, five-eleven frame stumbled down the hall toward his front door. He stubbed his little toe hard in the darkness. A second later, he grunted and cursed the sudden blinding spread of pain, but kept moving.

Oh, hell. No way out the front.

Dangerous ribbons of smoke curled violently through the metal front door frame and snaked up across the ceiling like an upside-down waterfall. The paint of the metal fire door already bubbled and blistered. David choked and swallowed hard.

If that door had been wood, his entire apartment might have already been completely engulfed. He might not have even come to. He saw no sense in touching the steaming door knob.

The apartment building stairs acted like a natural chimney, funneling the fire and heat straight up.

A window—climb out a window. He was only on the second floor.

His three richer roomies were already off on spring break for the next week, to the Bahamas or some such. Their parents could afford such junkets. David could not.

He suddenly realized two very important things. First, the fire hadn't spread to the back part of the apartment building yet.

Next, he was only wearing navy boxers and a gray T-shirt over his shaking frame.

Early April in South Bend, Indiana, could be any weather from sun and sixties to a flippin' blizzard.

Clothes. Only seconds to throw some on. Even in the dim, flickering orange light spilling out of the thick curtains, he spotted his laundry basket on the couch.

The smoke in the living room grew thicker. He put his precious picture, smartphone, and wallet down for only a few moments.

Jeans. On. Socks. On. He snatched up his thick blue, gold, and green hoodie from the back of the old couch where he usually left it, and pulled into its soft, warm comfort. Stocking cap. Popped on his head. Wool scarf.

Around the neck. He sat down and jammed on his old gray Nike running shoes, feeling a pair of thin gloves and keys in his hoodie pockets still when he bent over.

Ready to ride, or, at least, climb out the back window to escape burning to death.

He stuffed his folks' picture, wallet, and smartphone into his dark green Jansport backpack with his pad, gel pens, and a few books. He zipped it all up.

To the back window. He pulled the curtains aside and yanked the big panel open.

He jumped slightly at the sight of some guy who had already climbed down the back of the building from the third floor. Their eyes locked, only a window screen between them in the dim, pre-dawn light and the cold morning air.

The guy looked utterly terrified.

"Watch out!" he warned, trying to keep his voice low. "Those things are killing people. They're everywhere!"

"What things?" What was this guy freaking out about?

The guy jolted, wide-eyed, and then choked.

A bloody iron arrowhead jutted out the front of his throat. In the time it took them both to blink, another arrow punched through the front of his chest, out of his T-shirt. The poor guy's mouth gaped and worked. Then his eyes rolled up white. He fell backwards, head down.

David grabbed for him but missed, his hands blocked by the barrier of the screen. He tore it away and stuck his head out the window.

He spotted strange movement down in the darkness.

Two dark, twisted, hunched-over figures loped in on bandy legs and clawed feet wrapped in fur and rags. They were smaller than humans, about four to five feet tall, and very skinny and wiry.

Whatever they were, they were definitely not human.

One of them slit the dead guy's throat from ear to ear with a long, wicked-looking rusty knife.

Blood spurted bright black in the night.

The other creature sniffed the air and snarled up at David with a greenish-black, twisted, inhuman face. Long pointed ears stuck out of holes in its ragged hood. It had a big warty nose, and gleaming green eyes. It gave full draw to the same kind of short, black bow of jagged horn that the other one carried.

The creature took dead aim at David.

And fired.

Mergeworld 1 Amazon Link: http://amzn.to/1uboBDC

Mergeworld

Book Two

Amazon Link for *Mergeworld: Book Two*: http://amzn.to/1neuq0x

by Mason Elliott and Garan R. R Faraday

"Several of the enemy mage prisoners have escaped," a runner came to warn them. The young trooper looked terrified.

Mason drew his Spillers. They would have to be enough. After the bath, he didn't have all of his other guns. And there wasn't time to go after them.

It also worried him that he still felt–off his game, somehow. Something was still very wrong with him, but he couldn't figure out what. Perhaps that was merely what sorrow and depression felt like.

Blondie shook the terrified runner. "Calm down. Tell me what you know. Which prisoners? How many of them?"

"S-six, six, I think. They tried to free the rest, but the guards on the scene shot two down. Then the enemy mages fled this way, and started killing everyone they could find with magic."

Troops screamed, and close by to the west, magic blasts went off, and the sounds of battle and further bursts of magical rapidly sped their way.

The runner continued to stammer, "The tall n-n-necromancer is leading them. Five others. I don't know their names. As soon as they broke out, the duty officer sent me after you two and the Thul woman."

Blondie let the runner go. "Try to find the Thul. Go. Keep spreading the alarm."

"Yes, s-sir!" The young runner looked only too happy to keep running.

"They're coming for us, aren't they, Blondie?" Mason asked, hefting his Spillers.

Blondie clenched both fists, and violet magefire flared up to his elbows. "Yep. Just like I said they would. How do you want to do this, Mace?"

"Hmmm…too many to hit them head on. Let's go at them from the flanks. I'll hit them on the left."

His blond friend nodded. "Then I'll take them on the right. The necromancer's going to be the toughest of the lot. Let's peel off the other five, if we can, and then take him on together."

"Sounds good, Blondie. Let's ride."

They skirted around to either side, trying to stick to cover and stay out of sight. Mason quickly lost sight of his friend.

It did briefly occur to him that this would be an excellent time for Blondie to turn on them all, and help the mages make good their escape. But at this point, Mason had no choice but to keep trusting his good friend.

Blondie said that his abilities were returning.

He could tell them anything he wanted. How would they know if it was the truth or not?

From the sounds of things, the militia troops were putting up a pretty good fight and delaying the enemy at least somewhat. Each precious second they could hold them back, more troops would pour in.

Yet even as Mason got into position to attack, the enemy mages continued to push through, causing death and destruction all around them, and leaving many casualties in their wake.

Startled troops could slow the enemy down, but they would be hard pressed to stop six enemy mages bent on a rampage of devastation.

They were lucky that it wasn't all thirteen of the mage captives on the loose.

At Blondie's urging, Major Bill had spread several of the captive mages out to other nearby, secret locations–beyond the limited range of their prisoners' telepathy.

Mason spotted the enemy. The necromancer strode out in front with another sorcerer. A pair of enemy wizards marched slightly behind them on either side, guarding their flanks and watching the rear.

Blondie stepped up and raked the enemy left and the middle with violet lightning that knocked four of the six off their feet, and stunned the two flankers.

The first flanker on the other side turned to attack Blondie. The second one raised his hands and his eyes got big when he saw the Pistolero step out and aim both of his pistols.

Click! Click!

Nothing. Mason's guns wouldn't fire. He cocked and pulled the triggers again.

Nothing.

By then the one mage was charging Blondie, exploding anything that was made of wood around him. He sent the shards and splinters and whirling debris at Blondie, while the necromancer and the other sorcerer still looked dazed and tried to regain their feet. And the mage facing Mason shot greenish-yellow flames out of his hands at all before him.

Mason dove out of the way, tucked and rolled out of sight, and then crouched and ran. The enemy wizard would be on him in seconds.

Finally he came to a building and ducked inside. He scrambled out of sight into an adjoining back storage room and ducked down. He tried his guns again. Still nothing. Why was this happening,? Now of all times?

Blondie needed him out there.

Maybe if he reloaded. Yeah, that would do it.

Slowing his breathing, doing his best to stay calm, he broke out his spare cylinders for his guns and swapped them out. He was fast at it, but every second counted.

He went back out into the fight. As he expected, the fighting quickly turned Blondie's way, and blasts of magic nearby showed where the foes were pursuing Blondie hard and blasting everything around him. Blondie fought back as best he could, but from what Mason could tell, his friend was outnumbered four to one.

He raced that way, not even trying to stay under cover this time. He had to catch up quickly, and take them from behind, if possible.

Mason sped around a building and almost slammed into the same enemy mage as before. This one seemed to be holding back and protecting the rear of the other three while they stalked Blondie.

Mason had intended to shoot them on sight, but he clobbered the mage from behind now that he was right on top of him. The mage grunted and dropped, unconscious.

Pistol-whipping worked better in this instance. Mason dragged the mage back out of sight and quickly gagged him, and bound his hands and ankles behind him.

At this distance, Mason would not have any trouble taking out the other three with one or two shots, once he spotted them again. And their spells gave them away when they fired. Hopefully, Blondie was staying ahead of them.

Mason rushed forward once more, spotted several troops closing in with bows and crossbows, and motioned for them to go around and close in from one side or the other.

Finally he spotted the necromancer and the one wizard, crouched down and making plans of some kind.

Mason took aim at them with both barrels.

Click. Click.

Crap, not again. What the hell was going on?

Even worse, the necromancer turned and locked eyes with him.

"There's the other one. Let's get him!" All of their hands glowed with magefire.

Mason turned and ran for it. Dark lightning and exploding ice covered the area he had just been in.

His foes were right after him. Archers tried to fire upon the mages, but they swept the troops away from their positions with blasts of power.

A stone or outcropping of brick caught the toe of Mason's boot. He hurtled down upon his face, and tried to roll back up to his feet.

The third enemy mage stepped out right in front of Mason.

Now, the three of them had him fairly trapped.

"Kill him!" the necromancer roared.

The wizard still hesitated an instant. Then he prepared a spell, his hands beginning to glow brighter and brighter.

They were only a dozen or so feet away. Mason hurled his useless pistols at the wizard.

One missed as the fellow dodged to one side.

The other smacked him squarely in the face and dazed and bloodied him.

Mason expected to be cut down from behind by the other two enemies any second.

He glanced back just as the two stood ready to unleash their spells.

Amazon Link for *Mergeworld: Book Two*: http://amzn.to/1neuq0x

THE CITATION SERIES: BOOK 1

MASON ELLIOTT

NAERO'S WAR:

THE ANNEXATION WAR

THE
ANNEXATION
WAR

Annexation War Amazon Link: *http://amzn.to/1gmxGQk*

by Mason Elliott

Naero's flagship, *The Hippolyta,* was one of the latest, Dromon Class dreadnaughts. These warships were fashioned out of dense, iron-nickel planetoids, not less than half a kilometer in diameter. Incredibly tough and rugged on their own.

It took the most powerful mining plasma-borers–working in precise conjunction with construction fixers and an army of teks–months to hollow out armored crew quarters, lift and transport tubes, launching and loading bays. Next came space for power cores, sublight engines, jump drives, backups, gravitics, life support, sensor arrays, communications, navigation, weapons, main bridge and backup bridge.

Set in the exact heart of *The Hippolyta* were its signature big guns. A quad of the largest production guns ever constructed on any ship of war: Four, *16 meter*, rapid-fire, particle beam cannons.

Cannons any larger than that exploded, melted, or otherwise were not feasible within the limits of current tek and materials. Thirty-six secondary batteries, assorted specialized weapons and gun emplacements, and forty-five advanced fighters.

Seven hundred and forty able crew, including a full Rifle Company of two hundred and forty Spacer Marines, and all of their equipment, vehicles, and gear for ship's security and rapid response deployment. Strike Fleet Six's Marines came from the 3rd Spacer Marine Division– known as *The Death Eyes*–because of their superb snipers and their overall, excellent marksmanship ratings. Marines made up a third of the warship's complement.

Their motto: *If We Can See It...We Can Kill It!*

The main bridge was a massive armored dome constructed on top of the dreadnaught's big metal, rough-hewn orb, protected by heavy blast doors, and the latest, most advanced shielding in the fleet. Within, the circular bridge was laid out in four levels under the huge dome, a dome sixty meters high.

Each bridge tier was separated by the height of a few steps from one to the next. The inner three levels could rotate in any direction, independent of the others.

The fleet captain's command nanochair and station occupied the highest tier. Each bridge station had its own secondary shielding, in case enemy fire penetrated the shields, the blast screens, and the hull.

In combat, bridges were routinely targeted, for obvious reasons.

From that primary vantage point, the strike fleet captain could direct battles in three hundred and sixty degrees, through an advanced, battleholo display surrounding her, full zoom data-feeds, constantly updated by battle AIs. Naero could manipulate the displays by nanosensors programmed into the fingertips of her nanosuit gloves.

The battle display system also recognized her voice pattern, and would respond to voice commands, or commands punched in manually through pads on her command chair, or via other backups.

The next bridge level down from hers held the secondary bridge stations: Helm, Weapons, Communications, Navigation, and Scanning, spaced out equally along their ring.

The third ring held all of the twelve tertiary bridge stations, that monitored, controlled, and coordinated all of the ship's other important functions:

Engineering
Gravitics
Life Support
Power Supply
Security
Shields
Medical
Jump and Sub-light Drives
Damage Control
Alliance Fleet and Intel Communications
Main Computer
Launching Bays

The fourth ring went to the two powerlifts, leading from the bridge to the other movers, decks, and levels of the ship. All lift and access points throughout the ship were constantly guarded by two battle-ready Marines, stationed on either side.

If a warship was boarded by enemy assault craft during a battle, invaders could be cut off and eliminated between decks, before they could reach a vital area.

Today, Strike Fleet Six had a mission—a simple one.

Captain Naero Maeris and her fifty warships proceeded to probe the next system on the outer, port arcwall of the Alliance advance at Beleron-4.

A routine run. Current intel assured them to expect little or no Triaxian presence or resistance.

By any stretch of the imagination, Beleron-4 was a nothing world, in the middle of nowhere, with zero, nacha—absolutely no strategic or tactical value whatsoever.

Checking it off the list on the pacified worlds of the Alliance system-hopping schedule was more-or-less just a formality.

But it still had to be done. And Naero and her lot drew the duty at random.

So why did Naero's sense of warning go bonkers?

After they jumped in, simple three-stack, Delta-India-3 formation, the reasons for alarm grew perfectly clear.

They came in right on top of twenty Triaxian fleets of the enemy's latest warships.

And a gigantic new flagship—as huge as *The Hippolyta*—the advanced design of which did not even register as existing.

It had never been seen before.

Naero shot to her feet, kicked her command nanochair back out the way and sent it down into the nanofloor of her top-tier bridge control station.

She instantly called her battle display holos up in spinning, horizontal glowing ribbons and rings all around her.

Data relays went wild. Her fingers flashed among the highlighted screen arcs, taking control of them and their parameters.

Multiple warnings sounded, and with excellent reason.

Nothing about this was good in any way.

Haisha! Twenty enemy fleets could chop them into confetti—well before any other Alliance forces could even jump in to help.

No strategy, no formation could possibly save them against superior numbers such as these.

"All ships, full withdraw. Emergency retreat on this vector, in Charlie-Romeo-7, cone-ring formation. Shields and all weapons full front and hot. Maximize all targeting profiles on the lead attacking enemy elements–they'll be on us in seconds. Whatever happens–we fight until our carriers and some of our ships can break free and jump out behind us. Get the carriers out first!"

For a split second, everyone braced for the sheets of flame that would quickly overtake and overwhelm them.

The Annexation War Amazon Link: *http://amzn.to/1gmxGQk*

Please enjoy the following teaser from the next book in The Citation Series, Book Two:
The High Crusade

The Citation Series, Book Two
NAERO'S WAR:

THE HIGH CRUSADE

Amazon Link to *The High Crusade*: http://amzn.to/1DbFD5F

by Mason Elliott

General Walker's Marines from Bravo Command maneuvered into position under the cover of darkness using their stealth gear.

Naero agreed to slip in ahead and bait the trap, in her battlefield role as Shettana–*The Dark Angel of Death*.

Get ready, Om. The show's about to start.

I will need some time to prepare, concentrate, and focus enough of our energies in reserve, before you deplete them all.

Just get ready and keep us ready. I'm going to set our game plan in motion.

I will do all that I can to assist. Call upon me when you require me. Good hunting, Naero.

Thanks, Om.

The invaders would do anything to have a chance to destroy or capture her.

She was–in fact–the actual, literal bait, and the trap was being set for an entire invasion force of Ejjai elite, ravaging the Corps border world of Tholos-4.

No local planetary army, military, or militia had been able to stand before the horrific onslaught of the alien invaders.

The Ejjai hammered the local landers into submission with advanced artillery, orbital bombardment from Ejjai fleets, and close assault gunships and gravtanks.

Then the terrifying collection process began, and all the living, wounded, and dead were hurled into the shrieking, whining processing blades of the robotic meatships.

The horrible sounds of the meatships warred with the screams of their countless victims.

Given time, Ejjai mass cloning factories and robotic ship and weapon-building factories would also be established onworld.

The murdering bastards had already wiped three major cities and their mixed populations off the surface of the hapless planet, before Naero and the Marines could even deploy on world.

The enemy left those lost cities little more than red, blackened, burning scars and stains that could be viewed from orbit.

Nothing left alive.

Ejjai hyaenanoids loved carrion.

Every man, woman, and child of any kind, species, or age that the enemy captured was routinely tortured, killed, and processed into rotting ration blocks in the horrific, robotic meatships of the invading aliens. That included any sentients, pets, livestock—anything and everything that was meat.

The meatblock rations were only frozen to keep them from breaking down, and decaying completely.

Hatred was too gentle a word for what most humans felt for the Ejjai invaders and their extreme methods. Spacers, landers, and each of the other known races that encountered the Ejjai quickly learned to feel the same way.

This vile, uplifted, intrusive and opportunistic species needed to be completely exterminated, wherever it was encountered.

The invaders proved that they were incapable of co-existing with any other living things.

The Ejjai could only dominate, torture, and destroy all life that they encountered, anything they could sink their teeth and claws into. Uplifting them, and giving them advanced weapons and starships had only turned them into a galactic abomination, an interstellar menace, a virulent plague.

An utter nightmare.

One that needed to end for the poor people of Tholos-4.

Naero and her Marine allies were here to see to that.

It was amusing that the Ejjai always saw themselves as invincible, the supreme warriors.

Shettana and Bravo Command quickly intended to disavow the foe of such jaded notions, time and time again.

The Marines of Bravo Commander were the textbook picture of professional warriors. A legend among all the known systems.

Naero loved serving with the elite of the elite. Together they made a fantastic team.

Even the Ejjai had learned grudgingly to fear them from their initial engagements, and the proof was there.

Every invader force that came up against Bravo Command had been completely wiped out–in record time. And then Bravo quietly packed up and headed on to the next world, ready to do it all over again.

The enemy struggled to halt the Spacer advance and throw it back.

They tried everything they could think of.

Increased enemy numbers.

Different tactics.

New weapons–traps and tricks of many different kinds.

The Ejjai generals turned themselves inside out trying to find a solution–way to achieve victory against the Spacer advance.

Bravo Command slipped in and ruined the invaders' sick, twisted party, every single time.

And Shettana, The Dark Angel of Death, used all of her amazing, Mystic powers and abilities to help the Marines keep up the pressure, and drive the enemy to terror, madness, and distraction.

General Walker worked closely with Spacer Intel, always making sure his leathernecks had the latest high-tek toys, weapons, and armor that came online.

As a result, they landed an entire Marine Division on Tholos-4 and slipped into position, without the enemy even knowing they were there yet.

By the time the Spacer Fleets swept in to destroy the enemy naval forces–Bravo Command would already be implementing their plan to put the foe down hard and fast on the ground.

Three Marine infantry regiments, one artillery regiment, plus specialized units of meks, armor, and air-to-ground support.

The ghosts of Bravo Command spread the impending Shadow of Vengeance and Death over their foes like an unseen net, without any knowledge or awareness among the invaders themselves.

Bravo and Shettana prepared for another stunning series of lightning attacks.

All became poised and ready, while the heedless enemy celebrated their vile victories and atrocities.

Naero struggled to remain silent as she slipped in among the foe. Death and damnation to any invader who thought they could invade the human sectors with impunity, death, and Cosmicide.

On every world, the invader needed to be taught that bloody lesson.

Naero strode right into the belly of the beast.

Alone.

Defiant.

Confident in her skills and abilities and all of her comrades depending on her and backing her up.

Her cloaked combat armor made her virtually invisible. The Ejjai could not even smell her.

She used her gravwing to slip into the most heavily guarded command and control bunker the enemy possessed. With her skill and her tek, she could crawl upside down on the ceilings like an unseen insect.

Her miniature vidcams and audio collectors fed data to Intel in real time, covering everything she saw.

Naero's small contingent of cloaked Intel fixers and microdrones stayed close, ready to disrupt key enemy systems and communications when ready, planting microbombs and detonation devices as they went.

The Invader High Command celebrated their latest triumph with what one might expect from them—a huge, decadent, disgusting feast—held within a shielded bunker.

They set up their victory celebration within a huge underground arena, probably used by the Tholosians for some kind of urban or regional sporting event.

Ejjai got drunk on stinking, fermented grog made from human blood. They shipped it in from the meatships by the tankerful.

Under the bright lights of the hi-tek arena, tens of thousands of Ejjai feasted and celebrated their latest victories. The enemy generals praised their troops and used the huge arena vidscreens to plot out their next attacks on the three nearest Tolosian cities.

On the center of the playing field, Ejjai transports and appropriated trucks had also hauled in and dumped huge piles of human corpses from the local population for their undefeated troops to feed on.

Piles of fresh and not so fresh meat, diverted from the enemy meatships to help sate the troops in large numbers.

One of the piles was all dead children and infants.

Even worse, to Naero's horror, some of the bodies in the various meat piles were somehow still alive. They twitched or cried out in pain and terror. Some weakly attempted to crawl away, despite broken or missing limbs.

The Ejjai quickly seized them and began tormenting them even further, laughing hysterically at the sport. They stabbed, cut, and skinned them alive—or otherwise got creative.

As Ejjai were wont to do.

Ejjai were among the vilest, most disgusting creatures Naero had even encountered.

She resisted the very strong impulse to cut loose on them right then and there.

But she couldn't–not yet.

These monsters needed to die. Every single one of them.

And very soon, she would have a direct hand in launching the attack that would accomplish just that.

The timing had to be just right, so she steeled herself.

The generals. Reach the generals and stay ready.

Six Ejjai generals held court like warlords at huge tables overflowing with comconsoles, sensor stations, map screens, and piles of loot. And the bloody remains of horrific, eviscerated meals.

All Ejjai clone troops were female. Smaller male Ejjai concubines were kept around on leashes for fun, for the leaders. They even dressed them in human clothing and poorly fitting human lingerie.

As an oddity, one of the generals even had a human male dressed up as a concubine. But the poor guy apparently had to be kept in a heavily guarded pen off to one side–to keep all of the other Ejjai from devouring and murdering him, most likely in that order.

Naero circled around the generals and studied the arena, trying to devise the best way to take them all down.

She listened intently to the plans the enemy generals were making, feeding it all to Intel.

"So, are all of the atomics and genocide devices in place yet?"

Another general pulled up a mapscreen displaying all of their installation of such devices planet wide.

Naero instantly transmitted all of that data directly to Spacer Intel as well–priority alert.

Intel and Bravo Command were most likely already neutralizing the most vital elements of the enemy plot. These genocide devices could be scanned and located from orbit. But it was always good to be sure, and to know their exact locations.

The Ejjai generals scoffed. "We will be ready for anything the enemy can throw at us in less than a day," one of the other Ejjai generals boasted.

"They won't know what's going to hit them until it's too late."

"Good, very good. Speed things up if you can. Get it all up and ready."

"Don't worry, sir. We will be more than ready to deal with their so-called Bravo Command—and their spack witch."

All of the Ejjai generals had a good laugh and congratulated each other.

The lead general stepped up to a waiting podium and addressed the crowd.

"Great news, sisters! We have it on good authority that the spacks are sending their precious Bravo Command and their spack witch Shettana against us."

Lots of cursing and booing about that roared up.

Their lead general continued. "This time, we are more than ready for them!"

Huge rounds of applause to that.

"Let me just say that we have some heavy duty surprises of our own ready and waiting and in store for our enemies. We can't wait for them to get here—and have them all for dinner!"

That brought an even bigger round of cheering, cursing, and applause.

"We will engage the spacks in a matter of days, and with our increased numbers and new weapons—I say we're going to kick their asses and stomp them bloody. We will gut them! I want all my girls out there to feast on spack Marine flesh until you puke!"

Further rounds of cheering and vile responses.

"We will ferment their blood in our huge vats and get drunk on it!"

More horrendous rounds of cheering and applause.

"And once we have captured their filthy spack witch, all of you will watch as I personally cut her up and rape her with red-hot knives, and torture her to death over the course of an entire week. She'll sing to all of us with her screams. Then I myself will feast upon her guts, and eat her heart while the light in her eyes fades. I'll crack her skull open and eat her brains!"

The Ejjai went crazy.

"Wait until we post *that* on the webnets for the spacks and the skinners to watch! I promise you victory. We cannot be defeated. And we will sweep the human skinners and all the other inferior races into our meatships and out of all existence. They are our prey! Yet another galaxy that shall fall to us and our mighty masters!"

More about their mysterious masters. Interesting.

Furious cheering continued in waves.

"So my warriors. Feast on meat until you vomit, and then feast some more. Then prepare for battle as we crush our foes and ravage the rest of this world. We shall drown it all in blood and swim in it! Prepare for our ultimate victory! Our time has come. None can stand against us!"

They erupted in an orgy of celebration and vile gluttony.

Fights broke out among the meat piles, and the Ejjai fought with and murdered each other in their frenzy.

The lead general returned to the others, rubbing her claws together eagerly in the midst of the chaos.

"My sisters, I have a special treat that I've saved just for us, at this exact moment. Please, enjoy my precious gifts to you all." She motioned to a large knot of troops off to one side among some gravtanks.

A full squad of Ejjai in heavy battle armor led out six terrified human women, all of them naked, and extremely pregnant.

None of them had a mark on them. Yet.

But from the looks on their pale faces, they all knew very well what the enemy generals intended to do with them. Each of them was heavy with child in the later stages of pregnancy.

That they had remained unspoiled and unharmed up until now would quickly change for the worse–the worst fate imaginable.

Although they were unbound, there was no chance for any of these captives to break free or escape on their own against so many foes.

The generals each glared at them and gloated. The Ejjai generals slavered and drooled, snapping jaws and smacking lips.

Each general had a set of rusty, bloodstained butchering tools that they began to place out in front of them in heady, eager anticipation of their coming feast.

Then the squad of Ejjai troops guarding the six women suddenly staggered a few feet away as if drunk.

Some melted into slag where they stood.

Other Ejjai troops exploded.

The six human captives looked around in confusion.

The next instant, they all vanished.

The six Ejjai generals shot to their feet in stunned surprise.

They couldn't even speak, but a few flung cleavers and knives at the spot where the captives had stood.

Their weapons fell harmlessly to the ground.

All of this was captured and displayed on the big arena screens, and slowly attracted the attention of the astonished crowds.

Then Shettana appeared as if by magic, right before the lead Ejjai general, resplendent in her full Angel of Death mode. She was all dressed in black, shining black hair flowing in the wind, violet eyes burning above her mask.

Twin blood-red katanas crackled and hissed in the damp air, at the ready in either hand.

Every eye fixed on her—while the mini-gravpods from her fixers whisked the six cloaked, female captives away to safety.

Naero only had to buy few more seconds for them to make it out. Fierce Marines waited nearby to take charge of them and keep them safe.

With the six captives out of the way, at last Shettana could go to work.

"I have come for you, filthy Ejjai cowards. I am Shettana!" she cried.

She rammed both of her swords through the lead general's eyes and out the back of the Ejjai's scorched skull.

Two of the generals tried to run.

The other three tried to attack her.

It did not matter.

Bolts of scarlet lighting tore forth from both her blades, ripping and blasting the other five into charred pieces of meat and bone.

Naero cloaked and shot away, as the area around the tables was engulfed in torrents of enemy weapon fire the very next instant.

Then the gravtanks, gunships, transports and other vehicles lined up nearby began to explode.

Naero projected multiple holos of herself all over the arena and in the in the air, drawing fire in all directions.

She used *the voice*, her words booming and echoing from several directions.

"EJJAI FILTH. PREPARE TO MEET DEATH. FOR SHETTANA IS THE DARK ANGEL OF DEATH, AND HAS NO FEAR OF MURDERING COWARDS."

The Ejjai fired in panic from so many angles that they cut down each other by the hundreds—just as Naero planned.

Fear began to infect them.

Gouts of red lightning lashed into the arena stands from several directions like gigantic whips of destruction. The devastation flung dead and dying Ejjai everywhere in a cyclone of slaughter, adding to the total chaos and confusion.

"NO MERCY, EJJAI SCUM. NO ESCAPE. FEAR IS MY MOTHER, DEATH MY SIRE, AND I THEIR DAUGHTER! YOU CANNOT HARM ME. THERE IS NO ESCAPE FOR YOU!"

Just as the enemy started to figure out they were shooting at holos and murdering each other wholesale, Naero merged with one in her mirror images in the midst of hundreds of Ejjai in the arena stands.

Multiple thin rods of red Chaos energy shot out from her, fanning in a diameter of thirty meters.

First she impaled hundreds of the shocked invaders.

When she spun, the red blades chopped them all into smaller gory chunks and pieces.

Torrents of unleashed Ejjai blood suddenly gathered and swept down the arena, carrying others away in a sudden red rushing tide of gore.

Naero cloaked and flashed away again.

More enemy fire stormed and tore at her former position.

She took the place of another holo, and sent forth a sweeping hurricane of of Chaos bubbles and orbs of every shape and size into another section of the stands.

The explosions collapsed that entire section. Wreckage toppled inward.

Next she appeared on the field before the horrendous meat piles, in the midst of hundreds of more frantic enemies.

Half of them flung their weapons away and ran in terror before her as she raced toward them. So much for the valiant Ejjai.

"STAND AND FIGHT, SCUM!"

Naero surged and fought with the mob of foes, sweeping one way and then the other, cutting them down by dozens, by scores.

She moved among them so fast they could not focus their attacks.

Then she would abruptly change direction and sweep another way before they could hem her in.

She unleashed more scarlet lightening strikes.

She sent random Chaos blasts into packed pockets of foes.

At times she just whirled and passed through them with her swords fully extended, mowing them down in lines and bunches.

Once she had shattered them completely, she merely turned her back on them and began walking away quickly and with determination, toward the nearest exit.

Naero set her shield pod full on.

Three enemy tanks roared at her, cannons blazing.

Naero dodged and deflected their blasts into the stands.

Two gravtanks she exploded with Chaos bombs.

The last she sliced the last in half with her swords and kept walking calmly, straight through the burning wreckage as the gravtank exploded directly behind her to either side.

She ignored all enemy fire directed at her, kept walking, and cut down anything stupid enough to attempt to stand before her.

She crackled with destroying red lightning as she passed into one of the exit tunnels, laying waste to anything before her.

The enemy regrouped and poured into the tunnel in hot pursuit.

Just as Naero hoped they would.

Another kill zone. How convenient of them to all bunch up for her.

She turned at bay, just before exiting, and focused all of her energies in an intense Chaos blast cone.

The massive detonation tore the tunnel apart and blasted shredded pieces of the packed invaders out the other end, right before a massive fireball that followed hard thereafter.

Naero cloaked, and called out over her secure link.

"You guys ready? I've got them primed, but I'm also almost out of juice."

"We're in place and ready to join the show, Shettana. You okay? Do you need us to extract you?"

"Negative. I can finish my part. It just takes a lot of energy to sustain attacks at this level. You guys know that. Did Intel take care of those genocide devices?"

"Almost all accounted for."

"All right, I'm setting up for my final show. They'll take the bait, all right. You guys hit them hard when they do."

"Hard as we can, Shettana. You know us."

"I sure do, and I can't wait to watch it all go down–right from the front row. Copy that. Make the legends proud, Bravo."

She took up her position in the center of the fallen city nearby, just outside of the shattered arena.

She formed a Chaos construct around her that duplicated her and her every move.

Her construct became a scarlet, giant version of herself, semi-transparent and fifteen meters tall, red and glowing with huge blazing swords.

She stomped on a meat ship and slashed at it until it exploded.

Then she attacked the clone ship factory next to it.

"FACE ME, COWARDS. SHETTANA SHOWS YOU HER MIGHT. SHOW ME YOURS. FACE ME AND PERISH!"

Yet in actuality, her energies waned with each passing second.

It wasn't like being back on Janosha where there was limitless Cosmic energy to tap into. Away from the Mystic Homeworlds, Naero's energy levels and her abilities were not infinite or limitless. She made a good show of it, but even she could not sustain these levels of attacks for very long.

The entire enemy invasion roared to life , and locked on, bunching and sweeping her way, to engage her from all directions.

The Ejjai went insane with fury.

Up in the skies above and beyond Tholos-4, the Spacer navy sent the invader fleets spinning down in flames.

Thousands of Spacer Marines suddenly materialized out of the black at key points and positions.

Phantoms who owned the night.

The black was their domain, their element, and they surrendered it to no one.

Bravo Command unleashed a torrent of concentrated, interlocking fire against the bunched up invaders. Veils of destroying fire, artillery, and ordnance–a deluge of precisely timed destruction that no living thing could possibly survive.

Within a matter of minutes, a quarter of a million Ejjai invaders flashed and flared into a sweeping typhoon of white-hot death that overtook them.

Naero had done her job.

Completely drained of all her mystic energies for the moment, she could barely stand.

Even as she staggered away, a full platoon of gigantic Sterodans in phaze armor appeared all around her.

They piled on and overwhelmed her with their greater mass, and several shock charges that hit and rippled through both them and her. The shock charges rattled Naero's teeth in her skull.

The Ejjai and their mysterious masters still wanted her and the KDM alive and intact, apparently.

Naero grinned.

Yet another trap, and she had stumbled right into it.

This time, the enemy thought they had her at last.

Yet Naero knew something they did not, and called out into her own mind.

Om–you're up. They've got me.

Take these bastards down hard and fast!

Amazon Link for *The High Crusade*: http://amzn.to/1DbFD5F

Please enjoy the following teaser from the next Spacer Clans Adventure, Book 3:

NAERO'S FURY

NAERO'S FURY

Naero's Fury Amazon Link: http://amzn.to/1hLrPpO

by Mason Elliott

Naero still hadn't done it much, but going into a direct trance to enter the Astral Plane shouldn't be all that difficult. Master Vane had shown her how once. And she had gone there lots of times in her sleep, in her mind, to speak with Khai, using their astral crystals.

Before her friend Khai had vanished without a trace.

Yet she had never been completely trained in astral travel, and didn't know that much about exploring or moving around. Master Vane had taken her there once, just to teach her the basics and give her his marker. Many other times later to spar with her.

If nothing else, she could probably focus on his marker and locate him.

Zhen had roused Naero and reminded her it was time. And that she and Shalaen would monitor her while she was in the astral trance.

Naero focused her mind and abilities, controlling her breathing. Remembering the little she had recently learned.

Within several minutes of focused meditation, she open her eyes and found herself floating in the Astral Miasma, the nebulae of energy. She hugged her knees to her chest in her astral form.

Om spoke to her, even more easily here than in her own mind before.

I have accessed some of the Kexxian Matrix's data files on The Astral Plane. Like everything else, they explored it quite extensively.

Om, I'm naked here. I'm not complaining–but just tell me–how do I put astral clothing on again?

You control everything here by imagination, and force of will. Concentrate on your favorite clothing and they'll appear.

That's easy.

She looked down and saw her favorite Nytex flight togs, programmed just the way she liked them.

Naero blinked, spinning and twirling in one spot, turning upside down.

Why can't I move more than a meter at a time in front of us?

You're not used to this reality. So it's not clear to you.

The air around her looked opaque. Not mist. Not smoke or vapor. And it glowed slightly with its own bluish-gray light.

In the twilight she glowed softly blue-white with her own light. From within.

"I once heard rumors that the Mystics could travel and send messages this way, but I thought it was all just a myth."

Since the other planes are entire universes within themselves, it is said, they are all nearly infinite. Thus, it is difficult to pin point any kind of location or person unless you already know them.

Naero instinctively tried to stand up, but there was nothing to stand on.

Then she recalled Master Vane's Marker, and it appeared right before her. Where she found him, she would find the other High Masters.

At least she deserved a chance to be heard by them all. To try to explain herself and her actions. What happened with the obelisk was clearly not her fault.

But they would still blame her for it—especially Mater Vane, who seemed to blame her for everything since Hashiko's death.

Naero could not simply stand by and let the High Masters decide her fate without herself being present at her trial, in some way at least.

She focused on the crimson and black star more and swept forward, seemingly at great speed.

She came to an abrupt halt, like a starship coming out of jump at its destination.

The opacity around her partially melted away. She proceeded forward, opening her visual field far wider. She made out the area around her as the miasma peeled back.

Slightly below her, she saw spheres within glowing spheres, all spinning within greater spheres.

Her own sphere, glowing white-blue, suddenly surrounded her like a glittering soap bubble.

Yet it did not pop when she poked at it.

One sphere in particular, the largest, glowed and pulsed blood red, containing a withered old man with a long beard, pacing impatiently.

Burning eyes vanished and re-appeared at random all over his bald head. The red sphere absorbed Master Vane's marker.

Was this his true form? What he really looked like?

His scarlet sphere was also flanked by two smaller spheres with figures inside them.

Om made a calculated guess.

His current guardian adepts, no doubt. The ones you rescued from the enemy Darkforce generators on Janosha.

I think so, Om.

At most times, every High Master had at least two champion adepts protecting him or her, each of them very close to mastery themselves. Just as Hashiko had been.

Naero studied Vane's new guardians for the very first time, and tried to see into their spheres.

Something about each of them did seem strangely familiar.

One of Vane's adepts, the male, appeared to be so deep dark black, he could be a singularity. This adept's sphere was flat black on the surface and barely transparent.

If Naero had been able to breathe, she would have gasped.

Instead she simply raised her hand to her mouth.

She recalled that she had seen many of these adepts long before.

In her dreams, nightmares, and crazed visions. Perhaps even on the Astral Plane somehow.

Vane's other adept was the white female, the exact opposite of the other. So brilliant and blindingly radiant, she could be a pulsar. Her orb was like a high intensity bulb, blinding and almost completely crystal clear.

It occurred to Naero that during her initial testing, Klyne had male and female assistants as well.

She couldn't guess what the significance of that pattern was all about. Perhaps just some weird Mystic, egalitarian tradition.

Then why weren't any of the High Masters female?

Everyone seemed to ignore her where she floated.

The next larger sphere, farther away, glowed silver-blue.

If she focused intently on it, she discovered she could zoom in with her third eye—her mind's eye.

Within that silver-blue sphere, a silver man sat serenely, neither young nor old. Master Tree, in his purest form of order.

Two smaller guardian spheres flanked him.

Master Tree's female adept glowed with intense blue energy in a deep blue sphere.

The male likewise glowed with vibrant green force within a green sphere, a shining sword sheathed down his broad, athletic back. He seemed very familiar somehow.

Naero did a double-take. Long blond hair. Green skin. Big glowing sword.

Yep. In the flesh—or—astral form at least.

It was Khai! She was sure of it. He was alive.

Had he actually succeeded in his great task of forging his mystic sword in the heart of a gigantic pulsar? Was that it on his back?

Naero gasped again. Now that she knew what he looked like, Khai was also the dreamy green hunk from many past, pent up nightmares. The one who kept sticking his astral sword through her head.

What did it all mean? She wasn't nuts enough yet?

Now she knew for certain she needed serious help.

And to do some serious dating at some point, once-and-for-all.

If the Mystics continued to let her live.

Khai must have sensed her inner turmoil, or thoughts, or maybe just her concentration on him.

Mr. Green-god even glanced her way for a second, looking just as confused and puzzled by her sudden appearance.

Neither of them had ever met the other in person.

Naero covered her face with one hand and looked aside, withdrawing her sphere suddenly further away.

How fricking embarrassing.

She crept forward again. Slowly.

The third and final sphere glowed golden, and contained an equally golden child within, energetic and bristling with lightning. He bounced back and forth inside like a gigantic electron.

Master Jo of course.

Two flanking spheres.

One of his adepts had no clear form, eyes gleaming within a shifting, flickering miasma like the Astral Plane itself. His female counterpart shifted shape from one fantastic creature to another.

When she suddenly made out their voices, she could sense that an intense debate had been doing on. One that still continued.

"We cannot be certain in this matter," the golden child insisted. "We do not dare act in any rash way."

"Agreed, High Master Jo," the serene silver man added. "She might yet be another Trickster from what I can tell."

"Yes. Quite possible, High Master Tree."

The old man in the blood red sphere blustered impatiently. "Fools! Always conspiring against me. Taking positions opposite of mine for no reason but to anger me. I've been telling you all along, this child is clearly the Great Destroyer—long foretold. Our duty is clear. She is a threat to all existence. To multiple dimensions. She must be eliminated, at once, before she can grow even more powerful."

"High Master Vane," Tree said. "None of us can be sure of that fact. Including you."

"I am."

"You are always certain when it comes to destroying someone," Jo added. "Your pure Chaos answer to everything. Destruction or Creation."

"It works."

"No. It doesn't. It only delays and worsens the inevitable," Tree said. "The Universe shall have its way. We all know this. You were mistaken with the last savant when he appeared, and now he remains at large–a renegade beyond even our control."

Baeven? We're they referring to her uncle?

Vane rolled his eyes. "Idiots! The Renegade is the Trickster, I say. This child must in fact be the Great Destroyer. Just look at the powers roiling within her. They will surely corrupt and overwhelm her entirely and drive her mad in the end. She will go berserk on a scale that makes her recent outbursts feeble and puny by comparison. She must perish now, while we have a chance to put an end to her. While the only crimes she has committed include destroying an entire planet, and another of the vital obelisks!"

"We still don't understand the purpose of the ancient obelisks. And we've studied the mysterious disappearance of Janosha, and we still cannot be certain in any conclusive way, that she had anything to do with it."

"Really? Who else could it be then? Planets like Janosha aren't in the habit of just obliterating themselves suddenly for no reason at all. Everywhere she goes, destruction follows!"

I cannot allow this.

Quiet, Om. Don't do anything. I'm trying to listen.

Naero...they're discussing our destruction. The Chaos Master means to destroy us.

Master Jo continued to protest. "You can't just kill off every entity that manifests Cosmic Abilities such as these. Our universe is peppered with them. We must continue to locate and guide them–not find excuses to execute them. Like the Others have told us, Tricksters often appear to oppose Great Destroyers. Without the former, final victory is never possible. "

"High Masters," Tree said. "This young woman also possesses the Kexxian Data Matrix. We cannot destroy her without destroying it. Intel and The Spacer Council of Elders value our wisdom, but even they would not agree to such action."

"Regrettable," Vane said. "Yet I cannot take the risk. I have decided this matter on my own."

"You have no such authority on your own," Tree insisted.

"Idiots! I cannot stand by and allow our galaxy–perhaps our entire universe to be destroyed–just to satisfy your foolish, philosophical, and theoretical whims."

Master Vane turned to his adepts. "My finest students, obey me. Delay these fools. Keep them occupied whilst I act for the good of all existence."

More rapid than thought, the male dark ensnared the blue sphere and its satellites in coils and tendrils of darkness. While the bright female enveloped the golden sphere and its companions in waves of of pure light.

Naero tried to pull away, but in her panic she did not know where to go.

High Master Vane sped straight at her with impossible speed.

I must act, Naero.

No, Om. Please, this is already bad enough. Don't do anything.

I cannot comply. I must defend us!

Naero went down on her hands and knees before Master Vane. She called out, using *the voice* to project her words.

"Please, Master Vane. Do not attack me. I only wish to be trained to control my abilities. I have struggled hard to do so. I still don't understand what happened with the obelisk."

Vane bore down on her, arcs of pure scarlet energy bristling around him.

"Far too late for that, monster. Nothing is ever your fault, is it? Now, you must perish for the good of all. I told you this hour would come."

Instinctively, Naero drew back again, trying to evade his attack. She rose within her receding sphere.

Vane closed in once more, gathering his powers.

"Don't do this," Naero begged. "Please. Help me. I know I can't fully control all of my abilities yet. I'm trying as hard as I can. I can't be responsible for what will happen if you attack me. I can't control myself."

"Yes, and look at the results? Countless lives crushed and eradicated. Janosha vaporized–an entire planet. You must never be allowed to reach your full potential. Now–monster–hold still and embrace your fate."

Naero put her hands out before her, holding her palms out defensively. Pleading.

"No. Don't. I can't–"

"I know, Maeris. You can't help yourself. That is why you are *an abomination!*"

Vane smashed into her, piercing all of her defenses as if they were shattering glass.

In the distance, she sensed that Master Jo and Master Tree finally broke free.

Too late.

Master Vane attacked, trying to overwhelm her with raw power.

He pummeled her with impossible blows.

In the end, he beat her up badly, but only succeeded in knocking her around once more.

Om roared in their mind.

Kexxian defense protocols unlocked and on line.

An energized, glowing armor of some advanced origin formed around Naero like a hi-tek battle suit.

Naero saw out of her third eye as it awoke and burst into radiance like a blue-white star.

Master Vane came at her once more, all of his powers focused through his primary scarlet, burning eye, centered in his forehead.

All of his other flaming eyes closed as he concentrated, his skull wreathed in weird cosmic flames like a mane of cosmic fire.

"See how powerful you have already become? No adept could have withstood those lethal attacks. We must finish this now, before the others can interfere."

"Please, Master Vane. Please–I'm begging you–please, don't do this."

"Maeris, just as I foretold–you shall fall before the greatest of all Cosmic attack techniques. And I am one of the few who have ever learned to master it: The Eye of Annihilation!"

The same Chaos technique that had destroyed Hashiko–even she couldn't control it properly.

A massive blood red beam of destroying Cosmic force shot straight at her.

It all happened so fast. Naero heard Om screaming.

Reflection defense. Analyze incoming cosmic assault. Duplicate and reflect attack tenfold!

Just before the incoming blast vaporized her, a blue-white beam shot out of her own third eye to war against Master Vane's powers.

The Cosmic flows flared intensely.

Naero screamed as if her body and soul were being sucked through the eye of a black hole's needle.

The wide blue beam quickly drove the red beam back to its source.

At the last instant, High Master Vane cried out in terror.

"Impossible! There can be no such–"

The destroying energy ignited on contact.

A massive detonation on the Astral Plane blinded the area within a few light years.

High Masters Jo and Tree barely managed to withdraw and shield the others. All of their spheres shattered.

Pure cosmic energy punched into High Master Vane right before Naero's eyes.

It drove him back like a white-hot comet.

He struggled against it with all his might.

To no avail.

The reflected attack obliterated High Master Vane to glowing ash and dust, screaming in the wake of his own annihilation.

Vane's dying force of will echoed off into the universe.

Naero would have caught her breath if she had any.

The outcome left her completely stunned for a shuddering instant.

Om…what did we just do?

We had no choice, Naero. My sole purpose is to defend our current form.

Naero stared down at her hands in terror. Tendrils of Cosmic energy rippled and still curled off of her body and her sphere like smoke.

Om…*Haisha!* We just killed a High Master of the Spacer Mystics!

Naero's Fury Amazon Link: http://amzn.to/1hLrPpO

Please enjoy this teaser for The Citation Series, Book 3:

Naero's Trial Amazon Link : http://amzn.to/1oaMNE3

NAERO'S WAR:

NAERO'S TRIAL

Naero's Trial Amazon Link: http://amzn.to/1oaMNE3

by Mason Elliott

On the third day of Naero's trial, the Prosecution and the Defense made their final, closing statements.

Master Jo spoke first, for the Defense.

"In the final analysis, I would both conclude and insist that Naero Amashin Maeris has proven herself time and time again to be an honorable Spacer, and that her word is without question. She is also vital to the survival of her people in many important ways. Naero Amashin Maeris is a noble, invaluable warrior and a proven leader who has served the Clans and the Alliance well, in both peacetime and war. A Mystic Champion who is now part of the great and mysterious Cosmic Prophecy, long foretold. There is still so little that we do not know about those prophecies; who can say what her role will be in the end?"

Master Jo paced a bit. "And on a very basic level, she is a Spacer. As such, she has the right of all Spacers and all sentients to defend herself, to the death, against anyone who attempts to kill her. Reluctantly, she only resorted to lethal force when High Master Vane attacked her with the intent to destroy her, and take her life. Even after she had tried to get away from him, and begged him repeatedly not to attack her.

"She cannot not be convicted of murder for defending her own life against someone trying to kill her. Those are all many good reasons why you must see fit to exonerate her of these erroneous charges. We cannot take the life of this hero."

The Defense finally rested.

Master Tree was given the final word in the trial for the prosecution.

"Hero? First, let me also revisit the reckless side of this renegade, outlaw Spacer, who fled from justice and had to be brought back by force to face her crimes in shackles, in order to keep her from getting away once again. On several occasions, Naero Amashin Maeris has proven herself to be dangerous, unpredictable, and out of control. By her own words, she has more than once declared that if she ever lost control and became a threat to any of her people, that she herself agreed that she should be put down–and destroyed.

"The cold blooded murder of a High Mystic Master has not demonstrated this fact readily enough? Beyond all doubt? If she can slay a High Master of the Mystics so easily, how much more is she a danger to all? And she even admits that she cannot control her abilities. Her very existence has become such a clear and present threat that it cannot be ignored and must be dealt with. I repeat, she has admitted on several occasions that her powers can go out of control and be very dangerous.

"Next, she also clearly admits that she killed Master Vane. Now, of her own accord, she claims that she killed him in self defense. But she has thus far presented no single shred of proof of that. She claims that Master Vane attacked her, attempted to kill her, and that she killed him, as she now conveniently claims–in so-called self defense. And I remind everyone in this court, once again. It does not matter who she is, what she is, or whatever else she has done. No one is above Spacer Law.

"Not even the infamous, Naero Amashin Maeris."

Tree took in a breath and clasped his hands behind his back. "What are the facts, therefore? A High Mystic Master lies dead, murdered by his own student, who openly stated that she could not stand him. Who openly admitted that she killed him. Nothing else can be proven, beyond those facts. Nothing else exists as fact. And this case must only be decided, based solely upon the facts. Nothing else.

"A Spacer on trial for her life could readily claim and say anything. Merely stating something does not make it true. That does not prove it to be fact. According to the facts of what is known, Naero Amashin Maeris is clearly guilty of murder, and will undoubtedly say and do anything possible in order to get away with her crime. As anyone logically would, in order to escape punishment, justice, and execution."

Naero fumed. Haisha! What the hell did they expect her to say? Yes, I offed the asshole, I loved it, and I'm a fricking monster. Go ahead and kill me?

I wish that weren't so painfully funny, Naero.

Me too, Om.

Master Tree went on to demand that the jury uphold one of the key tenets of Spacer Law and Spacer society:

"Spacers do not murder other Spacers and take their lives! Naero Amashin Maeris is not above that law. Naero Amashin Maeris broke that solemn law. And like it or not, the law demands justice. There is no way around that law and no way to escape it. That law demands that she face the ultimate punishment for her being guilty of committing the ultimate crime!"

Tree emphasized his final point with a single, upraised index finger. "That punishment is immediate Death, by execution. To be carried out by beheading, at the hands and the blade of the Mystic Enforcer!"

The Prosecution rested its case.

Admiral Klyne looked slightly pale as he instructed the jury of Mystic Elders to decide the case and announce their decision after their period of deliberation.

Naero went back to her cell in silence feeling sick, unable to meet Khai's utterly heartbroken glance. She felt stunned and numb. She didn't know what to think. All that she could do was await the jury's decision, along with everyone else.

Yet it was her fate alone that was being decided.

But when she thought about it further it wasn't just her fate.

Everyone waited for eight long hours.

Naero could neither rest nor sleep.

Then everyone was summoned back to the court room.

A decision had been made. The jury had arrived at a verdict in her case.

Admiral Klyne announced, "All rise for the verdict to be read."

They did so.

The jury leader stood up and read their decision.

"According to Spacer Law, and based upon all of the facts and evidence presented, we the jury find the defendant, Naero Amashin Maeris, of Clan Maeris…guilty of murder in the death of another Spacer."

Naero gasped, nailed to the bedrock of the planet itself in almost complete shock.

Guilty meant…

Master Tree rose up. "This Mystic trial has ended; it is over. A verdict has been reached. Without question, this grim crime is punishable among our people by death. Under the circumstances, the sentence is to be carried out immediately and without delay."

Naero, I can–

Shut up, Om.

Naero gasped and covered her mouth with both hands as she sobbed and went down on one knee.

Then she dropped her hands to her abdomen and her eyes met Khai's in explosive waves of desperate horror and regret.

Their child from their love within that distant star barely grew within her. Now, no time remained to tell Khai all that she needed to before he performed his duty as the Mystic Enforcer.

Before he took her head…ended her life, and the lives of his own family.

Naero Amashin Maeris clenched her fists, and rose up with her head held high to meet her fate with her eyes clear and wide open, if that was what must be.

Amazon Link for Naero's Trial: http://amzn.to/1oaMNE3

Edition Notes

If you do not see this edition note here in this spot on the copyright page and on the very last page of your ebook or print version of this title, then you are not getting the final, polished version of this novel that the publisher, editors, and author intended for you to receive. Please contact either the publisher or the author via their emails or websites if you do not see the following update code:

High Mark Publishing Update Code K2428E